KU-027-496

USA Today bestselling author Katherine Garbera is a two-time Maggie winner who has written 108 books. A Florida native who grew up to travel the globe, Katherine now makes her home in the Midlands of the UK with her husband, two children and a very spoiled miniature dachshund. Visit her on the web at katherinegarbera.com, connect with her on Facebook and follow her on Twitter @katheringarbera

Avril Tremayne became a writer via careers in shoe-selling, nursing, teaching and public relations. Along the way, she studied acting, singing, pottery, oil painting, millinery, German and Arabic (among other things). A committed urbanite, her favourite stories are fast-paced contemporary city stories told with sass and humour. Married with one daughter, Avril lives in Sydney, Australia. When not writing or reading, she's thinking about food, wine and shoes.

After leaving her convent school, **Miranda Lee** briefly studied the cello before moving to Sydney, where she embraced the emerging world of computers. Her career as a programmer ended after she married, had three daughters and bought a small acreage in a semi-rural community. She yearned to find a creative career from which she could earn money. When her sister suggested writing romances, it seemed like a good idea. She could do it at home, and it might even be fun! She never looked back.

Tempted by the Tycoon

Tempted by the Tycoon
A Deal with the Devil

KATHERINE GARBERA

AVRIL TREMAYNE

MIRANDA LEE

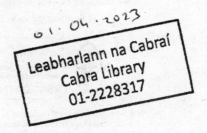
01·04·2023

Leabharlann na Cabraí
Cabra Library
01-2228317

MILLS & BOON

All rights reserved including the right of reproduction in whole or in part in any form. This edition is published by arrangement with Harlequin Enterprises ULC.

This is a work of fiction. Names, characters, places, locations and incidents are purely fictional and bear no relationship to any real life individuals, living or dead, or to any actual places, business establishments, locations, events or incidents. Any resemblance is entirely coincidental.

This book is sold subject to the condition that it shall not, by way of trade or otherwise, be lent, resold, hired out or otherwise circulated without the prior consent of the publisher in any form of binding or cover other than that in which it is published and without a similar condition including this condition being imposed on the subsequent purchaser.

® and ™ are trademarks owned and used by the trademark owner and/or its licensee. Trademarks marked with ® are registered with the United Kingdom Patent Office and/or the Office for Harmonisation in the Internal Market and in other countries.

First Published in Great Britain 2023
by Mills & Boon, an imprint of HarperCollins*Publishers* Ltd,
1 London Bridge Street, London, SE1 9GF

www.harpercollins.co.uk

HarperCollins*Publishers*
Macken House, 39/40 Mayor Street Upper,
Dublin 1, D01 C9W8, Ireland

TEMPTED BY THE TYCOON: A DEAL WITH THE DEVIL © 2023
Harlequin Enterprises ULC.

The Tycoon's Fiancée Deal © 2017 Katherine Garbera
The Millionaire's Proposition © 2015 Harlequin Books, S.A.
The Tycoon's Scandalous Proposition © 2018 Miranda Lee

Special thanks and acknowledgement are given to Avril Tremayne for her contribution to the *Sydney's Most Eligible...* series.

ISBN: 978-0-263-31849-4

MIX
Paper | Supporting
responsible forestry
FSC™ C007454

This book is produced from independently certified FSC™ paper
to ensure responsible forest management.

For more information visit: www.harpercollins.co.uk/green

Printed and Bound in Spain using 100% Renewable electricity at
CPI Black Print, Barcelona

THE TYCOON'S FIANCÉE DEAL

KATHERINE GARBERA

Sometimes we get lucky enough to meet people who will be more than acquaintances, more than friends… I've always thought of these people as kindred spirits, soul sisters. I've been very blessed to have these women in my life and on my journey, so this book is dedicated to them. Charlotte Smith, Courtney Garbera, Linda Harris, Donna Scamehorn, Eve Gaddy, Nancy Thompson, Mary Louise Wells and Tina Crosby.

One

Derek Caruthers was a badass. He knew it and so did everyone else he passed in the halls of Cole's Hill Regional Medical Center. He was one of the youngest surgeons in the country to have his stellar record and, aside from a few bumps along the way, he deserved his reputation as the best. Today he felt especially pleased with himself as he had been invited to meet with the overall hospital board. He was pretty sure he was going to be named the chief of cardiology as the hospital prepared to open its new cardiac surgery wing.

Mentally high-fiving himself, he entered the boardroom. Most of the members were already there but the new board member wasn't. The first item of business in today's meeting was to reveal who had been chosen to oversee the new cardiac wing. Derek had no idea who it would be, but given that Cole's Hill was a small town, and he'd heard that the new board member had a local connection to Cole's Hill, Derek was confident it would be someone he knew.

"Derek, good to see you," Dr. Adam Brickell said, coming over to shake his hand. Dr. Brickell had been Derek's mentor when he first started and the two men still enjoyed a close bond. The older doctor had retired two years ago and now sat on the board at the medical center. He had been the one to put Derek's name forward for chief.

"Dr. Brickell, always a pleasure," Derek said. "I'm really looking forward to this meeting. Something I usually don't say."

"Keep that enthusiasm, but there might be a wrinkle. What if the new board member has her own ideas about the cardiology department?" Dr. Brickell said.

"Her? I've yet to meet a woman I couldn't bring around to my way of thinking," Derek said. He didn't want Dr. Brickell to see any signs of nerves or doubt in Derek. Whoever this new board member was, Derek would win them over.

Dr. Brickell laughed and clapped him on the back. "Glad to hear it."

Derek's phone rang and Dr. Brickell stepped away to allow him to check his call. Given that he was a surgeon he never ignored his calls.

He noticed that it was from his friend Bianca. She and he had been besties for most of their lives. It had gotten a bit awkward on his side when he'd developed the hots for her in high school but all of that had ended when she'd moved to Paris to model, fallen in love with a champion racecar driver and married him.

But for Bianca, the fairy-tale romance and marriage had been short-lived; after only three years together, her husband had been killed in a plane crash, leaving her to raise a two-year-old son alone.

Well, because of that, Derek had once again made being Bianca's friend a top priority.

She'd been sort of fragile since she'd moved back to Cole's Hill. He knew it was the pressure her mom was putting on her to find a husband so that Bianca and her son wouldn't be "on their own."

He glanced around the room and caught Dr. Brickell's eye, gesturing that he needed to take the call. Dr. Brickell nodded and Derek stepped out into the hallway for privacy.

"Bi, what's up?"

"I'm so glad you're here. Did I catch you before the hospital meeting?" she asked.

"Yes. What's up?" he asked again.

"Mom has another man lined up for me to go out with tonight. Is there the slightest possibility you're free?" she asked.

No, and even if he were, he wasn't going to go there. They were friends by her design and probably for his sanity, he wasn't about to rock the boat by dating her. He would cancel for her but this was Wednesday and everyone in the Five Families area where they both lived knew that the Caruthers brothers had dinner at the club and then played pool on Wednesday nights. "It's pool night with my brothers and your mom will know that."

"Damn. Okay, it was worth a shot."

"It definitely was. I'm sorry. Who is it tonight?"

"A coworker from the network. He's a producer or something," Bianca said.

Bianca's mom was a morning news anchor for their local TV station. She'd been busily setting Bianca up on dates since she'd moved back to Cole's Hill.

"Sounds…interesting," Derek said.

"As if. Mom has no idea what I want in a man," Bianca said.

And that was a can of worms Derek had no intention of opening right now. "I've got to go. The board is almost all here."

"No problem. Good luck today. They'd be foolish not to pick you."

"They would be," Derek agreed. "Later, Bi."

"Later."

He disconnected the call and put his phone back in his pocket. He adjusted his tie as he looked down the hall for a mirror to check it and heard the staccato sound of high heels. He glanced over his shoulder, a smile ready, and his jaw dropped.

The woman walking toward him was Marnie Masters. Damn. She gave him a very calculated look from under her perfect eyebrows. Her blond hair was artfully styled around her somewhat angular face and teased to just the right height. She moved the way he imagined a lioness would when she sighted her prey and he didn't kid himself that he was anything other than the prey.

"Marnie, always a pleasure to see you," he said, though he'd been dodging her calls, texts and party invitations for the last eighteen months. So calling it a pleasure was a bit of a stretch.

"I would believe that if I didn't have to resort to taking this role on the board and leaving my practice in Houston in order to 'run into' you," she retorted.

"You're back in Cole's Hill?" he said, shaken. He knew he needed to get his groove back and put on the charm.

"Well, it's the new me. Daddy donated the money for this new cardiac surgery wing—at my suggestion—and the board agreed to his suggestion that I be hired to oversee the new wing. I just finished doing something similar in Houston and Daddy really wanted me to come home… So it seems as if you and I will be working together for the foreseeable future," Marnie said.

"I'm glad to hear the board has hired someone with your qualifications," he said.

"I imagine we will get to know each other much better now that I'm working here. It will give us a chance to spend more time together and get caught up."

Derek knew he couldn't just say hell no. But there was no way he was getting involved with her again. "I'm afraid that's out of the question."

"Why? There are no rules against it," she said, with a wink. "I checked."

"Of course there aren't any rules. It's just that I'm engaged," Derek said. "I wouldn't want my fiancée to get the wrong idea."

"Engaged?" Ethan Caruthers asked as he and Derek ordered another round of drinks at the Five Families

Country Club later that night. "Why would you say something like that?"

"You know Marnie. She wasn't going to accept a no. So I panicked and…"

"Said something over-the-top. Derek, that's crazy. I think when it becomes clear you don't have a fiancée, this could backfire," his brother said.

Ethan had a point. Already, his lie had added a wrinkle to his prospects for becoming chief of cardiology. Marnie hadn't been happy to hear about the engagement and had told the board that she was considering a few other applicants. Dr. Brickell had firmly been in Derek's corner, saying that the decision needed to be made sooner rather than later, but Marnie had stood firm. She'd insisted it would be two months before the final decision would be made and had enough support from other members to win the argument and temporarily table the decision.

The board had adjourned and Derek had gone back to work, doing two surgeries that had wiped the fiancée problem from his mind until he'd shown up here. Ethan was the only one of his brothers waiting when Derek had arrived.

"Tell me about it," Derek said. "If I could just find a woman…someone who needed a guy for a few months."

"Would Marnie believe one of your casual friends was your fiancée?" Ethan asked.

"No. I told her it was someone special and that's why it was under wraps."

Ethan took another swallow of his scotch and shook

his head. "Damn, boy, you always did have a gift for telling whoppers."

"I know. What am I going to do?"

"About what?" Hunter asked, joining their group. Hunter had recently moved back to Cole's Hill after spending the better part of ten years playing in the NFL and traveling the country promoting fitness while dodging the scandal of being accused of killing his college girlfriend. Recently the real murderer had been arrested and charged with the crime, which had enabled Hunter to finally break free of the dark cloud of suspicion. He was now engaged and planning the wedding of the century according to their mother and Ferrin, Hunter's fiancée. Everyone was in wedding fever in Cole's Hill.

"He needs a fiancée," Ethan said with a bit of a smirk.

Derek reached over and punched his brother. Of course Ethan would think it was funny. With only eleven months separating the two of them they were "almost twins," and as Ethan was the older of the two, he had always been a little smug.

"Do I want to know why?" Hunter asked, signaling the waitress for a drink as he sprawled back in his chair.

"Marnie Masters."

Hunter threw his head back and started laughing. "I thought you broke up with her years ago."

"It's been eighteen months," he said. He had broken up with her two years ago but had given in one night six months later when he'd been in Houston and slept with her again. It had just renewed Marnie's belief that he wasn't over her and that they should get back together. He'd been avoiding her ever since.

"So why do you need a fiancée?" Hunter asked.

"Marnie's the new board member brought in to oversee development of the surgical wing at the hospital. I panicked when I saw her and announced that I was engaged when she suggested we'd have a chance to spend time together."

"Ah," Hunter said. "Do you have someone in mind?"

"Not really," he said, but he knew that wasn't true. His mind kept pushing one face forward. She had nicely tanned olive skin, thick long black hair and the deepest, darkest brown eyes he'd ever gazed into. She was also not looking for marriage and needed a break from her matchmaking mother. He could provide her cover. But she'd have to be crazy to go along with his idea.

And she wasn't.

She was a single mom who needed her best friend to be there for her. Not come up with some scheme that would enable him to act out his long-held fantasies of calling Bianca Velasquez his.

Even if it was only for two months, three tops.

Damn.

Just then, Derek noticed her walk into the room with a guy who was a couple of years older than they were. She was smiling politely but he knew her routine. She'd brought him to the club for dinner so that when it was over she could politely bid him adieu and then walk the few blocks back to her parents' house in a nearby subdivision.

She was elegant. Graceful. The kind of woman whom

dashing A-listers fell for. Not the kind of woman who'd agree to a fake engagement.

"Uh-oh," Ethan said.

"What-o?" Hunter said.

"That has never been funny," Derek said.

"It's a little funny," Ethan pointed out.

"Not tonight," Derek said.

"I'm still not caught up. Where is Nate?" Hunter asked. Nate was their eldest brother and the last of three of them to arrive. He had recently married the mother of his three-year-old daughter, Penny. Derek liked seeing his eldest brother take on the role of husband and father.

"He's running late. Something to do with taking Penny on a ride before he could drive into town," Ethan said. "Being a daddy has changed him."

"It settled him down," Hunter said. "You two should try it."

"I am, sort of," Derek said. The idea of really settling down and getting married wasn't appealing. He was married to his job. It took a lot of focus and concentration to be a top surgeon and most women—even Marnie—didn't really get that. They wanted a man who paid at least as much attention to them as the job.

"What you're doing doesn't count," Hunter said. "Bianca deserves better than a fake proposal."

"It's probably as close as I'm going to get," Derek admitted. He knew that Ethan was hung up on a woman who was married to one of his friends. So that was probably not going to happen, either. "You know we're the ones who aren't letting the gossips of Cole's Hill down.

They like to think of us as the Wild Carutherses, which we can't be if we are all married up."

"I'll drink to that," Ethan said.

Derek toasted his brother and when Nate joined them a few minutes later the conversation thankfully changed from his fake engagement. Derek ate and drank with his brothers and kept one eye on the bar area where Bianca and her date were. He was ready to help her out. Like a friend would. That was all. Hunter had been right: there was no decent woman who wanted a fake fiancé.

Bianca Velasquez wasn't having the best year. She'd rung in New Year's by herself on the balcony of a royal mansion in Seville while Jose was en route to meet her. His plane had crashed and that had been…well, devastating. She'd never had the opportunity to finish her business with Jose. She'd been mad at him and had said to herself she'd hated him but the truth was he'd been her first love. They had a child together and no matter how many women he slept with while traveling the world on the F1 racing circuit, she…well, she hadn't been ready for him to leave her so abruptly.

She rubbed the back of her neck as what's-his-name droned on about a hobby he'd recently taken up. To be honest she had no idea what he was talking about. She'd zoned out a long time ago. And the thing was, he seemed like a nice man. The kind of man who deserved a woman who would engage in conversation with him instead of marking time and eating her dinner and dessert so quickly she gave herself indigestion. But Bianca couldn't be that woman.

"And I've lost you," he said.

She smiled over at him. He was good-looking and charming, everything she'd normally like in a man. "I'm sorry. This is a case of it really not being you, but me. I'm just…"

He shook his head. "I get it. Your mom mentioned this was a long shot but I couldn't resist seeing if you were as beautiful in person as you were in your photographs."

She blushed. She'd been a full-time model by the time she was eighteen and had gotten a contract that had taken her to Paris and launched her career as a supermodel. It had been in Paris where she'd met Jose and fallen for him. But she was older now and no longer felt like that carefree girl. "Those photos were a long time ago."

"Which photos? I'm talking about the one on your mom's desk," he said.

"Oh. This is embarrassing. I am totally not myself tonight," she said. "I'm sorry to have wasted your time."

"It wasn't a waste and if you ever feel like trying this again," he said, "give me a call."

He got up and left and she sat there at the table, staring out the windows that led to the golf course. The sun had long since set. She should head home but her son was already in bed and her mom would probably want to grill her about the date. And that wasn't going to go well.

So instead she signaled her waiter to clear away the dessert dishes and ordered herself a French martini.

"Want some company?"

She glanced up to see Derek Caruthers standing next to her table. He wore his hair short in the back and longer on top; it fell smoothly and neatly over his forehead. When they'd been kids his brownish blond hair had been unruly and wild, much like Derek himself. These days he was a surgeon renowned for his skills in the operating theater.

"I have it on good authority that I am not that charming tonight."

He pulled out the chair that her date had recently vacated and sat down. "Surely not."

"It's true. I was the most awful date. I felt like the worst sort of mean girl."

He signaled the waiter for a drink, and a moment later he had a highball glass filled with scotch and she had her martini.

"To old friends," he said.

"To old friends," she returned the toast, tapping the rim of her glass against his.

"How'd the meeting go today?" she asked. She envied Derek. He had his life together. He knew what he wanted, he always got it and unlike her he seemed happy with his single life.

"Not as I'd planned," he said.

She took a sip of her drink and then frowned over at him. "That's not like you. What happened?"

"An old frenemy showed up, making problems as is her habit and I had to shut her down," Derek said, downing his drink in one long swallow.

"How?" Bianca asked. "Tell me your troubles and I'll help you solve them."

It was nice to be discussing a problem with Derek. A problem that didn't involve her. The thirty-something who'd moved back in with her parents. She knew the gossips in Cole's Hill had a lot to say about that. From jet-setter to loser in a few short months. She pushed her martini aside realizing she was getting melancholy.

"Actually you can help me out," Derek said, leaning forward and taking one of her hands in his.

"Name it. You're one of my closest friends and you know I would do anything for you."

"I was hoping you'd say that," he said.

She smiled. Of course she'd help Derek out. He'd always been her stalwart friend. When she'd dreamed of leaving Texas and going to Paris to model, he'd listened to her dreams and helped her make a plan to achieve them. When she'd been lonely that first year, he'd emailed and texted with her every day.

"What do you need from me?"

"I need you to be my fiancée."

Two

Fiancée.

Was he out of his mind?

She shook her head and started laughing. Once she started she couldn't stop and she felt that tinge of panic rise up that she thought she'd been successfully shoving way deep down in her gut.

"Thanks, I needed that," she said. "You have no idea what kind of week it's been."

Derek leaned back in his chair, crossing his arms over his chest, which drew the fabric of his dress shirt tight against his muscles. Distracted, she couldn't help but notice the way his biceps bulged against the fabric. One thing that had been hard for her in the years of their friendship was to ignore how hot Derek was. He worked out. He had said one time that a surgeon had to be a precise machine. And that everything—every part of his body and mind—had to be in top shape.

"I'm not joking."

"Uh, what?" she asked. She was tired. Life hadn't worked out according to her plans and if she'd thought that once she reached this age she'd have everything all figured out, she was wrong. Really wrong.

She pushed her martini glass away, feeling a bit as if she'd followed Alice down the rabbit hole. But she knew she hadn't.

"I need a fiancée," Derek said. "The new board member who holds the fate of my career in my hands? It turns out she's a borderline obsessive I dated a while ago. The only way to keep her off my back is to make sure she knows I'm off the market."

"And how do I fit into this?"

Derek tipped his head to the side and studied her. "You could use a fake fiancé as well."

She still wasn't following. She was tired and her heart hurt a little bit if she were completely honest. Derek was one of her best friends and this sounded fishy to her.

"Why?"

"So your mom will quit setting you up on blind dates. You're too kind to tell her you aren't ready to date. If we are engaged then everyone will back off and leave us alone. I can focus on wowing everyone on the board at the hospital so that they have no choice but to name me chief. You can figure out what you want to do next without the pressure your parents are putting on you."

She put her elbows on the table and leaned forward.

When he put it like that she'd be a fool to refuse. "Are you sure about this?"

"I am," he said.

When wasn't Derek sure? She should have already known that would be his answer.

"If we're engaged, why would we have kept it quiet?" she asked.

He leaned in closer to her. "To give Hunter and Nate time in the spotlight. Hunter's wedding is really taking up everyone's energy."

"It is. And Kinley is busy planning it. She's going to wonder why I never even mentioned we were dating."

Bianca and Kinley were good friends. They both had been single mothers with toddlers the same age. Of course, Kinley wasn't single anymore and had found happiness with Derek's brother Nate.

Derek took her hand in his and a tingle went up her arm. "Tell her I asked you to keep it quiet."

"Hmm…it might work. Could I have until the morning to think about it?" she asked.

He nodded.

She pulled her hand away and then sat back, linking her hands together in her lap. Her palm was still tingling. She knew that saying yes would be the easy choice. But what about her son? Benito wouldn't understand that they were just pretending. Though given that he was only two years old he might not understand much of anything that was going on. He was good friends with Kinley's daughter…so he had been asking about his papa lately. He really didn't remember Jose at all.

"That sounds like it would be ideal but we live in the real world."

"Really? I hadn't realized that when I was operating on two different patients today," Derek said.

She recognized the sarcasm as one of his defense mechanisms and she didn't blame him. She was scared. The last time she trusted a man it had been Jose and his word hadn't been worth much.

"I'm not bringing this up to be difficult. I have a son. He's not going to understand why you are in our lives for a short time and then gone," she said. "We aren't twenty anymore, Derek, it's not like when you came to Monaco and we were wild. I'm a mom. You're in line to be chief of cardiology. We're...we are adults."

"Dammit. We can be adults and still be ourselves. You know me, Bi. You always have. I'm not going to disappear from your life when this is over. We're still going to be friends and I'd never cut Benito out. He's your son and just as important to me as you are."

Derek stood up. "Come on. Let's go for a walk where we can talk without worrying who might hear us."

She looked around and noticed they were gathering attention. She should have realized it sooner. "What about the pool game?"

"The boys can make do without me," Derek said. "This is more important."

There was a sincerity in his eyes; she wanted to believe in him. Well, that stunk, she thought. She'd thought she'd somehow become immune to the charm of handsome men. Of course, this was Derek and not some playboy whose parents she didn't know.

But still she'd like to think that her heart beat a little faster when he said she was important. She'd always liked Derek. He'd been one of her closest friends in middle school. He'd had the classic Caruthers good looks, but he'd been supersmart and once he'd graduated high school early and gone off to college and then medical school, they'd kept in touch first on AOL messenger, then on the different social media apps.

Years had passed before she'd seen him as an adult and she'd been blown away by how attractive her old friend had become. Of course, she had a different life by then, but there were times when it still surprised her. She never grew tired of the strong, hard line of jaw, his piercing eyes and the way his hair curled over this forehead. There was something about him that made her want to keep looking at him.

Dangerous.

As dangerous as listening to his idea for this fake engagement. Was there ever an idea that sounded dumber?

Maybe her mom setting her up with young men she knew in the South Texas area.

"What would this entail?" she asked.

Derek didn't allow himself to relax. This was Bianca. Bianca Velasquez. She'd been the prettiest girl at the Five Families Middle School. Though he'd taken an accelerated course in Houston so he'd be able to leave Cole's Hill and go to college early, they'd always kept in touch. At first he'd thought it was because of their families. Growing up there had been a lot of cotillion dances and Junior League events where their moms had thrown them together. But then as they'd both become adults, he'd thought the crush would fade.

It hadn't.

He knew that she wasn't the girl he'd dreamed about in middle school and high school anymore, but there was another part of him that wanted to claim her. That wanted to know that he had won over the prettiest girl from the Five Families neighborhood. That she was his.

Even just temporarily.

She was watching him cautiously. Almost as if she were afraid to trust him. That hurt.

More than it should have.

Granted, he was coming to her with a harebrained scheme, the kind that make his dad laugh his ass off at him. But she did need a break from the blind dates. And he did need a fiancée. He wasn't about to get involved with Marnie again and she would be relentless if he didn't provide a distraction.

"The hospital board has promised to make a decision in two months' time. So I'd need you to be my fiancée for about three months just so that you can attend the gala after I'm announced chief and the wing is opened," he said. Three months. That should be enough to convince him that any crush he'd had on her was well and truly dead. He could go back to being her friend and stop having hot dreams about her.

"Three months? Would we live together?" she asked. "I've been looking for a job and have some modeling gigs set up so I won't be in town continuously during that time. Would that be a problem?"

Derek leaned back in his chair trying to stay cautiously optimistic, but it seemed to him that she was almost on board with the idea. "I don't think so. In fact, I might be able to swing some time off and go with you. It would probably enhance the entire engagement story."

"Fair enough. What about the bachelor auction? I see you're already on the list. Would an engaged guy be on there?" she asked.

"Yes, because we were hiding our engagement. You can bid on me and win me now," he said with a wink.

"If we're engaged why do I have to bid on you?" she asked with a wink back. "My brother is already into me for a month of babysitting if I win him."

Derek had to laugh. The bachelor auction might have been one of the Five Families Women's League's largest fund-raisers but the men were always trying to get out of it. He just didn't like the idea of being at the mercy of someone who'd "won" him.

"I'm offering you three months of no blind dates," he said.

"That's something that Diego can't match."

"Yeah, I'm pretty sure people would not believe you were dating your brother."

"Thank God," she said, laughing. This time there wasn't the manic edge to her tone that had been there earlier when he'd first mentioned the whole engagement scheme.

"Yes. So what do you say? Are we going to do this?" he asked.

"Where would I live?" she asked.

"With me or not. Your choice," he said. "What do you want to do?"

He hadn't thought of anything beyond finding a woman who'd agree and then telling Marnie about her. But now that Bianca had mentioned living with him he knew he wanted her in his house.

Then he immediately had a vision of her in his bed. That thick ebony hair of hers spread out on his pillow, her chocolaty brown eyes looking up at him with sensual demand. Her limbs bare…

"Derek?"

"Huh?" His mind was fully engaged in the fantasy that had taken hold.

"I said, would you mind if I lived with you? I've been staying with my folks but we really need our own space."

He nodded. Living with him worked. "That sounds perfect. What do I need to do to get the place ready for you? Are we doing this?"

She leaned forward and he saw that same concern and uncertainty in her eyes and he realized that fantasies aside, he never wanted to put Bianca in a position where she was anything but a friend to him. He wanted her to be able to count on him. Even if that meant ignoring his own need for her.

"I want to say yes. Can I have the evening to think it over?" she asked, tucking a strand of her hair behind her ear. "I want to make sure I haven't missed any details and I want to run it by Benito. Make sure he's okay with another man in my life."

"He's two, right?"

"Yes, but he and I are very close and I just…after

losing his father, I want to make sure he's going to be okay," Bianca said.

Derek nodded. He wasn't going to force her. He was surprised she'd considered his offer and was willing to go along with it as far as she had this evening.

"That sounds fair," he said, pulling his phone from his pocket and checking his calendar. "I don't have any surgeries scheduled for tomorrow morning so I'm free. Would you and Benito like to come over to my place for breakfast? You can check it out and he can meet me."

"Sounds like a plan."

Too bad she didn't seem so convinced of that. He wasn't too sure how to convince her. This wasn't like the operating room where he knew all the variables and could make sure nothing went wrong. This was life where he tended to make mistakes, and he really hoped this didn't turn out to be a big one.

As she sat there with Derek, Bianca knew that one night wasn't going to be enough time to ensure she made the right choice. But then a two-year-long engagement to Jose hadn't really been beneficial in hindsight. This would work. She needed it to.

She had been struggling since she'd returned to Cole's Hill. She'd stayed in Spain for nine months after Jose's death and then just after Benito had turned twenty-two months old had decided to come back to Texas but she was no closer to figuring out what was next. She was the first to admit that her knee-jerk reaction of divorcing Jose when she'd found out about his mistress had been just her way of getting out of a bad marriage. She'd never thought beyond hurting him the way he'd hurt her. Now that he was dead, she'd hoped the anger would be gone, but she knew it was still there.

And not working, living with her parents where they had a cleaning staff and wanted to hire a nanny for her, just gave her too much time to think about—dwell on—the past. It was humiliating and not productive.

This idea of Derek's was a little bit on the crazy side, she knew that, but there was a part of her that really liked it. From certain angles, she saw it as the solution to all of her problems. She wanted to be out of her parents' house and out from under their overprotectiveness. She could research some career options besides modeling and give her a chance to be the kind of mom to Beni that she wanted to be.

"Yes. That sounds good to me," Bianca repeated. She realized she might have been staring at Derek. As their eyes met something passed between them that never had before.

A zing.

An awareness.

Oh, no. Had he figured out that she'd been secretly crushing on him for the last few months? How embarrassing. She gave him her cotillion smile—the one she always used to put boys in their place back in the day—and then pushed her chair back. "I think I should be getting home."

"I'll walk you back," he said. "Or we can steal one of the golf carts."

She shook her head. "I thought we both agreed to never speak of golf carts."

"No one will suspect a thing," he said.

"That's what you thought the last time. And I'm pretty sure that the groundskeeper knew it was us, even though he could never prove it."

"I'm pretty sure you're right. So, walking might be the safer option," Derek said in that easy way of his.

She felt silly thinking that there might have been something between them. It was probably all on her side. It had been a very long time without sex—since before Beni was born—and she wasn't dead. She had been hoping she'd at least feel okay hooking up with one of her mom's blind dates. But so far it hadn't worked out.

"You okay?" he asked, coming around to hold her chair while she stood.

"Yes. Sorry. Just tired. Being 'on' with a stranger is draining," she said.

Derek put his hand on the small of her back and she felt that zing again. This time a shiver spread up her spine and she stepped aside, fumbling for her handbag.

He followed her out of the dining room. She had an account at the club like all of the families who were members, so they didn't have to settle any bill.

"I need to let my brothers know I'm leaving," Derek said.

She nodded, still more in her head thinking about what he'd asked of her. His family was large, like hers, and she understood the dynamics of having siblings around.

The evening was warm; the unseasonable heat of the day hadn't dissipated yet. The parking lot was full of cars and though it was the middle of the week it felt like the weekend. The night was busy and full of life and she realized that was what she'd been missing.

She hadn't felt busy in a long time. She wasn't saying she had the whole mothering thing licked but she and Beni had fallen into a routine where she knew what to expect. And life had become routine instead of fun. She knew that was why she was thinking of taking Derek up on this idea. It was the first unexpected thing to happen to her since…well, for a really long time.

"I'm glad you're back in Cole's Hill," he said.

"Me, too. Remember how badly we wanted to get out of here?" she asked. "I really thought modeling was going to be the life for me. I mean I figured I'd be like Kate Moss and spend the rest of my life living in the jet set…but now, I'm sort of glad that I'm right here."

"Was Benito planned?" he asked.

"That's kind of personal," she said, but only because he'd stumbled onto an argument she and Jose had had many times.

"We're going to be 'engaged' and we're friends," he said. "Just asking because your dream life didn't sound like it included motherhood."

"It didn't. With all my brothers, I never thought about having a family of my own. I figured I'd be the cool auntie to my nieces and nephews," she said.

"So what happened?" he asked.

"Well…" She paused as they turned off the sidewalk onto the path that led to the manmade lake adjacent to her parents' house. She stopped on the bridge over the lake.

"Well?"

She put one hand on the railing and looked over at Derek. He was her good friend but there were so many things about her he didn't know. The embarrassing stuff that she shared with no one. And this was something that she never needed to tell him. This bit of humiliation had died with Jose.

She looked into Derek's eyes and started to tell him what she always did when she was asked about the baby. But in her heart, she remembered Jose saying that a baby and a family would stop him from looking outside of their marriage bed for company. That a family would ground him in a way nothing else could.

Three

Derek thought she'd have some sort of easy answer. Her modeling career hadn't been conducive to children, but she came from a big family as he did. It might be a bit old-fashioned but he had assumed she would end up wanting kids after she married. But her hesitance told him there was something more to it. He'd struck a nerve that he hadn't meant to and he should have just let it go.

But this was Bianca, and there was that look of sadness in her eyes that he didn't glimpse very often. He put his hand on her shoulder, felt that spark of awareness and shoved it down. She needed a friend not a guy who was turned on by her. That damned perfume of hers wasn't helping. It was subtle and floral and when the wind blew, he couldn't help inhaling a little more deeply.

"Bia?" he asked. "It's okay if you don't want to answer me."

She just glanced over at him with those big brown eyes of hers and he was lost. He realized this was exactly how he'd let himself get friend-zoned by her. She had very emotive eyes and he had always been suckered into wanting to comfort her, to be there for. To slay dragons for her. But Jose was dead so if he was the dragon there wasn't anyone to slay.

Besides she'd had the fairy tale: first-love marriage with Jose. That wasn't the problem.

"Hey, forget I asked. I was just making small talk," Derek said even though that was the farthest thing from the truth.

He heard his old man's voice in his head: *start out as you mean to go on.* Well, lying didn't seem like a really good place to start. But he'd asked her to be his pretend fiancée, not his real one. So maybe that meant they both were entitled to their secrets.

"It's okay. It's just that once I got married my life changed… I mean my priorities changed and then I got pregnant and once I held Beni in my arms, everything just sort of…" She paused, glancing over at him and arching one eyebrow. "Don't make fun of me."

"Why would I?"

"Well, when I had my son it was like a veil was lifted from my life and I realized how shallow I had been. When I considered that little face I wanted to be more. To be better. To give him the world—not material things—but experiences. It changed me."

He could see that. She pretty much glowed whenever she talked about her son. And Derek had seen her in town with the little boy and she seemed to be in her element when she was with him. He couldn't reconcile it but she almost seemed prettier when she talked about her son.

He remembered something his brother Hunter had said once…that women in love were more beautiful. And he finally saw that. He saw it on Bianca's face when she talked about her son. He had to be very sure that he was careful when she moved in with him. She might be his secret crush from adolescence but she was a woman now, a mother, and he couldn't afford to explore a "crush" unless she was looking for the same thing.

He took a deep breath, put his hands on the wooden railing and looked out over the lake. He'd grown up on the Rockin' C but he'd spent a lot of time with his dad on the golf course and hanging out at the club after school.

And as he looked at the moonlight reflecting on the water he thought about how much his town had changed. There was now a NASA training facility on the Bar T. Bianca was a famous supermodel, his brother a former NFL wide receiver. It was crazy.

"I don't think anything has lifted a veil from my life," Derek said out loud. He was still the same inside as he'd always been: determined to do whatever he had to in order to keep on track with his medical career. He'd left the ranch at fifteen and Cole's Hill to go to college, finished undergrad in three years and then gone on to medical school. There had been no stopping him.

"Maybe that's why this setback with being named cardiology chief has been such a shock. I just have always been focused on becoming a surgeon and then on making sure I was the best."

"You are the best," Bianca said. "You're lucky, Derek. You've always known exactly what your purpose is. Some of us stumble around until we find it."

"You? You never seemed to be stumbling."

She threw her head back and laughed, and he listened to the sound of it, smiling. She had a great laugh.

"That's just because I only let people see what I want them to."

"Like the Wizard of Oz?" he asked. They'd both been in the play in middle school. He'd been the Tin Man and she'd been Dorothy.

"Just like that. 'Pay no attention to the woman behind the curtain' should be the motto for my life."

"But not now, right? You have Beni," Derek said.

She shrugged. "I'm still faking it sometimes. I mean, he has given me purpose, but being a mom is tough. Every day as I reflect on what has gone on, I wonder if I've screwed him up...that's why I want to think this engagement over. I don't want to say yes and then realize that this decision is the one that ruined him."

Derek nodded. He was pretty confident in his personal life and in the operating theater but there were times when something went wrong and he had to keep going over the surgery to see what had happened. Had he missed something? Had the error been his? How could he keep it from happening again? He'd never thought that Bianca would be like that.

She seemed confident and able to conquer anything. Seeing that she wasn't perfect made him want her even more. It made her real. Not the image of the girl he'd had a crush on, but the real woman.

This night had taken a turn and she wasn't sure she was that upset by it. She had been saying that she wanted something different to happen. That she was tired of the Wednesday night blind dates set up by her mom that coincided with her dad taking Beni and her brothers out to dinner at the Western Two Step. Her father had missed out on bonding with Beni after his birth as they had been living in Spain. So her father was determined to make up for lost time. And the Wednesday nights with the boys were a long-established tradition in their family. It was a sports bar of sorts that had a huge gaming area in the back; they served what her father called "man food." Pretty much just burgers, steaks and fried everything. It was a tradition in their family for as long as Bianca could remember.

When she'd been in her teens every Wednesday she and her mom would have a spa night and go and get pedicures and manicures or facials or massages. And have a "girl's night out." Somehow her mom's desire to see her with a new man had taken over girl's night. Bianca knew that saying she was engaged to Derek would probably make her mom happier than just about anything else right now. The top of her bucket list was seeing her daughter happy again.

She'd said that to her.

And now she was standing next to the lake with the

cicadas singing their song in the background and Derek was watching her with that too intent look of his. It was something she associated mostly with him when he was in surgeon mode. But tonight, he was concentrating on her.

She knew how important being named chief of the cardiology department was to him. He'd laid out his life plans when they were fifteen; at the time, he'd been getting ready to leave for college and she'd just gotten her first modeling job in Paris. They had been sort of thrown together as the two outsiders. The two who were leaving. And here they were again.

There was a bubble of excitement in her stomach, something that she hadn't felt since Beni had started walking and talking. She shook her head and cursed under her breath.

"What? Are you okay?" Derek asked.

She nodded wryly at him. "I just hate it when my mom is right. I mean, it would be nice if she started screwing up sometime. But every time I rail against her interfering in my life, something happens to show me she's onto something again."

"What are you talking about?" he asked.

She realized she couldn't tell him how she felt. He wanted a friend. Not a woman who was feeling all tingly and very aware of the shape of his mouth. He had a great-looking mouth. Why was she noticing it now? And now that she'd noticed it why couldn't she stop wondering how it would feel pressed against hers?

"Nothing... I think I can make it safely home from here if you want to get back to your brothers," she said.

The sooner she got away from the temptation that Derek offered the better she'd be. Maybe it was just her reaction to being with a guy who—what? The nice man her mom had set her up with had been good-looking, too. So why was she attracted to Derek and not to him?

And shouldn't that be a mark in the con column for going through with the pretend engagement?

But she knew she wasn't going to say no. Not now. Not since she'd noticed his mouth and couldn't get out of her mind if he was a good kisser or not.

It was shallow, but for once the weight that had been on her since Jose's death seemed to be long gone. She didn't feel like the hot mess she'd been. She felt almost…well, almost like her old self and there was nothing that would make her walk away from this.

She'd forgotten how fun it was to not know what was coming next. How much she enjoyed the first flush of attraction. And this was safe. Right? Derek wanted a fake fiancée. She could do that. Be close to him, have her little infatuation but protect her heart. She wasn't going to fall for Derek Caruthers. The man was married to his job.

Everyone knew that.

There was no sense in pretending that he'd ever be interested in any woman for longer than a few months. It was precisely why he'd suggested a temporary pretend engagement.

"You have the funniest look on your face," he said. "I'm not going to abandon you before I see you home. My dad would whup me if word got back to him."

She smiled because she knew he meant for her to.

"You can see me to the sidewalk outside the house. If you come to the door my mom is going to grill us both and we haven't made a decision yet. You promised me time to think."

As if thinking was going to do her any good now that lust had entered the picture. She closed her eyes, desperately tried to remember what fifteen-year-old Derek had looked like. Tall, gangly, still wearing braces and with a little bit of acne, but it didn't matter because as soon as she opened her eyes she found herself staring at his mouth.

Adult Derek's mouth was lush; his lips just looked kissable. She'd kissed her fair share of men and some of the kisses had been disappointing but his mouth… he looked like he wouldn't disappoint.

"Bianca, I'm trying not to notice but you are staring at my mouth," he said.

"Mmm-hmm," she said.

"It's making me stare at your mouth and that is putting some decidedly different thoughts into my head."

"Like what?" she asked, throwing caution to the winds. Maybe he'd suck at kissing and she'd be able to walk away from him.

Or maybe not.

Derek knew he was treading very close to the edge of someplace that there would be no turning back from. He might be able to make the whole platonic-friends-helping-each-other thing work if he was able to keep his mind off the curve of her hips and the way she nibbled her lower lip when she was mulling over something.

But when she looked at his mouth, chewed her lower lip…it didn't take a mind reader to figure out what she was contemplating.

And for the first time since his ill-fated affair with Marnie he was on the cusp of doing something that might derail his career goals. Because he was afraid one kiss wouldn't be enough. He wasn't ready to settle down until he'd been established as head of cardiology. He wanted to keep his focus on medicine. He needed someone like Bianca because she was respectable, well-liked and not the kind of woman Marnie would ever believe he'd coerced into being his fiancée. A smart man would remember that instead of reaching out and touching a strand of Bianca's hair as it blew in the summer breeze—and possibly blow his chance of her going along with the fake engagement.

A smart man would be taking two steps away from her instead of one half step closer and letting his hand brush the side of her cheek. Her skin was soft, but really that wasn't a surprise. She looked like she'd have prefect skin. The scent of her perfume once again drifted on the breeze and he couldn't help himself when she tipped her head to the side and her eyes slowly drifted closed.

She wanted his kiss.

He wanted to kiss her.

He leaned in and felt the soft exhalation of her breath over his jaw just before he touched her lips with his. Just a quick brush. That was all he intended but her lips were soft and parted slightly under his and he found himself coming back and kissing her again. He angled his head slightly to the right and she shifted as well and the kiss deepened. His tongue slipped into her mouth. She tasted of Indian summer and promises.

He shifted his hand on her head, cupping the back of her neck as he took all that she offered in the kiss. She was like the sweetest addiction he'd ever encountered and he knew that walking away, just forgetting this, wasn't going to happen. He wanted her.

He felt the stirring in his groin and his skin felt too tight for his body. He started to draw her closer to him but stopped. He didn't want to rush any second of this. He wanted this embrace to last forever.

Because this was Bianca. The girl who'd always been too pretty, too smart and some would say too good for him. He didn't want the kiss to end and her to come to her senses.

Maybe it was the moon or the night or the warm breeze making her forget that they were friends. That she'd friend-zoned him a long time ago but he knew he wasn't going to want to let her go. Not tonight.

But he had to.

He pulled his head back, looking down at her. Her lips were parted, moist and slightly swollen from his kiss. Her eyes slowly blinked open.

"Derek…that was…"

He put his finger over her lips. He didn't want to discuss it. "Just a kiss between friends. We're doing each other a favor and tonight, seeing you here in the moonlight, I just couldn't resist."

She chewed her lower lip for a second and then nodded. "Do you think it was an aberration? That maybe it won't happen again?"

Lying to himself was one thing, but lying to her was something else. "Honestly, I think we'd be kidding ourselves—or at least I'd be kidding myself—if I said I wasn't going to be tempted to kiss you again."

"Me, too," she admitted. "I was sort of afraid that you didn't feel the same."

"That kiss was…"

"Magic," she said. "Like you intimated earlier it was probably the pale moon and the balmy night that are making us a little crazy. We're friends. We are doing each other a favor. Complicating things by kissing each other and thinking about each other in a non-friend way—"

"Non-friend way?" he interrupted. "I didn't realize friends couldn't kiss each other."

"You know what I mean," she said, crossing her arms under her breasts in a defensive pose.

"I do. But I wanted you to know that your friendship comes first. I have to admit I've thought about kissing you since you came home this summer. I hadn't realized how much you'd changed. You're prettier than I remembered, which is saying a lot, since you were so beautiful when we were teenagers."

"Thank you. That is one of the sweetest things I've ever heard. I should be getting home," she said.

He took her hand in his and led her up off the footbridge to the sidewalk in front of her house. She didn't say anything else and neither did he. He felt like there had been too much between them for this one night. He needed her.

For his career.

And he wanted her.

For himself.

And never had he been so conflicted about what he wanted.

"I guess this is good-night."

"Good night," he said. "I'll see you and Benito in the morning?"

"Yes. Probably around eight unless that's too early."

Normally eight on a day off would be too early but this was Bianca. And he had a feeling he was going to spend a restless night remembering that kiss. And trying to figure out how he was going to keep from repeating it once she moved in with him. Unless he could sleep with her and then let her walk away. But since he'd promised to stay friends with her and her son, Derek thought it would be wiser to try to keep them from becoming lovers.

And his gut seemed to say that her answer would be yes. That they were going to be living together.

He needed a plan to keep himself together when that happened.

"That's perfect," he said.

He stood there until she entered her house and then headed back to the club.

Four

Her mom was waiting for her in the formal living room when she walked in the door. Bianca took her shoes off and then walked into the room and sat down on the settee next to her mother.

"Another dud?" her mom asked.

"Si," Bianca answered her in Spanish. "But I did have something interesting happen."

"Good. Tell me all about it," she said.

"Not yet. Probably tomorrow. I'm tired and need to process it."

Her mom reached over and pushed her hair back from her forehead. "Are you okay?"

She shrugged. She'd kept the gory details of Jose's cheating from her parents but her mom had somehow figured it out. Somehow talking about it out loud had always made her feel like it would be more real. Bianca had almost been able to fool herself into believing that no one else knew if she kept it silent.

"I'm getting there," she said. And she was. "I think you might be right that dating is a good idea."

"Of course I'm right," her mother said with a smile. "Want something to drink?"

"Not tea. Maybe sparkling water with lime."

"I have to work early tomorrow," her mom said as they approached the kitchen. Their housekeeper always kept the bar cart stocked with sliced citrus, maraschino cherries and olives.

Her mom drove to Houston very early in the morning for work at the TV station. She could have requested that the family move to Houston to make her commute easier but she never had. The Velasquez family was rooted in Cole's Hill. Bianca's father's family had settled here with a land grant from the Spanish king generations ago. The fact that they now made their money from a world-class breeding and insemination program for thoroughbred horses instead of from actual ranching didn't make a difference.

"Beni will have me up very early, too. And I have an appointment in the morning."

"That little scamp does like sunrise," her mom said. "Sit down. I'll get our drinks. I gave Caz the night off. No sense having her in the house with just me."

"Makes sense. Do you and Dad think you'll downsize any time soon?" Bianca asked. She wondered how long her parents would keep the big house now that it was just the two of them. Having her and Beni here really hadn't made a difference in the huge house. Growing up with four brothers she'd never felt crowded.

"I don't know. Your poppa doesn't want to consider moving. Instead he wants to be here for our grandkids. Are you thinking of moving somewhere else?" her mom asked.

"I don't know. I am really happy being back here and am trying to find something I can do so that Beni can grow up here, too," she said.

Her mind drifted to Derek. His idea was a sort of solution. This was what she needed to mull over. Was the risk of the attraction she felt for him worth the chance she'd have to really figure out what she wanted? The fake engagement would give her space to think. She was afraid if she kept living with her parents she'd start to want what they wanted for her and Beni. Not what she wanted for herself.

Her mom talked about the housekeeper and her father's new idea to trade his pickup in for a Harley and Bianca listened with half an ear. She missed her son. It was only a little after eight o'clock but he had a late nap on Wednesdays so he could stay out until nine with his uncles and his grandfather. She wished he were home so she could stare into his little face and try to decide if going along with Derek's idea was the right thing or not.

It was hard to believe that she was considering it. Why wouldn't she agree to it?

After that kiss she had another reason to think twice about his proposition. This wasn't as straightforward as it had been when Derek had first sat down at her table in the club and made his offer.

But she didn't regret the kiss.

How could she?

"Don't you think?" her mom asked.

"What?"

"You aren't listening to a thing I've said. Are you okay, sweetie?"

She shrugged. "Yes. But I have a decision to make and I'm not sure what to do."

"Can I help?"

"No!"

"Well, I was just offering."

"Sorry, Mom, I didn't mean it like that. This is just something I need to decide for myself. And it's weighing on my mind. I didn't mean to ignore you. What were you saying? Something about Dad and a motorcycle?"

Her mom took a sip of her sparkling water and then reached across the table, putting her hand on Bianca's and squeezing it. "When I was trying to figure out if I should give up my job and be a stay-at-home mom like everyone expected me too, I spent a lot of time mulling things over. And in the end, well, you know I chose the morning news job."

"I know. That must have been hard, Mom," Bianca said.

"It wasn't as hard as living with the decisions afterward. The first three or four months I second-guessed everything. Should I have been home when Diego fell off his skateboard and broke his arm? Was my job the reason it happened? All of these were making me crazy and I was very unhappy. But your poppa pulled me aside one night and sat me down and said no matter what decision I had made, not picking the other choice was going to haunt me. He told me to commit to the decision I had made. And enjoy my life."

Bianca hadn't thought she needed to hear anything from her mom tonight but as always, her mom had found the exact right thing to say.

"Thanks, Mom. Every time I think I'm all grown up and know what you are going to say you surprise me."

"Good. Keeps you on your toes," she said with a wink. "Want to talk or watch a reality show?"

"Reality TV, please. I need some fake drama in my life," Bianca said.

They spent the rest of the evening watching TV until her dad and Beni got back home. Beni was dozing in her dad's arms and her father carried the little boy up to his bedroom. After her parents left, Bianca changed him into his pj's and then lay down on the bed next to her son, watching him sleep.

She wanted to say yes to Derek's proposition. And if she was very careful maybe he could be the transition between this and the next phase of her life. He wanted temporary and she had the feeling temporary was all she could really handle right now.

Plus, it was Derek. He was one of the few men she could count on always having her back and usually not expecting anything in return. And he had never asked her for anything before. She was intrigued and knew that she wanted to do it.

Why was she hesitating?

The last time she'd followed her gut, it hadn't worked out so well, she admitted.

* * *

Derek had taken the long way back to the clubhouse and now was headed to the billiards room—which was just what the club called one of the fancy private rooms that had a pool table.

"What'd she say?" Nate asked as Derek walked into the room.

What had she said? He hadn't thought of anything but that kiss and how complicated she really was. So much more than he'd anticipated when he'd first thought of asking her to help him out. But he realized now that even though they were friends there was a lot about Bianca he didn't know. He was intrigued— he'd be lying if he said he wasn't. And a part of him was worried that if she said yes she'd be a constant distraction. The other part of him was concerned if she said no that he wouldn't be able to stop thinking about the kiss and he'd go after her.

And his track record with long-term wasn't the best. So that would mean losing her completely from his life when they were done with their arrangement. He wasn't sure exactly what it was he did wrong with women but generally speaking he wasn't friends with any of the women he'd slept with.

"D? Something wrong with your hearing?" Hunter asked.

Derek gave him the finger while he opened a bottle of Lone Star beer and took a deep swallow.

"She's thinking it over," Derek said, turning to face the room and his brothers. Ethan and Nate stood near the table, while Hunter was racking the balls.

"That's not really much better than a flat-out no. Are you sure about this?" Hunter asked.

Hell, yes. If he'd had any doubts they had been amplified the minute her lips had melted under his. He rubbed the back of his neck, glanced at his watch and realized only forty-five minutes had passed since he'd left her. How was he going to make it until eight the next morning when time seemed to be moving so incredibly slowly?

But telling his brother that wasn't something Derek wanted to do.

"Yes. I've never been as sure of anything other than that I am the best surgeon in the world."

Hunter clapped him on the back. "Okay. But you know we are going to tease the hell out of you about this."

"How would that be any different than what you always do?" Derek asked. "You're forgetting that you have a honeymoon and a wedding night coming up. I think you're in for your share of teasing."

"But you also have the bachelor auction," Hunter added. "You and Ethan are going to be representing the Carutherses. Don't let us down. Or are you going to use your engagement to get out of it? I wouldn't blame you one bit."

"That's a good idea. I should line someone up. We need to bring in the big bucks like we always do," Ethan said. The auction raised money for the women and children's shelter.

"We don't always beat everyone else. The Velasquez boys beat us last year. And the Callahans think they are going to have a better shot this year because of Nate and Hunter being taken," Ethan said. "Liam was bragging about it over at the Bull Pit last night."

"How'd that go for him?" Derek asked. Ethan might be a lawyer and a damned fine one but he was also a Caruthers and they were all fighters.

"He left with a black eye and I'm wishing I'd listened to Dad and learned to lead with my left."

Derek laughed. Ethan was too much. He sensed there was something going on with his brother but right now he needed to concentrate on his own problems.

"Good," Nate said. "We only were behind the Velasquez brothers last year because Hunter wasn't here. Even if he's off the market now, he's good luck. He always brings the women with deep pockets. Remember that year you had that socialite from New York bid on you?" Nate asked.

Hunter grimaced. "Yes. She was interesting, to say the least. I'm glad I'm out of the running this year."

"Don't breathe a deep sigh of relief yet. Mom is talking about having an auction next year where wives bid on husbands to raise funds for the women's shelter."

"Ugh. Let's play pool and drink so we don't have to think about this," Hunter said. "Besides, we are supposed to be making fun of Derek and his fake engagement."

"Is it on?" Nate asked. "I thought she was thinking it over."

"I wouldn't have figured Bianca would stoop so low."

"Just proves you're not as smart as you think you

are, Ethan. She's considering it. We're friends, so it's not like it's that far of a stretch."

"Whatever you say," Ethan said. "Better you than me."

They played pool and ribbed each other until two in the morning. Ethan had too much to drink and decided to bunk at Nate's apartment in town. Nate dropped him off on his way home to the family ranch and Derek walked to his house on the other side of the country club from where Bianca's family lived.

He'd bought the house once he'd decided to come back to Cole's Hill and practice medicine. He could have had a bigger career in a bigger city but it wasn't about bigger for him. It was about doing what he loved and helping the people of his community.

He let himself into his house and his dog, Poncho, came running to meet him. The pug had been a gift from his parents last Christmas. The house was empty though and he thought about how nice it would be to come home and have Bianca waiting for him.

And maybe taking her to his bed and finishing what they'd started with that kiss.

Beni woke Bianca up at five with his little hand on her face and she opened her eyes and stared into his wide-eyed gaze and smiled. She hadn't meant to fall asleep in her son's room last night. "Good morning, *changuito*."

She called him her little monkey just as her father had called her when she was little. Beni had a stuffed monkey—whom he called Gaucho—they'd gotten at the Rainforest Café in London the last time they'd been in the city.

"Morning, Mama. Didya miss me?" he asked.

"I did. That's why I slept in here with you," she said, kissing the top of his head and then ruffling his hair. "Is that okay?"

He nodded. "I missed you, too."

She hugged him close for a minute and then shifted back. "This morning we are going to have breakfast with a friend."

"Yay!" Beni said, moving with lightning speed from under the covers to sit up. "Who is it? Penny?"

"Not Penny. But we are going to see her on Friday night for a movie in the square. This is a friend of Mommy's. He's…" She trailed off. How was she going to explain to her son that Derek had asked them to live with him for a little while? "He's asked us if we want to stay with him while we are waiting to live in our own place."

"What about *Abuelo* and *Abuela*?" Beni asked.

"They'd live here. It's not far from here. We are going to take the golf cart over to his house."

"What about my car? And Gaucho?"

Bianca let her gaze drift over to the motorized miniature F1 car that Moretti Motors had sent him for his last birthday. The car was an exact replica of the one that Jose used to drive for them. She ruffled her son's hair. "All of your stuff will be there, too. Even the stuff we have in storage."

"Yay!" he said, jumping to his feet and then bouncing around on his bed. It would be nice to have her own space. Her parents had had to make one of the guest rooms into a playroom/nursery for Beni. She hadn't wanted to impose on them especially since she hadn't intended to stay her that long.

Moving in with Derek would be the impetus she needed to really get moving on finding her own place. He wasn't going to want her to stay after he received his promotion. And overnight she'd realized that one kiss wasn't really that scary. She could handle the attraction she felt for him.

She'd reminded herself they were friends first. And she wasn't all that sexual. That was one of the reasons Jose had used for having a mistress. The kiss was a fluke. One that she was determined wouldn't happen again.

Beni bounced close to the edge and Bianca grabbed him around his middle, catching him midair. She turned and pulled him down on the bed next to her.

"Tickle time," she said.

He started laughing and she felt his little fingers moving over her ribs. She laughed along with him, tickling him until her heart felt too full. She hugged her son close and thought more about this move and realized that she really was going to say yes.

She couldn't stay here in her parents' house forever. Though they'd never ask her to leave outright, Bianca realized all the matchmaking might have been her mom's way of telling her it was time to start thinking about what she was going to do with the rest of her life.

Even though she and Jose had been headed for divorce when he'd died, Bianca realized that she'd never had a chance to deal with her anger toward him. They'd fought, of course, but she'd always thought she'd see him again. She'd been so mad at him for dying that she hadn't really wanted to move on. She had unfinished business and she guessed that was why she'd been hiding out.

But Derek had given her something new to focus on. So she'd do this. She'd be his fiancée for three months. And she'd keep her lust for the surgeon under wraps so that they could both get what they wanted. A promotion for Derek and some breathing room for herself.

Beni's tummy grumbled and she sat up. "Hungry?"

"Yes," he said.

"Why don't you use the potty and then meet me on the patio for breakfast," she suggested. The sun was just starting to come up.

"Can we swim after?"

"Yes," she said. "We have to be over at my friend's at eight so we have a little bit of time."

"Yay!" he said. He'd used to say *fantástico* whenever he was excited but his new friend Penny said yay. So he'd been using that a lot more. She noticed that his language was changing from mostly Spanish to English since they'd been back in Texas. Her family spoke some Spanish but mainly English at home, which was different from how it had been when Bianca and Beni had lived in Seville near Jose's family.

"I'll leave your bathing suit on the bed," she said to him in Spanish. Though it was early autumn it wasn't cold in Texas and her parents kept their pool heated.

"*Gracias*, Mama. I love you," he replied in Spanish.

She watched him run toward the bathroom and then

got out of bed. She found his racing bathing suit, a tiny Speedo that he liked to wear, and his water shoes and placed them on the end of the bed after she made it. Even though her family had always had a housekeeper her mom had insisted they make their own beds.

Bianca went into her room and donned her bikini and a cover-up. She pulled her hair up into a ponytail and then headed downstairs to get breakfast together for her and Beni. Even though it wasn't even six her mom had already headed out for work and her father had left a note saying he had gone to Austin to pick up something he'd ordered.

She and Beni had a light breakfast of fruit and then swam for an hour before she took him upstairs for his bath. She realized she was nervous and excited as she blow-dried her hair and put on her makeup. She took care using all the tips and tricks she'd learned from stylists during her years as a model to ensure she looked her best.

And only then did she feel like she was ready to go and see Derek.

She knew this was a fake engagement but the rest of the world wouldn't. Or at least that was what she told herself. Deep inside she knew that she wanted Derek to want her. Not to pity her. To see her as a woman he wanted by his side, not one he needed in order to keep his she-wolf at bay.

Five

Derek had never been around kids much. He had a new niece who was Benito's age—Penny. She was Nate's daughter but Nate had only found out about her a few months ago. So Derek and the rest of the Caruthers family were just getting to know her. Penny talked a lot. And now, as the morning progressed, Derek soon realized that Benito was a bit of a chatterbox as well.

He was adorable. He spoke English with a slight accent and he was very polite. It was also clear to Derek that Benito and Bianca had a close bond. The little boy never did anything without checking with his mom first.

While Derek had been awake most of the night waiting for Bianca to come over, this morning he'd thought a lot about her marriage to Jose and how this temporary thing he'd suggested could ever only be something between friends. Everyone—and he meant everyone in the world—knew that Bianca and Jose had been a fairy-tale love match. Her marriage had even been covered by E! and *InStyle* magazine. Not that Derek watched or read either of those things but his office manager did and she'd kept him up to date on the details.

How could she ever move on from the love of her life? And if she did, Derek suspected it wouldn't be with him. He was the rebound guy. The one who would make it easy for her transition to whoever was next in her life. And that was fine with him, he thought. He wasn't looking for more than that and neither was she.

He had brought them to the courtyard of his house. Built back in the 1980s, it was a large Spanish mission-style place with a central courtyard. There were two bedrooms on the ground floor that both opened onto the courtyard; the living room, kitchen and dining room did, too. He had a pool in the backyard and a large fire pit and outdoor kitchen. But the courtyard had a big fountain in the middle that had to be turned on. Benito had brought a stuffed monkey with him and Derek led him to the small stash of boats that Penny had played with the one time that Nate had brought her to his house.

He had asked his…well, butler sounded silly and housekeeper always made everyone think of a woman. Anyway, he'd asked Cobie, the guy who took care of the house and grounds and lived in the pool house, to make sure the fountain was on this morning and that breakfast was waiting for them on the table. It was just scrambled egg whites with spinach and turkey bacon, but Derek wanted to be able to offer Bianca and her son something to eat.

"Have you had breakfast?" he asked.

"Yes, but that was hours ago and we've had a swim, so we are hungry, aren't we?" Bianca asked her son.

"Si. Muy hambriento."

Benito ate the turkey bacon and a small portion of the eggs before asking if he could get down. Derek had noticed his eyes drifting to the fountain.

"There are some boats over by the fountain if you want to play with them while your mom and I finish eating," Derek said.

"Can I?" he asked Bianca.

"Si, be careful."

"Yay! I will be," Benito said. "Mama, will you watch Gaucho?"

"I will."

Bianca helped her son out of his chair. They placed the stuffed monkey in the center of the cushion on the chair and Bianca took her son over to the fountain. Derek listened as she gave the boy a few instructions, but he was distracted by watching Bianca. She was breathtakingly beautiful this morning. She wore a slim-fitting sundress, and when she knelt next to her son to talk to him, the skirt pooled around her legs. Her arms were lean and tanned. As she stood up and turned to walk back to the table, she noticed him staring at her.

He simply shrugged. She had to be used to men staring at her.

She arched one eyebrow at him but smiled.

He stood and held her chair for her so she could sit

down. Once he was seated again he took a sip of his orange juice and then folded up his napkin and placed it next to his plate. He wasn't hungry and pretending he was seemed foolish to him.

"Have you made your decision?" he asked as she carefully broke a piece of the bacon in half.

She put the bacon down on the plate and then wiped her fingers on her napkin. "I have."

He waited, expecting her to expand, but she didn't reply. Instead she pushed her sunglasses up on the top of her head, glancing over at her son, who was happily splashing the boat around in the water.

"And?"

She turned back to face Derek and nodded. "I'll do it. I think… I think we can make this work for both of us."

Something shifted deep inside his soul and he felt a surge of excitement. "Good. Very good. I will figure out how to ask you in public so we can announce it to our families. We can say the meeting at the hospital forced us to go public before Hunter's wedding."

"Okay. I don't want to leave it too long. I've already mentioned to Benito that we might come and live with you," Bianca said. "And he's a toddler so keeping secrets is pretty foreign to him."

"That works for me. How about a dinner here on Friday night? That's tomorrow so it only gives us a little time for me to plan it and see if I can get my brothers and parents here. Can your parents attend?"

Now that she'd said yes, he wanted to get things rolling and get her moved in and his ring on her finger.

Then he wanted to announce their engagement at work and at the hospital.

"I will have to change our plans. We were meant to go the movie in the square on Friday night, but I think this should take precedence. My brothers might want to come," Bianca said.

"Fair enough. My dining room seats twenty. Or I could rent a room at the club," he suggested.

"That might be more public," Bianca said. "Do you need it to be public?"

Having Bianca's agreement made him want to get everything moving. He wanted everyone in Cole's Hill to know she was his fiancée. He knew it was temporary, but that didn't mean they had to act that way in public.

And the more people who knew about the engagement the more likely Marnie would hear about them together and then he wouldn't have to do anything other than be awesome at his job.

Being in public made her uneasy when she thought about what would be her second engagement. Everything about her marriage to Jose had been fodder for the gossip websites and part of that had been her fault. Her manager had suggested that if they publicized the wedding then she might be able to transition her career from cover model into lifestyle trendsetter—writing blogs, doing videos talking about products that her followers would then buy and showing people a slice of her life. She'd gone along with it. She had thought that it would be the next logical step in her career.

And Jose had loved the spotlight so his first instinct

was to say yes. And they'd done it all. Cameras had followed them around as they made selections for the wedding ceremony. Nothing had been private and a part of Bianca had always wondered if that had been the beginning of the end for her and Jose.

"I don't need it to be public. I'm happy to have it here. In fact we could set up some tables here in the courtyard and have dinner out here," he said. His brow was furrowed and she wondered what he was thinking.

She felt that shiver of fear down the back of her spine and realized that she'd forgotten this part of relationships. Second-guessing and never really being sure she was doing the right thing. She didn't want to start this again. What had she been thinking?

Before Jose had died but after she'd made the decision to divorce him, she'd thought she'd never get involved with another man again. It had been unrealistic but she realized now why she'd made that decision. She reached for her glass of juice, missed it and spilled it on the table.

She stood up to avoid getting any on her legs and reached for her napkin to dab it.

"Sorry about that," she said.

Derek put his hand over hers and stood up as well. "It's okay. What have I done?"

"What?" she asked.

"Something I said triggered a look of panic on your face and I don't want that. Listen, we're partners in this. We're helping each other out," he said, his voice calm and assertive.

In fact, it was so reassuring that she remembered

this was her friend. Derek. She didn't have to worry that he was going to fall out of love with her and start cheating on her because they weren't in love. But they were in this temporary thing together. And a man who was trying to convince the town and his ex-girlfriend and potential new boss that he was engaged wouldn't be tomcatting around.

She took a deep breath.

"Sorry. I just remembered the craziness of my last wedding and engagement and I didn't want to repeat that."

"No problem. I prefer to keep it private. That's more our style anyway."

"We have a style?" she asked, slightly amused now that her panic had subsided.

"We do. And it's kid-friendly and family-focused," he said. "I'd like to invite my best friend and my brothers and their significant others and of course my parents but otherwise that's it."

"Same. Kinley's my best friend so she's already on the invite list. We don't have to invite her twice," Bianca said, smiling. "Let me clean this up and then we can start making a list."

"A list?" he asked, reaching around her and scooping up the plates after sopping up the juice with both of their napkins. "I got the cleanup. You stay here with Benito."

"Thank you," she said, realizing how different Derek was from Jose, who never would have touched a dirty dish. To be fair to him he had employed a fairly large staff for the three of them. But still.

"No problem. It's not the 1950s. I think I can handle

cleaning up. Would you be okay if I bring Cobie back to help out with the planning? He's probably going to do the bulk of getting the courtyard ready since I've got surgery tomorrow morning."

Every word out of Derek's mouth just was further confirmation of how different he was from Jose. And she felt the last of her tension melt away.

She nodded. "That would be great."

He turned toward the French doors that led back into the kitchen and she followed him, putting her hand on his shoulder to stop him. "Thank you, Derek. I hadn't realized how much baggage I was carrying around from Jose and the way things ended with him. And this... I think this fake engagement is going to be very good for me."

He tipped his head to the side and gave her one of those smiles of his that was sweet and true and reminded her of the boy he'd been before life had shaped him into the arrogant surgeon he was today. "That's exactly what I was hoping."

He continued into the house and she turned to see Benito splashing in the fountain. He was maneuvering the boat and making huge waves with his hands. She smiled and started laughing. The sun was shining, her little boy was happy and for once she didn't feel the shadow of her past, of her doubts and of her ennui, hanging over her the way it had been for too long now.

She went over to Beni, scooped him up and kissed him on the top of his head.

"Mama! I'm playing," he said, squirming to get down.

"I know, *changuito*, I just needed a hug."

He stopped squirming and wrapped his little arms around her neck and held her tightly. "It's okay. I like your hugs."

She set him down and watched him go back to his play before realizing that it had been a while since she'd seen Derek. She glanced over her shoulder and noticed he was watching her. And the look on his face made a shiver of awareness go down her spine.

Derek knew he had to keep things cool. But seeing the expression on Bianca's face at breakfast had given him the first clue that things maybe hadn't been perfect in her marriage to that F1 racecar driver. He knew it was none of his business. They had an arrangement, but this was Bianca and he had never been able to be cool around her.

Well, he'd been able to maintain appearances on the outside, of course, but inside she'd always had the ability to stir up his base instincts and make it impossible for him to think.

Again he had that fleeting thought that this might be a mistake but there was no way he wasn't going through with it. Bianca Velasquez was going to live with him. She was going to be his fiancée.

And even if that was temporary, he was okay with it.

He struggled to keep his eyes and his mind on the planning of the party where they'd announce their engagement to their friends and family. Instead all he could think of was how long her legs were and how hot that kiss had been the night before.

He wanted another kiss. In fact his libido was hinting

that they should probably practice kissing again before they had to do it in front of everyone tomorrow night. It made sense. It was logical. They had to convince the people who knew them best that this was a love match and his brothers...well, they knew the truth. He had to warn them not to say anything to anyone else.

Not that they would but he wanted to chat with them before the dinner. He didn't want to have any problems on the night of the announcement.

"You have a very serious look on your face," Bianca said. "If you don't want lights strung over the garden, it's okay to say no. Remember what you said, we're partners in this."

"It wouldn't be that hard to rig it up," Cobie said, who had now joined them in the living room. "We already have the anchors from the Christmas lights in the beams. I'm not sure if I can get all the lights we'd need in town but I could drive to Houston for more if I need them."

"I think Mom has some. I'll call and ask her if I can borrow them," Derek said. "I don't mind the lights. I was thinking about something else."

"The food? I am a pretty fair cook," Bianca said.

"No. You're not cooking the food for the party," Derek said. "Cobie, call that catering company we used for Christmas and see if they can do it."

"Cobie, would you mind giving us a minute?" Bianca said.

Cobie raised both eyebrows at her and then shrugged and turned away. "Hey, little dude, want to see the pool?"

"Mama, is that okay?" Beni asked her.

"Si," she said.

Cobie held his hand out to Beni, who took it. Derek watched them both leave.

"What's up?" he asked.

"I don't mind if you prefer a caterer but I will not have you tell me what I can't do. It sends the wrong message to Beni and personally I don't like it. I'm a grown woman and I can make my own decisions," she said.

Derek hadn't meant it the way she'd obviously taken it. "Sorry. I just meant it was a special night for you and I didn't want you working to prepare food for twenty or more guests."

"Fair enough. I think it was the delivery method. Maybe next time you could phrase it less like you were trying to boss the little woman around," she said.

"I'm happy enough to do that," he said. "Sorry if it came out that way."

"No problem. And now that I know where you're coming from, I believe a caterer would be a good idea. I think Mom has one that she uses and I know the club will cater in your home," Bianca said. "Since Cobie is handling the lights and decoration, would you like me to handle the food?"

Derek hadn't thought about asking her to plan any of this. "Sure. Do you have time?"

"Well, since I didn't get the job of receptionist at your medical group...yes, I have the time," she said. She'd applied for a job at his medical practice thinking that would give her something to do. But his office manager had pointed out that Bianca didn't have any skills to be an office worker.

"You didn't want to be a receptionist. I did you a favor," he said. "And you did a favor to Jess whom we hired because she needs the job and the money. She's going to college and had been working two part-time jobs and making less than what we're paying her now."

"That makes me feel better. But I'm still not working and could use something to occupy my time."

"I thought you had a modeling gig booked," he said. They had never really discussed what she'd be doing once they were engaged.

"I do. But it's not for a couple of weeks. We probably need to sit down and compare our schedules. That gig is in Paris. Normally I stop by Seville when I'm done with my work, to visit with my...with Jose's parents before coming back to Texas. Would you like to meet them?"

No. He most definitely didn't want to meet Jose's parents. But he had a feeling that was jealousy. "That would be fine. I'll have to check my schedule and see if I'm available. I have surgeries scheduled and of course I'm on the ER rotation. Most of my time off isn't until October."

"I had no idea," she said. "I've never really paid attention to a surgeon's schedule. I'll go by myself to Paris. And I'll make it a short trip. Might be better if you didn't meet them after all."

"Why?"

"Because this is temporary," she said. "It felt a little real for a minute and I need to remember it isn't."

He didn't want to dwell on the temporary part of it

or the jealousy he'd felt when she'd mentioned Jose's parents. But the truth was in three months she'd be back out of his life and he'd be right back where he was now, except he'd be chief of cardiology at Cole's Hill Regional Medical Center.

He ignored the part where she'd said it felt real. Because no matter how hollow he felt at the thought of her leaving, he knew she would leave. And that needed to stay in the front of his mind.

Six

Derek came out of emergency surgery and washed up at the sink. The day had been long. Longer than he'd anticipated. But being on call was by its very nature unpredictable and he couldn't complain since it was also invigorating. He knew better than to ever say it out loud but there was something about having a patient come in who no one had thought would make it and then saving the person.

His skills, training and natural ability made it possible. But now that he was out of surgery he was exhausted. He cleaned up and then turned to find Marnie standing in the doorway that led to the waiting area. He had to talk to the patient's family and he really didn't have the time to deal with her.

She looked thinner than when they'd been together

and she'd done something different with her eyebrows that made her look like she was scowling. She seemed so…defensive, and he hadn't even said anything to her yet.

"I have to see the family," he said. "I don't have time to discuss anything with you."

"We can talk when you're done," she said. "I have all night."

"I don't," he said.

"Oh, that's right, you have to get back to your fiancée," she said. "Who is the mystery woman?"

"We're having a dinner tomorrow night to announce it to our families and then I'll be happy to share the news with you," he said, brushing past her to walk to the waiting room and the family of his patient.

"Are you sure there is one? It doesn't seem your style to keep things quiet. I figured you'd have a skywriter do your names in a heart in the sky."

He stopped walking and turned to face her. "Really? Marnie, that sounds like something you'd like. I'm not that kind of guy. Besides, my fiancée's first marriage was very public and she'd like to keep this one quiet."

"Her first marriage? Are you sure you want to take a chance on a divorcée?" Marnie asked.

He sighed heavily. "I don't have time for this. And if I did I'd have to point out that following me around while I'm trying to work isn't exactly giving me space."

She held her hands up at shoulder level. "Sorry. I'm leaving. I look forward to hearing more about your mystery woman."

Marnie turned and headed down the hallway and

Derek went to talk to the family. The patient was a high school student who'd collapsed during football practice so the family was…well, it took Derek a while to explain everything to them. He stayed with them as long as they needed to talk. The mom kept hold of his hand and said thank-you so many times that Derek was starting to feel uncomfortable. Finally, his nurse came and rescued him.

"That took forever," he said to Raine as they walked away from the family.

"Sorry, the new board member stopped by and wanted some details and it took me forever to get rid of her," Raine said.

"Marnie."

"Yes. Didn't you use to date her?"

"Don't remind me. I'm going to shower and change. Is Dr. Pitman here?" Derek asked. Pitman was a partner in Derek's practice and they checked in on each other's patients when they did rounds at the hospital.

"He just arrived. He's ready to debrief with you," Raine said. "His nurse is running late. Her kid had something after school so I'm going to stay until she gets here."

"Okay. I'll see you in the office tomorrow morning," he said. "Oh, by the way, I'm engaged."

"Engaged? I thought you said one woman couldn't tame you," she said with a wink.

Raine might work for him but they'd always had a good relationship and she treated him like a kid brother. She was ten years older and Derek had relied heavily on Raine when he'd first started practicing on his own.

She had experience with people, which he'd lacked. He'd been a wiz in surgery but patients and their families had complained about his bedside manner—a lot. And Raine had been the one to help him figure out how to deal with them.

"Well, one did. Don't be surprised. I wasn't shocked when you finally roped a guy into marrying you."

She punched him in the shoulder. "Show some respect. I didn't even have to hogtie him."

"I'll remind Jer of that the next time I see him," Derek said.

"You do that," she said with a cheeky grin. "Who's the lucky girl?"

"I need you to keep it quiet. We are telling our families tomorrow night," he said.

"It won't be hard. You know I don't gossip," she said.

"I know," he said. "It's Bianca."

"Velasquez. Isn't she a model?" Raine asked. "She's the one whose husband died in the plane crash, right?"

Derek realized that everyone was going to know little pieces of Bianca's story. She was a pretty big deal in Cole's Hill because of the fame she'd found as a supermodel. "Yes. We grew up together and have been friends forever."

"Congratulations, Derek. I'm happy for you," Raine said. "Can't wait to meet her."

"Thanks," he said. Just then Raine got paged and he waved her off as he headed to the locker room to shower and change. He wanted to pretend that it didn't matter to him that everyone knew Bianca had married the love of her life. And that he could never be more than the second choice.

It was fake, for God's sake. He knew that. So why did it hurt?

Why was he upset that everyone was going to assume he was a runner-up for the woman who'd had it all?

He hated losing and he hated even more when people thought he lost. And he was still fuming, even after he'd showered, put on his clothes and got in his Lamborghini, speeding out of the parking lot and out of town toward the Rockin' C.

Bianca had arranged to meet Kinley and Penny at the coffee shop in town. The beverages were really nice and the pastries and bakery items were made here in town. Once the morning commuters were all at their nine-to-five jobs it became the place for young moms and their kids to hang.

Benito and Penny were sitting together in one of the padded armchairs. Penny had gotten a new book in the cowboy picture book series she was reading and together they were making up stories that went along with the pictures in the book.

Kinley had volunteered to go and get the drinks and as soon as her friend returned with the tray of iced tea for them all—the kids' drinks in cups with lids— Bianca glanced over her shoulder to make sure no one was close by.

"Why are you acting like a spy with some top secret info to pass?" Kinley asked.

Kinley was newly married to Nate Caruthers, the father of her child. The fact that Penny was almost three years old and that Nate—Kinley's new husband and Derek's brother—had just found out about Penny a few months ago had given the couple a few bumps but they were happy together now. Bianca noticed how easily Kinley smiled these days; it was like a weight had been lifted from her.

Which of course it had been. Keeping the secret from Penny's father had been a heavy burden for her friend.

"I have something to tell you, but don't want anyone to hear. Where's Pippa?" Bianca asked. Kinley's nanny usually accompanied her and Penny when they were in town.

"She's at home," Kinley said. "She needed some time alone today and since the bride I was supposed to meet canceled I'm free all day. So I told her to take the day. What's up with you?"

Bianca nodded. Kinley was one of the most in-demand wedding planners. She planned the weddings of A-listers and royalty, and was currently planning Hunter's wedding to Ferrin. They would be getting married at the end of the month.

"Lean in," Bianca said, putting her iced tea down and leaning forward.

Kinley did as she was told. "Okay, should we whisper?"

"I'm not being silly. I'm engaged."

"You're what?" Kinley asked, loudly.

"Kin."

"Sorry, it just took me by surprise," she said, leaning

back. She glanced around to see if anyone was paying attention to them and no one was. "Who is the lucky man?"

"Derek."

"What? How is that even possible?" Kinley asked. "I think I would have known you were dating."

"We kept it quiet and everyone was busy with your impromptu wedding and the planning of Hunter's big one," Bianca said. She'd been thinking about how she was going to tell her mom, and Kinley was sort of the test run. Her chance to test out the story she and Derek had come up with and to see if it was believable.

"Wow," Kinley said. "Does Nate know?"

"I'm not sure. So far, Derek and I have just kept it between ourselves," Bianca said.

"I bet he knows. Derek and he talk a lot. That rat. He should have told me," Kinley said.

"It's not his secret to tell," Bianca said.

"Fair enough. So when did it happen?" she asked. "Where's the ring?"

"Well, we are having a party for our families tomorrow night and after that I'll wear the ring in public," she said. Actually, she didn't even have a ring; she was going to need to do something about that. She made a mental note to talk to Derek about the ring thing.

"So that's what the dinner is for," Kinley said. "There is a lot of speculation about what was going on when you invited us all. Ma Caruthers is sure that Derek put you up to the party so he can weasel out of the Women's League bachelor auction."

"I wouldn't put it past him to try something like that. But that's not why we invited everyone to dinner."

Kinley grabbed her hand and squeezed it. "I'm so happy for you, Bianca. I love the idea of being sisters with you. Now I'm not trying to be mercenary but have you thought about a wedding planner."

"You know I want you to plan the wedding," she said because she knew that Kinley would expect her to. And she realized that the lies that she'd thought she'd have to tell by pretending to be engaged were bigger than expected. Each lie was leading to another one and she was going to be buried underneath them all.

In a way it was embarrassing that she'd lied to her best friend. She knew that her reasons were good but how was she going to fake-plan a wedding that she knew she was never going to have? She hadn't even considered this.

"Great. I can't do one for a few months. I'm slammed but I will make room for you," she said.

"That's okay. We want to let Hunter get married and then Derek is up for a promotion at the hospital so he'd have to settle in to a new job before we could marry and have a honeymoon. Just know when it's time to plan it, you're the only one I want to help with it."

Kinley nodded. "Are you sure about this? I remember watching your last wedding on TV."

"Yes. I am very sure. That was all for show and I never got to pick anything I really wanted. I had to use sponsors and what looked best in photos."

"Ugh. I mean from an industry insider I totally get

why they were insistent on stuff like that, but it was meant to be your special day."

In hindsight Bianca thought maybe the chaos of that first wedding was a harbinger of what her marriage had ended up becoming.

"Yes."

"Don't worry. Derek is a great guy and when you are ready to plan it, I know this wedding is going to be spectacular."

Kinley sat back and they chatted about other things, but Bianca was startled to have that out-of-control feeling again. She wondered if it was just because for once she had something going on in her life besides planning playdates for Beni or if it were something else.

Something more to do with Derek. An image of him in a tuxedo danced through her mind. She definitely wasn't going to do any pretend marriage planning because that made everything real.

Derek arrived at the Rockin' C driving through the big fence gates that he and his brothers used to climb on and ride when they swung open. The gates were always open these days since they didn't roam the cattle up this way anymore, and he sped past them.

Suddenly he realized he had no idea what he was going to say to his parents when he got out to the ranch. But as he turned his car toward the main house where Nate lived he decided to talk to his brother first.

He parked the car in the circle drive and hopped out, bounding up the stairs to the front porch in a couple of steps. He started to let himself in then remembered that

Nate and Kinley were married now and they might not want him just bursting in.

He rang the doorbell and listened to it chiming through the house. A few minutes later the housekeeper answered and directed him to the study where his brother was working.

"Why'd you ring the bell?" Nate asked as Derek came into the study and closed the door behind him.

"You're married now. Figured I shouldn't just barge in."

Nate laughed. "Very true. But Kin's in town with Penny so you're safe. What's up?"

Derek opened the little fridge in the credenza at the side of the room and took out a Dr. Pepper and offered one to Nate, who nodded. After he gave his brother his drink, Derek sat down on one of the leather guest chairs that were a new addition to the study since Nate had taken over running the ranch from their dad.

"I wanted to talk to you about tomorrow night. I need you and the boys to keep quiet about the fake engagement thing. I didn't tell Bianca that you guys know and I don't think she's going to mention it to anyone else."

"Not a problem. I'll make sure Ethan and Hunter keep quiet, too."

Derek knew his brothers would be okay. He wasn't really worried about any of them spilling the secret once they knew he wanted it kept hidden. They had always been good about having each other's backs.

"What else?"

"I need a ring for Bianca. I know it's not real but no

one else will know and if I were getting engaged…" He trailed off.

"You'd give her one of the family rings," he said. "Hunter didn't use one. But he wanted something new for Ferrin after his past troubles."

"I know, it made sense, but I've always thought when I did find the right woman I'd give her Grandma Jean's ring," Derek said. He realized that part of the reason he wanted that ring now was that it was for Bianca. If he'd asked another woman, someone whom he didn't care about the way he did Bianca, he would have gone into town to the jeweler's and picked out a ring. But this was Bianca.

"It's your ring to give to whomever you want," Nate said.

"What do you think? Is it stupid to give her that ring?" Derek asked his older brother.

Nate stood up and walked around the desk, leaning back against it. "I don't think so. You're going to need one of us to go with you to the bank to get it," Nate said. "I've got a breeder coming by in an hour so I can't go today. I might be able to do it first thing tomorrow."

"I have surgery at ten so I was going to call Pittman and see if he'd come in and open early for me," Derek said.

"That'll work for me. I don't have anything tomorrow morning except Penny. I'm taking her to school but I can bring her with me to the bank if you need to be there early so you can get to the hospital."

Derek loved that his brother had a daughter and that

being a father had made huge impact on Nate's life. He wondered if a real marriage would have the same effect on him. Nate wasn't really different, he just seemed… well, happier for one thing, and more mellow. He had taken the news of his daughter well and he'd changed completely the way he used to be.

They wrapped up their plans for tomorrow morning and Derek drove back to town at a more sedate pace. Thinking about Grandma Jean's ring had made him realize that even though his career had always come first, in the back of his mind there'd been the realization that one day he'd marry.

And the thought of putting that ring on Bianca's finger seemed right. Dangerous thinking, he reminded himself. He was just getting caught up in the same fever that was infecting everyone else in his family.

Hunter was getting married, Nate had settled into married life and fatherhood… Derek needed a night out with Ethan to remind himself that he was still one of the Wild Carutherses. And this thing with Bianca was temporary.

Temporary.

But it didn't feel temporary and when she called to ask if he wanted to join her and Benito on the tennis courts, he said yes. It was only a little after six in the evening.

It wasn't what he'd planned for the evening but he didn't dwell on it. He needed to be thinking like a fiancé if he had any chance of convincing the people who knew him best and the town gossips that this was real. Marnie was going to be looking for chinks in the story and only by playing it like it was real was he going to convince her and get that job he craved.

Though when he got to the tennis court thirty minutes later and saw Bianca in her cute tennis skirt with hair pulled up in a ponytail he realized he craved her even more than the job he'd been pursuing his entire life.

Seven

Bianca had been teaching Beni to play tennis, and she used the term loosely. He had a small plastic racket and he swung it in a clunky manner at the balls. Since they'd moved back to Cole's Hill, he needed something to do outside. They already swam most of the day at her parents' house, at least when it was warm enough. So she'd thought that tennis would be fun. Mostly she imagined she'd hit the ball and he'd chase it. Which he did. But he wanted to hit the ball, too.

And it wasn't her measly athletic skills Beni had inherited but Jose's abilities for sports. He was actually pretty good with the racket. She'd gotten him a child-sized one. And she was pretty confident that once he was older he'd be able to bat the ball over the net.

Inviting Derek to join them had seemed like a good

idea when she'd called him but then as she'd waited for him to show up she realized she'd done it so they could talk.

After her coffee with Kinley she realized how silly she was going to look when the engagement was over. While she didn't want to change the parameters of their arrangement, she did need to make sure that neither of them ended up being alienated from their families.

"Mama, your friend," Benito said.

She glanced at the entrance to the court they were playing on and saw Derek standing there. Benito waved at him as Derek walked toward them. The club didn't have a lot members using the courts at night and Bianca and Beni were the only ones out there.

"I'm your friend, too, Benito."

"I'm Beni. What's your name?"

"Derek. I'm Penny's uncle."

"Unca Derek," Benito asked.

Bianca rubbed the back of her neck. Uncle seemed the safest name. Or maybe just Derek. Derek looked over at her and she was at a loss.

She realized there were a couple of things she was going to have to sort out that she hadn't considered.

"Let's all go sit on the bench for a few minutes," she said.

"Okay, Mama," Beni said, skipping toward the bench in the shade at the side of the court.

Derek stopped her with his hand on her wrist.

"Is Uncle Derek a good idea?" he asked.

"Well you're Penny's uncle and our families are close. It's either that or just Derek or Dr. Derek."

"Dr. Derek sounds weird. And my brothers would make fun of me if they heard it."

"Are you coming?" Beni asked. He was sitting on the bench swinging his legs.

"Yes," Bianca said. "Listen, I'm not trying to make things harder than they have to be but we need to talk about this before tomorrow night. I want to make sure that Beni knows we're moving and when I talked to Kinley today… I just told her we're engaged. I didn't want to say it was fake." She put her head in her hands. "Oh, my God. I sound pathetic. This is a mistake."

The panic she'd felt when she thought he was going to try to manipulate her like Jose always had was nothing compared to what she felt at this moment. What kind of loser needed a fake engagement to jump-start her life? It didn't matter that she knew she wasn't doing it for any bad reasons. All of the things that Derek had said made sense. And he was her good friend.

He pulled her into his arms and just hugged her. Beni ran over. She felt his little arms around her legs and never had she felt more inadequate to be a mom than she did in this moment. She shouldn't be responsible for another person when she couldn't even get her own choices right.

"Mama," Beni said.

She pulled out of Derek's arms and stooped down by her son. Derek followed suit and soon they were a little circle of three on the tennis court. Beni had his hand on her shoulder and Derek put his hand on Beni's.

"Kiddo, your mom and I are really good friends and she and I are thinking about spending more time together. You and she would live with me, if that's okay with you," Derek said.

Beni turned to face Derek, his little face scrunched up as he studied him for a long minute. Then he nodded. "Like Penny's new papa?"

"Yes, just like that. Except I wouldn't be your papa. Your papa is watching over you from heaven so I'd just be…well, a good friend, and if it's okay with your mama, I'd be your daddy down here."

"Forever?" Benito asked, looking over at her for confirmation. She wasn't sure how to answer him.

"Yes. No matter what happens. If you and your mom move out of my house we will still always be friends and I'll always be your daddy down here."

Bianca felt her throat tighten and realized that already Derek was being more of a father to Beni than Jose had ever wanted to be. He only needed his son for photo shoots in the winner's circle. But Derek was making an offer to Beni that Bianca knew was real.

Beni turned to her and leaned in close, whispering in Bianca's ear. "I'd like that, Mama."

She nodded. She didn't feel like a loser anymore. She realized her son needed a male influence and not just his grandfathers and uncles. He needed a man who was his own, a father who was here and not in heaven.

"I'd like that, too," she whispered back to him.

"Now that we've settled that," Derek said, "tomorrow night there is going to be a party where we will talk to everyone in our families and let them know. But for tonight I believe we are supposed to be playing tennis."

"Mama's not very good."

"Well, thanks, *changuito*, who do you think taught you?" she asked, scooping him up in her arms as she stood and shifted him around to dangle upside down while she tickled his belly.

"You did," he said between squeals of laughter and she spun him around to his feet setting him down.

"That's right. But you are better than me."

"I know!"

Derek's attitude toward the promotion and the engagement changed after that moment with Beni. He'd made a commitment to the little boy and he'd honor it. Being friends with Bianca hadn't changed in the twenty years he'd known her; he didn't anticipate that ever changing. What had started as a gut reaction and, if he were being totally honest, anger at Marnie for trying to manipulate him had suddenly gotten real.

Just like the kiss.

He might need to start avoiding these two after twilight, he thought. There was a very real danger that he'd fall for them. Like, really fall for them, and this was supposed to be temporary.

His commitment to his profession was real, too. He had three things vying for his attention right now and he had always been a man of his word. That was one of the things that the Caruthers were known for. Their daddy hadn't raised his sons to be wishy-washy or to go back on their promises or shirk their commitments.

"You okay?" Bianca asked.

"Yeah. Just thinking."

"Well, stop it. You look like you are trying to obliterate the court with your stare."

"Sorry," he said with a shrug. "What do you say we stop playing and head over to the club for a cherry Coke and maybe I teach you how to play pool."

Derek knew actually learning the game wasn't something that Beni would be able to do now but his father had started doing things like playing pool and cards with them when they were toddlers and then as they had grown up it had felt natural to play.

"I know pool. Mama and I swim lots," Benito said.

"This is a different pool with balls and sticks."

He said something to Bianca in Spanish and Derek made a mental note to start listening to the Spanish language tapes when he worked out so he could talk to them both in that language.

"Okay," Benito said. "But not soda. I like juice."

"Juice it is," Derek said. "When your mom was little she only drank pineapple juice."

"That's my favorite," Benito said.

"I'm not surprised. Bia, I walked over to meet you. I don't have my car," Derek added.

"It's okay. We brought the golf cart so we can give you a lift to the club," she said.

"Can we ride in the back?" Benito asked.

Derek wasn't sure what that meant but Benito seemed pretty excited about it. When they got to the cart he realized that Beni wanted to ride in the seat that faced backward.

"Do you mind riding with him? He's too small to

ride back there by himself," Bianca said. "Or you could drive…"

"You drive. I'll ride with Beni," Derek said.

His promise to the little boy had been heartfelt but maybe a little bit impulsive. He realized that he didn't know Bianca's son at all. He was going to need to rectify that and a ride on the golf cart seemed a good place to start.

So he sat next to Beni on the back seat and put his arm around him. And when Bianca started driving the vehicle that couldn't have been going more than fifteen miles per hour he realized that there should be seat belts on the golf cart and lifted Beni off the seat and onto his lap, holding him securely with one arm.

Beni put his hands on Derek's forearm and he looked down at those tiny, chubby little hands. He'd never held a child's hand before, not even Penny's. He hadn't realized how small they were. Hell, that made him sound like an idiot but he'd never realized it.

"You two okay back there?" Bianca asked, not taking her eyes off the road.

"Yes, we're good."

Benito talked to him the entire time. Some of the words were hard to understand because he shifted between English and Spanish as he spoke. But the gist of it was that he liked speed and the wind on his face. And he laughed at lot.

When Bianca stopped in the special parking lot for golf carts in front of the club Derek was disappointed. He liked listening to Benito. But this was only the beginning.

He lifted him in his arms as he stood up, placed the little boy on the sidewalk next to him and turned to face Bianca. She looked cautiously at the two of them and then he felt Benito's hand slip into his and he knew why she was nervous.

He wanted to promise her that he'd never hurt her son. That he was a man who could make the world bend to his will. It was usually the case in life and in the operating theater but when it came to this woman and her child, he knew the stakes were higher.

She'd ceased being a girl he'd had a crush on and become a real flesh-and-blood woman to him when they'd kissed. She'd moved out of the realm of fantasy and into his real world that night. And now as her tiny son held his hand, he felt something, some emotion that was foreign to him.

It was as powerful as his connection to his patients and how he felt when he couldn't save them. There was the fear, disappointment, guilt and even a little bit of anger. He couldn't name but it felt the same in the pit of his stomach. It was something he couldn't control.

But then Bianca came over and touched his shoulder and it abated a little bit. They began walking toward the club together. He didn't allow himself to think of anything except showing Benito around the facility. He had a lot of stories about Bianca that he told to entertain the little boy and when they finally made it to the billiards room, Bianca was looking at him differently.

He thought maybe she finally saw him as a man, too. Not the awkward teenager who'd been her friend so long ago. For the first time he wondered if this might be something like love. Both of his brothers had fallen hard for women and were happy now.

But Derek had always felt like the odd duck in his family. He'd left home to go to college when he was fifteen. And though he could ride, rope and do ranch chores just like his brothers, he'd always been more of a bookworm. He was different.

But with Bianca he never felt different.

He felt…well, home.

Pool. She shouldn't be surprised that Derek wanted to teach her son to play pool. She was still grappling with how easily Beni had warmed to Derek but to be honest, she'd sort of sensed lately that he was a little bit jealous of Penny and her new father. The little girl had something that Beni hadn't been able to have until Derek.

Derek had ordered them a large pitcher of pineapple juice and had a step stool brought into the room. The pool tables at the club were all in private rooms and all themed. This one had been recently redecorated to honor the astronauts of the Cronus mission that would be blasting off to build a space station between Earth and Mars in the next year.

There was a mural of the solar system on one of the walls. Bianca noticed that the artist was clearly old school and had put Pluto into the design despite its demotion from planet status.

She could see Derek was relishing his role as tutor and when he offered to show her how to hold the pool cue, she couldn't resist pretending she needed some help. He was arrogant and his cockiness was showing through as he told Beni that someday he'd be a great player if he paid attention.

Next it was Beni's turn. Derek lifted him onto the step stool and kept one hand on the boy's back as he took the shot. The cue ball was in his hands and he rolled it slowly down the felt, stopping well before the triangle of balls that needed a break.

"Try again. This time push a little bit harder," Derek said, moving around behind Benito and putting his own hand over her son's.

Bianca couldn't resist the image of the two of them together and pulled out her phone to snap a quick picture capturing the twin looks of concentration on their faces as they both watched the cue ball. Derek counted down from three and with his help this time Benito broke the balls. The balls rolled around the table and a solid ball fell into the corner pocket.

"I did it."

"Of course you did. You have a very good teacher," Derek said, winking over at her.

"It's amazing there is room in here for the three of us and your ego," Bianca said.

"That's not ego, that's skill," he said.

"What's next?" Benito asked.

"Because one of the balls went into the pocket, you get to go again. Try to get all of the balls off the table."

She watched her son look over the table and she realized a split second before he moved what he was going to do. But she wasn't fast enough to stop him as reached for the solid ball closest to him and nudged it with his hand toward the pocket.

Derek caught his hand. "That's the trick. But try to do it with the cue—this one. Use this ball to knock them in."

"That's hard. Could we play different?" Benito asked.

She suspected her son was getting a little tired. It had been a long day with lots of time out and about. But Derek just nodded.

"We sure can. Actually when I was little that's how my dad taught my brothers and I to play. I was just showing off for your mom."

"What's showing off?"

Bianca waited to see how Derek would explain it and she wasn't disappointed when he said, "It's something a boy does when he likes a girl and he wants her to notice him."

"That's silly," Beni said. "Mama sees you."

"That's right, I do. He meant that he thinks he's better at playing this than I am. I don't think he was very impressed with my tennis game."

"Was that it?" Beni asked, looking back over at Derek.

"Something like that," Derek said. "It's getting late. Do you have time for ice cream before you head home?" he whispered to Bianca so that Beni wouldn't overhear.

Bianca shook her head. She wasn't sure what she was expecting when she'd invited Derek to join them but she was glad she had. But it was time for them to get home. "Not tonight. Can we give you a ride home?"

"No. A gentleman always sees a lady home. So I'll ride back to your place and then walk home from there."

"Are you sure?" Bianca asked. Her parents lived in the older section of the subdivision a good mile or so from Derek's home.

"Yes," he said. "I insist. I had a long day in surgery and could use the exercise."

"What else does a gennelman do?" Beni asked.

Derek lifted Beni off the stool and onto the floor. "He opens the door for her when he's the first one there like this."

Derek showed him as Bianca picked up her cell phone and the golf cart key and walked over to the open door.

"Thank you," she said.

"You're welcome."

Benito and Derek followed her. As they walked through the club together, she was aware that some of the patrons were watching them and she knew that it wouldn't be long before the gossip got back to her mom and to Derek's mom. It was a good thing they were having the dinner tomorrow night.

When they walked through the foyer toward the outer doors, Beni dashed around in front of her and with Derek's help, opened the heavy wood door.

She smiled down at her son. *"Gracias."*

"You're welcome," the little boy said, smiling up at her.

She wanted this little family to be real. She had to remind herself that it wasn't. That Derek could only ever be their friend. She had to remember that.

But just for tonight she was going to pretend that wasn't the case. That the man riding in the back of the golf cart with her son wasn't just her pretend fiancé but her real one.

Eight

Bianca's mom stood behind her in the bathroom, looking over her shoulder. "I don't know why we all have to go to this dinner at Derek's house. His mother doesn't know, either."

Her mom had been angling for the reason and Bianca had kept her silence. Mainly because after she'd told Kinley she'd started to realize how much confusion it was going to cause their families after they broke things off. She still wasn't sure how she was going to manage that.

She knew that she was going to have to keep her side of the bargain. Derek was proving to be a bit of an enigma. She'd gotten an email from him overnight with an invitation to a benefit at the hospital. It was to support the new cardiac surgery wing and he'd asked if she thought she could find a sitter for Beni.

It was the beginning of building a life together. And her battered heart was cheered by the invite. This was what she'd always thought couple-life would be like. It was what her parents had.

Nothing could have been further from what Jose had wanted with her than this. She realized that she was spending too much time thinking when her mom cleared her throat.

"You're going to have to wait, Mom," she said. "Just like Ma Caruthers. Derek and I will let you know what's going on once we are all together."

"It's just…"

"Ma. I promise you'll be happy about it," she said. "Oh, and I'm probably not going to be able to bid on Diego at the auction so he's going to have to find some other woman who is palatable to him to do his bidding."

"Are you and Derek dating?"

Bianca just shrugged. She suspected she was taking more joy from having this secret from her mom than she should. It was just that Ms. Bossypants was usually so in the know. She had started her career as an investigative reporter before her promotion to the morning news desk and during Bianca's teenage years her mom had shown her investigative prowess many times. It felt good to know something she didn't for once.

"Fine. Keep quiet. I can wait a few more hours to find out what's going on," she said. "Your father wants to take the big Cadillac that he just picked up two days ago."

No one would ever convince her father that anything other than a Chevrolet or a Harley was worth driving.

It had been a source of amusement for Bianca watching Jose try to talk her dad into driving an Italian sports car like the one from Moretti Motors that he'd gifted her dad when they'd first started dating.

She suspected the car was still in the garage under a tarp.

"Fine. That would be nice. We need to move Beni's car seat into it."

"Dad's already on that. And you can tell Diego the bad news about the auction yourself. He's spending the night over here instead of at his place in town. He said that the Caruthers boys were drinkers and he didn't want them to think he couldn't keep up."

She laughed. Her brothers and the Carutherses had always been in competition with each other. Actually it was that way with all of the town's heritage families, the ones who'd been here since the beginning and settled the town. Some of them were big ranching families, and some, like hers, were townies. But they were all constantly trying to one-up each other in a friendly sort of rivalry.

"I will talk to him. What do you think?" she asked her mom. "Do I look okay?"

"You look better than okay. Gorgeous," her mom said. Then she leaned forward in the mirror and did something that Bianca had never seen her do before. She pushed the skin on her temples back and sighed.

There were a few fine lines around her mom's eyes but she still looked younger than her age and beautiful. "Mom, what are you doing?"

"The station suggested I get Botox and…well, what

do you think?" she asked, pulling the skin taut again. "I didn't think I looked that old but with HD and all I guess I look different on air."

Bianca put her arm around her mom's shoulder. Of course, her mom looked fabulous but she worked in a medium that demanded perfection. "How serious was the suggestion? I think you look great but we know that sometimes we have no choice."

"It was truly a suggestion. Howard even said that it would be preventative before these lines started to show on camera. He also suggested I try not to smile so much," her mom said.

Howard was her mom's boss, and Bianca thought he was actually trying to help her mom, with that idea of his. She knew that. She was a model; she knew her days of modeling were numbered. After Beni's birth she'd actually been offered a few plus-sized gigs even though she wasn't truly plus-sized. When image was everything, life could be brutal.

"It's up to you. Actually, I think I might have a friend in Paris who has some products you can try before Botox. Want me to contact her? She's developing a new line."

"That would be great," Elena said. "Thank you."

Bianca squeezed her mom in a hug. "We are the only two Velasquez women. We have to stick together."

"Yes, we do."

Bianca had kept her name after her marriage to Jose because she'd had a career before their marriage. Beni's last name was a compound of hers and Jose's—Ruiz-Velasquez. They had followed the traditional way of naming using the father's surname first and then the mother's.

"So since we are the only two Velasquez women don't you think it would be a good idea to give me a heads-up on what's going to be happening tonight?"

Bianca just shook her head no and led her mom out of the room. She couldn't help feeling a tingle of excitement in the pit of her stomach.

Cobie had worked hard on the courtyard all day and it looked fabulous. As Derek took one last look at it before the guests arrived, he realized he'd wanted this night to be special for Bianca. Even though she meant more to him than he was willing to admit out loud, he had told her this was pretend. But pretend didn't have to mean something that wasn't classy and elegant. He realized that he was hoping it would impress her.

She'd made a few calls and they'd ended up with the catering service from the club. Cobie had even made sure that there was a table just for kids. To be fair there were only two children attending the party, Penny and Benito, but they had their own special area. There was even a buffet table that had been set at their level and food that had been prepared especially for them that only required fingers for eating and serving.

Ethan walked out on to the courtyard and whistled between his teeth. "Very impressive, bro. One might even think—"

"Don't say it. Didn't Nate talk to you?" he asked.

"He did. I was going to say one might even think you cared for her," Ethan said.

"Of course I do. We're friends," Derek said.

Friends. Just friends.

Even though it had been two days since that kiss. Tonight he was hoping for another one, which was probably not the smartest idea, but he'd always been known for being book-smart and not necessarily having the best instincts outside of the operating room.

Bianca was dangerous. He knew that and he liked it.

It was part of the reason why he'd fixated on her from the beginning. Once he said he was engaged, there wasn't another woman who would fit in his mind for a fiancée besides her.

Which was more telling than he wanted to admit, even to himself.

"Just friends."

"Shut up, Ethan," Derek said.

"Okay. But this place looks like something out of a dream. You did a really nice job," Ethan said at last. "I'm glad I came back from LA for this."

"You've been on the West Coast a lot lately. Everything okay?" Derek asked. His brother looked tired, Derek noticed. He reached for Ethan's wrist and then glanced at his watch. Ethan shrugged him off and Derek let him because his brother didn't seem pale. His health was fine. So something else was going on with him.

"Yeah. Just have a client who needs a lot of attention and it can't be dealt with on the phone or via email."

"Is it almost wrapped up?"

"Yeah, I think so. He's got a kid coming and he does a very dangerous job so I'm setting up all kinds of trusts and safeguards so that if something happens to him the kid will be covered," Ethan said.

"Sounds complicated. Just like the kind of puzzle you like to solve," Derek said.

"Yeah, it is. Some days when I'm jetting back and forth to Los Angeles or New York City I can't believe this is my life," Ethan said.

Derek nodded. "You and Hunter were always determined to get out of Cole's Hill."

"Well, Hunter more than me," Ethan said. "I like being home but I need a break sometimes, too."

"I'm feeling you," Derek said. "Last night we were up at the club and it was like the fishbowl effect as everyone watched us. It's the first time I've been aware of it. I mean, sometimes there will be something at the hospital but gossip doesn't really affect my ability to get the job done."

"You've always been a sort of wunderkind and in your own world. Focused on becoming the best surgeon."

He shrugged and nodded at his brother. "That's always been the most important thing to me."

"Still?" Ethan asked. "As I look around the courtyard, it seems like someone else might be in the running for your attention."

Derek didn't want to think about it. He'd flirted with the thought before but he'd been ignoring it. He didn't want to contemplate that Bianca and Beni might be changing his priorities. He had to be laser-focused; that was part of what made him such a good surgeon.

"Nope. This is pretend," he said with more bravado

than he felt. He wasn't about to tell his brother that Bianca had always been right there on the edge of his life and now she was closer to being in it. He wasn't sure what he'd do next.

Luckily the doorbell rang and Ethan went to the bar that Cobie had set up while Derek went to greet his guests. Cobie would have done it but Derek preferred to personally welcome everyone tonight.

He opened the door and his smile froze as he met Bianca's dark chocolate eyes. She wore a slim-fitting sheath in a silvery color that enhanced her tanned arms. A slit on the side showed off the length of her leg. She had on a pair of impossibly high heels, making her almost as tall as Derek.

She had her hair pulled up in one of those fancy ways women wore their hair for events but a tendril had slipped loose and curled against her cheek. He licked his suddenly dry lips and stood there as though he'd never seen a girl before.

And maybe he hadn't. He certainly hadn't seen a woman who took his breath away like Bianca did.

"Won't you come in," he said, stepping back to allow her to enter.

Seeing everyone together tonight made Bianca realize how many men there were in their combined families. She wasn't overwhelmed but she noticed that Kinley seemed…well, out of her element. She wondered if it was simply that she was getting used to being part of this large family.

She knew how much her friend had struggled on her

own after getting pregnant and giving birth to Penny. Kinley had asked if she could bring Pippa to the party and Bianca had agreed. Pippa now sat at the end of the table between Diego and Inigo. Whatever she was saying was keeping her brothers enchanted or maybe it was her British accent or the air of mystery about her.

Nate seemed to notice Kinley's unease and put his arm around her, whispering something in her ear that made her blush and then smile up at him. That was when Bianca, who'd been feeling pretty confident that she was okay with the whole fake fiancée arrangement, suddenly realized she wasn't.

Kinley had something real. Something that Bianca knew she'd always wanted. Something that everyone grew up believing they'd find as adults. Love. Didn't everyone? Didn't everyone want to be held and made to feel like they weren't alone? Bianca did.

She'd thought those dreams and desires had died with Jose but knew they hadn't.

Benito was close to what she wanted. She had poured her love into her little boy but she knew he'd grow up and someday be an adult on his own. She wanted a man to share her life with. She wasn't sure that pretending wasn't the way to get to that. But she wanted someone who was really hers.

Like that party invite that Derek had sent to her earlier. It meant blending their lives so when she attended an event she didn't have to wonder who would be there. If she'd have someone to talk to. A partner could be that. The right partner, she thought. Jose hadn't been that for her.

He definitely hadn't been that after they got married because he'd still been too busy proving he was the hottest guy on the F1 circuit. It was hard because the drivers were arrogant, spoiled and used to women falling all over them. Fair enough. There was something about all the rare masculine power that they exuded.

Derek had it, too. But her view of him was tempered by the fact that she'd known him as a boy. She saw past his arrogance and the cocky charm he wielded effortlessly. But that didn't mean he wouldn't hurt her.

He'd asked for temporary.

She had to remind herself of that fact constantly because of the way he acted at times. Last night in the club's billiards room. Tonight with his enchanting courtyard that looked like something out of a Hollywood romance movie set. Or when he glanced over at her and winked at her.

She felt something clench deep inside of her. She was falling for him. It didn't matter how many times she said "temporary" in her head.

Her heart didn't feel like this was make-believe.

Not at all.

Derek clinked his fork on the side of his wineglass to get everyone's attention and the conversation slowly stopped.

He stood up and then looked over at her, and she felt that nervous excitement again. It felt like there were butterflies in her stomach or more as though she'd swallowed the sun. She felt hot like she was blushing.

"Thank you everyone for coming here tonight on such short notice. I realize that we've kept you in suspense about why we wanted you all here. Bianca and I have a very special announcement."

He held his hand out to her and she took it and stood up. They hadn't rehearsed this and she wasn't sure what she was supposed to say. She tried to remember all of the things that she'd said to Kinley yesterday but her mind was blank. She was simply staring into Derek's blue eyes. She saw that curl that he tried to tame that had fallen forward on his forehead. And when their eyes met her panic stilled.

This was Derek. Her friend. The one man who wasn't a blood relative whom she could count on. She'd always been able to count on him and this was no different.

He lifted her hand and kissed the back of it. And then she felt him slipping something on her finger and she glanced down to see a charming antique engagement ring with a solitaire diamond set in a platinum band.

"I've asked Bianca to marry me and she's said yes. We've been keeping it quiet recently because of Nate's marriage to Kinley and of course Hunter and Ferrin's big day. We didn't want to steal anyone's thunder. But we figured it might be okay to let our families in on the secret," Derek said.

He put his arm around Bianca as everyone clapped for them. Her parents got to their feet as did Derek's and the two of them were surrounded by their folks and their brothers. Her mom hugged her close.

"No wonder all those blind dates didn't work out. You should have mentioned you were seeing someone," her mom said.

"I always thought there was more to the two of you

than just friends," Ma Caruthers said, hugging Bianca after her mom let go.

"Well, friendship is a great way to start a relationship," she said.

"Very true," her mom agreed.

"My sons have good taste in women," Mr. Caruthers said, hugging her close.

"We learned from your example, Dad," Derek said with a wink.

She noticed how her father stood back, though. He had always seemed to know that things weren't perfect in her first marriage and she went to his side. "I'm happy about this, Poppi."

He gave her a long level stare. "That's the important thing."

He kissed her forehead but didn't move toward Derek. Instead Derek came over to her father and held his hand out to the other man.

Her father reluctantly reached for it and shook it.

"I know that I have to prove to you that I'm good enough for your only daughter, Mr. Velasquez, and I promise over time I will make that happen."

Bianca was fooled by the sincerity in his voice. And she wondered at the ease with which Derek was making these promises. First to Beni and now to her dad. She wondered if he thought that this would go beyond temporary or if he had a way out of this for them both that would keep the peace between their families.

For her sake she needed everything between herself and Derek to be the truth. They were lying to their families, to the town, to everyone outside of each other so in order to keep herself in check, she needed to always remember that truth when she looked at him. And his promises were making it a little hard to remember this was temporary.

Nine

Derek pulled her into his arms as the music turned from Pitbull to Ed Sheeran and "Tenerife Sea." He didn't think too much about the lyrics, but just enjoyed holding Bianca in his arms. Beni and Penny had gone home with their grandparents and his brothers, Kinley, Ferrin and Pippa were still here along with Diego, Inigo and Rowdy. Pippa was dancing with Diego, which didn't seem like the best idea since he knew that Diego was a player and that Pippa had secrets she wasn't sharing.

The other guys were in the house either watching basketball on the big screen or playing cards. Since Ethan was at the table and dealing, Derek was very glad he was out here on the courtyard dancing with Bianca. His brother was a card shark and very good at winning.

"So you're making a lot of very convincing promises to Beni, to my father...you thinking something you haven't mentioned to me?" she asked.

He cursed under his breath as he danced her away from the other couples and then rested his forehead against hers and looked down into her eyes. "I think even if this is pretend, we need to make it look real. And any man who is going to try to claim you, Bianca, has to know that your father doesn't give his approval easily. Did he and Jose get on?"

She tightened her mouth and he wondered if he'd asked something he shouldn't, but he'd never been one of those guys to tiptoe around the uncomfortable questions. And tonight more than any other he needed to know what he was up against.

Because Bianca had just echoed the same sentiment that Ethan had expressed earlier. He had been making this real. Too real. And he'd already dismissed the excuse he'd been giving himself that it was okay to do this because she'd been his crush back in the day. He knew that she was so much more to him than that now. But he was supposed to be easing himself into her life.

Not throwing a party like this, he thought. One that left no doubt that he wanted this to last. Which was why she was questioning him and why he'd got his back up and asked her about Jose.

Jose was the one man that Derek would never be able to compete with. The guy was dead. The guy had fathered her son. The guy had been more at ease with romantic gestures than Derek ever would be.

He could only ever be a pale imitation.

Damn.

Screw that.

He imitated no one.

He was the best there was in Cole's Hill and pretty much in the top 1 percent in the country when it came to heart surgeons. He didn't live in the shadows.

And he wasn't prepared to with Bianca, either.

"Jose and my dad didn't get along. At first they seemed to be fine but then…well, about the time I got pregnant something happened and he and Dad stopped being chummy."

"What happened?"

She took a deep breath, looked around the courtyard and then grasped his hand, drawing him toward the glass doors right in front of them. Opening them, she stepped inside with Derek close behind. He knew she hadn't realized the doors led to his bedroom.

She glanced around and flushed.

"I just wanted to be alone."

"It's okay. I'm not planning on sweeping you off your feet and onto my bed…yet," he said with a wink. "I want to hear what happened first."

"It's…embarrassing, really."

"I doubt it," he said.

"No, it is. You know how we had that big wedding with all the cameras and media coverage and how everyone thought we were the romantic fairy-tale couple of the decade?"

He nodded, not really sure he wanted to hear this.

"Well, I thought we were, too. I was deeply in love with him and I couldn't see any faults. Marco Moretti, the head of the Moretti Motors Racing Team, and his wife tried to warn me that Jose was all show."

"Why did they try to warn you?"

"We are good friends. The team travels from country to country and some of the families go along, but I was an outsider and because of the modeling I'd done some of the other wives and girlfriends didn't welcome me. But Virginia, Marco's wife, did. Anyway, one day I was going on about how great Jose was and she said to be careful not to buy into that effortless charm he had with women."

Derek felt a stone in his stomach as he started putting things together. Little things she'd said and the way she'd reacted when Derek had mentioned her late husband. He realized that Jose had been a player.

"It's okay. You don't have to say anything else. I'm not going to cheat on you," he said.

"I know you won't, Derek. This is for three months. That's the part that I'm struggling with. You know? I'm beginning to think it's my fatal flaw. That I fall for guys who are just putting on a show. And this show... it's hard not to fall for it.

"I think Dad is reserving judgment on you until he can be sure you're the guy you claim to be," Bianca said at last.

He was. And he wasn't. He'd thought they would do each other a favor. They'd both get something they wanted and then life would go back to the way it had been. But having kissed her and seen beyond the image of who Bianca was, he knew they never could.

And he didn't want to hurt her the way that Jose

had. He didn't want to put another black cloud over her dreams. He wanted to tell her that maybe this wouldn't be temporary, but he didn't know that himself. Promising to be there for Beni had been easy. But promising her father not to hurt her might have been more than he could deliver. Making a promise to Bianca…he couldn't do that until he knew if he could handle both her and his career.

Nothing had ever competed with surgery for his attention. He'd dated but all of those relationships hadn't drawn him away from medicine the way he feared Bianca could.

She'd said too much; she knew it but it was time to clear the air. Now that their families knew about this engagement there was no changing her mind. Not that she'd really considered it but the time had definitely passed.

"Sorry. I shouldn't have mentioned that," she said, glancing around Derek's room. A lamp on one of the bedside tables was turned on, casting a soft glow around the room. It was large, with a king-size bed against one wall. There was a treadmill facing a flat-screen TV mounted on the wall next to the dresser. A seating area took up most of the opposite side of the room and there was a door that she assumed led to a private bath.

"Your room is interesting," she said.

He walked farther into the room to lean against the dresser. He had his long legs stretched out in front of him and then crossed his arms over his chest. He watched her with that enigmatic Derek stare. The one that she could never read.

"In what way?"

"Just very utilitarian," she said as she walked over to the seating area and noticed the bookshelf behind it. She scanned the titles: not a single work of fiction but a lot of medical journals.

"It's comfortable."

"I can see that," she said.

"You sound like you don't approve," he said, getting up to walk toward her.

She plopped down on one of the overstuffed leather armchairs and reached for the book that was on the side table between the chairs.

"This would put me straight to sleep."

"Are you sure?" he asked, taking the book from her. "It's about an experimental procedure for heart valve stents that has had some limited success. I'm thinking about possibly going to visit with the doctors who did the research to see some of their patients. If it works it would be an improvement on the operation we are using now."

There was that intensity that she'd always noticed in him when he talked about medicine. Any other guy would be trying to bum-rush her into bed and Derek was telling her why the book he was reading was interesting. It made her heart beat a little faster. She liked it when he got all serious and doctorly. "Why can't you just try it here?"

"It's risky. And some of the facts seem off to me. I want to see the actual research."

"Off how?"

"Some of the numbers and ratios don't add up," he said, tossing the book on the table. "But that's boring. I have exciting things in the room, too."

She glanced around it and then pointed to the treadmill. "The exercise equipment?"

He shook his head.

"Do you have sex toys in your dresser?" she asked with a wink. "I've read *Fifty Shades of Grey*."

"Hell, no. I don't need toys to please you," he said.

She flushed and cleared her throat, which was suddenly very dry. And now all she could think about was that big bed and him pleasing her.

She tried to push the images of his naked body moving over hers out of her mind but she couldn't. She had seen him at the pool and knew his chest was solid and muscly but now she wondered what it would feel like under her fingers. Did he have hair on his chest? She couldn't remember.

He arched one eyebrow at her.

"What?"

"I think you just realized the most thrilling thing in my room is me."

She shook her head. "That's a lot of talk, Caruthers."

"Again, with you thinking it's all ego. I promise you it's fact," he said.

"Another promise?" she asked.

"This one I'm happy to demonstrate," he said. "Remember that kiss by the lake?"

"I've thought of little else," she said. "I know that temporary means that we should keep our distance."

Derek stood up and drew her to her feet next to him. "Don't think. No more second-guessing any of this. Let's just see where it leads."

She bit her lip. She couldn't agree to that. They had a deal and she didn't want to shirk her side of it. "Do you mean that you want this to go beyond the three months?"

"I just mean let's take it slow and easy."

"That's not exactly an answer," she said. "I can't 'go with the flow.' I'm a single mom."

"You're an engaged woman who is in her fiancé's arms."

Bianca didn't really think she was, though. She felt those lies of fake and temporary weighing heavily on her and despite the fact that this was Derek and she wanted him more than she had wanted any man in a long time, she wedged her arm between them and stepped back.

"I'm not. This already feels way too damned real and it's not. I see this room and you are a surgeon first, Derek," she said. "There's a reason why you asked me to be your fiancée and it's not because you are waiting for the right woman. It's because no woman can compete with your career. I would love to go with the flow and if I was four years younger then I'd give in. But I'm not. I'm the woman that life has made me. I'm Benito's mom. I have to look beyond what feels good. I have to do what is right."

She hadn't meant to get so real with him but it needed to be said. She couldn't read him. She didn't know if he was faking this or if he thought that lust was enough for them. That an affair would be fine since they knew they'd be going back to their real lives in a few months. But she had already realized that she was in danger of believing every bit of this. And sleeping with Derek wasn't going to help her remember that he wasn't really hers.

The truth in her words cut through the thick lies he'd been telling himself. And it underscored the reasons why he'd been reluctant to make any more promises to Bianca. He had no idea if he could commit to a woman—even her—for more than three months. That was what he'd sort of been implying when he'd asked her to go along with it for now.

But Bianca wasn't that kind of woman.

She wasn't one who could be coaxed into half measures. He knew the reasons for her wariness were well-founded. He'd cut her off earlier because he didn't want her to say it out loud but he suspected she'd been about to tell him that Jose had hooked up with other women when he was married to Bianca bothered Derek. It made him mad as hell and want to find the guy and punch him.

But Jose was dead.

Derek hated him. He was glad that the man was out of Bianca's life but he was angry that he hadn't realized before now that she'd had such a crappy marriage. They'd been friends. Surely, Derek should have noticed.

But what would he have done?

That guy had done a job on Bianca and now he was gone. Maybe she felt relief or sadness... Oh, hell, what if she still loved him? Maybe that was the real reason for the failed blind dates set up by her mother and her agreement to this…idea that was seeming more and more complicated by the minute. He wanted it to be simple again. The way it had been when he'd first conceived it. But he knew that it would never be simple.

What had started out with the best of intentions was now making his gut ache. He wanted her. That was a given. They were young, good-looking and there'd always been a sort of what-could-have-been vibe between them. But now that he was alone with her in his bedroom, he knew he didn't want her to leave.

That even though they'd never discussed it he didn't want their arrangement to be platonic.

"I get that. But there is something more going on between us, Bia. And there always has been," he said. "Do you deny it?"

She shrugged.

"No. You can't get off that easily. I need an answer. If this is just coming from me that's one thing, but when we kissed by the lake the other night something stirred between us. Or was it just me?" he asked.

Three days. It seemed hard to believe that it had only been three days since he'd asked her to be his fiancée because he'd changed in that time. It was inevitable, he thought. They'd always been close and she was one of the few people who'd seen past his nerdy façade to the man beneath. She was special.

But right now he wasn't sure if most of those feelings should have stayed in the past.

"There is something between us. But I don't want to be a fool again. Love and me are adversaries. The last time I thought it was real, it wasn't. This time… I know it's fake. I know we are playing house to get you that chief of cardiology position and give me some breathing room to figure out what's next. But tonight felt real. And this ring…it's not a ring you give a fake fiancée."

He put his hand under her chin and tipped her head back until their eyes met. She'd kicked her heels off earlier when the dancing had started and was back to her normal five-foot, seven-inch height, which meant he towered over her in bare feet.

There were clouds in her eyes and fear as well. And he knew the pain of being hurt. Not of being in love, because he was honest enough to admit he'd been careful about his relationships and never pursued one with a woman who could touch him as deeply as Bianca. But he had been hurt.

He started to open his mouth. To make vows that he had no idea if he could keep or not. He wanted to say he'd never hurt her.

But he wasn't sure whether he was going to hurt himself.

"I… If I said this was a temporary affair, would that make it easier? I think we'd be fooling ourselves if we said we aren't going to sleep together," he finally said.

When he was unsure he always fell back on the bluntness that he'd used in his early residency days. It was just easier to detach when he was blunt. If she said no, it was fine. He'd wanted women before and not slept with them. But of course, they hadn't been living with him.

And she would be.

With her son, who was already starting to make Derek care for him. And with her swarm of brothers, who would probably beat him to a pulp if he hurt their sister. Two of her brothers lived in the Five Families neighborhood and the other two on the family's ranch.

"Maybe. I'm not trying to make this harder than it has to be. It's just that I seem to have the worst instincts when it comes to men. I really thought that since you were such a good friend this wouldn't happen."

"Really?" he asked, a tad disappointed.

She sighed, then shook her head. "No. Since I've been back in Cole's Hill, I have noticed you."

"What can I do to make this work?" he asked. "Drop the fake engagement? Sleep with you? Avoid sleeping with you?"

"I don't know. It would be so much easier if there was a crystal ball we could look into and see the future."

"It would be. Barring that, I think we should return to my suggestion that we sort of just see where this leads. We've been friends for as long as I can remember. I really don't want to think that I've done something that will lead to me losing you."

"I don't want that, either," she said. "Should we get back to our guests?"

"I don't think they'll miss us."

In the distance he heard the music change again. This time to Blake Shelton's "Sangria." He pulled her close and rocked them back and forth to the music. Her arms slipped around his waist and her hands held him tight. She sang under her breath and for now he told himself this was enough.

Ten

Derek moved to the music and she knew that they should leave his bedroom. But being in here all alone made her feel safe. She was in his arms and she felt like she'd found a man she could trust. With her heart and her body. She knew it might be the sangria she'd drunk at dinner or just the fact that he'd given her an heirloom ring. She couldn't put her finger on it but she knew once she left this bedroom she wasn't going to allow herself to be vulnerable around him again.

She had this night.

This chance to be with him.

She opened her eyes and saw he was looking down at her with intent. She tipped her head to the side and ran her fingers through that thick curly hair of his, pushing it to the left the way he liked to. His hair was silky and soft.

He moaned, the sound coming from deep inside of him, and he traced her fingers down over the side of his face and around his ear and then down his neck. She felt his pulse and as she kept touching him it started to speed up a little.

She raised both eyebrows at him, a slight smile playing on her lips. "Like that?"

"Hell, yes," he said, lifting his hand to rub his thumb over the pulse on her neck. He just slowly caressed her, moving his finger back and forth.

Shivers spread from where he was touching her over her collarbone and down her arms. Her breasts felt full and her nipples tingled.

"Like that?" he asked.

"Yes," she said, her voice breathy to her own ears.

He moved his hand to cup her neck and the back of her head. His fingers tangled in her hair and slowly drew her head back as he lowered his. Their lips met and an electric current made her lips buzz.

He parted his and she felt his breath and then the brush of his tongue. He thrust it into her mouth and their tongues tangled. Twisting her fingers into his hair, she held him to her so he didn't change his mind and pull back.

He anchored her body to his with one hand on her waist and the other one in her hair, holding her while he ravaged her mouth. She felt his erection thickening against her lower stomach and she shifted, rubbing herself against him.

He ran one of his hands down her arm, slowly and lightly caressing the outside of her arm, and then drew his hand back up the inside, the backs of his fingers brushing the side of her breast. It had been so long since a man had touched her that she realized that common sense had nothing to do with this.

She had felt empty and so undesirable for too long. And now Derek was holding her. Kissing her like he never wanted to stop as she shifted her hips, gyrating against him. Her eyes were closed, but there was no doubt of who was touching her. His cologne—spicy and masculine—perfumed each breath she took. His touch was precise, his hands sure.

He wrapped one arm around her hips and lifted her off her feet. He carried her across the room and then carefully laid her down on the bed, coming down on top of her. One of his legs bent to fall next to her on the bed while the other stayed between her spread legs.

She let go of him, her arms falling out to the side as she looked up at him and felt the emotion of the moment.

Tears burned the back of her eyes and she felt stupid because this was Derek and he was so sweet and caring and she wanted this to be real.

Oh, damn. Double damn. Just do the physical thing, she told herself. Forget emotions. They couldn't be trusted anyway.

But Derek wasn't Jose and he noticed immediately. He came down on the bed by her side and pulled her into his arms, rubbing one of his hands down her back. The other one wiped away the hot tears that fell on her face.

"What is it?"

She shook her head. She didn't want him to know

how long it had been since she'd had sex. Or that she had felt ugly and unfeminine after she'd given birth and Jose had pushed her away.

All the baggage she'd thought she'd stowed in a locker and buried deep inside of her soul was coming to the surface.

"It's been a long time for me," she said.

He gazed at her, those blue eyes of his full of an emotion that looked a lot like caring. She stopped analyzing and expecting to be hurt and decided to take Derek at face value.

"Sorry. It's just that after I had the baby it took me a while to get into shape and it affected my sex life with Jose. Wow, that's a mood killer, isn't it," she said. "What kind of man wants to hear about this kind of crap?"

"Me. Listen, I'm sorry you had a horrible time with Jose. But I'm not him and I would never hurt you. You are the sexiest woman I've ever seen. I have been crushing on you since I was fourteen."

"Fourteen?"

"Yeah."

"You should know I don't look like that poster of Jessica Simpson in that Daisy Duke getup you used to have in your locker," she said. "I'm real and not airbrushed."

"Good. I like real. I like you, Bianca. I want to make love to you," he said. "But I have no agenda here. If we don't tonight then it will happen when it's meant to."

"I'm afraid if I walk out of here tonight I'll do everything in my power to keep my distance from you."

"I can be pretty damned determined. And we're going to live together," he said. "Trust me—when the time is right it will happen."

Derek hadn't meant for things to heat up. She'd led them into his bedroom and then gotten way too real. But now that he had her in his arms and on his bed the urgency was there, of course, but he had long ago learned to control it. Control was everything to a surgeon and he applied it to every aspect of his life.

He shifted them until they were lying with their heads at the top of the bed. He piled the pillows behind his back and held her close to his side. She wasn't talking and that was okay with him as she kept running her hands over his chest. She slipped her finger between the buttons of his shirt and he had the first inkling that she didn't want this night to end.

But he waited.

She'd cried when he'd laid her on his bed. Any man worth his salt would know that things were going to take time.

"What are you doing?" he asked as he felt her nail scrape over the skin under his shirt.

"Touching you. Do you like it?"

"Yeah," he said. "Want me to take my shirt off?"

She sat up and turned away, only to look over her shoulder at him. She had a tentative expression on her face but she nodded. "Do you mind?"

"Not at all. You know what a big ego I have, so having a woman admire my body just feeds it."

She turned back to him and fake-punched him. "Don't be an ass."

"I'm not. Figured I'd beat you to saying it," he said with a wink. Then he tugged the tails of his shirt out of his pants and slowly undid the buttons. Not because he was trying to be coy but because his hands were shaking.

His surgeon's hands were shaking because Bianca Velasquez had asked him to take his shirt off. He'd pretty much already told himself that he was going to go slow with her. And every instinct in his body wanted to do the exact opposite. But he wasn't about to rush her or make her uncomfortable. It seemed to him as though she'd had enough of that in her marriage.

When he had his shirt unbuttoned she put her hand in the center of his chest. "I couldn't remember if you had a hairy chest or not."

"Just a little bit. Does that bother you?" he asked. One of the women he'd dated had wanted him to wax his chest, which had been the end of that relationship. But if Bianca asked…well, he'd consider it.

"No. I like it. I like the way it feels against my fingers when I do this," she said, rubbing her hand over his pectorals. She spread her fingers wide, the tip of one brushing over his nipple, which felt odd. He didn't really like it and brought his hand over hers to move it off.

She tugged her hand free and traced the hair from his chest along the narrow trail down his stomach. She stopped when she reached his waistband, running her fingernail along the edge. He had to shift his legs to accommodate his burgeoning erection. She noticed and ran her hand over it, stroking him up and down through the fabric of his trousers.

It was the most delicate torture to have her touching him. "I'd like to try this again."

"Now?" he asked.

"Yes," she said.

"Then come over here and kiss me," he said. She kept her hand on his erection and inched upward until she lay curved against his side. He lowered his head and kissed her. He kept the kisses as controlled as he could. He wanted to be ready to stop if she asked him to.

And that was going to be difficult because everything in him wanted to claim her. Wanted to make love to her and really make her his, so that she wasn't just his as far as everyone was concerned but the two of them would know she was his as well.

He skimmed his hands lightly over her side and when he reached the slit of her dress, he groaned. Her skin was soft, smooth and warm. He ran his finger along the edge of the fabric and then slowly inched it underneath around to her back to cup her buttocks in his hand and draw her closer to him. Then he moved her up and over his body.

She sucked his tongue deeper into her mouth and his penis jumped under her hand. She undid his zipper and slipped her hand into his pants, finding the opening in his boxers. Her fingers were long and cool against his erection. He felt his control slowly slipping away but he clung to it.

He reached for the zipper at the back of her dress and lowered it slowly. He was giving her time to say no if she wanted to but she sat up and rolled off the bed, standing up to take her dress off. It fell in a pool on the floor and he sat up to more fully see her.

She wore a balconette bra that pushed her breasts up and created a deep cleavage. He skimmed his gaze down her body, to the nipped-in waist, to her hips. She wore a tiny pair of bikini underwear in a nude color.

She held her arms out to her sides.

"This is me," she said.

He crawled across the bed and sat on the edge of it in front of her. Putting his hands on her waist, he drew her closer to him. He kissed her stomach and then her ribs and slowly worked his way over her entire torso. She was gorgeous. She was Bianca, and he had never seen a woman he wanted more.

"You're lovely."

"I think you're punch-drunk," she said. "But very nice."

"I'm not nice. I'm one big egomaniac, remember?" he said, drawing her down on his lap. She straddled him, wrapping her arms around his shoulders and pushing her fingers into his hair again.

She'd done that a number of times. She must like his hair, he thought. But really he was grasping onto any thought to distract himself from how good she felt in his arms. He told himself he'd take it slow. That he wasn't going to rush or pressure her. She was hard to resist but he did it.

He leaned forward to kiss the top of the globes of her breasts. They were full and creamy-looking in the muted light from his bedside lamp. He used his tongue to trace the lacey pattern of the bra that hugged her breasts and then wrapped his arms behind her back and undid the clasp.

She shifted around on his lap, pulling the fabric free from her body and tossing it on the floor. Her breasts were full and her nipples were pointed little nubs. He rubbed his finger over them as her hands moved lower on his body.

He felt her fingers fumbling for the button at his waistband. He stopped her before she went any further. "Are you sure about this? I think I could stop right now but if you take my pants off…"

"I'm sure. It was just…leftovers from my former life. I hadn't realized how much of myself I'd lost until now. In a way, you helped me, Derek," she said.

"Good. I'm glad to hear it," he replied. "One more thing."

"Yes?"

"Are you on the pill?"

She blushed; the color started at her breasts and went up to her cheeks. "No. I didn't even think… I'm not really that active."

"It's okay, I've got condoms."

"Good. I don't want to stop," she said.

"Me, either. Wrap your arms and legs around me," he said.

She did and he stood up, set her down on the bed and then turned away to take off his pants and boxers. He reached into the nightstand and took out one of the condoms he kept there.

He felt the brush of her fingers along his back and

turned to look at Bianca. She was touching the scarred flesh on his left side.

"Was this from the car-surfing incident?" she asked.

He nodded. During his early teenage years he'd been eager to prove himself as brave as his brothers and had earned a reputation for never turning down a dare. So he'd ended up on his skateboard being towed behind one of his friend's older brother's cars. But he'd slipped off and been dragged along for a few feet.

"Yes. Being dragged along asphalt leaves its mark."

"I'm sorry you were hurt. I remember when I came to visit you at the ranch and your father said that dumdums shouldn't have pretty visitors."

"Always so eloquent. But he was both pissed and worried. Not a great combination for him."

She ran he fingers lower to Derek's hip bone and then reached around to his front and took his erection in her hand again. She ran her fingers down his length and he turned to face her.

She smiled up at him and scooted back on the bed. He noticed she'd taken her panties off and was completely naked. His breath caught and all of the control he'd always taken for granted deserted him as he came down on the bed on top of her.

He needed to be inside her now. This was Bianca, the one woman he'd wanted above all others for longer than he could remember. He parted her thighs as he rubbed his chest over the tips of her breasts. She wrapped her legs around his waist and he felt the tip of his erection at the entrance of her body.

He cursed.

"What?"

"Condom. I forgot to put it on," he said.

She took it from him and as he shifted to his knees she tore the packet open and put the condom on him. Then she took his length in her hand and drew him forward.

He groaned. Putting his hands on the bed on either side of her body, he fell forward until he could trace her nipple with his tongue.

Now she moaned as she wrapped her legs around his waist again. He found her entrance and lifted his head to look up at her. He wanted to see the moment when he entered her.

Taking her hands in his and stretching them up over her head, he slowly pushed into her body. She was so tight he thought he wasn't going to make it all the way in before he came.

But soon he was buried hilt-deep in her body. Her hands tightened on his, her head rolled back and her eyes slowly shut.

He began to thrust into her, drawing out and then pushing back in. She clutched at his hips as he started, holding him to her, eyes half-closed and head tipped back.

He leaned down and caught one of her nipples in his teeth, scraping very gently. She started to tighten around him. Her hips were moving faster, demanding more, but he kept the pace slow, steady, wanting her to come again before he did.

He suckled her nipple and rotated his hips to catch her pleasure point with each thrust. Then he felt her hands clenching in his hair as she threw her head back and her climax ripped through her.

He started to thrust faster. He tipped her hips up to give him deeper access to her body. She was still clenching around his when he felt that tightening at the base of his spine seconds before his body erupted into hers. He pounded into her two, three more times, then collapsed against her. Careful to keep his weight from crushing her, he rolled to his side, taking her with him.

He kept his head at her breast and smoothed his hands down her back. He finally lifted his head as his breathing slowed and looked up at her to make sure she was all right. She smiled down at him. He held her close in the curve of his body and drew the edge of the comforter over them.

He might have started this as a reason to keep an old girlfriend off his back but as of tonight, he knew that he'd found a woman he wanted to keep. Now and forever.

Something that was underscored when they both got dressed and went back out to the party. She seemed to sparkle as she moved through their guests and occasionally glanced over at him with a secret smile.

He felt more daring than he had when he'd car surfed and he knew that it was because of her. Bianca.

A woman who held more power over him than he realized he had given to her.

Eleven

Bianca woke up in a strange room wrapped in Derek's arms. She carefully got out of the bed and looked back at him sleeping there. The music had long since stopped and the house was quiet. She glanced at the nightstand clock and saw that it was almost 3:00 a.m.

If she'd had any doubts that Derek was a special man to her, they were all gone now. And the word *temporary* had been shoved so far to the back of her mind that she was trying to figure out how to move forward. She knew there had to be a way.

She just had to figure it out.

Derek stirred on the bed and sat up, the comforter falling to his waist. He scrubbed his hand over his eyes and then looked at her.

"You okay?"

She nodded. "I… I need the bathroom and to wash this makeup off my face."

"Mind if I join you in there?" he asked. "Sorry for conking out on you like that."

"It's okay. I did the same," she said. "Let me pee first and then you can come in."

"Fair enough. I can use one of the bathrooms down the hall," he said.

"Nah. Give me a sec," she said, walking to the adjoining bathroom. Then she paused in the doorway and when she looked back, she noticed his eyes were on her butt.

"Do you have a T-shirt I can borrow?"

"Yeah," he said.

She hurried into the bathroom and did her business, calling out when she was done that he could come and join her. Derek had some decent face soap that was fragrance-free so it didn't irritate her skin. He came in and handed her a T-shirt printed with the San Antonio Spurs logo. She put it on.

It was a master bathroom that had two sinks. She went to the one that was clearly not being used by Derek. His toothbrush and razor were next to the other one.

She braided her hair into two plaits to keep it out of the water and then started to wash her face as Derek washed up as well.

"So…you okay?" he asked, his voice casual.

As she was drying her face on the towel he'd handed her, she remembered how unsure she'd been when she'd first come into his bedroom last night. And how she'd been crying.

The sex was…what needed to happen.

She lowered the towel and looked at him.

"Actually I'm pretty good. Thanks for that. I needed it."

He gave her the biggest, cockiest grin she'd ever seen from him. "Me, too."

She couldn't help it: she started laughing. She felt young and free in this moment, something that she'd lost somewhere in the last few years. There were moments when she held her son that she approached that feeling but it was nothing like this.

He started to walk toward her when his phone buzzed loudly from the next room.

"Crap," he said, brushing past her and stalking into the bedroom.

Her lover was gone and in his place was the surgeon. She'd seen him give a lecture at the hospital a few months ago when she'd attended a charity function and had been impressed by the difference in the personal and professional sides of the man she knew. Derek was by nature a bit of a charming rogue but when he was focused on his career he was intense and there was no time for frivolity.

He had that same intensity and focus speaking on his phone when she walked back into the bedroom. His questions were quick-fire and he had gone to his closet and started pulling out clothes. She realized he was going to have to go work.

It was three…in the morning.

This was something she hadn't considered. Derek tossed her a pair of basketball shorts with a drawstring waist and she drew them on. He was going to have to leave pretty quickly. Staying in his house alone wasn't what she wanted so she started gathering up her dress and clothes. Her purse was in the foyer on a table. By the time he was off the phone she thought she'd gotten everything.

"I have to go to the hospital," he said. "Sorry I don't have time to talk about it. Want me to drop you off at your parents' house?"

"Yes, please. Do you have time? I can walk," she said.

"I'll take you. The patient is en route to the hospital so I have a few moments to spare but we have to leave now."

He led the way through the darkened house. She grabbed her bag as he opened the front door. He had them in the car in a moment. Though he wasn't talking, she had a chance to see him in full-on doctor mode. She saw that he was already thinking about the upcoming surgery. He received an email and called the attachment up on the in-dash screen. It looked like an X-ray.

He pulled up in front her parents' house and she reached for the door handle but he leaned over and kissed her, hard and deep. "Sorry about this."

"It's your job," she said. "We can talk tomorrow."

"Yes," he said.

She let herself into the house and heard Derek speed away. She quietly made her way up to her room, dropping off her clothes before poking her head into Benito's room to check on him. He was sleeping with his mouth open. She stood over him and watched him for a few minutes before going back into her own room.

She took off the shorts that Derek had loaned her but left the tee on. She reached for her cell phone, which she'd left charging on her nightstand, and texted him to say good luck with his surgery.

She was surprised when she noticed the three dancing dots that signaled he was responding.

Thank you. Sorry the night had to end so soon. Looking forward to living with you.

Bianca quickly typed her reply.

Me, too.

She put the phone away and tried to go to sleep but her mind was buzzing. As she drifted off, she remembered the feel of Derek's arms around her, the Ed Sheeran song playing in the background of her mind.

Derek met Raine in the presurgery room where they scrubbed up. She briefed him on the additional information that the EMTs had sent on their way in. They were going straight into the operating room as the patient had shown all the symptoms of a heart attack and had undergone ten minutes of CPR and was failing. They'd finally revived him enough for surgery.

He worked carefully for the next six hours and when they emerged he knew he'd done all he could to save the patient. And it looked like the man was going to survive; Derek was cautiously optimistic. After cleaning up, he looked for Raine but she was with the family. Despite his exhaustion, his mind was buzzing from the surgery. He mentally reviewed every cut he'd made. Which was why he was distracted when he entered the lounge and bumped into someone who was standing there.

Looking up, he was surprised to see Marnie.

"You look tired," she said.

"I am. Surgery does that," he said. He wasn't being curt; his mind just wasn't back to functioning in the real world. He was still going over everything he'd done. He knew he'd done the best he could with a heart that was badly damaged.

"This was one of the things I hated about dating you," she said. "I thought if I worked at the hospital it would help me understand you. But I'm not sure it does."

He looked at Marnie. She'd done something different with her makeup today and she seemed softer. He walked over to the coffeepot and poured himself a cup. He had rounds and then he'd be able to head home and catch some sleep.

"I'm sure it doesn't. It's for the best that we're not together," he said.

"I heard about your fiancée this morning. Bianca Velasquez...very impressive," Marnie said.

"She is. We've been friends for a long time. She knew me before I was a surgeon."

"That might help her. Well, I hope it lasts," Marnie said.

Derek didn't know how to respond to that. "Why wouldn't it?"

"Because you aren't long on commitment," Marnie said. "Remember you started to get itchy about three days after we moved in together."

He wanted to tell her that it was all the junk she'd brought and the schedule she'd put on the fridge. How they both had to check in constantly with each other. But he held his tongue. There was no reason to start an argument with her. She was out of his life and they were both in a better place now.

"It feels different this time," he said.

She looked hurt and he realized that his words might have stung her. "We just weren't a good fit, Marn. You know it and I know it."

"I've changed," she said softly.

"I haven't," he said. "I've got rounds but I'll see you on Wednesday for the board meeting. Have a good Saturday."

He walked out of the room before she said anything else. The board was meeting every week for updates on the progress of the new cardio wing. He would be attending, and there would be no way to avoid her.

His encounter with Marnie made him miss Bianca. It was almost ten in the morning and he did have rounds to make but he pulled out his phone and texted her, and they began a back-and-forth.

Good morning. You awake yet?

I have a toddler. I've been awake since five.

Ouch. I have rounds but maybe this afternoon you and Beni can come over and start planning the move in.

I'd like that. I just got an email asking me to come to Manhattan on Tuesday for a photo shoot. I was thinking of going. Mom and Dad will watch Beni.

Should I wait until I get back to move in?

No. I think you should get settled this weekend.

Derek didn't want her to leave. He wanted them to get settled into living together. And he hated to admit that now part of it was about proving Marnie wrong about his ability to live with a woman. But he knew that he couldn't ask Bianca to not take a job. He'd never have stayed home this morning if she'd asked.

He knew surgery and modeling were different careers but hers was just as important as his.

OK. I'll take you to the airport.

Thanks. Text me when you want us to come over.

:) See ya later.

He pocketed his phone and finished his rounds, including a visit to the patient he'd done emergency surgery on overnight. Derek was pleased to see that he was responding well. He talked to the family and then left the hospital.

He drove home. As soon as he went inside, he headed to his bedroom. He could smell Bianca's perfume and saw the rumpled sheets that reminded him of last night. And there was an emptiness inside him as he looked around the house.

He wanted Bianca here. He needed her here in his house. Marnie had been right when she'd said that he hadn't been able to live with her. But Bianca was different. He took a quick nap, showered and then texted her that he was ready for her and Beni to start moving their stuff in.

He offered to pick her up but she said she was going to bring her own car.

He told himself that this was just a normal afternoon but he felt like a kid getting ready to go to bed on Christmas Eve. He was full of anticipation but when the doorbell rang he forced himself to walk slowly toward the door.

"Hello," he said opening the door.

"Hiya, Derry," Benito said.

He smiled down at her son, but his eyes never left Bianca's. There was something he saw there that made him believe that she had missed him, too.

He stepped back to let them enter, finally feeling like this house was about to become a home. And as much as that thrilled him he had to remember that he hadn't changed the parameters of their agreement.

Benito was pretty excited about having a "new dad." He'd talked of nothing else all morning and since his sentiment matched her mood she didn't say anything.

Derek looked tired but happy to see them. Cobie was in Houston visiting his girlfriend so it was just the three of them in the house.

"Beni, want to pick out your room?" Derek asked.

"Yes, Mama, you can have the room next to mine."

"Do you have any adjoining rooms?" she asked as Derek led the way to the stairs. In Texas, the master suites tended to be on the first floor and the other bedrooms and game rooms on the second floor.

One of the moms in Beni's playgroup had mentioned that not too long ago. Having grown up here it had seemed normal to Bianca but this mom who'd moved from Chicago had said her eight-year-old didn't like it and had been sleeping on the floor of her and her husband's bedroom every night. They were in the process of renovating the upstairs to accommodate the master suite.

She and Derek had slept together last night but she wasn't sure he'd planned on them moving into a room together. Besides they both were still trying to figure this out.

The notion that this was temporary had been put out of her mind but she had no idea if it had been for Derek as well. And it had only been one night. She knew... well, one night could change a lot of things but they hadn't talked so she had no idea where they stood.

Beni took her hand and then started singing a counting song as they went up the stairs. She sang along with him and noticed that Derek just followed behind. When they were all on the second floor, Beni dropped her hand to go explore the rooms.

"What was that?"

"Um…it's kind of embarrassing but I have a tendency to miss steps on the way down and slip on the stairs, so I count them as I walk down so I don't fall and Beni has always heard me because I really didn't want to fall when I was carrying him down the stairs. So when he learned the counting song at his day care he started singing it when we go up and down the stairs."

"I love it. You guys have a pretty close relationship," Derek said.

"We do. It's been mostly just he and I all of his life. He doesn't remember Jose that well. We have a lot of pictures of him and I tell Beni stories about his papa but it's hard." She paused before adding, "I think you should know he told *Abuelo* this morning that he has a new dad now."

Bianca wanted to make sure that Derek wasn't surprised in case Beni said anything to him. "I'll talk to him but he's small and so it's hard for him to understand that you are more like a friend."

"It's okay. We'll do it together."

She nodded. "I hope this isn't more than you intended when you asked me to do this."

"I think it already is," Derek said. "Things are changing but I have no regrets."

Hmm…well that didn't tell her anything. She wanted to pursue this topic further but maybe today wasn't the right time.

"How was surgery last night?" she asked.

"Good. The patient is responding well and I think he'll make a good recovery."

"I'm glad to hear that. I can't imagine what it's like to hold someone's life in your hands," she said. "I couldn't do it."

Derek stared at her for a long moment. "But you do it in a different way with Benito. And you do a wonderful job."

She was touched by his words and reached out to take his hand. "Thanks for saying that. But you haven't seen us in meltdown mode."

"I'm sure it's not as bad as you think."

"I'm going to let you keep believing that," she said.

Toddler-and-mom meltdowns weren't something that could be explained. They had to be seen to be believed. She and Beni were usually pretty good but sometimes he got tired and she got cranky. They weren't perfect.

"I think you should know that my track record with living with someone isn't the greatest," Derek said. "I… I'm not sure what I'll be like."

"I'm sure we'll be fine," she said, but that little dream she'd started to have about maybe making this permanent died a quick death. She didn't need a man, she knew that. Her happiness had never been dependent on one. But she liked Derek. She liked the idea of the two of them together.

She had bought into the advertising once again. She'd seen the party last night, experienced the tender lovemaking and thought, *This is it. This is real.*

The reason he hadn't expanded on what he'd said earlier was probably that he was still thinking that in three months they'd be out the door.

"Mama, I want this one," Beni said, poking his head out of one of the doorways.

Thank God for her little boy. She smiled at him and started down the hall. She was going to talk to him about Derek and she was going to have to make sure that even though they lived together she kept their lives separate. She already felt…well, like something had been taken from her but that was only an illusion.

She had wanted last night to be all physical and even though it hadn't been for her maybe it was good that it seemed to have been for Derek. She tried to reassure herself that it was much better to find out now before she allowed herself to care even more deeply for the man.

But the words rang hollow to her own ears and felt like a lie.

She smiled as Beni walked her around a room that connected to second one through a Jack-and-Jill bathroom.

She checked the room out and noticed the large walk-in closet. All the while, she tried to focus on the surroundings and not on the man who followed them quietly from room to room.

But that wasn't working.

Bianca had brought all of the stuff she'd been using at her parents' house over, mainly clothes, computers and Beni's favorite toys. Her brothers and Derek's had volunteered to get all of her stuff from storage so they were on their way.

The house was full of noise and men and Bianca wanted to hide out but she had to direct them as to where to put everything. Derek was helpful. She tried not to let it matter but he was so different from Jose. It seemed to her that everything that had been fake with Jose was real with Derek and vice versa.

She hoped she was deluding herself and would snap out of it soon.

Twelve

A month went by in a blur.

Bianca had been to New York and Paris for modeling gigs. Benito had taken over the downstairs area with his books and playthings and Derek was starting to get used to seeing his toy F1 car parked in the courtyard. But sometimes that was all he saw of either of his houseguests.

And they were definitely houseguests. Something had changed the day after he'd made love to Bianca and by the time he'd realized it, it had felt too late to change it back. He was busy at the hospital and she was busy with her son and starting a lifestyle blog and video channel. Some days all he saw of her were the videos she posted.

He watched them and wanted her. But it also made

him miss talking to her. But when he got home from the hospital she'd be at a family event or already in bed. It was hard to figure out how to get through to her and what he'd done to alienate her.

But today was the rehearsal dinner for Hunter's wedding to Ferrin so she couldn't avoid him any longer. They were staying in his old bedroom out at the Rockin' C together. Nate and Kinley had put them together and neither of them had wanted to say no, they couldn't share a room. Beni was having a sleepover in Penny's room. Pippa would be keeping an eye on the kids, including Conner, the son of Hunter's best friend, Kingsley. King and his new wife, Gabi were staying here as well. They were in town from California. The house was full of people and Derek hadn't seen his mom in such a good mood in a long time.

She'd hugged all of them more than once and kept saying how good it was to have all of her boys back on the ranch. It had made Derek realize that he should take more time to come and visit his parents.

He heard the bathroom door open and Bianca walked into the room wearing a jumpsuit with a halter neck that left her shoulders bare. The plunging neckline accentuated her cleavage. She had her hair up and her makeup was flawless as usual.

"I hadn't realized how big this party was going to be. I think there are going to be a few film crews here," Bianca said. "In case they ask about us, I'll try to downplay it. In fact, should I not even mention it?"

No.

"Definitely not. Listen, Bia, I'm not sure what I said

to you that day we were picking out rooms in my house but this isn't going the way I wanted it to. Let's talk."

"Don't we have a party to get to?" she asked, going to the dresser and fiddling with her jewelry bag.

"No. Tonight is the first time we have been truly alone. I want to discuss this," he said.

"Well, I don't," she said. "I have enough on my mind as it is."

"Like what? My brother is the one getting married," he said.

"Like my marriage to Jose. This reminds me of it," she said, but he could tell it didn't. She was trying to come up with a reason not to talk to him.

"I'm sorry but that's not going to fly," Derek said. He went over to her, putting his hand on her shoulder while watching her in the mirror.

She looked up and in her eyes he saw...well, he wasn't sure if he was projecting his own feelings but it looked like sadness. Maybe she was really upset about the high-profile wedding.

He squeezed her shoulder. "We're friends. And we haven't been talking at all. If this is bothering you then tell me about it."

She turned to face him and he stepped back to give her some space because he knew she needed it.

"It's not the filming. It's just me. I've been in a funk lately," she said.

Derek hadn't noticed. He hadn't really seen her so it would be hard to notice her mood.

"What's up?"

She shrugged.

"Well, I've been a real douche at work. Raine told me if I don't come back from this weekend with a better attitude I was going to need to find a new assistant."

Bianca looked up at him then and for the first time in weeks he felt like she really saw him.

"Why?"

"Well, my best friend stopped talking to me and is avoiding me," he said.

"I thought Rowdy was your best friend," she said.

"Don't be coy. You know I mean you," he said. He walked closer to her. "I've missed you. I can't figure out what it was I did that set us on the path we're on."

She chewed her lower lip. "It wasn't really you. I was feeling unsure of how we should proceed and that day... I heard your warning. That you don't really like living with someone else. And I knew I had to be careful to keep our lives separate."

"Why?"

"Beni was already thinking of you as a 'new dad' and that can't be. Not if we are going to be going our own separate ways in a short amount of time. I wanted to make sure I didn't start to believe in something that you never meant for us to have."

Derek rubbed the back of his neck and turned away to keep from cursing out loud. He'd done this. He'd shoved her away to try to make sure that he didn't get hurt.

"That wasn't my intention," he said.

She watched him with those big brown eyes of hers that seemed to see all the way to his soul.

"What did you intend?" she asked.

He took a deep breath. He didn't know. In a way she'd given him exactly what he'd asked for, but it was hollow. Not what he wanted. But he hadn't realized that until he'd spent a month living with a woman he cared for.

"I intended to let you know that I wasn't sure what I was doing," he said. "I just wanted you to know I might screw up," Derek finally replied after a long pause.

"Why?"

"I'd seen Marnie at the hospital before I came home that day and she pointed out how much I hadn't enjoyed living with her. Seriously, after three days I was ready to throw all of her stuff out of the house or move into Nate's condo downtown instead."

Bianca had been dreading getting through this weekend, knowing she'd be so close to Derek and not have an easy way to escape him. This conversation was confirming her worst fears.

Since she'd moved into his house, she'd kept busy and hoped the feelings she had for him would disappear. That was something that happened with Jose once they'd been married.

But she realized the differences between the two men immediately. For one thing no matter how little contact they'd had every morning when she came downstairs she always found Derek's little notes on the counter telling her when he'd be home and wishing her a good day. He'd leave them alongside two glasses of pineapple juice, which he knew she and Beni drank each morning.

It was sweet.

It had been hard to figure out why he didn't like living with a woman, why he was avoiding her, when he did things like that. She'd just figured that maybe he was being polite, that he had wanted them to feel at home in his house. But the gestures didn't stop. One night she had to meet with her attorney in town and Derek had picked Beni up from his day care and brought him home. She'd come home to the two of them making tacos and Beni showing him how to do the salsa. Something his *abuela* in Spain had been teaching him.

It had been sweet but Bianca had faked a headache and gone upstairs to keep from...falling for Derek. He'd said one thing—but his actions had shown her something else.

But she had been afraid to trust her instincts. She'd been so wrong once before and falling for a man had made her...well, not the smartest girl in the world.

And as Bianca mulled over what he'd just said, she realized something she shouldn't have forgotten. They were both coming into this afraid of what the future might hold. Afraid of how they were going to move forward. She wanted to make this work. If the last month had shown her anything it was that even pretending he wasn't important in her life wasn't enough to actually keep her from falling for him.

She wondered how much of his treatment of her was a reaction to what living with Marnie had made him feel. She wasn't sure.

She wrapped her arms around her waist. If there was a scarier thing than falling for another person she had no idea what it was. There was no way to protect herself. She knew that. Because even reminding herself every morning that she had to keep her distance hadn't helped her to stop caring about Derek.

And she didn't just mean caring for him as a friend. She cared about him the way she would a lover. She missed him in her bed.

She missed talking to him at night. And it wasn't as if they'd even had that many conversations, which should give her a clue as to why she was falling for him. It was the quality of those conversations. Derek always listened to her and made her feel like she mattered. Something Jose had never done.

"I'm not Marnie," she said at last.

"Thank God. Listen, you know I'm not the best at saying the right thing. I don't want us to continue on the way we have been. I like you and Beni and I want us to do things together. Can we start over?"

Could they? They only had two months left on their arrangement. Would that be enough to show her what they could really be?

"Yes. But what exactly will we do?" she asked.

"You should stop avoiding me," he said. "I do love watching your videos but I'd rather see you in person."

"You've been watching my videos?" She felt a little thrill despite herself. "Do I look silly? Pippa suggested I try it. She said she's been watching a few of them for years and that they seem to make some good money. So I asked around when I was in Paris and there is money to be made. Plus I have a built-in brand," she said. "I'm rambling. Sorry, it's kind of unnerving to know someone I know has been watching the videos. Especially you."

"I missed you," he said at last. "I like talking to you and you were limiting us to notes on the counter."

"I thought that was what you wanted," she said. "By the way, I love your notes on the counter. Did Marnie hate that?"

She was a little jealous of the woman he'd lived with. For one thing, he hadn't been with Marnie because he needed a fake fiancée. But Bianca also wanted to know what was different about the two situations.

"I didn't do that with her. She used to wake me up in the morning so I could exercise with her. You know I use the treadmill and review cases and read up on experimental stuff, but when I said that to her, she took it to mean that I wanted more space…which made her immediately give me less."

Bianca had a feeling his relationship with the other woman wasn't as good as Marnie might have believed. "I am never going to wake you up to exercise. I'm fine with a dip in the pool in the morning and chasing Benito around in his little F1 car."

"Great. I don't want you to do anything different. I think we should just stop avoiding each other and be ourselves," he said.

Someone knocked on the door.

"Yes?"

"Mom wants a picture of all of us boys and our women," Ethan said.

"Do you have a woman?" Derek asked, going to open the door.

Bianca followed him, trying not to let the fact that she was Derek's woman get to her too much. But it was exactly what she wanted to be. She was glad to know he'd been as dissatisfied with their arrangement as she had been. And that dream that she'd been trying to quash since she'd moved into his house suddenly seemed viable.

Her heart beat a little faster as she listened to Derek and his brother Ethan banter as they went downstairs.

Hunter and King were the life of the party. The best friends had lived for ten years under the cloud of suspicion of murdering Hunter's college girlfriend. Even though Hunter had been arrested and released without being charged, they'd been tried in the media and the damage was done. The scandal had followed them into the NFL and had even continued after their pro careers. It had only been last year when the murderer had been caught—an assistant coach on their college team who'd had a thing for drugging co-eds—and they both had been exonerated in the court of public opinion.

Derek, who'd watched his brother try to ignore the gossip for years, was glad to see him so happy. King had somehow gotten the microphone from the deejay at the party that had been set up in the backyard and was now telling stories about when he and Hunter had crashed a Superbowl party for their rivals. And Manu Barrett, the former NFL defensive lineman who was now a special teams coach on the West Coast, was joining in. Manu's brother was the astronaut Hemi Barrett who'd been chosen as part of the Cronus mission and trained outside of Cole's Hill on the Bar T land.

There were some TV cameras and a few video bloggers at the party. The crowd was a strange mix of college professors—Ferrin was an English professor at UT Austin—professional football players, astronauts, media folks, models, cardiologists, you name it. If Derek had one thought it was about how crazy his family was.

Ethan had been hanging back most of the night talking to Manu but once the defensive-lineman-turned-coach got up on the stage and started sharing football tales about Hunter's wild days, Ethan sought out Ferrin and whisked her away. Derek realized that his brother was trying to protect her from hearing any more stories about Hunter. All of them knew how hard Hunter had fallen for her and didn't want her to have second thoughts on marrying him.

"We need to get everyone dancing again," Derek said to Bianca.

"Agreed. Some of these stories should never have left the locker room. You go get the deejay to play something and I'll rally the guests. Have them play a song we can all dance to."

Derek left her and found the deejay but he had no idea what to request. He hadn't been to a "dance" that wasn't a charity event for the hospital or the Women's League in years. In fact the only song that came to mind was one he'd line-danced to back in middle school. But as soon as the music came on and he heard the laughter, he wasn't sure he'd made the right choice.

"'Macarena'? That's what you thought of?" Bianca asked as she took his hand and led him to the dance floor.

"I think the last time I was in charge of music was middle school."

She shook her head. "Well, it's working."

And it was. Everyone was laughing and dancing now and even all of Hunter's old teammates were on the floor. After the song was over they ended up dancing to "Gangnam Style." Watching a big former defensive lineman do that dance was one of the funniest things that Derek had ever seen. By the time they were doing the Electric Slide, everyone had forgotten about the stories that had been told about Hunter. Then the deejay slowed things down with a classic from Ella Fitzgerald that Ferrin had requested.

Derek pulled Bianca into his arms and slow-danced with her, noticing how all of his brothers were doing the same except for Ethan. Derek was glad he had Bianca. He was happy that he'd talked to her, too, because as the night progressed and the songs got slower and more sensual he realized he didn't want to be the only Caruthers besides Ethan on the outside watching this.

He wanted to be right where he was. In Bianca's arms. The last month had made him realize how much he wanted her in his life. Not temporarily, as he'd initially proposed, but for a long time.

He knew that he had one month, maybe two, to convince her that she wanted the same thing. And he didn't want to go overboard on her the way Marnie had with him. He didn't want to scare her off.

He held her close and his heart melted when she wrapped her arms around his waist and rested her head right over his heart. He was a heart surgeon; he knew that the organ didn't skip a beat or melt. But there was a part of him that would have sworn his heart did both of those things.

Soon they moved from dancing to drinking with his brothers and their friends. Bianca was sitting on his lap and she drifted to sleep while everyone was laughing and partying around them. It was time to call it a night.

Derek carried her up to his old bedroom and stood there watching her sleep. A part of him supposed he should go back out there with his brothers but he knew he didn't want to leave her. Finally he decided he should get her into something more comfortable.

He took off the halter top of her jumpsuit and then paused. He had no idea how to undress her without waking her up. And what if she did wake up and thought he was doing something...

"Derek?"

"Yes. I was trying to make you comfortable," he said. "Not being a creeper."

She started to laugh. "Thanks. Sorry I fell asleep. I know you're not a creeper. However it does sound like your brother might have known a few guys like that."

"It does. He had some wild days in the NFL," Derek said, going to sit down on the other side of the bed and take off his shoes. He heard her moving behind him as he finished getting undressed. He realized this was what he'd been hoping to find with Bianca. There was an intimacy that living together had brought to his life that he'd never had before. Something that he had always wanted but never thought he'd find.

Thirteen

Bianca watched him moving around getting undressed. He took his watch off first and then pulled his shirt from his trousers and toed off his shoes. This was the casual intimacy that she'd been looking forward to in her marriage but that she'd never had. Sex with Jose had always been on his terms and quick. He'd left her when it was over. The one time with Derek—and sleeping in his arms afterward—was the closest she'd come to spending the night with her lover.

Tonight she wanted more. She was tired of waiting and avoiding him. In their conversation earlier, Derek had seemed to suggest that he wanted more from her than just something temporary. She was buzzing from the champagne and the festivities. Tonight had changed everything.

She hadn't felt this hopeful about a relationship since she'd found out she was pregnant and thought that would fix her failing marriage. But this change was inspired by Derek.

He'd missed her.

He'd held her close when they danced, lighting a fire deep inside of her. One that would never be put out.

She stood up to get changed but decided that it had been too long since she'd had Derek. She knew it had been her own fault. But now that they were in this room together again, she wanted him.

And there was no reason she couldn't have him.

She striped down to her underwear. She'd worn a pushup strapless bra under the jumpsuit and left it on now. The tops of her breasts spilled out of the fabric. She wore a matching thong.

She turned to check her lipstick in the mirror, planning to touch up the bright berry color she'd used earlier, but when she looked in the mirror her gaze met Derek's. He watched her. His chest was bare and one hand rubbed down over his stomach. He'd taken his pants off and his erection poked through the opening in his boxers.

She canted her hips back and looked over her shoulder at him.

"See something you like?" she asked.

As opposed to the first time they'd been together, tonight she was herself again. The new Bianca, who had the confidence to know that this man wanted her and she could give him something no other woman could.

He sorted of grunted at her and a smile played around her lips.

She pouted as she turned and walked toward him using all the knowledge she'd gained on the catwalk in Paris. She knew how to move her body to draw attention to it.

"Do you think my lips need touching up?" she asked as she rounded the bed where he stood.

"Hell, no. I'm going to kiss the remaining lipstick off your mouth anyway," he said.

"Are you?" she asked. "I thought I was going to leave it on your skin. I was thinking I'd start here. With a kiss on the side of your neck. And then maybe work my way lower."

She touched him with her fingertip on the spot where his pulse beat rapidly and then walked her fingers downward. She skimmed over his nipple and watched him flinch as she continued moving lower. She stopped when she reached his belly button and swirled her finger around it, dipping her finger inside, and then bent forward to swirl her tongue around it. She felt his erection jump and lengthen against her breasts, which she'd deliberately leaned forward to rub against him.

She stood back up and put her hand on his shoulder, going up on tiptoe to bite the lobe of his ear. "Do you think you'd like that?"

He growled a response that sounded like yes and his hands came to her waist and then moved lower to her buttocks, grasping both of her cheeks and lifting her off her feet.

"Part your legs," he said in that low gravelly tone. "Put them around my waist."

"No."

She slithered down his body and away from him. "You sit down. Wait."

He growled deep in her throat when she leaned forward to brush kisses against his chest. Her lips were sweet and not shy as she explored his torso. Then he felt the edge of her teeth as she nibbled at his pecs.

He watched her, his eyes narrowing. Her tongue darted out and brushed against his nipple. She kept doing that to him and he began to realize where she was going with this. He arched off the bed and put his hand on the back of her head, urging her to stay where she was.

She put her hands on his shoulders and eased her way down his chest tracing each of the muscles that ribbed his abdomen and then slowly making her way lower. He could feel his heartbeat in his erection and he knew he was going to lose it if he didn't take control.

But another part of him wanted to just sit back and let her have her way with him. When she reached the edge of his boxers, she stopped and glanced up at him.

He held himself still, waiting to see what she was going to do next. She grabbed his boxers and carefully pushed them over his hard-on, easing them down his thighs and then leaving him to step out of them.

Her hands were on his erection and then he felt the brush of her lips against his shaft. She stroked him with her fingers and took the tip of him in her mouth. His hands fell to her head as she sucked him into her mouth and his hips canted forward. It had been too long since he'd been with her and he was on the knife's edge of his control.

He pulled her up and she let him. Sitting down on the edge of the bed, he drew her to him. He reached around behind her to undo her bra and when it fell off, he sat back to look at her. She took a half step back and put her hand on her hip, arching her eyebrows at him.

"Like what you see?" she asked.

"Stop teasing me, Bia," he said. "It's been too long and I'm about to lose it."

"Good. You're too controlled. I think you're trying to manage everything about this like you would in the operating room. But this isn't supposed to follow a script. This is supposed to be raw and honest."

"I feel raw," he said.

He pulled down her thong and she stepped out of it. He fingered the soft hair that covered her secrets and then drew her down on his lap, lifting her slightly so that her nipples grazed his chest.

"Now it's my turn," he said.

She nibbled on her lips as he rotated his shoulders so that his chest rubbed against her breasts. She put her hands on his shoulders and arched her back, her center rubbing over his erection.

"This is what I want," she said.

Blood roared in his ears; after months of waiting he wasn't sure of his control. He'd dreamed about this moment every night in the bed where he'd taken her, made her his. She was his fiancée as far as the world was concerned and now he wanted to leave his mark on her.

He was so hard, so full right now, that he needed to be inside of her body. He fumbled for the nightstand and the condoms he'd optimistically put in there earlier in the day. He couldn't get hold of the box but felt her reach around him and grab it.

"Is this what you're looking for?" she asked, holding a foil packet up.

"Yes," he growled.

"Let me," she said, scooting back on his thighs and ripping it open. She put the condom on the tip of his penis and slowly rolled it all the way down. She let her fingers linger lower, caressing him before she looked back at him.

There was a fire in his soul that was being fanned by Bianca. She was everything he'd always wanted but never thought he could have. He pulled her closer, his mouth slamming down on hers. All subtlety was gone. He plunged his tongue into her mouth and tangled his hands in her hair. The pins that held it up fell to the floor. He put one arm around her waist, lifted her up until he could shift his hips and found the opening of her body.

He drove up into her as she bit his tongue. When he was buried inside of her he stopped. He opened his eyes because he wanted to make sure this wasn't another erotic dream that he would wake from feeling frustrated and alone.

Bianca's eyes were open as well and there was fire in her big brown gaze. She shifted up and then slowly lowered herself back down on him. She put her hands on his shoulders as she started to ride him.

He pulled her head down to his so he could taste her mouth. Her mouth opened over his and he told himself to take it slow but slow wasn't in his programming with this woman. She was pure feminine temptation and he had her in his arms. All of the control he'd honed over the years was gone.

He nibbled on her lips and held her at his mercy. Her nails dug into his shoulders and she leaned up, brushing against his chest. Her nipples were hard points and he pulled away from her mouth, glancing down to see them pushing against his chest. Then she arched her back and he felt the brush of her nipple against his lips.

He caressed her back and spine, scraping his nails down the length of it. He followed the line of her back down the indentation above her backside, all the while taking control of the motion of her hips and driving her faster against him.

She closed her eyes and held her breath as he fondled her, running his finger over her nipple. It was velvety compared to the satin smoothness of her breast. He brushed his finger back and forth until she bit her lower lip and shifted on his lap.

He suckled her, used his teeth to tease her and then played with her other nipple with his fingers. She continued to ride him, her pace increasing but it wasn't enough for him. He wanted her.

He needed more.

He scraped his fingernail over her nipple and she shivered in his arms. He pushed her back a little bit so he could see her. Her breasts were bare, nipples distended and begging for his mouth. He lowered his head and suckled.

"You have very pretty breasts, Bianca," he said against her skin. She smelled good here as well, as if she'd spritzed her perfume in her cleavage earlier in the evening.

"Thank you," she said. "I always thought they were on the small side. That's why I wear push-up bras all the time."

He cupped them and looked up at her, their eyes meeting. "They are just right."

She leaned down and kissed him softly and gently. "I'm glad you think so."

He put one hand on the small of her back. With his other hand he pulled the remaining pins from her hair until it fell around her shoulders. He pulled it forward over the front of her chest. She sat straight with her shoulders back, which thrust her breasts up at him. He had a lap full of woman and he knew that he wanted Bianca more than…anything. She wasn't something he could win by working hard and studying, which had always been his way. And leaving her alone hadn't worked, either. It was only now that he had her back in his arms that he realized he was never going to let her go again.

She put her hands on his shoulders and he felt her tighten herself around his shaft as she shifted up on him and started to move again. Her eyes closed and her head fell back. He watched her for a moment until he felt like he was going to explode. But he needed to bring her along with him.

It had been too long and even though he wanted to make this last he knew that he was going to be hard-pressed to do that.

He leaned down and licked her nipple and then

blew on it and saw the goose bumps spread down her body. He loved the way she reacted to his mouth on her breasts. He kept his attention on them. She started to ride him harder and faster as he continued touching her there.

He leaned down and licked the valley between her breasts, whispering hot words of carnal need. She responded by digging her nails into his shoulders.

He bit carefully at the white skin of her chest, suckling at her so that he'd leave his mark. He wanted her to remember this moment and what they had done when she was alone later.

He kept kissing her and she rocked her hips harder against his length. He grabbed her hips and held her to him as he slammed up into her. Then he bit down carefully on her tender, aroused nipple. She screamed his name as her body tightened around his and he lifted his mouth to hers to capture her cries of passion.

She continued rocking against him and he slowly built her passion back to the boiling point again. He suckled her nipple as he rotated his hips to catch her pleasure point with each thrust, and he felt her hands in his hair clenching as she threw her head back the exact moment her climax ripped through her.

He varied his thrusts, finding a rhythm that would draw out the tension at the base of his spine. But she was having none of that and leaned down to whisper in his ear. Telling him how good he felt. And how deeply he filled her. Her words were like a velvet whip on him and he felt his orgasm coming a second before he erupted.

He didn't want this to end. The thought flashed

through his mind that the last time after they'd made love things had gone wrong.

"Bianca."

He called her name as he came. She arched over him again and then they collapsed back on the bed in a heap. He held her close and pretended it was just after-sex euphoria but he knew that she was in his heart now.

There was no leaving her. There was no turning back from this. And though he wasn't as sure of what the future would hold he knew that when the board made their decision about who would be chief of cardiology, he wasn't going to come home and break his engagement to Bianca. He wanted her to be his fiancée for real.

Which meant he was going to have to ask her to marry him.

And that was scary. Because she'd agreed to one thing—a temporary engagement. And the last time when he'd asked her for that, the answer hadn't been as important as it would be this time.

He carried her into the adjoining bathroom and they took a shower together. Neither of them talking.

When they climbed back into bed, he held her to him, cuddling her close and knowing that everything had changed. When they'd made love the first time it had fixed something broken in Bianca. This time it had fixed the pieces of him that had always been out of joint, leading him to an important realization.

That he'd finally found the right place for himself, right here in her arms.

Fourteen

The wedding weekend changed a lot between them but when they got back to their routines it was hard not fall back into old habits. But surprisingly, they didn't. The first morning they were back in the house Bianca went downstairs early to see Derek before he left for work. He and Beni were morning people, and she found them chattering away the entire time. They had started a new routine.

Derek changed a few of his other habits, too. Instead of staying home in the evenings when they went up to the club to play tennis he started joining them. As the weeks went by and the board meeting to name the new cardiology chief drew closer she started to feel like they were becoming a family.

So the day of the big announcement was a big deal

in her mind. She and Beni planned a special dinner for the three of them and she was pretty proud of the way that Beni had helped her decorate the courtyard.

Cobie was even helping them by hanging some lights she'd found online that were decorated with the caduceus, the symbol for medicine and surgery. She looked around the courtyard and knew that many of the most important moments in her life with Derek had happened here.

"Thanks for helping us get everything set up today," Bianca said to Cobie.

"No problem," he replied. "The little dude promised to help me with my Spanish so we're square."

"*Si*, Mama," Beni said. "Cobie is *muy bueno*."

She smiled as the two of them started speaking in Spanish and realized how Beni had really started to bloom here in Cole's Hill and in Derek's house. He liked having all of his stuff out of storage. She and Derek had taken him shopping in the outlets at San Marcos a few weeks ago to bulk up his room. This place was starting to feel like home.

And that felt right to her since Derek was definitely the man she'd fallen in love with. There was a niggling doubt in the back of her mind that wouldn't be eased until she asked him tonight to marry her. It was funny how everything here had started out temporary in theory but from the moment she'd started talking to Derek and they'd moved together, everything had been more real than it ever had been with Jose.

Being with Derek had shown her that what she'd felt for Jose had been infatuation and a little bit of oh-my-

God-I-can't-believe-this-is-my-life. There was none of that with Derek. There was just living in the town she loved and building a family with him and Beni.

She had something she'd never expected to find with anyone after Jose left. A part of her had been afraid that another man wouldn't be able to love her son the way she did. But Derek was really good with Benito. Even when the two of them had been keeping their distance, he'd still made time for her son. It had shown her that Derek Caruthers was a man of his word. And when he made a promise he kept it.

The doorbell rang, and since Cobie was helping Beni to wrap some lights around one of the trees, she waved for him to stay and went to answer it.

She opened the door to see Kinley and Penny standing there. Penny had on a cowboy hat, a pair of jeans and a T-shirt with a ballerina on it.

"Howdy," Penny said.

"Howdy," Bianca responded, stepping back and gesturing for them to come in.

"I got the cake you asked for from the bakery," Kinley said, handing the box over to her.

"Thank you. I wasn't sure I'd have time to get it before Derek comes home."

"Any word from him yet?"

"Nothing. I can only assume he's still in the meeting," Bianca said.

Kinley's phone pinged and she looked down at it. "That man. I told Nate we should turn on Find My Friends on our phones since he drives fast and I was worried about him having an accident on his way from town to the ranch."

"Okay. So what does that have to do with anything?" Bianca asked.

"He can see I'm at your place and wants to know if you've heard from Derek," Kinley said.

Bianca had to smile. One of the things she loved about the Caruthers family was the closeness between the brothers. She was glad that Beni would have more uncles.

"No, nosey, she hasn't," Kinley said out loud as she typed. "Okay, do you need me to help with anything?"

"Not really. I think everything is almost ready. Just waiting for Derek," Bianca said.

She patted the pocket of her pants where she'd slipped the ring box earlier. She had every last detail planned and now all she could do was wait. She decided to text Derek to see if he'd heard any news.

Any word yet?

Yes. Good news. I am the new Chief of Cardiology. Bad news three-car accident on the highway. Going into surgery now.

Congratulations. See you tonight.

Can't wait. <3

"Derek got the chief position," Bianca told Kinley.

"That's great," Kinley said. "Was there a chance he wouldn't get it?"

"Yes. I mean, he's brilliant and everything but he's still sort of young for the position. Plus, Dr. Masters joined the board to oversee the cardiac surgical wing and name the new head, and she and Derek had some past...relations."

"Relations?" Kinley asked with a laugh.

"I know that sounds dumb, right? They dated. And when they broke up she wasn't ready to move on. So she was sort of not happy with him on a personal level. I'm glad she's finally past that."

"Me too."

Kinley and Penny visited for a few hours, but by then, Bianca's elation had turned to worry. There was still no text from Derek that he was out of surgery. Her guests went home, Cobie retreated to the pool house and it was just her and Benito in the house. She tried to distract herself by watching him race his car around the backyard on the cone track that Derek had laid out for him. But when the time for dinner came around and there was still no word from Derek she was starting to despair.

She finally texted him to check if he was out of the operating theater. She got no response. And though she didn't want to be the type of woman who had to call around to find her man—she'd done that with Jose—she finally called the hospital and learned he was in surgery. The receptionist then forwarded her call to the cardiac wing so she could get an update from the assistant.

The fear and doubt that had been building inside of her dissipated as she heard the nurse's reassuring voice. It was hard to think that she was still dealing with trust issues. Derek wasn't interested in another woman. He had dedicated the last two months to her. Even the month when they'd been sort of avoiding each other.

"Could you let me know when Dr. Caruthers is out of surgery?" Bianca asked the nurse after they'd exchanged greetings. The nurse was pleasant and chatty, and Bianca decided she'd been worrying for nothing.

Until what the woman said next stopped her dead in her tracks.

"Ma'am, he left the hospital at least an hour ago."

Derek was exhausted as he and Raine left the operating room and went into the post-op area to clean up. They still had to see the family and talk to the other surgeon who would do the follow-up surgery for the other injuries sustained by his patient. The car accident had been pretty horrible and the medevac had brought three patients to their hospital and airlifted two others to Houston.

It had been a long day and he was looking forward to getting home to Bianca and Beni and having a low-key evening. He'd operated on the six-year-old girl who had been seated behind the driver. The driver was still in surgery. The point of impact had been on the driver's side and those passengers had sustained the most threatening injuries. The mother and two siblings had various fractures and lacerations but weren't being admitted to the hospital. When Derek walked into that waiting room and saw them sitting there, he had a flash of how he'd feel if it were Bianca and Beni in the operating room.

He sat down and updated them on the status of their

daughter and then let Raine take over so he could go home to Bianca. But then he had to answer a text from his brothers and he noticed one from Bianca as well. He told her he'd be leaving soon. He needed to see her and make sure she was okay. He didn't bother with a shower and just went to the parking lot. But he stopped when he saw Marnie leaning against his car.

"I take it your patient is doing well?" she asked as he approached.

"Yes. She'll make a full recovery."

"Good to hear. You really are a miracle worker when you're in the operating room," she said. "Sorry I made you jump through hoops before naming you chief."

"It's okay," he said. Actually, without Marnie's delaying tactics he would have continued on his path, never realizing what he was missing. He'd never have asked Bianca to be his fake fiancée. In a way, he thought he should be thanking Marnie.

"You made me realize how single-focus my life had become. I'm glad you forced my hand," he said.

She nodded and then gave him a hard look. "I hate it that you are marrying someone else."

"That's just because you don't like to lose," he said. "You don't love me."

She tipped her head to the side and studied him for a very long time. "You're right. I don't love you. You're too independent. I guess I tried to make it so you would need me but the more I tried that the farther away you got."

"We just weren't meant for each other," he said. "You'll find someone who will be right for you just like I have Bianca."

She nodded. "I hope so."

"I know so. The right man is going to fall at your feet, Marnie."

She gave him a quick smile. "From your lips to God's ears. 'Night, Derek."

"Good night, Marnie," he said, unlocking his door and getting into the car. As soon as he was behind the wheel, he took a deep breath. He wasn't ready to drive. He sat there, thinking. In the old days he would have gone to see Nate. That little girl had reminded him of Benito and he had never been so scared in the operating room. Once he started focusing on the heart and the operation his mind had cleared but when he'd first looked down at that little body, he'd realized how much his life had changed.

He had a family of his own now and keeping them safe was the only thing that really mattered to him. He took his phone out to text Bianca and let her know he was on his way home and saw he'd missed a text from her.

Where are you? The hospital said you left an hour ago.

He quickly typed his reply.

Sorry, got caught up talking to the family and then Marnie. On my way home now.

There was no further response and he scrubbed his hand over his face. He put the car in gear and drove home as fast—and safely—as he could. Within twenty minutes, he'd pulled into the driveway of his house and then let himself in.

Benito came running up to him and he bent down and scooped the little boy up. He was so happy to see him healthy. He glanced over Beni's head at Bianca and saw that she had her arms wrapped around her waist.

He knew she was upset about something but he only knew that his heart was so full of love for her that he needed to hold her and tell her.

He carried Benito in his arms over to her and hugged her close. She was stiff for a moment and then she relented and put her arms around them. He held these two people who had come to mean more to him than life itself in his arms for a few minutes until Beni squirmed to get down and excitedly told them to follow him to the courtyard.

The first thing Derek saw were the lights and the table. He stopped next to it and realized how very lucky he was to have decided to ask Bianca to be his fake fiancée. The only thing left to do was to make this real. She was already in his heart and in his mind he was planning a wedding for them soon.

Bianca saw the fatigue on Derek's face and she wanted to give him the benefit of the doubt. But he'd told her he had been talking with Marnie instead of just coming home to her. She wasn't sure how much of her jealousy and unease was from Derek and how much of it was left over from Jose.

Plus, what if he'd had to do something else in order to convince Marnie to give him the job? But she knew

Derek. Or at least she thought she had. He wasn't the kind of man who would betray her like that. Was he?

She and Benito led Derek out onto the courtyard patio where they'd set up dinner. The lights were on and the medical paraphernalia that she'd gotten to decorate the table were all in perfect position. She'd blogged about making every little thing in life special and her readers had given her some good feedback but now she was afraid she was a fraud. She was falling apart because her fiancé hadn't texted her right back.

"Wait!" Benito exclaimed. He ran back into the house and Derek looked over at her.

"What's he up to?" Derek asked.

"He has a surprise for you," Bianca said. Beni had wanted to dress like a doctor, like Derek.

"Poppi, look at me," the little boy said when he came back out on the patio. He had on a pair of scrubs and a stethoscope around his neck.

Bianca glanced at Derek and saw that moment of vulnerability and love on his face as her son called him Poppi.

"I'm like you," Beni said.

"I couldn't be prouder," Derek said. He scooped Beni up. The two of them chatted during dinner and Bianca sat there trying to reconcile the two images she had of Derek in her mind: the man who'd spent an hour with his former girlfriend and the guy who was learning Spanish and talking to her son about any topic the toddler wanted to discuss.

That love she felt for Derek grew stronger but her doubts held it trapped. She was afraid to let herself believe in him…believe in them. She watched him for a sign. Something that would show her that he was ready for the change that she wanted them to make as a couple.

At the end of the meal she was still waiting for a sign of what she should do next. She decided to keep the ring in her pocket. Asking a man to marry her seemed like a big risk when she wasn't sure if she'd fooled herself into believing in something that might not be real.

After Beni was bathed and put in bed she went back downstairs to find Derek. He was in the den talking on the phone and she hesitated in the doorway unsure if she should go in or not.

But he waved her inside and she came in and sat on one of the padded leather armchairs while he finished up his call.

"Sorry, that was Nate. He wanted to talk and this is the first chance I had," Derek said. "Did you get Benito put to bed?"

"Yes," she said. "He was very excited for you even though he has no idea what your promotion means."

"He's a sweet boy," Derek said, coming around to sit in the chair next to her. "I am starting to think of him as my son."

Those were words that would have warmed her heart earlier in the day, but now with doubts and old fears dominating her thoughts, it was hard.

"That's nice."

Derek leaned away from her and looked at her out from under that mop of bangs that had fallen forward. She didn't want to be charmed by how he looked but she always was. She always saw the boy who'd been her friend long before they'd been attracted to each other, when his hair was rumpled like it was now. She wanted to trust Derek.

She wanted to believe that he was just talking with his ex-girlfriend for some innocent reason instead of returning Bianca's texts and getting home to her. And a part of her knew all she had to do was ask him. Derek wasn't Jose, who would tell her sweet lies that she'd know better than to believe. Derek was blunt and honest.

"What's up? You haven't been yourself since I got home," he said. "Did something happen today? I'm sorry I've been so focused on my day I didn't even think to ask you."

She had that first inkling that her trust in him wasn't misplaced. "My day was fine. No bad news."

"What is it then?" he asked.

She took a deep breath and knew she had to just say it out loud. Now that she was sitting here next to him she felt almost silly about her suspicions but she couldn't just dismiss them.

"Why were you talking with Marnie?" she asked. "I was worried about you and called the hospital and they said you'd left an hour before you texted me."

Derek rubbed his hand over his face and she studied him. She was looking to see if he'd avoid making eye contact with her or get angry that she'd asked him.

"Sorry. She cornered me at my car. We talked. I realized that if it weren't for her and the pressure I'd felt I would never have asked you to be my fake fiancée. I wouldn't have even asked you out on a date, Bia."

She knew that. They had been friends but she saw now that they both had been careful to keep parts of their lives hidden. It had worked for them for a long time. "I know. Why was that?"

"I think I was afraid to see you as anything more than a friend," he said.

"Me, too," she admitted. "Being friends was so much easier than this. I was nice and safely living my life and pretending that you were still the boy who'd been my friend in middle school. But to be honest I'd noticed you'd changed."

"Same. So what's changed tonight?"

She took a deep breath. "I was jealous when I realized that you were with her."

Fifteen

Jealous.

He looked over at her sitting there in her short-sleeved blouse with the wide-legged trousers and realized how sophisticated she looked. He felt like a country bumpkin next to her.

And she was jealous.

She never had to be. He knew that but Bianca didn't. Could he convince her of that truth?

"Of Marnie? She's completely out of the picture," Derek said.

"I know that here," she said pointing to her head. "But my heart isn't so sure."

He leaned forward, putting his arms on his legs and his head in his hands. "I'm not that kind of guy, Bianca. I mean, I might have never been able to commit to a woman for the long term but I've never been the kind of guy who needed to date more than one woman at a time to prove something to myself."

He suspected her fears were based in her previous marriage and if he were being totally honest with himself he knew he'd contributed a little bit by the way he'd asked her to be his pretend fiancée instead of his real one. At the time he hadn't been capable of doing it any other way but now he knew it had been a mistake. He loved her.

He would do whatever he had to in order to make sure she understood.

"I know that. I mean, there's a part of me that can't believe that I even had to bring it up, but I do. I know it's not fair of me to ask you to pay for someone else's damage—"

"You're not asking," he said. "It's not a problem. I am the one who came over to you at the club that night. I'm the one who changed our dynamic. And I know that I've fallen in love with you."

He shifted around in his chair to face her and then reached over to take her hands. He wanted to make her understand that he was willing to give her as much time as she needed to feel safe with him. To believe in him and the love he had for her. She'd been conned by a world-class Casanova and he didn't want to do anything that would hurt her.

"You love me?"

"Yes. I didn't mean to blurt it out like that but I've known it since you moved in. I missed you every time you were gone, and Beni too. I started to realize what it meant to have a family of my own. But I also know that I asked you to do me a favor and now I'm changing that by telling you how I feel. I don't want you to feel trapped."

"I'm not trapped. I'm sorry about the jealousy. It took me by surprise because a part of me knows that you are nothing like Jose. But then I remembered the big show that our engagement was and how you and I started out as just…"

"Pretend. I think I was lying to myself even then," he said. With Bianca he didn't want to play games. When he'd seen that little girl on the operating table tonight he'd realized how fragile life was. He didn't want to waste another minute of his time with her.

He needed her to know how much she meant to him.

"This isn't going to change," he said, taking her hand and putting it over his heart. "My love for you has been a part of me for a long time. And at first it was the love of friends but it has grown and I want you to be my partner in life. I want to be Beni's father and I want us to give him brothers and sisters. I want everything when I look into your eyes, Bianca."

He felt her hand under his start to shake a little and she gave him the sweetest smile he'd ever seen on her face before pulling her hand free of his.

She stood up, and then went down on one knee in front of him.

"What are you doing?"

"I love you, Derek Caruthers. I never thought I would say this to another man but the last two months have showed me that the dreams I'd had of what life could be were possible with the right person."

"Get up," Derek said. "You've shown the same thing to me."

She shook her head and he shifted until he was kneeling next to her on the carpeted floor.

"What are you doing?" he asked her.

"Something that I should have done a while ago but I wanted to wait until we gave our temporary arrangement a real shot."

"Okay," he said, though he wasn't sure what she was getting at.

Then she reached into her pocket and took out a ring box. He felt his heart melt. The love he felt for her swelled and he couldn't quite believe what he was seeing.

"Derek Caruthers, will you marry me? Will you be my husband and partner and father to my children? Will you love me forever?"

"I will," he said. He leaned in and kissed her. He wanted to keep the embrace light but this was Bianca and they'd just decided to make their engagement real. When he lifted his head they were both breathing heavy. He stood up, drew her to feet and carried her into his bedroom.

He set her on the middle of his bed and remembered the first time they'd made love. That was the moment when he'd realized how much Bianca meant to him and that he was probably never going to be able to let her go.

"Wait a minute. You haven't put your ring on yet."

He opened the box and saw that it was a man's signet ring with a caduceus in the middle and a raised stone with their initials linked together in it.

He put it on his finger and then made love to Bianca. He had thought that his career was the one thing that would define him. But he found that living with Bianca and Beni had shown him who he really was. He was a surgeon yes and a brother and a son, but he was also a father, a friend and a lover. And it was more than he'd thought he'd ever call his own.

* * * * *

THE MILLIONAIRE'S PROPOSITION

AVRIL TREMAYNE

For Peter Alati – best brother ever.

CHAPTER ONE

SCOTT KNIGHT TOOK one look at the redhead standing over at the punchbowl and almost swallowed his tongue.

Tall, confident, beautiful…and dyspeptically cynical, judging by the look on her face. He liked every single thing in that package.

So…exactly what *was* the pick-up etiquette associated with divorce parties? Were they like funerals—no hitting on attendees unless you wanted to look like a slimeball?

He pondered that while he took another look at the redhead.

Strictly speaking, of course, this was a little more than a divorce party; it was a celebratory segue to Willa's new committed relationship with Rob. Scott wouldn't normally have advocated a jump from one hot pan right into another—even when the guy in the second pan was Rob, who was several thousand light years ahead of Willa's ex, Wayne-the-Pain—but he was suddenly cool with it if it lifted the party out of the funereal stakes and opened the way…

The redhead turned to the punchbowl for another dip. Scott noted that her body was divine. And he stopped worrying about anything other than getting his hands on it.

He headed over to the punchbowl with great purpose, grabbing a beer on the way—punch being way too girly for him. 'What's that quote about divorce…?' he asked, tilting his head towards her—but it was a rhetorical question.

She turned before the words had finished leaving his mouth and a slap of undiluted lust walloped him. She was even better close-up. A scorching mix of opulent looks, with slanted grey eyes, wickedly arched dark auburn brows, regal cheekbones…and a top-lip-heavy mouth painted blistering red.

She didn't bother answering. Clearly knew she didn't have

to. Knew he was already caught. He could tell by the way she waited, all self-possessed confidence, for him to continue, with the mere hint of a smile on her insanely sexy lips.

'Jean Kerr, it was,' he continued. '"A lawyer is never entirely comfortable with a friendly divorce, any more than a good mortician wants to finish his job and then have the patient sit up on the table."'

The sexy lips parted in surprise…and then the corners tilted up, just a little. She looked fascinated. He took that as a sign—a *good* sign—that his opening conversational gambit had hit the mark. She was with him. *Yes!*

She took a slow sip of her punch and examined him. Down, up. 'Are you in the market?' she asked, and the smokiness of her voice had his libido purring like a tomcat on the hunt.

Mmm-hmm. She'd not only caught him, she was well on the way to hog-tying him and dumping him in a babbling heap at her feet. And he wasn't complaining.

Scott gave her his *I am available for sex immediately* smile, which he liked to call his Number One smile, because it seemed to be the one that got the most use.

'Why, yes, I do happen to be in the market,' he said.

She laughed. Throatily gorgeous. 'I meant the divorce market.'

'I'm not married, if that's what you're asking. Or engaged.' Little step closer. 'Or partnered in any way, shape or form.'

She made a little moue with her luscious lips. 'Shame. Would have been fun.'

Scott wasn't often taken by surprise, but Cool-Hand Red had managed it with five little words. Why was his singledom a shame? Did she only do married guys?

'Still could be,' he said, rallying fast as he figured that simply couldn't be true. 'Fun, I mean.'

'With no money involved?' Little regretful sigh. 'I don't think so.'

What the *hell*? She not only preferred married men, but they had to *pay*? This was *so* not Willa's scene. It wasn't *his* scene either, and he'd thought he was up for most things—

except for all that hardcore S&M business. Inflicting pain—
and receiving it—thank you but no! Not his cup of tea.

She put down her punch, reached into the small and spar-
kly emerald-green evening bag draped via a chain over her
shoulder, took out an elegant silver card case, flicked it open
one-handed and handed him a plain, crisp white business card.

'"Kate Cleary",' he read. And then, 'Oh...' *Wince.* 'Ouch.'

Another of those throaty laughs. 'Divorce lawyer. Willa's,
in fact. And she's not only sitting up on the mortician's table,
she's leaping off it and twirling across the floor with a dance
partner. And I'm *very* comfortable with that. Now...what's
that *other* quote about divorce?' She raised a mischievous
eyebrow. 'Ah, yes. Zsa Zsa Gabor. "He taught me housekeeping; when I divorce I keep the house."'

He laughed. Delighted, relieved, intrigued—and *horny.*
'That explains how Willa got the house—who would dare
say no to *you*?'

'Lots of people dare—but there can only be one winner.
And I like the winner to be me.'

Scott's inner purr became a growl as his libido kicked
up a notch.

'Scott Knight—architect,' he said, holding out his hand.
'And expert inserter of foot into mouth.'

She took his hand in a firm, cool grip. Two mid-level
shakes—not wimpy, not crushing. Perfect.

'Nice to meet you, Scott Knight,' she said. 'And you're
more than welcome to roll out the lawyer jokes. Who knows?
There may even be one I haven't heard.'

'Ouch. Again. I'm going to need stitches.'

She retrieved her punch glass. 'Well, I have a needle and
thread.' Sipped. 'And a stapler too, if you prefer it a little...
rougher.'

His eyes skimmed her the way hers had him. She was
covered from neck to mid-thigh in snug black. Plain, plain,
plain—and off-the-chain sexy. Naked arms and legs. High

heels in nude. The little green handbag. Her red hair loose and gorgeous. And the lips—good God, the lips.

He felt a little shiver of excitement as he caught her scent. Tuberose. His favourite.

'You look like a tearer, not a repairer, to me,' he said, plucking the words more for their innuendo value than anything else. The only important thing was staying near her. He'd talk about knee replacements if that would keep her close.

'That's because I am,' she said. '"Ball-tearer" is the complete phrase, I believe.'

'You're not scaring me.'

'What *am* I doing?'

'You *know* what you're doing, Kate Cleary. You know very well. So let's cut to the chase. Are you hooked up with anyone? I mean, anyone I couldn't take out in a Rubik's cube tournament, obviously.' He held his breath, waiting for the answer. *No, no, no, please.*

'Is that your speciality? The Rubik's cube?'

'Well, I'm better with the cube than I am at hand-to-hand combat—although for you I could get a little gladiatorial. Certainly *with* you I could.'

'Then how fortunate that I am, indeed, single. So…do you need me to demonstrate my Rubik's cube abilities?'

'Exactly how limber are you with those nice, long, slim fingers?'

'Eleven seconds—limber enough.' The tip of her tongue came out, ran across her plump red top lip. 'But I can go slow.'

Scott's nostrils flared with the scent of her, the triumph of it. He edged closer, until they were almost but not quite touching. 'I'd like to see you go fast…*and* slow.'

She raised that eyebrow again. And, God, he knew—just from that—she would be awesome in bed. He was going to have to find out. Maybe tonight…

She tilted her head back. And there was a challenge in that. 'That's going to depend.'

'On…?'

'What you're offering.'

He was about to suggest they consider an early departure to negotiate the 'offer' when—*dammit*—Willa materialised, with Rob beside her. Okay, maybe she hadn't materialised—maybe she'd walked quite normally across the floor and he'd been too busy gagging with lust to notice. But, whatever, the interruption was so ill-timed he wanted to punch something.

'Kate, I'm so glad you've met Scott,' Willa said, all warm and thrilled and happy. 'He's not likely to be a client, though—he's the confirmed bachelor of Weeping Reef!'

Scott only just held back the wince. Because that made him sound either gay or like a player. Rob, at least, had the grace to wince *for* him and clap the hand of sympathy on his back.

Kate couldn't possibly think, even for a second, that he was gay. Not after the conversation they'd been having.

On the other hand… A player? Yeah, he admitted to that. But he liked to do his *own* warning off of women who had happily-ever-after in their sights—with charm and skill and softly negotiated ground rules that meant everyone had fun right up until the goodbye. He didn't need his friends making public service announcements to scare away prospective bedmates before he even got to the first kiss.

'Let's leave it at bachelor, shall we, Willa?' Scott suggested through slightly gritted teeth.

Willa, oblivious, turned to him. 'Oh, are you *not* a confirmed bachelor? I thought you said friends with benefits was as far as you ever intended to go? Not that there's anything wrong with that. At all. Of course.'

Scott stared at Willa, speechless. Rob blew out a *not laughing, I promise* breath. Kate was biting the inside of her cheek, in the same predicament as Rob.

'After what happened in the Whitsundays I—' At last Willa stopped. Blushed very prettily—as Willa did everything.

Scott was still staring, frozen, praying she was not going to finish that.

'Oh,' Willa said. 'Well. Anyway. Kate is the best family lawyer in Sydney, as well as being a wonderful, kind, compassionate—'

'Thank you, Willa,' Kate interrupted smoothly. 'But I'm not quite ready for sainthood.'

Scott, unfreezing, saw the flush of pink that slashed across Kate's high cheekbones—not pretty, *stunning*!—and decided it was time to take control of the conversation and get his seduction back on track.

Leaning into Willa conspiratorially, he said, 'I hear Kate's also a Rubik's cube champion.'

Kate choked on her punch, trying—again—not to laugh.

And somehow that made Scott want her even more. He needed to get her away from everyone immediately. Out onto the deck into that particular corner that he knew from previous forays at Willa's harbourside mansion was very private, screened by a giant pot plant.

But any chance of getting Kate alone was snatched from him by another of the old Weeping Reef gang, Amy, who landed in their midst—because Amy never merely *appeared* anywhere—accompanied by her flatmate Jessica, who'd become an honorary gang member despite never having been near the Whitsundays.

Seduction plans were officially on simmer—but not off the heat. Half an hour—that was all he needed. Half an hour and Kate Cleary would be his.

Amy gave Scott a smacking kiss on the cheek before enveloping Kate in a hug.

'Kate!' she squealed. 'It's been an age.'

Kate laughed as she returned the hug. 'Well, two weeks, anyway—you didn't drink so many mojitos at Fox that you've forgotten?'

What the hell...? Scott wondered if he was the only one of the group who'd never met Kate. Well—him and Willa's brother, Luke, who was still in Singapore. Was this some kind of Weeping Reef conspiracy? Would Chantal turn up at last—because God knew how he'd deal with that—and Brodie? He could picture Brodie sauntering over, snatching the heart of *another* of Scott's women...

Not that Kate was Scott's woman.

Jessica and Kate were hugging now. Okay—this was officially out of control. Even *Jessica* knew Kate?

'It wasn't the mojitos that were news at Fox,' Jessica said. 'It was one very particular martini.'

The blush was back on Kate's cheekbones. 'The less said about that the better,' she said with a theatrical shudder.

Scott was suddenly desperate to hear the story. 'You don't like martinis?' he asked—only to have Willa, Amy and Jessica burst out laughing.

He looked at Rob, who gave him a *don't ask me* shrug.

'It was a *dirty* martini,' Amy said, putting him out of his misery. 'Bought for her by Barnaby, my arch nemesis at work, who just happened to be drinking at Fox too. Blond, blue-eyed and gorgeous—that's Barnaby. Thinks he's God's gift to marketing. *And* to women. And to be honest, he kind of *is*. Just not to Kate.'

Kate shook her head, laughing, as though batting the subject away.

'It was the way he said "dirty",' Jessica put in, helping herself to a glass of punch. 'It's one thing being presented with a dirty martini. It's quite another to have it presented with a slimy pick-up line. *"Just how dirty do you like it, baby?"* Yep—that would make any woman want to jump you. *Not*.'

More laughing from the girls as Kate covered her eyes with a hand.

Rob was practically cringing. 'Seriously?'

Willa kissed Rob's cheek. 'Not all men are as evolved as you, Rob.'

Rob turned to Scott. 'You ever used that one?'

'Dirty martini? Nope. And, given the reaction Barnaby

got, I doubt I ever will. Although in my youth I did once embarrass myself with a comment to twin girls about a *Ménage à Trois*.'

Jessica's eyes bugged. 'Twins? Like…a real *ménage à trois*? Or is that the name of a fancy-pants cocktail?'

'It's a cocktail,' Scott assured her. 'And delicious, apparently—because, as it happens, they both ordered one and made very…*approving*…noises.' He cleared his throat, all faux embarrassment. 'As they sipped, I mean.'

'They ordered one apiece—with a side order of you?' Amy asked, batting her eyelashes outrageously.

Scott smiled. The lazy, teasing smile he reserved for flirty moments with women he wasn't ever going to take to bed. 'A gentleman never tells a lady's secrets.'

He saw something flash across Amy's face. Something like…distress? But it was gone so quickly he wondered if he'd imagined it. And the next moment she was laughing again.

'Well, anyway, enough with the "in my youth" talk. If I've got my arithmetic in order you're twenty-seven—one measly year older than me. And I'll have you know I still consider myself to be in my youth.'

An odd gasping sound from Kate had Scott turning to her. It looked as if she'd spilled punch on her dress, because she was brushing a hand over the bodice. It must have been only the tiniest drop—*he* certainly couldn't see any sign of it—but the next moment Willa was ushering Kate to the guest bathroom and Amy was asking Rob what exactly was in the punch, because she'd never seen Kate's nerves of steel so much as bend before, let alone be dented.

The punch, apparently, was a combination of vodka, white wine, white rum and champagne, with an occasional strawberry waved over the bowl—that did *not* sound girly! It was a miracle everyone in the house wasn't stumbling around breaking bits off sculptures, staggering into walls and pitching face-first into pot plants.

But Scott had a feeling the potency of the brew was not

the problem with Kate. She'd looked sort of *shocky*. Surely not because of that harmless *ménage à trois* talk? She was too sophisticated for that. It would take him two minutes, tops, to explain that away. Which would leave him twenty-eight minutes to charm her out of her panties.

But twenty minutes later Scott hadn't managed to get near Kate. Every time he took a step in her direction she moved somewhere else. As if she was on guard against him—which was crazy. Almost as crazy as what the sight of her loose-hipped, strolling, rolling walk was doing to his testosterone levels. Sexiest walk *ever*.

At the twenty-four-minute mark, as he made what felt like his hundredth attempt to reach her and she replaced the stroll with a dash—an actual freaking *dash*—towards a small group of people whose average age looked to be a hundred and four, he realised she really and truly *was* on her guard.

Oh, my God.

He was chasing her and she was running away. This had never, ever happened to him before.

And as he watched her, trying to figure out what the hell had gone wrong, the last six minutes of his self-allocated thirty minutes' seduction time ticked away...and she was gone.

Disappeared. Like Cinderella, but wearing both of her take-me-now shoes.

He fingered the card she'd given him.

Weird. Very, *very* weird. A mystery. What had he said? Done?

Well, Scott loved mysteries. And challenges. And women who wore red lipstick.

And he was suddenly very certain that this thing between him and Kate Cleary—because there was definitely a thing—was not going to end with a drop of spilled punch and no explanation.

He looked at her card again, noted the address—a block from his city office.

Easy.

CHAPTER TWO

KATE LET HERSELF into her apartment, tossed her bag onto the couch, kicked off her shoes, wiggled her toes…and let out a tortured groan that had nothing to do with her sore feet and everything to do with the divorce party.

Which had been a disaster.

She couldn't believe she'd been smut-talking about a stapler and a Rubik's cube. As bad as Dirty Martini Barnaby! Flirting with that hot, gorgeous hunk like a horny teenager.

And then to discover that the hot, gorgeous hunk practically *was* a horny teenager…

She let out another tortured groan.

Not that twenty-seven really *was* teenaged.

But she was thirty-two, for God's sake! A *my way or the highway* woman of thirty-two!

She opened the French doors and stepped onto the expansive terrace of her apartment. She'd chosen the apartment for the view—not the Harbour Bridge in the distance, even though that was her favourite Sydney landmark, but the boats. Something about them, bobbing gently in Rushcutters Bay, soothed her. The escape daydream, she called it. Sailing away from her troubles to a world of possibilities. A world of adventure…

She tried to bring herself back to earth by reminding herself of the time she'd forced the husband of one of her clients to sell his boat and hand over half the cash and he'd cried like a baby. But even the memory of that less than edifying spectacle couldn't stop her thinking about adventures and possibilities.

And tonight, very specifically, the possibility of an adventure with Scott Knight.

The image of him was so clear in her head. That killer body—tall, broad, strong. The slightly spiky mid-brown hair. The alertness of his cool, pale green eyes. That *I've got a secret* smile that was kind of calculating…and somehow intriguing exactly because of that. She'd wanted to twist him into a sexual pretzel the moment she'd heard his lazy, drawling voice—a voice so at odds with the alert intelligence in his eyes it was almost a challenge.

But…*twenty-seven years old*?

She covered her face with her hands and let fly with one more tortured groan.

Pent-up need—that was the problem. It had been a long time between…cocktails. Dirty Martini, Bosom Caresser, Between the Sheets, Sex on the Beach or any other kind. A *damned* long time.

Well, she clearly couldn't be trusted to see Scott Knight again until that pent-up need had been met. She would have to make sure any Weeping Reef gathering was Scott-free before attending. In fact, she'd go one step further and stick to girls-only catch-ups when it came to Willa. So just Willa, Amy, Jessica and the other girl she had yet to meet—Chantal—if she ever showed. No Rob. No Scott. Luke was in Singapore, and the other guy whose name started with a B—Brady? No, Brodie—hadn't turned up at anything yet. So the whole girls-only thing was definitely doable.

And in the meantime she would find some other man to twist into a sexual pretzel. Someone like Phillip, a barrister who was happily divorced, suave, cultured and—at forty years old—mature. In the right age ballpark.

Then she would let the girls know she was taken, word would find its way to Scott, and that would be that.

Yes, Phillip would do very nicely. She would give him a call on Monday and arrange to catch up with him at the bar near her office for a Slow Comfortable Screw. A Strawberry Stripper. A Sex Machine. Or…or *something*.

* * *

Monday morning for Kate began with an eight o'clock client meeting.

Kate always felt like cuddling this particular client. Fragile, timid Rosie, who crept into her office as though she'd like a corner to hide in. Rosie was so intimidated by her husband she couldn't even bring herself to tell him he was making her unhappy—so how she was going to raise the subject of divorce was anyone's guess.

It was not a position a *Cleary* woman would ever find herself in!

Her frustrating meeting with Rosie reminded Kate how happy she was not to be married. And that, in turn, prompted her to get to the task of calling the equally gamophobic Phillip to arrange that bar meeting. A highly satisfactory phone call that took four businesslike minutes.

Two meetings later she made herself a cup of coffee and opened her diary to recheck her schedule…and blinked.

Blinked, blinked, blinked.

She called her no-nonsense, indeterminately aged, absolutely superb assistant. 'What's this appointment at twelve-thirty today, Deb?'

'Hang on…' Keyboard clicks. 'Oh, Scott Knight. He called while you were with your eight o'clock. Said he'd mentioned a lunch appointment when he saw you on Saturday night.'

Kate slumped back in her chair, awed—and depressingly delighted—at the presumption of it.

'Oh, did he?' she asked, trying to sound ominous.

'So he *didn't*?' Chuckle. 'Well, I did wonder why you hadn't mentioned it to me, but he sounded… Well, let's keep it clean and say *nice*, so I made an executive decision and slotted him in.'

'Yes, he does sound "nice",' Kate said dryly, and smiled at Deb's sudden crack of laughter.

'Want me to cancel him, hon? Leave you to your takeaway chicken and mung-bloody-bean salad?'

Kate opened her mouth to say an automatic yes—but into her head popped an image of Rosie that morning. Diffident. Nervous. Panicky. Dodging her husband rather than telling him their marriage was over.

And hot on the heels of that came the memory of her own behaviour on Saturday night, dodging Scott at Willa's party. So unnerved by the force of her attraction to him she'd mapped out an actual plan for seeing only Willa, Amy and Jessica. *Crazy.* She should be able to see her friends whenever and wherever she wanted, without giving a second thought to whoever else might just happen to be in the vicinity.

As if she couldn't handle a *twenty-seven-year-old*!

And on her own turf…in her own office? Easy.

This would not be like the divorce party, where the kick of lust had taken her by surprise. She would be prepared for it today. And she could tell him directly, herself, that she was no longer in the market—so thanks, but no thanks.

'Kate?' Deb prompted. 'Shall I cancel him?'

Kate straightened her shoulders. 'No, that's fine,' she said. 'It will take approximately five minutes to conclude my business with Mr Knight. Plenty of time to eat chicken and mung-bloody-bean salad afterwards.' She nodded, satisfied. 'Now, can you grab me the McMahon file? There's something I need to check before the parties arrive to have another crack at a settlement conference.'

'Mmm-hmm. Settlement conference… That's what they're calling World War III these days, is it?'

Scott, no stranger to wooing women, brought flowers to Kate's office. Nothing over the top. Just simple, colourful gerberas that said *I'm charming so I don't have to bring roses.*

Not that he saw any softening in Deb's face as he handed over the bunch.

'Seems a shame to spend money on flowers when you're only going to be in there for five minutes,' she said.

'Oh, they're not for Kate,' Scott said. 'They're for you.'

'Even so…' Deb said, but he didn't miss the tiny sparkle that sprang to life in her eyes. 'Her meeting is running over time. Take a seat, if you'd like to wait.'

Scott angled himself so he could see through the glass wall of the boardroom. Could see *her*. Kate.

She was sitting at a long table, her back to him. Beside her was an overly blonded, expensive-looking woman wearing lime-green. The client, obviously. On the opposite side of the table was a man who epitomised lawyerdom. Pinstriped suit, white shirt, conservative tie. Beside Pinstripe was a man who looked as if he'd spent too long on the tanning bed, wearing an open-necked shirt with a humungous gold chain visible against his chest. Gold Chain was holding a dog. A furry little dog. Which he kept petting.

Amongst the four of them—five, if you included the dog— there were frequent vehement headshakes, very occasional nods, hand gestures aplenty. At one point Kate ran a hand tiredly over her hair, which was tied in a low ponytail. It made Scott want to touch her.

And that reminded him that their only physical contact on Saturday night had been a handshake. So it was kind of nuts to be so obsessed with her. But obsessed was what he was.

Suddenly Kate stood. She put her hands on the table and leaned forward—making a particular point, he guessed. She was wearing a cream skirt suit. Beautifully, tightly fitted.

Scott was appreciating the view of her really superb back-side when she stretched just a little bit further forward and her skirt hitched up for one split second. Just long enough to give him a tiny glimpse of the lacy band at the top of one of her…*ooohhh…stockings.*

She was wearing *stockings*.

All the blood in Scott's body redirected itself in one gush, straight to his groin. The sudden ache of it made him clamp his jaws together.

Stockings!

Stay-ups? Suspenders? Hell, who cared which?

Then she was back in her seat. Scott realised he'd been holding his breath and exhaled—very, very slowly.

He forced his eyes away from her—scared he'd start drooling otherwise—and saw Gold Chain give the dog a kiss on the nose while keeping his eyes on his wife across the table.

That seemed to incense Blondie—which Scott could understand, because it *was* kind of gross—who leapt to her feet and screeched so loudly her voice bounced straight through the glass wall. Next moment all four of them were standing. There were waved arms, pointed fingers, even a stamped foot. The stamped foot was from Blondie, who was then subtly restrained by Kate, who seemed serene in the midst of chaos. Pinstripe was using a similar restraining movement on Gold Chain, but was somewhat hampered by the dog snapping at him.

Scott heard a few words shouted—hurled. *Custody. Holidays. Missed drop-offs.* Interspersed with an occasional ear-sizzling foul-mouthed curse.

Shocked, Scott looked at Deb. Shouldn't she be calling the cops before someone threw an actual punch? But Deb just kept typing, unperturbed. Which would have to mean that Kate put up with such crap routinely, wouldn't it? Did that explain Kate's air of cynicism at Willa's divorce party? Because if this was divorce, it sure wasn't pretty.

He tuned back in to the screeches. A custody battle? Had to be. The antagonists were…what?…in their early thirties, maybe? So the kids had to be young. How *many* kids?

Scott wondered how his own parents would have handled a custody battle. Not that his parents would have done anything so undignified as get divorced. The joining of two old families, the merging of two fortunes, had been destiny working the way it was supposed to—even if he'd never seen his parents kiss, let alone hold hands. Their merger was too perfect ever to be classified as a mistake, so that sucker wasn't getting dissolved.

But if they *had* divorced he couldn't imagine them getting into a raging custody battle. Over *him*, at any rate. They would have come up with a simple, bloodless schedule of visits, complete with taxi pick-ups and drop-offs.

Custody of his older brother would have been a different story. There would have been nothing amicable about sharing the 'perfect' son. Maybe that was the real reason they'd stayed together—the inability to satisfactorily halve his brother.

And what an opportune moment for the boardroom door to be opening, so he could stop thinking.

Gold Chain was coming out, carrying the dog, speaking furiously to his solicitor. Pinstripe had a grip on his client's dog-free arm and was dealing admirably with dodging the growling dog's snapping jaws as he walked Gold Chain past Deb's desk and out of the suite. Kate and her client stayed in the room talking for a few minutes, but then they too appeared. Kate was nodding, her red-lipsticked mouth pursed in sympathy.

Kate caught sight of him—and slashes of pink zapped along her cheekbones as if by Magic Marker. And then she returned her concentration to Blondie.

'It's not good enough,' Blondie was saying. 'He keeps returning her late. If it doesn't stop I'll be rethinking the money. Make sure he knows that, Kate.'

A few soothing words, an unrelenting shepherding towards the suite exit. Out through the door.

And then…silence.

Deb looked at Scott. Raised her eyebrows. That little sparkle was in her eyes again.

Scott raised his eyebrows back, a little shell-shocked and a lot awed at what Kate had just put up with. And still somewhat gobsmacked that such a small dog could be so nasty. He'd back that dog against a pitbull.

And then Kate was coming back. Smiling coolly—very lawyer-like and professional.

'Scott,' she said, and held out her hand.

Scott shook it. 'Kate,' he said, and could hear the laughter in his voice. Less than forty-eight hours ago they'd been heading for sex. Today he got a handshake.

No. Just...*no*.

Kate gestured to the office next to the boardroom. Scott walked ahead of her, opened the heavy wooden door and stood just inside, taking in the dignified space. Carpeted floor. Big desk. Behind the desk a large tinted window on the outside world. Large window on the inside world too—untinted—through which he could see Kate speaking to Deb, because the Venetian blinds that were there for privacy were open. Neat, modern filing cabinets. Two black leather chairs in front of her desk. Vivid knock-out painting on one wall—the only splash of colour.

And then Kate was entering, closing the door behind her. He turned to face her. She was close. So close. Cream suit. Red hair. Those other-worldly grey eyes. Tuberose scent.

Just for a second the memory of the top of her stocking burst in his head.

And drove him wild.

Which had to be why he grabbed her by the upper arms, backed her up a step, pushed her against that nice solid door and covered her mouth with his.

CHAPTER THREE

FOR ONE FRANTIC SECOND he felt Kate stiffen.

God, don't stop me. I'll die if you stop me.

He licked her mouth—her gorgeous, red, luscious mouth—and with an inarticulate sound that was half-moan, half-whimper she opened to him.

Thank you, thank you, thank you.

His tongue swooped inside, tangled with hers...and she was everything he'd hoped she would be. Delicious, and hot, and desperate—as desperate as he was. She tasted so good. Smelled like heaven. Felt lush and ripe against him as he pressed her to the door. He wished he could get her closer—although that was knuckleheaded. If he pushed any harder against her they'd be through the wood, spilling onto the floor at the base of Deb's desk. And exhibitionism wasn't high on his must-do list.

Then Kate's arms circled him and he *was* closer. *Miracle.* She tore the shirt loose from his pants and then her hands were under the cotton, sliding up his back, down, then up. Rushing over his skin. No finesse, just raw, hungry possession. Restless, seeking, sweeping...

He heard her whimper, low in her throat, and it set off a flare in his head. He wanted every part of her in his hands all at once. Impossible lust. Outrageous. He grabbed the back of her head, bringing their mouths together so furiously their teeth clashed. But he didn't stop and neither did she. They were straining together. He could feel her heart thudding against his own rocketing beats. He wished he could see her naked. Needed to touch her bare skin.

Alone. He needed them to be alone.

Keeping his burning mouth fused to Kate's, he reached,

one-handed, grabbing for the cord that controlled the Venetian blinds. He scrabbled there, cursing inside his impatient head until he found it, yanked. *Close, dammit, close!* And then the blinds came clattering down and they were invisible—just him and Kate, wrapped together—and he was going to take her in some way, by God!

Next second they were spinning, fast and clumsy, and with one rough push it was *his* back jammed against the door, and he was sucking in gasping breaths with every tiny *get it while you can* break in their hungry kisses. Her hands were under his shirt again almost before the thud against the wood sounded his willing submission. Skating, racing up to his shoulders, over his chest, across his sides, down his stomach. Then she was reaching for his belt, undoing, unbuttoning, unzipping, her hands diving to touch, to grip him through his underwear.

He cradled her head, hands digging in to keep her mouth fused to his. Felt her hair—cool silk against his fingers. He must have wrenched the band from it because it was loose. They were almost at eye level—and that reminded him she was wearing high heels. The thought of those heels, her legs, made him groan. The memory of the top of her stocking— that one hot glimpse—was ferocious in his head. He wanted to see those stockings, wanted her legs wrapped around him.

His hands moved to her perfect backside. Tight and sexy and...*covered*. Not good enough. Not now. His hands went lower, down to her thighs. He stopped for a blinding moment as her hand squeezed him and he thought he'd lose it, but determinedly he moved on. The stockings. He had to feel them...touch them.

The instant his fingers reached the hem of her skirt he yanked it up. Out of the way. Out of *his* way. *God, God, God*, he'd reached that lacy edge. He could feel the band, snug against her slender thigh. *Oooohhhhh. G-o-o-o-d.* So damned *hot*. Fingers toyed at the edge for long moments, tracing the skin at the very top, then sliding up, over her bottom, now covered only by soft, slippery silk. He groaned into her mouth. He had to have her—*now*.

She spread her legs to accommodate his straining erection between her thighs, pulled him hard into the cradle of her, wordless and panting.

'I want to see you,' he said.

But before she could respond he was backing her further into the room. Step, kiss...step, kiss...step, kiss. And then they were at her desk, her thighs hitting the desktop. Her amazing, stockinged thighs. Just the thought of them had his fingers twitching to touch.

'Open your legs,' he said, and she did.

And then his fingers were there, feeling the damp silk. He was too desperate to be gentle, wrenching the covering aside so his fingers could dip into her. Urgently slipping inside her, then out, circling, then in, out, circling again. She cried out and he plastered his mouth to hers, bending her backwards at the same time as his arm swooped, scattering everything off the desk onto the floor.

He heard the thump and clatter—didn't care. Her back was on the desk, her bottom at the edge, her legs splayed and dangling, her feet in their sexy high heels just touching the floor. He was between her thighs, fingers still working, resolutely wringing wordless cries from her. He hadn't stopped kissing her, scared to break that mouth-to-mouth bond in case she told him to stop. He couldn't stop now—didn't want to stop.

Fingers still moving against her, he used his other hand to wrench her skirt higher until he knew—even though he couldn't yet see—that she was exposed to him.

He imagined the picture: pale fabric bunched around her hips, silky knickers covering her except for the slight skew at her core where his fingers played, the stay-up stockings in an understated nude that just made them that much sexier. *Steam.* He thought he must have steam coming out of his ears. Hell, he wanted to see that picture.

Okay—he would have to risk freeing her mouth just so he *could* see that picture.

He pulled back and Kate reached automatically to push her skirt down, but his hands stayed hers.

'No. I have to see. I *have* to, Kate.'

Throwing her head back, she let her hands drop to her sides, open to him.

He pulled back, looked long and hard, while his heart threatened to leap out through his eyeballs and he thought he might actually come on the spot. Violet. A flash of purple amongst the cream and nude. That delicious part of her just peeping out at the side. She was the most gloriously sexy thing he had ever seen in his life. He had a feeling the image of Kate Cleary on the desk, spread for him, would be the hottest memory of his life.

He made some low, growling noise—like an animal, because he *felt* like an animal—and knew he had to get at her the fastest way he could. No condom—because why would he need a condom just to see her briefly in her office on a Monday afternoon? *Idiot—don't leave home without one ever again.* So it would be his fingers and his mouth.

Even before the thought had finished he was on her, his fingers there, renewing their endless dipping slide. He dropped to his knees, watching each undulating movement of her hips. And when that wasn't enough he tugged that violet silk a little further off centre and put his mouth on her.

She bucked, cried out, as his tongue replaced his fingers, as his hands moved to grasp her hips and bring her closer to his mouth, angling her so he could explore every delicious fold and crease. The taste of her was intoxicating. The scent of her arousal, the feel of her as he suckled the pearly clitoris he'd freed from the silk...

'Delicious,' he said, between long, slow pulls. 'I knew you would be.'

And then she was whimpering in earnest, soft mewing cries as he alternated the pressure, building the fire in her with every scrap of skill and care he had, building, building... One last, long, endless, sucking kiss there and her hips bucked off the desk.

And then a low, throaty moan was torn out of her as she came and her hands fisted convulsively in his hair, dragging him into her moist heat, and he was breathing her in as he laved her with his eager, lusting tongue, so damned *hot* for her.

He stayed there, his mouth on her, until the waves receded.

And then her legs relaxed and she lay like an exhausted doll, legs spread, limp hands slipping from his hair as he stood back and looked at her. She was so wantonly beautiful to Scott's still hungry eyes that he had to cover his face with his hands—because he wanted to be inside her so badly the sight of her was painful.

A heartbeat later he heard the soft sounds of her getting herself together—sitting up, adjusting her clothes. He dropped his hands a millimetre at a time, gauging his control as he went.

Okay.

She was covered.

He could breathe.

Sort of.

That spectacular blush was on her cheekbones. 'What about...about you?' she asked. 'I mean...you. You know...'

Scott winced. 'That's what I get for not packing a condom,' he said, and pulled up his gaping pants, refastening the openings Kate had wrenched apart earlier. He tucked in his shirt. 'Not that I expected... Well, not that I expected *that*.'

Her eyes darted to the Venetian blinds as she edged off the desk and he read her relief as she puffed out a little breath. Had she not even noticed that he'd closed the blinds? That said something about the passion between them.

'So, Kate, I'd say you owe me,' he said. 'And I have an inkling you're not the kind of woman who likes to be in anyone's debt, so I'll collect tonight. Name the place. Name the time.'

She bent to pick up the various objects Scott had so unceremoniously shoved off the desk. Including her laptop, which she didn't even bother checking for damage.

Ordinarily he would have helped. But not now. Now he just watched. She was doing something inside her head. Calculating. Planning. So best to be a spectator, gathering clues from her demeanour. What was she thinking?

She picked up a box of tissues, but instead of putting it back on the desk she held it out to him. 'Lipstick,' she said, gesturing to his mouth.

He plucked a tissue from the box. '*Still* there?' he asked, giving her his most wicked smile. 'After my mouth was so busy between your—'

'Yes, still there,' she cut in.

Her voice was curt, no-nonsense...but he saw the shiver tremble through her body as she put the tissue box back in its place on her desk.

And then she checked her watch. Followed that with a stride over to the Venetians to open them with one sharp tug of the cord.

'Oh, no, Katie,' Scott said at that point. 'We don't get back to normal and move on to our next appointments after *that*.'

She looked at him. 'Kate. Not Katie.' She licked her top lip. Again. Eyes closed. Then opened. And then she threw her hands out with a *you win* sigh. 'All right—fair enough. Let's talk.'

She waved him to one of the black leather chairs as she walked around behind the desk and settled into her own intimidating, high-backed number.

'That was a mistake,' she said, very direct.

'I made one mistake—I didn't bring a condom. Otherwise that went pretty much as I would have liked.'

'I don't do relationships,' Kate said, ignoring that.

'Really?'

'Really.'

'Perfect.'

'What does that mean?'

'You don't do relationships. I don't do relationships. But I *do* do sex…and so, obviously, do you. And very well too.'

She stared at him for a long moment. Then that little lick of the top lip again—God, he wanted to be the one licking it.

'I have someone,' she said.

That brought a frown—fast and hard and very displeased. 'You told me at the party you didn't.'

'I'm seeing him tonight. We're working out an arrangement.'

'What kind of arrangement?'

She looked at him out of those clear eyes. 'A mutually satisfactory "friends with benefits" arrangement.'

'Work out an arrangement with me instead.'

'Phillip is forty.'

'Past his sexual prime.'

'Closer to my age.'

'How old are you, Katie?'

'Thirty-two. And it's Kate.'

'Then he's not closer to your age—I am. Five years versus eight years. And I want you more.'

'How could you possibly know that?'

'Because nobody could want you more than I do.' He leaned forward in his chair. 'And you owe me. One orgasm.'

'I'm not interested in having a toy boy.'

'And I'm not interested in being one.' He stared at her, wondering… And then he relaxed back in his chair. 'Aha! So *that* was it.'

'What are you talking about?'

'What happened at the party to make you run away. Amy said I was twenty-seven.'

'I don't do relationships.'

'Yeah—we covered that one.'

'People who are twenty-seven are in the prime age bracket for relationships.'

'Newsflash—so are people who are thirty-two.'

'I'm not like other thirty-two-year-olds.'

'And I'm not like other twenty-seven-year-olds. Remember? I'm the confirmed bachelor of Weeping Reef.'

'You said bachelor, but not *confirmed*.'

'I lied because I didn't want to scare you off.'

'Not exactly honourable.'

'That's because I'm not honourable. I have not one honourable intention when I look at you. Which won't bother you since you're not interested in relationships. So, Katie, you're going to have to tell your forty-year-old he's too late. Unless you didn't like what just happened...?'

Kate leaned back in her chair. Licked her top lip again, which was now almost bare of lipstick. It was heavy, brooding. He wanted it on his body.

'There's no reason I won't like it with Phillip just as much,' she said.

'What—you'd let Phillip go down on you on your desk during business hours, would you?'

'He wouldn't want to.'

'And that's why I'm the man for you. Because I would. I *did*. And I would do it again in a heartbeat, Katie.'

'Kate. And it's not a matter of liking. It's a matter of being clear what the end-game is so nobody gets hurt.'

'I don't get hurt.'

She looked startled. 'Everyone gets hurt.'

'Not me.'

'You've never been hurt?'

Scott's body tensed. *Redirect.* 'Let me put it this way. There's no need for either of us to get hurt. You mentioned the end-game. Why can't the end-game be sex? Pure and simple sex?'

Kate had picked up a pen and was tap, tap, tapping it on the desk. 'Pure and simple sex,' she said slowly. 'No strings?'

'You got it.'

Long moment. Tap, tap, tap. 'And if I were to lay some ground rules…? You wouldn't have a problem with that?'

'Lay away.'

'I'd need time. To think it through. Come up with an agreement.'

'I'm sure you already have the ground rules worked out for old man Phillip.'

'He's not old.'

'So your age fixation only works one way?'

No answer.

Scott smiled the Number One smile—*I am available for sex immediately*—as he got out his business card and tossed it onto her desk. 'You've got until I see you tonight to work out whatever rules you want—but, just to be clear, whether we come to an agreement or not, you owe me. If I leave this office and you suddenly have second thoughts about embarking on an affair with me, you still owe me. You. Owe. Me. And I'm not leaving until you give me a time and a place for tonight where you're going to pay me back. Katie. So let's have it.'

She was thinking—he could almost see her brain fizzing.

And then, 'Seven o'clock,' she announced. 'Come to my apartment.' She scribbled something on a sheet of paper and held it out to him. 'That's the address. And it's Kate.'

Scott reached for the paper, pocketed it.

Kate stood, walked around the desk to the door, opened it.

Scott got to his feet more slowly and followed her. But something about the controlled expression on her face got to him—so instead of walking out and heading merrily on his way, he stopped beside her, grabbed her upper arms, tugged her close and slammed his mouth hard on hers. Long, hot moment. Framed in the doorway for anyone who happened to be in the suite to see.

He released her just as suddenly, and smiled to see the combination of shock and desire on her face as he drew back.

'You've got no idea how much I'm going to need that debt paid when I see you at seven tonight,' he said softly.

And with that, he turned to wink at the unabashedly staring Deb and sauntered towards the exit.

As he reached it he heard Deb's voice. 'That was some five minutes, Kate. So, what will it be? Chicken and mung beans? Or do you need something more substantial—a chunk of raw meat, perhaps—to get your strength back?'

CHAPTER FOUR

RACING HOME AFTER WORK that evening, Kate was kicking herself for not going with her first instinct and simply supplanting Phillip with Scott at the bar. A quick twist of an arrangement already in place. Same bar. Same purpose. Just a different model.

She didn't know why the invitation to her apartment had popped out of her mouth instead.

Although, thinking back to that hot scene on her desk—God, her *desk!*—she figured it was probably just as well she'd gone for a more private option. If she couldn't control herself with Scott in her place of work, with Deb sitting just outside the door, how could she trust herself not to perform her payback sex act in the bar, on her knees under the table?

An image that got her so turned on she switched the water temperature of the shower to cold before getting under the spray.

Lust was still fizzing under her skin when she got out, so choosing something to wear took on a whole new meaning—because it had to be something that could come off easily.

Forgoing underwear, she grabbed a loose, tissue-thin shift in a rich russet colour. *Very* easy to take off when the moment came. And she hoped the outline of her body under the fine silk would drive Scott a little crazy in the meantime—payback for how crazy he'd driven *her*.

She left her hair loose. Put on a minimum of make-up. No lipstick—her mouth was going to be all over him, and she didn't want to leave a trail over his clothes or his skin.

She was so full of nervous energy, she caught herself pacing the floor while she waited for him. At this rate one touch of his clever fingers would have her unravelling—and she was *not* going to unravel twice in one day! She poured herself a glass of very cold white wine and forced her fidgety limbs onto the couch, trying to summon at least a semblance of composure.

The intercom buzzed at six fifty-nine p.m. and she closed her eyes, taking a deep breath. *This was it.*

As she let Scott in she ran her eyes over his body—white T-shirt, jeans. Very cool, very gorgeous. Her eyes kept going. Down to his…

Oh.

Converse All Star sneakers.

Cool, gorgeous…and *young*.

Those sneakers were *not* something forty-year-old Phillip would wear.

Twenty-seven. Okay, wake-up call. What the hell had she been thinking? She forced her eyes away from his feet, up to his eyes, preparing to tell him the deal was off.

But the look on his face gave her pause.

Kate had never seen such taut grimness—and she'd seen some very grim faces in the courtroom. His look got more taut and even more grim as he ran his eyes over her dress, all the way down to her bare feet and back up.

'Is something wrong?' she asked, alarmed.

'Yes,' he said, and his voice was every bit as grim as his face. 'I've been replaying that scene in your office in my head all afternoon, and I'm so desperate to get my hands on you I can't think straight. So let's skip the pleasantries.'

He nodded at the glass of wine on the coffee table.

'I don't want the drink you're probably going to offer me. I'm not into mood music, so don't bother asking me what I want to listen to. No need for a tour of the apartment—I can see it's nice and modern and open-plan. Don't give a rat's about the view. And the only thing I want to eat is you. *Again.*' Strained smile. 'Now, are we doing the ground rules before or after I get my orgasm?'

'Before,' Kate said, any thought of backing away from

their agreement obliterated by the heat of his words, the wild rush of desire that bolted through her.

'Then let's do it fast. Before I explode.'

The air was thick with lust as she guided him to the dining table, handed him the pages she'd prepared for their signatures.

'So we're—what?' he asked. 'Signing a contract?'

She nodded. 'With a contract we'll both know where we stand, what we can expect. It keeps things uncomplicated.'

Scott laughed, but didn't refuse, so Kate started running through the clauses.

She didn't even make it through the first one before Scott cut her off. 'Katie—you want a contract, then a contract it is. But it's a sex contract—not a pre-nup or a business merger. And it's not even legally enforceable, as we both know. So can you just give me the basics? Then I'll sign—there's no way I won't—and we can move on to implementing it. Because if I have to see your nipples poking against that dress for much longer without touching you, I am going to go freaking insane.'

The sudden throb between Kate's thighs had her squirming on her chair.

'I see I'm not the only one eager to get to the implementation stage,' he said, and with an inarticulate *I give up* growl reached out to cup one of her breasts through the silk.

She felt her nipple tighten even further. He pinched it gently, once. She gasped, he groaned, and then he wrenched his hand away and shot out of his seat.

'Going to need a drink after all,' he said. 'No—don't get up. Faster if I get it myself while you start going through the rules.' He headed for her kitchen, with a final prompt. 'Come on, Katie. Get it done for pity's sake. I can hear you, I can see you—go.'

'Right,' she said. *Basics.* Basics were good. Fast was good. The sooner they agreed on the terms, the sooner she could have him.

Cupboard opening…clacking of a glass on the kitchen counter.

'Two nights per week,' she said.

Fridge door opening…closing. 'What if I want more?'

'Two per week is the minimum. We can negotiate additional days as required.'

He was pouring. 'Okay. Next.'

'Any costs incurred in pursuit of mutual sexual pleasure to be split fifty-fifty.'

He was back with his wine. 'I can live with that.'

'No public displays of affection.'

He was sitting. 'Done,' he said. 'Nauseating stuff, PDAs.'

'No kissing unless it's sex-related.'

Scott held up a 'stop' hand. 'Hang on. When is kissing between an unrelated man and woman ever *not* sex-related?'

She was blushing—she could feel it. Because this was an embarrassing clause. It presupposed he would *want* to kiss her outside of sex. But kisses led to affection. And trouble lay down that road. So, embarrassing or not, it was best to have it covered in advance.

'I mean no kisses hello, goodbye—that sort of thing,' she said. 'Only kisses that lead to or are the result of sex.'

Scott looked at her mouth for a long moment. She thought he was going to object. But then he shrugged.

'Okay,' he said. 'Go on.'

'Fantasies,' Kate said, and felt the blush deepen.

'We get *fantasies*?' Scott asked reverently. 'Yee-ha!'

Kate rolled her eyes, but she was smiling. 'I thought you'd like that part of the deal. There are still rules, however. I'm suggesting a start phrase—if one or the other of us decides to enact a fantasy, a text message with "Play Time" is all that's required—along with the date, time and place. And, of course, any outfits, devices and accessories will be provided by the fantasy's owner.'

'If you could see inside my mind…'

Kate laughed. 'I'm sure I'll be seeing what's inside it very soon. But in addition to a start phrase we'll need a trigger word which, when said, will stop the activity should one of us become uncomfortable with what's happening.'

'Why not just "stop"?'

'Because that might be part of the fantasy—either a version of "stop" or "don't stop". Or it could mean "pause" or "wait" just as easily as it could mean "no more". Better to have something unambiguous. Like…maybe…a name? Something that couldn't be mistaken for anything else and wouldn't have anything to do with sex.'

Scott smiled—a particularly cool smile that made his eyes look like ice. 'Let's go with "Hugo", in that case,' he said.

'Hugo?'

'I can assure you that will stop me in my tracks.'

'Fine,' Kate agreed. 'I don't know any Hugos, so it won't be confusing for me.'

'What else?' Scott asked, hands clenching and unclenching with impatience.

'We're up to confidentiality. The details of this contract must remain confidential.'

'Okay. Are we done?'

'Last point. Fidelity is assumed—'

'Absolutely,' Scott agreed promptly. 'I don't share.'

'I haven't finished. Fidelity is assumed, but should an unforeseen sexual encounter occur with someone other than the two parties covered by the agreement—if you or I—'

'Yes,' he interrupted. 'I know what you mean. If you sleep with someone other than me; if I do someone other than you…'

'Yes. If that happens it must be confessed prior to the resumption of any contracted sexual activity between us.'

But it seemed Scott had reached his limit.

He whipped the pages out of Kate's hand, grabbed the pen, flipped to the final clause, scratched out some words, added something and initialled the changes.

'That's my input,' he said. 'No infidelity or the contract is null and void.'

Kate thought about insisting that it remain, because fidelity was for real relationships and this was not one of those—but in all honesty it was a relief. She'd seen too much of the aftermath of infidelity to be sanguine about it under any circumstances.

So… 'All right,' she said. 'Should one of us seek our pleasure elsewhere, the agreement is broken.'

'You won't need to look elsewhere, Katie. I'll keep you so busy you'll be begging for a break.'

He picked up the pen again, ready to sign.

'Wait,' Kate said, snatching the pen from him before he could put it to paper. She licked nervously at her top lip. 'Scott, I think you should read the contract properly before you sign. You've found one clause you didn't like—there may be some wording that's unclear, or something else you're uncomfortable with when you have time to think about it. And I don't want to feel like I'm taking advantage of your youth.'

Scott's eyes narrowed. 'I'm twenty-seven—not stupid,' he said. 'And I hope we're not going to waste a lot of time talking about my age. Otherwise I'll be calling "Play Time" pretty damned fast and spanking you—and that's not even a fantasy of mine.'

'Not? Really?'

'Really. Not into pain—giving or receiving.'

'No spanking. Got it. Good. But, back on topic, you're not as experienced with the law as I am, so—'

'Boring subject. And not *germane*—there's a lawyer word for you, to prove that not all twenty-seven-year-olds are ignorant morons. I just love lawyer words.'

'Yes, but—'

'Am I deeding my firstborn child to you?'

'No.'

'Am I beholden to you for the rest of my life?'

'No—just a month. Through to the twenty-eighth of February.'

'Maybe I'd better read the contract, then, because that's not going to work for us unless there's an automatic rollover in there. Considering the size and intensity of my hard-on all three times I've been near you, I'm going to need longer than a month to do you every way I want to.'

Kate took a long, slow, silent breath. She'd never been with a man who talked so blatantly about sex. It should have been a turn-off—so why did it have the opposite effect? She had the feeling that if Scott Knight had bought her a martini and asked *'Just how dirty do you like it?'* she would have offered to show him on the spot.

'Yes,' she said, 'there is a rollover option in there.'

'Right—so give me the damned pen.'

Kate watched as he scrawled his signature.

It made a funny feeling erupt in her stomach—almost as if she owned a part of him with that one dashed name. For a moment it frightened her. She didn't want to own him. Didn't want him to own *her*. Not in any way, shape or form.

He handed her the pen and she hesitated.

'They're your rules,' Scott said, reading her easily. 'So sign.'

She signed.

And then Scott pushed his chair back from the table, looked across at her. All that grimness was back, tenfold.

'Now, come here,' he said.

CHAPTER FIVE

KATE WALKED OVER to him.

'I love that dress,' he said. '*Love* that dress. But take it off.'

Kate forced herself to go slowly as she reached for the sides of the dress and started to roll the fine silk between her fingertips, raising the hem gradually. Their first experience, in the office, had been frantic and fast, sudden and shocking and blind. This time she wanted to control it. To offer herself to him one piece at a time. Tease him. Wow him.

Payback.

Scott leaned forward in his seat, eyes intent on the hem inching upwards, until she reached her upper thighs. She paused there as Scott's breathing became harsher, choppier. One more roll. Another. Bringing the hem higher up, up—until she was exposed from the hips down.

She saw Scott swallow as his eyes focused. 'Like fire...' he whispered. 'Come closer.'

Kate took two steps until she was standing an arm's length away. He reached out to touch, smoothed his fingers over the narrow strip of dark red hair.

'Let me in.'

She adjusted her stance and Scott slipped his fingers between her legs, playing there until she was gasping.

He looked up at her. 'Keep going. I want to see all of you.'

With that, Kate lost any desire for taking things slowly—so much for control!—and reefed the dress up and off. She tossed it to the floor and stood naked before him.

He kept his fingers moving in the moisture between her thighs while he looked up at her. He swallowed again as she pulled her hair back over her shoulders. The movement tightened her breasts, as if she was offering them to him.

His fingers stilled, slipped out of her, and Kate almost protested.

He sat back, eyes all over her. 'You are the sexiest thing I've ever seen,' he said hoarsely, and with a determination that was almost intimidating bent to remove his sneakers.

He got to his feet, reached into his back pocket for a condom, held it out to her.

She took it and instantly started ripping the packet. Scott—with sharp, efficient movements—took off his T-shirt, unzipped his jeans, pushed them and his underwear down and off.

And, God, he was gorgeous. Hard. Huge. Perfect.

He reached for her, pulled her in, groaned long and low as their naked bodies connected, slid together.

'I'm sorry, but this won't take long,' he said. 'We're not going to make it to the bedroom. Not this first time.'

He pulled back, jaw clenched tight. Nodded at the condom in her hand. 'Put that on me and I'll try not to come while you do it.'

Trembling, eager, Kate complied, while Scott uttered a string of low-voiced curses. And then he basically stumbled back, pulling Kate with him, until he was sitting on the chair again.

'Straddle me,' he said. 'I can get more deeply into you from this position. And I want to go deep. Deep and hard. Okay?'

'Okay,' Kate said, in a breathy voice she hardly recognised as her own.

She slid onto his lap, wrapped her legs around him, around the chair. He held her hips, settling her, then shifted so her bottom was in his hands, manipulating her so she was more perfectly positioned for his entry. Another groan, this time against her neck, followed by a sucking kiss there. Then, with one almost vicious thrust, Scott was inside her, pulling her closer, closer. Another sucking kiss on her neck and then his mouth was on hers, kissing her deeply, tongue plunging within, licking her top lip, back inside her mouth.

'Best—the best ever—to be inside you,' he said against her lips.

And somehow those not very romantic words pushed Kate over the edge and into orgasm. She grabbed his face. Pulled his mouth closer, too close for words, and fed him gasping kisses until he followed her, with one long, last, deep thrust, into an explosive orgasm.

Best. Ever.

Those two small words were all Scott could think of as he came back to earth after the most mind-blowing release of his life.

Kate. So jaw-droppingly sexy. Looks that were almost taunting, they were so hot. She'd met him thrust for thrust, taken him as deep and as hard as he wanted to go, kissed the wits right out of his head.

He snuggled her close for a long, quiet moment, stroking her hair gently now that the first rampage of lust had passed. He felt her heartbeats and his, in unison, starting to slow. But he figured he'd never have a normal heartbeat around Kate. She fired his blood like nothing he'd ever experienced. Everyone else he'd ever been with paled in comparison. Every other one was a girl. But Kate was a woman.

And, for now at least, *his* woman.

At the thought, he felt himself start to harden again, still inside her.

She laughed, low and deep. She'd felt that, then.

She pulled back and looked into his eyes. Kissed him again, lush and soft, and he got harder still.

He stood, bringing Kate with him. Her legs wrapped automatically around him.

'Bedroom's back there,' she said with a head movement.

'I hope it's a single,' he said with a laugh as she squirmed against him. 'Because anything wider than that is going to be a waste of space.'

* * *

Three hours later Scott got quietly out of Kate's bed, pulled on his jeans and T-shirt, and looked down at her.

She was deeply asleep, no doubt exhausted after what he'd put her through. Even when he hadn't been able to get it up after that third time he hadn't stopped touching her. Mouth, hands…all over her.

Best. Sex. Ever.

He thought about leaving and going home—but that felt… wrong. Sneaking away as though he'd got what he came for and didn't have to linger. Not that Kate would mind, given the contract. Sex—just sex. The end-game. He could sneak away and it wouldn't be regarded as sneaking by either of them.

But they hadn't had dinner and he was too hungry to leave. She would be too if she woke before morning. He padded into the kitchen, checking the contents of the cupboards and fridge. Not overly stocked, but he could fix omelettes.

Making himself at home—as he always seemed to do in kitchens—Scott got busy with eggs and whisk and was soon sliding his perfectly cooked omelette onto a plate. He grabbed a glass of wine—making a mental note to bring some beer to leave in Kate's fridge—and pondered where he should sit to eat.

But it was no contest—and he knew it in his heart.

He'd said earlier that he wasn't interested in the view from Kate's apartment. And in that first hot burst of screaming desire it had been true—she was the only thing of interest to him.

But he knew what the view was, and now that the edge had been taken off his caveman libido he wanted to see it.

Rushcutters Marina, where he'd boarded his first yacht as a child and learned to sail. Sailing had become a passion. His one and only rebellion had been taking that year to sail in the Whitsundays rather than go straight to university the way his parents wanted, the way his perfect, by-the-book brother had. For Scott, sailing had been…*freedom*. And even though he'd given up sailing, there was something about boats that just kept pulling at him.

So he settled himself at Kate's girl-sized outdoor table and looked out at the water as he ate. It should have been peaceful but, as ever, he found peace elusive.

He finished his omelette and walked over to the edge of the terrace, looking out at the water, listening to the gentle lap of it against the boats.

It was so different from the Whitsundays, and yet it made him remember that time eight years ago at Weeping Reef. The six of them—Willa, Luke, Amy, Chantal, Brodie and him—had formed what they'd imagined would be a lifelong bond, when their lives had been just beginning, only to see that bond disintegrate before that one summer was over.

All because of a love triangle.

One moment Chantal was Scott's girl; the next she was Brodie's. No words needed. Because everyone had been able to see it, just from the way they'd looked at each other.

Brodie was the only person Scott had ever confided in about all his childhood crap—and it had been hard to deal with his best friend slipping straight into the place his brother usually occupied in his tortured mind: the best, number one. As the white-hot knowledge had hit, Scott had lashed out, and everything had crashed and burned.

Scott and Chantal, both stuck working at Weeping Reef for the summer, had never recovered the friendship that had been between them before they'd become lovers.

Brodie had simply disappeared.

And Scott had missed him every single day. He *still* missed him.

The fight seemed so stupid, looking back. But that was what happened when you combined too many beers and too much unseasoned testosterone.

Chantal was just a girl—albeit it a smart, beautiful, wonderful girl—and what they'd had was a romance of proximity. They'd arrived at the resort before the others, and everyone had automatically assumed they were an item because they looked perfect together. A default relationship. With occasional sex that had been fun but hardly earth-shattering.

The fight hadn't been about Chantal. Scott knew that with hindsight. That fight had been all about *him*. About never being quite good enough to win the prize. Never being quite good enough to *be* the prize.

At least he'd learned from the experience. Learned not to trust. Learned to take control of his emotions and hang on to that control at all costs. Learned to keep his pride intact. Learned not to care too deeply. About friends…or lovers.

Now, if only he could work out how to deal with the restlessness that had followed him ever since, he'd be happy. But it was as if he was in a constant battle with himself: *let go and just be; don't ever let go; let go; don't let go; just be…*

'Couldn't you sleep?'

The soft question from behind him startled him out of his heavy thoughts. Scott took a moment to school his features. And then he turned, dialled up a smile—one that was a little bit naughty, a little bit *sex me up*—which he routinely used on women he'd just laid.

Kate was wearing a loose, light dressing gown, and looked tousled and natural and lovely.

'You wore me out, Katie,' he said. 'I needed fuel, so I made myself an omelette. I'll make one for you too—because if you tell me I didn't wear you out in return, I'll die of shame.'

She chuckled. 'Oh, I'm worn out, I promise. We're equal.'

She came over to stand beside him and he found himself drawing her close, tucking her against his side, under his arm.

'I think that qualifies as a PDA,' Kate said.

'We're not in public, so how can it?'

He felt her sigh at his dodge-master answer but she didn't say anything, so he kept her there, under his arm. It was… restful, somehow.

'I love this view,' she said after a long moment.

'Best harbour in the world.'

'Yes,' she said slowly. 'But it's more about the boats for me. The thought of sailing away from your troubles, beginning a wonderful adventure. The freedom of it. I've often dreamt about stealing a yacht and just going.'

She must have felt the slight jerk he gave, because she turned her face up to his, frowning.

'What?'

'A lawyer? Stealing? *Sacré bleu.*'

Her eyes narrowed. 'Yes, but that's not really it, is it?'

Pause. And then he laughed—even managing to make it sound natural. 'What you said just reminded me of my own sailing adventures, that's all. And not that I want to burst your bubble, but reality will bite you on the arse wherever you are.'

'Ah, of course—I forgot you were a sailing instructor at Weeping Reef. You and the other guy I haven't met yet. Brodie?'

That was all it took for Scott to tense up. Brodie's name coming out of Kate's mouth. He didn't want to talk about Brodie. It was too personal, too…raw. God, *still*.

'So what part of it bit you?' Kate asked.

'Let's just say I was too young to appreciate the experience,' he said, and forced himself to smile down at her. This smile meant *go no further*—and he didn't have to use it often because he didn't let people get close enough to push his buttons.

'And, no,' he added quickly, thinking to nip in the bud any other question she might have brewing, 'that's not an invitation to tell me I'm still too young. I'm old enough to have made the sensible choice: sail back to Sydney, go to university, become an architect. All grown-up—just like you. Now, are you ready for your omelette?'

He could sense her slight hesitancy. Another question…? A comment…? But Kate finally shrugged, smiled. And thankfully gave up.

'How lucky am I?' she said. 'A man who sizzles in bed *and* in the kitchen.'

'I like cooking—the orderliness of it. You put a set number of ingredients together and, as long as you combine them in the right order, they come out at the other end in perfect formation.'

Kate grimaced. 'My cooking doesn't do that!'

'Mine does. I insist on it.'

He leaned down and kissed her.

'No kissing,' Kate said, pulling away awkwardly after a moment. 'Not outside of sex. Remember the rules.'

'Oh, yeah, the rules.'

Well, Scott happened to think parts of her contract were ridiculous, as *well* as not being legally enforceable. So not only was he *not* going to be controlled by her rules, he was going to enjoy flouting them. The kissing clause was a case in point. He liked kissing Kate, so he was going to keep kissing her. Simple.

'You know, Katie, a kiss isn't a declaration of honourable intentions, if that's what's bothering you. I assure you my intentions are still *entirely* dishonourable—so relax. It shouldn't surprise you, as the owner of that sexy-as-hell mouth, that men want to kiss it.'

'But—'

Scott swooped before she could get another word out, kissing her again, drawing from the deep well of expertise he'd amassed during an impressive career of seduction. And this time it took her longer to pull away.

'Scott!'

'Hey, this is pre-contract,' he argued. 'We're still on payback sex, by my reckoning.'

'I owed you one orgasm. And I paid that back on the dining room chair. We're on the clock now—and I can't believe you're blurring the rules on day one.'

'Then if it makes you feel better,' he said, grabbing her hands and pulling her in close, '*this* kiss is going to lead to sex.'

And with that, he lowered his head once more, put his mouth on hers. He felt her melt, melt, melting into him. *That* was control. He would control this. Control *her* through her precious contract. Take what he wanted when he wanted it with a clear conscience and no hard feelings when they said goodbye at the end. He'd finally achieved perfection in a relationship!

Not that this was a relationship.

Scott nudged her legs apart, settled himself between them, thrust against her. 'See? I'm ready for you already.'

'Is that perma-erection of yours a benefit of youth?' she asked, leaning into him.

'I could be a hundred years old and five days dead and still want you, Katie,' he said in return. 'Let's go to bed and I'll show you how much. And *then* I'll make you an omelette before I head home.'

CHAPTER SIX

KATE DIDN'T KNOW if it was youthful vigour or if Scott just had more testosterone than the average man, but he'd been at her apartment nine nights in a row. He'd only skipped the tenth night because he had a pre-scheduled poker night—and he'd bemoaned not being able to get out of *that*!

Each time they'd both been insatiable, from the moment he stepped inside to the moment he staggered out, bleary-eyed, in the wee hours.

By tacit agreement Scott never stayed the night. That would have been too…intimate. And, okay, that seemed ridiculous, given the extent to which they'd examined each other's bodies—she'd seen the kitten-shaped birthmark on Scott's right butt cheek, for God's sake, so cute it hurt—but there was something 'next step' about sleeping together. And the contract didn't allow for next steps.

Their nine encounters had included two Play Times.

The first Play Time Scott had turned up as a doctor making a house call. Doctor/patient had been hilarious, to start with. But it had quickly progressed to hot, hot, hot as he'd gloved up and examined various parts of her body, sounding cool and professional with his 'How does that feel?' and 'Is that helping?' while she squirmed and gasped and orgasmed in a long, crazy, unending stream.

Their second Play Time, on their ninth night together, he'd opted for master/slave—but with a midway role-swap.

For the first part of the evening Kate had been the master. Which was just as well, because her phone had been running so hot she would have made an unsatisfactorily preoccupied sex slave. Her client Rosie was in crisis mode, having finally asked for a divorce, and was calling Kate every fifteen minutes for advice. Another client was desperate for help because his ex-wife was threatening to move interstate with their two children. And a colleague wanted advice on a property settlement.

None of it had seemed to faze Scott, who'd taken to his slave role like a duck to water and lavished attention on her as she'd stressed on the phone. Making her tea, massaging her shoulders and feet, rubbing her back, stroking her hair...

And when the phone had finally stopped ringing he'd reduced her to a state of orgasmic bliss. By which time she'd been *dying* to be his slave and would have agreed to anything he asked.

But Scott had issued only one command: that she accompany him to the Visionary Architect Awards dinner.

Which was how now, two nights later, Kate found herself in her best evening gown—a modernised cheongsam in royal purple satin—her hair pinned into a complicated bun, her face flawlessly made-up, essentials stuffed into a glittery silver evening bag...

And feeling all kinds of weird.

A date that wasn't a date.

With a lover who wasn't a boyfriend.

And, despite her being Scott's 'slave' tonight, he'd insisted on coming to her door to get her, like an old-fashioned gentleman caller.

It was...*confusing*. And Kate knew she wouldn't be any less confused by the end of the night. Because not only was Scott a master manipulator, adept at getting her to do whatever he wanted, he was also a champion question-deflector. If she asked him something he didn't want to answer he would just kiss her! And if she complained about kissing being against the rules he would insist the kiss was going to lead to sex, and the next moment they'd be in bed.

Kate had never had so much sex in her life! Or so few answers.

And the upshot was that she wanted to know...well, *everything*!

She was even insanely curious about what Scott would be wearing tonight—something she'd never, ever contemplated ahead of dates with other men...*not* that this *was* a date. How ridiculous was that? It was a black-tie event: ergo, Scott would be in black tie. No need to be curious because all men looked pretty much the same in black tie.

A thought that went straight out of her head—along with the rest of her grey matter—when she opened the door to him and her heart did a thudding swoon.

He was just *so* gorgeous.

Tux in navy blue. Formal shirt in black, not white. He'd forgone the bow tie. Shoes that were buckled, not laced. He looked modern and edgy and scrumptious. Exactly the way an award-winning architect should look.

'Wow!' she said, after a moment of stunned silence.

'Wow yourself!' he responded, and kissed her. 'I wish I'd come over after the game last night, because now I think I'm suffering withdrawal symptoms. I don't know how I'm going to keep my hands off you during dinner.'

And as Kate's heart swooned again—at the kiss, at his words—she wondered if she could invoke *her* first Play Time and whisk Scott off at some stage of the evening for some restroom sex. And she'd *never* wanted to try that before.

Scott took her hand—hmm, PDA or just giving her some support for her five-inch heels?—and didn't let go until they reached his car. When Kate did a double-take, because it was a red Mini—not at all what she would have expected. Not that she'd given a lot of thought to what car Scott would drive, but shouldn't it be a little less...well, *cute*? A little more macho? Like maybe a black off-road truck. Something that did not remind her that he had a kitten-shaped birthmark she would love to see *right that second*.

Scott opened the car door for her and helped her in before getting behind the wheel.

'I hate these events,' he said as he buckled his seat belt. 'So thank you for not leaving me sad and dateless.'

'I'm your slave, remember? I didn't have a choice.'

'Hey, yeah—I forgot!' he said. 'So in that case I would like a kiss for the road.'

'Your wish…my command,' Kate said, and leaned over to give him a steamy, lingering kiss. Even though that kiss was not going to lead to sex. *Uh-oh.* She was getting as bad as him.

But at least he was looking suitably scorched when she eased back.

'Definitely not going to keep my hands off you during dinner,' Scott said fervently.

Kate laughed. 'Not that I believe for a moment that a phone call to the first name in your little black book wouldn't have snagged you a date.'

'Not wishing to sound like an egomaniac, but that is true. The fidelity clause, however, is a killer,' he said. 'How ungallant it would have been, beating off my lascivious companion at the end of the night.'

'You're not telling me your dates always end in sex?'

'Aren't I?'

Kate dutifully laughed—but the idea of him even thinking about sex with another woman was somehow unsettling. And the fact that it unsettled her was…well, *that* was unsettling too.

'You're the one who got fussy about that fidelity clause,' she reminded him, aiming for a nonchalance she just couldn't make herself feel. 'If it's a hardship to give up all those women out there panting for you, you only have to say the word.'

'I'm not risking you ditching me that fast.'

'Who says I'd ditch you? Maybe I wouldn't care.'

He shot her a curious look. 'You honest-to-God wouldn't have minded if I'd done the deed elsewhere tonight?'

'We'll never know, will we?'

'Yeah—not buying it,' he said. 'You wouldn't have liked it. And—just to remind you—I definitely *would* mind, so no going there for you.' Quick, cheeky grin at her. 'Not that you need to.'

'Oh, the confidence of youth.'

Another grin. 'Not youth—*skill*, Katie. And, for the record, it's not that I couldn't have resisted Anais—she's the first A in my black book, by the way—because I could have. It's that I didn't want to hurt her feelings with a knockback she wouldn't have been expecting. So, you see, you had to come to spare the poor girl's feelings.'

'Oh, so this is all about me doing Anais a favour!'

'Well, you can't deny you've got a soft spot for the oppressed.'

'Has Willa been talking about my imminent canonisation again?'

'Nope. I just know, Saint Kate. When you were on the phone two nights ago I sensed weeping aplenty and a fair amount of teeth-gnashing at the other end of the line—and I heard how you dealt with it.' Scott reached for her hand, brought it to his mouth, kissed it. 'All class.'

Kate, uncharacteristically flustered, had to swallow twice before she could force herself back into banter mode and once more to actually find her voice.

'And poor Anais is oppressed *how*, exactly?' she asked—and was relieved the question had come out light and amused.

'All right, you got me,' Scott said, rueful. 'Anais is not oppressed. In fact, she tried to oppress *me*!'

'You? Oppressed? *Puh-lease.*'

'She *did*! Bondage and discipline. *Ouch.* Evil. I cried like a baby.'

Kate couldn't help it. She laughed. 'So that's what I have to do to keep you in line, is it?'

'No. I told you—I'm not into all that. All you have to do to keep me in line, Katie, is redirect your soft spot where it's needed.'

'And where would that be?'

'Well, to me, obviously. Haven't you been listening? I'm oppressed.'

'You need a little more oppression,' Kate said dryly, and when he laughed, sounding boyish and completely irresistible, she found herself wanting to kiss him again.

She decided a subject-change was required for her own sanity.

'So, what are the chances of Silverston taking the prize tonight?' she asked.

Scott waited a moment. 'Did you look it up?'

'Well, yes, of course. What kind of slave would I be if I didn't know what award my master was up for? Creative Residential. Five finalists.'

'I'm not expecting to win.' He sounded offhand—but his hands had tightened on the steering wheel.

'Why not?' she asked.

A shrug, but no answer. Just one of those smiles that she thought he must have stacked up like a jukebox—pick one and play it.

'I hope the food is good, because I'm starving,' he said. 'What's the bet it'll be smoked salmon out of a packet, followed by overdone steak with three vegetables on the side, then chocolate mousse?'

Which, of course, was not an answer. And it seemed she wasn't going to get one, because Scott kept the conversation flowing around a host of boy subjects—which Kate suspected had been deliberately chosen—for the rest of the drive.

Sports results—*please, kill her*—action movies, gory television shows.

By the time they arrived at the five-star hotel where the event was being held, Scott had a new jukebox smile pasted on—a smile that said *I'm here! No big deal!*

But it became obvious very quickly to Kate that his arrival was, in fact, a *very* big deal—to everyone except him. As pre-event cocktails were served outside the ballroom people made their way to Scott in a steady stream, drawn as though by a magnet. But although Scott smiled, chatted, shook hands, kissed a score of female cheeks, he held everyone at bay…and they didn't even realise he was doing it. He was effortlessly, carelessly charismatic, and people clearly wanted to be in his orbit, but he was essentially untouchable.

What the hell...?

Kate remembered what he'd said that day in her office. *I don't get hurt.* She was starting to believe it was true. To get hurt you had to be close to someone. And dial-a-smile Scott wasn't close. To *anyone*. The question was: why not?

'Bored?' Scott asked her, leaning in close.

'No. Why?'

'You were staring off into space.'

'Oh, just...thinking. But not bored.'

'Well, *I'm* bored. Slave or not, I'm going to have to think up a way to reward you for sacrificing your night to this tedium.'

'Just win the prize,' she said.

Instantly his eyes shuttered. 'Hmmm.'

That was all he said. *Hmmm.*

What the hell...?

'Have the organisers already notified the winners?' Kate asked, puzzled. 'Is that why you're so sure you're not going to win?'

'No. It's not— No.'

'Then...what?'

One of those dismissive shrugs. 'I just don't.'

'Don't what?'

'Win. That's the way it is, Katie.' He looked over her shoulder. 'Ah, the doors are opening. Let's go in and try not to...' His eyes widened, his voice trailed off. Then, 'Damn,' he said under his breath. 'He *is* here.'

Kate turned to see what he was seeing. 'What? Who? Oh! He looks like—'

'Me.'

'Only—'

'Taller.'

'Well, yes, but—'

'Better-looking.'

'I was going to say "older".'

His eyes zoomed to her. 'Are you going to tell me he's more

age-appropriate for a thirty-two-year-old? Because if you are—don't. I'm not up to another discussion about my age.'

Kate could only blink. She seemed to be thinking *What the hell?* a lot tonight but...well, *what the hell...?*

His eyes roamed behind her again. 'Oh, for the love of God!'

Kate turned again as Scott's lookalike descended on them.

'Who *is* he?' she asked.

'My brother. His house is one of the finalists.'

That was all he had time to say before he was enveloped in a bear hug.

'Scottie!' his brother boomed out.

Scott stiffened, before giving his brother an awkward pat on the back.

Edging back as fast as he could, he took Kate's elbow and brought her closer. 'Kate—my brother Hugo.'

Hugo? As in Play Time? The word that would stop Scott in his tracks? *What the freaking hell...?* This evening was turning out to be very...instructive.

The resemblance between the two men wasn't as strong close-up. Hugo was like a more refined version of Scott. His eyes were brown, not green. And he spoke with a slightly British accent—very different from Scott's Aussie drawl. Kate thought the accent was an affectation until Hugo confessed, with the fakest attempt at self-deprecation Kate had ever heard, that he'd been to medical school in England.

He looked more conservative than Scott—from his sharp, perfect haircut to his traditional black-tie get-up. Hugo was more talkative, more...accessible. But there was something missing. That indefinable something Scott had in spades— that mix of charm and wit and sexy intrigue. Hugo was obviously smart. He was good-looking. A little stuffy, maybe, although he seemed like a decent guy. But nobody would rush to Hugo's side the way they rushed to Scott's.

Kate was on the point of filing that description away when Hugo raised the subject of the award, with a look at Scott that could only be described as *pitying*—and Kate's hackles rose, sharp and hard. Okay, description revised. Hugo was *not* a decent guy; Hugo was a bastard.

'So—Creative Residential! Who would have thought we'd end up competing *again*, Scottie?' Hugo asked, with a heavy clap on Scott's back. 'I checked out Silverston on the website. Good job, Scottie. *Really* good job.'

'Thank you,' Scott said with a smile that was definitely forced.

Kate, *hating* that smile, blinked innocently up at Hugo. 'You're not a doctor *and* an architect, are you, Hugo?'

'Well, no, but—'

'So your *architect* is the finalist?' More wide-eyed *I don't understand* innocence.

'Yes, my man Waldo.'

'Oh, your *man*. I see. Scott's client is leaving the honours to him. Credit where it's due, right?' Kate asked, and hoped Scott's client wouldn't embarrass her by appearing out of nowhere!

Hugo chuckled, oblivious to any insult. 'Ah, but I had considerable input into Waldo's design,' he explained. 'So when I asked if I could come along this evening, of course Waldo was only too happy. Especially when I told him there would be a little friendly family rivalry for the prize.'

Scott, whose eyes had frosted in a way that did not look at all friendly, raised his eyebrows. '*Waldo* let you have a say? Waldo *Kubrick*?' He turned to Kate. 'Waldo is brilliant—actually, the best. But he's more temperamental than a busload of French chefs.'

Hugo gave Scott another pitying look. 'Yes, he *is* the best, isn't he?' Then came an apologetic and yet not *at all* apologetic cough. 'Sorry, Scottie.'

'Sorry?' Scott asked. 'Why?'

There was something in Hugo's eyes that Kate didn't like. Something malicious.

'Let's just say Knightley is pretty special,' he said. 'The buzz is there.'

Kate felt a laugh building and had to bite the inside of her cheek hard. Knightley? His house was called *Knightley*?

'Yes, it is,' Scott said coolly, and gestured towards the ballroom. 'Well, good luck, Hugo. We're heading in.'

And then Scott turned to Kate—who was trying not to laugh and at the same time silently communicating to Scott that she knew why the name *Hugo* would stop him in his Play Time tracks—and something lit in his eyes as he took in the expression on her face. And his smile, for the very first time, was in his eyes.

And it was absolutely devastating.

Scott felt a little off-balance.

It had been a lightning-fast emotional shift—from the normal feeling of inadequacy he always experienced around his brother to wanting to take Kate in his arms right there in front of Hugo, to whom he never, ever introduced *anyone*. And not only take her in his arms but breathe her right into his body. All because she'd wanted to laugh. It didn't seem to matter that he didn't even know what had amused her. Not that Kate didn't usually laugh—she did, a lot, and he loved that. But there was just something different about it tonight.

'What's so funny?' he asked as he pulled out her chair.

She sat. Waited for him to sit beside her. 'Not that I want to disparage your brother, *Scottie*—'

He groaned.

'Sorry, but I owe you for all the Katies,' Kate said.

Wince. 'Yeah. I get it. No more Katies. Hand-on-heart promise.'

'But what is *with* that house name? Is Hugo an *Emma* fan? Or maybe his wife? Naming the house after Mr Knightley, perhaps?'

'Emma who?'

Kate rolled her eyes. 'Never mind. I think the explanation is simpler. He named it after *himself*, didn't he? Like one of those British stately homes?' She was biting the inside of her cheek again. 'Maybe he got the idea at med school...'

'Knightley,' Scott said slowly. '*Knightley.* Oh, my God. I didn't even think— It never occurred— I mean—God!' He sat, stunned, for a moment, and then he started laughing. *'God!'*

'It's not a laughing matter,' Kate admonished, but Scott could see she was struggling to keep a straight face. 'It's *de rigueur* to name your home after yourself, you know.' Her mouth was starting to twist. 'My own apartment is c-called C-Castle C-Cleary.'

And then Kate was laughing too, and the sound of it was just so sexy he had to touch her. Needed to share this delicious absurdity with her physically.

He reached for her hand and she twined her fingers with his, still laughing. Even her eyes were laughing. What must that be like? To have eyes that laughed? Eyes that were warm like molten silver. Beautiful.

His throat closed over and the laughter jammed. Stuck in his throat. All he could think about was kissing her until she was breathless. As breathless as he felt just looking at her. Breathless. And perfect. For once, perfect...

Kate stopped laughing too, and then she reached out with her free hand. Touched his face as if she felt it too. The connection.

And then panic hit.

No! No connection. He didn't want that.

He jerked back, away from her touch.

He looked at their joined hands, and the sight of their linked fingers jolted him like an electric shock. He let go.

He picked up his wine glass, took an urgent swallow. And then, eyes sliding away to some distant point, he cleared his throat.

Kate cleared her own throat, picked up her own wine glass, sipped. He heard the quick breath she took.

'So...um...what's it like?' she asked, putting the words out hesitantly into the sudden, excruciating void.

Wine. He needed another sip. Took it. Put the glass down. 'What's what like?'

'Knightley?'

Shrug. 'I know as much as you do about Knightley. Just what I've seen on the awards website.' He waved at someone across the room.

'So it must be... Is it...? Is it brand-new, then? I mean that you haven't seen it?'

'No,' he said. 'I just haven't. Seen it, I mean.'

Their first course arrived, and Scott almost sagged with relief. He pasted on a cheerful smile, and at last he could look at her again. 'Well, Kate—as you can see, I was on the money with the smoked salmon.'

From that point the seemingly endless procession of award presentations, cheesy entertainment and bland food courses proceeded exactly as Scott had expected. Except for one thing: a burning awareness of Kate beside him. Something he'd never felt with Anais or any of his other black-bookers at one of these insipid evenings.

And that bothered him.

Even the way she was captivating the architect on her other side was getting to him. Thank God Miles Smithers was sixty years old and happily married, or he'd probably want to smash the guy's tee—

Whoa! Pull up. There was no thanking God required. Or teeth-smashing. It didn't matter if Kate was captivating a sixty-year-old married architect or a thirty-two-year-old billionaire Greek god! If she was physically faithful she could captivate whomever the hell she wanted to captivate. None of his business.

And it wasn't as though he was being a scintillating conversationalist himself. If not for Miles, Kate would be catatonic! He was being a first-class boor, barely grunting a reply when she asked him anything.

All because of that...that moment. That intense connection which he hadn't bargained for and didn't bloody well want.

Having Hugo sitting two tables away, already looking every inch the victor, wasn't helping either.

Scott had known his brother wouldn't be able to stay away tonight, wouldn't be able to vacate the space, just for once, and let Scott occupy it. But he'd been anticipating a hand-wave and a superior nod across the room—that was their usual interaction. It must have been the sight of Kate that had prompted Hugo to dial it up a notch.

Kate. So glamorous and secure and beautiful. Out of his league. Which Hugo would have seen at a glance. So he probably should have guessed Hugo wouldn't have been able to resist coming over in person to foreshadow his win.

And Knightley *would* win.

Because Hugo *always* won, even if he had to win via a third party like Waldo.

When the Creative Residential category was announced Hugo looked directly at him. There was a tiny narrowing of his eyes, an oh-so-poignant smile—a look Scott had being seeing all his life. A look that said *Sorry, I just can't help it that I'm so much better than you, little brother.* Even more insufferable than usual because Kate saw it. And, God, how he wished he could get her out of there so she didn't have to see it again when he lost. Why, why, *why* had he brought her?

Knightley was the second finalist announced. Pictures flashed up on the huge screen at the front of the room and—yes—it was a knockout. Hugo turned to clink glasses with Waldo, who had the grace to look uncomfortable about such precipitate celebration.

Two more finalists.

Then Scott's name was announced. Silverston was being described in admiring detail and Kate turned to him, radiant, looking as if she was proud of him or something. She took his hand in hers as though that were entirely natural, held on.

PDA, Scott wanted to say—but couldn't get it out of his tight throat. This was embarrassing. He wasn't going to win. Kate would be giving him one of Hugo's pitying looks in a minute, and having her hold his hand while she did so would only make it harder to stomach.

He wanted to disengage his hand, but couldn't seem to let go. So he concentrated, instead, on making his hand go slack and dead. Let her interpret that. She'd be letting go of his hand any moment now. Any moment... Any...

Nope.

She wasn't letting go. And everything was starting to blur in his head until he forgot why he shouldn't be holding her hand.

Flashing images on the giant screen... The MC leaning into his microphone, saying something... A short blare of music... Spotlights swirling...

Scott found that, far from going slack and dead, his hand was gripping Kate's. Hers was gripping right back.

And then she leaned in and kissed him briefly on the lips, and he thought, *What?*

And the applause was ringing out.

And the spotlight—it had stopped on him. It was shining on him. On *him*!

He blinked. Shook his head.

Kate laughed. Nodded.

And Scott knew. He'd won. He'd really won.

He was too shocked even to smile, let alone move. But Kate nudged him and somehow he got to his feet, started heading towards the stage—only to realise he was still holding Kate's hand. He looked down at it, looked at her. She was laughing as she raised his hand to her lips, kissed it—the way he'd kissed hers in the car. And he needed exactly that, right at that moment. *Exactly.*

And then he was walking to the front of the room, up onto the stage.

'Wow,' he said when he got to the microphone. 'Like... *wow!* Okay, this is like one of those moments where the award-winner says they never really expected to win...and then pulls out a *just in case* speech.'

General laughter.

Deep breath.

'But I don't have a *just in case* speech. So…so…um… thank you. I mean—to my client, to the team at Urban Sleek. The other finalists! So amazing. And…and Kate. Just…for… well. Thanks again. And…well, wow.'

Trophy in hand, Scott made his way back to the table, where Kate kissed him again, and he sat in a daze for the rest of the presentations, embarrassed at having given the worst speech in the history of all awards ceremonies everywhere in the world. But he'd just never expected to win. Why would he have prepared a speech? He never won. *Never.*

It wasn't until the final award was being presented that he remembered Hugo. He looked over at Hugo's table, saw his empty seat—bathroom visit?—and then forgot all about Hugo as formal proceedings gave way to the dancing and socialising part of the evening and what felt like a horde of people headed over to congratulate him.

He figured Kate must be longing to escape by the time the throng of well-wishers had dissipated, but when he opened his mouth to suggest they make a run for it, she smoothed a hand over his lapel and smiled at him—and his brain cells scrambled.

'Don't you think we should have a celebratory dance?' she asked.

Scott looked from her to the dance floor, then back.

'Scott?' She smiled. 'Dance?'

'Er…'

Really? 'Er…' is the best you've got? Get it together.

Clearing of the throat. 'Actually, I'm not much of a dancer, Kate.'

'That's all right, neither am I.'

'No—I mean I don't. Dance. Ever.'

She seemed startled by that. 'You mean you never *have*?'

He checked his watch. 'I was thinking… It's late. I should get you home. You've suffered enough.'

Kate was watching him. Curious, a little wary. She seemed

on the verge of asking something… But then she gave her head a tiny shake and said, 'Sure.'

Scott was silent on the drive to Kate's. Because the tension he'd been feeling all the way up to the announcement of his win was back. Tenfold. And it must have rubbed off on Kate because she was silent too, staring through the windscreen.

He pulled up outside her building and Kate unbuckled her seat belt. Then she just sat there, looking at him, waiting for him to turn off the ignition.

'Aren't you coming up?' she asked at last.

'I thought…it's late…I thought…'

'*I* thought you said all your dates ended with sex?'

Silence. Awkward.

'Ah, but not tonight,' Kate said. 'Well, we only specified two nights a week, didn't we? And we've hit that target. But, just so you know, slave girl ends now.'

With that throaty laugh he loved a little too much, she opened the car door and got out. But then she leaned down to look in at him. 'Congratulations again, Scott. That was some house you designed.'

'Thanks. And…and…' Shrug. 'Goodnight, Kate.'

Door closed.

Night over.

Thank God.

Scott drove off, up the street, around the corner, heading home.

Ordinarily he would have helped his date out of the car. That was what he always did, because that was the gentlemanly thing.

Ordinarily he would have walked his date to her front door—again, gentlemanly.

Ordinarily he would have followed his date inside, all the way into her bed. Gentlemanly? No. But expected. On both sides.

Ordinarily.

But with Kate…?

Well, it wasn't a *date*.

It was supposed to have been just an easy fix for the night. Because he really *hadn't* felt like going the black-book route and he really *hadn't* wanted to do the sexual brush-off at the end—which he definitely *would* have done, because fidelity really *was* a sticking point for him and he really *wasn't* interested in having sex with anyone except Kate. *For now*, he added, just to be clear on that. And, aside from all of that, it had been fun to manipulate Kate's rules by negotiating her role tonight as part of Play Time.

An easy fix, a non-date, a fun manipulation.

But it had turned into something…*else*.

Because with her there, the award had been somehow more important than it should have been—and that had surprised him.

Because Hugo had tried to show off to her and she hadn't thought he was anything special—in fact, she'd thought he was a little bit ridiculous.

Because they'd laughed together like…like *that*.

Because she'd had to go and get all proud and lovely about his award.

None of which had anything to do with the end-game.

And it was the end-game he wanted—not the something… *else*.

So it was best to re-establish some distance between them before he had sex with Kate again. And as for walking her to her front door…? He just hadn't trusted himself to get that far and no further. Not with her.

Anyway, it wasn't as if she was his responsibility. He didn't have to usher her protectively behind locked doors. She wasn't some vulnerable girl who couldn't take care of herself. She *could* take care of herself. She *wanted* to take care of herself. She'd been arriving home from all kinds of dates—and this wasn't even a date—for years. She'd laughed when he'd insisted on going to her door to pick her up tonight. She hadn't looked at all put out that he wasn't getting out of the car to walk her to her door at the end of the night. She didn't want that kind of attention. She didn't need—

Oh, dammit to hell!

Swearing fluently and comprehensively, Scott did a U-turn and sped back to Kate's. He screeched to a stop, leapt from the car, raced to the apartment block and followed a semi-familiar resident into the building without having to press the intercom. Which was fortuitous, because he had no idea yet what he was going to say to explain his reappearance.

His heart was thumping when he reached Kate's apartment and knocked on her door.

He still had no idea what to say, but he was suddenly so desperate to see her he was happy just to wing it. *So answer... open the door...come on.*

Kate opened the door cautiously.

Well, of course she was cautious! He could have been anyone.

'You shouldn't open the door without knowing who it is,' he said. Yep, he had lost his freaking mind.

Her only response was to raise her eyebrows. God, he loved the way she did that—all haughty and amused.

She was still wearing that stunning dress, but her hair was half down and her feet were bare.

Scott cleared his throat. 'I should have walked you to your door.'

'Why?'

'Because it's the right thing to do.'

She shook her head, laughed as though to say *silly boy*— and that riled him.

So he reached for her, pulled her close and did what he'd been wanting to do all night.

He kissed her.

CHAPTER SEVEN

SCOTT WAS STILL kissing her as he backed her into the apartment and kicked the door closed.

And Kate really wished he didn't have the ability to turn her to mush—because *she'd* wanted to be the one closing the door. *Slamming* it. Right in his face.

Because…because… Well, because how *dared* he make tonight the first date in his life that wasn't ending with sex? *Not* that it was a date, but still!

Pride might have forced her to laugh it off out there in the car, but she was furious. His first date not to end in sex and it was *her*? On *this* night of all nights? An important night he'd *shared* with her? A night when he'd finally shared *something*?

Yep—one hundred per cent furious.

But with Scott kissing her as though he wanted to suck her right into his soul, she felt the anger drain away. Because she could feel that it was more than a kiss. There was something there—something he wanted from her that he couldn't, wouldn't, articulate. Something that made her ache for him, *long* for him.

'Scott, what's wrong?' she asked when he broke away to take a breath. 'Tell me. Please tell me.'

But he kissed her again. 'Just let me…' he said. *Kiss.* 'I want…' *Kiss.* 'I just…'

He didn't finish those sentences. Kate wondered if he'd even finished them in his own head. Because he kept kissing her, for the longest time, as though there *were* no thoughts, just the kissing.

And for tonight, she decided, it was enough.

'Come with me,' Kate said, and led him to the bedroom.

Scott undressed her. First, the cheongsam—falling to the floor in a purple crumple. Next came her underwear. Her most expensive, coffee-coloured silk and lace, removed like an inconvenience. She smiled, remembering the excitement with which she'd donned that underwear, thinking to drive him wild tonight—and now he just didn't care.

He reached into her hair, gently removed the remaining pins, tossed them to the floor. Ran his fingers through the red mass of it, seemingly more interested in her hair than the sight of her naked body.

It felt strange…and thrilling. The way his eyes stayed on her face, her hair.

'Take my clothes off,' he said, and his voice was a throb.

Kate chose first to put her mouth on his, to let it cling there. She took a moment to snuggle against him, feeling both vulnerable and wicked as his arms closed around her and she was held, naked, against his fully clothed body.

Not until he started to shake did she step back, slipping her hands under his jacket, over his shoulders, smoothing it back and off so that it dropped to the floor behind him. Next came his shirt buttons, slipped through their holes as Scott breathed out a long, slow prayer of a breath. Then she eased his cufflinks out.

They looked expensive, so she glanced towards her dressing table, thinking to put them somewhere safe—but Scott stopped her before she could step away.

'Don't leave,' he said.

'But I only—'

He took the cufflinks from her and tossed them over his shoulder as though they were no more valuable than her hairpins. He didn't even blink as they hit the wall.

Kate slid the shirt from his body, stopped to kiss him again, her breasts against his chest, almost moaning at how wonderful that felt.

Next, she undid his pants. Eased them down. Knelt at his feet, unbuckled his shoes. She paused, rose on her knees.

Perfect position for taking him in her mouth. She wanted to do that so badly.

But Scott, reading her mind, drew her up. 'Not tonight,' he said.

A minute later his shoes were off, his pants and underwear kicked away, and she was back in his arms, being held against him, while his hands smoothed down her back, over and over, as he breathed her in, his mouth against her hair. 'Kate…' he said. 'Kate.'

But Kate didn't think he even knew he was saying her name. He seemed to be in a kind of trance.

So she let him lead her to the bed, let him pull the covers back, draw her gently down beside him. He kissed her again, so softly. And then he eased slowly back, taking Kate with him. Wrapped her in his arms. Kissed her eyelids, her mouth, her neck, nuzzled into her hair.

She simply held him, opening to him in any way he wanted. Even the simple act of sliding a condom onto him, his hands lightly covering hers while she did it, seemed like a sensual discovery.

And when at last he positioned her beneath him and slid inside her welcoming heat, it was as though his body sighed and relaxed and just…*was*. For the longest moment he stayed still, taking her face between his hands, laying his mouth on hers, kissing her with an intensity that pierced through to her burning heart.

Tears started to Kate's eyes and she didn't even know why. She closed her eyes, knowing it would change things if he saw her cry. And she wouldn't have changed this slow, sweet loving for anything.

She knew what was happening, and she wanted it. She was giving herself to him: *I'm here, yours.*

His. For tonight she was his. And Scott was hers. Hers alone. For tonight.

And when he spilled himself inside her, with a gasping, luscious groan into the mouth he was kissing so deeply, Kate held him tight, so tightly against her, and wrapped her legs around him, let herself join him in her own flowering release.

'Thank you,' he whispered into her ear.

For what? she wanted to ask, but she dared not break the spell by seeking answers he wouldn't give.

And in any case Scott was holding her close, kissing the top of her head, stroking her back. And it really was enough.

So beautiful… Soothing… Lovely…

Ahhhh…

When Kate woke early the next morning she turned, smiling, to face Scott—only to find his side of the bed empty.

A quick walk through the apartment showed that all he'd left behind was a note, on the kitchen bench.

Saturday night?
S

Two words. One question mark. One initial.

Which brought home to Kate that last night had been just…well, just last night.

He hadn't stayed until morning, the way she'd thought he might. She wouldn't see him tonight, the way she'd hoped. And their relationship hadn't metamorphosed into anything other than what it was: contractual sex.

Which brought her to Saturday night. Yes or no?

She sighed as she looked at the calendar on her fridge. Today was Friday the thirteenth—hopefully that wasn't an omen!—and Saturday, tomorrow, was…

Oh.

Ohhhhh.

Saturday. The fourteenth of February.

Not that the momentousness of that date would have entered Scott's head. He wasn't a Valentine's Day kind of guy.

And in this instance it was a moot point. Because her sister Shay, and Shay's partner Rick—who *were* Valentine's Day kind of people—were leaving their two gorgeous daughters with Kate while they went out for a romantic dinner.

So she should just get straight on the phone and tell Scott she was busy on Saturday. No need to embarrass herself by mentioning Valentine's Day. She didn't want him to think she was angling for something other than sex. Something like… Well, something Valentine-ish.

Even if she had a lump in her throat about the whole stupid day.

A lump so big it was physically impossible to get a word out of her clogged-up throat. Which made a phone call impossible.

Okay, she would email.

Got your note, Scott.
I'm babysitting my nieces, Maeve and Molly, on Saturday night. I'm free Sunday if that suits?
Kate

There. Cool, businesslike. Contract-worthy.

Three hours later, back came a two-word response: No problem.

And Kate released a big, sighing breath.

Right.

Good.

Good…right?

Because Valentine's Day actually sucked. If Kate had a dollar for every now-divorced couple who'd managed either their proposal or their actual wedding on February the fourteenth, she'd be retired already! Valentine's Day was all about spending too much on wilted roses and eating overpriced restaurant dinners.

Stupid.

The worst possible day for scheduling a date with a sex-only partner.

Valentine's Day? *As if!*

Kate went to her kitchen, looked again at the calendar stuck on her fridge.

Yep, there it was. February the fourteenth. With a nice big red heart on it, courtesy of whoever printed stupid refrigerator calendars. A big red heart. A *love* heart.

And, to her absolute horror, Kate's eyes filled with tears.

Kate had a hectic day of meetings, followed by a catch-up with the girls for drinks after work, and by the time she clambered into bed that night, she was sure she was over the whole weepy Valentine's Day phenomenon that had blindsided her.

So when she woke on Saturday morning to find that depression had settled over her like a damp quilt, she went the whole tortured-groan route. What had happened to her brain during that awards dinner on Thursday night to have resulted in her losing all her common sense?

Sex-only partners *did not celebrate Valentine's Day*. Sex-only partners scheduled sex on days like the *fifteenth* of February. A perfectly legitimate, much more appropriate day for having no-strings sex with guys who left two-word notes on your kitchen counter.

A *two-word* note. And a *two-word* email. That encapsulated her relationship with Scott very nicely—two words: *sex contract*.

Imbued with a burst of *damn your eyes* energy, Kate got out of bed and on the spot decided to clean her apartment. An activity that was *not* some kind of displacement therapy twisted up in her need to wash that man right out of her hair, but a simple household activity. A spring clean—just in summer.

She got underway with gusto.

Gusto that lasted approximately fifteen minutes.

Which was how long it took for the first memory to sneak in.

Kate was wiping down the dining table—and there in her head was the memory of that first night…Scott reaching across to hold her breast...and then the whole dining chair thing. *Ohhhhhhh.*

It was like a switch, throwing open the floodgates—because the memories started pouring in, room by room, after that. Plumping up the couch cushions—that night when he'd thrown the cushions off and dragged her on top of him... Cleaning out the fridge—Scott, coming up behind her, hands all over her... Bathroom—three separate shower scenes.

Her bedroom—*holy hell.* So vivid it was painful. And the most painful of all that last time... Scott drawing her gently down onto the bed...kissing her as if he wanted them to merge.

Okay, enough cleaning.

She hurried to the laundry to dump the housekeeping paraphernalia, only to be hit by another memory. *Oh. My. God.* Had she—? Yes, she had! She'd had sex with Scott Knight in *every single room* of her apartment—*including* the damned laundry room! What normal person had sex in the laundry room? Sitting on top of the washing machine, with the vibrations adding a little extra hum to proceedings as you wrapped your legs around—

Arrrggghh.

She had to get out of the apartment. Maybe even *sell* the apartment.

She took a cold shower, changed into *I am not in need of antidepressants* clothes and hurried out of the building.

The boats were what she needed. Up close and personal. Escape. So she crossed the road to the marina and breathed out a sigh of relief as she reached the jetty. The boats would float her stress away as they always did—on a tide of dreams. Adventure. Possibilities.

One day she would hire a sailing instructor and she would learn... She would learn...

Uh-oh.

Her eyes darted from yacht to yacht...and on every deck she could picture Scott Knight eight years ago, young and free, teaching people to sail. Scott as he was now, teaching *her* to sail.

One of those now-familiar tortured groans was ripped out of her and she turned her back on the boats.

Coffee—she needed coffee.

She hurried to the marina cafe and was horrified when Dean the barista's eyes popped at her as if she was a crazy person. 'You okay, Kate?'

What the hell did she *look* like?

'Fine, fine, fine,' she said reassuringly—before realising that two more 'fines' than were strictly necessary did not denote 'fine'. 'I just need coffee, Dean.'

'Really? Because you seem a little wired.'

Forced smile. 'Really, Dean. Just the coffee.' Subtext: *Give me the damned coffee and shut up.*

But as she took her coffee to one of the tables and sipped, Dean kept giving her concerned glances from behind the coffee machine. As if she had a neon sign flashing on her forehead: *Beware of woman losing her marbles.* Thank heaven her coffee of choice was a nice little macchiato. If she'd had to put up with a cappuccino's worth of *Are you okay?* looks she might have gone over and slapped Dean!

As it was, she could chug it down quickly and flee back to her apartment. Where she would look up the official definition of 'pathetic'! Just to be sure she *wasn't*.

Fifteen minutes later she had the dictionary open, her finger running down the column…*paternalism*…*paternity*…*paternoster*…

Aha!

Pathetic: arousing pity, especially through vulnerability or sadness.

In other words, *Kate Cleary: sexless on Valentine's Day.* The usually imperturbable Dean, the barista, had instantly clocked her out-of-character vulnerability. And she didn't need a dictionary to know that she was arousing pity—in *herself*!

How very...well, *pathetic*.

Although at least she could dispute the 'sad' part of the definition. Because she was not *sad*. She was sexually frustrated! Completely different from sad. Not that two whole nights without sex was going to kill her. She'd gone way longer than two nights before! *Waaaaaay* longer. She wasn't a nymphomaniac! Or...hell! *Was* she a nymphomaniac?

Nylon...nymph...nymphalid...nymphette... Nymphette? Good Lord—nymphette? *Nympholepsy...*

Nymphomaniac: a woman who has abnormally excessive and uncontrollable sexual desire.

Ohhh, crap. Maybe she *was* a nymphomaniac. At her age! That was just...sad.

Oh, God! Sad!

She was a fully-fledged pathetic nymphomaniac.

Kate fled to the terrace—the only place in the apartment she hadn't had sex with Scott. And the only reason she hadn't had sex with him on the terrace was because exhibitionism wasn't exactly his 'thing'. And, even though it wasn't her 'thing' either, the realisation that she probably would have gone there, *in full view of any passersby*, flashed through her mind and shocked her.

Depraved pathetic nymphomaniac! That was her. And it was Scott Knight's fault. Because she'd never been this desperate for sex in her whole life.

And now she wouldn't even be able to enjoy the view from her terrace, because one quick look at the boats confirmed that Scott was now firmly entrenched as part of her escape daydream.

When the intercom finally buzzed that evening and she heard her sister's calm voice, she almost cried with relief.

Her family always anchored her. And you *had* to get it together when you had two children to entertain.

When Shay and Rick had left she pushed the coffee table out of the way so the girls could take up their preferred positions on the rug—seven-year-old Maeve leaning back against the base of the couch, engrossed in a book about cake and cookie decorating, and five-year-old Molly stretched out on her stomach, leaning on an elbow and drawing her version of a fairy house in her sketchbook.

Kate was just about to pick up the phone to order pizza—the girls' favourite meal—when the intercom buzzed again. Shay and Rick should be sipping champagne at the restaurant and surely could have telephoned if they were having a last-minute panic—but nobody needed to tell a family lawyer that parents could be irrational!

She pushed the 'talk' button. 'Yes, Shay?' she said with an exasperated laugh.

'Um…nope. It's me, Kate.'

CHAPTER EIGHT

SCOTT.

Kate's vocal cords froze. *God help me, God help me, God* help *me.*

'Kate? Come on—buzz me up. My arms are going to fall off in a minute.'

Kate buzzed the door and then just stared at it, paralysed.

Something was swelling in her chest—a mixture of joy and yearning and uncertainty. What did it mean that he'd come when she'd told him not to? He shouldn't be doing this. She was glad he was here. No, she wasn't—because they had rules. But it was Valentine's Day. No, that meant nothing. She couldn't let him get away with breaking the rules. No matter how glad she was that he was doing it.

Mmm-hmm. She sure was making a lot of sense!

She heard Scott's voice vibrating through her door like a tuning fork. That disarmingly lazy drawl, addressed to some stranger. A laugh. Yep—he'd hooked a new fan in under a minute.

She rested her palms against the door, could almost *feel* him through it.

Breathe. Just breathe.

One knock.

Breathe!

She opened the door and Scott stepped over the threshold as though he owned the place.

'What are you doing here?' she managed to get out.

'Why wouldn't I be here?'

He handed her two bottles of wine—a white and a red— and carried a six-pack of beer and a paper bag containing who knew what into the kitchen.

Kate followed him, put the red wine on the counter, the white wine and beer in the fridge.

'You can't just buzz the intercom whenever you feel like it,' she said, in her *Don't disturb the children* voice.

Scott shrugged. 'If the intercom annoys you, give me a key.'

Which, of course, was *not the point*. 'I am *not* giving you a key.'

Another one of those shrugs of his. 'Then it's the intercom.'

'You can't stay,' she said. 'I'm just about to order pizza.'

'I love pizza.'

'Not for you, Scott. You shouldn't be here. I told you I was babysitting Maeve and Molly tonight.'

'And I emailed you back to say that wasn't a problem.'

'That wasn't—? I mean… Huh?'

'Oh,' he said. 'Were you trying to tell me not to come? Tsk, tsk, Kate—you have to be more specific, in that case. Lawyers shouldn't be leaving loopholes. So, to be clear…it's not a problem that you're babysitting tonight, which is why I'm here. And, yes, Sunday is fine too.'

Kate thought back to her email, his reply, acknowledged the ambiguity…but knew very well he was playing her.

'You knew what I meant, Scott. And we're supposed to negotiate if we have a problem with dates.'

'Okay, let's negotiate.'

She closed her eyes, took a deep breath. Opened her eyes to find him looking all woebegone.

'Don't you like me any more?' he asked.

She stared at him as laughter and frustration warred inside her. 'No.'

'But why?'

'Because you're—' She broke off, laughed because she just couldn't help it, damn him. 'Just because. And I hope you like entertaining children—because that's the only action you're getting tonight. I can't—won't—leave two little girls eating pizza while you and I go for a quickie in the bedroom.'

He leaned in close, snatched a kiss. 'One—that's just a kiss, not a proposal of marriage, so don't complain. Two—I'm not *asking* you for a quickie in the bedroom while the girls eat pizza. And three—it won't be quick; it will be nice and slow...*after* Maeve and Molly's parents have picked them up.'

One more rapid-fire kiss.

'You really have the most sensational mouth in the world.' Another kiss—quick and scorching. 'And make mine pepperoni.'

He had the nerve to laugh at the tortured look on her face.

'What? Is it the money? I'll pay you half, as per our contract, if that's what's worrying you. Honestly—you lawyers are so tight!'

And with that, he liberated three red foil-wrapped chocolate hearts from the paper bag and presented one to her. 'Happy Valentine's Day.'

And there she went—crumbling. 'Oh, you...you *know* it's Valentine's Day?'

'Well, *yeeeaah*! Multiple cards. Even one present—a cute little cat o' nine tails from Anais that you and I will *not* be trying out. But nothing—*nada!*—from you. And, Kate, I'm warning you—if you haven't had the common decency to buy me a chocolate or a cupcake or at the very least a soppy card, I'm eating half of that chocolate heart.' Quick unholy grin. 'And I'll take mine molten...off your tummy.'

And with that gobsmacking pronouncement, Scott swaggered into the living room while the last of her resistance disintegrated.

'Which one's Maeve and which one's Molly?' he asked. 'No, don't tell me. My friend Willa told me Maeve is seven, so that would be...you.' He pointed to Molly, who giggled. He did an over-the-top double-take. 'Not you?'

Head-shake from Molly.

'I'm Maeve,' Maeve said, and Scott plonked himself down on the rug and leaned back against the couch next to her.

'Okay—will you be my Valentine?' he asked and handed over one of the hearts.

Her eyes lit as she shyly took the heart and nodded.

'Ohhhhh!' That came from the rug. 'What about me?'

Scott nodded sagely at Molly. 'Well, it just so happens I'm in the market for two Valentines tonight.' He produced the other chocolate heart and a beaming Molly came over for long enough to take it from him and give him a sweet little hug before she resettled on the rug.

He turned to Maeve. 'So, Maeve, what's so interesting?'

Maeve flashed her book's cover.

'Ah, you're going to be a chef,' he said.

Maeve nodded, still shy.

'I'm not bad in the kitchen myself,' Scott said, and proceeded to talk about biscuits.

Biscuits? That was just so…random. Biscuits! And chocolate hearts on Valentine's Day. And asking Willa about the girls. Kate didn't know what to make of it all. What to make of *him*.

Unless it was that he was completely irresistible.

She called for pizza, then set the dining table, while Scott charmed her nieces—looking absolutely nothing *like* a confirmed bachelor as he did it.

The man knew his baking. The pros and cons of shortbread, ginger snaps, honey jumbles, chocolate chip cookies and macaroons were all discussed at length. And the absolute deliciousness of…what?…whoopie pies?…was being extolled? Kate had never heard of a whoopie pie.

'They're like little chocolate cookie sandwiches, with a creamy filling,' Scott explained to Maeve—who'd never heard of them either. 'Next time you're here, we'll bake them together.'

'Can I bake too?' Molly asked.

'You sure can. Three of us can make three times the pies! What have you got there, Molly?'

In no time Scott was lying next to Molly on the floor, having the picture explained to him. Maeve abandoned her book to lie on Scott's other side.

Scott gave a bit of improvement advice, explaining that it was his job to design houses, and as Kate paid for the pizzas she heard the girls asking him to redraw the house for them.

'I'd be honoured,' Scott said, and then got to his feet and helped the girls up. 'But first—pizza!'

It was adorable the way he got the girls drinks, helped them choose the biggest pizza slices, chatted about the most beautiful houses he'd designed in a way that made them sound like magic castles. After dinner he stayed with Maeve and Molly while Kate cleared up, drawing in Molly's sketchbook and making the girls *ooh* and *ahh*.

Yep, bona fide adorable.

And Kate just *had* to see the drawing. So she peeked over Scott's shoulder.

Oh. *Ohhhhh*.

It was the perfect little girls' house. Towers and turrets. Winding paths. A secret entrance to an underground treasure cave, a private elf garden, a sunken pool with a waterfall. He'd sketched two bedrooms, labelled 'Molly' and 'Maeve', with fairytale beds and magic mirrors and spiralling staircases.

When Kate took the girls off to clean their teeth and get ready for bed, each of the girls kissed Scott goodnight—one per cheek—and he blushed.

Scott Knight, who could talk more boldly about sex than any man she'd ever met, *blushed*.

Kate felt her heart do one of those swoons inside her chest, and thought, *Uh-oh. This is bad. Very, very bad*.

She read to Maeve and Molly until they drifted into sleep, and then—a little apprehensive—went to find Scott.

He was on the terrace, where he gravitated every time she left him alone.

'I poured you a glass of wine. It's there on the table. And sorry, Kate, but that table's going to have to go, along with the chairs,' he said. 'It's so fragile I feel like I'm going to break something every time I'm near that furniture.'

She had to agree it looked like a children's toy set next to Scott's imposing frame. Everything did. But she forbore from pointing out that she was not going to change her furniture for a man who wouldn't be in her life for long.

Whew. That hit her. This was finite. It had a start date and it would come to an end. She couldn't let herself forget that just because he'd smiled at her once as if he saw something wonderful in her. Or because he'd made love to her once as if he was embedding himself inside her.

Scott took a long pull of beer from the bottle in his hand, gazing out at the marina as Kate fetched her glass and joined him at the edge of the terrace.

'What's it like? Sailing?' she asked.

'It was fun.'

'Was?'

'I don't sail any more.'

'But…why? I mean, why not?'

'It was just…' Shrug. 'Time to concentrate on the important things in life.'

'Fun is important.'

He looked down at her. 'I *am* having fun. With you,' he said, and leaned down to kiss her.

'I know why you do that,' she said, when he pulled back.

'Do what?'

'Kiss me.'

'Well, *duh*, Kate! I do it because I like kissing you.'

'You do it to distract me. So you don't have to answer my questions.'

'And does it? Distract you?'

'Yes. But why are such simple questions a problem for you?'

Pause. 'Prying into my past is not part of the deal, Kate.'

Kate felt it like a slap—not just the words but the *keep your distance* tone. She found she was gripping her glass too hard, so put it on the broad top of the terrace railing.

She heard Scott sigh. Then he was smoothing his hand over her hair like an apology. 'Kate, the sailing… It's just something I set aside to focus on the realities of life—like studying and working. And look at me now—I'm an award-winner!' Low laugh, with all the self-deprecation his brother lacked. 'It's enough for me.'

'If it were enough you wouldn't spend every moment I leave you alone out on the terrace, watching the boats.'

'Pry-ing…' he sing-songed.

'It's not prying to ask questions about a person you… you're…'

'Having sex with,' he supplied. And sighed again. 'You drew up the contract, Kate. There wasn't a clause for fire-side chats in there.' Slight pause. 'Right?'

'Right.'

'So has anything changed for you?'

She wanted to say yes. That things *had* changed. Because of the way they'd made love two nights ago. The way he'd presented her with a chocolate heart. And blushed when two little girls had kissed him. The way he tried to pretend that the boats bobbing on the harbour held no fascination for him when she knew they did.

But if things changed he would go. She knew it instinctively. *Not yet. Not…yet.*

'No,' she said quietly, and picked up her wine glass, sipped. 'Nothing's changed.'

They stood in silence, side by side, staring across at the dark water, the city lights in the distance.

And then Scott cleared his throat. Just a tiny sound. 'Good. Because the whole fireside-chat thing… It would be like me asking you…' Shrug. 'I don't know…' Shrug. 'If you wanted…maybe…to have children. One day, I mean.'

Another clearing of the throat. 'Because you're so good with the girls anyone would wonder about that.'

What the hell? Kate slanted a look at him. He was looking out at the Harbour.

But then he turned, looked at her. Eyes watchful. 'And you wouldn't want me to ask you that, would you?'

'If you wanted to ask me that, Scott, I'd answer. Because it's no big deal.'

'Ah, but I don't need to ask. I already know the answer is yes.'

And for the first time in a long time, Kate thought, *Yes.* The answer, very simply, *was* yes. Except of course she'd lost that simple answer somewhere along her career path.

She turned back to the boats. Long moment.

'You know, Scott, I've seen fathers who say they've been tricked into pregnancy and shouldn't have to pay child support. Divorcing parents using child custody as carrot and stick to punish or bribe. Surrogates who decide to keep their children when those children are the last hope of desperate couples. Fathers pulling out all the stops to avoid their children being aborted. Twins separated and fostered because of financial pressure. Unwanted children, abused children, ignored children. I'm not sure that's an enticement to parenthood.'

'But you wouldn't be like any of those parents.'

'No. But a lot of women are good at choosing the wrong man.'

'Then don't choose the wrong man.'

'Oh, simple!' She turned to him. 'So simple that I suppose if you found the right woman it would be a case of *Bingo, let me impregnate you immediately!*'

He laughed softly. 'Since the longest I've been with a woman is two months, I'd say I'm hardly father material.'

Two months. The equivalent of one contract rollover. *Consider yourself warned, Kate.*

'Well, at least you've got the uncle routine down pat,'

she said. 'Judging by how you were with Maeve and Molly. Where did you learn that? Does Hugo have children?'

'Yes, he does. One girl. One boy. Twins. A perfect set. My brother does all things to perfection.'

Kate caught the wryness—but before she could even wonder at it Scott had tugged her under his arm, leaned down for another *that's enough talking* kiss.

'I can't wait to touch you,' he said.

'You *are* touching me,' she said, all breathless—because that was what it did to her every time he kissed her.

'I'm calling another Play Time next week, Kate.'

'What do you want to do?'

'Uh-uh. Secret. But you're not keeping up. Come on—don't you have a fantasy *you* want to try out? I'd love to indulge you.'

'I do have something in mind for next week,' Kate said, because since it was a damned sex contract, and she'd put that stupid clause in there herself, it would look strange if she didn't have even one scenario in mind. But the truth was she could think of nothing she wanted more than just taking him into her body, holding him close.

'Woo-hoo, I'll be hanging out for that,' Scott said. 'But remember—no S&M, no B&D. I wasn't kidding about that stuff. It creeps me out, the pain thing. I don't enjoy it, and I sure as hell can't see myself inflicting it on you. Oh—and while fruit and veg is acceptable, under certain circumstances, no wildlife, no livestock. I'm not *that* kinky.'

'Wildlife?' Kate spluttered out a laugh. 'That is just disgusting. Is your black book annotated? Because maybe I'd better take a look at what you expect. I might have to rein you in.'

Scott grinned at her. 'Just making sure we're on the same page after seeing the way that guy in your boardroom was patting and kissing his little dog like it was his girlfriend.'

Another spluttered laugh. 'Please! You're going to give me nightmares. And Sugarplum isn't a dog. She's a shih tzu.'

'The dog is called *Sugarplum*?'

'Yep.'

'Well, *that* is an abomination.'

Kate bit the inside of her cheek. 'Actually, I have another name for her. *Hostis humani generis.*'

'Is that a legal term?'

'It is. It means "enemy of the human race". Which I think is very apt in Sugarplum's case.'

'I'm going to have to kiss you for that. Because legal terms get me so damned *hot*! Can you say something with *functus officio* in it?'

She was laughing helplessly. 'Not offhand, no.'

'Then *hostis humani generis* it is.'

Kate was still laughing as Scott planted his mouth on hers…but not for long. By the time he slipped his tongue inside her mouth, she was tingly and dazed. And Scott seemed equally affected.

'I love kissing you,' he breathed against her lips.

'People do tend to love doing things they're particularly good at.'

'You're no slouch yourself—but even if you were, Kate, one look at your mouth is all I'd ever need to get me ready to dive inside you.'

She shivered. Closed her eyes briefly. He could turn her on too easily. So easily it was dangerous.

Change the subject.

'Anyway, Sugarplum's family is sorted. You won't be seeing her around the office again.'

'Who ended up getting the kids?'

'Kids?' Kate asked.

'That couple. You know—the kids?'

'Ah,' Kate said, and winced.

'Not kids?'

Another wince.

'You're not telling me that fight was about that evil little yapper, are you?'

She could see the horror—almost comical and yet not. The disbelief.

Kate shrugged.

'So they don't have kids?' he asked.

'I'm not saying that.'

'So they *do* have kids, but the fight was over...' Stop, stare. 'You're not serious?' he said.

She raised her eyebrows.

He shook his head, stunned. 'I hope they're paying you a lot, because from where I'm standing your job sucks.'

'Lately...yeah, it *does* suck.'

'At least your family must be proud of you, though. Lawyers are like doctors—they've got the parental-pride market cornered.'

'Actually, my mother would probably prefer an architect to a lawyer! She's an artist, so creative stuff is more her speed.'

'Your mother's an artist?' And then his eyes widened. 'Oh! *Ohh!* Cleary! *Madeline* Cleary? Yes! Of course! The painting in your office and the one in your bedroom. Wow.'

'Yes—wow. And my father is a playwright, but not as well known. What about *your* parents?'

'Doctors times two. So...your mother... She's not happy about you being a lawyer?'

'She thinks I get too emotionally invested in my cases. Whenever I stress out, she says, *"Kaaaaate, I warned you how it would be."* And then she adds something about thanking heaven for divorce—which is her way of telling me I'm doing the world a favour, and to just get on with the next uncoupling. It's the Cleary way, you know—fight like hell, then move on.'

'Now, you see, *my* mother would see divorce as an admission of failure. Which is why Knights don't divorce. Failure is not an option.'

'Even if the alternative is to stick with someone who's horrible? Someone abusive? Divorce has got to be a better alternative.'

'Then why do you stress out about it, Kate?'

'I've just…' She paused, sighed. 'I've had a run of nasty ones lately. And seeing people ripping each other apart, seeing the kids on the sidelines…' Another pause. 'It can make you cynical.'

'Cynical. Now, *that* I understand.'

'Which is when I start thinking about boat theft.'

'I'm surprised you haven't done it already.'

'Maybe I would have—except for one small thing.' She slanted him a glinting smile. 'I can't sail!'

He touched her face. Gentle, soft. 'Ah, well—definitely a problem!'

'And, you know, my job has compensations.'

'Money?'

'Yes, that's one.'

'And meeting handsome architects through your clients.'

'Handsome *egomaniacal* architects, even,' Kate said, and laughed. 'But I'd definitely classify meeting Willa as compensation. It was…*satisfying* to fight for her.'

'Yeah, I get that. From what I know of Wayne-the-Pain, he would have tried to screw her out of everything just to pay her back for wanting to be something more than an arm bauble. She said you fought like a demon. That it was your way—to fight to the death.'

'Yes, like I said—the Cleary way. And definitely *my* way. Even more so for people I love—and I love Willa. She's… special. Strong. So much tougher than people think. I admire her more than I can say. She deserves everything good and fine in the world. Joy. Peace. Security. And love. She deserves love.'

'I think you're a secret romantic, Kate.' He nudged her playfully. 'So where's my Valentine's Day card?'

'It's in the mail,' Kate said, nudging him back. 'Along with a few tools of oppression—handcuffs and hot wax to go with Anais's whip, because I think she's on to something there.'

Scott gave an exaggerated shudder. 'I promise you, she

is *not*.' Pause. 'Mind you, for a B&D aficionado, Anais has some remarkably pedestrian notions about love.'

'What's pedestrian?'

'Let's just say the idea of a straight up and down sex contract would never have entered her head. You and I… We're… *different*. We know what we want and what we don't. And we go for it.'

Kate thought about that for a moment. 'Are you saying Anais believes in love, and that that's pedestrian? Because I hate to break it to you, Scott, but I'm pedestrian in that way too. It's impossible *not* to believe in love in my family. They throw it at you in great gooey clumps, whether you want it or not.'

'Ah, but that's a different kind of love to the romantic stuff.'

'The principles are the same. Real love, of *any* kind, glories in a person's strengths and talents and…and their flaws too. *Especially* their flaws. It accepts and it…it heals. It lets you just…*be*. Be who you are. A lot of divorces happen because that's *not* the kind of love on offer.' Stop. Breath. 'And that's when the lawyers come in—earning thousands of dollars negotiating whether it's Mr or Mrs X who gets five hundred dollars' worth of groceries in the settlement. And that's a true story.'

'But it's not about the groceries, is it?'

'No. It's about power. Punishing someone because they can't love you enough, or don't need you enough, or won't give you enough.' She shivered. 'It makes you wonder…'

'Wonder?'

'Why you'd ever let someone have that power over you.'

'And that is why you and I—two sex-crazed cynics—are meant for each other.'

'For the grand total of two more weeks.'

'Rollover clause, remember?' He eyed her closely. 'You're not finished with me yet, are you, Kate?'

'No, I'm not finished with you.' She clinked her glass

against Scott's beer bottle. 'Here's to not having to get divorced. Not that Clearys get divorced any more than Knights.'

'But—' He broke off, shook his head. 'You said your mother's in favour of divorce.'

'And so she is—for all those people silly enough to get married in the first place.'

'You mean…? Hang on, I'm not getting this.'

'Clearys don't get divorced because they don't get married.'

'You mean like…ever?'

'Not in recent history.'

'Your mother?'

'Nope.'

'*Her* mother?'

'Absolutely not—Gran was all about free love.'

'Molly and Maeve's parents?'

'No. It's easier, you know, not to rely on a man. Or, in reverse, a woman. But don't misunderstand me—our fathers were in our lives as much as they wanted to be, and it worked very well.' She smiled. 'Gus—my father—and Aristotle—Shay and my other sister Lilith's father—even get along well together.'

'So it's one of those weird, blended, out-there families that are going to be the ruin of civilisation? The Knight family would be horrified!'

'Are *you*? Horrified?'

'I said the Knight family. I'm not really part of that.'

She looked at him sharply. 'What does that mean?'

He shrugged. 'I need another beer,' he said, and went into the apartment.

Kate followed him inside. Waited while he grabbed a beer from the fridge.

'What's your family like, Scott?'

'Doctors.'

'No—I mean, what are they *like*?'

'Well…doctors.' He hunched a shoulder. 'You've met

Hugo. He's pretty up and down perfect. That's the standard. My family is *not* weird, blended and out-there. More like stultifyingly conventional.'

'So you're…what? The black sheep?'

'More like the sheep with second-grade wool.'

'Okay, what does *that* mean?'

He took a pull of his beer. 'Nothing. Just that growing up as a Knight is… Well, it's nothing a Cleary would understand.'

'Try me.'

He paused. Looked at her. Opened his mouth. Closed it. Shook his head. 'Forget it, Kate.' One of those infuriating smiles that meant nothing. 'It's not *germane*. And— Ah, the intercom. Better go let your sister in.'

If Shay and Rick were surprised to find a man at Kate's they didn't show it. And Scott—well, he was all smooth charm. But in that closed-off, *keep your distance* way. A way that made Shay, who was unusually perceptive, narrow her eyes at him.

As Shay and Rick went to get the girls there was silence.

Kate racked her brain for a way to break it—a way to break through the sudden wall of reserve that was between them.

But in the end Scott was the one to break the silence. 'So, Kate, I owe you.' He reached in his pocket for his wallet.

'Wh—What?'

'Money for the pizza.' He handed over some notes.

Kate stared at the money in her hand as he returned his wallet to his pocket. 'Scott…?'

'Fifty-fifty, remember?' he said with a meaningless smile. 'And now I'd better hit the ro—'

He broke off as Rick and Shay reappeared, carrying Maeve and Molly, who were drowsy and tousled and lovable.

Kate kissed the girls. And then watched, fascinated, as they each in turn leaned towards Scott for him to kiss them too. She saw Scott blush as he did so. The cool reserve was gone for those few moments, replaced by something perilously close to tenderness.

Scott…and children.

Something he couldn't have because he never stayed with a woman long enough? Or because he was a Knight. Or… or what?

Shay, won over in that instant, smiled at him, and Scott blushed again.

And then Kate and Scott were alone again, and she wondered what was going to happen next. Given the way he'd kissed her out on the terrace, by rights she should have been flat against the door with Scott all over her the moment it closed behind her family…but Kate had a feeling that was not going to happen.

Scott took her face between his hands and she waited, breathless and curious.

'You're so beautiful, Kate,' he said, but that fact didn't seem to make him happy.

He leaned close, put his forehead on hers and just stopped. Not moving, not even breathing.

Kate wanted so badly to wrap her arms around him and tell him everything would be all right, even though she didn't know what was wrong. But she stayed exactly as she was. Soaking in this moment where nothing happened, nothing changed.

And then Scott released her, stepped back. Smiled one of those smiles that didn't reach his eyes.

'I hope you appreciate that I did *not* kiss you then,' he said. 'Please note for future reference that I am capable of obeying the rules. No kissing if it isn't going to lead to sex, right?'

'But I thought—'

'I just—I just think I'd better go home tonight.'

'But you can still go home tonight. I mean, after…'

But at the look on his face—closed-off, determined— Kate forced herself to stop. She wasn't going to beg. Not any man. Ever. And especially not this one, who was already running rings around her in every possible way.

Ring-running. For her own mental health, it was going to have to stop.

So she smiled, as remote as he was. 'Yeah, we're over our target, right?'

'Right,' Scott said. 'I'll see you tomorrow, then—new week, new target.'

'Not tomorrow,' Kate said.

'But you said Sunday.'

'And now I'm saying no.'

His eyes narrowed. 'That sounds like pique, Kate. And we don't have room for pique in our contract.'

'No, we don't have any allowances for pique in our contract, Scott,' she said, very cool. 'This is not pique. I wasn't expecting you tonight—as you know very well. I was, in fact, planning to do some work once I'd put the girls to bed. Now I have to play catch-up tomorrow. So thank you.'

'Ouch. I'm going to need that stapler,' Scott said.

Then with a mock salute he was gone.

Kate looked at the door, wondering exactly what had happened out there on the terrace.

She crossed her arms against a chill premonition that things between them were not going to work out the way either of them expected.

CHAPTER NINE

THE NEXT MORNING Scott was back at Rushcutters Bay, his finger frozen just short of the intercom buzzer, wondering what the hell he was doing.

Kate had made it clear she was going to be busy today, doing the work she'd planned to do the previous night if not for his inconvenient arrival. Code—and not exactly secret—for *I don't want to see you*.

And yet here he was, trying to work out how to charm his way into her apartment, how to apologise for the way he'd run away last night. The way he *kept* running away.

But how did you tell someone you'd run because you were in too deep and wanted to pull back—even as you were fronting up for more?

He hadn't intended to see her last night after she'd sent that irritatingly dismissive email about babysitting, but... well, he'd *wanted* to see her, dammit!

And he'd also known that if he *didn't* see her he'd be looking down the barrel of another sleepless night. Because his frazzled brain kept circling round and around everything that had happened on Thursday night, urging him to prove to himself that the way he'd been feeling was a one-off, all caught up in the unforeseen angst of the occasion—Hugo; that shared moment when they'd both just *got* it; his winning—*winning*! *That* was why he'd smiled at her—okay, he smiled a *lot*...he even smiled at *her* a lot...but not like that. And *that* explained the sex too—so straighty one-eighty that it should *not* have seared him like a barbecued steak, and yet it had been on fire, plated up, skip the garnish, *delicious*.

So, yeah, last night, he'd intended to prove the one-offness of it all to himself. To turn up off-schedule, joke about Valentine's Day, dazzle her with a little light-hearted banter, with the girls there to run interference and put the kybosh on anything emotional. Then they'd have sex in a manner in keeping with their contract—he'd thought of something highly technical that would mean they'd have to concentrate on not breaking a bone, so no time for losing themselves in the moment—and *voilà*: back to normal. Head back in the right place, heart untouched.

No watching her sleep or tracing his finger over her eyebrow, no sniffing her damned perfume when he was alone in her bathroom. None of that creepy stuff.

But instead his dumbass brain had started shooting off on tangents until he'd started thinking about kids. Redheaded, grey-eyed kids. How it would be to bring up kids the Cleary way, with people flinging gooey clumps of love at you—not the Knight way, where you had to prove yourself every damned day just to get a frosty nod. And then had come the blinding knowledge that he'd have to be married to the mother of his kids, so maybe the Cleary way would never work for him.

And then it had hit him that he was really, actually, contemplating fatherhood. *Fatherhood! Him!*

In too deep—caring too much—needing more—*run*.

He should have been happy to be barred today, so he could get his brain out of his gonads and back where it was supposed to be. But after one more sleepless night, thinking about that look on her face as he'd left, here he was.

Because... Well, what had that remote smile of hers meant? That she was finished with him? Well, no. Not happening until *he* was ready. So he was going to charm her into *not* finishing with him—while simultaneously stepping away from the too-deep chasm that was yawning at his feet.

Simple, right?

Yeah, simple. Sure.

Oh, for the love of God, man up!

He let his finger land on the buzzer. Waited, drumming his fingers on the wall.

By God, she'd better be at home after spinning him that line about work. She'd better not be out somewhere, with someone, doing something. Or he would— Would— Well, he'd…explode! Or…or something.

'Hello?' Her voice, husky and gorgeous—and for a moment his breath caught.

Get a grip. Get a damned grip!

'It's me,' he said, and winced—because that aggressive tone of voice was not charming.

Long pause. Followed by an arctic, 'Yes?'

'Can I come up?'

'Why?'

'Because I want to see you.'

'You saw me last night. That will have to tide you over until I can spare the time.'

Pause. Pages being riffled. What the hell—? Was she checking her schedule?

'Probably Tuesday.'

Yes, she'd been checking her schedule! Scott felt his temper start to simmer.

'No,' he said, and there was *absolutely* nothing charming about that snapped-out word.

'I beg your pardon?' Past arctic and heading towards ice age.

'Let me come up and explain.'

'The contract doesn't require explanation.'

The freaking *contract*. They didn't *need* a contract to have sex. He hadn't *asked* for a damned contract, had he? She'd *forced* it on him.

'All right, I won't explain,' he said through clenched teeth. He made a mammoth effort to rein in his slipping temper. Charm. Charm, charm, *charm*. 'So…since I'm obviously not coming up, why don't you come down and keep me company while I have a cup of coffee at the cafe across at the marina? Ten minutes and you can get back to work.'

Long, long moment. He heard the breath she sucked in. Waited for the breath out—waited, waited…

And then the breath whooshed out and she said, albeit grudgingly, 'All right.'

Not exactly effusive, but Scott closed his eyes in relief.

Five minutes later she was there, wearing a maxi-dress in sky-blue and a pair of flat silver sandals, her hair swinging in a ponytail. Delectable Sunday-morning fare.

His temper disappeared as if by magic just at the sight of her. He wanted to kiss her so badly he automatically leaned in—but Kate flinched backwards.

'No kissing, remember?' she said.

'Sorry, Kate,' he said, trying to look chastened but not quite managing it. He was just so happy to see her. God, what was happening to him?

They walked in silence to the cafe. Ordered coffee at the counter. A long black for him; a macchiato for Kate. Took their cups to one of the tables closest to the jetty.

'About last night…' Scott said, diving in.

Kate stirred sugar into her coffee. 'I thought you weren't going to explain.'

He ignored that. 'It just got a little…a little…heavy. Talking about children—'

'A subject *you* raised.'

'And about… Well, about all that stuff.' Shaky little laugh. 'Love.' Grimace. 'And…and stuff. I didn't sign up for deep and meaningful. Neither of us did. So I'm not sure how all that came spewing out.'

'It happens,' Kate said. 'It's normal.'

'No, it's not. Not for me. It's not what we—'

'Signed up for,' she cut in dryly. 'Got it. No need to labour the point. And no need to explain, remember?'

'Anyway, I thought we needed a breather—that's all,' he mumbled, and hurriedly picked up his coffee, took a sip, burned his tongue and refused to show it. Because people in control didn't burn their tongues on coffee. And he was. In control. Definitely.

'And yet here you are, the very next morning. That's a breather, is it?'

'I just— I wanted to—'

'Explain. Yep. Got it.'

Kate looked at him—the epitome of inscrutability. She drew in a breath. Seemed on the verge of speaking. But then something behind him caught her attention and her eyes widened.

'Isn't that…? Yes, surely…'

But it was a murmur directed at herself, not him.

She refocused on Scott. 'That's Brodie, isn't it? He really is as gorgeous as his photo.'

CHAPTER TEN

BRODIE.

Gorgeous Brodie.

Instinctively Scott hated that combination of words coming out of Kate's mouth.

But then the reality of her words hit.

Brodie. Here.

They were about to come face to face. *If* he could make himself turn around.

But for that first moment he was robbed of the ability to breathe, let alone move, as eight years of feelings rushed at him.

That one hot moment. The sense of betrayal. The bitterness. Shame at what he'd done. Regret at what he'd lost. And…loneliness. A confusing, potent, noxious mix he just couldn't seem to control the way he'd since learned to control everything else.

Kate was watching him. Any minute now she'd ask him what was wrong. It was a wake-up call to get it together—because he did *not* want to be asked.

He took a breath, pushed the feelings away, forced himself to turn.

Recognition in a split second. Brodie's walk. Unmistakable. A loose-limbed, relaxed amble. He was as beach-blond as he'd always been. Tanned. Wearing sunglasses. Boat shoes, jeans, pale blue shirt with the sleeves casually rolled up to the elbows. And a tattoo—an anchor—on the underside of one forearm.

Scott remembered that tattoo. He'd been impressed by it. And a little bit jealous. Because Knights didn't get tattoos—and yet when he'd seen Brodie's he'd wanted to be the kind of guy who *did*. Not that he couldn't have had one—

then *or* now. But deep down he'd always known it wasn't his thing. It was the rebelliousness of a tattoo that had appealed to him, not the reality of ink in his skin. Everything about breezy, laidback Brodie had appealed to Scott—who was the exact opposite.

He knew the instant Brodie recognised him from the slight hitch in his stride. The sunglasses were whipped off, the eyes widened, a smile started...then stopped. Replaced by wariness. Then the sunglasses were shoved into the pocket of his shirt—Brodie was not the kind of guy to hide behind sunglasses or anything else—and Brodie walked on, heading straight for them. He stopped at their table.

'Scott,' he said.

'Brodie.'

Okay, it was all a bit ridiculous. *Scott. Brodie.* Kate would be coughing up her name in a minute. Maybe the barista would pop out and give them a *Dean.*

Scott laughed—couldn't seem to help it. And he had the satisfaction of seeing surprise replace the wariness. It felt good.

'Join us for coffee?' he asked.

'Sure,' Brodie said, recovering from the surprise, and snagged a spare seat from the next table.

Kate reached out a hand to shake. 'I'm Kate. A...' Tiny, tiny pause. 'A friend of Scott's.'

Brodie smiled as he took her hand, said nothing—but Kate blushed.

She flicked a glance at Scott, then back to Brodie. 'I'm a friend of Willa's too. And Amy's.'

'Ah, you're *that* Kate.'

'Oh, dear, you're not going to make a lawyer joke, are you?'

'Fresh out of lawyer jokes, sorry!'

'Well, isn't *that* a breath of fresh air?' she said with another of those flicking looks. At Scott, then Brodie.

Scott felt the sting. So he'd made one lawyer joke—just

once! That didn't put him ahead of Dirty Martini Barnaby in the woeful pick-up line competition, did it?

'I'll go and get the coffee,' Kate said. 'What'll it be, Brodie?'

'Black. Same as Scott.'

Nod. Smile. And she was off.

'Girlfriend?' Brodie asked, once Kate was out of earshot.

Scott crossed his arms over his chest. Shook his head. 'Nothing like that.'

Pause. A long one.

Okay—they were back to ridiculous.

Time to suck it up and move on.

'Are we going to get all girly and talk about things?'

Brodie winced. 'God, I hope not.'

'Right. Good. Great.'

Arms were uncrossed. His hand held out. Brodie took it. Shook.

'That's it?' Brodie asked.

'Well, let's see…' Scott frowned, looking as if he was thinking deeply. 'We were best friends. A girl who never loved me—a girl I didn't really love—fell for you. I punched you. You got an attack of nobility and took off. She stayed and was miserable.' He shrugged. 'I'd say between the three of us we royally screwed that up. It's sure felt screwed up for the past eight years, and I'm kind of over everything about it. So, yeah—that's it. From my perspective at least.'

'I've missed you, you know—you bastard.'

'Hey—we're not getting all girly, remember?'

Brodie laughed. 'That's why I added the "bastard".'

'Yeah, well, "bastard" doesn't make it any less girly.'

'Still an uptight control freak, then.'

'And you're still…what? King of the hair braids?'

'The sisters have outgrown the braids.' Brodie shuddered, but he was laughing too. 'Thank God.'

Slight pause. But not uncomfortable.

And then the question just came out of Scott's mouth, as though it was just…time. 'So, have you seen her?'

'No.'

'Do you want to?'

Long pause. 'Eight years,' Brodie said.

And somehow Scott understood the world in those two words. 'Okay, enough said. But just so you know—it wouldn't bother me. Not any more.'

Brodie jerked his head backwards towards the cafe counter. 'Because of Red?'

Brodie looked over Scott's shoulder, saw Kate coming towards them with a coffee-laden tray. That rolling walk. So damned sexy.

He blinked. Swallowed a sigh. Shook his head. 'That's just an…arrangement.'

Kate arrived, distributed the coffee. Sat down. 'So, how's the luxury yacht touring business?' she asked Brodie. 'In Queensland, right?'

'I should warn you,' Scott broke in. 'Kate's main goal in life is to steal a boat and sail off on an adventure—except she can't sail.' He smiled at Kate, expecting her to share the joke. But she merely looked steadily back at him.

Brodie was smiling at her too, and she *did* smile at him— and Scott found himself gritting his teeth. *A contract. Just a contract—and this is why.*

'Well, Kate, I'm down for a couple of weeks,' Brodie said. 'I'll take you sailing. Unless…?' He glanced at Scott. 'Are *you* going to teach her?'

Scott shook his head quickly. 'I sold my boat.' He looked at Kate; she was still smiling at Brodie. *Just a contract.* 'She's all yours.'

He caught—just—an infinitesimal flinch, the blink of hurt on Kate's face, and wanted to call the words back. But it was too late. Her smile went megawatt—straight at Brodie. And Scott wanted to claim that wide, gorgeous mouth of hers right there and then, in front of Brodie and everyone else in the vicinity. Screw the no-kissing rule.

'If you're still here next Saturday, Brodie, I'll take you up on that,' Kate said, and then she was tossing back her macchiato—and that *had* to burn her damned tongue. Not that you could tell from the next blinding smile she beamed at Brodie!

Brodie and Kate discussed timing, swapped numbers, while Scott sat there like a statue—ice on the outside, volcano on the inside.

And then Kate put some money on the table and Scott had to grit his teeth again. Because—come *on*!—couldn't he even buy her a damned cup of coffee?

The contract. Fifty-fifty. No, you can't buy her a damned coffee.

'Work calls,' she said, all cheery and unconcerned. 'Bye, guys. See you Saturday, Brodie.'

Gone.

Brodie looked at Scott, who had yet to take a sip from his fresh cup.

'Are you insane?' Brodie asked conversationally.

Scott laughed, and if it had a slight edge of insanity he wasn't going to acknowledge it. 'Tell me about your business,' he said instead.

When Kate got back to her apartment she was so furious—and disillusioned, and...and *hurt*, she couldn't think straight.

God, she hoped Scott hadn't seen the hurt.

Not that Scott, who didn't *get* hurt, would ever understand it. He'd just think she was *piqued*. The way he had last night just because she'd finally taken a stand and told him not to turn up today.

Well, that had sure worked!

And she really *must* be a pathetic nymphomaniac. Because she'd been so glad to see him when she should have been annoyed. So very glad...right up until he'd told her he hadn't *signed up* for deep and meaningful.

Nobody signed up for deep and meaningful. It just…*happened*.

But not, apparently, to Scott.

Well, what had she expected? That two weeks of rock-your-hormones sex would somehow make her special? That the guy she was sleeping with might want to teach her to sail rather than palming her off on someone else? That he might actually introduce her to his friends so she didn't have to introduce herself, when she didn't have the remotest idea how to categorise their relationship for public consumption? That he might, somehow, claim her as someone just a little bit special?

The way she wanted to—

Ooohhhh.

She shuddered out a breath as reality hit her like a truck. She wanted to claim him. *Mine, mine, mine.*

Great! Just freaking great. Because Scott had made it pretty clear this morning that he was reading from a different script—and it wasn't a romance. To Scott she was a collection of body parts, transferable to his friend for any non-bedroom stuff!

She's all yours!

Well, *quid pro quo. There* was a legal term for Scott to mull over.

If she was nothing but a collection of body parts to him then he would be nothing but a collection of body parts to *her.*

Scott Knight: Kate Cleary's stud.

No more kissing. No dates that weren't really dates. No unscheduled drop-ins. No fireside chats. Nothing except sex. Only twice a week, because she was no longer in a negotiating mood. Starting with a Play Time that would fry his nether regions!

Before she could think twice she grabbed her phone, pulled up Scott's number and got texting.

Play Time. Tuesday. 9 p.m. Ellington Lane.

That would shock him. He'd be sitting there with Brodie, never dreaming she'd text him so soon after that dismal coffee catch-up. He probably expected her to be lying face-down on her bed, crying into her pillow because she was *piqued*. Well, he could just—

Ding.

Text message. She grabbed her phone. Opened Scott's text message.

Roger that.

With a smiley face.

A…a *smiley face*?

Now, you see—that was why he wasn't the right man for her.

Or maybe why he is.

'Yes, thank you, subconscious. Not helpful.'

Scott was champing at the bit as he approached Ellington Lane on Tuesday night.

He had no idea what fantasy Kate had dreamt up to carry out in this dingy, narrow, deserted laneway, but hopefully it didn't involve his murder—because Ellington Lane certainly looked as if it regularly saw a dead body, and Kate surely must want to kill him after Sunday.

He wasn't even certain she was going to turn up, given she hadn't bothered answering any of his thousand calls since then.

But he was here waiting anyway—he who *never* had sex in public places—so hungry for her he'd do anything.

He was going to make tonight *so* damned good for her. Use his body to show her he didn't mean what he'd said—because clearly he couldn't trust his malfunctioning brain to choose the right words.

He still couldn't believe he'd said it. *She's all yours.* Just because she'd smiled at Brodie and he'd wanted to grab her and demand she stop. Because she was his, his, *his*, and she was supposed to smile at *him*—got it?

God, he was a moron! *You're mine—so go with that guy instead, why don't you?*

He *deserved* to be standing here, lust-starved and desperate, in an ill-lit, deserted alley, wondering if she'd turn up, shivering at the thought of what she'd do to him, and just... well, *longing* for her.

He took a deep breath, trying to steady himself.

And suddenly there she was.

CHAPTER ELEVEN

SCOTT'S HEART LURCHED as Kate took one step. Stopped.

She was backlit by a street lamp just outside the lane. Standing with her legs slightly apart, looking tough. Tight pants, high boots, hands on hips, wearing some kind of cap.

She started walking towards him—very slowly, very deliberately. Halfway, he could see she was wearing a police uniform—but a sexed-up, skintight version.

His mouth went dry—so dry that when she asked, 'What seems to be the problem?' he couldn't answer.

And then she was in front of him, and he could smell tuberose, and he wanted to throw himself at her feet and beg.

'Not talking?' she asked, and there was a snap in her voice. 'Then I'd say you're up to no good. Turn around, hands wide on the wall.'

He did as he was told.

She kicked between his feet. 'Spread 'em.'

He *spread 'em* with alacrity, and then breathed out a long, silent sigh of surrender as she plastered herself against his back.

'So… Are you behaving yourself?' she asked, and chuckled, low and breathy, right in his ear.

'Yes, Officer,' he said—or at least he tried to, but it came out as a half-strangled gargle.

'Now, why don't I believe you? What's in your pockets?'

'Nothing.'

'I think I'll check for myself.'

Next moment her hands were diving into the back pockets of his jeans.

'Condom,' she said. 'Not exactly "nothing". Not soliciting, are you?'

'No.'

'No *what*?'

'No, Officer.'

'I'll hold on to this,' she said, and he imagined her sliding the condom into the back pocket of her tight, tight pants.

'Right. Let's check your other pockets,' she said.

And her hands were *there*, digging into his front pockets, making his heartbeat go off like a cracker as she 'accidentally' nudged against the erection straining fiercely against the denim.

'All clear,' she breathed against his ear. 'So—why don't you just tell me what you've been up to so I don't have to keep searching?'

'But I've done nothing wrong, Officer.'

'So let me ask you, buddy: do you know the meaning of the term *ignorantia juris non excusat*?'

Oh, God. God, God, God.

'No. But it sounds…sexy.'

'Well, it's not sexy,' she said, despite the fact that she was unbuttoning his jeans, sliding his zipper down, sliding her hands inside, over his erection, squeezing, stroking. 'It means ignorance of the law is not an excuse.'

He groaned.

'Am I hurting you?' she asked.

'No. No, Officer, you're not hurting me.'

'Then why are you groaning?'

'Can't…*ahh*…help it. Sorry. J-Just what law am I ignorant of?'

'The law that says you're not allowed to bribe a police officer.'

'But I'm not,' he said, just as her hands went beneath his underwear, cool and silky and freaking *wonderful*. Another groan slipped out. Could a man die of lust? Because he was on the way.

'Then maybe you should *think* about bribing me, so I'll let you off the hook.'

'Um… Um… Um…' Seriously, his brain was fricasseed.

'Something that doesn't involve a condom, since I've confiscated that,' she said.

'Um…'

'Turn around.'

He turned fast enough to give himself a corkscrew knee injury. Reached automatically for her.

'No touching an officer,' she barked. 'Just stand there. Stand there and take it like a man.'

Before he knew what was happening she'd shoved him against the wall. And then she was on her knees in front of him, dragging his jeans down, just low enough to free him. Holding the base of him with one hand, cupping his balls with the other, she licked the very tip of him. Delicate, fluttery…gradually moving down the shaft, back up, down, then up. Alternately kissing and licking. Gradually increasing the pressure of her tongue, her lips.

He wanted to touch her hair, but she'd wound it up under the police cap. And looking at that cap as she worked on him was getting him more excited than he'd ever been in his life.

She tilted her head back, replaced her mouth with her hands, looked up at him, parted her lips, licked that heavy top lip…and with a quick, wicked smile closed her mouth over him.

Scott let loose with a whole string of groaning cries as she sucked him, using her lips, her tongue, her teeth, even the roof of her mouth. Stretching him, laving him, devouring him. Her hands were moving everywhere her mouth wasn't until he was half insane with need. He felt the orgasm building, clawing to get out.

And then she did something with her tongue, and he looked down at the police cap, caught a glimpse of pale skin as she angled her head and her mouth performed a twist he'd never experienced before, and it was rushing at him.

'Kate! Kate, I'm going to come!' he said in urgent warning.

But she just kept right on going, shifting so that her hands were gripping his hips, keeping him inside her mouth, and he thought for a moment he was going to pass out with the pleasure of it. She kept up the pressure right through his explosion of a release, as his hips jerked under her hands and he spilled himself to the point of exhaustion.

And then she got to her feet. Looked at him as she licked that top lip again. 'So, whatever you were doing tonight before I caught you—' as though she'd just written him a ticket '—don't do it again.'

And then she turned, started walking away.

Scott couldn't believe, at first, that she would just leave him like that—but she kept going.

'Kate!' he called out, pulling up his jeans.

Stop. Turn. 'It's Officer Cleary.'

'I'll come with you. I owe you.'

'Is that another bribe?' She shook her head. 'Now, you see, that's why I don't associate with criminals.'

'But—'

'You'll receive a message from the station in a few days, once I've cleared your name, and then we'll see.'

She turned again, walked briskly down the lane. And was gone.

He finished tucking in his shirt. Feeling both incredibly sated and hugely unsatisfied.

Because she was gone. Without having let him touch her once.

Gone. Just like Sunday morning.

Gone.

One thing Scott knew was that he wasn't a fan of this 'gone girl' thing. He was going to have to let her know he didn't appreciate her just leaving. Like, *bang*, leaving.

Even if it *was* essentially what he'd done to her on Saturday night—and without giving her any kind of release at all. But he'd had a *reason*. Self-preservation! Her? Tonight? What possible reason could she have had?

Bang. Gone.

Nope. He didn't like it one bit.

The next day Scott left two phone messages for Kate.

Her response was to text him back.

Play Time. Thursday. Your house. 7 p.m.

He swore long and loud. Play Time was all very well, but he wanted to talk to her. That interrupted conversation from Sunday morning was still heavy on his mind and he wanted to fix it. Because things didn't feel…*right*.

He tried to call her again—she didn't pick up. So he called her office, spoke to Deb. Received the message that Kate was interstate, working on a child custody case.

'And it's a messy one,' Deb told him. 'So you've got no chance of getting hold of her and please don't try. She's…'

He could feel the hesitation. Teetering, teetering… *Go on, tell me, tell me.* But no.

'Look, just leave her to it,' Deb said, and hung up.

He found himself hanging on to the phone, reluctant to let it go. As if it was some line of communication he didn't want to snap.

Which was just plain stupid.

He forced himself to disconnect.

He worried about what Deb had said. *'She's…'* Just the one word. Hesitant, hanging, worrying.

She's…what? She's…not interested in you any more? She's…having a meltdown? Having a biopsy? Eating chicken for lunch. What, dammit? *What?*

He paced around his office, needing to speak to her, knowing he couldn't.

Focusing on the first thing that had popped into his head—that she wasn't interested in him any more—calmed him a little. Because if that were true she wouldn't have sent him that Play Time text.

And they had a *contract*—which might be stupid but at least meant that even if she was over him she still had to see him for another week and a half. So he had time to work on her, get her back onside. Time to make the sex so phenomenal she'd be sorry she didn't have a clause demanding seven nights a week instead of a lousy two.

Starting Thursday, when he saw her again. At *his* house, this time. In *his* bed.

He never brought women home, because…well, *because*. But Kate…?

He sucked in a breath as the image of her in his house shimmered in his head.

Would she like it?

In his bed?

How would she look there?

Not that those thoughts were *germane*! The *germane* thing was that it would be the perfect opportunity to gauge whether the wattage of their sexual attraction needed to be amped up. Although, frankly, much more wattage might just finish him off.

A new image popped into his head. Kate on her knees in that dark alley, going down on him. Refusing to allow him to touch her. Just leaving him there.

Okay, so he *hadn't* calmed down.

He wouldn't be calm until he spoke to her. Until he knew what was going on with her.

He wouldn't be calm until *she* was calm.

Because he knew, *knew*, she wasn't calm. He'd heard the worry in Deb's voice. A child custody case. The kind that hit Kate the hardest. She would be stressed. And…and *grieving*. Interstate—on her own. With nobody to hold her and tell her it was going to be all right, even if it wasn't. Just to *be* there. With her—for her.

And then he stopped himself. She had a family to turn to. A large, loving family. She didn't need him.

Sex. No strings. That was what they had. She'd made that plain by responding to his voicemail messages with a text. She was going through hell...but for him she offered Play Time. Because that was the deal. He'd teased her that she was falling behind on the fantasies, so she was dishing them up. Twice in one week. Any man would want that. Phillip the aged barrister would be *thrilled* with that.

Scott found that his hands had balled into fists and determinedly unclenched them. Flexed them. Took a deep, calming breath.

Better.

It was no good getting bent out of shape over Phillip. Over Play Time. Or over Kate being alone dealing with hell. No damned good.

So he would take Deb's advice. He would wait until Thursday. He would see what fantasy she came up with. He would respond sexually.

And that would be all.

CHAPTER TWELVE

KATE TOOK EXTRA-SPECIAL care getting ready for Play Time on Thursday. Her hair was swinging loose, artfully dishevelled, and she had on her favourite red lipstick—which was fine for today because there would be no kissing.

She was wearing her sexiest underwear. Nude mesh and lace, complete with suspender belt—and she'd gone for ultrasheer black stockings as a contrast. Achingly high black stilettos. A taupe trench coat, tied but not buttoned.

That was it. Not one thing more. Perfect for the role she was playing.

A role that would not involve any of those pesky *deep and meaningful* fireside chats.

Scott would be happy about that. And, frankly, she was happy about it too. Having spent two soul-destroying days fighting to get her client's little boy back, 'Kate Cleary' deserved the night off. Tomorrow she would take up the legal cudgels again—but tonight, Kate wanted to be someone else.

When Kate arrived at Scott's house in East Sydney she had to recheck his business card to make sure she had the right address—because she was standing in front of an old church. She'd already guessed Scott's house was going to be special, if Silverston was anything to go by. But this was something else. She couldn't wait to see inside.

No! She caught herself up. She wasn't a starry-eyed girlfriend, about to get a guided tour of her boyfriend's architectural wonder of a home. Scott—who hadn't even invited her here—was probably in there pacing the floor, hating the idea of her invading his private space. So she wouldn't give him the satisfaction of being interested.

She noted the intercom in place of a doorbell, which reminded her that his house doubled as a second office. Perfect, since she was here on 'business'.

She waited outside for seven o'clock to hit, using the time to layer on the persona she'd chosen, mentally steeling herself to resist the first heart-melting look at him, the first touch. And then, on the dot, she pushed the button.

Instant answer.

'Kate?' Sounding anxious. 'There in two seconds.'

'Oh, Mr Knight, has there been a mistake?' she asked, all breathy and flustered.

Pause. And then, 'Kate? It *is* Kate, right?'

'It's *Lorelei*, Mr Knight. Don't you remember? You booked a home visit. Are you going to buzz me in?'

Another pause. Longer.

He would be processing that. Kate's voice giving a name he'd never heard, referring to a job he hadn't booked.

And then the intercom clicked off. So…was he *not* going to buzz her in?

But less than ten seconds later the door opened and he was there. He took her arm, drew her in. Tried to kiss her.

'Oh, sorry, Mr Knight. Miss Kitty doesn't like her girls to kiss the clients.'

His jaw tightened, but he said nothing.

Despite Kate's best efforts she couldn't help giving the space just one sweeping glance. Soaring arched ceilings, like a…well, like a *church*. Stained-glass windows, stark white walls, honey wood floors, a staircase that provided a pop of colour, with steps painted a vivid red, leading up to a mezzanine.

Enough! Stop!

'Where do you want me, Mr Knight?' she asked.

He gestured to the staircase. 'Go up.'

She walked quickly to the stairs and ascended. She paused at the top, needing direction—and had to close her eyes to stop herself peering over the half-wall. She was not going to look again. Not, not, *not*.

'There,' Scott said from behind her—and she opened her eyes to find him pointing to a long, intricately carved wooden screen at one end of the mezzanine floor.

Her heart started to race as she approached the screen. She was so excited to see what was behind it. And when she stepped around it she gasped. Just couldn't keep it in.

More stained-glass windows—taking the place of a fancy bedhead—dominated the space. The walls were painted a dull gold. A huge bed of dark wood with a blood-red coverlet sat on a raised stone dais. There were Persian rugs on the wood floor surrounding the dais. Antique chairs—grand and austere—were positioned either side of the stone slab, with candlesticks as tall as Scott beside them. The room was heartbreakingly, unexpectedly beautiful.

Kate schooled her features to show nothing as she turned back to Scott and smiled—a professionally vacant smile.

He was watching her with a hint of disapproval that she forced herself to ignore. Conservative Scott Knight *would* disapprove of a prostitute—but that didn't mean he wouldn't enjoy the experience.

She undid her belt, held the coat wide. 'Do you like what you see, Mr Knight?'

He swallowed, hard, as his eyes slid down her body and stuck at the tops of her black stockings. 'Yes,' he said. 'I want to touch you.'

'You can touch. Just no kissing.' And with that, she shrugged out of the coat and went to lay it on one of the chairs.

But she didn't make it that far. Because Scott was after her in a heartbeat.

Kate shivered as he grabbed her, as he spun her to face him, as he yanked her hair back to give him access to her neck, as he licked the pulse beating there.

And then he lowered his head, going straight for her nipple, taking it into his mouth through the mesh of her bra, sucking hard, harder, until she cried out. He didn't stop, just moved to the other nipple, then back again. Back and forth.

She was a quivering mess of nerves and need by the time he stepped back, took her coat and threw it at the chair.

He swallowed hard again as his eyes dipped to her breasts. Her nipples were dark and distended, the mesh covering them wet. His hands moved to her breasts, fingers pinching where his mouth had been. Pinching, rolling. And then he was digging into the thin cups, tearing them down so that her nipples popped over the tops, and his mouth was back, suckling and nipping and licking her.

Her hands were in his hair, pulling hard enough to hurt—but to keep him there, not to drag him away. She could feel the unbearable wetness between her thighs, wanted his hands there, his mouth.

As though he'd divined that, he dropped to his knees, kissed the tops of her stockings—one, then the other—and licked, *slooowly*, along the top of each, where her thighs were naked. Kate was scared she'd collapse on the spot, it was so erotic.

And then, completely at odds with the languor of that, he yanked her panties down to her knees and shoved his tongue between her legs. Her tangled underwear trapped her and limited Scott's access, forcing him to concentrate his tongue in one ravaging line. *So...damned...good.* She heard his ragged breathing, felt his fingers digging into the backs of her thighs, hard enough to bruise.

He growled something, impatient, and next moment was dragging her down onto the rug, ripping at her underwear, manoeuvring her onto her hands and knees. And then he was behind her, his mouth on her again, sucking her, forcing his tongue inside her until she was panting and whimpering with need.

A quick rustling sound, but his mouth didn't stop. Condom. She heard the packet tear. Zip opening. She imagined him sheathing himself. Knew he would be inside her soon.

She pushed herself back against his mouth, urging him word-lessly to hurry, to fill her.

He moved, covered her, his mouth at her ear. 'You're going to have to ask me,' he breathed.

'Please…*please*.'

'Please what?'

'I want you inside me. Do it. Inside—*now*.'

The words weren't even out of her mouth before he'd shoved himself into her. Holding her hips, screwing into her as though he had to get close, closer, closer still. Up to the hilt. Over and over. Pounding, pounding, pounding. And then he tensed, coming with a loud cry. His hands reached for her waist, yanked her upright, her back against his chest, and he was feeling for her clitoris, fingers forking either side, perfect pressure.

Ah, ahh, ahhhh.

'Come for me, Kate. Come now…come.'

And, in a blast of almost excruciating pleasure, she ex-ploded into orgasm.

Slowly, Scott withdrew from her. Sat back, turned her, hoisting her onto his lap

He tried again to kiss her, and she drew back. 'No kiss-ing,' she said, but was horrified to find her voice wobbling.

Even worse—he'd heard it too.

He looked at her—sharp, concerned. 'What is it, Kate?'

'Lorelei. And no kissing.'

'I'm not kissing Lorelei. I'm kissing Kate,' Scott said.

He coaxed her to open her mouth, took his leisurely time, letting his tongue move from licking her lips to sliding inside.

After a long, delicious moment he stopped, edged a frac-tion away, smiled into her eyes. That smile she'd only seen once—that night—but it was even more devastating now, because it was layered with gentleness.

I am in such trouble here.

'Kate…' he said, and his voice shook.

Such trouble. And she didn't need trouble.

Steeling herself, she smiled back. 'Lorelei,' she corrected. 'And that will be two thousand dollars, Mr Knight.'

The shock on Scott's face had her shrinking inside, but she forced herself to hold his eyes.

And then he smiled again—but it was back to the juke-box, pick a smile and whirl. 'Your prices are too low. I would have paid five. In fact, I *will* pay five. Because, as I recall, I booked Lorelei's services for a full night.'

'We don't stay overnight, Scott...you and I.' *Uh-oh*, the wobble.

'Miss Kitty says Lorelei *does*. And if you want your five thousand dollars that's what you're going to have to do.' He gave her a boost off his lap. 'So up you go. Whatever you've still got on, get it off. Then get into that bed.'

The next morning, after *Lorelei* had belted herself into her trench coat and left, Scott threw down three cups of coffee. He needed the caffeine to get his brain and his body func-tioning again.

But it didn't work.

Something was bothering him. Very deeply.

And it was... Well, it was Play Time.

The whole 'Lorelei' thing was eating at him. After that one frenzied bout of lovemaking on the rug, when he'd kissed Kate, he'd felt such an overwhelming burst of joy. Kate...in his arms, in his house, and he'd wanted her so damned much.

And she'd responded by asking him for her fee.

So he'd decided to get his money's worth. All night long he'd been at her, taking her with lips, tongue, fingers, his never-ending hard-on. And she'd met him move for move, always receptive—as 'Miss Kitty' expected—never saying no, opening her arms, her legs.

Everything but her mouth.

Because he'd tried to kiss her many times, and each time she'd pulled away with a coyly admonishing slap on the wrist, the shoulder, the butt, and a reminder of Miss Kitty's rules.

He'd tried to talk to her in those respite periods while they'd recharged their burnt-out batteries. About the child custody case. Her mother's art. Maeve and Molly, Shay and Lilith, Gus and Aristotle. Even about Deb. But every time he'd been frozen into crunchable cubes by her vacant 'Lorelei' stare.

The end result was that although he could have written his own sex manual after experimenting so comprehensively with Kate's body during the night, he wasn't satisfied.

And the flat fact was he didn't *like* Play Time.

There. He'd admitted it.

He must be certifiable, but he couldn't seem to whip up enthusiasm for any more fantasy-land stuff. It was like the sexual version of Brodie's tattoo—nice in theory, but just not him. He must be more of a Knight than he'd thought. Conservative. Boring, even.

Did Kate find him boring? In bed? Out of it? Both? Because she was suddenly very interested in Play Time. No kissing. No talking. Just role play. Was Play Time the nonnautical equivalent of a yacht heading to the Whitsundays? Taking Kate away from humdrum in the bedroom?

He put his coffee cup down with a clatter.

She'd made him *pay* for it! He almost hadn't believed it when Kate had demanded his cheque for five thousand dollars—and then had actually taken it when he'd jokingly written it out, before breezing out of the house.

A house she hadn't expressed the slightest interest in.

And his house was worth *some* level of interest from the woman he was exclusively sleeping with, dammit.

Not good enough, Kate.

He wanted to know what she thought about it. And he was going to force her to tell him. Did she like it? Hate it? Want to change it? *What?*

Scott gave her three hours—time to slough off that annoying Lorelei—then called her mobile. No answer. So he called her office.

Deb picked up the phone—and told him in no uncertain terms he wouldn't be getting a look-in that day because Kate was in back-to-back meetings.

Well, he wasn't going to put himself through the embarrassment of having his call go to voicemail, as had been happening with monotonous regularity. He would email her instead. And if she didn't respond he would… He would… He would do something as yet undetermined! But *something*, at any rate.

Calmly, rationally, unemotionally, he tapped out a message suggesting they catch up for dinner that night and fired it off, knowing she'd pick up the email on her smartphone whether she was in a meeting or not.

And then he waited, refreshing his emails every thirty seconds, working himself into a lather over the fifty-fifty rule she'd probably insist on when the bill came tonight. Well, screw her stupid fifty-fifty rule—*he* would be picking up the tab. Like a normal guy who *wasn't* a complete arsehole would do when he took a woman out for dinner.

Refresh, refresh, refresh…

Come on—respond!

Fifteen minutes later his phone buzzed.

Text message.

His stomach clenched as he reached for his phone. Because he just knew.

And, yep, there it was.

Play Time. Sunday. Noon. My apartment.

Scott hurled the phone across the room.

CHAPTER THIRTEEN

KATE SAW THE Whitsundays girls in their usual corner table at Fox on Friday night, cocktails already in hand, and thought, *Thank heaven.* A rowdy, uncomplicated girls' night out was exactly what she needed.

Jessica, who was facing the entrance, was the first to notice her across the crowded floor of the bar area, and she waved enthusiastically as Kate squeezed her way across the floor.

Willa slid a Manhattan—Kate's favourite cocktail—to her as she collapsed into her seat.

Kate, surprised and touched by Willa's prescience, kissed her.

'I knew you'd need it.' Willa's smile was full of sympathy. 'How did the case end up?'

Kate eased the elastic from her hair and ran a tired hand through the strands. 'Victory for Team Cleary.'

'Fantastic!'

'But it was harrowing, even for a jaded cynic of a lawyer.'

'You're not a jaded cynic,' Willa said. 'Or you wouldn't care so deeply.'

Kate felt a little prickle of tears—and that just underscored how wrung-out she was, because she never let her emotions show in public. She blinked the tears away, smiling determinedly.

'Whatever I am, I sure need this!' she said, picking up her glass and half draining it. 'And now—a *fun* topic of conversation, please.'

Amy laughed. 'Well, you're just in time to hear Willa tell us about her most romantic moment with Rob. Will that do?'

'That will do very, very nicely!' Kate said. 'But first...' She drained the rest of her Manhattan and signalled to a passing server for another round of drinks for all four of them. 'Better! Okay, Willa darling, spill it!'

'I'm not sure you guys will think it's romantic, but…oh, God, it *is*!'

'Don't make us beg!' Amy said.

'Well…Rob recommended me to a chief financial officer…'

'And…?' Amy urged.

'For a vitamin distribution company.'

'And…?' Jessica prompted.

Willa sucked her mojito through a straw. 'Rob told him I was super-bright!'

'And so you are, my darling,' Kate said.

'And…and brilliant!'

'Nice,' Jessica added.

'And that I knew about foreign-owned entities, so maybe I could help find a creative solution to a problem the company was having.'

Kate laughed. 'Okaaaay… That's not exactly floating my boat just yet, but I'm hoping something juicy is coming up.'

Willa beamed around at them, glowing with love. 'The CFO said they'd had a dozen accountants try to find a solution and fail. He said Rob had assured him I would be able to help. And I *did*! And I got *paid*!' She sighed, all satisfaction, and sucked up another mouthful of mojito. 'Isn't that romantic?'

Kate, Amy and Jessica stared at her, and then Amy burst out laughing.

One by one the others started laughing too.

'Hey, it's not funny,' Willa protested, but she had a smile lurking too.

Jessica said, 'Well, it's not exactly rose petals strewn over the bedcovers.'

Amy looked at Jessica. 'Seriously? *That's* your romantic fantasy? I would never have picked it, Miss I-can-play-basketball-and-change-a-car-tyre-when-the-game's-over.'

'Well, I *can* change a car tyre,' Jessica said. 'But I'd like a rose-petal-strewn-bed for afterwards. With candlelight. And being hand-fed ripe strawberries in the midst of it all. Lovely.' She raised her eyebrows at Amy. 'Why? What's yours, Miss Personality-plus?'

'Easy. A defender,' Amy said definitely. 'Someone who will ride in like a medieval knight on a destrier, catch me up and save me from…from…' She stopped, smiled a little sheepishly. 'Well, from danger,' she finished, then sighed. '*That's* romance.'

All three looked expectantly at Kate.

'Oh, no,' she said.

'Come on,' Amy begged.

Jessica sniggered. 'I'll bet it has something to do with Big Burt the handy vibrator.'

Kate felt herself blush—and then blushed harder when three jaws dropped simultaneously as the girls took in her colour change.

'No way!' Amy said.

'Not…not exactly,' Kate said, and then she threw in the metaphorical towel. 'Okay, you asked for it. It *does* happen to involve Burt. Not *Big* Burt, but his namesake. Burt *Lancaster*. And Deborah Kerr. And, no, Jessica, that does *not* mean I want to be in a three-way with Burt and Deborah, who are, in fact, both deceased. And, no, I never wanted to have sex with Burt Lancaster when he was alive either.'

'So what *does* it mean?'

'It means— Oh, dear, this is kind of embarrassing! Okay, it's all about my obsession with *From Here to Eternity*, which I really need to outgrow. And you have *got* to watch that movie, Jessica! It should be mandatory viewing for all women.'

'Okay—it's on the download list!' Jessica said promptly.

Kate ran a finger around the rim of her empty glass. 'When you get to the scene at the beach their passion is just so…so *strong*… And there's nothing they can do about it except acknowledge it and know that it's going to happen. They've been swimming, and they're at the shore, and she's lying on the sand, and then he's there with her, and she's in his arms. And he's kissing her like he can't help himself, with the waves breaking over them… And when she runs for drier ground he follows her, and drops to his knees, and basically…basically *falls* on her—like he's so damned hungry for everything about her… Well, *whew*!' She waved a hand in front of her heated face. 'That is *some* scene.'

Jessica was, likewise, fanning herself. 'It beats Willa's chief financial officer and my rose petals, that's for sure. And it gives Amy's destrier a nudge too.'

Kate laughed. 'Well, suffice to say if a man kisses me like that in the surf I'm his. From here to eternity.'

There was a moment of respectful silence.

And then Willa smiled. 'There's one thing I need to add to my own account,' she said, all smug. 'When Rob spoke to that vitamin-company CFO he said…' Pause. Blink. 'He said…' She paused again, went all dreamy-eyed. 'He said he'd trust me with his life.'

'Oh…' said Amy.

'Oh…' said Jessica.

'Oh,' said Kate. Deep breath. 'In that case, you win.'

Willa was glowing. 'Yes, I do, don't I?' she asked, delighted.

'I wonder what Chantal would say?' Amy mused. 'About *her* most romantic moment, I mean.'

Willa pondered that, eyes half closed. 'It would be something to do with dancing. The romance of swaying against a man, having him hold you close, showing you just by the way he looked at you that you were his…'

Four sighs as their fresh round of drinks was deposited— and then four dreamy sips.

'So Chantal's in your camp, Willa. She's already had her moment,' Amy said. 'With Brodie, I mean, at Weeping Reef.

Because that's what happened, right? The dance, the look that everyone could see?'

'It *was* sizzling,' Willa said.

Amy drained her glass. 'No wonder poor Scott got bent out of shape.'

Kate felt the blood drain from her face. What? *What?* 'Scott?' she said, and thanked all the saints in heaven that her voice had come out halfway normal.

'Oh, yeah—you don't know the story,' Willa said, sounding sad. 'Scott and Chantal were an item at Weeping Reef. *The* item. Until Brodie came on the scene. Actually, they were an item even after Brodie arrived. Chantal and Brodie didn't seem to like each other—except that they *did*, if you know what I mean, and just didn't recognise it. I think I was the only one who saw what was happening. Scott certainly didn't, and he was blindsided. Chantal was dancing with Brodie—which was no big deal. She loves dancing. Lives for it. But she could never get Scott onto the dance floor, and he never had a problem with her dancing with other men. But that night it was...*more*. Like a...a flash. The way they moved together...the way they looked at each other. Everyone knew in that one moment that Chantal and Brodie belonged together.'

Kate remembered asking Scott to dance at that dinner. Him telling her he didn't. Ever. Remembered him insisting on absolute fidelity in their contract.

'So what happened?' she asked through her aching throat.

'A huge argument—which ended with Scott slugging Brodie. Brodie took off, leaving Scott and Chantal at the resort together...but *not* together. Not *at all* together. Looking back, it all seems so needlessly dramatic, given nothing actually happened between Chantal and Brodie. But Scott and Brodie haven't spoken since.'

Uh-oh. Awkward. 'Actually, they...they *have* spoken,' Kate said, and took a quick silent breath to steady her nerves for the inquisition.

The three girls stared at her, waiting.

Kate took a slow sip of her Manhattan. 'I was having coffee with Scott, at the marina across the road from my place, on Sunday morning. And Brodie walked past. His boat's moored there.'

'Oh, my God!' Amy squealed. 'I don't know what part to ask about first. Coffee with Scott? How did *that* come about?'

'We've seen each other a couple of times since Willa's party.'

There was a long pregnant pause.

'It's nothing,' Kate said.

More silence.

'Really nothing,' she insisted. 'There was an…an attraction there, and we wanted to see if there was anything worth exploring. That's all.'

'And is there?' Jessica asked.

Kate took another sip. 'No. There really isn't,' she said, and felt the truth of that, the pang of it, pierce right through her heart. It took her a moment to recover from that certainty, to find her voice again. 'Anyway, Sunday morning he was in the area, so—'

Amy choked on her drink. '*In the area?* Are you *sure* there's nothing worth exploring?'

'Yes, in the area, and, no, there's nothing worth exploring,' Kate insisted, but she could feel the heat slash across her cheekbones. 'He buzzed my apartment and I went down to meet him.'

Very important to get the message out that he hadn't stayed the night at her place. She was a little embarrassed about hiding what was a straightforward arrangement from her friends, but she couldn't seem to up and confess. And it wasn't only the confidentiality clause stopping her. It just felt too…*painful*, somehow, to share.

'And what happened?' Amy asked.

'While we were sitting there drinking our coffee along came Brodie.'

'And then…? Come on, Kate,' Amy urged. 'The suspense is killing me.'

'All right. I'm just trying to remember it.' *As if she didn't!* 'There was some…tension. Yes, now that I think back there was definitely tension between them to start with. But I left them talking while I went to order, and by the time I returned, it was all quite amicable between them.'

'Thank God,' Willa said. 'They were so close, back in the day. Closer than brothers. It hasn't felt right, their estrangement.'

'So what happened next?' Amy asked. 'Is Brodie still here? I'd love to see him. And did they talk about Chantal?'

Chantal. The name whipped through Kate's bloodstream, breath-stealing.

Jealous. She was jealous—of something that had happened *eight years ago*. Because one woman had sneaked past Scott's defences, where *she* couldn't go. Where she was resolutely *blocked* from going. She picked up her glass to take another sip of her cocktail, realised it was empty but had no recollection of drinking it. Too much, too fast.

'I don't know what happened then because I left them to it,' she said. 'I knew they hadn't seen each other in a while, and I…I had work to finish. I haven't spoken to Scott since.'

Which wasn't strictly correct…but was still true. Officer Cleary and Lorelei had spoken to Scott—not Kate.

'Nobody was throwing punches, if that's any comfort to you,' Kate added. 'And one thing I *do* know is that Brodie is still in Sydney, because he's giving me a sailing lesson tomorrow.'

'Oh! You are *so* lucky!' Jessica said. 'I'd love to learn to sail.'

'Well, it's only one lesson,' Kate said. 'All I can really expect is to find out if I've got what it takes or if it will be like the time I tried Tai Chi—nice idea, but not going to happen. Why don't you come too, Jessica?'

Jessica sighed. 'Nah—I've got kickboxing tomorrow.'

'Why don't you ask Scott to teach you if you're really interested, Jess?' Amy suggested. 'He's the absolute best. Better than Brodie—even though Brodie's the one who's made it his career.' She turned to Kate, looking quizzical. 'In fact, Kate, I don't know why *you* don't ask Scott to teach you. At least he lives in Sydney, so you'll get more than one lesson out of him.'

Kate busied herself snagging a server and ordering more drinks. By the time she'd done that, she had her poker face on. 'From what I've gathered, Scott doesn't sail any more.'

'That's true,' Willa said. 'You know, Weeping Reef was so beautiful, and we were all so excited to be there, but a lot of things went wrong. Things that…that changed us, I guess.'

'Ain't that the truth,' Amy murmured. And then she took a deep breath, seeming to shake off a thought. She smiled— very brightly. 'But that was then and this is now, so let's drink to moving on. Onwards and upwards, ladies. Onwards and upwards.'

The girls clinked glasses, although Kate wondered if her empty glass actually counted.

'The music is starting and they're opening the bar off the dance floor,' Jessica said. 'The crowd should spread out soon.' She looked at the packed bar area. 'I wonder if there's a rose-petal-sprinkler in amongst that lot who might be persuaded to ask me to dance.'

And then Jessica gasped, her eyes wide as saucers.

'Well, bite me!' she said. 'Maybe I *will* come along tomorrow, Kate. Because Brodie looks mighty hot.'

'Huh?' Amy swivelled in her seat and squealed.

Willa was the next to look. 'Oh, my God. I told Rob to join us here, but…but…how…?'

Kate turned very, very slowly as a cold finger of dread trailed its nail down her back.

Rob, Brodie…and Scott. Heading across the floor towards them.

CHAPTER FOURTEEN

'Look who I roped in!' Rob said as the three men reached the table.

And then everyone was standing, exclaiming, hugging, laughing. Even Jessica, who'd never met Brodie, was in there.

Everyone except Kate, who stayed in her seat with a fixed smile on her face, watching the reunion.

There was a general scrabbling for chairs while Brodie went off to the bar for beer and the next round of cocktails was delivered.

Rob sat and drew Willa onto his lap. 'Scott called to see if I wanted to go for a beer with him and Brodie, but I persuaded them to join us here instead,' he explained.

'I'm so glad you did,' Amy said. 'Because we were just talking about them.'

Scott sent Kate a brooding look, which started her heart thudding.

But all he said was, 'I'll go and find some extra chairs,' before stalking off.

Brodie was soon on his way back, carrying three beers as he cut across the small, still deserted dance floor rather than squeeze through the crush of drinkers spreading out from the bar.

He slid the beers onto the table and Rob snatched one up.

Jessica looked up at Brodie conspiratorially. 'We've been talking about our favourite romantic moments, Brodie. What do you think is better? Impressing a CFO with your business acumen—and no prizes for guessing who *that* one belongs to—strewn rose petals on a bed, a knight on a charger or *From Here to Eternity*?'

Brodie laughed. 'Are they the only options?'

Amy slapped her hand over Jessica's mouth—no doubt staving off any mention of dancing cheek to cheek in the Whitsundays.

'Can't take her anywhere,' Amy said, and quickly redirected the conversation.

Kate was relieved. Not only did she not want to hear the Chantal story again—not with Brodie at the table and Scott on approach—but she didn't want to let any red-blooded male into her guilty *From Here to Eternity* secret. And especially not Scott, who would laugh himself into apoplexy over it.

Scott had one of his false smiles in place as he handed a chair to Brodie. 'I had to promise to go back and have a drink with a group on a hen-night bender to get that chair, Brode!'

Brodie laughed as he took the chair. 'Don't pretend that's a hardship,' he said, and then grimaced an infinitesimal apology as his eyes flickered in Kate's direction.

Great. Brodie had seen her with Scott for all of ten minutes and yet he knew. Or maybe Scott had shared all the salacious details—perhaps with an offhand *And soon she'll be all yours, Brodie*.

Scott carefully didn't look at her—just positioned himself between Amy and Willa.

Brodie slotted his chair in beside Kate. 'Ready for tomorrow?' he asked, raising his voice a little over the rising sound of music that was being cranked up to encourage dancers to take to the floor.

'I'm still game if you are,' she said, leaning in close so she could be more easily heard.

'Oh, I'm game,' he said with an easy smile.

Such an *easy* smile. A *natural* smile. A smile that reached his eyes. Green eyes, like Scott's—but deep and warm, not cool and cautious.

Amy nudged her shoulder against Scott's. 'I told Kate she should have asked *you* for lessons.'

Scott cast Kate another brooding look and she felt herself blush almost by reflex. Everyone at the table would be working it out any minute if he kept that up.

'I sold my boat,' he said.

'Well, you could hire one, couldn't you?' Amy asked. 'What would it cost? To hire you and a boat and learn how to sail?'

'Well…' Scott said, and rubbed a jaw darkened by raspy shadow.

It was the first time Kate had ever seen him anything but clean-shaven. His eyes looked strained too. Tired. And she was an idiot, with no instinct for self-preservation, because she wanted to hug him, and kiss him, and tell him to take better care of himself—

'I'd say…' Scott began again, with another look at Kate '…five thousand dollars? Or the barter system is okay. Trade a service for a service.'

—and kill him. She wanted to *kill* him.

Amy looked shocked. 'Man, that's expensive.'

'But worth it,' Scott said. One more look at Kate, and then he turned to Willa to say something.

The conversation ebbed and flowed around Kate as, silent, she pondered the way her evening had started—four friends sharing their secret longings for romance. But Willa's was real. Whereas Kate's…? Pure Hollywood. Never going to happen.

And it was probably time she admitted that she wanted it to be real. Wanted what Willa had. Wanted someone to trust her with his life.

Because she *could* be trusted.

People trusted her with their lives every day. They trusted her to extricate them from bad marriages with a whole skin and the means to live. They trusted her to do the best thing for their children. They trusted her to find a way for them to achieve closure, and keep their dignity, and get a fair deal.

They trusted her…before moving on with their lives without her.

And that wasn't enough any more.

She wanted someone who trusted her but didn't *want* to move on with his life without her. She wanted someone complicated and creative, and strong and principled, and smart and funny, and sexy and…and…*hers*.

She wanted love. She wanted, specifically, *Scott Knight* to love her. Not just the scent, the taste, the feel of her…but the whole of her. Wanted to trust him with her life and wanted him to trust her with his.

She wanted him to tell her about growing up never feeling quite good enough, and she wanted to make sure he knew that he *was*. Good enough for anything—for everything.

She wanted *Scott* to tell her about Weeping Reef. About Chantal and Brodie. How he'd felt, what it had meant, what it had done to him to feel so betrayed, if it still ate at him.

She wanted to tell him she would never, ever hurt him like that. That she would never betray him. *Couldn't* betray him. That she—

'Kate?'

Brodie—pulling her back.

'Refill?' he asked, nodding at her glass, which was empty again.

'No,' she said, and tried to smile. 'And that's my last—so don't worry. There'll be no heave-hoing over the gunwales tomorrow.'

'It wouldn't be the first time I've held a girl's hair out of the way, so don't sweat it for my sake, Katie.'

Scott clunked his beer glass on the table. Loud enough to make Amy, sitting beside him, jump.

'Kate—not Katie,' he said. And then he turned back to Willa as though he hadn't just bowled that out loud and livid enough for everyone to marvel at, and asked, 'When's Luke coming home?'

After a stunned moment, Willa gathered herself enough to speak. 'No immediate plans, as far as I'm aware. He's in the middle of a deal in Singapore he won't tell me anything about. Confidential, apparently.'

'Confidential,' Amy repeated, but the tone of her voice—all dark, when Amy was basically the brightest, shiniest girl in the world—made Kate wonder if perhaps she wasn't the only one hitting the cocktails a little too hard.

'Yeah,' Willa said, a little uneasily. 'He's like a clam about stuff like that.'

Amy looked straight at Scott. 'But *you* know.'

'About Singapore?' Scott asked. 'Nope.'

'Not Singapore. I mean what happened at Weeping Reef.'

Kate wondered what she was missing and looked around at the others. Willa was looking startled—everyone else confused.

Scott half sighed, half laughed, winced. 'I think we all know what happened at Weeping Reef.'

'I *knew* he'd told you. You know—at Willa's party—when you said that…that thing about a gentleman never telling a lady's secrets.'

Nobody spoke.

'Amy,' Scott said into the awkward pause, 'if you think I have a lady's secret to tell—one that *doesn't* involve me getting up to no good with a hooker called Lorelei…' He waited while everyone at the table except a cringing Kate and a startled-looking Amy laughed. 'Then please fill me in. Otherwise I'm going to go and fulfil my obligation to that clutch of hens—or flock, or brood, or whatever the hell a group of chickens is called. The ones who donated a chair to our cause when I first arrived.'

He waited, watching Amy, who was blinking, stunned.

'Right, I'll take that as a no, then,' he said, and stood. 'Give me fifteen minutes,' he said to the group at large.

'Yeah—as if!' Jessica said as he was sucked into the crowd. 'It will only take him five minutes, max, to sort out his next one-night stand. He has the gift.'

But Amy was looking at Willa, dazed and confused. 'Luke really didn't…?'

Willa slid off Rob's lap and into Scott's vacated chair,

right next to Amy, and took Amy's hand. 'No, Amy. He really didn't.'

'Well…*wow!*' Amy said.

Brodie turned to Kate. 'We seem to be a little out of this loop, Kate. Shall we join the few brave souls venturing onto the dance floor?'

Kate had a feeling Scott wouldn't like her dancing with Brodie.

But, then again, Scott was in the process of picking up a drunken bed partner on a hen night.

And he'd told Brodie she was *all his*.

And Scott didn't love her.

And he never would.

And she wanted to die.

What was one dance stacked against all that?

'Sure,' she said.

Brodie led her onto the small dance floor. Without any hesitation—and completely ignoring the fact that every other couple on the floor was dancing without touching—he took Kate in his arms.

'What's going on?' Brodie asked, without preamble.

'What do you mean?'

'You and Scott. Am I going to get my teeth smashed in for dancing with you?'

'No. But I don't think the threat of that scares you or you wouldn't have asked me to dance, would you?'

No answer. He simply pulled her a little closer.

'So, Brodie, why *did* you ask me to dance?'

'Because I love Scott.'

'I don't—'

'And don't tell me you don't know what I mean, because you do.'

There was a pause as she silently acknowledged the truth of that. 'He won't care that I'm dancing with you. He's not the jealous type. Not with me anyway.' She sighed and settled her head on Brodie's comfortable shoulder. 'We're not…*meant*.'

'Why not?'

Kate ran through the reasons in her head and chose the least painful one she could think of. 'For a start, he's too young for me.'

She heard the laugh rumble through Brodie's chest. 'Scott hasn't been too young since he popped out of the womb—when he no doubt emerged *not* crying, just calmly looking around and wondering how to get fed without having to ask for help.'

Kate choked on a sudden giggle. 'That does sound like him.'

'Yep—everything calculated, everything his way, no drama, no demands, keep your distance. He has more self-control than anyone I've ever met. Too much.' Pause. 'I've only ever seen him lose it once.'

'I know about Chantal,' Kate said, looking up at him.

'Yeah, I figured you did. And if he told you that—'

'No,' Kate interrupted. 'He didn't tell me. He doesn't get personal. Not with me.'

'Ah.'

'Yes, "*ah*".'

'But you want him to?'

'What would be the point, when he's off picking someone up for the night?'

'Except that he's not.'

'Well, who knows?'

'I do. Because if he was doing that he wouldn't be heading this way looking like he's about to deck me, would he?'

'What?' Kate squeaked, and Brodie spun them so she could see Scott as he approached.

'I wonder if he's about to cause the second scene of his life?' Brodie asked, not seeming at all concerned. 'Let's hope so.'

CHAPTER FIFTEEN

SCOTT HAD NO IDEA what he was doing, but he was doing it anyway.

He reached Kate and Brodie, then stood there like an idiot while he tried to contain the savage burst of possessiveness that was urging him to tear Kate out of Brodie's arms. This was beyond that drunken punch at Weeping Reef. Because this wasn't about Brodie, either as a love rival or as a Hugo substitute. This was about Kate and him. About wishing he *did* dance so it could be him dancing with her. Wishing it was *him* teaching her to sail. About hating himself because of all the things he wasn't—but wanting to demand, anyway, what the *hell* she thought she was doing dancing with another man when she belonged to him.

He barely noticed Brodie melting away as he reached for Kate, yanked her into his arms and kissed her. Right there on the dance floor. A scorching kiss, which he hoped said *I want you*, but suspected said something else. Something about need and desperation and all the things he didn't want to risk.

When he stopped, pulled back, looked down at her, she shivered. He felt it rip through him as though they were connected.

'I think that qualifies as a PDA,' she said.

'That had nothing to do with affection. That kiss was not *affectionate*, Kate.'

'That kiss is not going to lead to sex either.'

'Yes, it is.'

'No. We have an appointment, and it's not for tonight.'

'We can negotiate, remember?'

'You don't negotiate. You do whatever the hell you want, whenever you want.'

'That's because your rules are stupid.'

'You agreed to them.'

'I shouldn't have.'

'But you did. And now you've gone and broken the confidentiality clause.' She nodded towards their table. 'Because your friends just saw you kiss me.'

His only response was to grab her hand and drag her off the dance floor, out of the bar, into the night, around the corner into an alleyway that was only a step above Ellington Lane in terms of desolation. Without a word he took her in his arms again, kissed her almost savagely. He wanted her so much—so *much*.

Her hands grabbed the front of his shirt, clutching fistfuls of it, anchoring her as she kissed him back, and he thought, *Thank God*. She wanted him. She still wanted him. Everything else would fall into place as long as that fact held. Because without it why would she keep seeing him?

There was a burst of sound as the bar's main doors opened, disgorging a group of people into the night, and sanity returned. The doors closed again. A low conversation, a trill of laughter from the departing patrons. Scott pulled back, waiting to see if he and Kate would be discovered, but the group passed by. All was quiet again.

And Scott suddenly felt utterly, utterly miserable.

He stepped away, shoved his hands in his hair, looked at Kate.

'What was *that* about?' she asked—as usual, going straight to the point in the way he just bloody loved.

'I wanted to kiss you, that's all.' Could he sound any more defensive?

'So what happens if I ask you—now—to come inside and dance with me, in public, in front of your friends?'

Tight, fraught pause. Scott stuck his hands in his pockets. 'I don't dance.'

'No, you *don't* dance, do you? But that doesn't mean *I*

don't, Scott, if I'm lucky enough to be asked. And I *was* dancing. Why did you drag me out here?'

'Because—' He broke off with a muffled curse.

'Because…I was dancing with *Brodie*, perhaps?'

One heavy heartbeat…two, three.

And then, 'Why is that a problem, Scott?'

No answer. Because how could he explain without revealing everything that was wrong with him? All the reasons she would soon find someone better—whether it was Brodie or that barrister or someone else? How could he tell her that he needed to push it? Push it while he still had it in him to get over her when the inevitable happened?

'Do you think I prefer him?' Kate persisted.

He shrugged as his hands dug a little deeper into his pockets. 'If you do, that's okay. Women…lots of women…do.'

He said the words but his heart was threatening to leap into his brain and cut off his blood supply, oxygen, his synapse control—everything. Because it *wasn't* okay. It would kill him.

'Not *lots of women*, Scott,' she said. '*Chantal.* And that's what this is all about, isn't it? Chantal. The only woman who ever got to you. Enough to make you lose that prized control.'

Scott registered the fact that she knew about Chantal. Who'd told her? Did it even matter? He tested that in his brain. No, it didn't. Because Chantal didn't matter. It had been *Brodie* who'd mattered all those years ago, not Chantal. And now…only Kate mattered. *Only Kate.*

'I'll teach you to sail,' he said, which was so far from an adequate response as to be classified as a non sequitur.

'You don't have a boat, remember? And I don't have five thousand dollars since I ripped up your cheque—which, in case you're too stupid to realise it, was only ever a Play Time prop. So no need to trade sailing lessons for my services like I'm a *real* prostitute. I'm already under contract. You're getting the goods for free. Until the twenty-eighth, anyway.'

She turned to walk away and his temper surged, hot and

wild. His hands came out of his pockets and he grabbed her, spun her, gripping her upper arms, furious. 'Don't talk about yourself like that.'

'Then stop making me feel like that by trading me to your friends,' she shot back. '*"She's all yours."* Remember?'

'All you have to do is tell him no. No, you're not going sailing tomorrow. Tell him, Kate,' Scott said, wanting to explode with the emotions churning in his gut, but hanging on…and on, and on.

'I *am* going sailing tomorrow,' she said. 'As planned. Because he *offered*, without having to be shamed into it. But don't worry, Scott. If anything happens between me and Brodie I'll advise you. As I expect you to tell me if you hook up with one of those giggly hens. And that will be that, won't it? Agreement null and void, as per the contract. Okay?'

They stared at each other. Scott's hands unclenched, slipped down her arms to her hands, held. The words were there in his chest. *Not okay. Don't do it to me. Don't. Please, please don't.* Choking him.

'Kate. Oh, God, Kate. I just—'

But the bar doors opened again and Scott let go, stepped back, re-jamming his hands in his pockets at the sudden burst of sound. People were walking past, talking, laughing.

And up popped his shield, like some automatic reflex. 'Okay,' he said.

'*Okay?*' she said, incredulous. And then, 'Okay…'

Her eyes closed.

Long moment, and then she opened her eyes. 'I don't understand any of this. Why did you let Rob talk you into coming here when you knew I'd be here? It's not what we're about, is it? Drinks with friends?'

'I wanted—' Stop. Swallow. *Confess.* 'I wanted to see you.'

'You're seeing me on Sunday. At noon. Remember?'

'I remember. But who'll be opening the door? Kate? Officer Cleary? Or Lorelei?'

'Who do you *want* to see, Scott?'

Silence. Because the answer had stuck in his throat. The way words always did.

He saw her shoulders slump, as if she was defeated. Knew he wasn't handling this. Wasn't handling *her*. Wasn't handling *anything*.

'Surprise me,' he said, and forced a smile. His *I'm cool with that* smile.

Except he *wasn't* cool with it. He wanted her to call him on what he'd said. To fight with him. Rage at him. Slap him if she had to. To demand more. *More!* To tell him that she *deserved* more and she *wanted* more. And she wanted it from *him*. To say, *So step up to the plate, Scott Knight, and if you can't give it to me I'll find it somewhere else. I'll find someone else. Someone...else.*

Say it—say it, Kate. You want someone else. Say it!

But she gave him smile for cool smile instead. 'Fine,' she said. 'I'll make sure it's memorable for you.'

And then she patted her hair into place. Twitched at her dress.

'But now I'm going to go back inside to get my things. I've had a big week. A bad week. And I need to go home.'

He wanted to take her hands again, but he couldn't seem to get them out of his pockets. 'Tell me. What happened with the case?'

She looked at him. And the tears in her eyes almost undid him. But when she spoke her voice was like crystal. Clear and smooth and cold.

'No fireside chats, remember?'

'But I—'

'Stop, Scott. Just *stop*. I came out to relax with a few girl-friends and instead I'm standing in a dark alley with a man who's not saying anything that makes sense. I just want to go in, pay my bill, grab my things and leave. You go back to that hen party, and text me before Sunday if you've been unfaithful.' Short, strange laugh. 'How quaint that sounds. Let's say, instead, if you've adhered to the clause.'

And with that, she stalked out of the alleyway.

By the time Scott had himself enough under control to return to the table, Kate had been and gone.

He picked up the fresh beer that was waiting for him because Brodie, who had his back like in the old days, had known he'd need one.

'Want to borrow my boat in the morning?' Brodie asked.

Scott smiled—his *all okay here* smile. 'No, I'm good. She's all yours.' *Oh, God, no!* He'd said it again. *All yours.*

'I think we both know, Scott, that she's all *yours*. But if you'll take my advice you won't take too long to claim her—because Kate doesn't strike me as the type to wait forever.'

CHAPTER SIXTEEN

KATE WOKE ON Sunday with full-blown jitters.

Because she didn't have a clue what she was going to offer Scott for Play Time at noon.

It was almost more than her tired, slightly sunburned body could manage just to get out of bed, let alone plan a fantasy, because yesterday's sailing lesson had been the most full-on physical three hours she'd ever spent.

Sailing was as freeing, as exhilarating, as wonderful as she'd always thought it would be—with an excellent side benefit: all that hauling of sheets and dodging of booms, being ordered around and shoved all over the deck by Brodie and his two cohorts, had left her with no time to think about Scott. Or about their upcoming Play Time either.

The guys had taken her out for a congratulatory drinking session afterwards, because apparently she had what it took, and by the time Kate had got home, she'd been so tired she'd fallen into bed.

She'd slept for a full three hours before thoughts of Scott had niggled her into wakefulness. And then had come the night-long tossing and turning she was learning to expect.

Fractured sleep, painful dreams, tortured thoughts. Wondering how Scott had felt, knowing she was on the water with his best friend. Rethinking every look, every word from Friday night. Trying to figure out what was behind the anger Scott refused to unleash—was it the way he felt about her, or residual mistrust from the eight-year-old Chantal/Brodie situation? Hoping he hadn't—*please, please, please*—voided their contract by touching another woman.

After all that it was no wonder she was devoid of ideas.

Arabian nights, pirate and tavern wench, boss and secretary—all of which she'd considered—just seemed stupid.

How she wished she'd never thought of writing fantasies into the contract. She hated Play Time. *Hated* it!

So much so that in a fit of pique—yes, *pique*!—she decided to wear her most complicated dress. Buttons *and* zips *and* ties, with an exotic fold or two. An origami nightmare of a dress. Because Scott *deserved* to have to fight his way through to her for a change, rather than have her laying it all out for him to take.

He'd said the first time they met that for her he could get a little 'gladiatorial'—so let him prove it by fighting his way past her dress! In fact, she would make it harder. She would blindfold him! And what was more, she would give him a time limit.

That was a good enough Play Time for her.

Scott buzzed on the dot of noon—he was nothing if not punctual—and she let him into the building without waiting to hear his voice.

'We only have an hour,' Kate said, all brisk and business-like as she opened the door to him, holding two silk scarves at the ready.

His eyes narrowed. 'Why?'

'Nothing to do with Brodie, if that's what you're wondering.'

'I'm not wondering. Are you wondering?'

'About Brodie?'

He just looked at her.

'Oh, do you mean am I wondering about you and the hens on Friday night?' she asked, and eked out a tinkling laugh. 'No. You would have texted me, wouldn't you, if anything had happened?' She was forcing the panic back. 'And anyway…well, *pacta sunt servanda*, right? Agreements must be kept. And as I recall, that was your sticking point. Fidelity.'

'*Pacta sunt servanda,*' he repeated. 'You *do* remember how that legal talk turns me on, don't you?'

Her breath caught in her throat. 'Yes.'

'Is that why you're doing it?'

'The more turned on you are, the faster we'll be, right?'

He didn't like that—she could tell by the way his whole face tightened. He walked past her and laid a flat parcel on her dining table.

'Stand still while I do this,' she said, coming up behind him.

And, although he stiffened, he let her tie the scarf over his eyes.

'Play Time,' she announced.

The set of his mouth was grim as she led him carefully into the bedroom, over to the bed. 'Sit,' Kate said.

But Scott did more than sit. He flopped onto his back, lying there as though he didn't give a damn what she did to him, and Kate hesitated, wondering if he didn't want her today. If he didn't want her any more, period.

Pulse jittering, she looked at his body, laid out on the bed for her, wondering how she would be able to bear that...and saw that he was hard. She hadn't even touched him and he was aroused—whether he wanted to be or not.

It took the edge off her sudden panic to know that whatever his *I give up* attitude was about, it wasn't a lack of desire. She could work with that. She would make this so good for him he wouldn't be able to pretend he didn't want her.

'I'm going to blindfold myself now,' she told him, knowing how disorientating it must be for a control freak like Scott not to know what was happening. 'No peeking today—by either of us. And no speaking either.'

'No—?' Short, tense pause. 'No *speaking*, Kate?'

'No. Just...feeling...'

Scott's lips tightened but he said nothing.

And then Kate tied her own scarf and felt her way onto the bed. She lay next to him, turned to him, kissed him. A long, lush moan of a kiss. Not being able to see, she was even more conscious than usual of the uncompromising firmness of his mouth as he stayed stock-still for her to explore. The warmth of it, the taste, the way it fitted so perfectly against her own.

Slowly the tension left him, and at last he kissed her back, his tongue sliding into her mouth, and then he was taking over, reaching everywhere. Thank *God*.

A moment later his hands were wandering over her fully clothed body. Traversing the cotton of her dress. Pausing, testing, assessing the fastenings, the barriers.

Kate's task was easier. She slid her hands under his T-shirt, smoothing them over his chest. She loved his chest. The breadth and strength of it, the texture of his warm skin, the spread of hair. The picture of him, flat on his back on her bed, was so strong in her mind…but the fact she couldn't see it with her eyes somehow made the drug of touching him more potent. As if she could reach right through his chest and into his heart with nothing but the pads of her exploring fingers.

A push, a nudge, and his T-shirt was up, over his head, off. She checked quickly that the scarf was still secure around his eyes, and then her hands moved to his jeans. Unbuttoning, unzipping as his breathing turned harsh and laboured. She loved the way his breaths came like that when he was excited, almost past bearing but trying to control it—control himself, control everything.

She straddled him, facing his feet—which might have felt weird if they hadn't both been masked, but now felt perfect. Her core was on his warm skin, just above the band of his boxer briefs. Just that was enough for her to long to have him inside her. She started pushing his jeans down his legs, hands stroking as she leaned further forward with each push. She loved his legs. Long, hard, strong, the perfect amount of hair. Down, down, down. And then—*stop*.

She'd forgotten about his sneakers. Well, blindfolded or not, she could undo a shoe. She fumbled with the laces, wrenched the sneakers off, threw them. They landed on the floor with a soft thud. Next she pushed his jeans off, threw them too. Started to turn around.

But Scott kept her exactly where she was with a hand on her back. She got the message and stopped, on her knees, one either side of his hips. Stayed...waited. What was he going to do?

And then the hand on her back was gone and both Scott's hands were under her dress, reaching between her spread thighs, snagging against the French knickers she'd put on today before she'd come up with a plan that meant he wouldn't actually *see* the frothy pink lace.

He didn't seem to care about the lace, because his fingers were impatient, almost rough, as he yanked the knickers aside, his fingers sliding into her drenching wetness, in and out, until her breaths were nothing more than rasps and she was trembling. She felt so hot, so lush, aching as those fingers continued to dip in and out of her while the fingers of his other hand joined the action, circling her clitoris, precise, constant, inexorable.

She hadn't removed his underwear, but that didn't stop him thrusting hard against her bottom as he circled and slipped and probed every millimetre of her sex until she was coming in a luscious roll.

She didn't know how it had happened, but a moment later she found herself flipped onto her back. She waited, breathless, for what Scott would do—regretting the damned dress, deciding she would help with her own unwrapping.

But before she could lift a finger to even one zipper, Scott had gripped the cotton at her neck and torn the dress right down the front, spreading the two halves wide.

'Scott...' she whispered, shocked.

'No talking,' he said, and reached for her bra straps, accurate despite the blindfold.

He yanked them down her arms until her breasts were bared. Unerringly, his mouth found her nipples, sucking, licking, building the pressure from barely there to strong and demanding, unrelenting as his cotton-clad erection strained against her.

She reached down to try to push his underwear off him, clumsy because of her bra straps, but he knocked her hands aside and kept up the suckling. Next moment he was scooting down her body, between her legs. The French knickers were shoved down and his mouth was there, licking fast and frantically, and she was coming again with a loud cry.

He kept his mouth there through the last undulation of her hips and then he came back up her body, kissing her almost brutally. He fumbled with the scarf over her eyes, ripping it away. Rising up over her, on his knees, he tore off his own blindfold. Stared down at her for a scorching moment.

Before Kate could reach for him he was off the bed, throwing his clothes on helter-skelter.

'But— But— What about you?'

'Owe me,' he said, zipping up his jeans.

'I can do it now.'

'You should have grabbed a condom before the blindfolds went on. Because now I've ripped the masks off, Play Time's over. We're seeing…we're talking. And that's not in the rules for today, is it? You don't want to *talk* to me today. You don't want to *see* me today. I'd say you didn't even really want me to *touch* you, or you wouldn't have worn that chastity belt of a dress. You wanted it over with *quickly* today.'

He grabbed his sneakers, shoved his feet inside them, yanked on the laces.

'Well, you're done—all sorted, all serviced with time to spare—and now I'm going.'

'Scott…'

But he was out of the room, and her curse was floating behind him.

'Scott—wait,' she said as she got off the bed, impatiently shedding her ruined dress, wrenching up her bra.

The door slammed before she was even out of the bedroom.

He was gone.

Eyes swimming, she walked over to the dining table, picked up the parcel he'd left there. Opened the brown paper. Removed a...a *plaque*? Yes, a simple metal plaque. Black type on dull silver. Two words: *Castle Cleary*.

Her swimming eyes overflowed.

To hell with Play Time, Scott thought savagely as he got into his car. And to hell with being made to feel like a male prostitute with an allocated time slot.

Not that the whole blindfold experience hadn't been intense. He'd been insane with need by the end of it. So needy it had made no sense to run out when he did. She would have serviced him even without the blindfolds.

Serviced him.

And didn't that say it all?

She would have *serviced* him. The way he'd *serviced* her. *Scott Knight, Escort Service, at your beck and call.*

So what? his sane self asked.

It was perfect, wasn't it? Exactly what he'd wanted? A sex contract. Month to month. No strings. No emotions. Complete control. No pretending they were forever. No need to call her unless it was to schedule a hot bout of sex. No deep and meaningful conversations. No conversations at all, lately—not with Lorelei, not with Officer Cleary. And not with Kate.

And today not only no speaking, but no looking either!

Just feeling—which was a good enough euphemism for *just sex*.

Just sex.

Perfect.

And he was a freaking idiot not to just take that and run with it.

Scott pulled out his phone. Stabbed the buttons.

Play Time, my house, Tuesday, 7 p.m.

Half a minute later, back came a reply.

Fine.

'Right,' he said out loud to his face in the rearview mirror.

But something about his face wasn't normal. He looked like a freaking psycho killer!

Well, to hell with that too! He was *not* going to see that every time he glanced in the rearview mirror on the drive home. He'd have a crash if he had to see that.

He had to calm the hell down.

Cursing, he banged out of the car, strode across to the marina, focused on the boats.

Which made him feel even crazier. And just miserable again.

Kate had had her first sailing lesson yesterday. With Brodie. How had it gone? What had they talked about? Fireside chats aplenty with Brodie, for sure. Because Brodie was easy to talk to—easier than Scott. Easier, kinder. Better all round.

Everything inside Scott clenched—including the growl that he wouldn't let loose from his chest.

And then he put his face in his hands—because the sight of the boats was suddenly unbearable.

CHAPTER SEVENTEEN

KATE WAS PREPARED for the Monday morning *What the hell was that kiss about?* calls from Willa and Amy. She offered up a perfectly nuanced laugh as she blamed the lethal combination of Scott's beer and her Manhattans, positioning it as a Dirty Martini Barnaby moment gone a step too far. And if the girls didn't sound exactly convinced, at least they let the subject drop.

She was *less* prepared for Deb's darting, anxious eyes as she kept a steady flow of peppermint tea—her favourite stress remedy—pouring into Kate's office—while very carefully *not* asking about 'that nice Scott Knight'. Not that Deb had to ask; Kate was convinced she had psychic powers.

And she was not *at all* prepared for her mother's visit on Tuesday morning.

Madeline Cleary swept into Kate's office the way she swept through life: grandly, wearing a caftan, hot-pink lipstick and high heels.

She took a seat, fixing Kate with one of her *don't mess with me* stares. 'Okay, Kate, what's this Deb's been telling me?'

Deb! Psychic and *traitor*!

'"This"?' Kate asked, closing the door sharply—knowing it would drive Deb crazy not being able to listen in, which served her right.

'Scott Knight,' her mother said.

'He's an architect.'

'Well, isn't that lovely? Much more interesting than a barrister. But not really the pertinent fact at the moment, is it, Kate? Don't bother with any of your legal obfuscation. Just tell me what's happening.'

'No.'

'Okay, then bring him to dinner on Sunday and I'll ask him instead.'

'That won't be happening. It's not like that with us. I mean the...the family thing. It's just...just...' The words trailed off and she shrugged.

Her mother looked at her—very long, very hard. 'It's just that he's the one, perhaps?'

Kate tried—failed—to laugh. 'Nothing that romantic.'

'So *make* it romantic.'

'You can't make these things happen.'

'Not if you're pussy-hearted. Which, of course, is *not* the way I raised my daughters. I raised lionesses.' She leaned forward. 'Kate, remember when I tried to dissuade you from going into family law?'

Eye-roll. 'Yes.'

'Not because I don't like lawyers—'

Another eye-roll. 'Although you don't!'

'But because you're so tender-hearted. I knew you'd be running yourself ragged, fighting for the downtrodden and then bleeding all over the place when you lost a case.' She sat back again. 'And do you remember what you told me to do?'

Kate smiled—it blossomed despite her hideous mood. 'I told you to shove it.'

Her mother beamed at her. 'And I was so proud of you.'

Kate ran her hands over her face, laughing helplessly. 'You're a weirdo, Mum.'

'It's an artistic thing. So what?'

'So I love you.'

'And I love you. And I think you deserve a reward for all the crap you put up with day after day. And if he's the reward you want, then you're going to have him.'

'He doesn't want...that. The whole forever thing.'

'From what I hear, he's had plenty of what *he* wants.'

Arrgghh. Going to kill Deb. Boil her in a vat of peppermint tea.

'So, Kate, it's time for what *you* want. Which just might turn out to be what he wants too.'

'He doesn't.'

'How do you know? Have you asked him?'

'No, of course not.'

'Why "of course not"? Because he's a boy and they have to ask first? Don't make me slap you. Just *ask* him.'

Silence.

'Kate, the reason I was so proud of you that day when you told me so eloquently to shove it was because you threw it all at me. How you felt, why you felt it, what it meant to you. You said you would move heaven and hell to do it. And that if it all came to nothing, or you couldn't hack it, at least you'd have no regrets about not *trying*. And, really, Kate? If it's *you* asking for something, fighting for something...' She smiled—a smile so completely proud and understanding and just so *family* Kate wanted to cry. 'Well, Kate, who would ever say no to you?'

Who would ever say no to you?

Oh, God. God! Scott would say no. *He* would.

'So, Kate, *tell him*. What you feel. Why you feel it. What he means to you. And move heaven and hell. Because, of all of my daughters, *you* can. And then, whatever happens, at least you'll have no regrets.' She paused again, shrugged. 'The alternative is that I tell your father what he's done to you—and he and Aristotle have been playing with a new set of throwing knives, so I'd prefer not to go that route. At least not yet.'

Kate arrived at Scott's on Tuesday ten minutes late.

She stayed in her car for another ten minutes, with her mother's words going through her mind. *Tell him, tell him, tell him.*

But she couldn't help feeling it would be like pulling the rug out from under him. *I said it was only going to be sex, Scott, but it's love.*

What would he say?

Big sigh. Because she had no idea.

He'd sent so many mixed signals her way she was beyond knowing what he expected of her, what he wanted from her, how he felt about her. He'd been everything from distant to demanding, from impassioned to indifferent. From flippant to furious. Agreeing to the rules—and breaking them.

The way he'd looked at her in that alley on Friday night, when he'd taken her hands in his—that was not about sex. And that last Play Time, when he'd been so angry with her— irrational, emotional…

Wasn't that a bit like love?

She sucked in a breath, because just saying that in her head made her heart flutter. Running a hand over her stomach, which was similarly fluttery, she wondered, maybe, if she *should* ask him.

But *after* Play Time. Because if Play Time involved her getting into a PVC cat suit or wielding some kind of implement…? Well, she couldn't see herself talking about love after a dose of kink.

Sighing, she started to push the intercom button—but Scott opened the door before the chime even sounded. He took her in his arms, kissed her as though he'd been waiting a year and was starving for the taste of her.

And *everything* in her fluttered. Nervous and hopeful and a little bit terrified.

Releasing her slowly, Scott gestured for her to move into the house, and she was struck again by the magnificence of what he'd achieved—even more so today, when she was seeing it as Kate, who'd been invited, not Lorelei, who'd invited herself.

It was stylish, lavish, unusual. A manifestation of all those parts that made Scott who he was. The coolness, the control, the hidden fiery core.

Kate cleared her throat. 'So… Play Time?'

He put his arm around her, led her into what she supposed was the living room—or living *space*, more correctly, since there were no internal walls, only strategically placed columns.

'Yep,' he said. 'I'm calling it "The Architect and the Lawyer".'

She halted as her hopes started to soar. 'That sounds… normal.'

'Ah, but with a twist. The way I'm seeing it is that the architect gives the lawyer a tour of his house. Along the way the lawyer tries to find a legal term appropriate for each space—extra points for Latin. And if the lawyer likes what she sees, she gets to touch the architect. And if the architect likes what the lawyer says…same deal. He gets to touch her. And then the architect—because he is multi-talented—prepares dinner. And they eat. And drink wine. And then, if all that touching has meant anything at all, they go upstairs to bed and negotiate the rollover of their contract for another month.'

'Oh,' she said as her hopes stopped soaring and started plummeting. The contract. One more month. Not exactly forever.

Scott took her briefcase, threw it onto his glamorous coffee-coloured couch with no regard for the potential damage its buckles could do to the fabric, and slowly turned her to the living area. 'So—what do you think?' he asked.

She tried to smile. 'I guess I'll start with…*ab initio.*'

'Well, I'm going to have to kiss you for that.'

'Do you even know what it means?'

'No.'

And then he drew her close and kissed her cheek. Just her cheek…but she felt it tingle all the way through her body.

'So what *does* it mean?' he asked when he released her.

'"From the beginning",' she said. 'It's commonly used to refer to the time a contract, statute, deed or…or marriage becomes legal.' *Oh, God—why had she mentioned marriage?* She cleared her throat. 'But in this instance we'll use it for the start of the house tour.'

'Suits me,' Scott said. '*Ab initio*. We can use it for the start of our new month too.'

'Hmm…' Kate said. A vague, *nothing* noise. 'Where to next?'

'Library—which, you will be interested to note, used to be an altar.'

She could already see it, and walked slowly across the wooden floor and up the three steps. So beautiful. Coloured rugs. A fireplace—unlit in the heat of February. Books nestling in custom-made shelves; armchairs—some leather, some fabric—low wooden tables. She turned to face the main space, looking out at the expansive floor, partitioned into discrete zones via the columns—all spectacularly clean and modern, which made the library feel like an oasis of plush comfort.

'It could do with a few of your mother's paintings, but otherwise what do you think?' Scott asked.

Mother. Her mother. *Tell him, tell him*. 'Umm…' She turned to him. '*Ad coelum*.'

Scott drew her in and kissed her eyelids. First one, then the other.

'If you like it…aren't you going to touch me?' he asked, all husky.

Kate reached a hand up, cupped his face, ran her thumb over his cheekbone. 'Want to know what it means?' she asked.

'Yes, as soon as you touch me again—you owe me for the living room.'

She brought up her other hand and now both hands cradled his face. She leaned up, kissed him gently on the mouth. And then she smiled into his eyes.

'To the sky. It's actually abbreviated from *cuius est solum eius est usque ad coelum et ad inferos*—which basically means whoever owns the soil owns that space, all the way up to heaven and down to hell. And this is just heavenly. Which seems apt for a converted church.'

'You've got no idea how much you are turning me on, Kate.'

'That's the whole idea of Play Time, isn't it?'

He frowned slightly, but said nothing. Simply took her arm and continued the tour.

Scott showed her all over the masterpiece that was the lower floor. And it was obvious why his renown as an architect was growing.

The huge arched panels of stained glass juxtaposed against the ultra-modern use of materials and neutral colours in most of the spaces were startling and lovely. The structure of the zones, flowing one into the next, was incredible. Scott's stark office and the state-of-the-art kitchen and guest bathroom were top-notch contemporary. The surprising pops of colour, like the scarlet staircase and the chartreuse relaxation nook off a plant-filled atrium, were brilliantly eccentric. How could such disparate elements combine into something so blow-your-head-off gorgeous? But that was...*Scott*.

Kate had to concentrate hard in order to be able to spit out Latin legal phrases, only to have her thoughts scatter every time Scott chose a different part of her to kiss. It was agonising, this falling in love. Feeling it dig itself more deeply inside her with every gentle, lavishing touch of Scott's fingers, his mouth, on her lips, her cheeks, her ears, her eyebrows—her damned *eyebrows*!—and her hair. Wishing so hard it meant something, the way his eyes closed, the way he held his breath as she touched him in turn. Shoulders, hands, neck, chest.

She was in torment by the time they circled back to the library, where Scott settled her with a drink while he finished preparing dinner. He was so jaunty as he left her—even whistling, as though he had everything he could possibly want.

But then, Scott *did* have everything he wanted. *Exactly* what he wanted. *She* was the one who didn't have what she wanted. And she still had no idea how to get it—except to ask for it...and risk losing even the little of him she had.

Kate didn't know how long had passed when Scott came to escort her through to the dining area. But she could feel time just generally slipping away. Four days until the twenty-eighth of February. When their contract would be terminated—or rolled over.

Scott held out a chair for her at the sleek wooden table and waited for her to sit.

'You didn't have to cook dinner,' Kate said.

'Well, you see, Kate, the fifty-fifty rule wasn't working for me. So this—' charming little shrug '—is my way of taking you to dinner. And before you tell me I'm breaking the rules, I'm going to remind you that extras are allowed in Play Time.' He sat opposite her. 'Cucumber soup. Perfect for a Sydney summer.'

But Kate was beyond taste as she silently filled her spoon, raised it to her mouth, swallowed. Time after time. Until her bowl was empty.

Scott—who'd done an excellent job of keeping up a flow of small talk—cleared the plates, then returned with something that looked so delicious Kate's heart sank. He'd taken such care—but how was she supposed to eat it when her heart had swelled so gigantically it threatened to choke her?

'Korean-style pork tenderloin with wild and brown rice pilaf and steamed pea pods,' Scott announced.

As Kate doggedly forced the food down Scott explained a house design he was currently working on. Presumably she offered appropriate rejoinders, because he didn't make an issue of her lack of vocal enthusiasm.

But then, why would he? It wasn't *conversation* he wanted.

He cleared the plates a second time, and while he was gone Kate had a mini-meltdown, remembering her mother's words. *Make it romantic.* How did a person turn a contract into something romantic? *Move heaven and hell.* How? What was the trigger? What would it take to make him love her?

And then he was back, carrying a tray. On the tray was a plate piled high with cookies of some kind and two exquisite boxes—one pink, one purple—decorated with fluttery fairies, shimmering with glitter, finished off with gauzy bows.

'Whoopie pies,' Scott said, depositing the tray in front of Kate and taking the seat beside her.

Unable to stop herself, Kate reached for one of the boxes, ran suddenly trembling fingers over the top, pulled the end of the ribbon through her fingertips.

'Do you like those boxes?' Scott asked.

She looked at him, said nothing.

'They're for Maeve and Molly. Because…' He shrugged, blushed. 'Well, you know… I spoke to them about baking whoopie pies and I… Well, since I didn't know when I was going to see them again, and I was baking anyway, I thought they… Ah, hell, I thought they'd like them. That's all. And I saw the boxes in a store near my office, so I…' He cleared his throat. 'I bought them. No big deal.'

Nice and defiant. Still blushing.

And everything surged in Kate—wrenching at her heart, racing through her blood, shattering every thought in her brain…flooding her with absolute crazy love. She was insanely, wildly in love with him.

She couldn't pretend any more. Not for one more moment.

And the next moment of her life started precisely *now*.

'Hugo,' she said.

CHAPTER EIGHTEEN

SCOTT REELED BACK in his chair. 'What's he got to do with anything?'

'I don't know, Scott. Why don't you tell me what he has to do with you, with us, or indeed with anything? Because you've told me precious little so far. So—Hugo.'

'Oh, I get it. Is this—? This is about…about Play Time. Stopping Play Time, right?'

'Yes, Scott, it is.'

'But…why? What was so bad? Do you want to…to go back and start again?'

'No.'

He blinked. 'Okay, then, let's skip it altogether and just go upstairs and—'

'Hugo,' Kate said again.

He tried to smile, but didn't nail it. 'You don't know what I was going to suggest.'

Kate didn't bother even trying to smile. 'The fact that you said we should go upstairs—to bed, no doubt—tells me all I need to know. It tells me we don't have a relationship.'

'Sure we do.'

'No, Scott, we don't. We have a contract.'

'You're the one who wanted the contract.'

'Semantics. With or without the signed piece of paper, we have an *arrangement*. An arrangement is *not* a relationship. And if you're happy with that then I'm calling "Hugo". As in *enough*. No more Play Time. No more anything.'

Scott shoved a hand into his hair. 'Kate, if it's the subject of my brother that's bothering you—'

'Didn't you listen? Hugo—as in *I'm finished*.'

'—he has nothing to do with us.' Right over the top of her. 'I never thought you'd meet him.'

'Well, I did meet him, Scott, so how about you explain now?'

Silence. Scott's jaw tightened.

'Scott?'

'You're the smartest person I've ever met, Kate. I'm sure you worked it all out the night of the architect awards. Why do you need to wring the words out of me?'

Kate stared at him.

He stared back.

And then he shoved *both* his hands into his hair. 'Dammit—all right. It's no big deal.'

He took a moment. Placed his hands on the table, palms down. Very specific. Controlling them.

'Very simply: my brother was the perfect child. Better than me at school, better than me at sport, better than me at everything. My parents let me know it in a thousand ways when we were growing up. And when Hugo hit the doctor target…? Big bonus points, there. Now he's hit all the personal targets too—getting married, providing grandchildren. Long story short—Hugo is *family* all the way. And I'm…*not*. I'm number two. All the way.'

Kate reached for his hand but Scott pulled it back, out of the touch zone.

'All the way,' he repeated. 'Want an example, Kate? What about that time I was in the Whitsundays, goofing off, teaching holidaymakers to sail, making a fool of myself over a girl who didn't love me? What do you think my brother was doing?' But the question was rhetorical. 'He was one-upping me spectacularly by sailing solo around the world.'

'So what?' Kate asked, but it was hard to get that out because she wanted to cry.

'So *what*?' Scott laughed—harsh and awful. 'So sailing was *my* thing. Why did he have to take that too? I swear, if he knew I liked cooking he'd go and get himself a publishing deal for a cookbook.'

'Hugo didn't win the architecture prize. You did.'

'Wait until next year's awards,' Scott said. 'He'll pull a rabbit out of someone's hat.'

'Exactly, Scott! Out of someone *else's* hat! Unlike you, wearing your *own* hat. Because you can't tell me you simply follow blindly—not your parents, not your brother, not anyone. Otherwise you'd be a doctor like the rest of your family—you're certainly smart enough.'

'There's no mystery there, Kate. I just wanted to be an architect.'

'I know that. And I know why. Because it's *you*. Creativity—and order. The perfect career for *you*! And I think your brother hates how good you are at it. Because you can bet that although you could be a doctor if you wanted to—'

'Not as good as Hugo.'

'Maybe…maybe not—but you could be *some* kind of doctor. Hugo, however, could never be *any* kind of architect.'

'You can't possibly tell that.'

'Sure I can—because he wasn't the one in the navy blue tux that night. He doesn't have it. *It*. That thing you have. And what does it tell you that he didn't even have the grace to come over and congratulate you when you won that award?'

Scott said nothing.

'That he was jealous,' Kate said. '*Is* jealous. Of you.'

Scoffing laugh. 'He has nothing to be jealous of.'

'Really? Because the way I see it, you have something Hugo wants badly but will never, ever have. I'll bet your parents don't have it either. I'll bet none of them even understands it—which is why it's three against one in the Knight family. You have creativity, and charisma, and wit, and decency, and…and adventure in your soul, and so much more. *That's* why you went to the Whitsundays, and why Hugo had to make do with what he *thought* was one better. Except it *wasn't* one better. He had to *follow* you to one-up you. And he had to one-up you because that's the only way he can feel better than you. He can't bear your success because he wants it *all*—all for himself. He can't *be* you, so he *steals* from you. But he can't steal the one thing he really wants because that would make him…you. And, no matter what he tries, he never *will* be you.'

Scott shook his head, wearing one of those smiles that meant nothing.

'And the sailing thing?' she said urgently. 'I'd tell you to make it your thing again, if it bothers you, but you don't *have* to make it your thing. Because it *is* your thing. It always was—and it will be waiting for you when you're ready to let it all go and just be, Scott. Just *be*. Without comparing yourself to anyone.'

'I've given up comparing myself, Kate.' Scott took a deep, visible breath. 'Number two is fine with me.'

Heart. Breaking.

'You're not number two. Not with me, Scott.'

'Not yet. But give it time. Someone else will come along. Someone older, like that Phillip guy. Someone smarter, like Hugo. Someone not as stitched-up and closed-off and conservative, like Brodie. That's why you danced with him. Why you went sailing with him. I'll bet you even told him about your custody case.'

She was silent.

'Did you, Kate?' he asked, and she heard the edge of danger in his voice.

'I don't talk about my cases. Not in…in detail.'

'Obfuscation? How very…*legal*.' He shook his head, disgusted.

'You sound like my mother. She really would like you, Scott.'

'Did you tell him, Kate? It's a simple question—one of those simple questions you say you don't have a problem with.'

She took a quick breath. 'Then, yes. That's the answer. I did. I told him.'

Scott's hand fisted, banged on the table, and Kate flinched.

'Why?' The word shot out like a bullet.

'Because he asked. As a friend.'

'I can't *believe* this.' Scott shot to his feet, paced away, then back. 'What the hell am *I*, Kate? I've been trying to talk to you about it for a week.'

He banged both fists on the table this time.

'Tell *me*!' Another bang. 'Tell *me*, Kate, dammit!'

Kate's heart had jumped right into her throat as his fists hit the table, and for a moment all she could do was stare at him. He looked a heartbeat away from breathing fire.

Out of control—at last.

And now she had to find words, when all she wanted to do was fling herself at him and wrap herself around him and beg him to let her love him, to love her back.

She realised she'd left it too long to speak when, cursing, Scott started to pace away again. One step…two.

'Wait,' she said, standing, grabbing his swinging arm so fast her chair toppled backwards. 'I'll tell you.'

He was shaking his head as he turned, wrenched his arm free. 'Don't bother, Kate. Just…just *don't*. It's too damned late.'

'I'm representing the father,' she rushed out. 'Who's been sitting on the sidelines going slowly out of his mind while his ex-wife's new boyfriend slaps his three-year-old son around. Something he's reported over and over and over. But nobody believes him. Because there's been enough mud slung to cast all sorts of doubts about him. His little boy screams and begs every time he has to go back to his mother after a scheduled visit.'

Kate's breaths were heaving in and out and she'd started to shake with the fury of it.

'My client ended up so desperate he kidnapped his own

child to protect him. And what did he get for caring like that? No more visits. At all. That's what.'

Her throat was clogged and swollen. The injustice of it was raging out of her, even though she'd won. Why? *Why* did it still get to her? No answer—it just did. And it was all too much. The case…Scott…her damned life.

'So you want to know why I didn't tell you, Scott?' she asked as the tears started. 'Because you didn't sign up for deep and meaningful, remember? And that's deep and meaningful to me. I needed you. But how could I tell you? What could I say? When you said—made it clear— Oh, God. I can't. I…can't. I…'

But she couldn't go on. She was choking on tears. And suddenly she gave in to them, sobbing into her hands.

And then she was in Scott's arms, held tightly against his chest. 'Shh, shh, Kate…I'm here.'

'No, Scott, you're not,' she sobbed into his shoulder. 'You're not here. Your body's here—that's all. Just your body.'

She tried to pull away but Scott held on. 'I'm not letting you go, Kate, so stop struggling.'

'And if I do? If I stop struggling?' She looked up at him. 'Then what? You'll ask me to spit out a few legal terms and take me to bed?'

'Yes,' he said simply.

'That's not enough,' she cried, and buried her face in his shoulder again. 'I want more.'

'So do I. That's why we're rolling it over.'

'No, Scott, we're not.'

'You just said you wanted more.'

'Not more sex! More…*more*.'

'I don't— I don't—'

'No, you *don't*,' she cut in, half-despair, half-rage, as she pulled out of his arms. 'That's the problem. Well, I'm not hanging in limbo any more, like a suspended piñata, waiting to have the crap beaten out of me.'

'A piña—?' He stopped. Incredulous. 'I'm not beating anything out of you. I would never hurt you.'

'Oh, you're hurting me, all right.'

'I'm *not* hurting you,' Scott said furiously. 'I *won't* hurt you. You won't hurt *me*. That's the whole point!'

'And I'm telling you—you *are* hurting me. Because I love you. And you don't love me back.'

The shock of it was plain on his face. 'You don't love me. Kate, you *know* you don't.' Pleading, almost. 'You can't. You don't want love.'

She laughed, shrugged, helpless.

Waves of panic were emanating from Scott. 'You said you'd never give someone that kind of power over you.'

'Except that now I would give it to you.'

'Cynical. We're both cynical. It's what made us perfect. *Makes* us perfect.'

'I'm *not* cynical, Scott. Or if I am it doesn't last—not if I have someone…' she swallowed '…someone who'll say to me, "Shh, I'm here", like you just did. Putting things right for people is what I do, what I *want* to do, even if sometimes it gets too much. And perfect…? I don't want to be perfect. And I don't want you to be perfect either. I want to be *im*-perfect—with you. I want children who are perfect or im-perfect—who are *anything* as long as they're yours. And I want to say to *you*, *Shh, I'm here*, when things get too much for you. Because I'm in love with you. And I would do any-thing—*anything*—for you to love me.'

His eyes were wild. 'I…can't do this.'

'Why not?'

'I don't. Do this.'

'You loved Chantal. Why can't you love me?'

'I didn't love Chantal, Kate. And I don't blame her for choosing Brodie. I never did. Anyone would choose him.'

'Not me. Because I chose you. I'm *choosing* you. No—it wasn't even a choice. It just happened. Love. I didn't even know I was waiting for it. But I was. I was waiting for the right man to come along. Then there you were. And suddenly you were mine. The perfect imperfect man. The right man for me. Uptight…beer not cocktails…hell, no, to dancing…sport and poker games…with a kitten on your backside…wearing a blue tux and driving a red Mini…baking for two little girls. How could I *not* love you? And now, Scott, I want us to just…just *be*.'

He was shaking his head. His face was white, stark fear in his eyes. 'I'm not the right guy for anyone, Kate. I'm the "friends with benefits" guy, with a bulging black book. I've never had a relationship—don't you see? *Never!* And there's a reason for that—because I know what I'm good at. Sex—no strings. My speciality. I've got more tail than I know what to do with. That's me. And I'm fine with that.'

It was like a punch direct to Kate's heart, killing it—that was how it felt. As if her heart was dead. A swollen lump she wished she could rip out of her chest.

'T-T-Tail?' Kate stammered over the word, her teeth chattering with reaction.

He looked at her, all hard-eyed. 'Tail,' he repeated.

God, the ache of it. Crushing. Ravaging. 'So here I am, opening myself to you, telling you I would move heaven and hell and everything in between—*everything*—to have you—*you*, Scott. Not Brodie, not Hugo, not Phillip, but *you*. And your response is to tell me I'm a piece of *tail*?'

He stood there like a block of granite, silent.

'Right,' she said, and swallowed. 'Right.' She looked blindly around, head spinning. 'Right.' Was the blood draining out of her? That was what it felt like. 'Saturday is the twenty-eighth of February. End of contract. We've had one session this week—Sunday. And we have tonight. We'll make this the last one, because I'm not inclined to negotiate any extras for the week. *Cadit quaestio*—a settlement for our dispute has been reached. Sex—once more—and the issue is resolved.'

'It's not resolved.'

Agony twisted through her. He didn't love her, but he wouldn't let her go either. 'What more do you want from me?'

'I want... I want...' His hands were diving into his hair again. But no more words emerged.

Kate took an unsteady breath. 'Well, given everything you've just said to me, and all the things you can't seem to say, I finally know what *I* want. I want out. I'm saying no to the rollover option. No to everything.'

'You can't do that.'

'Now, you see, you should have read the contract when I told you to. Because I *can* do that. I *am* doing that. I'm not going to turn into one of those bitter people I see in court—hating you, trying to punish you because you don't love me or need me the way I love and need you. If you don't love me then I don't want you.'

'You do want me. I know you do.'

Kate started removing her clothes.

'What the hell—? Kate, what are you doing?'

'Getting undressed.' She was down to her underwear in record time. 'I'm taking back my "Hugo" and we're restarting Play Time. As I recall, it was a dining experience you offered me—you bent the fifty-fifty rule to get it...clever you. So I'll get on top of the dining table, you can put those whoopie pies all over me, and then—'

But whatever she'd been about to say was whoomped out of her as Scott grabbed her by the arms. 'You're not lying on top of anything except my bed.'

She greeted that with a nice, brittle laugh. 'How conservative of you.'

'Yes, I *am* conservative. And I'm over all this Play Time stuff. I don't want you on your knees in alleys, or stripping for me like a hooker, or blindfolding me like we're in a B&D room, or any other kooky stuff.'

'That's exactly what you wanted—why do you think I was giving it to you?'

'Well, I don't want it now. Got it, Kate?' He shook her, once. 'Got it? I. Just. Want. You. As agreed. In bed. Okay?'

'As agreed,' she repeated. And the tears came. 'No, Scott, it's not okay.'

'Why not? Why *not*, dammit?'

'Because I love you. And loving you hurts like hell.'

He let her go, stepped back as though she'd struck him.

'Come on, Scott. Look on the bright side. You never liked all those rules. Anais is going to make you a much more *beneficial* friend.'

'I don't want Anais.'

'And after tonight I won't want *you*. So here I am, offering you one last time. Take it...or leave it.'

'They're the only two options?'

'Yes.'

'Then I'm taking it. Get on the table, Kate. Let's say goodbye in style.'

CHAPTER NINETEEN

SCOTT KNEW HE would never forget the sight of Kate lying on his dining table, letting him take her as tears leaked from the corners of her eyes.

He'd been so sure she would stop crying. That he could *make* her stop crying with the power of his depthless passion for her. But even as she'd succumbed to his body, as she'd soared with him into orgasm, her tears had kept coming… slow and silent.

Scott had been frantic. Scooping her off the table afterwards into his arms, holding her against his shaking body.

Wordless, she'd tried to leave. But he'd whispered that he wanted more, that he *needed* more. So she'd let him carry her upstairs to his bed. He'd kissed her for what felt like forever. But the tears had just kept coming. And even hating himself for her pain and his own desperation, he hadn't been able to let her go.

He'd watched her as she slept. The frown on her face. The tear tracks. The divine mouth, swollen from the way he'd devoured her.

She hadn't spoken one word to him—not since that last, 'Take it…or leave it.'

And he'd taken it, all right. Taken, taken, *taken*. Hoping, selfishly, to sate himself at last. Hoping he would wake up and not want her any more. Hoping he'd be able to let her go in the morning.

But when he'd woken she was already gone and he'd had no choice to make; she'd made the choice for both of them.

He hated his bed—because she wasn't in it.

So he went downstairs.

Where he decided he hated his house—because she wasn't there.

In the dining room were the girls' glittery boxes, waiting to be filled with whoopie pies. But the whoopie pies were nothing but a heap of broken biscuit and smeared cream on the floor, surrounded by shards of shattered plate. The plate he'd shoved off the table in his urgency to get to Kate.

As he looked at the mess and remembered how joyful he'd been, waiting for Kate to arrive, it hit him that what he hated most of all was his *life*—because she'd walked out of it.

And ringing in his ears, over and over, were her words. *'I would move heaven and hell to have you.'*

That was just so...*her*. Direct. Laying the argument out. Fighting to win. The way she always fought. To the death. To win the prize.

To win...the prize...

His breath hitched as he repeated that in his head. *Fighting to win the prize.*

The prize—*her* prize—was...him.

His heart started to thump. Loud, heavy, dull.

Why was he so scared about being her prize when she was everything that was wonderful? When *she* wasn't scared to claim *him* even though he wasn't anything wonderful at all?

But wasn't that exactly it? That time on her terrace, when they'd talked about love, she'd said that real love—of *any* kind—gloried especially in a person's flaws. She'd told him last night that she wanted to be imperfect...with him. She wanted them to just...*be*.

She knew everything. Chantal, Brodie, Hugo, his parents. Knew about all the times he'd lost. Had been with him when he'd finally won. She'd seen the very worst of him—because, God, he'd shown it to her—and she loved him anyway. He didn't have to be perfect. He just had to...*be*.

Eyes stinging.

She'd said she would move heaven and hell to have him.

Chest aching.

That had to make him the best man in the world. Not second-best—*the* best.

Sweat ran down his back.

There might be smarter men, funnier men, better-looking men, more successful men, easier men—but not for Kate.

Breaths coming short and hard.

She would move heaven and freaking *hell* for him.

Whole body throbbing.

Exactly what he would do for her. Move heaven and hell.

Because she was his. Only his. And he wanted, at last, to reach for the prize, to claim the prize for himself—the only prize worth having. *Kate.*

The simplicity of that, the peace of it, burst in his head and dazzled him—but then the enormity of what he'd done to her, what he'd said, hit him and he staggered, grabbing for the closest chair.

Was it even possible to fix what he'd done?

Terrified, he grabbed his phone, called her mobile.

No answer.

Called her office.

Got Deb. Who had only two words for him: *'Drop dead!'*

He emailed Kate. Texted. Called her again.

He risked the wrath of Deb and called her again. *Three* words this time: *'Drop dead, arsehole.'*

So he tracked down Shay, because for sure Kate would have told her sister—she was a Cleary, not a Knight, and they were close—and maybe he could grovel by proxy.

And, yep—she'd told her sister, all right.

Dropping dead would have been a kindness compared to what Shay told him to do to himself, with a casual reference to Gus and Aristotle throwing knives at his corpse wrapped around a collection of four-letter words. She followed that up by telling him the most diabolical thing he could possibly hear. That Kate had never been in love before—but she was a Cleary, so that wouldn't stop her from ripping the love out of her heart and stomping it to a violent death. The Cleary way: fight like the devil—but when you lose, move on. No second chances. No going back.

Shaken, Scott hung up and did the manly thing.

He called Brodie and suggested they get drunk.

It was only beer number one but Scott didn't mince his words. There was no time to wait for the anaesthetising effects of booze. No time for tiptoeing.

'I'm in trouble,' he said.

Brodie took that with equanimity. 'I think what you mean is *I'm in love*.'

'Yep,' Scott said, and swallowed a mouthful of beer.

Brodie took his own long, thoughtful sip. 'I don't see the problem—unless she doesn't love you back.'

'She said she does.'

'And the problem, therefore, is…?'

'I told her I had more tail than I knew what to do with.' He grimaced. 'And that that was how I wanted it to stay.'

Brodie said an enlightening, 'Aha…'

'Well?' Scott demanded belligerently.

'Well, basically…' Pause for a swig of beer. 'You are an idiot.'

'Yeah, but what do I *do*?'

'Call her.'

'Tried. All day. Tried everyone. Her…her office…her sister. Her assistant told me to drop dead. And I won't tell you what her sister told me to do with myself because it's anatomically impossible but will still make your eyes water. I tried Willa. Then Amy. Just subtly, to see if they knew where she was going to be tonight. At least they don't seem to have any idea there was anything between us, so I haven't ruined *that* for her.'

There was a moment of stunned silence, and then Brodie hooted out a laugh. 'Are you *kidding* me? Nobody who saw you kiss Kate on that dance floor is in any doubt that you're a goner. The *bartender* knew, you moron.'

'Well, why didn't *I* know?'

'Idiot, remember?'

'So what the hell am I going to do?'

Long, thoughtful pause. 'Scott, I'm going to share something with you, even though you don't deserve it—you big clunk. Four words: *From Here to Eternity.*'

'Huh?'

'That night at the bar, before we got there, the girls were talking about their idea of romantic moments.'

'And...*what*?'

'Four scenarios were mentioned. One was Willa's—so let's discount that, because it was something financial.'

'Yep, that's Willa.'

'Then there was one about rose petals being strewn around the bedroom.'

Scott snorted out a laugh. 'God!'

'Yep. You wouldn't say *that* was Kate, would you?'

'Er—no!'

'What about a knight on a white charger?'

'What the—? I mean— *What?*' Scott burst out laughing.

'Not Kate?' Brodie asked, his mouth twisting.

'Hell, I hope not.'

'Sure?'

Scott shook his head. Definitive. 'No—that's not her.'

Brodie gave him a sympathetic look. 'Then I'm pegging her for *From Here to Eternity.*'

'What the hell *is* that?'

'A movie.'

'About what?'

'How the hell would I know? It's got to be a chick flick. I mean, come on—*eternity?* But I'm guessing there's a clue in that movie.'

'How's that going to help me?'

'Well, dropkick, I'm going to download the movie and we're going to watch it together. And—sidebar conversation—you are *so* going to owe me for this!'

'Okay, okay—I'll owe you. But what exactly are we going to do *after* we watch it?'

'I don't know—not yet. Which is why we're watching it in the first place. To figure out what her most romantic moment is. And then, mate, you're going to *give* her that moment—because words are not going to be enough. Action is what's needed.'

Two hours later—mid-bite of a slice of seafood pizza— Brodie paused the film. 'And there you have it,' he said.

'Have what?' Scott asked warily.

'That's the scene.'

'That? I mean...*that*? Seriously?'

Brodie replayed it. Nodded, very sure of himself. 'That. Believe me. I know women, and that's it.'

'Looks...sandy...'

'Suck it up, buddy. Suck. It. Up.'

'I can tell you right now I am *not* writhing around in the surf on Bondi Beach surrounded by a thousand people.'

'If that's what she wants that's what you're going to do.'

'Aw, hell...'

Brodie laughed. 'I'm just messing with your head, Knight. Nothing that public will be required. I have a friend down the coast who, as it happens, lives near a beach that is chronically deserted.'

'And just *how* am I going to get Kate to drive for hours along the coastline with me when I can't even get her to pick up the phone?'

Brodie held up a hand for silence. Grabbed his phone off the coffee table. Dialled. Then, 'Kate?'

Scott leapt off the couch, waving his hands like a madman and trying to grab the phone out of Brodie's hand.

Brodie punched him in the arm. 'Nope—haven't seen him.' Lying without compunction. 'Why?'

Scott made another mad grab—got another punch.

'No,' Brodie said, holding Scott off with a hand on his

forehead. 'I just wanted to offer you another sailing lesson on Saturday.'

Pause while Scott almost exploded—but in silence.

'Great,' Brodie said into the phone. 'Eight o'clock. See you then.'

Brodie disconnected and turned to Scott, grinning.

'*I* want to teach her how to sail,' Scott said.

'So do it.'

'Do it *when*, *genius*?'

'After the beach clinch. I'm going to drop Kate off at a particular inlet down the coast on Saturday, just after lunch. You—having bought a neat little yacht I happen to know is for sale—will have sailed down there and will be waiting to drive her to that deserted beach.'

'If I sail down there I won't have a car.'

'So *hire* one!'

'And then what?'

'And *then* you will roll around like a dumbass in the surf with her.'

'And…?'

'And you will sail her back to Sydney, teaching her the way you should have offered the first time she mentioned sailing to you. Honestly—do I have to do *everything* for you?'

Scott stared at Brodie. A grin started working its way across his face as he picked up a piece of pizza. 'I should have known a guy who'd order a seafood pizza would know all about girly stuff,' he said. 'Pepperoni is where it's at, mate. *Pepperoni*.'

'Shove your pepperoni where the sun doesn't shine, *mate*—and get me another beer.'

Scott laughed, and started to get off the couch to go to the fridge.

But Brodie stopped him, one hand on his forearm. 'You're it for her, you know? Don't let that mangy brother of yours keep getting away with making you feel like second-best. Because he is *not* better than you.'

Scott gripped Brodie's hand where it rested on his arm. 'I know he's not. She wouldn't love me if he was.'

Brodie smiled. 'And neither would I.'

'Brode—mate—*please*!' Scott said.

'You are *so* uptight—I'm not at all sure I shouldn't try to cut you out with Red,' Brodie said.

'You can *try*,' Scott said, and then he laughed.

CHAPTER TWENTY

KATE COULDN'T DRUM UP any enthusiasm for the sailing lesson, but she was waiting at the jetty on the dot of eight o'clock, with a fake smile worthy of Scott himself pasted on.

Because it wouldn't do for Brodie to report back to Scott that she was looking wan and miserable.

She climbed aboard and darted a look around the deck. Half expecting… Maybe hoping just a little…?

'He's not here, Kate,' Brodie said.

She looked at him as the hope died. 'You know?' Short, unhappy laugh. 'Of course you do. Best friends, right? You don't have to badger confidences out of him.'

'Are we going to talk about it?' Brodie asked.

'No,' Kate said, and heard the dangerous wobble in her voice.

'Okay, then.' He took her bag, stowed it. 'Remember I said we were sailing down the coast and going swimming when we got there?' He gestured to her long cotton pants, her long-sleeved T-shirt. 'You got your swimmers on under there?'

'Yes,' she said.

'Then we're off.'

Kate tried to recapture some of the joy of her first sailing lesson, but that sense of freedom, of escape, was elusive. She was just so…so heartbroken.

Nevertheless, she threw herself into it—and if Brodie was a little less didactic this time around she wasn't going to complain about getting special treatment. He was that kind of guy—the kind who read anguish and allowed for it. Not the kind to tell a girl she was a piece of tail…even if she *was*.

Hours passed, and Kate started to wonder if they were going to turn around any time soon—because at this rate they wouldn't make it back to Sydney before Sunday morning. But they finally stopped at a calm, protected inlet for lunch.

Slowly Kate started to relax. But with relaxation came those horrible, useless, helpless tears. She hurried over to the bow of the boat, away from the others, trying to stem the flow. But it was no use. They welled in her eyes, clogged the back of her nose. Thank heaven she was wearing sunglasses, so Brodie wouldn't see.

But almost before the thought had formed Brodie was there, standing just behind her. She knew it, but she couldn't turn. Just couldn't move. Because the tears were flowing freely.

'He's not good with words,' he said. 'Not the *important* words.'

Kate covered her face with her hands, dislodging her sunglasses.

Brodie turned her, took off her sunglasses, hugged her. 'At least he didn't punch you. That's what he did to me the first time I told him I loved him.'

Kate started laughing then—and it was the weirdest thing, mixing laughter with tears.

Brodie tilted her face up. 'You going to give him another chance?'

'No. That doesn't happen in my family.'

'Well, at least you gave him *one* chance, I guess,' Brodie said. 'It's more than his own family gave him.'

'Oh, God. Don't say that.'

'It's true. He needs a family, Kate. A new one. A *real* one.' She was crying again.

'And he's over there on the shore, waiting for you to be it.'

Kate, stunned, turned to look.

And there he was. Tall and bulky, in jeans and T-shirt and aviator sunglasses, hands jammed into his pockets. Waiting for her.

Waiting…for *her*…

But waiting for what?

Kate didn't even notice when Brodie took his arms from around her. Barely heard him call to one of the guys on the boat. Dinghy... Something about a dinghy...

Next thing she knew she and her bag were *in* the dinghy, heading towards the shore. Scott took off his sunglasses as she got closer, flinging them away as if he didn't care what happened to them.

And then she was there, and he was reaching for her, helping her out of the dinghy, holding out his hand for her bag, wrapping her in his arms, holding on to her, holding tight. It felt electric—like a massive, hungry jolt—so different from the calm comfort of Brodie's embrace.

And she knew it would always be like that with Scott. Because he was *it*. The only one for her. It was a thought that scared her so much she almost couldn't breathe. Because it meant that without him she would be alone—forever. And she didn't want to be alone any more.

But being alone was better than loving a man who didn't love her back.

She took a deep breath, pulled out of his arms. 'Scott, I meant what I said.'

'Kate, please—just bear with me, okay? You'll see.'

Without waiting for her to respond, he took her hand, led her away from the water, up to the road.

He opened the door of a nondescript car—where was his Mini?—and helped her in.

'Where are we going, Scott?' she asked tiredly as he got behind the wheel, started the car.

'Don't ask, Kate. I'll stuff it up if I talk.'

So Kate simply sat as Scott drove—a total mess, almost ill from the way her heart was hammering.

He parked, got out of the car and came around to her side to help her out. He took her in his arms again and she couldn't bring herself to pull away. She felt him shaking. Like a leaf.

'Scared, that's all,' he said with an embarrassed shrug as she looked up at him.

'Why?'

Short half-laugh. 'You'll see,' he said again, and led her off the road towards a patch of scrub.

Her eyes widened. 'In *there*?'

Scott winced. 'Yep. In there. God help us.'

He led the way in until the thick scrub morphed into sparsely vegetated dunes. She could hear the roar and rush of surf, and then it was there. A tiny jewel of a beach, waves breaking in a constant sucking stream.

'A surf beach?' she said, poised on top of a dune.

'Yeah, a surf beach,' he said, grimacing, and trudged with her down onto the sand.

'It's beautiful,' Kate said, trying to understand the grimace—trying to understand *something*. Anything. 'And not a soul here except for that one surfer. Amazing.'

'It's a local secret,' he said. 'And apparently a little dangerous for swimming.'

'So why are we here?'

Scott screwed his eyes shut and blushed. *'From Here to Eternity,'* he said.

Kate's mouth dropped open. It took her a moment to find her voice, but at least by the time she did Scott had opened his eyes.

'Is this a joke?' she asked icily.

'No.'

'Who told you?'

'Brodie.'

She sucked in a tortured breath—felt the heat rush along her cheekbones. 'And who told *him*?'

'He figured it out. Something Jessica said that night at Fox.'

'Jessica?' she said ominously.

But Scott wasn't listening. He looked a heartbeat away from a nervous breakdown.

'Well, Kate, we're here,' he said. 'Let's do it.'

He stripped down to a pair of well-worn board shorts—in

which he looked mouthwateringly good. And then he came to her, took her face in his hands. Licked slowly along one cheekbone, then along the other.

'I've wanted to do that for the longest time,' he said. 'You are so absolutely beautiful when you blush.'

'Scott, this is not going to work,' she said a little desperately, hanging on to her resolve by a thread. 'I told you. No rollover. I'm done.'

'It's not about the rollover and we're not leaving until we do it—so get your gear off.'

'That surfer—'

'I can handle one surfer.'

'But anyone could come past.'

'Yeah—I know. It's a bit like the night Officer Cleary frisked me in Ellington Lane.'

'That was different.'

'How so? Did you know we wouldn't be caught?'

'No, I didn't know. But it was dark and I…' She huffed out a breath, aggravated. 'Really, I just didn't care.'

'And there I was, thinking you were law-abiding!'

'I am. But I'm not conservative. And *you are*, Scott.'

He touched her hair. 'And yet here I am, trying to get you out of your clothes on a beach in broad daylight,' he said, and smiled—and his whole face lit up with it.

Her heart lurched. That smile. *Devastating.*

'Scott, don't do this to me,' she said shakily. 'Stop doing this to me.'

'I have to do it. Kate, please. You've got to let me. Just this one thing. For you. Please, Kate. Please let me.'

Kate looked into Scott's eyes—they were warm and serious and…and *desperate*. Looked at the waves. Back into Scott's eyes.

Why was she fighting it? The man she was in love with was offering to make her a gift of her ultimate fantasy. She'd be like Willa and Chantal—her most romantic moment would be real. And she could pretend, couldn't she, that it was love?

'All right,' she said, and wondered if he'd finally driven her mad as she stripped down to her one-piece black swimsuit.

Scott took her hand. Gave her a look redolent of bravery. 'Shall we?'

She nodded, but wondered if this memory—precious though it would be—was going to be worth it, given that every time it surfaced in the future her heart would break all over again.

Scott led her into the surf, just far enough for them to duck under the water and get wet.

'No further,' he said. 'I can feel the water tugging, and this is going to lose all its romance value if we get swept out to sea and either drown or get eaten by a shark.'

He pulled her into his arms.

'And in any case...' he said, backing her towards the shore. Backing her, backing her, backing her, and then dragging her to her knees, where the waves were breaking. 'This is the money shot, right?'

And with that, he eased her flat onto the sand, and then he was on top of her, kissing her as if he'd happily drown as long as his mouth was on hers.

The water surged over them. Receded, surged, receded. For the longest time they stayed there, waves breaking over them, Scott's mouth on hers, tongue thrusting, mirroring the breaking of the waves over their bodies. Over, over, over. Way longer than the scene in the movie.

Eventually he pulled back, just a fraction, smoothed her hair off her face, gazed down at her. And something was shining in his eyes that made her long to have him inside her. She wasn't supposed to want it any more—she was supposed to have ripped him from her heart—and yet she did want it...did want him. She ached with need.

A sudden strong wave took Kate unawares and she choked on sea water. Scott grabbed her hand, dragged her out of the wash and up the beach to dry land, where she dropped to the sand and rolled onto her back, spluttering, laughing, coughing, eyes streaming.

And despite the fact that she was half drowned, deranged, probably a little snotty, Scott dropped to his knees beside her and looked at her as though she were the most wondrous thing he'd ever seen.

He was smiling, and there were tears—*tears!*—in his eyes as he rolled with her on the sand until she was on top of him.

She snaked her fingers into his wet hair, wanting him so much she thought she might seriously burst with it.

He looked up at her, so serious. 'So, Kate, what's the Latin for *And so endeth the contract*?'

She froze. *And so endeth...?*

Oh. Ohhh. Her breath caught as the pain hit.

It all made sense. Today was the twenty-eighth of February. The last day of their contract. She'd given herself to him at his house on Tuesday, fulfilled the contract to the letter, but he had to wring that little bit extra out of her—even after breaking her heart. Probably thinking she'd let him get away with this latest manipulation because he was using her secret fantasy to do it. And who *wouldn't* want their ultimate Play Time, right?

Hating herself for letting him do this to her—hating *him*—Kate shoved herself off him, got to her feet, started pulling on clothes over the dampness and sand.

Scott had felt the change in Kate that split second before she'd rolled off him.

'Did I stuff it up?' he asked, getting to his feet. 'Because I thought… I mean I watched the movie… I…I thought that was…'

The words tapered off as Kate skewered him with a glare.

Was this the part where she told him he was too late? That she didn't love him any more? No, he couldn't face that. Didn't—*wouldn't*—believe it.

Scott started dressing, just to keep his hands occupied

while he waited for her to speak, to give him a clue about where he'd messed up. But she didn't speak and he couldn't take the silence.

'Are you going to tell me what I did wrong, Kate?'

'You know.'

'No, I don't.'

'The twenty-eighth of February,' she said coldly.

Scott looked at her blankly.

'February *twenty-eighth*!' she snapped. 'You couldn't re-sist having the last word, could you, Scott? One last Play Time—and using my deepest, most secret fantasy to do it. Good job. For someone who said he would never hurt me, you sure wield a sharp knife.'

What the hell—?

She picked up her bag. 'So when is Brodie coming back for me?'

'Brodie's on his way to Sydney,' Scott said. 'I'm taking you back.'

The blood drained out of Kate's face.

'What?' he asked urgently. 'What did I do?'

She laughed—and it wasn't the joyful laughter they'd shared in the waves. 'Today. Last day of the contract, right?'

'Yes…' Still bewildered.

'I've spent three days tearing you out of my heart, and thanks to your little stunt today all that work is lost. I'll have to start over.'

Scott's mouth went dry—a dryness that had nothing to do with the ton of salt that had swirled in and out of his mouth with all that sea water. 'I thought you wanted the contract to be over?'

'I did. But not like— Oh, just forget it.'

He grabbed her arm. 'No, tell me, Kate. If you don't tell me, how can I explain?'

She wrenched free. 'Under the terms of our contract you don't have to explain.'

'Dammit, Kate, I've had a gutful of the contract. It's over! *Over!*'

'It was over on Tuesday, but that wasn't good enough for you, was it? Because *I* decided that. I decided it out of love. But you had to control the ending—out of…of…*pique*! And so here you are, controlling it—like you've controlled everything since the moment we met.'

'That's *crap*, Kate. I've *never* been in control. Not from the first moment I saw you. I don't— I don't *want* to be in control with you. And that—' He shoved irritably at his hair. 'That is not an easy thing for me to admit.'

'Oh, you've been in the driver's seat all the way along. Running rings around me. Flouting the rules. Turning up any time you wanted. All those calculated kisses to get me to shut up when I asked you a personal question—when I *told* you kissing was dangerous.'

'You never told me that!'

'It was *implied*! Because it's obvious! To everyone except you. Kissing—no problem for Scott Knight, because Scott Knight doesn't care and Scott Knight doesn't feel.'

'But I did—I mean I *do*—'

'Shut up, Scott. Just *shut up*. Because I *do* feel. And every time you kissed me I felt more—and more and more. Wanted you more and more. But all you wanted was Play Time! So I gave that to you too, because I figured I could *sex* you into loving me. I would have done anything. *Anything!* But you wouldn't even let me protect myself by sticking to a few simple rules.'

'Kate, stop. I—'

'You know what's the stupidest thing of all? I started to think that maybe you were breaking all those rules because you didn't *want* the contract.'

'I didn't. I wanted—'

'I thought you just wanted to kiss me, see me, be with me—take it however it came. The more you broke the rules, the more I hoped. But you were breaking them because it was a game to you. *I* was a game.'

'No, that isn't—'

'And that last night—what you said to me. *Tail*. A piece of tail. That's what I was. *All* I was. All the way along. And you, with more tail than you know what to do with, could have anyone—so why me? Why did you still take and *take* from me that night? When you knew how…how painful it was for me to love you like I did? You knew I wanted to leave and you wouldn't let me go.'

'Okay, that's *enough*, Kate!' He grabbed her then, dragged her in. 'I didn't let you go because I couldn't. I can't, Kate. I *can't*.'

'But you will—because tomorrow is the first of March and we are done.' She jerked out of his arms. '*Done!* Do you get it? *A mensa et thoro*—legal separation without divorce.'

'Don't talk Latin to me now.'

'*Res judicata*—the final adjudication. No further appeals. Goodbye.'

Scott blanched. His shoulders were tight enough to snap his spine. Head drumming. Heart hammering. Hands clenching and unclenching.

'Except for one thing, Kate,' he said. 'You love me.'

'Well, you see, I'm going to let Phillip the barrister help me get over that. Tomorrow—the first of March—when there will be no possible suggestion that I am still under contract to you. Time for a *new* contract. This time I might even get the *friend* part of "friends with benefits". Someone who w-won't h-hurt me.'

'I won't hurt you.'

She turned away, breath hitching. 'You already have, Scott.'

'Then I'll make it up to you.'

'You can't. You wouldn't know how. Because you've never been hurt and you've never been in love.'

'I have been hurt. When you left me. When you wouldn't

speak to me. More hurt than I thought was even possible. And you're hurting me now. And I'm letting you because I deserve it. Hurt me all you want. Any way you want. But just don't leave me, Kate.'

He came up behind her.

'Because I *am* in love. Right now. With you. First love. Last love. All in one. I'm here with my heart bleeding, aching for you, so in love I can't even find the words to tell you how much.'

She turned slowly. 'No...' she breathed. 'You don't love me.'

'Kate, if you think *anyone* else, in their wildest dreams, could have got me to watch a damned chick flick, let alone re-enact a scene from one... Well, you're insane—that's all I'm saying.'

'That was Play Time.'

He glared at her. Shouted. 'Newsflash, Kate. I. Hate. Play. Time. *Hate* it. Got it?'

'Then why—'

'And if you think rolling around in the surf like a lunatic is my idea of a sexual fantasy, you are wide of the mark, my girl. I've got sand in every nook and cranny of my body and it's bloody uncomfortable. A piece of seaweed is sticking somewhere I don't even want to think about—it may require medical intervention to get it extricated. And it's driving me nuts. But you know what? I will go back and roll around in that surf until we shrivel into prunes—with salt water pouring out of my ears, and snot streaming out of my nose, and that surfer out there laughing himself into convulsions, if it's what you want. Hell, I'll take you to Hawaii and we'll try it on the original beach!'

'I didn't *ask* you to roll in the surf!' Kate shouted back.

'You didn't have to ask! I did it because I'm not good with words, so I had to *do* something. I watched that movie for you. I'm on this beach because I love you. I *love* you! And, so help me God, if you don't call that weasel Phillip and tell him to back the hell away and stay the hell away, I am going to *kidnap* you.'

'Kidnap me?' she sputtered.

'On the yacht I bought.'

'You bought a yacht?'

'And I bought *music*—so I can dance with you on it. And I'm going to teach you to sail, and take you to the Whitsundays, and…and… What's so funny?'

'You,' Kate said, and laughed so hard she dropped to her knees. 'The way you said "m-music". Like it was p-poison.'

'Kate,' he said dangerously, 'you *do* realise how many women would swoon to have me tell them I love them, right? But you're the only one I'm ever, *ever* going to say it to.'

'Egomaniac,' Kate said, and kept laughing.

'It's not funny.'

'No, it's not. It's a serious condition, egomania,' she said, and laughed again.

Pause. He was confused. But…hopeful.

'Is laughter…? Is it good under these circumstances?' he asked tentatively.

'Accedas ad curiam.'

'Yeah, smartarse—going to need a translation,' he said, but a smile had started to stretch his mouth and he could feel it—*feel* it!—in his eyes too.

'You may approach the court,' she said. 'That's all I will say for now. And, Scott—just so you know—I have sand in every nook and cranny too.'

'Well, I think I'm going to have to take a look at your crannies, in that case,' Scott said, and dropped to his knees beside her.

He kissed her, long and hard, until they were both breathless.

'Are you going to take me to see your yacht?'

'It's not a *yacht*—it's a Jeanneau 36. If you're going to be a sailor you need to know these things.'

'Does it have a name? Like…you know…a *real* name?'

'It does,' Scott said, and started laughing.

'Which is?'

'Which is…drumroll…*Scottsdale*.'

Kate started laughing again and it reminded Scott of that night—the awards dinner—when they'd laughed about Knightley and he'd wanted her more than he'd wanted to breathe. He should have known right then that she was meant to be his. That she *would* be his.

'Wait until Hugo hears I've copied *him* for once,' Scott said, and then he stopped. Cleared his throat. 'Kate, just one thing… About my family…'

'That would be me,' she said softly. 'Just me.'

'Oh, God, Kate, I love you,' he said, and pulled her down to lie with him on the sand again. 'But you have to know that I have a bit of a conservative streak, like all the Knights.'

'You don't say?'

'So…divorce parties, break-ups, custody battles… They don't apply to us.'

'Don't they?'

'Because Knights don't divorce. And I will not let you go.' He stopped to kiss her. 'If you try to end it I'll make your life hell. I will fight tooth and nail—move heaven and hell and everything, *everything*, in between—to keep you. Exactly the way *you* fight. To the death. So better not to go there. You get all freaked out when marriages end badly. We don't want you stressing.'

'No more stress. Got it. But…Scott? Was that a proposal? Because we're not exactly marriage-minded in my family.'

'But I am. And, sorry to break it to you, but I have to be married to the mother of my children—conservative, I'm telling you, I hope your mother is going to cope. And one more thing. You're not getting any younger, so we'll have to get cracking on the kid thing.'

With that, Kate pushed him away, got to her feet, ripped her T-shirt over her head. 'My *age*? Are you seriously going there? Because if you are we're going another round of *From Here to Eternity*.'

Scott didn't argue. He simply stood up and took off his clothes. And then he turned to Kate and held out his hand. 'Or, as we like to say in legal circles, *ad infinitum*,' he said. 'Which means—'

'Forever.'

And then Scott grinned. 'Okay, let's put on a show for the surfer dude, and see how much more sand we can pack into our nooks and crannies.'

* * * * *

THE TYCOON'S
SCANDALOUS
PROPOSITION

MIRANDA LEE

CHAPTER ONE

BLAKE STOOD NEXT to the groom, wondering what the hell he was doing, being best man at this wedding. He knew this marriage wouldn't last—knew it was just a matter of time.

He'd tried to reason with Lachlan. But nothing could dissuade him. Not even Blake's argument that he himself had married at the same age—twenty-four—and the marriage hadn't lasted six months.

At least the bride wasn't an actress, Blake reasoned more positively. Also on the plus side, it wasn't as though marriage—even a temporary one—harmed a movie star's popularity these days. Gone were the days when the power-brokers of Hollywood had dictated who a star could marry. *And* when.

The rise of social media had changed all that. The public couldn't get enough of celebrity relationships. They especially enjoyed break-ups and divorces, and any whiff of scandal. Such was life in the spotlight.

Thankfully Blake's own life wasn't so much in the spotlight—though he'd gained a little more attention in the press since moving Fantasy Productions from Sydney to LA fifteen months ago. Still, movie-makers—even very successful, very wealthy ones like himself—didn't grab the headlines the way actors did. Especially those like Lachlan, with his golden boy looks, buffed body and bedroom blue eyes. Add to that buckets of boyish charm and you had a prize publicity package.

Blake had first recognised Lachlan's potential when he'd attended a performance at Australia's much lauded National Institute of Dramatic Art a few years ago. He'd instantly signed him up. And the rest, as they said, was history. Three years and four movies later Lachlan was an established star, whilst *he'd* become Australia's most successful film writer/director/producer.

Blake suspected, however, that their working relationship would not last for much longer. It was only a matter of time before something—like this marriage—would make his star move on.

'There she is,' Lachlan whispered suddenly, snapping Blake out of his cynical thoughts.

Blake followed the groom's enthralled gaze past the seated guests and up the sweeping staircase down which the bride would eventually descend, and into the large living area, which had been filled with several rows of chairs divided by a strip of red carpet.

Blake spied a froth of white up on the gallery landing. White dress, white hair, white flowers. Behind the bride, attending to the long white veil, bustled the one and only bridesmaid, wearing something long and svelte in jade-green. Blake couldn't see her properly—didn't have a clue who she was. He hadn't even met the bride, having been too busy with his latest movie, plus several other new projects, to fly back to Australia for Lachlan's engagement party, and only jetting in to Sydney late last night.

The only contribution Blake had made to this wedding had been getting billionaire Byron Maddox—who was a good friend as well as a business partner—to offer his very lovely harbour-side home as a venue for the wedding and the reception afterwards.

The original venue had rather inconveniently burnt down six weeks ago, throwing Lachlan into a panic after getting a phone call on location from his hysterical bride-to-be.

Thank heaven for rich friends, Blake thought, and threw Byron and Cleo a grateful glance.

When they smiled back at him his own face cracked open into a wide smile. God, but they were a great couple.

If ever a man and woman were made for each other it was those two. They almost made him believe in true love.

Finally some music started up. Not a traditional bridal march but a rather romantic piano rendition of 'The First Time Ever I Saw Your Face'.

It was at that moment that the bridesmaid in jade-green moved round from behind the Barbie doll bride and came into full view.

Blake's dark eyebrows lifted in surprise. She wasn't a stunner. But she was extremely attractive. Tall, with a slender figure and pale skin which suited the off-the-shoulder style of her gown. Her hair was a golden-brown colour, drawn straight back from her high forehead and falling in a softly waved curtain down her back, held in place by a simple circlet of pink and white flowers. It was her face, however, which Blake kept returning to—a face any camera would love.

Blake had a habit of looking at faces as though through a lens, especially on a first meeting. It was a long-ingrained habit, and one which didn't do any harm, really. No one knew what he was thinking at the time, so Blake didn't feel any guilt as he continued to assess the bridesmaid's looks from every camera angle.

He knew from experience that high cheekbones and a well-defined jawline photographed well in any light and from any angle. This woman's nose wasn't starlet-small, but it suited her, giving her face character. She didn't have pouting bee-stung lips either, although it was all the fad these days. Her mouth was actually rather wide, but still well formed. And expressive. So were her almond-shaped eyes.

Blake frowned as he tried to fathom the reason behind the sadness he kept glimpsing within their dark brown depths as she made her way slowly—and stiffly—down the staircase. Along with the sadness lay undeniable tension, he noted. Her knuckles were white as she clasped the posy of pink and white flowers at her waist with unnecessary force.

At last she reached the bottom step. It was at this point that she sucked in a deep breath, as though trying to gather all her courage. The gesture touched him, evoking an uncharacteristic surge of compassion. Something was bothering that girl about this wedding—something much more emotional and personal than Blake's cynical view.

'Who's the bridesmaid?' Blake muttered under his breath, so that only Lachlan could hear.

'What? Oh, that's Kate. Maddie's sister.'

'Older sister?'

'Older? Yeah. God, doesn't Maddie look incredible?' he exclaimed, clearly awed by the beauty of his bride, who remained standing at the top of the staircase, all eyes on her.

Not Blake's, however. He'd had his fill of Barbie doll blondes—especially those manufactured in Hollywood by plastic surgeons and ambitious mamas. His eyes were all for the bridesmaid, with her natural-looking figure and lovely but oh, so sad eyes.

Her chin lifted as she took her first step along the makeshift aisle, her focus straight ahead during what seemed to be a very difficult journey for her. She didn't look at him, or at Lachlan, or at any of the guests. She seemed frozen now—a robot with no feelings on show any more. But that didn't mean they weren't there.

Smile, sweetheart, came the sudden wish from deep inside Blake. *Don't let the world see that you're hurting. Don't give people the chance to hurt you further.*

And they would if she let them. People could be cruel—especially once they'd sensed weakness. Fortunately, no one was looking at her. All eyes were still on the beaming bride, who was now approaching the bottom of the staircase. The music changed to 'Isn't She Beautiful?' Which the bride was. Even Blake had to agree that Maddie was drop-dead gorgeous. But such beauty was often only surface-deep, he'd found, the same way Lachlan's was.

The same way Claudia's was...

The thought didn't hurt him the way it once had. But that didn't mean he'd forgotten the lessons his one and only marriage had taught him.

The main one was, *Don't, for pity's sake, believe anything that ambitious young actresses do or say to you. Sleep with them, by all means, but don't fall for their flattery or their brilliant fakery. And never marry one. Lord, no.*

In truth, marriage was not for him—even with a non-ambitious non-actress. Not yet, anyway. Aside from his scepticism over the lasting power of romantic love, he wasn't good husband material. He was way too obsessed with making movies, working seven days a week, often twenty hours a day. What time did that leave for a wife, let alone children?

Maybe when he was forty he might consider both. But he was only just thirty-two. Plenty of years left to think about such things.

Meanwhile, his attention returned to the attractive but bleak-looking bridesmaid.

Damn. She looked as if she was going to cry now. Her bottom lip was definitely quivering, accompanied by a flash of true panic in her eyes. Clearly she didn't *want* to cry. Just in time she got control of herself, her nostrils flaring as she sucked in another deep, desperate breath.

Blake wondered what on earth was going on in that girl's mind. He knew that women often cried at weddings, but they were usually tears of happiness. He could be wrong, he supposed, but he was absolutely certain that whatever she was thinking they weren't happy thoughts!

Maybe this Kate knew what sort of man her kid sister was marrying—knew that he was a player. Maybe she feared for Maddie's future happiness. Well, she had a right to be scared on *that* particular score! Not that he could be a hundred percent positive that was the reason behind her grim face. He could only guess.

In actual fact Blake often found himself speculating on the various emotions he noted on the faces of perfect strangers. He was a people-watcher—an essential talent for a writer-cum-movie-maker. After all, motivations and emotional conflicts were the backbone of all storytelling.

His gaze returned to Kate's stiffly held face and robotic walk. At last she reached the end of the aisle, flashing him a frowning glance before moving sideways to her left, where no one could see her face except the celebrant. And *he* was busy ogling the bride. Now all Blake could see was her profile. Her head and shoulders drooped for a split second, then lifted abruptly, the muscles in her throat standing out as she once again took rigid control of herself.

His heart went out to her. As did his admiration. Whatever was bothering the bride's sister, she was a brave soul. Brave, but still rather fragile.

When the posy of flowers she was holding began to shake Blake determined not to let the evening end before he found out what was upsetting her so much. He could be charming when he wanted to be. And quite good at getting people to open up. Yes, he would worm the truth out of her. Women did love to confide. And hopefully, sooner rather than later, he would bring a smile to her face.

He imagined she would be quite lovely if she smiled. Already Blake found her attractive. And intriguing. And extremely desirable.

Much more desirable than the Barbie doll bride.

CHAPTER TWO

KATE GRITTED HER TEETH, still stunned at how much she was hating this, how sick she felt to her stomach. Yet she'd known for ages that this day was coming. She'd had plenty of time to prepare herself mentally. All to no avail, it seemed.

She clasped her bouquet even tighter and willed her mind to go blank. But her mind refused to obey. It whirled on and on, tormenting her. *Torturing* her.

Because today was the end of the line, wasn't it?

The end of all her hopes and dreams where Lachlan was concerned. Today the man she loved would marry her sister. And that would be that. No more stupidly hoping that he might wake up one morning and realise Maddie wasn't right for him and that *she* was a much more suitable wife. No more fantasising—as she had during their three years studying together at NIDA—that he might finally see her as a potential girlfriend and not just as his good mate and acting buddy.

There was nothing worse, she realised, than the death of hope.

Kate sighed, stiffening when she realised just how loud that sigh had been. As much as she was wretched to her core, she'd determined earlier today not to let anyone— particularly Maddie—suspect the truth. And she'd managed—'til the moment that sickening music had started up and she'd had to step into the spotlight on those stairs. At which point she'd frozen, the sheer futility of her feelings washing through her.

She knew she should have smiled but she simply hadn't been able to. Not that it had mattered. No one had been looking at her. No one except the man standing next to Lachlan. Blake Randall, the best man.

He had kept on looking at her. And frowning at her. Wondering, probably, why she looked so forlorn.

Kate would have liked to tell him why—would have liked to scream that if it hadn't been for *him* all their lives would have taken a different course and she wouldn't be standing here today, having her heart broken.

A slight exaggeration, Kate. Your heart was broken last Christmas, when you optimistically brought Lachlan home for dinner.

They'd both just graduated from NIDA, and Lachlan's parents had gone away on a Christmas cruise. Plus he'd been between girlfriends at the time. Which hadn't happened too often. She'd thought it was her chance to snare his sexual interest. And it had seemed at first that she had. Lachlan had actually flirted with her in the car during their drive from his flat at Bondi to her parents' home at Strathfield.

But all that had changed the moment he'd met her very beautiful and very vivacious blonde sister.

Something had died in Kate when she'd seen how quickly and easily Maddie had captured Lachlan's sexual interest. By the end of Christmas dinner Maddie's almost-fiancé had been firmly dispensed with and she'd gone off with Lachlan, moving in with him the very next day.

So, in reality, Kate had had ten months to get over her broken heart. Ten long, soul-destroying months during which her own acting career had stalled and she'd been reduced to working weekends in a local deli whilst going to endless auditions during the week.

If she hadn't been living at home she wouldn't have survived. The only acting job she'd managed to snare in that time had been a part in a play. It had been quite a good part, too. But the play hadn't proved commercial or popular at the box office. Despite garnering reasonable reviews, it had closed after six weeks.

She'd tried out for various movies and television shows, but had so far been unsuccessful, usually being told that she wasn't 'quite right' for that particular part; didn't have the 'right look'—or the right height, or the right something. Sometimes she wasn't given a reason at all. Her agent said she needed to be more positive when meeting producers and directors, but any positivity she'd possessed seemed to have disintegrated.

In truth, Kate had always been on the shy side, with social skills not her strong point. The only time she felt truly confident was when she was in character, playing an outgoing role. Then she *exuded* confidence. If only she could be more like Maddie, whose social skills were second to none and whose confidence was out of this world.

A nudge at her elbow snapped her out of her thoughts, and Kate turned to see Maddie glaring at her before shoving her bouquet into her hands. The glare disappeared once she'd turned back to beam at the male celebrant. Kate felt a sudden urge to throw the bridal bouquet onto the floor and stamp on it.

She didn't, of course. But the unexpected burst of anger did achieve something, shoving aside her self-pity and replacing it with a determination to stop letting unrequited love ruin her life. It was way past time for her to get over Lachlan and move on.

Steeling herself, Kate turned her body to the right in order to watch the ceremony, seeing immediately that Blake Randall had done the same and was looking straight at her. No, he was *staring* at her, as if he was trying to work out what was going on in her head.

If she told him he would probably laugh. Whilst she'd never actually met the man, she'd seen him interviewed on television several times. Despite having made a career—

and loads of money—making movies about love and romance, he'd come across as a cynic about both, stating bluntly on one occasion that he was just giving the audience what they wanted.

Of course he had been a popular topic of conversation amongst the students at NIDA—especially after making Lachlan into a star. Kate knew Blake Randall had been married once to Claudia Jay, an Australian actress who'd starred in one of his early films. The marriage hadn't lasted long, and Claudia had claimed her new husband had neglected her shamefully once the honeymoon was over. Kate suspected there was more to their divorce than met the eye, Claudia having moved to Hollywood soon after the breakup.

She didn't feel sorry for either of them. They were both tarred with the same brush, in her opinion. Both of them ruthlessly ambitious, leaving little room to really love anyone other than themselves. Blake had gone from strength to strength after his divorce, whilst Claudia had gone on to have a successful career in Hollywood, her name linked with a succession of high-flying producers and directors.

Kate herself didn't dream of Hollywood success. Or necessarily of being in movies. She loved acting on the stage most of all. But she wouldn't knock back a decent role in a movie or a television series. *If* she was ever offered one.

Kate was about to sigh again when she remembered her agent's advice to be more positive. And a little more proactive. It occurred to her that any other aspiring actor would take advantage of being in a wedding party opposite a brilliant movie-maker like Blake Randall. She shouldn't be ignoring his interested glances. She certainly shouldn't be standing around looking like a wet weekend and sighing all the time. She should be making the most of this rather amazing opportunity by smiling and flirting and projecting Little Miss Confident and Available, not Little Miss Miserable and Vulnerable.

All she had to do was pretend. No, *act*. She *was* an actor, wasn't she?

But it was no use. She simply couldn't summon up a smile. Maybe if he'd been more pleasant and approachable-looking she might have managed it. But his looks matched his reputation as a demanding tyrant to work for. He had gleaming black hair—worn unfashionably long. Thick black brows. Deeply set piercing blue eyes. An arrogant aquiline nose. Slightly hollow cheeks. And a rather cruel-looking mouth.

The press described him as 'handsome'. Kate thought him scary-looking. And very intimidating.

She was in the process of abandoning any idea of even *talking* to him later when he smiled at her. Just a small smile, really—a slight lifting of the corners of his mouth—but it was accompanied by a wicked twinkle in his eyes. They did strange things to her, that smile and that twinkle. Made her feel more confident. And quite sexy. Which was astonishing given her libido seemed to have died ten months ago, along with her heart.

Before she could think better of it she smiled back. A small smile and possibly without any accompanying twinkle. But it was a start. His smile widened, his eyebrows lifting, taking away his scariness and making him look quite handsome. Not handsome the way Lachlan was handsome—but then, no man Kate had ever met was *that* handsome.

He mouthed something at her and she frowned, not sure what he was saying. He repeated it more slowly and she finally understood the words.

You...look...lovely.

Kate honestly didn't know how to react, blinking her surprise before looking away. She wasn't used to men of

Blake Randall's ilk coming on to her. They went for the Maddies of this world. Or for stunning actresses like Claudia Jay. Admittedly she looked the very best she could today—thanks to Maddie and her mother bullying her into hours of work at the beauty salon—but she doubted she could compete with the sort of women who usually vied for this man's attention.

Kate was still trying to work out how to respond when there was a burst of applause behind her. Kate was taken aback to realise that the ceremony was over, and Lachlan and her sister were now legally man and wife.

She waited for a jab of devastation to overwhelm her but it didn't come. Instead all she could think about was Blake Randall flirting with her.

How odd.

There was Maddie in Lachlan's arms, being kissed very thoroughly, and even whilst she couldn't bear to watch at the same time it made her wonder what it would be like to be kissed by that hard, cruel mouth which was once again smiling at her. No, *grinning* at her.

It was infectious, that grin, as was the wry gleam in his eyes as he nodded his head towards the couple who were still locked together in an exhibitionist kiss.

Without thinking this time, she grinned back, and suddenly lightness lifted her previously heavy soul, making her see that there was definitely life after Lachlan.

How silly she'd been to imagine that the world had stopped turning simply because the man she loved did not love her back. There was still plenty to live for. Her career, for starters. Kate adored acting—loved inhabiting another character's skin and making her audience believe that she really was that person. It was the ultimate high when she pulled that off. The ultimate adrenaline rush.

The besotted couple finally wrenched themselves apart, and a flushed Maddie turned to Kate to retrieve her bouquet.

'What a pity Lachlan and I can't leave right now,' her sister grumbled. 'I can hardly wait I'm so turned on. Oh, God, don't look at me like that, Katie,' she hissed impatiently. 'You know how much I like sex. And my Lachlan is just the *best* at it.'

Kate smothered a groan of despair. Or was it disgust? Whatever it was, that feeling of devastation she'd so valiantly pushed aside was back with a vengeance.

CHAPTER THREE

OH-OH.

Disappointment swamped Blake as he caught sight of Kate again, her face having been obscured by the bride turning to collect her bouquet. Gone was her lovely smile, and in its place her former bleak expression.

What the hell had happened in the last few seconds? What had the Barbie doll said to her? Something not very nice, judging by the unhappiness in Kate's eyes.

Blake knew from first-hand experience that siblings were not always the best of friends—especially those of the same sex. Rivalry and jealousy often raised their ugly heads, making true friendship impossible. His own brother was a case in point. James had always been jealous of him, despite there being absolutely no need. James was the first-born son, after all, and his parents' favourite—especially since he'd followed in his mother and father's footsteps to become a doctor, like them.

On the other hand Blake had been regarded as the black sheep of the family since he hadn't even gone to university, since he'd done something considered very left field by embracing the entertainment world—first as a DJ, then shooting music videos for a couple of years before finally plunging full-time into making low-budget independent movies.

Both his parents and his brother had given him dire warnings about his future. And Blake found it telling that now he'd made it big they were all hurtfully silent on the subject of his success. Blake had used to let it bother him, but he no longer cared. Or so he told himself. They all had small minds, in his opinion, James the smallest of them all.

Blake rarely saw his family these days, only visiting at Christmas and on special occasions. Now that he'd moved to Los Angeles to live and work he suspected he might not even do that. Just send the occasional card. He no longer kept in contact through social media or email, nor with phone calls, having resolved not to give them any further opportunity to deliver snide remarks about his lifestyle or his movies. Which they did, if given the opportunity.

Blake had no evidence that Kate's sister had just made some kind of nasty remark to her except for the look on her face. But that wasn't jealousy he was seeing in her expressive blue eyes. It was hurt. And dismay.

Why her unhappiness bothered him so much he could not fathom. He'd never been a particularly empathetic soul. Perhaps it was because he found her attractive and didn't like the idea of there being some hidden impediment which would hinder his pursuing his interest in her. Whatever the reason, Blake resolved not to rest until he'd solved the mystery of that unhappiness.

And it *was* a mystery. Because on the surface of things Kate had nothing to be unhappy about. She was gorgeous! Okay, she didn't have the in-your-face blonde beauty of her sister. But she was still highly desirable.

Of course being physically attractive was no guarantee of happiness. Maybe she was unhappy because she was still unmarried, despite being the older sister. Though not much older, surely. Blake knew Lachlan's bride was only twenty-three, which made Kate what? Twenty-five? Twenty-six, maybe? Hardly a marital use-by date in this day and age.

'Get with the programme, Blake,' Lachlan said, grabbing his nearest elbow. 'We have to sign the marriage certificate.'

As the groom ushered him over to where the paperwork had been set up on a side table Blake cast a surreptitious glance back at Kate. She seemed to have gathered herself, and her expression was not wretched any longer. It was, however, utterly devoid of emotion once more—a totally blank mask. How on earth did she manage that? When *he* was upset everyone knew about it. He didn't throw tantrums, exactly, but his face always reflected his feelings— as did his voice.

He watched her watching the happy couple sign the register, but her eyes betrayed nothing now. Which was telling in itself.

When it was their turn to step forward as witnesses, he waved for her to go first. After throwing him a closed look, she picked up one of the provided pens and signed quickly, with only the slightest tremor in her hand. He glanced at her signature before he signed his own name.

Kate Holiday, he read, and realised that until that moment he hadn't known the bride's surname. So of course he hadn't known Kate's. He'd never met the bride's parents either, or anyone else in her family. Strange, really, given he was the best man.

Blake wondered all of a sudden why Lachlan had asked *him* to be his best man. He would have thought a young Aussie male with his looks and personality would have had at least one best mate—a pal he'd gone to school with or studied at NIDA with.

Obviously not. Either that or he preferred someone famous to stand by his side at his wedding. A celebrity. Lachlan was very much into celebrity.

It hadn't occurred to Blake until that moment that he was being used—that this wedding was little more than a publicity stunt, with a trophy bride, a glamorous Sydney setting and a rich and famous best man. Lachlan was no better than Claudia, really.

Whilst the thought did bring a sour note to the proceedings Blake knew he would have the last laugh. Because in actual fact Lachlan wasn't so great an actor, and his range was decidedly limited. Once he was seduced by the big boys in Hollywood and started making movies that weren't tailored to his specific brand of looks and charm his career might very well sink like a stone. Major studios were very unforgiving once the box office results rolled in. Lachlan's past successes in Blake's movies would not carry him for ever.

A slight smirk curved his top lip as he put his signature to the marriage certificate. It was still there when he put the pen down and turned to face his intriguing partner.

'So, Kate Holiday,' he said, doing his best to hide his underlying irritation, 'we haven't been properly introduced. But I dare say you know who I am.'

'Yes, of course I do,' Kate said. 'Lachlan has spoken of you a lot.'

'Well, you have one up on me, then—because he's told me nothing about you.'

She seemed quite taken aback. 'You mean he's never mentioned that we were students together at NIDA? We were in the same class,' she went on, obviously peeved. 'We graduated together last year.'

'Sorry. He's never mentioned it,' he told her, doing his best to get his head around this news.

Kate was an *actress*! Who would have believed it? Still, it went some way to explaining her ability to hide her emotions. Though she wasn't hiding them at the moment. She was looking decidedly upset. On his part, he was just perplexed.

Why hadn't Lachlan told him that his future sister-in-law had been at NIDA with him? He knew Blake held an enormous respect for their graduates. On top of that, he was always on the lookout for fresh talent—especially actors with Kate's unique and very interesting face.

He wondered if Lachlan was jealous of her acting talent. That would be just like him. He would hate anyone to steal his thunder. Narcissistic devil!

'All I know is that you're Maddie's older sister,' he admitted. 'I don't even know how much older.'

'I'm twenty-five,' she confessed, almost as if it was a crime.

Twenty-five was a good age for an actress, he thought. And for other things...

Finding out that Kate was an actress didn't dampen his desire for her in any way. If anything, it increased it—along with his sudden resolve to help her career in any way he could. Blake suspected it might not have taken off, since he'd never heard of Kate Holiday. And he would have if she'd done anything of note. Blake had his finger on the pulse where rising stars were concerned.

Just then they were shepherded outside by the photographer—a rather officious fellow who was very full of himself.

'So, what have you been in lately?' he asked her as they trailed past the huge marquee which had been set up in the gorgeous grounds of Byron's home. 'Anything I might have seen?'

'I doubt it,' she said. 'I was in a play earlier this year, but it closed rather quickly. I was brilliant, of course,' Kate added, throwing a self-deprecating smile his way. 'But not brilliant enough, apparently. One of the reviews said I was "very decorative".'

Blake laughed. 'Which you are,' he said. 'Very.'

She looked startled, her high cheekbones pinkening a little. Acting? he wondered. Or was she genuinely taken aback by his compliment? Blake decided he didn't care either way. She enchanted him. And intrigued him. He was going to enjoy finding out more about her this evening, and at the same time putting a spoke in Lachlan's ego by giving her career a boost.

He would offer her a part in one of his upcoming movies. Nothing too large. She was an unknown, after all.

Of course Blake anticipated that his offer to help her out would come with the bonus of taking her to bed in the fore-seeable future. Which he very much wanted to do. More so than he had in a long while. Whilst sex was something he enjoyed, he wasn't a sex addict. He could do without—especially when he was working long hours. Which he had been for several weeks now, finishing up Lachlan's latest movie and getting it ready for distribution.

Possibly this longish stint of celibacy was responsible for the rather urgent wave of desire he was currently ex-periencing. Hopefully there wasn't any extraneous rea-son why Kate shouldn't respond to his pursuit. The only hurdle he could think of was a boyfriend in the wings. Or, worse, a fiancé.

A swift glance at her left hand detected a total absence of rings.

Good. A boyfriend he could handle, but a fiancé was another matter entirely.

'I am *so* going to hate these photographs,' Kate mut-tered when the photographer started giving them orders.

'I don't know why,' he commented as they were force-fully arranged in a group in the well-lit gazebo, with the harbour and the bridge in the background. 'With your bone structure I bet you're very photogenic.'

Even if she wasn't the best actress in the world, she would look good on screen. Blake felt confident that the camera would love her.

'It's very nice of you to say so.'

'Not at all. It's the truth. I never say things just to be nice.'

Not until tonight, that is. For some weird and wonderful reason Blake felt uncharacteristically compelled to be nice to Kate. *Very* nice. And it wasn't just because he wanted to have sex with her. Right from the first moment he'd set eyes on her sad-looking self she'd brought out the gallant in him. Which was unusual. Because a white knight with women Blake was *not*—especially since Claudia's betrayal.

Quite frankly he could be a bit of a bastard where the opposite sex was concerned. Especially if the girl was an ambitious young actress who made it obvious when they met that she was his for the taking—not because of a genuine attraction but because sleeping with him would further her career.

Kate was different, though. A different sort of girl. A different sort of actress.

He'd given her every opportunity to flirt with him. And flatter him. But she'd done neither. He liked that. He liked that a lot.

'Would the bridesmaid please *smile*?' the photographer snapped impatiently. 'This is a wedding, not a funeral.'

CHAPTER FOUR

BUT IT IS a funeral, Kate wanted to wail. It was the death of her dream to marry Lachlan herself one day.

A stupid dream, really. Stupid and futile—especially once he'd met Maddie.

Of course she should never have taken him home. But she'd honestly thought it would be safe, with Maddie practically engaged. How had she been supposed to know that they would take one look at each other and fall head over heels in love?

Well, you should have known, you idiot!

Not that it would have made any difference.

Get real, you fool. Even before he met Maddie Lachlan had three years to notice you in that way. But he didn't and he never would have! You're not his type—which is blonde and beautiful, with buckets of self-esteem and a sense of self-entitlement to rival royalty. Somehow that description doesn't fit you, dear heart. Not even remotely.

A very strong male arm suddenly wound around her waist, pulling her firmly against his side and propelling Kate out of her self-pitying thoughts. Glancing up at Blake, she encountered narrowed blue eyes giving her a warning look.

'If you don't start smiling properly,' he whispered into her ear, 'I'll start thinking you can't act your way out of a paper bag.'

Kate blinked, then swallowed and straightened her spine—after which she rewarded him with a beaming smile. Because no way did she want Blake Randall thinking she couldn't act. Hadn't she resolved earlier to try to use the opportunity of meeting him to her advantage? It would be utterly foolish to ignore a man of his influence and contacts. If she couldn't have Lachlan's love, then at least she could have a career.

'That's better,' he said, smiling down at her.

Her spirits lifted again, as they had earlier when he'd smiled at her. Kate couldn't quite understand why he was as interested in her as he seemed to be—but who was she to look a gift horse in the mouth?

The photos were still a trial—especially when she and Blake mostly had to stand to one side and witness Maddie and Lachlan having endless shots taken of just the two of them in all sorts of romantic poses and clinches.

Maddie had confessed to Kate that morning that they'd already sold their wedding photos to a well-known tabloid—which wasn't surprising. Her sister was very money-hungry. Celebrity-hungry, too. They were certainly a well-matched couple in that regard; Kate was well aware of Lachlan's love of fame.

She winced as she watched him kiss his blushing bride for the umpteenth time.

If she'd been alone with Blake, Kate might have been able to distract herself by chatting about movies. But, no, fate wasn't going to be that kind. Her parents were now hurrying over to them, demanding to be introduced, and gushing like mad over the bride and groom.

After what felt like for ever, but was probably only a few minutes, Blake suddenly took her arm and said, 'You must excuse us, folks, but we really have to speak to Byron ASAP.'

He didn't explain further, just swept a relieved Kate away.

'Are they always like that?' he growled as he snatched two glasses of champagne from a passing waiter, pressing one into Kate's hand.

'Like what?'

'Raving about your sister like she's a bloody princess. They never said a word about how gorgeous *you* look. It was all about Maddie—Little Miss Perfect and oh, so clever to have snared herself a husband like Lachlan.' He snorted at that. 'They won't be saying that in a couple of years' time.'

'What do you mean?' she asked, a little flustered by his saying *she* looked gorgeous.

'Damn it,' he said, gulping his glass of champagne before giving her a slightly sheepish look. 'I probably shouldn't be saying this. Though maybe you already suspect?'

'Suspect what?'

'That where the opposite sex is concerned Lachlan is a rat. No, more of a cat. A tom cat. He can't keep it in his pants for long. Trust me when I say that being married won't stop him from sleeping around. I walked in on him having sex with a make-up girl just a few weeks ago. Long after his engagement to your sister.'

Possibly Kate shouldn't have been shocked—Lachlan had garnered quite a reputation during his years at NIDA—but she was.

'Poor Maddie,' she said, and downed half of her glass of champagne.

'I agree with you. If she truly loves Lachlan then she's in for a bumpy road.'

What an odd thing to say, Kate thought. *If she truly loves him.* Of course Maddie truly loved him. Lachlan was the sort of man who inspired love. Every time Kate looked at him she felt that tightening in her stomach, that wave of longing. So nowadays she tried not to look at him. It was easier that way.

She did go and see his movies, though. Which was the worst form of masochism since they were all love stories and always had at least one sex scene. But she simply could not resist.

'Is that why you were upset earlier?' Byron asked her. 'Because you're worried about your sister's future happiness?'

Kate stared up into his deeply set blue eyes, which held a surprisingly sympathetic expression at that moment. And there she'd been, believing he was some kind of ruthless bastard. Not so, it seemed.

'Yes,' she lied, for how could she tell him that it was her own future happiness that had been worrying her?

He reached out to touch her wrist lightly. 'No point in worrying about other people's marriages. What will be will be.'

Kate didn't know what to think. Her thoughts were somewhat scattered. How could Lachlan do something like that? It had certainly tarnished her opinion of him. Not her love, however. That didn't tarnish quite so easily.

Suddenly she frowned at Blake. 'Why did you agree to be Lachlan's best man when it's obvious you don't like him very much?'

He shrugged. 'Don't get me wrong. I don't dislike Lachlan. He's not a bad fellow. Just weak when it comes to women throwing themselves at him. Which they do. All the time. Look, he asked me to be his best man and I said yes. Call it a business move rather than a measure of close friendship. The publicity will be good for our next movie, which should be coming out in the New Year. Too late, unfortunately, to be up for any awards this year, but I couldn't get it edited and distributed any earlier.'

'I see. And is that also why you organised for the wedding to be held here? For the added publicity?'

'No. I didn't think of that at the time. When the other venue burnt down we still had a couple of weeks' shooting to complete in Hawaii, and I couldn't afford for my leading man to keep getting hysterical phone calls from his fiancée. So I stepped in and fixed things. Now, I think they're waiting for us to go into the marquee for the reception. We'll be on the same table, but I doubt we're seated side by side—worst luck. Still, there'll be a party and dancing afterwards. Then we can talk some more.'

He put a firm hand in the small of her back and gently pushed her towards the entrance to the marquee. It felt good, that hand. Very...*reassuring*. Also very intimate.

She sneaked a quick glance up into his deep blue eyes, startled when they bored back down into hers with the sort of lustful look men usually reserved for Maddie.

The realisation that Blake Randall lusted after *her* was flattering, but also very flustering. Her whole body tightened in response, which threw her. She couldn't *possibly* lust after Blake Randall in return, could she? Surely not. She was just shocked, that was all.

And yet...

She glanced over at him again, this time focusing on his mouth and recalling how she'd wondered earlier in the proceedings what it would be like to kiss him.

Exciting, she decided, her heartbeat quickening. Exciting and risky. *Very* risky. Because he wouldn't want to stop at kissing.

Kate knew in theory that love and lust didn't have to reside together. But she'd never experienced one without the other. Which was why her very limited forays into sex had been such disasters—and why, for the last four years, she hadn't had a proper boyfriend or been to bed with anyone. How could she after falling so deeply in love with Lachlan?

Yet as she stared at Blake Randall's perversely sexy mouth she could not dismiss the notion that she just might enjoy going to bed with him despite not loving him. Not that she would. She wasn't that sort of girl. She wasn't like Maddie, who'd been jumping into men's beds at the drop of a hat since she was sixteen.

Besides, you don't really want to go to bed with him, Kate told herself firmly. *You're just flattered that he fancies you. That's what this is all about. Not true lust. Just your poor pathetic ego, desperate for someone to show some interest in you. Now, stop ogling the man and get some perspective!*

Just in time she wrenched her eyes away from his mouth. But it was too late. His lips were drawing back into a knowing smile. He'd already seen her staring at him.

'First dance is mine,' he said with a devilish twinkle in his eyes. 'Don't forget.'

Relief claimed Kate as the wedding planner bustled over to them, interrupting what was becoming an awkward situation.

Her name was Clare. She was about fifty, a sleekly attractive blonde with an air of self-importance somewhat like the photographer's. They were in business together, Maddie's mother having hired them because they were supposedly 'the best'.

'*Do* come along, Kate,' the woman said, and glanced at her watch. 'You too, Mr Randall. We are now running behind schedule.'

Blake rolled his eyes at Kate after Clare had departed to hurry up some of the other guests.

'Irritating woman,' he muttered as he steered Kate over to their table. 'Do you know she had the hide to ask to see my speech? Claimed she needed to check if it was too long.'

'How rude!'

'That's what I thought. Lord knows how people like that stay in business. Anyway, I didn't show it to her because I haven't written one. I just assured her it would be the shortest best man's speech in history. Which it will be. I detest long speeches.'

Kate gnawed at her bottom lip. 'You're not going to say anything…revealing, are you?'

'About Lachlan being a player, you mean?'

'Yes.'

'Of course not. That's not my place. My role tonight is to be complimentary and charming and funny.' Blake laughed at the doubtful look on her face. 'Don't worry. I can be all of those things when I need to be. I'm actually a very good actor myself.'

CHAPTER FIVE

BLAKE WAS AS good as his word, keeping his best man's speech very short and very witty, heaping gushing compliments on the bride and hearty praise on the groom, refraining from any of the usual tasteless *double entendres* concerning the groom's past behaviour with the opposite sex, and finishing up by toasting the happy couple with gusto.

I really am a good actor, he decided when he sat down to huge applause less than five minutes after he'd stood up. Because it had certainly gone against the grain for him to say the overly nice things he had. He hadn't lied for Lachlan's sake, of course, or for the bride, but for Kate, whom he could see had been upset by his revelation about Lachlan's lack of morals.

He regretted telling her now. It had been unnecessary. He'd achieved nothing except to increase her anxiety over the future of her sister's happiness. Clearly she was fond of her sister, despite her parents' obvious favouritism for the younger girl.

He cringed when he recalled the father of the bride's over-effusive speech about his perfect younger daughter. It had been sick-making. If he'd been Kate he would have walked out. Or thrown something at him. But she'd just sat there, sipping champagne and smiling, even laughing at some of her father's gushing stories about Maddie as a little girl.

She was an incredibly generous and sweet-natured soul. Odd, given her chosen career. Aspiring actresses were rarely sweet. Unless they were faking it. And Blake felt confident she wasn't.

He smiled when he thought of her smallish breasts and her lack of false eyelashes. No. Nothing fake about Kate Holiday.

Which was one of the reasons he found her so attractive.

She found him attractive too.

Blake was an expert in female body language, and he'd noticed her reaction to his none-too-subtle compliments. She liked them, but didn't quite know how to react to them. Didn't seem to know how to flirt.

Not like her sister. He might not have met the bride before, but he'd seen her in action tonight—both with the celebrant and the photographer and also himself, to a degree. Not that she'd actually said anything to him yet. There'd been no opportunity. But she'd fluttered her false eyelashes at him whenever she'd had a chance, her smile both sweetly coy and smoulderingly sexy at the same time.

She was a piece of work, all right. Lachlan just might have met his match with Maddie Holiday.

Finally the interminable meal and the speeches were over and the happy couple rose, leaving the table to go and cut their three-tiered wedding cake.

Blake immediately moved into the bride's vacant chair so that he could talk to Kate. 'So what did you think?' he asked her on a teasing note. 'Did my speech meet with your approval?'

She smiled at him, her expression wry. 'You're right. You're a *very* good actor. You didn't mean a single word of it, did you?'

'I meant the bit I slipped in about the beautiful bridesmaid. I didn't think the groom complimented you enough in his speech. Now, the dancing will start soon. I've been to a few weddings in my time, so I know the routine. First the bride and groom will do the bridal waltz, and then we'll all be invited to join them on the dance floor.'

'Yes, I know,' she said. 'I have been to the odd wedding or two as well. Though never as a bridesmaid.'

'Never?' That surprised him, given her age and her niceness. 'But you must have loads of girlfriends. Haven't any of them got married yet?'

'Actually, no,' she said.

'No, you haven't got loads of girlfriends? Or no, none of them have got married yet?'

'I do have a few girlfriends from my years at NIDA, but no one so close that they would ask me to be a bridesmaid.'

'What about from school?'

'No. I wasn't popular at school. I was considered a nerd. And not very cool.'

'I find that hard to believe,' he said, but he was lying.

He could see that she was on the reserved, rather introverted side. *He'd* been very popular at school—perhaps because he'd been a rebel. There was no rebel in Kate. Not a great deal of confidence, either. How on earth did she expect to succeed as an actress if she didn't exude confidence?

Still, she had *him* to help her now. She just didn't know it yet. It was probably not the right time or place to offer her a part in one of his movies tonight. Or to try to seduce her, either.

But he couldn't let the grass grow under his feet. He was flying back to LA in a few days. And Blake had no intention of going back without having some delicious sex with this delightful creature, as well as giving her career a much-needed boost.

He would invite her out to dinner tomorrow night. Somewhere seriously good. After which he would take her back to the city penthouse he was staying in. It belonged to Byron, but he wasn't using it much now that he'd moved into this absolutely gorgeous harbour-side mansion.

'What about boyfriends?' he asked, wanting to know

the lie of the land before he got his hopes up too high. Not that a boyfriend would stop him now. The more time he spent with Kate the more he wanted her.

'What?' she said, blinking up at him.

God, she did have lovely eyes. And so expressive. Perfect for the camera.

'You said you don't have loads of girlfriends,' he went on, 'but you've surely had loads of boyfriends. There must be one at the moment.'

A strange cloud dulled her eyes. Strange, because he couldn't read the emotion behind it. What *was* it? Not distress. Or dismay. Sadness again? Yes, that was it. Sadness. A very deep sadness. He wondered if she'd had a serious boyfriend and something dreadful had happened to him. He couldn't imagine any man worth his salt dumping Kate, so what else could it be?

Only death, Blake decided, warranted this depth of sadness. A very recent death, possibly. That would explain everything that had puzzled him about her tonight. It might also explain why she hadn't responded all that strongly to his none-too-subtle overtures. Perhaps by finding him attractive—and he was pretty sure she did—she felt she was betraying her loved one.

Blake pulled himself up sharply before he got carried away. Which he did sometimes. Nothing worse than being a movie-maker. He found drama in every situation. The reality was probably nothing like what he was imagining.

'Actually, no,' she said, a rueful little smile hovering. 'I do not have a boyfriend at the moment. I have had boyfriends in the past, of course.'

Well of course she had. If she hadn't she wouldn't be normal.

'Then there's no one to object if I ask you out to dinner tomorrow night?' he went on.

She didn't look totally surprised, just a little wary.

'No,' she said, but there was reservation in her voice and reluctance in her eyes.

He knew then that she wasn't going to be easily seduced. One part of him admired her for it, but that other part—the part which was aching and hard and more conscienceless than it had ever been—refused to be deterred.

So he decided to play his trump card. Too bad if it was a bit premature. A man had to do what a man had to do.

'I want to talk to you about a part in my next movie which I think would be perfect for you,' he added, dangling what he knew would be a powerful carrot.

There was no doubting her surprise. No, her *shock*. Genuine, ingenuous shock. God, she really was irresistible.

'But why would you do that?' she asked, jerking her head back a little as she blinked up at him. 'Surely you would need me to audition for you first.'

Damn it all, why did she have to be so difficult? He respected her for it, but it was irritating.

'I don't need to see an audition from a graduate of NIDA,' he dismissed. 'Their programme produces the most talented actors.'

'Yes, but...but...'

'Kate Holiday,' he said sternly. 'Do you want to be a successful actress or not?'

'Of course I do,' she replied, looking quite offended. 'It's what I want most in the world.'

'Then stop looking a gift horse in the mouth.'

She smiled then. Which pleased him no end.

'You'll come to dinner tomorrow night?'

'Yes.'

'Good. Now, let's go and dance.'

CHAPTER SIX

How AMAZING, KATE thought a little breathlessly as Blake swept her onto the dance floor and into his arms. Dinner tomorrow night and a part in a Blake Randall movie.

Amazing, but also a little worrying. She'd heard casting couch stories, knew that it still happened, and wondered if Blake was of that ilk. Would he expect her to have sex with him at the end of the evening?

Kate knew he fancied her—had seen desire in his eyes. And even more worrying was the suspicion that if he made a pass at her she might just say yes to whatever he wanted. Which was not like her at all!

But this was her chance, wasn't it? she reasoned desperately. Her chance to get her career off the ground. And she did find him attractive. Very attractive. And sexy. *Very* sexy. It was that mouth of his. And the hot, hungry gleam which fired up his eyes whenever he looked down at her. Which he was doing at the moment. He made her feel sexy in return. And terribly tempted.

A thought suddenly came to her, however—one she didn't like at all.

'This part you have in mind for me,' she said as he whirled her round, thankfully at arm's length. 'It's not in one of Lachlan's movies, is it? I honestly don't want to be in one of his movies.'

'No, it's not a rom-com. More of a family drama. A character-based script which I wrote a few years ago but hadn't got round to making. But it's all systems go now, and we start shooting in late November. Look, keep this under your hat, but I think Lachlan and I will be parting company in the near future.'

'But why?' she asked, totally taken aback.

Blake glanced over at the man in question before answering. Fortunately the dance floor was big enough for them not to be too close. Nevertheless, when he spoke he kept his voice low.

'Mr Rodgers has an exalted opinion of his acting abilities. He doesn't really understand why his movies with me have been so successful. He thinks it's solely due to him. He might do one more movie with me, but he'll go with the money in the end. He recently got himself a new agent—one who's buddy-buddy with the big production companies. They've already offered him a very lucrative contract for three movies. He says he's just thinking about it, but I can see the writing on the wall.'

'That's not very loyal of him,' Kate said, feeling upset for Blake. Though he didn't seem that upset himself.

He shrugged. 'There's no such thing as loyalty in Hollywood. Just box office figures. I'll survive without him, I can assure you. I have several new projects already in the pipeline—none of which rely on Lachlan Rodgers.'

'That's good.'

Good, too, that she wouldn't have to work with him. That would have been just awful. And so would her acting have been, with her new brother-in-law's presence being both distracting and upsetting.

Still, Blake might be right about Lachlan's acting abilities being limited. When they'd been at NIDA he certainly hadn't come top of the class. He'd been good, but not as good as some of the others. She herself had been singled out by their teachers for more praise than he had.

'Let's not talk about Lachlan any more,' Blake said. 'I'd rather talk about you. So, tell me, if you've only had that one part in a play since you graduated, how have you been surviving financially?'

'Well, I do live at home, rent-free. And I've been working at a local deli at the weekends. That pays for my clothes and fares, and leaves me free to go to auditions during the week.'

'Do you have a good agent?'

Kate sighed. 'I thought I did. But I'm beginning to have my doubts.'

'You need to get yourself a new one, then.'

'I think I will.'

The music changed from a waltz to a faster, more throbbing beat. More people got up to dance, at which point Blake pulled Kate very close and told her to put her arms around his neck. After a slight hesitation she did so, and felt Blake dropping his hands down to her hips. His grip was firm, pulling her lower half against him, making Kate quickly aware of something hard pressing against her stomach. It was impossible to ignore.

Blake's eyelids grew heavy with the contact, and a tense silence enveloped them as their fused hips swayed to the music. On her part she felt mesmerised—both by the obvious evidence of his desire for her and her own shocking thoughts. She began imagining how it would feel to have his flesh buried deep inside hers, to have his mouth on hers, kissing her, only lifting to whisper hot, hungry words in her ear.

Her mouth went dry.

Not so another part of her anatomy.

Suddenly she needed to go to the bathroom. ASAP.

'I'm sorry,' she said, flustered by the urgency of that need, not to mention what was going on in her head. 'But I... I have to go to the Ladies. Too much champagne.'

A total lie. She'd only had one glass during dinner, worried that if she drank too much she might do something she'd regret, might somehow make a total fool of herself.

It had taken every ounce of her acting ability not to react to her father's speech, not to let jealousy for Maddie take her over. She loved her sister. She always had. But she did so hate it that everyone else loved her so *much*, with no love left over for her. Lachlan's speech had been total agony, and Kate hadn't been able to look at him even when he'd toasted *her*, as was his duty.

'Sorry,' she repeated, and then hurried away out of the marquee, almost running back to the house and up the staircase to the bedroom and en-suite bathroom where she'd dressed earlier.

There was probably a powder room or two downstairs, but she didn't know where they were and she simply couldn't wait. But, perversely, when she sat on the toilet she didn't do all that much, and yet the odd feeling of pressure remained.

She'd never felt anything quite like it. Not painful, exactly. No, not painful at all. Just weirdly tight and tense. Her belly was as hard as a rock, whilst elsewhere she was hot and embarrassingly wet. Once again her thoughts took flight, her fantasies definitely on the R-rated side.

'Good grief, Kate,' she groaned aloud, confused by the way she could want any man like this, when she was in love with someone else.

She certainly hadn't done so for the last four years. Never. Not once. Blake Randall, however, seemed to have broken through her frozen libido and brought it to life in a startling way. More than startling when she considered that even when she'd first fallen in love with Lachlan he hadn't evoked so violent a physical reaction.

Her feelings about him had always seemed more softly romantic than starkly sexual. She sighed over him. And dreamt about him. But she'd never been consumed by explicit sexual fantasies. Which she had been a minute ago.

Kate shuddered as she recalled that moment when she'd literally ached to have sex with Blake. She was still aching.

Oh, Lord, whatever was she going to do?

You're going to get a grip, that's what you're going to do. Then go back downstairs and...

And what?

She honestly had no idea. She'd probably leave it up to Blake to make the next move. And he would. She felt sure of it. And the prospect was sending an excited shiver down her spine.

After she'd washed her hands she stared at herself in the vanity mirror, seeing her over-bright eyes and flushed cheeks. Glancing down, she checked to see if her nipples were on show. Thankfully they weren't, courtesy of the corset-style underwear she had on. Maddie had chosen it for her, insisting that it would give her some shape. Which, right now, she was grateful it did.

Kate couldn't deny that she wanted Blake to pursue her. What she *didn't* want was for her own desire to be embarrassingly obvious, or for him to think any response of hers was because he had offered to give her a part in one of his movies. Because what she was feeling at the moment had nothing to do with her career and everything to do with herself as a woman.

It was quite thrilling to be the centre of attention for a change. To feel special, and attractive, and truly desired.

At the same time Kate still felt flustered by the strength of her own sexual response to Blake's overtures. She didn't quite know what to do next. Flirting didn't come naturally to her. She wasn't like Maddie. She didn't have her sister's sexual boldness. Or her confidence. What if she was misreading the situation?

This last thought brought a laugh to her lips. How could she possibly have misread that erection? Unless, of course—she giggled a little—Blake had a gun in his pocket.

Kate had a smile on her lips as she left the bathroom—a smile which was wiped away when she encountered Lachlan standing in the bedroom, with a dark scowl on his beautifully shaped mouth.

'Lachlan!' she exclaimed. 'What are you doing here? Where's Maddie?'

'Dancing with your father. She won't miss me for a minute or two. I told her I was going to the Gents. Look, I saw you duck out of the marquee and I followed you.'

Kate frowned. 'But why?'

'I wanted a word with you in private. I wanted to warn you.'

'Warn me? About what?'

'About Blake bloody Randall.'

Kate sucked in sharply. Why on earth was Lachlan speaking about his mentor and best man with such disrespect? 'What…what about him?'

'About his modus operandi with pretty women—especially ones who have acting in their blood.'

Kate was torn between being flattered by Lachlan calling her pretty and worrying about what this dreaded 'modus operandi' could be. Though she was beginning to suspect…

'First things first: does he know you went to NIDA with me?'

'Well, yes, he does. I told him.'

'*Damn.* That's stuffed things good and proper, then. No doubt he's already offered you a part in one of his movies? That's one of his moves when he fancies an actress. And you're looking extra-fanciable tonight, Kate. Frankly, I've never seen you looking so good. Blake only goes for the good-looking ones. So, *has* he offered you a part?'

'Well, yes,' she admitted, feeling a little bit sick. 'A small one.'

'I don't doubt it's just a small one,' Lachlan scoffed. 'Mr Perfectionist wouldn't risk spoiling one of his movies by giving an unknown a seriously *good* part. You'll probably only have a few words here and there. Just enough to make sure you have to be on location with him so that he can shag you every night. But once the movie is wrapped up you can bet that will be the end of it. He has a reputation for seducing his female stars, but once the movie is over so is the affair.'

He came forward and curved his hands over her shoulders—a gesture that shocked Kate rigid because it forced her to look up into his eyes...those beautiful blue eyes which had entranced her from the first day they'd met.

Perversely, however, neither his touch nor his proximity sent her weak at the knees, as she might have expected. All she felt was a confused wariness.

'I wouldn't like to see that happen to you, Kate,' he went on. 'You're far too nice a girl to be used by that bastard.'

Goodness. Such strong words! 'Is that why you didn't tell Blake I was in your class at NIDA?' she asked, trying to make sense of Lachlan's present attitude, not to mention his past actions. 'You were trying to protect me?'

That startled him, and his hands dropped away as he stepped back in surprise. It took him a few seconds to school his face into an expression of concern. 'Well, yes. Yes...yes, of *course* that's why,' he said, hurriedly but not convincingly.

Kate wasn't sure what to believe now—both about Blake's so-called bad reputation with actresses and Lachlan's using it as an excuse for not mentioning her to Blake at any stage. Nothing rang true.

Okay, so Blake offering her a part without auditioning her had been surprising. In all honesty, however, she couldn't see Blake having to bribe girls into his bed. He was the sort of man women would throw themselves at. She herself was already wildly attracted to him.

'I find it hard to believe Blake is as bad as you say he is,' Kate said.

Lachlan's bedroom blue eyes softened on her and he

once again reached to curve his hands around her shoulders. 'Oh, Kate, Kate… Trust me when I say you don't want to get tangled up with Blake Randall. He can be a twisted bastard. That bitch Claudia throwing him over totally screwed him up. He likes breaking hearts—especially when that heart belongs to an actress. He's bad news, sweetheart. Promise me you won't take him up on his offer—that you'll be having nothing further to do with him after tonight.'

Kate shook her head from side to side, her thoughts more muddled than ever. 'Why did you ask him to be your best man if you despise him so much?' she asked, in an echo of what she'd asked Blake earlier.

Lachlan shrugged. 'It was a good publicity move to promote our next movie. On top of that he was chuffed by my asking. Look, you can't afford to get on the wrong side of the right people in the movie-making world, so don't go telling him I said any of this. Just don't accept that part, for pity's sake. Tell him you don't want to make movies… that you'd rather act on the stage. That's what you always said you wanted to do.'

'I do. But I haven't been very successful at it, in case you haven't noticed.'

'What? Oh, yes. That's bad luck. Still, if you show up at auditions in future looking the way you look tonight you should be in like Flynn. Now, I really must go. Lord, but you *do* look delicious…'

He bent and gave her a peck on the cheek before dashing out of the room and running down the stairs back to his beautiful bride, leaving Kate's head in total turmoil. Because she simply couldn't believe in Lachlan's sudden concern for her. He'd hardly even spoken to her this past year, and had never asked her how things were going for her career-wise.

Not that she'd seen him all that often, but there had been the odd occasion. A family dinner last Easter. A Mother's

Day luncheon in May. Then his and Maddie's engagement party a few months ago...

Maybe his dislike of Blake's behaviour with women *was* a credible reason why he hadn't told his mentor about her. But she didn't buy it. She was beginning to suspect that Lachlan didn't want to share his success—that he wanted to be the only one in his class to make it big in the movies.

Kate's love for Lachlan didn't blind her to his faults. Behind his charm lay considerable arrogance, a selfish nature and a rather ruthless ambition. She was glad now that she hadn't made him any rash promises, because in all honesty she didn't *want* to turn down the part. It was a chance to show someone with lots of connections and contacts that she could act.

Okay, so Blake could be a devil with women. That didn't really surprise her, given his success and his power. But forewarned *was* forearmed. And she didn't have to sleep with him if she didn't want to. The trouble was...she *did*, actually. If Kate were strictly honest with herself, the idea of Blake Randall seducing her was not altogether an unattractive prospect. As for him sending her on her way with a broken heart... Well, that part was laughable. Impossible. Her heart had already been broken.

So to hell with being sweet and nice, plus a total failure. It was time to take a few risks. Time to be proactive, the way her agent kept telling her to be. Time to stop being lily-livered and put her best foot forward!

CHAPTER SEVEN

WHERE ON EARTH *was* she? Blake began thinking when Kate didn't return after ten minutes. How long did it take for a girl to go to the toilet?

Lifting his champagne to his lips, he took a deep swallow, thinking all the while that if she didn't show in the next thirty seconds he would go in search of her.

'Not like you to be standing alone at a party,' Byron said as he wandered up to him, looking splendid in his tux.

But then, Byron would look good in anything. The man had everything. Looks. Money. Charm. And more recently a gorgeous wife and a delightful baby girl. Blake would have been jealous of the man if he didn't like him so much. And if he wasn't such a solid investor in his movies.

'I'm waiting for my dancing partner to come back from the powder room,' he grumbled. 'She's been gone ages.'

'I presume you're talking about Kate?'

'Yes, Kate.'

'Sweet girl. Much sweeter than her sister,' Byron observed drily.

'Too true,' Blake agreed. 'I wouldn't want to be married to *that* one.'

Byron laughed. 'You wouldn't want to be married to *anyone*.'

'You know me so well. Ah, here she is. Kate, sweetheart, what took you so long?'

Kate had no intention of telling him the truth. Certainly not in front of Byron. Or ever, actually.

She grabbed a glass of champagne from a passing waiter and smiled at the two men over the rim as she took a long swallow. They were the sort of men that women must smile at a lot, she conceded. Both very attractive, though in entirely different ways. Byron was fair-haired and traditionally handsome, with clean-cut even features and a smile which might out-dazzle Lachlan's. He was a true gentleman. Whereas Blake looked more like a gypsy, with his wayward black hair, his dark beetling eyebrows and deeply set and very intense eyes.

They pierced her now, those eyes, making her quiver inside. *Lord, but he wouldn't have to try too hard to seduce me*, came the shocking thought.

'Kate's an actress—did you know?' Blake asked Byron, whilst not taking his eyes off her.

Byron's eyebrows lifted. 'No, I didn't know.'

'Neither did I until tonight. She's a graduate of NIDA. Was in the same class as Lachlan.'

'Really? How come he didn't mention it?'

'I have no idea.'

Once again Kate kept silent. After all, what could she say? She really wasn't sure what reason was behind her supposed good friend not mentioning her acting aspirations. But she suspected it had nothing to do with protecting her virtue. Or her heart.

The thought angered her. And made her all the more determined to take whatever help Blake could give her.

'Blake's offered me a part in one of his movies,' she said brightly, at which Byron's eyes widened considerably.

It crossed Kate's mind that maybe Byron knew of his friend's modus operandi with actresses as well. A momentary concern tightened her chest, but it was quickly dismissed—as quickly as she swallowed the rest of her champagne. The alcohol fizzed down into her near empty stomach—she hadn't eaten much of the formal meal— going straight to her head and giving her some much-needed Dutch courage.

She wasn't by nature a rash person. Or a reckless one.

Yet she wanted to be both tonight. She *needed* to be both tonight—needed to throw off her earlier wretchedness, needed to ignore her broken heart and surge boldly and bravely into a new future: a future in which her futile feelings for Lachlan had no role to play.

She had to move on. *Had* to. There was no alternative. Kate was tired of feeling depressed. And of being rejected both personally and professionally. It was time to tap into her acting skills. Time to channel Maddie and just go for it.

'I think, darling Blake,' she said, with a decidedly flirtatious sparkle in her eyes, 'that I am in desperate need of some more dancing.'

Blake almost did a double-take. Even Byron shot him a startled glance. This wasn't the Kate who'd dashed off to the Ladies. This was a different Kate. A saucier, sexier Kate. Maybe she had more of her sister in her than he'd realised.

In a perverse way, he wasn't sure he liked it. His body did, however, and his erection returned with a vengeance before he'd even taken her into his arms.

Without prompting she slid her own arms up around his neck and pressed herself against him. Blake swore under his breath, knowing she had to be aware of his arousal. It discomfited him, for some reason. As much as he wanted Kate, he had never been the kind of guy who shagged sozzled bridesmaids at weddings, however much they wanted it.

'Sweetheart...' he murmured, noting her over-bright eyes with their dilated pupils. 'How much have you had to drink tonight?'

She blinked up at him, then laughed. 'Not all that much. But I could do with some fresh air. It's rather warm in here. Fancy a walk in the garden? It's lovely down by the water.

Not cold at all. We could go and sit in the gazebo whilst you tell me about this wonderful part you have for me.'

Kate knew she was prattling on, but she really wasn't comfortable in the role of vamp, or seductress, or whatever it was she was trying to be. Not that it mattered. Blake already fancied her. She'd felt the evidence more than once. She didn't have to act like this. It wasn't her.

She had no doubt that once they were alone in the gazebo he would make a pass. Kiss her at least.

But what if he wanted to go further than that?

As attractive and sexy as she found him, Kate didn't really want to have sex with Blake tonight. So tacky to act like that at a wedding! Her *sister's* wedding, no less. No, she couldn't throw caution to the wind to that extent. And to go outside with him—to be alone with him in the vast, rather romantically lit grounds—was dangerous in the extreme.

Because she wasn't sure that if he started kissing her she would want him to stop. The way he kept looking at her was powerfully seductive. His hot gaze bored into her like a laser beam, searing her insides and making her want to be even more reckless than she'd vowed to be. She couldn't recall ever feeling quite so...*stirred*.

'Let's go, then,' he said firmly, a possessive hand on her elbow, steering her towards the exit of the marquee.

Fortunately—or perhaps unfortunately, as it turned out—they were interrupted before they could make their escape. It was her mother, still looking like the very proud mother of the bride, all puffed up and flushed in her very pretty and very expensive pink suit, an older version of Maddie with her bottle blonde hair, but just a little too much make-up for a woman of fifty.

'Maddie sent me to get you, Kate,' Janine Holiday said somewhat breathlessly. 'She wants you to help her change into her going-away outfit.'

'What? So soon? But it's still quite early and—'

'The poor love says she's terribly tired,' Janine cut in. 'As you know, she's been up since the crack of dawn.'

Kate *did* know. She'd been got up as well, and then dragged off to the beauty salon so that she could be plucked and primped and polished until she hardly recognised herself. But she supposed it had been worth it in the end. Blake thought she looked lovely.

Kate didn't believe for a moment that Maddie was 'terribly tired'. That girl was like one of those batteries which never ran down. She knew exactly why Maddie wanted to leave. She'd whispered the reason to Kate earlier. She wanted to have sex with her new husband.

An hour or two ago Kate would have been overwhelmed with jealousy. Now her only feeling was distaste. She might still be in love with Lachlan, but she no longer liked him or wanted him. After what Blake had told her about his cheating behaviour Maddie was welcome to him.

'You'd better go,' Blake said, a wry note in his voice. 'I'll catch you later.'

Kate threw him an apologetic glance before allowing herself to be drawn away by her mother.

'Maddie's already gone upstairs,' Janine said as they headed for the house together. 'I think, Kate, that after she and Lachlan have left your father and I will go home too. I'm pretty tired myself. It's been a long day. Marvellous, but exhausting. What about you?' she added. 'I suppose you won't want to leave that early.'

'No.'

In truth, Kate was horrified at the thought of listening to her parents rave on about Maddie's wedding all the way home. Strathfield was an inner Western Sydney suburb which was a good half-hour drive from Byron's harbourside mansion.

'That would be rather rude. The party's only just started.

We can't *all* leave early. Besides, Cleo said I could stay the night if I liked, so I think I'll take her up on that offer.'

'Cleo?'

'Byron's wife. You must have met her.'

'I suppose I must have. I've been a bit distracted today. What does she look like?'

'Brunette. Burgundy dress. Very stylish. And very nice. Look, I'll catch a taxi home in the morning. I'll bring the dresses with me when I come.'

'Oh, all right. But perhaps I'd best take Maddie's wedding dress home with me tonight. I wouldn't like anything to happen to it.'

'What on earth could possibly *happen* to it?' Kate asked, amazed and a little hurt.

Janine looked irritated. 'I don't know. I just think it's better to be safe than sorry. Now, off you go. I need to get back to your father before he gets himself into trouble.'

Kate almost laughed. Her father was not the type of man who ever got himself into trouble. An insurance assessor, he was as conservative as his job, his only passion in life a collection of rare stamps. And, of course, his second and much adored daughter, who'd played Daddy's girl to perfection from the time she was just a tot.

Whenever Maddie perched herself on her father's knee and wrapped her arms around him he could deny her nothing. And he never had. Whatever she wanted, she got. Toys. Clothes. Expensive school excursions. A boob job. And finally, when she turned twenty-one, a car. Which she had promptly wrecked, losing her driving licence as well. This hadn't overly bothered Maddie, because by then she'd always had some obsessed boyfriend very eager to drive her wherever she wanted to go.

Kate trudged up the stairs, sighing as she went. She wished she could hate Maddie. But she didn't. She just couldn't. Yes, her sister was vain, and manipulative, and terribly self-centred. But, despite all that, she was an engaging personality, irrepressible and outgoing, and very, *very* charming. Kate couldn't help admiring her, in a way. And loving her.

More was the pity.

CHAPTER EIGHT

'OH, *THERE* YOU ARE!' Maddie exclaimed as Kate walked in.

She'd already taken off her wedding dress and tossed it carelessly onto a nearby chair. She was standing by the bed in nothing but a strapless white lace corset, her double D cup boobs almost spilling over the top. Her stockings and shoes lay in an untidy heap on the floor.

'Join me?' she said as she swept up the bottle of champagne which was sitting in an ice bucket on the bedside table.

Next to it were two flutes, delivered to the room when they'd been getting dressed earlier. Neither of them had felt like drinking at the time. Maddie had been too excited and Kate too wretched.

'For pity's sake, watch what you're doing!' Kate groaned when the cork popped off and champagne started fizzing out of the bottle. Hurrying over, she rescued the precious wedding dress in time, returning it to the plastic cover where it had been residing for the last two weeks.

'Oh, don't be such a worrywart. It's not red wine. Champagne won't even stain. Besides, it's not like I'll be wearing the damned thing ever again. Mum will put it into her treasure box so that she can bring it out and drool over it every now and then. She's got all our grad dresses in there too. Even our christening dresses. Here—have some champers. You might need it.'

'What do you mean, *I* might need it?' Kate asked as she took the glass.

Maddie flashed her one of her mischievous glances. 'Blind Freddie could see that Blake Randall is very taken with you, darls. All thanks to *moi*, of course. If you'd turned up today looking like your usual drack sack he wouldn't be all over you like a rash the way he was on that dance floor a little while ago. Now, does he know you graduated from NIDA?'

'I told him.' Kate took a deep swallow of the cold champagne. 'Your dear husband never even mentioned it to him. Which I find quite odd, since we were supposedly good friends there.'

Maddie laughed. 'Never underestimate the male ego, darls. Lachlan wouldn't want any of his NIDA buddies stealing his thunder, so to speak. Especially not you, Kate. You're too good an actress. And then there was that other matter...'

'What other matter?'

'Your crush on him,' she stated with bald honesty.

'My *what*?'

Maddie rolled her eyes. 'Please don't pretend you don't know what I'm talking about. It was obvious—even at home. You never stopped talking about him from day one at NIDA. Lachlan tells me it was quite embarrassing... the way you followed him around like a puppy. He said he couldn't even go for coffee without you inviting yourself along.'

Kate could hardly believe what she was hearing. *Lachlan* was the one who had kept inviting *her* for coffee. His wanting to talk to her all the time had been very flattering. It hadn't been just his looks which had made her fall in love with him. But now she saw that he'd just been picking her brain, as most of their conversations had revolved around her acting methods.

A very real fury welled up inside her. Fury plus a degree of humiliation. How could she have been so taken in by him? But she had. Oh, yes, she *had*.

In her defence, *all* the attractive female students at NIDA had gone ga-ga over him. And most of them had become a girlfriend of Lachlan's at some stage—each of them dated for a while and then dumped, not harshly but cleverly. Lachlan had used buckets of his boyish charm to smooth over each break-up, with the result that they had never had anything bad to say about him, even after he'd moved on.

Kate had waited and waited for him to move on to *her*. She was the only one he hadn't dated, and whilst she knew she couldn't compare with Maddie, she wasn't a total dog. Lots of people said she was quite attractive. But he had never asked her out. Not once.

Just thinking about those wasted years had Kate finishing her first glass of champagne in no time and seeking a refill.

'Oh, come, now,' Kate said as she put the bottle down. 'I wasn't as bad as that. And I wasn't the only girl at NIDA to be impressed. I mean, he is so *very* good-looking. But we all got over that once we realised how up himself he is.'

Kate felt rather proud of her well-delivered lie. Studying acting had come in handy more than once today.

'I certainly don't have a crush on him any more, I can assure you,' she said with a straight face as she lifted the glass to her lips again.

'So you say,' Maddie said, putting down her own glass on a side table and standing with her hands on her hips, eyes narrowed and lips pursed. 'I guess I'd be more inclined to believe you if you had a boyfriend. Look, Lachlan is my husband now, and I don't want to go through my life thinking my sister still has the hots for him. *Do* you?'

Kate drew herself up tall, squared her shoulders and fixed Maddie with uncompromising eyes. 'Now you are being seriously silly. Okay, I admit I did have a small crush on him. Once. But trust me when I say I don't any longer.'

Maddie gave her a long hard glare before shrugging dismissively. 'Well, I'll just have to take your word for it, I suppose. But I did wonder why you seemed so uptight earlier. If I thought that—'

'Maddie, please stop! You've totally got the wrong idea. The reason I was uptight earlier was because I was nervous.'

'Nervous! What about?'

'About being a bridesmaid. I've never been one before.'

'For heaven's sake! I've never been a bride before and *I* wasn't nervous.'

'You're never nervous about anything.'

'True…' Maddie preened. 'Okay, now that's all sorted, let's get back to what I originally wanted to talk to you about. Blake Randall's obvious interest in you…'

'Oh, yes?'

'Yes. Now, I don't want you to waste this opportunity,' Maddie said as she went over to the walk-in wardrobe and came out carrying the very stylish ice-blue woollen dress which her mother had chosen and for which her father had paid a small fortune. 'That's why I said you might need to get a bit tipsy. To give you some Dutch courage,' Maddie added, unzipping the dress and laying it out across the bed. 'Because I *know* you, Kate. You let opportunities go by because you simply won't go for them. So go on—drink up.'

Kate did as she was ordered, glad that the alcohol was already hurrying through her veins and reaching her brain, bringing with it a much-needed devil-may-care attitude.

'You have to have tunnel vision in this world,' Maddie rattled on, stepping into the blue sheath and pulling it up onto her shoulders. 'You can't wait for things to just happen. You have to *make* them happen.'

This was hardly news to Kate. She'd thought exactly the same thing earlier this evening.

'Now, I have a confession to make,' her sister went on, doing up the side zipper and then slipping her bare feet into the pair of nude high heels which were sitting ready for her at the foot of the bed. 'When you brought Lachlan home last Christmas even though I'd almost decided to marry Riley I knew I didn't love him. But I liked him, and I knew he'd give me a good life money-wise. He owns his own plumbing business and everyone knows that plumbers earn heaps. But then I took one look at Lachlan and saw an opportunity for a much better life—a life which would be very exciting and very glamorous, with a husband who was gorgeous and brilliant and seriously sexy. I realised suddenly that I couldn't settle for Riley, even though he was very good in bed. I wanted more. I wanted Lachlan and what he could give me. I mean, the temptation to go for him was overwhelming.'

She hesitated briefly and sent Kate an apologetic glance. 'I know you liked him, Kate, and I'm sorry. I dare say you were hurt when we left together that day. But I simply had to try to get him to fall in love with me. And he already wanted me, don't you see? He didn't want you. You weren't his type.'

'Yes, I'd already gathered that,' Kate said, thankful now that she was becoming, if not merry, decidedly numb. Without thinking she lifted the glass to her lips and took another deep swallow.

'So…you're not in love with Lachlan either, then?' Kate said, trying not to look and sound as shocked as she was.

'Love?' Maddie scoffed, smoothing down her skirt before walking over and picking up her champagne once more. 'What's love?' she said dismissively after a sip. 'A very temporary state—especially where the male sex is concerned. Their idea of love is usually all about sex. A woman has about eighteen months at best to get what she wants from a man before he goes off the boil. If you want marriage then you have to get him to propose during the first twelve months. I'm under no illusions. I know that

Lachlan will stray. He's too handsome and sexy to stay faithful—especially in the movie world. But I'll always be his wife—or at least his very rich *ex*-wife.'

Kate was appalled. And suddenly she must have looked it.

'Don't get me wrong,' Maddie went on as she stepped over to the dressing table to attend to her make-up and hair. 'I *do* care for Lachlan. Very much. And we have great chemistry in bed. I couldn't stand to marry a man who wasn't a good lover. Makes up for a lot of things…great sex. It also makes a man amenable to doing what *you* want. Which brings me back to my advice to you about Blake Randall,' she said, turning round to look straight at Kate as she sprayed herself liberally with perfume.

'And what advice would that be?' Kate asked. Her emotions were still outwardly under control, but inside she was dissolving. Maddie didn't even *love* Lachlan. All she wanted was the good life. *Dear God…*

'Get him into the sack ASAP. Don't wait. He'll be off back to Hollywood in a few days. Strike while the iron is hot. And his iron *is* hot. For *you*, darls. Lachlan says he's a sucker when it comes to pretty young actresses. And you *do* look pretty tonight, Kate. More than pretty. I actually feel a little jealous.'

Kate had to laugh. 'Now, *that's* not true,' she said, turning to fill her glass again. How had it become empty so quickly? 'You've never been jealous of me.'

'Oh, I wouldn't say that. I envy your acting ability. It's brilliant.'

And so is yours, Kate thought with a touch of malice.

'Blake Randall is going to get a real shock once he realises how good you are,' Maddie went on. 'But he won't ever realise that unless you keep him around long enough to see it.'

'Maddie, he's already offered me a part in one of his

movies,' she stated, bypassing her distress and surrendering to irritation. 'I don't *have* to sleep with him.'

'Oh, God—don't be so naive.'

'I'm *not* naive.'

'Yes, you are. Hopelessly. It's a man's world, Kate. They have all the power. Our only power comes from sex. I found that out years ago. Now, how do I look?'

Kate sighed. 'Like you always do. Gorgeous.'

'Thanks, darls. I love you—you know that, don't you?'

Kate did know that—which was perverse. Somehow she smiled and came forward to give her sister a hug. 'I hope you'll be very happy,' she said, and tried to mean it.

'Oh, I will be. I know it. Now, where did I put my bouquet...?'

CHAPTER NINE

BLAKE WATCHED FROM the sidelines as the beaming couple said their goodbyes, the bride making a big fuss over her parents before throwing her bouquet straight at her sister.

Kate laughed, but the laughter didn't touch her eyes. Blake still wasn't sure what was going on in that girl's head. She'd come back downstairs shortly after the bride, sipping a full glass of champagne as she made her way a bit shakily down the steps, her spare hand gripping the banister for support. She'd looked lost and decidedly tipsy.

Blake would have gone to her then if Cleo hadn't suddenly appeared by his side, striking up a conversation and leaving Blake no opportunity to do anything except surreptitiously watch Kate's rather unsteady progress.

Once at the bottom of the stairs Kate had scanned the crowd of guests for a few seconds, then walked over to stand with her back against a nearby wall, her lips no longer sipping but drinking fast.

Fortunately by the time the bride threw her bouquet her glass was almost empty, otherwise champagne might have gone everywhere. Despite acting as if she was thrilled, Blake suspected she was on the verge of tears—which sent him striding over to her side, where he slid a firm arm around her waist and pulled her against him.

'I think you've had way too much to drink,' he murmured.

'*I* don't,' she said, lifting big brown eyes up to his.

They were very glassy, but still very lovely.

'I don't think I've had *nearly* enough. Let's go and find another bottle of this delicious champagne.'

'Not right now, darling heart. Let's go for that walk down to the gazebo instead. Get you some much-needed fresh air first.'

'Whatever you say,' she said, with a nonchalant shrug of her slender shoulders. 'Just wait while I give this bouquet to my mother. She might want to take it home with her... have it cast in gold.'

Blake smiled at the unexpected sarcasm. Or was it jealousy? Was *that* what her changeable moods tonight had been all about? Jealousy over her sister?

He was tempted to ask her, but then decided best not. He didn't want to start talking about Maddie. He wanted to talk about *her*. Kate. The deliciously sexy and intriguing Kate.

If only she'd realise that not every man liked the obvious. *He* certainly didn't. He couldn't wait to take her to dinner tomorrow night, and to get her by herself afterwards in a romantic setting befitting their first time together. He'd already asked Byron if he could use his city penthouse for the next few days. It was a fantastically glamorous pad and Kate would be suitably impressed.

And Blake wanted to impress her. Impress her and protect her and make her happy—which he could do by giving her career a leg-up and getting his leg over at the same time. It wasn't as though she wouldn't enjoy sex with him. It certainly wouldn't be a case of her just lying back and thinking of her career. Blake *knew* he was a good lover. Always had been.

God, you're an arrogant devil, Blake conceded inwardly. *Has it even crossed your mind that she might say no to you? The bed part, that is, not the movie part?*

It was a novel thought, but not one he took seriously. Kate wouldn't say no to him. He'd seen the desire in her eyes on the dance floor earlier—felt it in her deliciously uptight body. It was just a matter of finding the right place and the right time. And making the right moves, of course.

Blake had every confidence that nothing would come between him and success.

A wave of relief flooded Kate after they'd all left—Maddie and Lachlan first, and then her parents, her mother taking with her Maddie's wedding dress and veil. Kate certainly didn't want to be responsible for them, or even to see them ever again. Thank God she'd handed over the bouquet as well, or she just might have thrown it into the harbour.

In truth, her broken heart had lightened considerably with their departure. Out of sight was out of mind. To a degree. Of course it helped that she was just a little bit drunk. No, a long way drunk, she accepted with an uncharacteristically naughty giggle. It helped her be able to return to the seriously attractive man who clearly wanted *her*—Kate Holiday. Not her blonde bombshell sister. *Her*.

God, she adored the way Blake looked at her. So hot and so hungry. It made her feel weak at the knees, and yet perversely powerful at the same time. She smiled flirtatiously as she walked slowly back to him, unconsciously acting the vamp, swinging her hips and licking her suddenly dry lips.

Bloody hell, thought Blake, his body leaping into action. If she didn't watch it they'd be taking things a lot further down in the gazebo. Only her obviously drunken state would stop him. But, damn it all, resisting her was going to be difficult.

Keep the touching to a minimum, then, he warned himself. *And definitely no kissing. In fact it would be much better if you went back into the marquee and just danced*, he told himself.

Yes, and perhaps get her some more champagne. Give

her something to do with that mouth of hers instead of doing what she was doing.

Actually she didn't wait for him to do anything—just came up very close, slid her arms up around his neck, right then and there, and planted those tempting lips right on his.

What was a red-blooded male supposed to do? One with a hard-on the size of Nelson's column?

Without thinking it through he kissed her back for a few seconds before common sense returned. Then, taking her firmly by the hips, he eased her away and speared her with a reproachful look.

'Naughty, Kate,' he murmured, aware of other people staring at them. 'Come on—we're off to the gazebo. And we'll pick up a bottle of champagne on the way.'

Kate giggled. She liked being called naughty. Liked *being* naughty. God, but he was a good kisser. She couldn't wait for him to kiss her some more. For longer next time. She'd only briefly felt the tip of his tongue. She wanted more of it, diving in deeper, making her head swirl again. She wanted...

Oh, she didn't know what she wanted. Oblivion, she supposed. Oblivion from the horrid thoughts which kept jumping into her head.

Maddie doesn't love Lachlan...
Lachlan doesn't want you...he wants Maddie...
You're not his type...

She needed to block those thoughts out—needed to replace them with wild, wonderful thoughts; needed to have this man's arms around her again. Not just on the dance floor, or during a brief kiss, but all night. In bed.

Kate grabbed Blake's hand and squeezed it tight. 'I do *so* like you,' she said.

He smiled down at her. 'Good.'

It was cold down in the gazebo, a sea breeze having sprung up. When Kate shivered Blake took off his jacket and draped it round her shoulders.

'Such a gentleman,' she said, appreciating the warmth.

'Not always.'

'Oh. You forgot to get some more champagne.'

'You've had enough.'

'Don't be such a spoilsport.'

'I'm just protecting your virtue.'

She laughed. 'I'm not a virgin.'

'I should hope not. But what's that got to do with protecting your virtue?'

'Maybe I don't *want* you to protect me. Maybe I want you to ravage me senseless,' she said, a wild glint flashing in her eyes. 'Not here, of course. I understand we can't do it here. It's cold and uncomfortable. But I'm staying the night at Byron's house. Are you?'

'Yes...' he said.

Kate ignored his frown. 'In that case we could spend the night together. In *your* room, preferably,' she added, knowing the other bedroom would still smell of Maddie's perfume.

Blake knew they were getting into dangerous waters here. The alcohol was making her reckless. The really dangerous part was that he rather *liked* reckless. Yet he knew being reckless wasn't in Kate's true nature. She was going to regret this in the morning.

But, hell on earth... He was only human. And a long way from being a saint.

'Kate,' he said, clutching at what conscience he *did* have where women and sex were concerned. 'I can't. I'm sorry. You're drunk.'

She stared at him, shock and confusion in her eyes. 'What? You don't *ever* go to bed with a woman who's had a few glasses of champagne? I find that hard to believe. From what I've heard you're the very *devil* with women.'

'Not always,' he returned. 'It depends on the woman.'

Tears suddenly filled her eyes. Tears and a type of rage. 'The truth is you don't really want me, do you? Not enough. I thought you did. I thought… Oh, what does it matter *what* I thought?' she cried, jumping up and throwing his jacket at him. 'You're a total bastard and I hate you!'

CHAPTER TEN

BLAKE STOOD OUTSIDE the bedroom door, listening to the sound of Kate sobbing inside. Cleo crossed her arms and glared at him, having joined the chase when she'd spotted Blake racing after a fleeing Kate. Both of them had followed her back into the house and up the staircase, unable to catch her before she'd slammed the bedroom door in their faces.

'What on earth did you do to her?' Cleo demanded. 'You were both getting along fine earlier in the evening. She was glued to you when you were dancing, and then later you were kissing down in the foyer.'

'We went for a walk to the gazebo,' he said, sighing.

'And?'

'I refused to have sex with her.'

'*What?* Good Lord—that's a new one.'

'Look, she was drunk. I don't have sex with seriously intoxicated women, no matter how much I fancy them.'

'That's very commendable of you, Blake. But I'm not sure if I totally believe you. You *do* have a rather ruthless reputation where the ladies are concerned, you know.'

'No, I *don't* know,' Blake snapped. 'Just because I enjoy a bachelor lifestyle it doesn't mean I treat women badly.'

He supposed his so-called reputation was a hangover from those few months after Claudia had left him, when he had indulged in some thoughtless revenge sex. With actresses, of course. But those days were long gone. Okay, so his girlfriends were still usually actresses, or people involved in the movie industry. But that was only logical. Who else did he meet?

'Fair enough,' Cleo said. 'Don't get angry with *me*. I'm

just telling you what I've heard on the grapevine. Obviously Kate has heard something similar. Still, it was a strange re-action on her part. I would have thought she'd be impressed by your gallantry.'

'Obviously not. I don't understand her, Cleo.'

'I think you should go in there and talk to her.'

'She'll probably scream at me to get out.'

'If you really like her, you have to try. Don't wait. Wait-ing never works where women are concerned.'

'You're right.' He tried the doorknob and found it wasn't locked. Still, he hesitated.

'I really must get back to the party,' Cleo said. 'Byron will wonder where I've got to.'

'Tell him you had to check on the baby.'

'He won't believe that. April's at her godmother's to-night.'

'Well, say you had to call and check that she was okay.'

Cleo laughed. 'I can see you're an accomplished liar.'

'Hardly. I'm usually accused of being brutally honest.'

'That's not always a virtue, Blake—especially when it comes to women. Kindness is what we value most in a man, which might involve the occasional white lie. Any-way, I must go. I'll catch up with you later and see what you achieved.'

She was gone in a flash, leaving Blake mulling over what she'd said about kindness.

I can be kind, he told himself as he slowly turned the knob. *Can't I? Yes, of course I can.* And he pushed open the door.

Kate was lying face down on the bed, weeping into a mountain of pillows.

'Kate?' he said gently as he approached the bed.

'Go away,' she blubbered. 'Leave me alone.'

He ignored that and sat down on the side of the bed. 'Not until you tell me what I did that was so wrong.'

'You don't understand,' she cried in muffled tones.

'No, I don't. Not unless you tell me.'

She rolled over and showed him her pitiful face, her flushed cheeks stained with mascara and tears, her eyes swollen with weeping. 'I… I can't,' she blurted out. 'It's too…humiliating.'

'Kate, I like you. A lot. And I fancy you. A lot. I have every intention of making love to you tomorrow night, after I've taken you out for a suitably romantic dinner and then taken you back to a suitably romantic place, befitting what a lovely girl like you deserves. Does that sound like I don't really want you?'

She shook her head from side to side, then buried her face in her hands. 'It's nothing to do with you, really.'

'Then what's it to do with?'

'I can't tell you.'

Blake took her hands away from her face and held them, forcing her to look up into his eyes. 'It's something to do with your sister, isn't it?'

Her puffy eyes widened.

'I'm a fairly observant character,' he went on. 'I noticed that every time you had something to do with your sister today you became upset. Unhappy. Different. When you came downstairs after helping Maddie with her going-away outfit you were *very* different. I couldn't put my finger on it at the time, but in hindsight I think you were extremely upset and that you tried to hide your feelings behind a rather reckless façade. As much as I hate to admit it, I don't think you really *wanted* to have sex with me. Not me personally. You were just craving distraction. That's why you drank so much as well—to dull whatever pain it was that your sister caused you.'

He stopped talking then, and she just stared at him, her expression bewildered at first, and then just bleak. 'If I tell you, you're going to think me a fool.'

'I doubt that very much. We're all capable of foolishness. So what is it, Kate? What's been bothering you so much today?'

She blinked, then sighed, and then shook her head again. 'I can't believe I'm going to tell you this. I… I never wanted to tell anyone—never wanted anyone to know, especially my family.'

'Well, I'm not family. Sometimes it's good to tell outsiders. They can give you objective advice.'

Though, damn it all, he wasn't feeling all that objective where Kate was concerned. She touched him as he had not been touched in years.

'Just blurt it out,' he insisted. 'Stop thinking about what I might think of you and tell me this awful truth, whatever it is.'

Her face filled with anguish. 'That's very easy to say. Not so easy to do.'

'Just *do* it, Kate.'

She sighed again—a heavy but resigned sigh. 'All right, I will. The thing is…the awful truth is…that I'm in love with Lachlan.' And she hung her head in a gesture of shame. Or possibly humiliation.

Blake supposed later that he should not have been so shocked. After all, practically every female who'd seen one of Lachlan's movies was in love with him. Young. Old. Married. Single. They all adored him. That was why his romantic comedies were so successful.

'I see,' he bit out, angry with her at first, for being so stupid as to fall in love with someone so shallow, and then sympathetic—because hadn't he done exactly the same thing at her age? He'd fallen in love with Claudia, who was probably even worse than Lachlan.

'You *don't* see,' she cried, sitting up and wringing her hands together. 'And you *do* think I'm a fool.'

'No,' he returned slowly. 'I don't think that at all. I can

understand why you might have fallen in love with him. He's very good-looking, and extremely charming when he needs to be. So how long have you been in love with Lachlan?'

'What? Oh, since the first day we went to NIDA together.'

'Love at first sight, then?' Blake said, thinking it was more like lust at first sight. Even *he* hadn't fallen in love with Claudia at first sight.

Blake had always been a bit of a cynic where true love was concerned. Claudia had had to work hard on him in order to convince him of her love. And she had—convinced him, that was—which had made the speed of her betrayal after their marriage all the more devastating.

'Yes,' she said sadly. 'But he didn't ever return my feelings. He liked me okay, so I thought I was in with a chance—especially when he was between girlfriends. He was always nice to me…often seeking me out to help him with assignments. But Maddie told me tonight that he found my crush on him quite embarrassing. That's what he called it. A crush…' Her laugh was slightly hysterical, her hands still twisting in her lap.

'And when exactly did she tell you this?' Blake asked gently.

'Oh, when I came up here tonight to help her change. Though she didn't really want my help. She just wanted reassurance that I was over my crush and that I didn't still have the hots for her precious husband. Which I assured her I didn't. After that she proceeded to give me a lecture about you.'

'About *me*?'

'Yes, she advised me to sleep with you. Said it would be good for my career.'

'Which advice you followed to a T,' he said ruefully.

Her face twisted. 'No—no, you've got it all wrong. My

coming on to you wasn't about my career. It was because you seemed genuinely attracted to me and I was flattered... especially after what Maddie said about Lachlan wanting her and never wanting me. Apparently I simply wasn't his type. So I thought...well... I must be Blake's type. So when I came downstairs and saw you, waiting for me and smiling at me, it made me feel a bit better. Then, when I kissed you, I felt a lot better. Yes, I know I'm drunk, but I needed you, Blake. Needed to feel desirable. I wanted to be wanted. By someone. *Anyone!* So when you turned me down I just felt so bad. I... I couldn't handle it.'

Blake watched as her already fragile control began to shatter.

'And the worst thing is,' she added, her eyes filling with the most heartbreaking distress, 'she doesn't even love him. Not really. Of course she's sexually attracted to him. Who isn't? But the reason she married him was to live the good life—whatever that is. Oh, God...'

Kate couldn't go on, feeling a tight ball of emotion gather in her chest as all the hurt, misery and frustration of this past year overwhelmed her. A cry such as she'd never heard before punched from her lungs. It sounded like a wounded animal—a wounded *dying* animal.

She froze, her shoulders stiffening with the effort to hold on to herself, her eyes wide with shock. But it was no use. There was no stopping the avalanche of pain once it broke free. Whirling away from Blake's startled face, she threw herself back onto the pillows and let go, sobbing her heart out with even more fervour than she had earlier.

It was horrible, humiliating, but she had nothing left of control or courage. She told herself that she didn't even care that Blake was witnessing her breakdown.

It was odd, then, that underneath her almost hysterical weeping, plus her dizzy and decidedly alcohol-infused thoughts, she had enough brainpower left to worry that he probably wouldn't want her in one of his movies now—let alone anything else. It bothered her greatly that he would see her for what she was. A stupid fool and a total failure!

CHAPTER ELEVEN

BLAKE WAS USED to women's tears. Good actresses could summon them up at the drop of a hat. But these weren't just ordinary tears. Kate was sobbing like nothing he'd heard before. If she kept this up she would make herself ill.

He wondered if he should go and find Cleo and Byron—get them to call a doctor, someone who could give Kate something to calm her down. Though Lord knew the possibility of getting a doctor to make a house call at this hour on a Saturday night was highly unlikely. Perhaps they might have something in their medicine cabinet which would be useful. A tranquilliser of some sort.

Whilst he mulled over this possible solution he tried placing his hand on the back of her head and stroking her long hair, murmuring the sort of soft, soothing words which he often put into a script but had never actually said before.

'Now, now—don't cry...there, there...'

How soft her hair was. How silky and soft and sexy.

Must not think about sex now, he told himself sternly. *Time to be kind. Time to just be a good friend.* Clearly Kate needed a good friend—someone who would comfort her and then talk sense to her, when she was capable of listening. Which probably wouldn't be tonight.

But still... Fancy falling in love with Lachlan! What a total waste of time *that* was. It probably wasn't true love, either. Just an infatuation. He was the kind of guy girls got infatuated with very easily. His golden boy looks, of course, and that brilliant smile, that overpowering charm.

How ironic that Kate's sister didn't really love him—that she'd just married him for the good life. Not that she didn't put on a good act. She played the besotted bride to perfection. And she had the looks to carry off the role. She might even make the marriage a success. After all, if she didn't love him she'd probably be prepared to tolerate his infidelities. Either that or she herself might move on to someone even more successful, the way Claudia had.

Claudia...

Blake thought of Claudia as he stroked Kate's hair. What a bitch! A selfish, ambitious, cold-blooded bitch. He'd always hoped she'd fall flat on her face once she'd dumped him for that aging Hollywood producer. But she hadn't. Her career—whilst not top drawer—had been very successful.

She was now married to one of the executives at Unicorn Pictures. Blake had run into her at a party not that long ago, and she'd been sickeningly nice to him. Admittedly, he'd been sickeningly nice back—even chatting away very amicably with her reasonably handsome and annoyingly clever husband. No point in making enemies in Hollywood. Not good for business.

Quite frankly, he was well and truly over her. A good feeling, that, after spending years being bitter and somewhat cynical—especially where aspiring young actresses were concerned.

The fact that Kate was an aspiring young actress did not escape Blake, but she wasn't like any aspiring young actress he'd ever met before. Besides, he was *glad* she was exactly that. It gave him the opportunity to get to know her better and to do what he'd been aching to do all night.

Stop thinking about sex!

Blake gritted his teeth and continued stroking her hair, valiantly ignoring his very active hormones and concentrating on giving Kate what she needed at that moment. Which was gentle words and a soft touch.

Hopefully by tomorrow night her needs would be different. It didn't escape Blake that she'd had a very mixed agenda when she'd offered herself to him in the gazebo.

No doubt there was some rebound and revenge in there somewhere. But he still felt confident that she was genuinely attracted to him. He knew she hadn't faked that kiss.

Finally the sobbing subsided into the occasional shudder, and Blake's hand fell away when Kate abruptly rolled over.

'I... I have to go to the bathroom,' she choked out, scrambling off the bed and dashing for the nearby en-suite.

Blake groaned when he heard the sound of Kate throwing up, torn between offering further help and keeping a compassionate distance. In the end he decided on compassionate distance. He heard her flush the toilet a couple of times, then turn on a tap. Possibly to rinse out her mouth. He heard the tap snapped off but she didn't emerge. He heard her mutter something under her breath, followed by a sigh and some rustling sounds.

When a few minutes had passed and all had fallen ominously silent in the bathroom he made his way reluctantly over to the shut door. His hand had actually lifted to knock when the door opened.

Blake sucked in a breath sharply. *Bloody hell!*

She wasn't naked. But she'd removed her bridesmaid's dress and was standing there dressed in a strapless black satin corset which was so sexy it was criminal—especially when worn with flesh-coloured stay-up stockings and high heels.

'I had to take my dress off,' she explained shakily, looking both sheepish and embarrassed. 'I got some vomit on it. Mum's going to be furious with me,' she added, wincing. 'I... I would have had a shower, but I didn't know I was going to stay here overnight and I didn't bring any nightwear with me. I'm not trying to be provocative. Truly.'

She swayed on her high heels, grabbing the doorknob as if her life depended on it.

'Oh, God, will someone please stop the room from spinning around?'

Blake took a firm hold of her and led her back over to the bed, sitting her down and doing his level best to keep his male mind from corrupting his good intentions.

Kate didn't need him ogling her. But her body was exactly the kind of body he admired on a woman—tall and slender, but with enough curves to be unmistakably feminine. Still, he already knew that—had thought it when he'd first seen her walking down the staircase. She had great skin too. Clear and almost translucent, indicating that her honey-gold hair was probably natural and not the result of hours of painstaking dyeing.

'What you need,' he said gently as he removed her shoes and then her stockings, without once looking at the V between her thighs or her tiny waist…or her very nice cleavage, 'is a big drink of water followed by a good night's sleep.'

'I did drink some water in the bathroom,' she told him.

'And you kept it down?'

'Yes.'

'Good. Now, into bed with you.'

Again without really looking at her, he pulled the bed-clothes back and angled her in between the sheets before swiftly covering her, right up to her neck.

But just when he thought he could safely make his escape her head lifted from the pillow, the bedcovers slipping a little—*darn it*.

Her puffy eyes sought his, their expression plaintive. 'Please don't go. Not 'til I've fallen asleep.'

'Oh, but I…um…'

'I won't jump on you, I promise.'

His smile was wry. *What a shame.* He wouldn't mind one bit if she did. Like they said, the road to hell was paved with good intentions.

'Very well,' he agreed, and lay down next to her. On top of the quilt, not under it.

She rolled over and stared at him with wonder in her sleepy eyes. 'You're really a very nice man,' she murmured. 'Very…kind.'

'There are a lot of people who would disagree with you.'

'Then they don't know the real you.' She yawned. 'They say men should be judged by their actions, not their words. You're a gentleman, no matter what other people might think.'

Blake wondered exactly what 'other people' she was talking about. Was his reputation with women really that bad? Then he wondered what she'd think of him tomorrow night, when he took her to dinner and set out to seduce her with every weapon he had in his considerable arsenal.

He rolled over and looked her straight in her heavy-lidded eyes. 'You should go to sleep now,' he advised. 'You're going to have a seriously late night tomorrow.'

'Am I?'

Was that a quiver of excitement in her voice?

Blake gave in to temptation and bent forward to kiss her—not on the lips, but on her slightly clammy forehead. 'You'd better believe it, sweetheart. We have a dinner date, remember?'

'Oh, yes,' was all she said, with what sounded like a satisfied sigh.

'Roll over the other way,' he advised thickly. 'I'll stroke your hair until you drop off.'

She obeyed him, sighing again when he started stroking.

Touching her—even her hair—was agony. But he did it, thinking all the while that she was worth the effort.

It was a relief when she fell asleep and he could creep out of the room, telling himself all the while that he wouldn't have to wait too long before he could satisfy the lust she kept on evoking in him. Less than twenty-four hours.

But as he stood in the doorway and glanced back at her it crossed Blake's testosterone-fired brain that once the alcohol was out of Kate's system and she didn't have to watch the man she loved marry her sister she might not be quite the same person who'd thrown herself at him tonight. Tomorrow morning she might be filled with shame and embarrassment. She might actually say no to him.

What a horrific thought!

Blake closed the door and walked slowly towards the staircase, pondering such a possibility. Not for long, however. Confidence in his own abilities had never been a problem for Blake. He had always achieved what he'd set his sights on. And he'd set his sights on getting Kate into his bed.

She wouldn't say no to him. He'd make sure of that!

CHAPTER TWELVE

'IT'S GOOD OF you to drive me home,' Kate said with stiff politeness once they were out of Byron's driveway.

Blake glanced over at her from behind the wheel of his borrowed Lexus. She looked vastly different from the glamorous bridesmaid of last night. Just a simple girl this morning, wearing dark jeans, trainers, and a grey sweatshirt which had a picture of the Opera House on it. No make-up, and her damp and very straight hair pulled back into a ponytail, not a curl or a wave in sight. Not a hint of perfume, either.

Blake wondered if this was some ploy to get him to lose interest in her. Fat chance of that happening. He'd thought of little else all night. Besides, he adored the way she looked. So natural, yet still so sexy.

'My pleasure,' he replied warmly.

She didn't say anything further, gazing out of the passenger window like some tourist taking in the sights. Blake doubted it was anything like that. He suspected, as he'd feared, that she'd woken this morning feeling pretty bad about what had happened the night before.

Cleo had taken a breakfast tray up to her room around ten, reporting back that Kate seemed somewhat subdued.

'There's no need to feel embarrassed,' he said at last.

Her head whipped round and her expression was totally devoid of embarrassment. Or distress. 'I'm not,' she denied. 'I was for a short while this morning. But not any longer.'

'Good.'

'I know I made a fool of myself last night, but that's all in the past now. I have to move on.'

'You definitely do.'

'I dare say that sooner or later I'll get over being in love with Lachlan, but until that happens I'm not going to waste any more of my life mooning over him or wishing things were different. I'm going to concentrate on my career—one hundred and ten percent.'

'Atta girl.'

She threw him a droll glance. 'That doesn't mean I'm going to jump into bed with *you*, just because you've offered me a part in one of your movies.'

Blake almost ran into the back of the car in front of him, braking just in time. He hadn't noticed that the lights ahead had turned red, bringing the traffic to an abrupt halt. As, it seemed, were his plans for tonight.

'Are you saying that your being attracted to me last night was all about the drink, then?' he asked casually. Oh, *so* casually. If there was one thing Blake had learned about the female sex since the debacle with Claudia, it was never to let a girl know you wanted her like crazy.

Kate scrunched up her face. 'I didn't think so at the time. But in hindsight I suppose it did play a part. Look, I want to be strictly honest with you, Blake. I was in a pathetic state last light. Your attention flattered my rather fragile self-esteem. You're a good-looking man. You're also powerful and successful. I'm not used to men like you coming on to me.'

'Then more fool them,' he said, and smiled over at her.

She didn't smile back. 'Please don't,' she bit out.

'Don't what?'

'Don't keep flattering me. I don't appreciate it. Now, I have a couple of questions to ask you about this part you've offered me. Unless, of course, you've changed your mind about that now you've seen how I usually look,' she added with a steely glance his way.

Brother, that 'fragile self-esteem' of hers seemed to have taken a back seat. There was not a hint of vulnerability in her eyes at this moment. Kate had suddenly turned into one tough cookie. Blake suppressed a smile. He liked her tough almost as much as he liked her tipsy.

The lights turned green and he drove on. More slowly this time.

'I actually like the way you look today,' he told her. 'I'm not into Barbie dolls. So the offer still stands. It would be a wonderful addition to your résumé and will get you more work. Not here in Australia, however. You'd have to move to LA and get yourself an American agent.'

'Move to LA!' she exclaimed, her eyes widening for a split second before she got control of herself again. 'I didn't realise— I…um…forgot you'd moved over there.'

'I'll probably make the occasional movie back here in Australia, but not the one I'm offering you. Look, we don't actually start shooting until late November, so you've got plenty of time to get yourself organised and over there. We're still in pre-production and I've a few more minor characters to cast.'

'I see,' she said thoughtfully. 'And how will you go about doing that?'

Blake shrugged. 'I'll have a couple of the casting agencies I use send me some likely candidates and I'll give them all an audition. Then I'll choose.'

'In that case that's what I want to do too,' Kate said firmly. 'Go for a proper audition up against other people.'

Blake suppressed his frustration and kept his voice calm. 'But, Kate, there's no need. The role's yours.'

'Why? It doesn't make sense. Unless what Lachlan said was true. That you give the girls you fancy small roles in your movies just so you can shag them every night.'

'Lachlan said *what*?'

'You heard me.'

'Bastard.'

'Is it true?' she demanded. '*Do* you do that?'

Bloody hell. What did he say to that?

'I have done,' he admitted reluctantly. 'Once or twice. In the long-distant past when I was hurting after Claudia divorced me. I'm not proud of it, but I haven't done anything like that for many years. I can't understand why Lachlan would say such a thing. These days I would never risk the success of one of my movies by offering actresses roles on the strength of how much I fancy them.'

'That's what Lachlan said too. That's why you only ever offer the girls you fancy really *small* roles.'

Blake's temper rose. 'So when did Lachlan say all this to you?' he demanded through clenched teeth.

'Last night.'

'Yes, of course. It *would* have been last night. *When*, exactly, last night?'

'When I left you briefly to go to the Ladies. He followed me. He said he cared about me and was worried about me getting tangled up with you.'

'Yeah. Right. And you believed him?'

'I believed what he said about *you*. After all, you'd already offered me a small part in one of your movies without knowing if I could act or not.'

'Firstly, madam, I *do* know you can act. You're a graduate of NIDA, for heaven's sake! Secondly, it is *not* a small role. It's a very good supporting role. Thirdly, I didn't offer you the role because I wanted to "shag" you,' he insisted. 'God, I hate that term. It sounds disgusting. I much prefer to say "have sex", or "sleep with", or even "make love". Anyway, wanting to have sex with you isn't the reason I offered you that job.'

'Oh? What was, then?' Both her question and her eyes were full of scepticism.

Blake sighed. 'I just wanted to make you happy. To make you smile.'

She stared at him for a long moment. 'So you offered me a job out of pity?' she bit out, angry now.

'Absolutely not! I'm not into pity—especially where my movies are concerned.'

'What *are* you into, then?' she asked, a challenging note in her voice.

'Success. And satisfaction.'

'What kind of satisfaction?'

His smile was rueful. 'What do you want me to say, Kate? Okay, so I want to have sex with you. That's hardly a hanging offence. I'm single. You're single. You haven't got a boyfriend and you're not a virgin. I assume you *do* have a sex life? I honestly thought you might enjoy going to bed with me. I'd certainly enjoy going to bed with you. But, aside from all that, I wasn't lying when I said my main motivation for all the things I did last night was to put a smile on your face. That was God's honest truth and it still is. I'm sorry if I've offended you. That was the last thing I wanted to do. Look, if it makes you happy I'll give you a proper screen test for the role. We can do it tonight. I'm sure I've already told you that I'm staying in Byron's city penthouse for the next couple of days. We could go there early this evening, before I take you out to dinner. Or are you reneging on that as well?'

'I'm not reneging on anything. I just need to get some things sorted in my head.'

'Such as what?'

'Such as if my audition's all right, and you still offer me the role, does the offer come with strings attached? Will you expect me to sleep with you at some stage?'

He looked at her long and hard. 'Only if you want to,' he said.

She didn't answer straight away, just turned her head to stare out through the passenger window for a while before glancing back at him.

'Fair enough,' she said, and rewarded him with a small, rather enigmatic smile.

He wondered what it meant, that smile. Whatever, he took some comfort from it. And some confidence. Which was strange, given that confidence was never usually a problem with him—especially with members of the opposite sex.

But Kate rattled him in ways he had yet to fully understand. Blake knew he was very attracted to her, but she stirred other emotions in him besides lust—emotions that were both uncharacteristic and unfamiliar.

In the past few years his relationships with women had basically been selfish ones, his only concern what pleasure they could bring to his life. Sex. Companionship. Compliments.

Oh, yes, he enjoyed the way the women in his world flirted with him, and flattered him, and, yes, were only too willing to go to bed with him. Which suited Blake just fine. He never felt he had to bend over backwards to please them. Didn't need to declare love or promise commitment to enjoy their company.

Kate, however, brought out the gentleman in him. Yes, he wanted her—but not quite so selfishly. His tendency to think only of himself was tempered by a compulsion to try to make everything right in her world. To make her… Yes… to make her *happy*. Of course that didn't mean he wouldn't try to seduce her tonight. He would. But he would stop if she made it clear that she didn't want him to. The trick was to make sure she *did* want him to…

'You might have to make a slight detour,' she said suddenly. 'I'd like to drop off my bridesmaid dress at the dry cleaner's. No way am I taking it home the way it is. Do you know your way to the big shopping centre at Burwood?'

'Not exactly.' He wasn't as familiar with the western

suburbs as he was with the eastern, having being brought up there.

'We're not far away now. I'll give you directions, if you like.'

Half an hour later they were back in the Lexus and heading for Strathfield, which was the next suburb going west.

'It will do you good to move away from home,' Blake said, after seeing how stressed Kate had been at the dry cleaner's, despite the lady there assuring her that the dress would be as good as new once cleaned properly. 'Your mother sounds like a pain. And it's perfectly obvious that Maddie is the family pet.'

Kate sighed. 'You're right on both those counts.'

'Then why are you finding excuses not to come to Hollywood and make a new life for yourself? You said you wanted to move on. So do it!'

'I'm not making excuses. I just want to make it on my own. I don't want charity.'

Lord, but she was one difficult girl. Any other actress would have jumped at the chance.

'Don't you believe in your acting ability?' he challenged.

Her chin came up and her eyes flashed. 'Yes, I do. I'm very good. *Damned* good, actually.'

'Then be "damned good" tonight and you'll be on your way to LA.'

CHAPTER THIRTEEN

'WHERE'S YOUR BRIDESMAID DRESS?' were her mother's first words when Kate walked into the family kitchen shortly after midday. 'Don't tell me it's stuffed into that silly little bag!'

Kate counted to ten, then said, 'It's at the dry cleaner's. Someone knocked into me and I spilt some wine on it.'

'Oh, for pity's sake, Kate. Couldn't you have been more careful? Just as well I brought Maddie's dress home with me or that would probably be ruined too.'

'My dress is not ruined,' Kate countered, quite calmly, hugging the hope that soon she wouldn't have to put up with this kind of thing. 'The dry cleaner said it would be as good as new.'

'I hope so. Did Maddie finally get you? She rang me from the airport and said she'd tried to ring you but your phone was turned off.'

'Yes. Yes, it was.' And would remain so for now.

The last person she wanted to talk to was Maddie. She didn't want to hear how wonderful her wedding night had been. Neither did she want to hear a blow-by-blow description of every moment of her honeymoon. Kate had told her sister yesterday not to ring her, but to put her news on social media.

Her mother rolled her eyes in exasperation. 'What's the point of having a mobile if you don't turn it on? Anyway, Maddie sent you a message via me—though I have no idea what she was on about. She said she hopes you did what she told you to last night and that everything worked out. Does that make sense to you?'

'Perfect sense,' Kate replied, and searched her mind for

a half-truthful answer which wouldn't shock the pants off her mother. 'Maddie suggested I suck up to Blake Randall and see if I could get myself a part in one of his movies.'

'Goodness. Such language. I'm sure Maddie wouldn't have said it like that. And did you do that? Er…"suck up" to the man?'

'I sure did.'

'And what happened?'

Various images flashed into Kate's head, none of which she could relate to her mother.

'Blake said that since I was a graduate of NIDA he would gladly give me a screen test.'

'Oh, my. What a clever girl your sister is.'

Kate almost lost it then. Truly, did Maddie have to get the credit for *everything*?

Another count to ten.

'So when are you having this screen test?' her mother asked eagerly.

'Blake is organising one for early this evening,' she informed her mother, thinking to herself that she really would have to turn her phone back on in case Byron wanted to ring her. 'He flies back to LA in a couple of days, so time is of the essence. Now, I'm going to go and have a lie-down. Last night has exhausted me. Oh, and don't worry about cooking me dinner tonight, Mum. I won't be coming back here after the audition. Blake's taking me out to dinner.'

'Blake Randall is taking you out to *dinner*?' she said, mouth agape.

'Yes. Do you have a problem with that?'

Her mother tossed her head, the way she did when she couldn't think of what to say for a second or two. 'Well, you're not the sort of girl men like him *usually* take to dinner,' she finally managed. 'There again, I suppose you *did* look surprisingly attractive at the wedding yesterday.'

Her eyes narrowed on Kate's outfit.

'Make sure you wear something better than what you've got on, though. And put on some make-up and do your hair properly. Truly, Kate, it's no wonder you haven't had a boyfriend for years. You simply don't try.'

Kate didn't tell her that Blake had said he liked the way she was dressed today. Her mother probably had no idea he'd driven her home. Blake hadn't come inside. No doubt she thought Kate had taken a taxi home.

'Maybe I don't *want* a boyfriend,' she fired back.

'More likely the one you want you can't have,' her mother muttered.

'Oh, not you too, Mum,' Kate said, hiding her hurt behind irritation. Did *everyone* in her family know about her infatuation with Lachlan?

Yes, of course they did. Time, then, to put things to right.

'If you're talking about Lachlan, then you're way off the mark. Yes, I did have a crush on him once—but I got over that ages ago. Frankly, I feel sorry for Maddie being married to him. He's not the type to stay faithful.'

'Oh, rubbish! Lachlan adores Maddie. And why would he look elsewhere when he has a wife as beautiful as she is to come home to? They make a brilliant couple. You're just jealous, that's all.'

'No, Mum, I'm not,' she said, with the kind of calmness which came with stating the truth.

Because, as amazing as it seemed, Kate didn't feel jealous of Maddie marrying Lachlan any longer. Not one iota. Her breakdown last night seemed to have somehow banished all the self-destructive emotions which had been affecting both her life and her career for ages. Her depression was gone this morning, along with her lack of spirit. She felt stronger, and a lot more confident.

Kate suspected that her love for Lachlan was on the wane. Her rose-tinted glasses were off where he was concerned and she was finally able to see him for what he was. Not a charming golden boy, but a selfish, arrogant and narcissistic individual, whose only aim in life was his own success. She doubted he loved Maddie any more than Maddie loved him. They were both just trophies for each other. If their marriage lasted two years she'd be surprised.

'Time will tell, I guess,' she added, and walked out of the kitchen.

By the time she reached her bedroom she'd totally dismissed her mother's annoying remarks, plus all thoughts of Lachlan and Maddie. They were not what she wanted to think about right now. She had other things on her mind. Like what *was* she going to wear tonight?

Kate wasn't all that worried about the screen test. She suspected it was just a formality. Blake had said he was going to give her the part anyway; it was only she who had insisted upon a screen test to save her dignity.

She would be wonderful tonight. Her pride demanded it. The same pride that had claimed she would not jump into bed with him just because he'd promised her a job.

His reaction to her making that stand had been very telling. Lord, he'd almost crashed into the car in front of them. Clearly he *had* expected her to sleep with him. But he'd been clever enough to pretend that he hadn't assumed as much.

'Only if you want to…'

What a devious and devilishly tempting invitation *that* was. Because she did want to. Had known it immediately he'd said those words. She hadn't dared look over at him lest he see the heat in her eyes. So she'd looked away until her reaction could be controlled and she could reply with a brilliantly nonchalant remark.

Not that he'd seemed put out by it. No doubt he still thought it was just a matter of time before she gave him what he wanted.

Which was her. In his bed.

The realisation still astounded her. Why *her*? She just didn't understand the ongoing attraction on his part—and certainly not today, when she looked anything but attractive. But she would tonight. Oh, yes, her pride wouldn't let her go for the screen test and then out to dinner with Blake looking, as Maddie would have said, 'like a drack sack'.

She did have some smart outfits—most of them bought for special occasions and nearly all of them chosen for her by Maddie, who admittedly did have good taste and was always on trend with fashion. One particular outfit came to mind. It had been in a shop window, on a tall mannequin with honey-coloured hair rather like hers. Maddie had dragged Kate out clothes shopping back in May, insisting that Kate buy something decent for her engagement party.

'That'd look good on you,' she'd pointed out.

'Maybe…' Kate had replied. 'But it's hardly a ball gown.'

It certainly hadn't been a ball gown, but a knee-length dark red satin cocktail dress, with finger-width straps, snugly fitted, and paired with elegant stiletto shoes. Hanging around the mannequin's neck had been an oval-shaped diamond pendant on a long, fine silver chain.

'No matter. We can look for a ball gown later. We've got all day. Let's go in and try that on you.'

It had suited her, and Maddie had insisted she buy the whole outfit—pendant as well. Thank God it had only been costume jewellery. As it was everything had come to over five hundred dollars. When Kate had dithered about the price Maddie had blithely used her credit card to pay for it all, telling her not to worry, that she wanted her to have it.

'Call it an early birthday present,' she'd said.

Kate had thought the gesture terribly generous of her at the time. Now she wondered if there had been some guilt involved. Whatever—it was a stylish outfit, and one in which she would feel good tonight.

Walking over to her wardrobe, she drew it out and hung

it on the door. Then she turned her phone back on—surely Maddie would be in the air by now—lay down on her bed and tried to get some rest.

But her mind wouldn't let her. She kept thinking about Blake lying next to her last night, telling her that she was going to have a very late night tonight. She wondered if he still meant to seduce her, regardless of what he'd said in the car today.

Surely he wouldn't. A *gentleman* wouldn't. A gentleman would keep his word.

But he wasn't *really* a gentleman, was he? It would be naive of her to pretend that he was. Yes, he'd been very kind to her last night. Quite the white knight. But she suspected that gallantry wasn't his true nature; more likely he was a clever and ruthless devil who wasn't beyond using bribery to get a girl into his bed.

He'd used sweet words as well.

I just want to make you happy. To make you smile...

Could she really believe that? Why should he care whether she was unhappy or not? He didn't even know her!

Lachlan had warned her about him—said he was bitter and twisted after what Claudia had done to him, that he used women and treated them badly. But that didn't ring true either. There *was* kindness in him. And compassion. Oh, Lord, she wished she could work him out. He was a conundrum, all right. Still, she really should stick to her guns and not let him seduce her tonight...even if her heart beat faster at the thought.

CHAPTER FOURTEEN

KATE COULDN'T BELIEVE her luck when her mother popped her head around her bedroom door just after four, announcing that she and her father had been invited out for dinner with some friends. They hadn't been guests at the wedding and they wanted to hear all about it.

Off she went, without another word, leaving Kate feeling both grateful and slightly miffed. Which was perverse, she thought as she rose and started getting herself ready. The last thing she wanted was her mother making critical remarks about how she looked. But she might at least have thought to wish her luck with the screen test.

Six o'clock saw her pacing up and down in the front room, watching and waiting for Blake to arrive. By five past six she was beginning to panic. By ten past six she felt sick. He wasn't coming. He'd changed his mind. But if that was so then why hadn't he rung?

It was at this critical point that she remembered he didn't have her phone number. She hadn't given it to him. She didn't have his, either. What if he'd had an accident? What if…?

And then there he was, pulling in to the kerb, jumping out from behind the wheel and striding round the front of the silver Lexus. God, he looked gorgeous, dressed all in black. Black trousers and a black silk shirt, black belt and shoes. Black as his hair. He was frowning, though, his thick dark brows drawn tightly together as he hurried through the wrought-iron gate along the path and up onto the front porch.

Kate resisted flinging open the door before he'd actually rung the bell, but it was a close call. She made him wait a few seconds before she finally turned the knob, doing her best to stay calm and composed and not act like a teenager on her first date.

Actually, it *was* her first date for some years—a fact which should have been depressing. But she had no time for depression tonight. She was having a screen test with the brilliant and wickedly sexy Blake Randall and then going out to dinner with him. How fantastic was *that*?

His deeply set blue eyes gave her one long thorough once-over. 'Good God, Kate, you make it hard on a guy, don't you?' he growled.

'What do you mean?' she asked, pretending not to understand.

'You know exactly what I mean, you bad girl. You could have at least put your hair up into a prissy bun thing instead of leaving it down. I have to tell you now that I have a thing for long hair—especially long, straight, silky honey-coloured hair. I also have a thing for silk dresses and sexy stilettos.'

His sigh was rather melodramatic.

'I thought you wanted me to keep my hands off tonight? Oh, don't bother to answer that,' he swept on, whilst rolling his eyes. 'I'll do my best but I can't promise you anything. Now, let's get going. We're already running late.'

'I have to just get my purse and lock up.'

Kate glanced in the hallway mirror as she hurried past. Her cheeks were flushed and her eyes shining. Lord, he really was a devil. Because she didn't *want* him to keep his hands off, did she?

'So, where's Mommie Dearest?' he asked as they made their way out to the car.

'Visiting some friends.'

'Does she know you're out with me tonight?'

'Oh, yes. I told her. About the screen test *and* the dinner.'

'And?'

'She was surprised at first, and then not very interested.'

'You know, she's just like *my* mother,' he said as he opened the passenger door.

'Oh? In what way?'

'I have an older brother—James. He's the apple of her eye. Can do no wrong. I'm the black sheep in a family of doctors.'

'So you understand, then?' Kate said with a sigh as she climbed in and buckled up.

'I certainly do.'

She closed the door.

'Hold on to this,' he added after getting in behind the wheel and handing her a tablet. 'I've copied the three scenes you're in and brought them up, ready for you to read. You can study them during the drive to Byron's penthouse. That way you'll be prepared by the time we get there. Your character is a secretary who's having an affair with her married boss. She's actually a bit of a closet *femme fatale*—dresses very conservatively in the office and has a witty turn of phrase. I'm sure you'll get the gist once you've read the scenes.'

It hit Kate suddenly that very soon she was actually going to audition for *the* Blake Randall—movie-maker extraordinaire. Up until now it had all seemed somewhat hypothetical. She'd just presumed she would do well. Her confidence was at an all-time high today.

But what if she *didn't* do well? What if she totally stuffed it up?

Nerves gathered in the pit of her stomach as she read through the scenes. The first one wasn't too difficult. Just an office scene with a boss and his PA, with some clever *double entendres* in the dialogue. She thought she could handle the third scene as well. Back in the same office, with the boss breaking off the affair and saying he was going to try to make his marriage work. The PA then told him she'd already got another job and quit, throwing at him the fact that she had bigger fish to fry.

Kate quite liked the idea of playing a bitch. Those sorts of roles were often remembered. But the second scene worried the life out of her.

In a hotel bedroom, it required her character to be in bed, obviously naked under the covers, watching her lover get dressed. She was described as having 'sated, heavy-lidded eyes', with 'a blistering sensuality' in all her movements. In the scene she reached for a cigarette and smoked it slowly, praising her lover's performance and claiming she'd never had better.

'So what do you think?' Blake asked, perhaps sensing her unease.

'I think,' she said slowly, 'that I am going to have difficulty pulling off this role.'

'And why is that?'

Kate knew she had to be honest with him. Or risk making a total fool of herself. But, God, it was going to be hard telling him the truth.

'Well, the thing is…when I act I can usually tap in to some personal experience to help me with the emotions involved. I'm afraid I haven't anything to tap into for this second scene.'

His forehead bunched into a frown. 'What are you saying, Kate? Spell it out for me.'

Kate sighed. 'Well, if you must know, I've never lain in bed watching my lover get dressed. I've never experienced what it is to be sexually sated. I've only ever had three serious boyfriends, and they *were* just boys, really. And I wasn't ever in a bed—just in the back of a car or on a lumpy sofa. The first time was during my last year in high school. He was a total nerd and hadn't got a clue. Same as me. My other two boyfriends were at university, where I was doing an arts degree and waiting to get into NIDA. They were a bit better than the nerd, but not much.'

'I see,' Blake said thoughtfully. 'So why didn't you have sex with anyone once you went to NIDA? Surely there were some older more experienced chaps there who asked you out?'

'Yes. But I didn't want to go out with them.'

Blake rolled his eyes at her. 'Don't tell me. By then you were madly in love with Lachlan.'

His derisive tone brought an embarrassed heat to Kate's cheeks.

'Oh, Kate, that is just *so* pathetic.'

'I know,' she said in a small voice.

An awkward silence fell, and Kate was startled when she realised they were in the middle of the CBD. Blake suddenly shot across the road and down a ramp which led to an underground car park, braking hard at the bottom so he could activate the security gate. It rose slowly, during which time he threw her a frustrated glance.

'I suppose you haven't dated anyone this year, either?' he ground out.

She shook her head, her mouth having gone dry.

'Truly?' he exclaimed, then muttered very rude words under his breath the whole time it took him to park.

He stomped around to the passenger side of the car, wrenched open the door, snatched up the tablet from her lap and threw it onto the back seat before practically dragging her out of the car and over to the bank of lifts in the corner, glaring at her all the while.

'Not another word,' he snarled when her mouth opened to protest at his caveman-like handling.

Kate backed away from him in the lift, crossing her arms in a huddle of misery when he didn't explain what was going on. Clearly she wasn't going to be doing the screen test. Maybe he was going to give her a lecture about her futile love for Lachlan. He sure as hell was angry with her.

When the lift door opened on the top floor he strode out without looking to see if she was following him or not. She did, of course. What else could she do?

Byron's penthouse was exactly what Kate had expected of a billionaire owner. The rooms were massive and lavishly furnished, and the views from the terrace almost as good as those from the Centrepoint Tower. Everything that proclaimed Sydney one of the most beautiful cities in the world lay before her.

But Kate wasn't in the mood to be impressed. Neither was she interested in being lectured.

'I think,' she said as she stood in the middle of the main living room, her arms crossed once again, but this time with stiff resolve, not misery, 'that you should just take me home. I'd call a taxi, only my purse and my phone are still in your car.'

CHAPTER FIFTEEN

BLAKE WAS TORN between seducing her and slapping her. 'Don't be ridiculous,' he snapped.

'Don't call me ridiculous,' she fired back at him. 'You wanted the truth and I told it to you. I'm sorry if you find it "pathetic" to love someone enough not to want to be with anyone else. No doubt when Claudia dumped you, you went out and shagged everything in sight. But I'm not like that. My feelings run a little deeper.'

'Should I get the violins out now?'

'Oh!' she said, stunned by his insensitive attitude.

Her fingernails dug into her upper arm whilst she struggled with the urge to actually stamp her feet. The only thing stopping her was the fact that he would think her pathetically childish if she did.

'Might I remind you that you would have been quite happy for me to shag you last night?' he threw at her.

Her arms unfolded in a flurry and she strode up close to him, her dark eyes flashing with fury. 'Trust you to bring that up. I was drunk. You *know* I was drunk.'

'Not at first, you weren't. That only came later—after you'd been screwed up by your sweet sister. You wanted me when we were dancing, sweetheart, and don't pretend you didn't. You *still* want me.'

'I do not. I definitely do not. I… I…'

He'd had enough of this—enough of wanting this girl and having to wait until she accepted the fact that she wanted him back. Without hesitation he pulled her into his arms and kissed her, his mouth quite brutal with frustration and a wild, flaring passion.

She froze at first, but then she melted into him, moaning as her arms slid up around his neck, her high, softly rounded breasts pressing hard into his chest. Her gesture of surrender calmed his fury and his mouth gentled on hers, his hands sliding up under her jumper to caress the bare flesh of her lower back. He felt her shiver, then felt himself swell to alarming proportions.

I'm going too fast, came the stern warning. *I have to slow down. Have to. Going too fast isn't going to work with this girl.*

She might not be a virgin, but she was close to it.

Kate groaned when his head lifted. She didn't want him to stop. She'd never been kissed like that in her life. And it had been mind-blowing.

'So,' he said with a wry smile, 'before I go on I have a question I must ask you.'

'What?' she asked, her voice sounding dazed.

'Do you want to?'

'Do I want to what?'

He laughed. 'Have you forgotten already the deal we had? The one where we would only have sex if you wanted to.'

'Oh. Oh, yes. No. I mean, yes. I did forget about that.'

'So *do* you want to?'

'Yes,' she said, her heart pounding in her chest.

'You won't accuse me later of taking advantage of you? Or bribing you into bed with a part in one of my movies?'

'No.'

'Good. Now, I think this is cause for celebration. I'm sure I saw a bottle of champagne in the fridge earlier. Follow me.'

Kate blinked, then followed him into one of those kitchens that often featured in house and garden magazines. All white and stainless steel, with stone benchtops and no visible drawer handles.

'What are we celebrating?' she asked breathlessly as he retrieved the champagne and found a couple of glasses.

'You discovering that love and great sex don't have to go together.'

The cork popped and he filled the glasses, handing her one before lifting the other to his lips...those cruel-looking lips which only a couple of minutes earlier had rendered her mindless.

'Have you ever had an orgasm?' he asked her, his focus unblinking.

Oh, God, how to answer that?

'Yes,' she admitted, and then swallowed. 'Just not when I'm *with* anyone.'

'Right. Okay. I can work with that. At least you know what a climax feels like.'

Kate could only shake her head at him. 'This is a very intimate conversation.'

'But a very necessary one if I'm to give you what you want. And what you obviously need. Now, let's take our champers along to the master bedroom and get this show on the road.'

'This *show*?' she echoed, appalled and excited at the same time.

'Just an expression, sweetheart. Don't take offence. Sex can be fun, you know. A form of entertainment followed by the most delicious feeling of relaxation. It doesn't have to be all serious with lots of heavy emotion. Being in love can be very disappointing, because when you're in love you try too hard. And trying too hard is the kiss of death where good sex is concerned.'

'I wouldn't know,' she choked out, her stomach suddenly in knots.

'Drink up,' he advised. 'You're looking a little green around the gills.'

'I'm nervous, I guess.' She took a deep swallow, hoping that the alcohol would do the same job as it had last night.

'You weren't nervous when I was kissing you just now. Once we get started again you'll be fine. Trust me.'

She did, letting him lead her down to the most magnificent bedroom she'd ever seen. He turned to shut the door, leaving her to wander over to the king-sized bed which was dressed all in white, with a fluffy grey throw draped across the foot of the bed.

She took another swallow of champagne as she stared at the bed and tried to imagine being naked in it with Blake by her side.

'Here, give me that,' Blake said, taking the glass from her trembling hand and putting it down with his on one of the bedside tables. 'You're thinking too much,' he said, and drew her into his arms, his eyes darkening as they roved over her probably anxious-looking face.

Just kiss me, she thought breathlessly. *Kiss me and take me again to that place where the real world recedes and there's nothing but your mouth on mine and your hands all over me.*

He kissed her, but slowly this time, tenderly, his lips roving over hers until they gasped apart. She sucked in sharply when his tongue-tip met hers, moaning for more. But he didn't ravage her mouth as she'd thought she wanted him too. Instead he made love to it, giving her pleasure and frustration in equal parts. His hands were gentle as well—not delving boldly under her top as they had before, but running up and down her spine on top of her clothes.

When he stopped, she groaned in protest.

His head lifted and he smiled down at her. 'Softly, softly, catchee monkey,' he murmured.

'What?'

'Nothing. Come on. Sit down.'

'Sit down?'

'Yes. I want to get rid of those heels for starters.'

She sank down on the side of the bed, stunned when Blake knelt at her feet and slowly removed her left shoe.

Once it was disposed of he glanced up at her, his smile wry. 'I'm always removing your footwear.' Then he bent his head and slipped off her right stiletto, easing it off and tossing it aside.

'Now,' he went on as he stood up, 'as gorgeous as your top is, I want that gone as well.'

Kate immediately thought of her simple white cotton bra—which, whilst not old, wasn't very new either. Or very sexy.

Before she could worry too much about it he'd removed her pendant, dropping it on the bedside table before slipping the thin straps of her dress over her shoulders.

'If I'd known I was going to d-do this,' she stammered, 'I would have worn some s-sexier underclothes. Not that I have any…' she muttered under her breath.

'Come now, Kate,' Blake said with laughing eyes. 'What about that black number you had on last night? That had me salivating, it was so sexy.'

'Maddie bought that for me.'

'Oh, yes—Maddie the sex kitten. Or at least she thinks she is.'

'You don't think so?'

'I already told you, Kate. She's not my type. Now, *you*…' he continued as he reached around and unhooked her bra. 'You are definitely my type.'

Kate's heartbeat stopped when he peeled off her bra and left her sitting there naked to the waist. Yet, oddly, she felt more excited than embarrassed. And totally breathless. After a few dizzying seconds she began breathing again, hard and fast, her chest expanding as she sucked in much-needed air.

Blake's eyes dropped to her breasts with their fiercely erect nipples, all tight and hard and eager for his hands, or his mouth.

'Oh, yes,' he said thickly. '*Definitely* my type.'

Just when she thought he was going to do what she craved he knelt down again, reaching up under the skirt of her dress and pulling down her white cotton panties. And then he was pushing her back onto the bed and lifting her dress, putting his mouth not to her aching nipples but to that part of her which she hadn't realised until that moment was far needier.

She gasped, then groaned. His fingers and tongue were doing things to her that had never been done before. They made her burn for him, made her incapable of stopping him. She was mindless. Tortured. Rapturous. All she knew was that she couldn't bear it if he stopped. She was so close to coming. *So* close.

He stopped.

'No, don't stop!' she cried out.

'Have to, sweetness,' he said, standing up and pulling her skirt down again.

'But I was about to...you know—' She broke off and sat up, feeling flustered and frustrated.

'Yes, I know. But so was I.'

'Oh,' she said, only then noting his ragged breathing.

'Never happened to me before,' he ground out, and stared at her as if it was *her* fault.

'I'm sorry,' she said, which was crazy. What was she saying sorry for?

'I suppose it has been several weeks since I've had sex,' he muttered, as if he was looking for a valid reason for his lack of control.

'Really?' That surprised Kate. She'd always thought powerful, good-looking men like Blake never did without sex for long. She'd imagined they always had women throwing themselves at them.

'Really and truly.' He sighed a heavy sigh, at the same time running his hands agitatedly through his hair. 'Under the circumstances, best we move on to the real thing.'

CHAPTER SIXTEEN

'I JUST NEED to go to the bathroom first,' Blake lied. 'Meanwhile, why don't you get into bed?' He made his escape, desperate for a minute or two by himself.

Blake closed the door firmly behind him, still rattled by what had just happened. He simply couldn't believe he'd almost lost it, having always prided himself on his sexual skills—especially his ability to control his body and not act like some horny teenager whose only aim was getting his rocks off.

It was especially embarrassing given Kate's sexual history. He'd been determined to give her the time of her life, and what had he done? Almost blown it—that was what he'd done.

Maybe he'd been trying too hard to please her.

That last thought bothered him. He wasn't usually a try-hard.

He glanced at himself in the bathroom mirror, shocked by what he saw. Not his usual cavalier self, but someone who was beginning to care too much. About her. That was the problem. It had been the problem from the first moment he'd seen her, walking down that staircase, looking haunted and terrified.

It annoyed the hell out of him that she was in love with Lachlan—that she probably fantasised about him when she made herself come in her lonely bed at night. He wanted to obliterate that bastard from her mind...wanted to give her something or someone better to dream about.

And that would be you, would it, Blake Randall? You—a man who doesn't even believe in love, or romance, or any of the things that seem to matter to women? What can you give Kate that would really matter to her? That would be a positive influence in her life? That would make her happy? Or at least happier.

The chance for a successful acting career, he supposed. And a healthier attitude to sex. Sex didn't *have* to be connected to love. Much better to be just about physical pleasure. And fun. That was what he had told her, and that was what he was going to deliver.

So he cared about her as well? So what? He was allowed to care, wasn't he? There was no crime in that.

'Right,' he told himself sternly, and turned to flush the toilet before heading for the bathroom door.

Kate stiffened when she heard the toilet flush. She had taken off her dress and dived naked into the bed, shivering a little at the coolness of the sheets. Not that the room was cold, the penthouse obviously had ducted air-conditioning and heating.

Her heart jumped when he emerged, but his ready smile calmed her a little.

'Sorry about that,' he said, and whipped his shirt up off over his head.

Kate hadn't really thought about what his body might look like without clothes. She'd known he was tall and slim, with nice shoulders and olive skin. But the reality was better than she could have imagined, with his well-toned arms and chest, and a smattering of dark, sexy curls arrowing down to his navel.

'You must work out a lot,' she said, just for something to say. Better than sitting there ogling him.

He shrugged as he took his wallet out of his pocket and placed it by the bed. 'I have a gym in my home. Everyone works out in Hollywood. Everyone except the really fat-cat producers. All they have to do is go to lunch and show their credit cards.'

'I jog sometimes,' she said, trying not to stare. But it was getting harder now he'd taken off his trousers. 'And I walk a lot. I don't have a car.'

'You have a great figure,' he complimented her, sitting down on the side of the bed in his black underpants and taking off his shoes and socks. 'I adore it. I like natural.'

'Well, I'm certainly that.'

Maddie had had a boob job when she was twenty, which her parents had happily paid for. But Kate didn't mind her B-cup breasts, believing they went with her more athletic shape. Her agent had once criticised her smallish bust, but she'd ignored him. Thank goodness she had. She rather suspected Blake wouldn't have fancied her if her breasts had been surgically enhanced.

Relief swamped Kate when Blake kept his back to her as he took off his underpants. Hopefully he would just dive into bed the way she had and she wouldn't have to look at his penis.

But he didn't oblige, turning to pick up his wallet and extract a condom first. He was fully erect. Impressively so. Her mouth went dry at the thought of what was to come. Her heartbeat quickened.

She looked away while he drew the condom on, not turning back to face him until she felt the mattress dip.

'Don't go shy on me,' he told her as he put his arms around her and drew her close.

She looked up into his eyes. 'I'm not shy so much as nervous. I need you to kiss me again.'

'And *I* need to kiss you again,' he replied, and did so.

It was even better with their naked bodies pressed against each other. So exciting and intimate, making her quickly hungry for more. Not just more kissing. More bodily contact. She wanted him inside her. No, *needed* him inside her. Her leg lifted to curve over his hip, giving him access to her body, urging him without words to take her. Now. *Now!*

He did her silent bidding, his body surging into hers, rolling her onto her back and going even deeper. His mouth moved away from hers, his eyes hot and hungry as he began to move. She moved with him, lifting her legs high onto his back, clinging to him and almost sobbing with pleasure. Her heart was squeezed tight in her chest, her flesh gripping his like a vice.

She was just beginning to think she might have a heart attack when she came with a rush, her release so brilliant and violent that she screamed out. 'Blake! Oh, Blake!'

His climax quickly followed hers, and his own cry of release was loud and primal, his whole body shuddering as he came. Finally he collapsed across her and buried his face in her hair.

Kate revelled in the feel of his weight, holding him tight lest he try to withdraw. She didn't feel all limp and sleepy, like she'd read in books. She felt more awake and alive than she'd ever felt before. She could hardly wait to do it again. And again. She wanted to try everything with him—every possible position—and not just in this bed.

Her fantasies were endless and wild. She was envisaging herself doing the sort of things Maddie did with Lachlan.

Lachlan...

It came as a shock to Kate that she could think of Lachlan whilst in bed with another man and not feel a single bit of regret that it wasn't him in bed with her. If anything, the thought of him vaguely repulsed her. How odd. Was she over him at last? She rather suspected she was. Whatever—she'd certainly reached a point where her feelings for her brother-in-law were not going to stop her from enjoying life. From enjoying Blake.

Kate stirred beneath him. Blake lifted his head and smiled down at her. She smiled back at him—a slow, sensual smile which echoed her satisfaction and hinted at her on-going desires.

'Methinks,' he said, with a sexy glitter in his eyes, 'that you won't have too much trouble with that movie role after all.'

CHAPTER SEVENTEEN

'YOU'RE DOING *WHAT*?'

Kate ignored her mother's horrified reaction—at least on the surface. She'd known what to expect and had steeled herself accordingly.

'You heard what I said, Mum,' she replied coolly. 'I'm going to Hollywood. My screen test went very well last night. Blake said the part is definitely mine.'

Lord, she really *was* a good actress. Not a hint of irony on her face. Nor shame. Not that she intended to feel shame over what she'd done with Blake last night. Or what she intended to do in the future. He'd opened a whole new world to her—one she wanted to explore and enjoy to the full. And she wasn't just thinking about her career.

'He's also kindly offered to let me stay at his place until I get on my feet.'

She couldn't wait to live in the same house as him, to be with him every night. Even if it only lasted a short while.

Janice Holiday's eyes narrowed on her daughter. 'Now, why would he do something like that?'

'Why not? He's a kind and generous man. Look at the way he stepped in and organised that lovely and totally free venue for Maddie's wedding, saving Maddie from a nervous breakdown and saving you and Dad an absolute fortune. He didn't have to do that.'

'We *did* pay for the marquee,' Janice huffed. '*And* the catering. Besides, it was Lachlan he was helping out—not us. *He's* the one who's making Blake Randall a small fortune.'

'I think the shoe is on the other foot, Mum. It's Blake who's making *Lachlan* a small fortune. Without him Lachlan would still be a struggling actor, trying to make ends meet.'

'Oh, rubbish! Anyone with any brains can see it's Lachlan's talent which has put Blake Randall on the map. Without him that man would be an also-ran, making boring little movies which no one would go to see.'

Kate had no intention of arguing with her mother. Experience had taught her it was a total waste of time. She always had to have the last word.

'Don't think I don't know what's going on,' her mother continued, her tone caustic. 'Men like that always want something in return for their so-called generosity. You slept with him last night, didn't you?'

Kate drew herself up to her full five foot nine inches, setting reproachful eyes on her mother. 'I did not,' she denied, quite truthfully.

They hadn't slept one bit—either before or after dinner.

'Well, it's just a matter of time. When are you seeing him next? Today, I'll bet.'

'No, I'm not.' *Worse luck.* 'He's playing golf with Byron today, and has an important business dinner tonight. Then he's booked to fly back to LA early tomorrow morning. I plan to follow as soon as I can. I checked the visa situation online and Australians can get their visa waivered—but you have to wait three days after applying. I'm allowed to stay for ninety days before reapplying.'

Her mother looked doubtful. 'Surely that would only cover tourists? Not people who are going to work in the country?'

'No, it says you can be going there for business or pleasure. And Blake said once I'm there and have a contract in my hand I can apply for some other visa which I will eventually need.'

'So you haven't signed a contract yet?'

'No. Not yet. But I will once I get over there.'

'And who's going to pay for your plane ticket to get you over there? *You* don't have that sort of money. Or is our generous Mr Randall going to pay for that as well?'

Blake had offered to do just that, but Kate had refused. She didn't mind temporarily staying in his house as a guest, but she wasn't going to let him pay for other things. That would make her feel like a kept woman. All she wanted from Blake was a helping hand with her career. Oh, yes, and lots of lovely sex.

'I was hoping that you and Dad would buy me a return ticket. After all, I've never asked you to buy me anything before.'

'We give you free board and lodging. I would have thought that was enough.'

'You gave Maddie free board and lodging too,' Kate pointed out, keeping her temper with difficulty. 'Yet she was earning good money as a receptionist. On top of which you bought her a car *and* paid for her to have a boob job. Not to mention a thousand other expensive items over the years. I have never asked you for *anything*, Mum,' she said, her voice rising a few decibels. *'Never.'*

Her father suddenly appeared in the doorway, surprising Kate. She'd thought he'd be at work by now. Possibly he had a flex day. He sometimes took one on a Monday, and he was still in his dressing gown.

'What are you two arguing about?' he asked wearily.

'Kate wants us to buy her a plane ticket to go to Hollywood. A return ticket, no less. She's had this ridiculous offer of a movie role from Blake Randall and she thinks he's doing it out of the goodness of his heart. She doesn't realise there's no such thing as a free lunch. He'll want his pound of flesh in return. And it's not as though she has a contract in her hand. On top of that, she's going to stay at his house. Well, I *ask* you. It's as plain as the nose on your face what he wants. Though Lord knows why. I mean, it's not as though Kate is a raving beauty, like our Maddie. I could understand it if Blake Randall wanted *her* for a part in one of his movies. What do you think, Neville?'

'What do I *think*, Janice?'

He answered in a tone that Kate had never heard before. It was rather cold and very firm—not what she'd expected from her hen-pecked father.

'I think we should not only support our daughter and buy her a return ticket to LA, but that we should make it business class. It's a long trip, and I wouldn't want her getting there looking all tired and drawn. Unlike you, I have every respect for Blake Randall, and I don't think he has some dastardly ulterior motive in offering Kate a part in one of his movies. Why should he when she's such a brilliant actress? Have you forgotten how wonderful she was in those plays they put on at NIDA? *She* was the star—not Lachlan. I dare say Blake Randall was already aware of her talent, even before her screen test.

'And by the way,' he added, whilst his wife's mouth was still hanging open. 'Kate might not be what *some* people call a raving beauty, but she is very attractive, with classic features which will last long after most women's faces fall apart. Now, I am going back to bed. I'm not at my best this morning. Please give Kate our credit card, Janice. And Kate? Well done. You're a hard worker and a fine actress and you deserve all the success in the world.'

'I have to confess, Blake,' Kate told him when he rang her later, as promised, 'that I didn't know whether to laugh or cry. I mean, it was amusing to see my mother stuck for words for once, but...but...' She felt suddenly choked up and couldn't go on.

'But you were touched by your father's magnificent defence of you?'

'Yes. Yes, I was.'

The things he'd said about her had meant so much. Kate hadn't realised how hurt she'd been all these years by his seeming to favour Maddie. Now she saw that it had been more her mother doing the favouring than him. He'd just gone along with what his wife and Maddie wanted to keep the peace. Of course Maddie *was* very charming—and very manipulative. It was awfully hard to say no to her. Kate also conceded that she herself had been silly to stay in the background all the time…not asking for anything, and playing the victim, in a way.

No more of that, she decided. She was done with playing second fiddle to her sister.

'How was your golf game with Byron?' she asked, lying down on her bed and stretching out. 'Did you win?'

'Did I win, she asks? Of course I won. In the end. I let him get close to me in the first nine, but I slaughtered him in the second.'

Kate smiled. He really was terribly arrogant. But she still liked him.

'Poor Byron…'

Blake laughed. 'Hardly poor. He just keeps on getting richer. That man has the Midas touch when it comes to investments. I'm always happy when he comes aboard as co-producer on one of my movies. They never bomb. Not that I *ever* make duds, of course. Anyway, I told him about the movie you're going to be in and he's agreed to put a good chunk of money in it. In the past he's only ever wanted to invest in Lachlan's movies, but he's willing to take a chance now on anything I recommend.'

'Maybe he thinks *you've* got the Midas touch?'

'There's nothing magical about *my* success. It took me years of trial and error to work out what worked in movies and what didn't. Even so, you can never be one hundred percent sure of a positive reception. Film audiences can be very fickle.'

'Speaking of movies,' Kate said, 'I've been thinking about my part and I have a suggestion to make. I hope you don't mind.'

'Good grief! Her first movie role and she's already trying to change the script,' he said, but he was laughing.

'Not at all. I just don't like the part where I reach for a cigarette. I mean, I *hate* smoking, and so do most people now. I know I'm supposed to be a bad girl in this movie, but her smoking doesn't really add anything to the role and I'd rather not do it. Couldn't I reach for a glass of champagne instead? That would be just as effective.'

'I don't see why not. Is that all?'

'Oh, yes. Absolutely.'

'Good. I'm not a man who likes it when actors try to change my scripts.'

'I wouldn't dare.'

He laughed. 'I think perhaps you would. In time. God, I wish I didn't have to go to this dinner tonight. I'd much rather be in bed with you.'

'*I'd* rather you were in bed with me too.'

'Have you booked your flight yet?'

'Yes. I fly out late Friday evening and I get into LAX around six Friday evening your time. Australia is seventeen hours ahead of you, so I found out.'

'It's a non-stop flight, then?'

'Yes.' She gave him the flight number.

'I'll just write that down,' he said. 'You'll be glad you're flying business class.'

'I still can't believe Mum and Dad forked out that much money. Maddie's going to be so jealous.'

'How will she know? She's in Europe on her honeymoon for the next month or so.'

'That won't stop her ringing Mum every day.'

'I will never understand this obsession women have for talking on the phone all the time. I can't stand it.'

'You're talking to *me* on the phone right now.'

'You're the exception to my rule. I like talking to you. Of course I'd prefer to be talking to you with your naked body next to me, but since I can't have that, then I have to settle for this. Damn—it's just occurred to me that I won't be enjoying that privilege again for over four days. You wouldn't consider catching a taxi here at around eleven tonight, would you? I should be finished with my business dinner by then. You could stay the night, perhaps?'

It was tempting. *Very.*

'I'm sorry, Blake, but I can't do that. I told my mother I didn't sleep with you last night and I couldn't stand the next few days if she found out I'd lied. Which she would if I did what you're asking.'

'Fair enough. It'll probably be better for the waiting. Anticipation is one of the best forms of foreplay.'

She could believe that. She was already turned on, just thinking about being with him again.

'Your silence betrays you, sweet Kate. Just think what we could have got up to tonight. There are so many things I want to do to you and haven't done yet. We could have had such fun.'

Kate was glad he couldn't see her red cheeks. Or hear her thudding heart. But something—a kind of pride, perhaps—demanded that she did not let him think he could do whatever he liked to her and she wouldn't object.

Last night had been amazing, sexually, showing her how good it was to move on with her life, to put Lachlan behind her and find pleasure in another man's body. But that didn't mean she was going to become Blake's mindless plaything. She did have a mind of her own and she aimed to use it.

'There are things I want to do to *you* too, Blake,' she countered coolly. 'But, as you just said, it will be all be better for the waiting.'

Now *he* was the one who was silent. But then he laughed—a low, sexily sardonic laugh.

'I'll meet you at the airport,' he said, letting the matter drop.

Kate's independent mode was not easily dropped. 'Won't that be a bother? You'll have to pay for parking, and maybe wait if the flight is late, or customs are slow. I could just as easily catch a taxi if you give me the address.'

'*Cab*, Kate. In LA they're called cabs.'

'Oh. A cab, then.'

'No, I'll meet you,' he insisted. 'Carlos can drive me and wait somewhere until we're ready to be picked up.'

'You have a chauffeur?'

She shouldn't be surprised, but she was, which showed her that she hadn't truly absorbed just yet how wealthy Blake was. The penthouse she'd spent last night in hadn't been his, after all.

'Not exactly,' Blake replied. 'Though I often use Carlos to drive me places. Carlos is my housekeeper's husband. Her name's Juanita. She does the cooking and cleaning. Carlos is handyman, gardener and sometimes chauffeur. They're from Mexico, though they've lived in the USA for over twenty years. They came with the house and I thank God every day for them both. They're a great couple. Good workers and always cheerful. I feel very blessed to have them.'

Kate was taken aback by this last statement.

'I didn't know you were religious,' she said.

'What? Oh, the "blessed" thing. No, I'm not—but most of America is. I dare say I've picked up a few phrases.'

'I rather like it. It's sweet.'

'Americans *can* be sweet. But sometimes their sweetness is only on the surface—especially in Hollywood, and especially in the movie business. Thankfully Carlos and Juanita didn't come to LA to try their hand at acting. All they wanted, they told me, was a better life for themselves and their children.'

'They have children?'

'Unfortunately, no. They weren't lucky that way. Juanita said they left it too late before they tried and then it didn't happen. But they're not bitter about it. They're thankful for what they have.'

'They sound like a great couple.'

'Yes, you'll like them.'

'I'm sure I will. And I'm sure I'll like Hollywood—no matter what dire warnings you give me. I can't wait to get there.'

'And I can't wait for you to get there too,' he said, with heavy irony in his voice.

Kate laughed. 'Will you stop that? Let's talk about something else besides sex.'

But even as she said the word it occurred to Kate that a man like Blake would rarely have to wait for the pleasure of a woman in his bed. Maybe he *wouldn't* wait. Maybe when he got back to LA he'd ring up one of his lady-friends—he was sure to have heaps—and have her fill the gap in his sex life until Kate arrived on the scene.

Jealousy jabbed at Kate. Yet it wasn't the same kind of jealousy she'd used to feel about Lachlan and Maddie. Strangely, this was more disturbing—and infinitely more confusing. Because she didn't love Blake the way she'd loved Lachlan. She didn't love Blake *at all*! She liked him a lot—found him terribly sexy and quite fascinating. But she didn't want to marry him or spend the rest of her life with him. She didn't romanticise her feelings for him in any way. She saw them for what they were.

Why the jealousy, then?

Kate decided it was just her newly found feminine ego— the ego that thought her performance in bed last night had been oh, *so* good.

Silly Kate. Don't go thinking you're anything special to Blake, because you aren't. Your mother is right. There's no such thing as a free lunch. Yes, Blake might want to help you with your career—he probably gets off on the idea of being a magnanimous mentor—but there is a price to be paid. In his bed.

Just because you'll love every minute of it, that doesn't mean sleeping with Blake is without danger. What if you do fall in love with the man? It could happen now that Lachlan seems to be history.

Never forget that Blake doesn't want a real relationship with you, came the stern warning. *There is no future with him—no prospect of you becoming a proper girlfriend. And if you can't come to terms with that before you go to LA then you're a fool and you shouldn't go.*

Kate resolved not to be a fool. Because nothing was going to stop her going to Hollywood.

'What would you like to talk about?' Blake asked.

'Movies. What else?'

CHAPTER EIGHTEEN

BLAKE STOOD IN the arrivals area, close to the gate where Kate was due to emerge. Her flight had landed a good twenty minutes ago, but still there was no sign of her. Patience was not his strong suit, and his agitation was increasing with each passing second.

And then suddenly there she was, pulling a black suitcase behind her, her eyes scanning the crowd for him. She didn't see him straight away, giving Blake a thankful few seconds to drink her in unobserved.

She was a sight for sore eyes, despite being dressed in sensible travelling clothes—stone-washed grey jeans, a white T-shirt and a black jacket. Hardly an outfit which would usually fire up his male hormones. But it did. As did everything else about her. Her hair was bundled up on top of her head in a haphazard style which he found extremely sexy, and her face was freshly made-up, bringing attention to her lovely dark eyes and wide, luscious mouth.

Blake could not wait to get her home and alone. He'd had enough of just talking to her over the past few days, having spent more time on the phone to Kate than he had with any woman in his life—including his ex.

Aside from their long discussions about movies and acting, he now knew more about Kate than he'd ever found out about Claudia. She'd told him all about her upbringing—including her not very happy days at school, when she'd been totally overshadowed by her younger's sister vibrant personality, her self-esteem plummeting until she'd discovered acting in the school's drama class. Once portraying another character, her confidence had soared. Though it had always shrunk again once she was off the stage.

There had been no boyfriends for her—not until she'd met Tom, the boy who made the sets for the drama class, who had basically been as introverted as she was. Blake already knew that sex with Tom had been ordinary, at best. But at least she'd had a boyfriend for a while.

Her meagre sexual experiences at university had been of a similar ilk. Then, of course, had come the fiasco with Lachlan. It pleased Blake that Kate could talk about Lachlan now with more pragmatism. Her rose-tinted glasses were well and truly off. Who knew? Maybe she was finally getting over the guy? He sure hoped so. She deserved better than a self-obsessed narcissist who would never love anyone as much as he loved himself.

Suddenly she spied him, her face lighting up, her expression a mixture of joy and relief.

He moved forward, all smiles, taking the case away from her. 'You made it,' he said, and bent to peck her on the cheek. Blake was not a big hugger and kisser in public.

'Only just. My shoulder bag sparked off some machine and I was taken aside like I was a criminal. They emptied out all the contents and checked it over for drugs. It came back clear, of course. I mean, I would *never* do drugs. Still, I almost wet myself with terror whilst I was waiting.'

Blake nodded in sympathy. 'That happened to me once. Puts the wind up you, doesn't it? Still, store that emotion for when you have to act a part that requires terror. Nothing is wasted when you're an actor. Or a scriptwriter, for that matter.'

Kate took the bag off her shoulder and sighed as she stared into it. 'They just threw everything back in. My make-up is all over the place. And they've squashed up the magazine I bought.'

She pulled it out. Blake recognised the beaming couple on the cover immediately. He would hardly forget *that* bride and groom in a hurry. Clearly Maddie hadn't either, no matter how pragmatic their conversation over the phone. The headline caught his eye too: *Hunky Aussie Actor Weds*.

'I couldn't resist,' she said a little sheepishly. 'I saw it on a stand at the airport in Sydney and just had to buy it.'

An emotion Blake wasn't overly familiar with grabbed at his insides. It took him a split second to recognise it as jealousy.

Blake had experienced jealousy when Claudia had dumped him for that Hollywood fat-cat—along with fury and confusion and a whole raft of other conscience-blasting emotions.

He hadn't been able to think straight, but his arrogant male ego had refused to let him cry, or get counselling for his hurt. Instead he'd behaved badly, working his pain out by indulging in revenge sex with a couple of actresses who had made a play for him.

Thankfully, neither of them had been the type to suffer from a broken heart afterwards, but one of them had told him in no uncertain terms what she thought of his callous attitude the morning after. It had been a sobering experience, and one which he'd taken to heart. After that he'd been more careful with women, always making it clear that dating him wasn't a long-term proposition. He was into flings and affairs, not relationships.

He had had what might be termed a girlfriend or two since his divorce, but nothing serious. He certainly had never invited a girl to stay at his place for more than a night.

Or he hadn't until Kate had come along.

It worried him now…what he was getting himself into with this girl. If he didn't know better he might think he was falling in love. Which would never do. If and when he was foolish enough to fall in love it wouldn't be with someone who'd spent the last four years of her life dreaming of another man. For all he knew Kate was still dreaming of him. She might talk big about moving on, but she'd bought that magazine, hadn't she? Had probably spent hours during the flight admiring photos of him and wishing she were in Maddie's place.

'Not that I really wanted the damned thing,' Kate went on. 'I was just curious. I also hoped there would be some pictures of you and me—but, no, they were all of Lachlan and Maddie. Typical.'

And without a backward glance, she tossed the magazine into a nearby bin, before throwing him a remorseful glance.

'You didn't want to look at it, did you?'

Blake could have kissed her. She wasn't pining for that fool, and the thought brought him a type of joy which might have worried him if he hadn't been so relieved.

'I've already seen the photos, Kate. As soon as that magazine came out they were all over social media.'

'Oh, yes. I imagine they are. I'm not into social media. But Maddie is.'

'And Lachlan as well. He's an incorrigible show pony. Can't say I'm overly keen on the way technology has gone. But it's the way of the world, Kate. Speaking of technology,' he went on ruefully, and whipped out his phone, 'I'll just text Carlos and tell him to make his way to the pick-up point.'

'And I'll text Mum and Dad—let them know I've arrived safely.'

They both finished together, and Kate turned her phone off before dropping it back into her bag. Blake slipped his phone into his pocket, then took her elbow.

'Let's go.' Blake pulled her suitcase along behind them. 'I have a web page, of course,' he continued as they walked companionably together. 'And various other links which my PA attends to. But that's for business only. I like to keep my personal life to myself.'

'I do too. I don't understand why ordinary people—not celebrities—take photos of everything they do, even the most mundane things, then post it somewhere on the internet for people to see. I just don't get it.'

'I suppose it's a form of entertainment. And it makes them feel important. Like they're celebrities.'

'But it opens them up to criticism and bullying.'

'True. But that's become a fact of modern life, too. Social media isn't going to go away, so you might as well embrace it. You have to develop a thick skin, Kate, if you want to be a success in Hollywood. Because if and when that happens you'll be criticised to death over everything from your clothes to your weight and whoever you have by your side. You'll be stalked by the paparazzi and your life generally won't be yours.'

Kate stopped and stared at him. 'You make success sound so attractive!'

Blake shrugged. 'It's a sink-or-swim existence, being in the spotlight, but it can be very exciting. Though only if you don't let it go to your head...like someone who will remain nameless.'

'Oh, I suppose you mean Lachlan.'

'Lachlan who?' he said, with just a touch of malice. 'Ah, here's our ride.'

CHAPTER NINETEEN

KATE GAPED WHEN a white limousine braked abruptly at the kerb, next to where they were standing.

'Oh, my goodness!' she exclaimed, both impressed and slightly overawed.

Blake grinned at her. 'When in Rome, you know...'

The driver—a short, middle-aged man with black curly hair and swarthy skin—jumped out from behind the wheel, flashing Kate a welcoming smile before grabbing her suitcase.

'Better get inside, boss,' Carlos said, with only the slightest accent. 'The Indians are circling.'

'What does he mean?' Kate said as Blake yanked open the back door.

Just then a photographer stepped forward from Lord knew where and snapped a couple of shots of them both. Blake didn't say a word, just hustled Kate into the limo, throwing the photographer a big smile before climbing in after her and shutting the door. By this time Carlos was back behind the wheel and they were soon off.

'Carlos, this is Kate,' Blake introduced. 'Kate, this is Carlos.'

'Hello, Carlos.'

'Welcome to LA, Kate. Sorry I was a bit slow picking you up, boss. Friday evenings, you know... Lots of comings and goings.'

'No sweat, Carlos. If I didn't want to be photographed then I shouldn't have had you drive up in a limo.'

Carlos laughed.

'You didn't mind us being photographed?' Kate asked Blake.

'Hell, no. It's good publicity for me—and for you. Those photos will be all over the internet somewhere within the hour—with a caption something like *Blake Randall meets mystery woman at airport. A new star or a new girlfriend?*'

'Goodness!' Kate exclaimed, not sure if she was thrilled or anxious.

She didn't like the thought of her family seeing it—especially her mother. But even if she didn't see it, Maddie would. And she rang her mother every day. Being on her honeymoon wouldn't stop her. She could just imagine their conversation. Maddie might have urged Kate to make a play for Blake, but she wouldn't have dreamt that her sister would end up in LA, staying at his house.

Actually, Kate was finding it all a bit surreal herself. She could hardly believe that she was here. The last few days had seemed endless. Blake had rung her every day, which had been wonderful, but it had made her crave to be with him again. She'd almost forgotten her career for a while, her focus more on the sexual side of things. Yet they were both entwined, weren't they?

'Don't let it bother you,' Blake said, perhaps sensing her sudden unease. 'The Hollywood publicity mill runs on endless speculation. Best not to fight it or it only gets worse. Go with the flow. Have fun with it.'

'Fun?' she echoed.

He grinned over at her, then picked up her hand and kissed it like a gallant gentleman of old. *'Oui, mademoiselle,'* he said, sounding like Maurice Chevalier in *Gigi*.

Their eyes met over her hand and the air around them thickened with instant desire. How handsome he was—and very sophisticated-looking, dressed in a charcoal-grey business suit, white shirt and silver tie. Her heart had fluttered when she'd first sighted him at the airport. It had also pushed firmly aside any qualms she'd had over this trip. For she'd seen real affection in his eyes. Real caring.

Now all she saw was hunger—a raw, animal hunger which threatened to transcend her own.

A highly erotic shudder rippled down her spine and he saw it, his eyes darkening. He enfolded her hands in both of his and pulled her hard against his side. She dropped her head to his shoulder with a sigh. This would have to do. *For now.*

'If photographers are going to pop out from behind every pole or door,' she said, after a couple of minutes wallowing in the warmth of his body, 'I'll have to watch how I look when I go out.'

'You always look gorgeous,' he told her.

She smiled up at him. 'I really don't. But it's sweet of you to say so.'

'Did you bring some going out clothes with you?'

'Sort of…'

'What does that mean?'

'I suspect that my version of "going out" clothes falls a little short of the Hollywood version.'

'Maybe. Maybe not. People don't always get dressed up to the nines here. It can be a very casual city. But if you like I'll take you clothes-shopping tomorrow.'

'Will you?' she said, smiling wryly to herself as she recalled a scene from one of her favourite movies. 'In Rodeo Drive?'

'Of course.'

Her eyes slanted up to his. 'Thank you, but I think I should make do with what I have until I earn some money,' she said, knowing that that would be taking things a step too far. As it was, the balance of their relationship was a bit iffy. No way was she going to let him start buying her clothes. 'Actually, my wardrobe is not too bad at the moment. Dad forked out some more money for me—behind Mum's back, of course—and I went shopping this week.

Also, fortunately the weather here is similar to that in Sydney at the moment.'

'So it is. Your spring is much the same as our fall.'

'Fall? Oh, you mean autumn.'

'Yes.'

'You seem to have become very American in the short time you've been over here.'

'Actually, I *am* half-American.'

Kate sat up straight and stared at him, the action pulling her hand out of his grasp. 'How did that come about?'

'My mother's American. My dad met her when they were both studying medicine at Harvard. I was born over here—in Boston. They moved to Sydney just after I turned one. I have dual citizenship.'

'You still sound like an Aussie to me,' Carlos piped up. 'More so than Kate.'

'For which I am grateful,' Blake said.

Kate settled back in the seat and put her head on his shoulder again. 'The teachers at NIDA insisted that we get rid of any strong Australian accent. They said it was a negative when it came to getting work.'

'That's absolutely correct. Especially in Hollywood. They like an international-sounding voice. Not too many roles over here for Australians. By the way—did you bring all your references from NIDA?'

'What? Oh, yes—yes, of course.'

'Good. We'll need those to help get you the necessary visa for you to work here.'

Kate frowned. 'There won't be a problem with that, will there?'

'I doubt it. I've hired the best lawyer in LA to process your application. Now, no more work talk. We're almost home.'

'Already?' Kate's head swivelled to see where she was.

'West Hollywood isn't that far from the airport,' Blake explained.

The limousine wound its way up a rather steep road, with houses set back behind high security walls and often behind tall trees. Not that she could see them very well. Night had fallen, and whilst there were street lights they were few and far between. Up and up the road went, and one side of the road was now higher than the other.

Kate was craning her neck to peer up at the spectacular properties on the high side when Carlos pulled into a wide driveway in front of some tall wooden gates fixed into an equally tall stone wall. She couldn't see through that either, but she could see over it.

Up high, on a hill beyond, sat a house which took Kate's breath away. Whilst possibly not the biggest house in the world, its contemporary architecture could not help but impress. Over the wall she could see two rectangular-shaped floors, white in colour and cement rendered, the top one smaller than the one below. Both had wide covered decks which were lit up and no doubt provided splendid views of the surroundings.

Kate suspected, however, even before the gates opened, that there would be another floor out of sight. And she was right.

The bottom floor was even larger, encompassing a six-car garage, a fully equipped gym and a separate two-bedroom apartment which Carlos and his wife Juanita occupied—this information supplied by Blake as the limousine rolled into the huge garage next to a black sports car and a white sedan.

'So what do you think?' he asked her.

'I think,' she replied, 'that you are a very lucky man to live in a house as amazing as this.'

'And *I* think,' Carlos added with a cheeky smile over

his shoulder, 'that I am an even luckier man to have a boss like Señor Blake.'

Blake just laughed, but Kate could see he was pleased. Proud, too, of his house.

After meeting Juanita—who was as welcoming and cheerful as Carlos—Kate was given the grand tour by Blake. They started on the middle floor, which encompassed two large living areas, a bespoke kitchen, a home theatre, three en-suite guest bedrooms and another powder room for the use of guests, as well as a solar-heated pool which was entertainment heaven, with an indoor-outdoor barbecue and a cute cabana, complete with comfy lounge setting, a washroom and a built-in bar.

But it was the deck that led off the living area at the front of the house which took Kate's breath away.

'Oh, Blake,' she said, leaning against the wooden railing with a wondrous sigh. 'This is some view.'

That was an understatement. She could see for miles across the lightly timbered valley and over to the hill on which stood the famous HOLLYWOOD sign.

'The view upstairs is better,' he said.

'Really?' She found that hard to believe.

'I'll show you. Then we'll come down and have some dinner. Juanita's cooked something special for you. I knew you'd be too tired to go out.'

Kate actually didn't feel tired, despite not sleeping all that much on the plane. She'd been too excited. And too afraid. Not of flying. Or of Blake. But of what she had done, leaving her home and her country behind to be with Blake and pursue a career not on the stage, as she'd always intended, but in the movies—which was much more daunting to her.

Stage work was safe in Kate's eyes. Her looks weren't on display so much as they were in movies. She'd never been an overly confident or a bold person, but since meeting Blake she'd begun to change. He made her feel beautiful for starters. And now, tonight, in his company, she was changing again. No longer afraid, she felt both alive and confident. And, yes, free. Free of past failures. Free of her futile love for Lachlan. Free to really move on.

It was a delicious feeling.

'I hope you like chillies,' Blake said as he took her hand and led her up the thickly carpeted stairs to the top floor.

'I *love* chillies. I love all hot spicy food.'

'Good.'

The top floor was totally devoted to the master suite, consisting of the hugest bedroom Kate had ever seen, a bathroom which looked like a picture she'd once seen of a Roman bathhouse, and a spacious separate sitting-room-cum-study, complete with an enormous flat-screen TV on the wall.

But it was the wraparound deck which seduced and entranced Kate, with its view way beyond what she'd been picturing. She'd expected a better view of the Hollywood Hills, but when she walked round to the other side the city of Los Angeles lay before her, its many and colourful lights rivalling even those of Sydney on New Year's Eve. And beyond the city lay the ocean, dark and serene under the night sky.

'I don't know what to say,' Kate said, and smiled over at Blake. 'It's so gorgeous up here. Your whole home is splendid but, honestly, I could look at this view for ever.'

CHAPTER TWENTY

BLAKE HAD THE sudden urge to tell her that she could do that. All she had to do was marry him.

Crazy, really. Thank God he hadn't opened his mouth and said as much. Because he would have regretted it. And she would only have said no.

He told himself that it wasn't *love* compelling him to voice such idiocies. Just a temporary infatuation. And frustration. She was an enchanting creature and a highly desirable one. Give him a few weeks with her in his bed and he would come to his senses.

'So, are you going to stay with me in there?' he asked, nodding towards his bedroom.

Her eyes widened a little, but then she smiled. 'Do you want me to?'

'But of course.'

'I shouldn't…' she said, but her eyes were sparkling.

'But you will…'

'Of course.'

Of course, he thought ruefully as he swept her into his arms and kissed her, his head reminding him that she was still an actress even if she *was* different. And she was ambitious. If she hadn't been she wouldn't be here. Because she didn't love him. She probably still loved that idiot show pony, with his golden boy looks and sickeningly seductive charm.

His mouth worked hard to make her forget him—at least for now—and Blake didn't ease up until he felt her total surrender to the heat of the moment. She was a naturally sensual creature—he'd discovered that during the time they'd spent together in Sydney—and her celibacy over the past few years had made her ripe and ready for his attentions.

And attend her he would. Every day and every night. He would fill her body and her mind until she was incapable of wanting or even thinking of any other man. And he would spoil her rotten, seducing her with a lifestyle which few women would turn their backs on. And then, when the time was right, he just *might* ask her to marry him.

Okay, so it was still a crazy idea. But, crazy or not, the idea refused to be dismissed.

His mouth gentled on hers whilst his mind began working out how he could persuade her to throw her lot in with him. He reasoned that he could legitimately argue that marriage between people who liked and desired each other had a better chance of succeeding than those marriages entered into out of romantic love. He could point out that they would have a good life together. She would have *the* good life—a better one than her materialistic sister would have with lover-boy.

Blake suspected that getting one over Maddie would appeal to Kate. But his all-time winning argument might be that they didn't have to be married "til death do us part'. If it didn't work out they could divorce, and Kate could walk away with a very nice settlement.

When love wasn't involved there would be no bitterness. And no children, of course. He would never expose a child to such a marriage.

Thinking about the 'no children' aspect forced Blake to accept that Kate would never go for such a proposal. The girl was a romantic of the first order. The best he could hope for was that she would agree to live with him. At least for now.

For some reason that eluded him Blake felt somewhat disgruntled with this solution to his current obsession with Kate. But it would have to do.

He lifted his head, satisfied to find that she was breathing heavily and her eyes were glazed.

'Sorry, sweetheart,' he said, and touched a tender fingertip to her softly swollen lips. 'As much as I would like to continue, Juanita will be upset if we let her food over-cook.'

Which was a lie, Juanita having informed Blake earlier in the day that their entrée and dessert were pre-prepared and cold, with a main course that would not take long to cook. But it was better than telling Kate the truth; that he was so hard for her he might not last if he went ahead and had sex with her right at this moment.

'Well, we can't have that, can we?' Kate said, her eyes clearing. 'She's much too nice to upset.'

Blake liked it that Kate liked his housekeeper. And Juanita seemed genuinely to like Kate back. She fussed over their meal, returning often to the table to see that everything was okay. Which it was. Juanita was a brilliant cook. Her guacamole was second to none, as were all her other Mexican and Spanish-inspired dishes.

Not that Blake ate at home all that often. He networked over lunches and dinners, both at fashionable restaurants and at the various golf clubs he frequented. When working in his office he often skipped lunch entirely, living only on coffee. Today he'd been too busy to eat much, so he was appreciative of the three-course meal—especially the seafood paella which was followed by his favourite dessert: fried ice-cream, which had a delicious coconut and cinnamon flavour.

Kate, he noted, ate everything as well—a lovely change from most women in Hollywood who hardly ate at all.

'If you keep feeding me gorgeous food like this, Juanita,' Kate complimented her over coffee, 'I'm going to put on weight.'

'You are not the type to get fat,' Juanita replied. 'Not like me.'

Juanita was an attractive woman, with wavy black hair and flashing brown eyes. She was, however, pleasantly plump.

'You are *not* fat,' Kate said.

Juanita smiled. 'And you are a lovely girl. Australians are very nice people, I think. Or most of them are. I am not so keen on that fair-haired actor who comes here sometimes. You know the one I mean, Blake?'

'Indeed I do.'

'He is rude to me. He has no respect.'

Blake frowned. 'I didn't know that. What does he say or do that's rude?'

She scowled. 'He is clever, that one. He waits until you are out of the room… It is not what he says so much. It is the way he looks at me—like I am beneath him because I am Mexican.'

Blake decided then and there that Lachlan would never enter his house again. Neither would he contract him for any more movies. It was time their relationship—such as it was—was at an end. And if at the back of his mind he knew this decision was all about Kate, he steadfastly ignored it.

'I'm sorry, Juanita,' he apologised. 'You won't have to put up with that ever again. He won't be back.'

'What do you mean?' Kate asked in shocked tones once Juanita was out of earshot.

Blake shrugged, then picked up his coffee cup. 'It's time Lachlan and I parted company. Aside from the lies he told you about me at the wedding, he's become too big for his boots. And, like *I* told you at the wedding, he's not that good an actor. He suits a certain type of part but he has no versatility. I want to move on from making romantic comedies. I have a hankering for some more serious movies— like the one I've offered you.'

'Do you think that's wise?' Kate asked, frowning. 'You

made your name with those movies starring Lachlan. *The Boy from The Bush* has an enormous cult following.'

Blake tried not to react badly to her remarks, but found it impossible. 'Yes—silly female fans who think a handsome face, a good body and a dazzling smile is the be-all and end-all.'

He knew immediately that he had hurt her feelings. Her face told the story. Her face told him lots of stories—none of which he wanted to hear.

'I think you're wrong,' she defended, her cheeks flushing. 'Lachlan might not be Laurence Olivier, but he does have *some* talent. *And* star quality. I know he's vain and shallow, but I dare say lots of other movie stars are as well. Claudia Jay for one,' she added, with a curl of her top lip.

'True,' he conceded. 'Okay,' Blake went on, finding an apologetic smile with difficulty, 'he's not as bad as I'm making out. I'll admit that. But I don't like racists. Or philanderers.'

'Then perhaps you're in the wrong business,' Kate pointed out tartly. 'Hollywood is hardly renowned for treating minorities fairly. Or for its stars being faithful.'

Wow, Blake thought. *That's telling me.*

Kate might look and act quiet at times, but she knew how to voice an opinion. And, whilst it irked him that she might be defending Lachlan because she still had feelings for him, she was speaking a whole lot of truth.

His smile this time was full of admiration and respect. 'So you won't mind if I hire Lachlan for the occasional movie?' he asked, watching her closely to see how she would react.

'Why should I mind?' she shot back at him. 'If you think I'm still in love with the man, then you're dead wrong. I can see now that I was no better than those "silly female fans" you described. Who think "a handsome face, a good body and a dazzling smile is the be-all and end-all". I confess I used to watch his movies and drool with the rest of them. But I assure you I wouldn't drool now.'

Wouldn't you? Blake wasn't so sure about that. What was that saying about fearing a woman doth protest too much?

'I still won't be inviting him here to my home ever again. If and when we do business it will be at my office.'

'That's your prerogative, Blake. And your decision.'

Juanita coming in at that moment interrupted what was becoming an awkward conversation.

'More coffee?' she asked.

'No, thanks,' Kate said, and gave Juanita a warm smile.

Blake hadn't quite finished his yet, and said so.

Juanita nodded. 'Carlos wants to know what guest bedroom to put Kate's suitcase in.'

'None of them,' Blake told her. 'Tell him to put it up in my bedroom.'

Juanita smiled. *'Si,'* she said, and hurried out to tell her husband the news.

Kate glanced at Blake. 'Juanita seemed pleased.'

'She likes you.'

'Hasn't she liked any of your other women?'

'I have never had a woman stay here with me before—not even for a night.'

'Really? So where do you have sex, then? At their place?'

He had to laugh. It was a long time since he'd been with a girl who was so direct.

'Sometimes.' *And sometimes in trailers on location or in hotel rooms.* 'If you must know, my love-life has been very limited since I moved to America. In actual fact I hadn't had sex for several weeks before I met you.'

'Really? Why not?'

Why not, indeed? Maybe he was bored with the kind of women he'd been sleeping with. Maybe he was sick to death of one-night stands and ships that passed in the night.

Maybe I was waiting for someone like you, he wanted to

say, but didn't. As a very experienced scriptwriter, he instinctively knew when something was too much too soon.

Blake shrugged. 'I'd been very busy working on Lachlan's last movie. It wasn't turning out as well as I would have liked. I needed to rewrite a couple of scenes and reshoot them. Then the editing afterwards was a nightmare. Most of it ended up on the cutting room floor. Thank God the movie's got a good score. Good music can do wonders. It won't lose money, but I doubt it will set the world on fire. Now, enough of this chit-chat, my love. I'll just finish up this coffee and then it's off to bed for us.'

CHAPTER TWENTY-ONE

'WHAT'S KEEPING YOU so long?' Blake called out to her from the bed.

Kate had insisted on having a shower first. *Alone*, this time—unlike when she and Blake had showered together during that sex-crazed night back in Sydney. She didn't want to do anything kinky with him. She just wanted to *be* with him, to have his arms around her and to have him make love to her as if she was really his love. It was silly of her, she knew, to feel like this about him. But she couldn't seem to help herself.

Was this true love at last? she wondered as she dried herself.

Her feelings were certainly different from what she'd felt for Lachlan. But she couldn't be sure yet. It was way too soon. But, oh, he made her so happy.

Kate smiled at this last thought. Because that was what he'd said he wanted to make her. Happy. Well he'd succeeded all right. And how!

'If you don't get yourself out here pronto, madam,' Blake called out, 'I'm going to come in there and ravage you on the spot.'

'You are such a beast,' she said laughingly, and emerged from the bathroom demurely covered by a huge bath sheet.

'Take that damned thing off,' he demanded testily. 'Then get yourself in here.'

Kate liked it that she didn't feel nervous or shy with him, slowly unwrapping the towel and letting him feast his eyes on her naked body. She'd returned to the beauty salon the day before her flight was due and had every scrap of hair waxed off her body. And she meant *every* scrap.

Blake's eyes smouldered with desire as they raked over her. 'How did you know I like that look?' he said thickly.

'I didn't. I just hoped you would. And it makes me feel sexy.'

'You *are* sexy—with or without clothes.'

'You say the nicest things.'

'Not always.' And he threw back the bedclothes, showing that he was not only naked but armed and ready for action.

She dived in and snuggled up to him, pretending to be shocked when he said what he wanted to do to her in rather crude terms.

'Such language,' she chided, and kissed him on the neck.

'Well, it's a much better word than *shagged*.'

'I agree with you. But I would prefer *make love*—do you mind?'

'Not at all. It's a lovely expression. Let's make love, then.'

'Yes, please.' And she lifted her face to his.

His kisses were gentle to begin with. But not for long. Kate welcomed the passion of his mouth. And his hands. Her breasts swelled in readiness for his caresses, her nipples aching to be played with. And play with them he did—sometimes tenderly, sometimes roughly. She gasped, then sighed, then gasped again.

'I love these,' he said, and pulled at them until they were even longer and harder.

When she thought she couldn't bear it any longer he moved on, one of his hands dipping down between her thighs to torture her there. But, oh, how she loved it. Loved it that he seemed to know exactly what to do. Loved it that he kissed her mouth at the same time…invading her in twin places.

He was a master magician with her body. But also with her head. For there were no bad thoughts to haunt her during his lovemaking. Nothing but the here and now, which was both blinding and blissful.

She cried out when he entered her at last, her body lifting to his, soaring higher and higher until it splintered apart. His name flew from her panting lips when she felt him come along with her. For what felt like ages she was suspended on a plateau of wild throbbing pleasure. And then she was falling, as though from a great height. But there was no fear...nothing but the sensation of freedom and, yes, love.

It was the last thought Kate had before sleep claimed her. That she loved this man who'd set her free—free to be the woman she'd always wanted to be.

Bloody hell, Blake thought as he held her sleeping body close. *If this isn't love then what is it?*

Whatever it was, it scared the living daylights out of him. Because it was almost out of his control. But only *almost*. He could still think, he supposed. Blake had always been of the belief that if he could still reason then he hadn't fallen into that particular honey trap. Not yet, anyway.

Easing her out of his arms, he withdrew, then practically staggered into the bathroom. His legs felt so weak. Yet he'd only had her once. Maybe it was the build-up of the last few days which had made his orgasm so momentous, so overwhelming. Or maybe it was just *her*. She did things to him—made him feel things and plan things which were quite alien to him.

Once he'd got over the fiasco with Claudia he'd lived a very independent lifestyle, not needing or wanting anyone in particular. He'd had the occasional girlfriend, but nothing serious. Sex for him had become nothing more than the scratching of an itch, so to speak.

Yes, his bed partners were still usually actresses, but that was only natural. In his line of work he met lots of actresses. They were invariably attractive girls, intelligent and amusing—and *very* keen to be seen with him. Sex with them was easy and satisfying, but instantly forgettable. He never made them promises he couldn't keep, never let them think there was any kind of future with him.

Blake hadn't lied to Kate when he'd said no other woman had stayed with him up here. After he'd moved into this house fifteen months ago he'd decided that it was going to be his private domain—a sanctuary where he could work and write and fantasise…not about sex, but about being lauded as the greatest movie-maker of the present day.

Success was very important to him. As it was to Kate, Blake reminded himself. He should never forget that. As wonderful as she was, she'd still had her eye on the main chance when she had accepted his offer of help plus his invitation to stay here at his house.

Yes, there was no doubt she found him attractive. Lots of women did. And, yes, she enjoyed sex with him. But she was still in the recovery phase after being in love with Lachlan. It would be foolish of him to imagine there was more to her feelings than gratitude and a whole heap of rebound lust.

Which was fine by him. He didn't really want her to fall in love with him, did he?

Did he?

Blake scowled as he flushed the toilet, washed his hands, then padded back to bed. She was still dead to the world, curled up in a foetal position under the quilt, cuddling her pillow as if it was her favourite teddy bear.

How young she looked. Young and vulnerable.

Be careful with her, Blake's conscience warned as he climbed into bed. *Don't hurt her. If you do you'll hate yourself. And you haven't hated yourself in quite a while.*

He didn't touch her again that night, despite his postcoital exhaustion quickly becoming a distant memory. He lay there next to her for ages, fiercely erect, before finally falling into a troubled sleep.

He woke before dawn and still he lay there, trying to relax—envying Kate, who hadn't moved a muscle. In the end, he rose, quietly pulled on a tracksuit and headed downstairs to the gym.

CHAPTER TWENTY-TWO

KATE WOKE SLOWLY, her eyes remaining closed whilst she wallowed in the warmth and comfort of the bed. It seemed *extra* comfortable this morning, she thought drowsily, wondering if her mother had put clean sheets on the previous day. Kate *loved* the feel of clean sheets...loved the—

Her eyelids shot up like a suddenly released blind. Kate sat up just as quickly, her rapidly clearing mind remembering everything in an instant. She was startled rather than shocked, because everything that had happened to her since she'd arrived in LA last night had been good. *Very* good. She regretted nothing. Absolutely nothing. Not even falling in love with Blake—who was, she'd already noted, no longer in bed with her.

Her eyes darted around the bedroom, which seemed even larger in the daylight, the curtainless windows and the sunshine having the effect of extending it out to the deck and the view beyond. There was no sign of Blake anywhere. He wasn't in the bathroom—its door was wide open. So was the door to his study. Perhaps he was downstairs, having breakfast.

Kate's stomach growled, but it was her full bladder which demanded immediate attention. Jumping out of bed, she headed for the bathroom, sweeping up the discarded towel from the floor on the way, planning to use it as a cover until she could unpack and find the robe she'd brought with her.

No way did she want Blake returning to find her prancing around naked. She didn't mind being without clothes when he was making love to her—that seemed perfectly all right. But an exhibitionist she wasn't. Or maybe she just didn't want to act like Maddie, who seemed to enjoy walking around in the nude—especially since she'd had her boob job.

Emerging from the bathroom with the towel wrapped around her, Kate went in search of her suitcase, which she knew was in one of the walk-in wardrobes. There were two. His and hers, presumably. One was filled with Blake's clothes, the other empty, confirming Blake's claim that he'd never had a woman stay here before her—a thought which pleased Kate no end.

She wasn't under any illusion that Blake had somehow fallen in love with her. He didn't seem a 'falling in love' kind of man. But she was obviously special to him. And he obviously trusted her to let her stay with him in his bedroom. She could see that since his disastrous marriage he'd become somewhat of a cynical loner, using women just for sex and not letting any of them get too close.

Whilst she went about the business of unpacking, Kate wondered what it was about her exactly that he liked so much. It wasn't as though she was a great beauty. Or super-smart. Or highly experienced in the erotic arts. Though maybe that in itself held some kind of attraction. Maybe Blake fancied himself in the role of sexual tutor, getting off on showing her all the different forms of foreplay as well as many and varied positions for intercourse—most of which they hadn't tried yet, but all of which Kate had read about.

She was widely read, and her choice in books was quite eclectic, from biographies to historical sagas and lots of contemporary fiction, some of which included quite explicit sex scenes. She'd always known exactly why her limited sexual experiences in the past had been disappointing, and had once upon a time hoped that Lachlan would give her what she secretly craved.

That hadn't happened, of course. And, amazingly, she couldn't care less. He meant nothing to her any more. Her only regret was that she'd wasted four whole years believing he was the love of her life. The reality was that her feelings had probably been nothing but a youthful infatuation. Puppy love, spawned by Lachlan's golden-boy looks and his blistering charm.

When she thought about it in hindsight Kate felt somewhat foolish, though she consoled herself with the fact that most of the other girls at NIDA had fallen under his spell as well. None of *them* had seen him for what he was, either. But at the same time none of them had seemed all that heartbroken when he'd dated them, then dumped them.

Obviously they hadn't deluded themselves about his character as much as she had. Or maybe, once they'd spent time with him one-on-one, they'd seen the *real* Lachlan, not the good-looking charmer. Now that her rose-tinted glasses were well and truly off, Kate appreciated just how much he'd used her to help him with his acting. It had been cruel of him to take advantage of her like that. *Very* cruel.

Maddie was welcome to him, she decided. They were well matched, those two—both vain and selfish and horribly shallow. Not worth thinking about any more. Back to unpacking.

Kate retrieved her dressing gown and toilet bag, hurrying back into the bathroom to clean her teeth before hanging up the towel and then slipping into the robe. That done, she quickly brushed her hair, put it up into a topknot, then returned to finish her unpacking.

She hadn't brought a lot of clothes with her, only the things she really liked, as well as the new clothes she'd bought this week.

Kate smiled as she drew out her favourite new jacket. It was made of black velvet, which was very 'in' this year— or so she'd been told. It was cropped at the waist, with no lapels, and had silver zips decorating the pockets. Very stylish—and rather sexy when worn with her new tight white jeans and black high heels. The salesgirl had also talked her into adding a silvery grey silk cami, which she'd said made the outfit *'pop'*.

Kate couldn't wait to wear it all for Blake.

'And what are *you* smiling at, madam?'

Kate spun round at the sound of his voice. Blake stood in the open doorway, dressed in a navy tracksuit, a dark grey towel hanging around his neck.

Her smile was enigmatic. Or so she hoped. 'That's for me to know and you to find out.'

He grinned as he dabbed at his damp forehead with one end of the towel. 'I do love a mystery. *And* a challenge.'

She laughed. 'I don't think I've ever presented you with either. I've been putty in your hands from the first.'

His own smile was wry. 'You think?'

'I *know.*'

'You know nothing, sweetheart,' he said, in an enigmatic tone of his own. 'Now, I have to have a shower. I'm hot and sweaty. Have you showered yet?'

'No.'

'Good. Stop doing that for now, then, and have one with me.'

When she hesitated—she wasn't sure why—he raised his eyebrows at her. 'Come now, Kate, you're not going to start playing games with me, are you?'

She frowned, suddenly unsure of herself. It was one thing to fall in love with this man… Another thing entirely to let him think she would jump to his command *all* the time. It was tempting to say yes, but was that the kind of woman she really wanted to be?

Definitely not. But, oh, it was difficult to say no.

Her pride struggled to her rescue—though it had a fight on its hands. Because when he went all masterful like that she wanted to obey him…wanted to do whatever he wanted her to do.

'I'm not sure what sort of games you're referring to,' she said, with only the smallest quaver in her voice. 'I'm a very straightforward kind of girl. But I don't appreciate your ordering me into the shower like that. It's not...respectful.' Even as she said the word she thought how old-fashioned and prissy it sounded.

He stared at her for a long moment, then nodded. 'You're right. I apologise. It's just that you look so deliciously sexy in that silky thing you're almost wearing. Forgive me?'

Kate glanced down at her black and white robe, which wasn't silk but polyester and had cost her all of fifteen dollars on sale. It was quite a modest garment, reaching past her knees, and it had three-quarter-length kimono-type sleeves. The sash belt, however, had come loose, and the neckline was gaping. But, since she didn't have much of a cleavage without a bra, she wouldn't have thought she looked at all sexy.

Kate yanked the lapels together and tightened the belt, aware that her nipples felt like bullets under her robe. 'Of course I forgive you,' she said, already regretting her stance. What was that she'd said about being putty in his hands?

'Would you *please* join me in the shower?' he asked politely, his dark eyes glittering with wicked intent.

She hadn't forgotten what he'd done to her the other night in Sydney when they'd showered together. The experience had been both thrilling and utterly seductive. She sighed, then shook her head at him, her own eyes glittering as well. She'd claimed she didn't play games, but this one was such fun. And wasn't that what he'd promised her from the start? That sex could be fun?

'I shouldn't,' she said. 'You will only take wicked advantage of me.'

'What if I promise not to, on the proviso that *you* take wicked advantage of *me*?'

Kate wasn't given to having lurid sexual fantasies, but

her turned-on mind was suddenly filled with a clear image of how she could do just that. She could see herself now, taking a soapy sea sponge and slowly washing Blake all over. *All* over. She would order him to turn this way and that, so that not an inch of his body was unknown to her. Only one area would be neglected.

Kate would refuse to wash him *there* until he was going crazy with need…until his erection was hard and painful and, oh, so impatient, quivering wildly for her touch. Only then would she press the hot wet sponge around its base, squeezing it tightly and sliding it up and down. He would gasp at first, then groan, and finally he would come—right there in the shower. The violence of his release would send him lurching back against the wall, his outspread palms bracing himself against the wet tiles. His breathing would be ragged and his eyes glazed as they stared at her with shocked pleasure…

Of course it didn't quite work out that way. It started well, with Blake happy for her to wash his body, and amused at first when she bypassed his penis. But he was not a man to let *any* woman take control of things indefinitely.

'I thought you didn't play games?' he growled when she turned him around and began washing his buttocks.

'When in Rome…' she quipped, echoing what he'd said the previous night.

He sucked in breath sharply when she turned him around again and brushed the sponge across the tip of his swaying erection. His eyes darkened and his right hand shot out to grab her wrist, forcibly bringing the sponge to where he wanted it to be.

'You seem to have lost your sense of direction,' he said, his voice thick and his eyelids heavy.

Using his superior strength, he forced her to do at once what she'd planned to do eventually. But he stopped her before he came—stopped her and tossed the sponge away.

Then he took her face in his hands and kissed her 'til she was lost in a haze of desire. It was Kate, then, who found herself pushed back against the wall, bracing herself whilst Blake sank to his knees before her.

'Oh, God,' she moaned when he spread her legs wide, because she knew how good he was at this. She had no hope of holding out—no hope at all. But she had to try. She didn't want to come like this.

So she lifted her eyes to the twin shower heads and watched the water gush out, trying not to think about how glorious it felt to have his lips and his fingers doing what they were doing, how her insides were twisting tighter and tighter, how she was already balancing on the edge of the abyss.

Her mouth had already fallen open in readiness for her release when Blake abruptly wrenched away from her and stood up.

'You can't stop now!' she cried out, her frustration acute.

He just smiled. 'Don't be greedy.'

He snapped off the water and bundled her out, grabbing a towel from a nearby rack and rubbing her roughly dry before doing the same to himself. Her hair was still dripping wet when he pulled her over to the double vanity unit and wrapped her hands over the edge, showing her flushed face reflected in the overhead mirror.

She could have protested...could have refused. But she did neither, just staying where he'd put her whilst he rummaged in one of the drawers and extracted a condom.

His entry was rough, but not painful—her body was supremely ready for ravaging—and their climaxes were simultaneous, their release more violent than ever.

He pulled her upright whilst their bodies were still shuddering together, holding her hard against him and nuzzling his mouth against her ear. 'God, Kate,' was all he said.

She didn't reply, her mind too dazed for her to make coherent conversation, her eyes tightly shut.

Never in her wildest dreams had Kate imagined sex could be like this. Because that was all it was that they'd just shared. It hadn't been making love. It had been just sex. Yet she'd thrilled to it all the same.

Her eyes opened and she stared at their reflection in the mirror, stared at his hands as they roved languidly over her breasts, down over her stomach, then between her legs.

'No,' she groaned when he started touching her in her most sensitive place.

He ignored her, and soon she gave up any hope of protest...

'You're very quiet,' he said to her over breakfast.

'I was just thinking,' she replied.

'About what?' He picked up his coffee and searched her face over the rim of the mug.

'About my screen test,' Kate lied. She'd actually been thinking that she wanted him again. 'When will I actually be doing it?'

'Probably Monday,' he said between sips. 'I'll organise an actor and a studio today.'

'I wish you didn't have to go to work,' she said, quite truthfully.

She would have loved to spend the whole day in bed with him. Or wherever he might want to have sex with her. The bathroom again. Or on the sofa in his study. She didn't care where. Kate suspected that if Juanita hadn't been hovering in the kitchen she might have tried to tempt him right here and now. She was only wearing her robe, nothing on underneath, and it was making her hotly aware of the moistness between her thighs.

She moved restlessly on the chair, desire squirming in her stomach. And lower...

Oh, Lord!

Love had turned her into a sex addict. Or maybe it wasn't love. Maybe it was just lust. Maybe she was deluding herself.

'Have to, I'm afraid,' he replied, putting his coffee down. 'I'm juggling several projects at the moment, all of which need my personal attention. Now, speaking of work, I'll need to get my lawyer on to your visa ASAP. I hope you were able to get everything I asked you to bring? Not just your references from NIDA, but the reviews of that play as well.'

Kate blinked at him, her mind having wandered to other things. Like how gorgeous he looked in that business suit. Gorgeous and sexy and...

'Kate?' he prompted, frowning at her.

'What? Oh, yes—yes. I got everything, and more. I remembered that the director of that play actually filmed our last dress rehearsal. I contacted him and he gave me a copy of the DVD.' She'd meant to tell Blake yesterday but she'd totally forgotten.

'That's fabulous. Because seeing is believing. Much better than a letter just saying you're good. Something like that DVD could tip everything in your favour.'

'Only if my acting is good, though.'

'You know it is.'

She sighed. 'I thought so. But maybe people over here won't be impressed.'

'Now, don't start with that negative talk. Negative talk never gets you anywhere. Come on,' he went on, standing up. 'Let's go and get everything.'

After Blake had left Kate had another shower, then dressed in dark blue jeans and a lemon cotton top which suited her colouring and was not too warm, although the ducted air-conditioning was keeping all the rooms at a pleasant temperature.

It was only when she went out onto the deck or into the pool area that she felt cool. And then, not too cool. No doubt the day would warm up. There were no clouds in the blue sky. The weather reminded her of spring in Sydney.

Kate talked to Juanita for a while, offering to help her, but Juanita refused.

'No, no—you are a guest,' the housekeeper said. 'And you must be tired. Flying that far is very tiring. Or so I am told. I never fly anywhere. The thought terrifies me. Go and have a lie-down. Or watch a movie—Señor Blake has thousands.'

It was only then that Kate remembered Blake had left a printed copy of her script on the desk in his study upstairs, suggesting she read the whole thing through in order to fully understand the context of her part.

After getting herself another mug of coffee, Kate carried it upstairs and went into his study, settling herself onto a comfy leather sofa and placing her coffee on its built-in side table. She had just begun to read when the tell-tale ring of her phone infiltrated faintly, from where she'd left it on the bedside table.

Thinking it might be Blake, she hurried to answer it.

But it wasn't Blake.

It was Maddie.

CHAPTER TWENTY-THREE

'MADDIE!' KATE EXCLAIMED. 'What are you doing, ringing me? You're supposed to be on your honeymoon.'

'Honeymoon? *Huh*. Darling Lachlan spends more time on his phone than with me. His new American agent is negotiating some big movie deal for him. A franchise, apparently, all with the same hero. Rather like James Bond, only sexier. Not sure how it *could* be sexier… Anyway, he's very excited about it. Can't say *I* am. The money's fabulous, but all the films are going to be shot in Europe and he says I can't go on location with him. I'm supposed to stay home in Sydney like a good little wife.' She laughed. 'As if I'm going to do *that*. Anyway, that's not why I'm ringing you…'

Kate had an awful suspicion that she knew exactly why her sister was ringing her.

'I know all about your going to LA,' Maddie rattled on. 'Mum told me everything. And I know you're staying in Blake Randall's house.'

'Yes…' It was only one word but it carried a whole heap of meaning. Such as *It's none of your damned business, Maddie*.

'Look, I'm not against what you've done. Hell, sis, I was all *for* it. Remember? But Lachlan's appalled. Lord knows why. I moved in with *him* the day after we met. Maybe things are different in America. Anyway, he wanted me to warn you about what people will soon be saying.'

'What people, exactly?'

'Hollywood people. Lachlan says they can be very small-minded and downright malicious. He said they'll be nice to your face but they'll snigger behind your back. They don't like unknowns like you getting the star treatment just because they're sleeping with the boss. He said you haven't paid your dues and that'll get right up their noses.'

'Well, thank you for the warning, Maddie,' Kate said, sounding much cooler than she was feeling. Why couldn't Maddie be *happy* for her? *She* had everything *she* wanted. 'But I don't much care what Lachlan says. As for my getting star treatment—Blake's only offered me a supporting part in this movie. It's not like I have the main role.'

'And you won't get one, either. Lachlan says he'll screw you 'til the movie's finished and then he'll toss you out on your ear. Lachlan says that…'

'I don't give a monkey's uncle what Lachlan says,' Kate bit out. 'He's just jealous. And possibly so are you.'

'That's not true!' Maddie denied. 'I'm just worried about you. I don't want you to get hurt.'

'Oh, really? Were those your sentiments when you honed in on the one man you knew I had a crush on?'

'I've already apologised for that.'

'At the same time admitting that you don't even love him,' Kate swept on angrily. 'You just want the good life, you said. Well, I'm having a better life now—with a man I *do* love,' she threw down the line without thinking. 'And you obviously don't like it one bit!'

Kate might have said more if Maddie hadn't hung up on her. She stared down into the silent phone, swamped by a mixture of frustration and fury. Finally she turned off the phone and threw the damned thing on the bed, determined never to speak to her sister again.

It was only when she sat down in Blake's study and picked up the script again that she realised her hands were shaking. No—her whole body was shaking.

It was then that she started to cry.

Blake tried Kate's phone again but it was still turned off. *Damn it*. She'd probably turned the darned thing off and gone back to bed for that rest he'd advised. Yet he really wanted to talk to her. Excitement was still fizzing through his veins.

What to do? He couldn't go home yet. He had a meeting with the head of Fortune Films this afternoon. To cancel at this late stage would not be wise. They were the only distribution company worth having, in his opinion.

Blake glanced at his Rolex. It was twenty past one. No way could he get home and back in time for the meeting at two-thirty. A light suddenly popped on in his brain, solving his problem. *Juanita*. He would ring her and have her go in search of Kate.

If she was asleep then it was high time she woke up, otherwise she wouldn't sleep tonight. It was a thought which brought a wry smile to his face. Maybe he should let her stay asleep…

But, no, his news simply couldn't wait.

Kate was sitting out on the deck, dry-eyed, when Juanita found her a second time. She'd come up an hour ago, insisting Kate come down for some lunch. But Kate hadn't felt like eating, and had told Juanita she would be down a little later.

Now she was back, looking at Kate with concern in her dark eyes.

'Señor Blake has just rung me,' she said. 'He said he has been trying to ring you but your phone is turned off. He said he has good news and could you please ring him?'

Kate sighed, but did not move. She could not imagine any news which would make her feel better. It was silly of her to believe anything Maddie had said, but she was only human and doubts had crept in. Doubts about what she was doing. Doubts about Blake. Doubts about everything. On top of that, she hated it that Maddie had hung up on her—

hated herself for trying to hurt her sister. Revenge was *not* good for the soul.

Juanita hovered. 'Señor Blake...' the housekeeper went on. 'He...he is a good man but not always a patient one. Please... He will think I did not give you the message if you don't ring him straight away.'

Kate heard the worry in Juanita's voice and immediately stood up. Juanita's relieved smile made Kate feel guilty. It wasn't like her to be so thoughtless.

'Sorry, Juanita. Please don't worry. I'll call him now.'

'That is good,' Juanita said, and bustled off.

Kate hurried into the bedroom and retrieved her phone and turned it on. Within a few seconds Blake was on the line.

'I hope I didn't wake you,' were his first words.

'No, no. I wasn't asleep. What's up?'

'I watched that DVD of your play and I have to tell you, Kate, I was more than impressed. You were *fantastic*. In fact I was so impressed I had a copy made and had it couriered over to the agent I think will suit you best. He promised to look at it this very afternoon and get back to me.'

'Oh,' she said, somehow unable to react normally, with her old friend depression having taken hold of her. 'That is good news.'

'You don't sound very enthusiastic.'

'Sorry. I think I might be a bit jet-lagged. I tried to read through that script, like you told me, but my eyes kept glazing over.'

'Then you really should try to get some sleep. I want to take you out to dinner tonight. To celebrate. Because there's no *way* they'll knock back your working visa once they see you in that play. You're a shoe-in, sweetheart.'

Kate couldn't tell him she didn't want to go anywhere. So she said nothing.

'Kate?' he said after a few moments' awkward silence. 'What is it? Something's wrong. I can tell.'

Kate sighed. 'Maddie rang me.'

Blake swore. 'And what did your darling sister say to upset you *this* time?'

Tears suddenly swam in Kate's eyes. 'It wasn't what *she* said so much. It was what Lachlan had told her to say.'

'About what?'

'About me coming to Hollywood with you.'

Blake swore again. 'That bastard needs sorting out. Tell me what he said. And I want to hear every single word.'

Kate swallowed the lump in her throat. Then she repeated every single word of Lachlan's warnings. But she didn't tell Blake what she'd said back to Maddie about loving him.

He didn't swear this time. He just listened.

'When I accused them both of being jealous,' Kate finished, 'Maddie hung up on me. That's why I turned off the phone. So she couldn't ring me back.'

'I see. And do you believe what Lachlan said about me this time?'

'No...'

'You don't sound so sure.'

'I... I thought he had a point saying that people will believe I'm sleeping my way to success. They *will* think that, Blake.'

His sigh was heavy. 'You can't spend your life worrying about what other people think.'

'I suppose not. It's just that I want to feel I'm succeeding as an actress through my own efforts.'

'That wasn't working so well for you when we first met, was it?'

'That's because I was not in a positive frame of mind at the time. Maddie getting together with Lachlan had affected me badly. I coped whilst I was doing the play. It was the perfect escape from my melancholy, playing an upbeat girl who refused to let anything get her down. But when the play folded I lost what was left of my confidence. I was terrible at all my auditions. And I *looked* terrible. I can see that in hindsight. I wouldn't be terrible now. I *know* I wouldn't.'

'So are you saying you don't *want* this part in my movie?'

She hadn't thought that. Not until this moment. 'I think perhaps it's best I decline, Blake. I'm sorry. It was very generous of you to offer it to me, but…well…it just wouldn't feel right. Not now.'

'You mean since bloody Lachlan poisoned your mind about everything,' Blake snapped.

Kate could not deny that she'd begun having doubts about what she was doing here in Blake's house…what role she was playing. As much as she had enjoyed their interlude in the bathroom this morning, it had highlighted to her that Blake's feelings for her were probably largely sexual. His generosity and caring might not be real—just a means to an end. Falling in love with him might have blinded her to his true character.

'I wouldn't say "poisoned",' she said slowly. 'But he's given me food for thought.'

'You still love that bastard, don't you?'

'No,' she said truthfully. 'No, I don't. I told you that already.'

'I know what you *told* me, Kate.'

His scepticism shocked her.

'Love doesn't die that quickly,' he growled.

'It does when it wasn't true love in the first place.'

'If only I could believe that…'

Kate hated it that he didn't believe her. She ached to tell him that *he* was the one she truly loved, but she doubted he'd believe that, either. And if by some fluke he did, then it would just give him more power over her.

Not a good idea, Kate. She was having enough trouble sorting her head out as it was.

'I think it would be best if I went home, Blake,' she said shakily.

'No, it would *not*!' he roared down the phone. 'You hate it there.'

'I don't *hate* it.'

'Bull-dust. Your sister and your mother might not mean to, but they suck all the life out of you. Your family will make you feel like a failure if you go back now. And you're *not* a failure. You're a beautiful and talented actress who just hasn't had the right break yet.'

Blake's lovely compliments sent tears pricking at her eyes.

'You *have* to stay here, Kate. Okay, don't take the part I offered if it bothers you. Though damn it, girl, you're looking a gift horse in the mouth. I suppose that's why you don't want it? You think it's charity on my part, or something much worse. You don't realise just how fantastic an actress you are. I would *kill* to have someone like you in any of my movies. Hell, Kate, watching you in that play practically blew my mind.'

'But, Blake, you offered me that part *before* you saw me in the play,' she pointed out.

He was silent for a few fraught seconds, then he laughed. 'Okay, so you've caught me out. Yes, I wanted you, Kate—almost from the first moment I saw you—and I wasn't above using your ambition to get you into my bed. But I wasn't lying when I said I want to make you happy. I honestly do. You've touched something in me, Kate—something that is rarely ever touched. I'm not known for my empathy, or my compassion. And as for passion—the only passion I've had for years is for my movies. Until I met you. God, but I want you with *passion*, girl. And I need you. I won't let you go home—not whilst there's breath in my body. You're to stay here with me—not as a guest, but as my girlfriend. A proper live-in girlfriend. Then, once your visa comes through, you can knock yourself out going to endless auditions until you get yourself an acting job. And once you've made it on your own you will do a movie for *me*. Not some minor role but the lead, in a script I will write especially for you!'

Kate sucked in breath sharply. Lord, how did an aspiring actress in love say no to all *that*?

'And if you're worrying about how much money I'll have to spend on you until you're earning money on your own,' he charged on, 'then I'll keep a tally. You can pay me back as soon as you can. What do you say to that idea?'

'I'm pretty speechless right now.' *And brimming full of emotion.* Okay, so he hadn't said he loved her, but he did care about her. Passionately so.

'We can't let other people spoil what we have together, Kate. It's special—our connection, our chemistry. Don't you agree?'

'Yes…' she choked out.

'So you won't go home?'

'No.'

His sigh was a sound of total relief. 'Thank God.'

'But promise you won't try to change my mind about doing that part,' she said with a sudden rush of worry.

'I promise. It wasn't quite *you*, that role, anyway. You need to be the heroine of the story, not some slutty other woman. Now, I must get off this phone. I have an important meeting this afternoon. But I'll be home by six at the latest. If I'm going to be any later I'll ring you, so don't turn off your phone. And if your stupid sister rings you again *you* be the one to hang up.'

'I just might do that.'

'Good girl. I've booked dinner for us at seven. I won't be taking you to any of those celebrity restaurants—just a local steakhouse which does fabulous food. Wear something nice, but nothing over the top. The dress code at Jimmy's place is quite casual.'

'I've got just the thing.'

'Good. Have to go. Bye.'

He'd hung up by the time Kate said goodbye in return.

She sat for a long time, thinking about what he'd said. And what *she* had said.

She was proud of herself for deciding not to let Blake present her with her career on a silver platter. The temptation had been there to do just that. Face it, she'd been *well* on the way down that particular road. But, honestly, if she had she would never have felt good about any success which might have come her way.

Kate wasn't overly concerned about what perfect strangers thought of her, but she *did* care about what her family thought. Silly, really, but that was the way it was. Maybe one day she'd be able to be like Blake, not needing or caring about anyone back home. But that day hadn't come yet.

Kate already regretted being stroppy with Maddie over the phone. Maybe she should ring her back. Or text her.

And maybe not.

Best leave things for now.

Glancing at the time on her phone—it was after two—Kate decided to go in search of Juanita and that lunch she'd offered her. At the same time she aimed to find out where everything was in the main kitchen, so she could get herself her own breakfast and morning tea and lunch. She wasn't used to being waited on hand and foot and, whilst it was a deliciously pleasurable experience, Kate didn't want to become one of those spoiled rich women who wouldn't lift even one precious finger unless it was to get her nails done.

Not that she was *rich*. But she was living with a very rich man.

This was still the part which didn't sit well with Kate.

Because it made her feel like a kept woman. A mistress. Being *any* man's mistress had not been in her life plan at all. Love did make a woman weak in some ways, but hopefully not in others.

Kate reaffirmed her determination to keep that tally Blake had mentioned, of what he spent on her. And to pay him back once she got herself an acting job. She also resolved to do some research on the internet, find out what was hot now in television series. She knew that several young Australian actors had found work in LA that way. Being unknown hadn't worked against them in *that* field. It was, in fact, often seen as a plus. The television industry loved new faces and fresh new talent.

With these resolves fixed firmly in her mind, Kate stood up, slipping her phone into the pocket of her jeans before heading downstairs in search of Juanita.

CHAPTER TWENTY-FOUR

'SORRY I'M A bit late!' Blake said as he dashed in shortly after six-thirty.

When Kate had heard him running up the stairs to the top floor she'd emerged from the bathroom, where she'd been titivating for the last half-hour.

He stopped to stare, his eyes turning hungry as they raked her over from top to toe. 'God, don't *you* look gorgeous?'

'Not too casual?' she asked as she hooked silver hoop earrings into her ears. Her hair was up in a loose knot, with a few wispy bits around her face.

'Not at all. I love girls in white jeans and heels. And I *love* that jacket.'

'So do I.' She flipped it open and shut, giving him a better look at the sexy silver cami, not to mention her bra-less breasts.

'Damn it, girl, you *really* make it hard on a man,' he growled, his dark eyes glittering. 'I desperately want to kiss you, but if I do we'll never get to the restaurant.'

Kate's heart started racing with a hunger of her own. 'Would that be such a disaster?'

'Not a disaster. But perhaps unwise. Because I'm starving. And starving is never good if a man wants to make love to his woman all night long.'

'All night long?' she choked out as her whole chest squeezed tight.

'Absolutely. Tomorrow's Sunday. I'm not going to work and I've cancelled my morning golf game. Which—and trust me on this—is not something I do very often. I love my golf. But I love making love to *you* even more.'

'Oh…'

His eyes narrowed on hers. 'You're not going to cry, are you?'

Kate swallowed, quickly pulling herself together. But that had been so close to him saying that he loved her. So heartstoppingly close…

'No, no. Absolutely not.'

'Good. Now, I'm going to have a quick shower. *Alone*. But I don't have time to shave or we'll be late. Do you mind me with a stubbly chin?'

'Not at all. It suits you. It's sexy.'

And it was. *Very*. It made him look like a pirate. Kate loved movies with pirates in them. Their characters were always masterful. And whilst they could be wicked, it was never in a horrible way. They just dared to do what a modern man wouldn't. Like kidnap women and then force them to fall in love with them…

A bit like what Blake had done to her.

Blake rubbed his chin. 'Sexy, eh?'

'Yes. *Very*.'

He laughed. 'You're not trying to seduce me, are you?'

'Could I?'

'*Could* you?' He shook his head at her, smiling a wry smile. 'Oh, that's funny, Kate. You've no idea how funny. Now, I suggest you go downstairs and have a pre-dinner drink. There's plenty of wine in the fridge. Or champagne, if you prefer. I won't be long.'

Blake slammed the bathroom door shut, sighing as he started reefing off his clothes. Lord, but she didn't know how close he'd come to reefing off *her* clothes—her very sexy clothes.

His plan to seduce Kate with sex was really backfiring on him. *He* was the one totally seduced and obsessed, and so in love with her that he could hardly contain the words.

I love you! he wanted to shout out. *I love you and I want to marry you!*

Once again the idea of marriage had jumped into his head, and it was beginning to annoy him. He didn't need to *marry* Kate just because he'd fallen in love with her. Why marry her? It was unnecessary in this day and age. They could just live together, as he'd already suggested, which would be so much easier, and much less complicated.

But it was no use. Marriage was what he wanted—along with her love. Nothing else would do.

'Stupid bastard!' he ground out, and stepped in under a cold shower, gasping as icy shards of water beat down on his overheated brain and body, bringing him back to reality with a rush. To a reality that was as sobering as it was sensible.

Because it was still way too soon to say such things to her. He *had* to give her more time. Had to let her get over that other stupid bastard before she was capable of falling in love with him.

Meanwhile he had to be patient. *Not* his favourite activity.

CHAPTER TWENTY-FIVE

JIMMY'S STEAK HOUSE was not a large establishment. Neither was it a place whose popularity rested on celebrity patronage, like lots of other Hollywood restaurants. Or so Blake told Kate on the way there.

'You'll like it,' he said. 'The food is great and it's quiet. There are no bands playing, nor even a piano player. They have booths as well as tables, so you can get some privacy, and you can actually hear yourself talk. I hate eating in places where you have to shout to be heard.'

Kate couldn't have agreed with him more.

'This is great,' she said, once they were seated in a booth well away from the door.

Of course she would think anywhere was great if she was with Blake. But she did genuinely like the quiet ambience and the decor, which was all clean lines and simple. White walls, wooden floor and tables, no tablecloths.

They hadn't been stared at when they'd come in, though all the ladies present had given Blake a few second glances. And why not? He looked devilishly handsome in black jeans, a white silk shirt—open at the neck—and a sleek lightweight black jacket. His casually sexy clothes, combined with his five o'clock shadow and his slightly rumpled black hair, gave him that bad-boy image women found so attractive.

Kate was no exception.

'Do you like red wine?' he asked as he picked up the drinks menu.

'It's okay,' she replied. 'But I prefer white.'

'You can't drink white wine with steak,' he pronounced, with his usual arrogance.

He ordered red wine, and Kate discovered to her surprise that she did like it. Or at least she liked this particular red wine, which she suspected was hideously expensive. It had a French label, and the waiter treated the bottle as if it was made of gold.

'Well?' Blake asked after she'd had a few sips.

'Lovely,' she replied.

'I told you so. You *must* widen your horizons, Kate.'

She smiled. 'I've widened them quite enough already, don't you think?'

He frowned. 'What do you mean?'

'You *know* what I mean.'

'I suppose you're referring to throwing in your lot with me?'

'Yes. I suppose I am.'

'Best thing you ever did. You were losing your way back in Sydney.'

Kate sighed. 'Don't you *ever* have doubts, Blake?'

He looked at her hard, then laughed. 'Everyone has doubts, Kate. But you have to learn to ignore them and just go for what you want. Otherwise you'll spend your whole life regretting your lack of courage.'

'Is that what you've always done? Just gone for what you wanted?'

'In the main. I was seriously derailed once—but you don't need to hear about that.'

Kate presumed he was referring to his divorce. *Horrid* thing, divorce. Especially if there were children involved...

'How long did it take for you to get back on the rails?' she asked him.

'How long?' he mused, lifting his glass to his lips for a long sip. 'Not too long. But I was terribly bitter for a while. Which I now regret. Bitterness is as self-destructive as revenge. And it gets you nowhere. You have to learn to move on and not dwell on the past.'

'You're talking about Claudia, aren't you?'

'Partly.'

'What do you mean by that?'

'I was talking in general—not just about Claudia in particular. I harbour no animosity towards Claudia any more. I met her the other week at a party and we had quite a pleasant chat. She's not too bad when you're not in love with her.'

Kate hated to think that he'd *ever* been in love with her. Which was pathetic, really.

Their steaks arrived at that fortuitous moment—Blake's medium rare and hers well done. Both were accompanied by French fries and salad, plus a side dish of herbed bread. The steaks covered half the plate.

'My goodness,' she said. 'I wish you had a dog. Then I could take him home some of this steak. I'll never eat it all.'

'You might have done, if you'd had it medium rare like me. Goes down much easier that way.'

'No, thanks,' she said, crinkling her nose at him. 'I don't like eating meat with blood in it.'

'Have you ever tried it?'

'No…'

'Then don't knock it 'til you try it.'

'Okay. Give me a mouthful of yours, then.'

He did—and she did like it. It was very tender…more tender than hers.

'See?' he said smugly. 'You shouldn't be afraid to try new things, Kate.'

'Yes, boss.'

He laughed. 'You sounded just like Carlos, then.'

'And *you* sounded like an old schoolteacher of mine. Not one I overly liked.'

'*Ouch*. That's not good.'

'No—so cut it out with the life lessons. I'll get there, Blake. In my own good time.'

He cocked his head to one side. 'You've become quite an independent little miss during the past week, haven't you?'

'I hope so.'

'Good. I like that. Now, eat up or the food will get cold. Nothing worse than cold steak.'

They both tucked in, and Kate realised how hungry she actually was. She ate ninety percent of the steak and all of everything else—including the herb bread.

'I like to see a girl with a good appetite,' Blake said as he dabbed his mouth with a serviette. 'Rare thing in Hollywood, I can tell you.'

'I'm lucky that I can eat whatever I like and not get fat. I have a fast metabolism.'

'That *is* lucky. And good for your career. You'll stay slim and at the same time you won't get all skinny and fragile like some of the actresses I know. Speaking of your career... I was talking to Steve late this afternoon and—'

'Who's Steve?'

'Steve Kepell. The agent I think would suit you. The one I sent the DVD of your play. Anyway, he was as impressed as I was—both by your acting and your looks. Said you were very photogenic. But he *did* suggest that whilst you're waiting for your working visa to come through you have some lessons from a dialect coach. Get rid of your Australian accent entirely. Oh, and he also suggested you have a few sessions with an audition coach. He gave me the name of a good one. Anyway, I'll line up both for you on Monday so that you can get started ASAP.'

Dismay swamped Kate, and her forehead bunched up into a troubled frown.

'What?' he asked.

She shook her head at him. 'I'm sorry, Blake, but it's all getting a bit too much.'

'What is?'

'Everything you're doing for me.'

He sighed. 'You're not going to say no again, are you?'

'Coaches like that are very expensive. I'm not dumb. I know what they cost.'

'But I can afford it,' he told her, her voice tight with obvious frustration. 'My movies are raking in heaps.'

'That's not the point. People will say I'm a freeloader, or a gold-digger. I know you said I shouldn't worry about what other people think, but I do.'

Blake scowled. 'They wouldn't say either of those things if you were my wife.'

'Your *wife*?' Kate exclaimed.

CHAPTER TWENTY-SIX

BLAKE COULD HAVE cut his tongue out. He'd done it now, hadn't he? But, damn it all, he was beginning to see everything he wanted getting away from him. And he couldn't bear it.

The shock on Kate's face just about killed him. Clearly marrying him was the last thing she wanted, or would ever do. And whilst one part of him found pleasure in this undeniable proof that she was nothing like Claudia, the rest of him was plunged into the most alien despair.

True to his nature, however, Blake refused to admit defeat. With a will of iron he climbed out of the pit and put his intelligence to finding the right words to say to her, finally adopting what he hoped was the right expression. One of mild exasperation.

'Yes, yes,' he said, with a flourish of his left hand, 'I know exactly what you're going to say. We've only known each other a week. You don't marry someone you've only known for a week.'

'I… I wasn't going to say any of that at all,' Kate denied, feeling both flushed and flustered.

Because of course she would marry him in a heartbeat if he loved her. The brevity of their relationship didn't matter. She already knew more about him in a week than she'd learnt about Lachlan in four years. Kate knew down deep that Blake was a decent man. Caring and kind and above all fantastically good in bed.

'I was going to *say*,' she went on, having to force out the words, 'that I would only marry you if we were both madly in love with each other.' Blake's not loving her was a deal-breaker. Kate needed her husband to love her. 'I'm sorry, Blake, but marriage without love is not for me.'

'I see,' Blake bit out. 'Well, that's it then.' He looked at her for a long moment, his dark eyes searching hers as the corner of his mouth lifted in a strange smile. 'You wouldn't consider it even if one half of the couple was madly in love with the other?'

The truth behind his statement hit Kate with a squall of anxiety and embarrassment. 'Oh, no!' she wailed, her stomach churning. 'You rang Lachlan, didn't you? And he *told* you. Or Maddie told you. I *knew* I should never have told her. Oh, God...'

And she buried her face in her hands momentarily, before looking up at him again with anguished eyes.

Blake shook his head at her. 'Kate, I don't know what in hell you're talking about. I haven't rung Lachlan. Though I will. Soon. He needs to be sorted out. But I haven't yet. And I certainly haven't talked to your sister.'

Kate blinked in confusion, then blinked again—until suddenly she realised what this meant. If he hadn't talked to Maddie or Lachlan then he didn't *know* she loved him. So he had to have been talking about himself.

Her heart flipped right over at the enormity of her discovery.

'Are you saying that you're actually in *love* with me?'

His smile carried amusement. 'Not "actually" so much as madly. Yes, Kate, my sweet. I'm madly in love with you. Is that so surprising? Now, what on earth were you going on about just now? What was it you told Maddie that she shouldn't have told me even though she didn't?'

'Oh. Yes. Oh. No. Oh. Well...' God, she was babbling like an idiot.

'Out with it, woman. No lies, now.'

'I... I told her that I love you.'

Blake seemed stunned. 'You *love* me?'

'Yes. Yes, I love you. Very much.'

'Wow... I never dreamt...' His hands lifted to run rather shakily through his hair. His gaze searched her face with an air of wonder. 'I thought it was too soon. I thought...'

'I know what you thought, but you were wrong. Lachlan means no more to me now than Claudia does to you. The moment you came into my life I saw that he was just a cardboard cut-out hero, whereas you are the real thing.'

'I'll have to remember to use that line in one of my movies.'

'You will not!' she said. But she was smiling.

'Right. Now, can we go back to that earlier part of our conversation where I suggested you become my wife?'

'Oh, *that* part.'

'Well, what do you say?'

The temptation to just say yes was acute. But...

'You need to ask me properly first—with an engagement ring in your pocket. And the wedding won't be taking place until after I get my first independent acting job, gained by my own efforts and no help from you.'

'Done!' he agreed, grinning as he whipped out his phone.

'What are you doing?' Kate asked breathlessly. She was still in a bit of shock at the speed of everything.

'I'm calling Carlos.'

'Yes, boss?' Carlos answered. 'You ready to be picked up?'

'Yep. But we won't be going straight home. I need to do some shopping first. Oh, and bring Juanita with you.'

'Juanita?'

'Yep. I know how much your wife likes jewellery. She'll know exactly where we should go to buy an engagement ring.'

'I'm sure she will,' Carlos replied gleefully. 'See you outside in about ten minutes, boss.'

'Perfect.'

CHAPTER TWENTY-SEVEN

BLAKE LAY BACK in bed with his fiancée in his arms, feeling happier than he could ever have imagined. His original quest to make Kate happy had been achieved—she hadn't stopped smiling or admiring her engagement ring for the last hour—but his own happiness exceeded anything he'd ever experienced before.

Who would have believed that an old cynic like him could find true love—and with an actress, no less? It was the ultimate irony. But a logical one in a way. Who else would he have so much in common with? Who else would understand him the way Kate did?

Byron was going to be surprised. Or perhaps not. Since marrying Cleo and becoming a father Byron had become an old softie. He would rejoice in their news and give Blake his heartiest congratulations and best wishes. Blake vowed to ring and tell him in the morning.

He wouldn't, however, be ringing Lachlan. If the rumour mill was correct he'd soon be severing his connections with Fantasy Productions anyway. Blake didn't bother to hope that Lachlan's new venture would fail because it probably wouldn't. Action heroes didn't have to be great actors. Blake didn't really care either way, but he vowed not to have anything more to do with the man—either personally or professionally.

'Will you stop admiring that damned ring?' he said now, pretending to be angry, 'and give your new fiancé some much-needed attention.'

'Rubbish. You've had plenty of attention. I still can't believe we're engaged.' And she wiggled her left hand back and forth, the five-carat brilliant-cut solitaire diamond glittering under the light of the bedside lamp.

'Well, Carlos and Juanita believe it. They wanted to throw us a party tomorrow night, but I said no because Sunday is their day off. Instead I'm going to take my wife-to-be out for the day. I've booked lunch for us at the Polo Lounge at the Beverly Hills Hotel, and then we're going to drive down to my favourite country club and I'm going to start teaching you how to play golf.'

Kate grimaced. 'That'll be a disaster. I'm not very sporty, you know.'

'With *your* build? You'll be a natural.'

And, surprisingly, she was.

Kate smiled during the whole drive home. They hadn't gone in the limousine, instead taking Blake's Porsche.

'I *was* good, wasn't I?' Kate said smugly as they walked hand in hand up the steps into the house.

'You sure were. *Too* good. In no time you'll be beating me. Well, perhaps not. But you could probably beat Byron.'

'Darling Byron. He seemed genuinely happy for us over the phone, didn't he? And not at all shocked.'

'Men like Byron never get shocked. Not like mothers.'

Kate was taken aback. 'You told your *mother*?'

'Hell, no. That can wait until after we're safely married. Same with yours. Then they can't spoil anything, can they? Not once we're a *fait accompli*.'

Kate flashed him a questioning glance. 'How long do you think it will take me to get a job?'

'No time at all once your visa comes through.'

'I can't wait.'

'We don't *have* to wait, you know. We could fill in the marriage licence form online tonight and be in Vegas for a wedding tomorrow. What do you say?'

Kate shook her head. 'No. Let's not be silly. Let's wait. Do you want coffee?'

'Yes, but I need to go to the bathroom first. Be back in a jiff.'

Kate put on the coffee machine. after which she toddled off to the nearby guest powder room. When she returned to the kitchen Blake was there, humming as he took down two mugs.

'You know, I rather like the idea of a Vegas wedding,' Kate told him. 'Provided I have a proper wedding dress and you wear a tux. We have to have decent photos to show our children.'

'Children!' Blake exclaimed, having not thought of their having children until that moment.

'Well, of course. Don't you *want* children?'

Blake considered the idea, and then decided he did. Kate would make a wonderful mother. He wasn't so sure about his own fathering capabilities, but he would give it his best shot—like he did with everything he attempted in life.

'Yes, I'd like children. Though I don't want a big family. Two would be enough. Though perhaps one would be better,' he added drily. 'No sibling rivalry then.'

'True. Okay, we'll settle on one until we see how the land lies. Of course I have to warn you that I might change my mind and eventually want six.'

Blake laughed, then turned and drew her into his arms. 'That's a woman's privilege, I guess. Though you're not to change your mind about marrying me.'

'As if I would.'

'Tell me again that you love me,' Blake urged, and pulled her even closer.

'I love you, Blake Randall,' she said, her eyes going smoky.

'And I love *you*, Kate Holiday.'

'Perhaps you should show me how much,' she suggested saucily.

'What about the coffee?'

'It isn't going anywhere.'

Blake smiled, then bent his mouth to hers.

EPILOGUE

Four and a half years later...

KATE SAT AT her dressing table, putting the finishing touches to her make-up and doing her best to keep her nerves under control. Tonight was a big night for her. And for Blake. It was the premiere of the movie Blake had once promised to write especially for her—a romantic drama, with Kate as the heroine and not a nasty line in the whole script.

Which had come as a huge relief!

Up until now Kate hadn't done any movies at all, concentrating on the television series which had been the first job offered to her, and which had gone on to be a huge success. She had already done several seasons, with more to come.

It was part of what was called the *domestic noir* genre, and Kate's character was a black widow type who was wickedly amoral, going through a new husband each season—one murdered, one dead of natural causes and the rest divorced—whilst having countless affairs on the side.

According to the producer, she'd been chosen for the part for two reasons. She was a total unknown and she didn't look the *femme fatale* type, which added an ironic edge to her actions and made her character compellingly fascinating to watch, making the audience wonder *What next?* all the time.

Of course her character—Amanda—only ever married rich men, and she was always dressed to kill. And when Kate had fallen pregnant for real, towards the end of the first season, the writers had just written a pregnancy into the second season—though of course they'd made sure

Amanda's new husband wasn't the father. More drama that way.

The show was called *The Career Wife*, and it had already won several awards.

'When can I start wearing make-up, Mummy?'

Kate smiled at her daughter in the dressing table mirror. Charlotte—already nicknamed Charlie by Blake—was lying face down on the nearby bed, with her pretty face propped in cupped hands. She'd only turned three a few months ago, yet she seemed so much older. Though thankfully not too spoiled. Her English nanny had seen to that. And so had Juanita, who loved Charlotte dearly but refused to let her act like some pampered princess.

'Not just yet, darling,' Kate said gently. 'Perhaps when you're—'

'Eighteen,' Blake said firmly as he emerged from the bathroom, looking very suave in his black tuxedo.

'Eighteen?' Charlie squealed, sitting up and scowling at her father. 'Oh, Daddy, don't be so silly. I think seven is a good age—don't you, Mummy?'

'Er…' Kate didn't know what to say.

'Over my dead body,' Blake growled. 'Thirteen, my girl. And that's my final word!'

Kate smiled, noting how smug their daughter was looking, though she tried to hide it.

She even came up with a sulky pout. 'You *are* a meanie sometimes, Daddy.' But, having said that, she added sweetly, 'But a very *handsome* meanie.'

He laughed. 'Oh, go on—get out of here, you little minx. Your mother and I have things to talk about.'

Charlotte scrambled off the bed and ran out of the room.

'You *do* look handsome,' Kate said as she stood up and headed for her walk-in wardrobe.

Blake's hand shot out to grab her as she walked by, spinning her round into his arms.

'No, don't!' Kate squawked before he could kiss her. 'You'll ruin my make-up.'

'Bloody make-up,' he grumbled, but let her go. 'Wait 'til I get you home later,' he threw after her.

She smiled over her shoulder. 'Promises, promises...'

Kate was still smiling as she reached for her outfit. It wasn't a typical glamorous gown of the kind that most actresses wore to premieres and award nights. It was much simpler. Some would say conservative. It was a long cream crêpe skirt with a matching jacket, nipped in at the waist and then reaching down past her hips, giving her slim figure an hourglass shape. But Kate did add a touch of Hollywood glamour with a star-shaped diamond brooch and matching drop earrings, shown to advantage with her hair elegantly up.

'You look utterly gorgeous,' Blake said. 'I love that outfit. Where did you get it?'

'I had it made especially. I didn't want to wear anything like I wear on my TV show. I wanted to look classier than that.'

'Well, you certainly do. But sexy at the same time. Sometimes less is more.'

'No more compliments or I might let you kiss me.'

When he came forward with that look in his eyes she laughingly warded him off, snatched up her clutch purse and hurried towards the door.

Blake sighed and hurried after her.

'Thank you so much for minding Charlie for us tonight, Juanita,' Kate said.

Blake had give Charlotte's nanny two tickets to the premiere, and she was coming with a fellow nanny whom she'd met in a local park and who had become her best friend. Juanita and Carlos had already seen the movie, at an early screening which Blake had organised to get audience reaction. They'd loved it—and so had everyone else.

Kate still felt horribly nervous, her mouth dry and her heart racing. It was her first movie, after all. And what made her even more nervous was the fact that her parents and Blake's parents were going to be there, Blake having generously paid for the four of them to stay for a few nights in one of the hideously expensive bungalows at the Beverly Hills Hotel, only a short walk from the theatre.

'Money well spent,' he'd declared when she'd protested at the expense. 'You don't honestly think I'm going to have them all staying *here*, do you? Heaven forbid!' And he'd literally shuddered.

Both sets of parents had eventually come to terms with Blake and Kate eloping to Vegas, but none of them had exactly been happy at the time. Kate could still remember the dire warnings which had come from her mother.

'It won't last, you know. Still, I suppose you can always get a divorce and come home...'

Blake's parents had been equally negative in their prognostications.

'Not *another* actress, Blake. Oh, dear. Some people just don't learn.'

The arrival of Charlotte a little over a year later had certainly helped smooth things over—as had both Kate and Blake's ongoing success. And a visit home to Sydney last Christmas had been a big hit. Charlotte had been at her adorable best and no one had been able to resist her charm.

Even Maddie had fallen in love with her—dear, irrepressible Maddie, whose marriage to Lachlan had ended two years ago after Lachlan had been widely reported on social media as having affairs with every single one of his leading ladies. Though pretending to be heartbroken at the time, Maddie had happily taken a huge settlement—along with the house in Sydney they'd bought together—and promptly got back with Riley the plumber.

Leopards really didn't change their spots, did they?

Lachlan certainly hadn't. But his comeuppance was on the horizon. His career had faltered after his last movie, which had had some not too stellar reviews.

The movie business was a risky business—Kate knew that. And an actor's popularity could disappear overnight.

Such thinking sent a nervous shiver down her spine, made her hands twist together.

'Everything is going to be fine,' Juanita said, and clasped Kate's trembling hands in both of hers. 'You are a great actress. That is a great movie.'

Carlos said much the same on their way to the theatre. But the kind words didn't lessen Kate's escalating anxiety. They were friends, after all. And all those other people who'd come to the pre-screening had been fans of Blake's work. They might not have wanted to tell him the truth: that the movie wasn't great and Kate was simply awful as a romantic heroine as opposed to playing the conniving villain she played in *The Career Wife*!

'Are you all right?' Blake asked her as they pulled up outside the theatre.

Huge crowds had gathered on the sidewalk, along with lots of paparazzi.

Kate refused to load her anxiety onto Blake. No doubt he was feeling a little tense himself.

'No, no. I'm fine,' she said.

'Good—because there's nothing to be nervous about. Byron rang me while you were getting ready. He and Cleo had just watched the copy of the movie I sent him and they were over the moon about it. Said it was going to make us all a small fortune. The only reason they aren't here in person to celebrate is because their son is due in two weeks' time.'

'Yes, I know. But let's not forget Byron and Cleo are biased. They're friends.'

'And very canny investors. Byron doesn't wear blinkers when it comes to money. Trust me when I say you're about to become an even bigger star than you already are.'

'Promise?'

'That's not a promise. That's a fact.' And he leant over and kissed her on the cheek.

Kate's anxiety eased slightly at his confidence, and his love. Somehow she found a smiling face for the photographers, but didn't linger in the foyer, hurrying into the theatre, where she smiled some more at the already seated guests before thankfully sinking into her own seat.

Finally, after considerable delays and endless advertisements, the movie started—by which time Kate thought she was going to be sick. She tried to concentrate but her focus seemed blurred. Suddenly all she cared about was what the audience was feeling and thinking. She had to force herself not to look around and stare at people's faces.

She did sneak a few surreptitious glances at her parents, who were sitting on her left. They seemed wrapped up in the drama, and her mother's mouth was slightly agape. Was that a good sign or a bad sign?

Finally, after what felt like an eternity, the movie ended and the credits started rolling. For a few seconds there was a deathly silence. Kate didn't know what to think. And then, as one, everyone in that theatre stood up and started clapping. Clapping and shouting *Bravo!*

Even Blake seemed surprised. And touched—especially at the sight of his dad, clapping the loudest.

Kate was just stunned, and her eyes filled with tears when her mother turned to her and said, 'Oh, my dear. You were just wonderful. I'm so, *so* proud of you.'

Kate and Blake stood up to more cheers, and Kate turned to the man she knew was responsible for this moment— the man responsible for every happy moment in her life.

MILLS & BOON

THE HEART OF ROMANCE

A ROMANCE FOR EVERY READER

MODERN

Prepare to be swept off your feet by sophisticated, sexy and seductive heroes, in some of the world's most glamourous and romantic locations, where power and passion collide.

HISTORICAL

Escape with historical heroes from time gone by. Whether your passion is for wicked Regency Rakes, muscled Vikings or rugged Highlanders, awaken the romance of the past.

MEDICAL

Set your pulse racing with dedicated, delectable doctors in the high-pressure world of medicine, where emotions run high and passion, comfort and love are the best medicine.

True Love

Celebrate true love with tender stories of heartfelt romance, from the rush of falling in love to the joy a new baby can bring, and a focus on the emotional heart of a relationship.

Desire

Indulge in secrets and scandal, intense drama and plenty of sizzling hot action with powerful and passionate heroes who have it all: wealth, status, good looks…everything but the right woman.

HEROES

Experience all the excitement of a gripping thriller, with an intense romance at its heart. Resourceful, true-to-life women and strong, fearless men face danger and desire - a killer combination!

To see which titles are coming soon, please visit

millsandboon.co.uk/nextmonth

Reaching up, she kissed him softly on the mouth and whispered, 'Thank you, my darling. For everything.'

Blake's dark eyes were full of love and admiration as he took her hand and lifted it to his lips. 'No,' he murmured. 'Thank *you*.'

* * * * *

Introduction

The year 1997 marks the 25th anniversary of the establishment of the British Airways Board in April 1972, although it was to be a further two years before the complex task of merging Britain's two major state-owned airlines and their many subsidiaries into a unified organisation with its own corporate identity was completed. In the intervening 25 years British Airways itself has undergone a massive transformation from a state-owned monolith into a dynamic and successful public company which has become a world-beating symbol of British entrepreneurial skill and technical expertise.

The pace of change within the airline can be gauged by looking at some of the changes evident from this second edition of abc British Airways when compared to the original edition published in 1993. In the intervening years the fleet has been modernised by the addition of the new Boeing 777 as well as further deliveries of established types such as the Boeing 747-400 and the Boeing 767, while older aircraft such as the BAC-111 and the Lockheed Tristar have finally retired. The organisation of the airline has been rationalised by the strengthening of the British

Airways Regional subsidiary and the establishment of British Airways (European Operations) at Gatwick. On the other hand, British Airways has distanced itself from the volatile inclusive tour market with the sale of its Caledonian subsidiary in 1995. At home, virtually every significant airport in the UK is now served by the British Airways Express network, a highly innovative and successful franchise operation, and abroad the airline has made further investments and agreements, helping it towards its stated intention of becoming a World Airline in every sense.

In fact, British Airways is, by a handsome margin, the world's biggest carrier of international airline passengers and has a scheduled route network covering around 170 destinations in almost 80 countries. On average, a British Airways flight departs from an airport somewhere in the world every 90 seconds, contributing to a total of over a quarter of a million flights in a full year carrying over 30 million passengers and half a million tonnes of cargo. This global operation is carried out by a fleet of over 250 modern aircraft flown, serviced and supported by a staff of 48,000 who are dedicated to keeping

Below: **British Airways is offering an increasing range of services from its Birmingham hub as evidenced by this selection of aircraft, including a Boeing 757, Boeing 737 and ATP on the ramp at the Eurohub terminal.** *L. Marriott*

Above: **Imperial Airways was the forerunner of BOAC and was formed in 1924. The Handley Page HP42 shown here was the pride of the fleet when it entered service in 1932 and was used extensively on routes to Africa, India and the Far East, carrying passengers in great comfort and safety, but at the abysmally slow cruising speed of 90kt. It was hopelessly outclassed by contemporary American airliners.**
ASM via I. James

their airline one step ahead of its competitors. And competition there certainly is. The widespread trend towards deregulation and the build-up of international megacarriers has meant that British Airways has constantly to improve its services to passengers and to expand its fleet and route networks if it is to remain a world leader. Many years ago the British state-owned airlines were regarded unfavourably in comparison with the supposedly more efficient American airlines, but today this has changed completely. British Airways is widely admired for its technical expertise and levels of service, and, most of all, for its hard-headed commercial success. With some of the major US airlines and most international carriers running at a loss, and the remainder struggling to secure a small profit in the difficult period following the Gulf War in 1991, British Airways continued to bring home record-breaking profits which by 1994/95 had reached £250 million. However, the air transport world is now shaking off the slump of the early 1990s and many airlines are now showing healthy balance sheets, enabling them to order new aircraft and develop new routes, presenting a double-edged threat to British Airways.

With the cash available from its profits, British Airways has been able to move forward with its plan to become a truly global airline and has acquired major shareholdings in airlines such as Deutsche BA, TAT European, Air Liberté and QANTAS, although a shareholding in US Air has been relinquished. In addition, it has marketing agreements with many airlines across the world such as Canadian Airlines and America West, giving its passengers access to routes not flown by British Airways aircraft. However, these are all eclipsed by a far-reaching agreement with American Airlines announced in 1996 which, subject to government approvals, will put in place the world's largest airline alliance and, for marketing purposes, could ultimately lead to a new name such as British American Airlines! In other areas the British Airways logo, livery and unsurpassed standards of service have been introduced to many new passengers through the creation of the British Airways Express franchise in 1993. Initially applied to British domestic operators such as CityFlyer Express and Brymon Airways, the concept has now been applied to international routes flown by Maersk Air (UK) and GB Airways. In addition, domestic operators in other countries have also signed up for the British Airways franchise, which is now widely recognised as

4

providing tangible benefits for British Airways and the franchisee airline and, not least, for their passengers.

A modern airline is a complex organisation and requires its staff to have a wide variety of trades and skills. Apart from the flightdeck and cabin crew, there are the engineers and maintenance staff, the passenger and customer service staff, ticketing agents, accountants, caterers, cleaners, drivers, baggage handlers, computer programmers and operators, and public relations staff — to name but a few. Most of these have to be organised into shifts to cover 24 hours of operation at many locations and much of the work is covered in great detail by legal requirements and standards. On top of this are the various factors which are outside the control of the airline, such as weather and ATC delays, which can cause carefully planned schedules to be disrupted, necessitating changes of plan at short notice and requiring extra effort from staff to ensure a minimum of disruption to passengers. British Airways is generally recognised as one of the world's most efficient airlines and invests heavily in staff training and customer service, having won countless awards based on the excellence of its various service brands. It has, for example, been awarded the accolade 'Airline of the Year' by the influential US magazine Air Transport World on two separate occasions in recent years.

In mid-1997 the airline introduced a widely publicised new livery which was intended to emphasise its concept of being a world airline, sensitive to the needs and perceptions of peoples from around the globe, rather than being a purely national airline. However, this was more than a mere cosmetic change as behind the new paint lay a £6 billion programme to improve services, products, aircraft, facilities and training. These wide-ranging schemes will equip British Airways to compete on a global scale in the new millennium.

This book is intended to give some idea of the scale and nature of British Airways and its associated companies. Although the emphasis is on the airline's fleet of aircraft, with details of each specific type, other aspects of the airline are also covered to give the reader a full appreciation of 'The World's Favourite Airline'.

Below: **Loganair has now been absorbed into British Regional Airlines, itself owned by the Airlines of Britain Group. The ex-Loganair fleet of Islanders, Shorts 360s and a Twin Otter now flying in British Airways Express colours serve Scottish internal routes under BA flight numbers.** *British Regional Airlines*

1. British Airways — A Brief History

In simple terms, British Airways was formed by the merger of its famous predecessors, British Overseas Airways Corporation and British European Airways, and operations under the new title formally commenced in April 1974. However, this momentous event was the culmination of many years' work, going back to the 1960s when the government gave considerable thought to the problems and future shape of the British airline industry. In May 1969 the result of a formal government inquiry was published in the Edwards Report which recommended the establishment of a British Airways Board to oversee the activities of BOAC, BEA and British Air Services as well as to encourage the growth of a 'second force' independent airline in which the board would also hold a share. At this stage it was expected that BOAC and BEA would continue to operate as separate airlines but there was considerable political pressure for a full merger. Following the provisions of the Civil Aviation Act (1971), the new British Airways Board was established on 1 April 1972 and took over control of the assets of the two airlines. One of its first actions was to reorganise the airlines into seven operating divisions which became effective as from 1 September 1972. These were:

BOAC Division: Effectively all operational aspects of the long-haul airline
BEA Division: The operational part of the short-haul airline and subdivided into Mainline, Super 1-11, Cargo and AirTours divisions.
BAS Division: The former British Air Services regional fleets of Cambrian, Northeast, Scottish and Channel.
British Airways Helicopters: The former BEA Helicopters.
British Airways Engineering: Engine overhaul based on the established BOAC facility at Treforest, Wales.
British Airways Associate Companies: Incorporating the various associate and subsidiary companies such as hotel and tour groups formerly owned by BEA and BOAC.

International Aeradio: A jointly-owned company originally set up to provide ATC services and communications networks required by the airlines.

Following on from this reorganisation the board also recommended that the single name 'British Airways' be adopted to cover the activities of the seven divisions and this title was formally adopted on 1 September 1973. The last recommendation, made in November 1972, proposed the long-expected total merger of the airlines and this was accepted without delay by the government so that British Airways was finally born, after a long gestation, on 1 April 1974.

In considering the story of British Airways it is relevant to look briefly at the history of BEA and BOAC, the two state-owned corporations set up during and after World War 2 and themselves the result of government-inspired mergers. BOAC was formed in 1940 as a result of the nationalisation and combining of Imperial Airways and the original British Airways. Of the two, Imperial was the older, having been formed in 1924 from the amalgamation of several smaller airlines, and was also the larger. Its fleet of aircraft, including the magnificent C class flying boats, flew services around the world providing vital links throughout the British Empire which was then at its zenith. British Airways was more of a newcomer, having been formed in 1935 from the merger of Hillman's Airways, Spartan Air Lines and United Airlines, and its main base was at Heston — just north of the present Heathrow. After World War 2 BOAC concentrated on the rebuilding of its long-haul services and a new state-owned corporation, BEA, was established on 1 August 1946 to operate domestic and European flights. There was also a third state-owned airline, British South American Airways (BSAA), which was set up to operate services to South America and the Caribbean using a fleet of Avro Tudors but operations ceased in 1949 after the unexplained loss of two aircraft. Initially, BEA

took over European transport and passenger flights which had been flown by the RAF from the closing stages of the war but in 1947 a large number of independent airlines were nationalised and their aircraft and routes absorbed into BEA.

In the 1950s both airlines expanded considerably and were responsible for many pioneering innovations in the field of civil air transport. After experience with a converted DC-3 powered by Rolls-Royce Dart turboprops, BEA went on to become the world's first airline to fly regular scheduled services with turboprop airliners when the first world-beating Viscounts were delivered in 1953. In the meantime, BOAC were blazing a trail with the world's first jet airliner, the de Havilland Comet, with passenger services commencing in 1952. Unfortunately, a series of tragic accidents led to its grounding in 1954 and jet services did not recommence until 1958 when the much improved Comet 4 entered service and BOAC regained some of its lost prestige by being the first airline to fly transatlantic jet services in October of that year, beating Pan American by three weeks.

Despite many attempts by the British aircraft industry to meet BOAC's requirements, the airline generally ended up ordering US equipment for its long-range fleet. Thus,

Above: **British Airways is the world's leading international airline with a fleet of around 250 modern aircraft including the immensely prestigious Concorde — the world's only supersonic airliner.** *ASM Photo*

Below: **Ancestry. British Airways' current predilection for American equipment dates back to the 1940s and '50s when its predecessor, BOAC, operated aircraft such as the Lockheed Constellation, the Boeing Stratocruiser and the Douglas DC-7C. An example of the latter (G-AOIE) is shown here at Heathrow.** *Ian James Collection*

Stratocruisers, Constellations and DC-7Cs outlasted the British-built Hermes in the 1950s, and Comets and Britannias were later replaced by Boeing 707s. In 1964 the British Vickers VC-10 entered service, followed by the stretched Super VC-10 in 1965, and this latter version was probably superior to the 707 in almost every respect but did not attract enough orders

to be a commercial success. By comparison, BEA adopted a staunch 'Buy British' policy and rapidly moved from piston-engined DC-3s and Elizabethans onto the turboprop Viscount and its successor, the Vanguard. These were followed in 1960 by the short/medium-range Comet 4B and the specially designed Trident in 1964. In 1966 the airline ordered a fleet of BAC-111-500s for use on its German services from Berlin and for regional services from Manchester. BEA's last significant act prior to the formation of British Airways was to place orders and options for up to 18 Rolls-Royce-powered Lockheed L.1011 TriStars, although the first of these was not delivered until 1975 when it appeared in British Airways markings. (The airline's first choice had been the projected BAC-311 but this did not go ahead due to a lack of government support.)

In the late 1960s BOAC initiated orders for two aircraft types which were to play a significant role in the developing fortunes of the modern British Airways. The first of these was the Anglo-French Concorde, in whose development BOAC was closely involved, and which first flew in prototype form in 1969, although passenger-carrying services did not commence until 1976, and then under British Airways colours. The other was, of course, the wide-bodied Boeing 747 which was to revolutionise the economics of long-haul airline operations. BOAC's initial order was placed in 1968 and deliveries began in 1970 with no less than 15 in service when British Airways took over in 1974.

After the formation of British Airways in 1974, the original seven operating divisions continued to exist and were joined by two additional organisations responsible for passenger product sales (British Airways Travel Division) and cargo handling and sales (British Airways Cargo UK). At this time the airline had a fleet of around 215 aircraft and employed over 58,000 staff and, from an operational point of view, was still run as two separate airlines. However, in 1977 a fundamental reorganisation was carried out with the aim of achieving more integration and centralised control. The previous Overseas, European and Regional divisions were

combined into a single unified operating structure with centralised departments responsible for commercial operations, flight operations, engineering, planning, catering, personnel and other services. Airline operations were organised into six (later reduced to five) separate route structures, three long-haul, two European and one domestic. British Airtours continued as the charter subsidiary and British Airways Helicopters also retained its autonomy. In the meantime there had been exciting developments on the commercial side with the first European shuttle operation having been inaugurated in 1975 on the Heathrow–Glasgow route. Pioneered in the United States, the shuttle concept introduced the idea of high-frequency flights on busy routes using simplified ticketing procedures with seat availability guaranteed by the use of standby aircraft. The instant success of this operation led to its adoption on the London–Edinburgh service in 1976 and subsequently to other routes. In the same year British Airways, jointly with Air France, became the first airline to offer supersonic passenger services with Concorde flights to Washington and the Middle East. On the domestic front British Airways was giving serious thought in 1981 to closing down the loss-making Glasgow-based Highlands and Islands services and handing the routes over to smaller airlines. However, a staff proposal which involved significant staff cuts and re-equipping with HS.748s was accepted and a new autonomous Highlands division was set up and has been consistently profitable ever since. A similar situation occurred at Birmingham where, again, the enthusiasm of local staff was responsible for keeping services in place. The year 1982 saw a further rationalisation and reorganisation of all other operations which were now divided between three new self-contained divisions — Intercontinental (long-haul flights), European (combining all domestic and short-haul flights) and Gatwick Services. The latter was responsible for all British Airways flights operating from Gatwick, including those of British Airtours whose main base was at the airport. As a result of this reorganisation and the steady elimination of duplicated resources stemming from the original structure inherited from BEA and BOAC, British Airways staff numbers had fallen dramatically by this time to around 35,000. In 1983, while retaining the three flight operations divisions, the commercial and accounting network was broken up into eight self-contained route centres.

British Airways Helicopters, which had continued as a self-contained operation since the 1974 merger, was sold off in 1986 to the Mirror Newspaper Group to become British Independent Helicopters. This sale, and the earlier airline reorganisations, were among many measures taken in the mid-1980s in preparation for the privatisation of British Airways which took place in February 1987 when the sale of 720 million shares raised a total of £900 million. Freed from the restraints of state control, the airline immediately began a programme of expansion and acquisition ultimately aimed at turning it into a world force. In July 1987 it made a surprise bid for the entire share capital of rival independent British Caledonian and after much hard bargaining with the Monopolies Commission and other interested parties, the deal was finalised by the end of the year. BCAL's fleet of five Boeing 747-200s, eight DC-10-30s and 13 BAC-111-500s was quickly absorbed and repainted, although the General Electric-powered 747s were not retained as they were not compatible with BA's Rolls-Royce-powered fleet. In addition, British Airways also took over a BCAL order for 10 Airbus A320s which became the airline's first and only Airbus type.

In the wake of the BCAL takeover, British Airways' Gatwick operations were substantially enlarged and reorganised with a fleet of 14 Boeing 737s and a number of long-haul aircraft. The charter subsidiary, British Airtours, was renamed Caledonian and adopted a new livery based on the previous BCAL colours and retained the distinctive tartan uniforms of the cabin crews. Also, in 1988, all British Airways activities were transferred to Gatwick's newly opened North Terminal which offered greatly improved passenger facilities. In the wake of the downturn in traffic experienced after the Gulf War, plans were announced in January 1992 to reorganise operations at Gatwick by means of revised schedules calculated to appeal to business travellers, together with various moves intended to reduce costs and improve efficiency. These plans received a considerable boost following the takeover of rival independent Dan Air in October 1992 with the addition of several new scheduled routes and the acquisition of a fleet of modern Boeing 737-300/400 aircraft. British Airways then proceeded to set up a new low-cost, short-haul operation based on the merging of its own and Dan Air's former Gatwick scheduled routes which has resulted in a network serving 56 destinations in 31 countries by over 400 flights a week. This is now organised as a separate division under the title British Airways (European Operations) and has its own dedicated fleet of Boeing 737s, now enhanced by the addition of several Boeing 757s to service routes to Baku, Moscow and Tel Aviv. This disposition has been made possible by the introduction of the Boeing 777 at Heathrow which has displaced Boeing 767s onto other routes previously flown by the 757.

In addition, British Airways has built up a considerable long-haul operation at Gatwick and currently approximately nine Boeing 747s, five 767s and the whole DC-10 fleet are based here, the latter operating many of the US and South American routes taken over from British Caledonian. Today, following a further recent reallocation of routes, the Gatwick Operation has grown to such an extent that there are now more destinations served from that airport by British Airways than from Heathrow, with more than 1,000 flights a week now flying to 116 city destinations.

Although scheduled operations from Gatwick have increased substantially, a policy decision to withdraw from the unpredictable inclusive tour market resulted in the sale of Caledonian Airways to the Inspirations travel group at the end of 1994 for the sum of £16.6 million. During its last year as part of the British Airways group, Caledonian had carried over 2.2 million passengers and has continued to operate successfully since being transferred to its new owners on 1 April 1995.

In recent years British Airways' policy has been dominated by attempts to negotiate partnerships and takeovers with other airlines in an effort to build up a worldwide airline network. In 1988 a marketing agreement was made with United Airlines giving BA passengers access to a major US domestic network. An offer to buy out United was rejected by the US government and the agreement subsequently lapsed. Opposition also led to the withdrawal at the end of 1992 of a bid for 49% of US Air, although British Airways subsequently negotiated a 24.6% shareholding which was approved in May 1993 leading to close co-operation between the two airlines. However, despite some benefits to British Airways in terms of increased passenger revenues, the relationship was not a happy one and US Air's continuing financial and staff problems led eventually to a formal termination of the alliance and the sale of British Airway's shareholding early in 1997. In Europe a bid to take a shareholding in Sabena was rejected in 1991 and a year later a proposed merger with Dutch carrier KLM also fell through. However, British Airways has successfully bought 49% shareholdings (100% since 1996) in the French regional TAT and the German airline Delta Air Regionalflugverkehr, the latter being renamed Deutsche BA and its aircraft repainted in BA-style colours, while in the important Pacific and southeast Asia region a deal to purchase 25% of the Australian flag carrier QANTAS was completed at the end of 1992. Back in Europe, British Airways took over the financially troubled French independent Air Liberté in November 1996 and has set up a joint management board to cover the activities of this airline and TAT European, with the intention of eventually merging the two concerns by the year 2000. Following the break-up of the former USSR, British Airways was involved in the establishment of a new airline, Air Russia — a joint venture with Aeroflot in which services were expected to commence in 1994. Although this project did not reach fruition, British Airways is still involved in training programmes with several CIS airlines to assist them in bringing their service, maintenance and operations up to western standards. However, the most significant move to establish a worldwide

Below: **Railway Air Services (RAS) began flying in 1934 and built up an extensive domestic route network before World War 2. Operations recommenced towards the end of the war, when this photo of a still camouflaged RAS Dakota was taken, but the airline, together with several others, was nationalised and taken over by the state-owned BEA in 1947.** *ASM via Ian James*

Above: **The world-beating Vickers Viscount formed the backbone of the BEA fleet in the 1950s and '60s, but by the time this photograph was taken at Southampton in the early 1970s it was used mainly on domestic routes by subsidiary divisions such as BEA Scottish Airways and BEA Channel Island, both of which are represented in this line-up. The third Viscount, in the background, belongs to Cambrian Airways which formed part of British Air Services and was absorbed into British Airways in 1974.** *Ian James Collection*

network occurred in early 1996 when British Airways and American Airlines announced a programme of code sharing and co-operation which would unite two of the world's air transport giants (American is the second busiest US carrier). At the time of writing, this programme is still subject to approval by the various governments and regulatory authorities, but seems likely to go ahead despite the vociferous opposition of rival airlines such as Delta and Virgin Atlantic.

At home, an extensive reorganisation of regional services based at Birmingham, Manchester and Glasgow has resulted in a new subsidiary company, BA Regional, which was formed in 1992. This has entailed the withdrawal of the long-serving BAC-111s previously based at Manchester and Birmingham and their replacement by Boeing 737-200s carrying the new Regional title. The Scottish services were operated by a fleet of 13 new British Aerospace ATPs which replaced the BAe.748s previously used. In addition to flying domestic and European services from the regional centres, the new subsidiary also operates transatlantic services which

commenced in 1993 and uses Boeing 757s and 767s leased from the parent company. However, many of the regional domestic routes are increasingly being served by commuter aircraft flown by the various British Airways Express operators, details of which are contained in this book. The concept of the British Airways Express franchise was inaugurated in August 1993 and has now been expanded to include a number of overseas airlines.

The air transport business is one of the most competitive in the world and as more governments adopt a policy of deregulation it will be the largest and most efficient which will survive. These pressures have led to a reappraisal of the airline's organisation under its new chairman, Robert Ayling, and early in the next century British Airways may well become a 'virtual airline', contracting out many services such as accounting, passenger handling, catering, maintenance and training. The airline may not even own its aircraft and premises but lease them from other agencies, leaving only a core of essential staff and management services actually working directly for the airline. This may sound far-fetched but a start has already been made with the transfer of 4,000 jobs in administration and accounting to India where the costs of skilled personnel are considerably less than in the UK. If this trend continues, British Airways will become a world airline in a very real sense and the first moves in this direction became apparent in June 1997 when British Airways unveiled its revolutionary new livery. Unlike conventional liveries whereby a uniform design is applied to all aircraft in the fleet, the latest concept features a basic blue and white colour scheme with a range of world images decorating the tail sections. These images are drawn from communities and ethnic groups around the world and are intended to portray British Airways as a world airline based in Britain rather than as British airline primarily serving the needs of its UK customers only. In fact research shows that over 60% of its customers are of non-UK origin, a figure which supports the move to creating a worldwide image. The new livery is part of a £6 billion programme which will involve the purchase of 43 new aircraft over the next three years including 29 Boeing 747-400s, nine 777s and five 757s. It also includes the cost of a new corporate office complex currently under construction at Harmondsworth near London Airport, and the new World Cargocentre, also under construction at Heathrow. In addition, there will be a considerable investment in training staff to improve services to the airline's customers

of every race and creed from around the world. However, even now British Airways ranks among the world's leading airlines and its recent history, particularly since privatisation, has shown that it intends to stay there. With an expanding fleet of modern aircraft, dedication to passenger service, and worldwide connections, it has every intention of being not only 'The World's Favourite Airline' but its biggest and best.

Above: **British Airways Helicopters, formerly BEA Helicopters, operated a substantial fleet in support of North Sea oil operations, including six Boeing Vertol BV234 Chinooks one of which is shown here taking off from Sumburgh. British Airways sold its helicopter operation to the ill-fated Maxwell Group in 1985 but the company still operates today under the title British Independent Helicopters.**
Malcolm Bradbury

Left: **BEA drew up the specification for the de Havilland (later Hawker Siddeley) Trident which entered service in 1964 and was the first commercial aircraft to be certificated for automatic landings. Developed versions of the Trident remained in service with British Airways until 1985.** *ASM Collection*

2. Aircraft

British Airways has a fleet of over 250 aircraft serving routes as diverse as short-haul regional services in the Scottish Highlands and intercontinental long-haul flights around the world; from high-density, short-range shuttle flights to weekly flights to rarely visited distant cities. In order to meet the conflicting requirements of a worldwide route network the airline seeks to achieve a balance between having aircraft ideally suited to the density and length of each sector while at the same time avoiding an unnecessary proliferation of aircraft types. Given that the operational life of a modern aircraft may be in excess of 20 years, selection of the right aircraft type is essential as the results of any policy change take years to work through. Thus it is only recently, over 20 years after British Airways was formed, that some of the aircraft originally ordered and flown by BOAC and BEA have been phased out of service. A typical example is the BAC-111, which gave sterling service from when it entered service with BEA in 1968 until it finally retired from the British Airways fleet in 1994; even then, it has made a reappearance in British Airways colours when operated by the Birmingham-based BA Express franchisee, Maersk Air (UK). Also

gone from the fleet is the last of the graceful Lockheed TriStar wide-bodied trijets. On the other hand, the supersonic Concorde is still the glamorous flagship of the fleet despite having been originally ordered by BOAC in the 1960s. However, now that British Airways is responsible for ordering its own aircraft on a purely commercial basis, it has become apparent that Boeing is very much the favoured supplier and the airline has accrued many advantages, both financial and operational, from its close liaison with the manufacturer. Boeing offers a range of aircraft which can meet virtually any requirement and in many cases these share common systems and components which reduce pilot training and engineering costs. It is likely that the mainline divisions of British Airways will eventually standardise on an all-Boeing fleet,

Below: **Concorde at night. A busy scene as G-BOAD is prepared for a charter flight from Cardiff Wales Airport.**
Malcolm Bradbury

although BA Regional and other subsidiaries may well take aircraft from other sources, an example being the British Aerospace ATP flown by BA Regional in Scotland. The takeover of BCAL in 1988 led to the unplanned introduction of two new types into the British Airways fleet: the McDonnell Douglas DC-13 10-30 and the Airbus A320. DC-10s are still used mainly on the ex-BCAL routes out of Gatwick but some are leased to the now independent Caledonian. However, the A320s were based at Heathrow as the 10 aircraft of the BCAL order were delivered and used on various domestic and European routes. Despite the success of the aircraft in service and intense political pressure, British Airways has not ordered any further Airbus types but has preferred to stay with Boeing when ordering new aircraft.

Aircraft of the British Airways Mainline, European and Regional Fleets

The following pages present a review and specification of each of the aircraft types currently operated by (or on order for) the British Airways Mainline, European and Regional fleets. These are:

- Aérospatiale/British Aerospace Concorde
- Airbus A320
- Boeing 737-200
- Boeing 737-400
- Boeing 747-100/200
- Boeing 747-400
- Boeing 757
- Boeing 777
- British Aerospace ATP
- McDonnell Douglas DC-10-30

Aircraft owned and operated by British Airways Express franchisees are briefly described in a separate listing.

Left: **The major proportion of the British Airways fleet is made up of Boeing aircraft. This view shows a 747-436, a 777 and a 767 lined up at Boeing's Seattle plant and clearly illustrates how the new 777 fills the capacity gap between the other two aircraft.** *Boeing*

Aérospatiale/British Aerospace Concorde

Dimensions and Weight

Length:	20ft 9in	Max Take-off Weight:	408,000lb (185,070kg)
Span:	83ft 8in	Operating Empty Weight:	189,400lb (85,900kg)
Height:	37ft 1in	Max Fuel:	94,750kg
Wing Area:	3,856sq ft (358.25sq m)		

Powerplant

Four Rolls-Royce/Snecma Olympus 593 turbojets. Each 38,050lb thrust with reheat

Performance and Payload

Max Cruising Speed: 1,176kt

Economic Cruising Speed:

Range (Max Fuel):	3,550nm	Range (Max Payload):	3,360nm
Passenger Capacity:	100	Cargo Capacity:	1,300lb (590kg)

Concorde is absolutely unique and provides British Airways with a high-profile flagship for its prestigious transatlantic services which no other airline, apart from Air France, can match. Taking just over three hours for the 3,000-mile crossing to New York or four hours to Washington, the graceful supersonic airliner flies well above the slower conventional jets at altitudes up to 60,000ft while its passengers relax in sumptuous comfort, pampered by British Airways' renowned service. Concorde is something special!

It is therefore all the more sobering to realise that the prototype first flew as long ago as 2 March 1969, although an exhaustive 5,000hr test programme to thoroughly investigate the untried concept of safe commercial supersonic flight delayed the inauguration of scheduled services by British Airways until January 1976. Changing circumstances in the intervening years caused a dramatic downturn in Concorde's fortunes and airlines which had flocked to place options for up to 74 aircraft gradually fell by the wayside in the face of

Below: **With its unique graceful lines, Concorde is instantly recognisable. This is G-BOAA on approach at London Heathrow with undercarriage down and the nose visor lowered for landing.** *ASM Photo*

Above: **Another view of G-BOAA, this time taking-off. Despite its supersonic performance, Concorde's ovoid delta-wing design means that the complex arrangements of flaps, slats and other high-lift devices which are a feature of conventional aircraft are not required.** ASM Photo

rising fuel prices and growing environmental pressures. It was not until June 1972 that British Airways placed a firm order for five Concordes, and these were all delivered in the course of 1976/77. Due to action by US environmental groups Concorde was initially not permitted to operate into American airports and consequently the first supersonic schedules were to Bahrain. However, services to Washington started in May 1976 and to New York in the following November. Subsequently, British Airways entered into agreements with other airlines in an attempt to broaden Concorde's route structure. At the end of 1977 a joint service to Singapore via Bahrain was inaugurated in conjunction with Singapore Airlines but this was abandoned after a few flights due to problems connected with overflying Malaysia. Eventually the service was restarted and ran for almost two years from January 1979 but as much of the flight was overland, there were few opportunities for supersonic flight. In 1979 a leasing agreement with Braniff resulted in the Washington service being extended to Dallas/Fort Worth but this lasted only until May 1980.

In 1980, under an agreement reached with the government who decided to write off all

Concorde development costs so that the aircraft could operate on a purely commercial basis, British Airways took delivery of two further aircraft and in 1982 set up a new Concorde Division which today is entirely responsible for all aspects of the aircraft, including its commercial profitability. Scheduled services are now concentrated on the all-important transatlantic routes to New York and Washington, and in winter direct flights to Barbados are flown at weekends. In addition, the aircraft has been available for charter and some spectacular flights have been made, breaking numerous records in the process. Despite a few well-publicised incidents, Concorde has an excellent safety record which bears comparison with any conventional subsonic airliner and has already carried well over 1 million passengers. The interior of the cabin is split into two compartments — of 40 and 60 seats respectively — by a central bulkhead and is sumptuously fitted out so that the 100 passengers recline in luxurious seats upholstered in grey leather. The whole Concorde fleet has recently been refurbished and fitted with new galleys, improved cabin lighting and a new high-quality audio entertainment system, this work being completed in 1993/94.

Following on from the two development prototypes (001 and 002), two pre-production (01 and 02) and 14 production aircraft were built. Both prototypes are now in museums while the pre-production aircraft are stored by the manufacturers, leaving the remainder evenly split between British Airways and Air France. By the end of this decade the aircraft will have been in service for over 20 years and will be nearing the end of their useful lives. However, Concorde has shown that there is a market for high-speed travel at premium fares and all the

major airframe manufacturers, including British Aerospace, are looking at the specification for a possible successor. If this is built, it will be larger than Concorde, seating around 250 passengers and will be powered by quieter and more fuel-efficient engines but it is unlikely to be in service before the year 2005. In the meantime Concorde flies on, still regarded by many as the most beautiful aircraft ever built.

Unlike most other aircraft in the British Airways fleet, Concordes do not carry individual names.

Airbus A320

Dimensions and Weight

Length:	123ft 3in (37.57m)	Max Take-off Weight:	158,700lb (72,000kg)
Span:	111ft 3in (33.91m)	Operating Empty Weight:	85,000lb (38,900kg)
Height:	38ft 7in (11.76m)	Max Fuel:	19,159kg
Wing Area:	1,318sq ft (122.4sq m)		

Powerplant

Two CFM International CFM56-5 turbofans. Each 25,000lb thrust

Performance and Payload

Max Cruising Speed:	487kt at 28,000ft	Economic Cruising Speed:	454kt at 37,000ft
Range (Max Fuel):	3,750nm	Range (Max Payload):	2,300nm
Passenger Capacity:	Up to 149 passengers	Cargo Capacity:	1.8 tonnes (100 series), 2.3 tonnes (200 series)

The A320 is the only Airbus product in the British Airways fleet and was obtained as a result of the takeover of British Caledonian who, as one of the launch customers, had placed an order for 10 aircraft. The first of these, G-BUSB, had already been rolled out in

BCAL colours and was hastily repainted in British Airways livery before delivery in March 1988. Another three aircraft had been delivered by the end of the year and a further three followed in 1989, with the remainder in 1990. The first five were actually Series 100

models, the remainder being the higher gross weight Series 200. Initially based at Gatwick, A320 operations were transferred to Heathrow in October 1988 and they are currently used on short- and medium-range services to a variety of European destinations, but may be seen occasionally on UK domestic routes. The aircraft are configured in a one-class 146-seat layout although the cabin can be divided by temporary partitions to allow use of a Club class section when required on the European sectors.

Although well received by passengers, the most significant feature of the aircraft is the flightdeck with its distinctive sidesticks instead of conventional control columns, pointing to the fact that this aircraft employs a computer-driven fly-by-wire control system. When the pilot applies pressure to the sidestick (which actually moves only very slightly) the flight control system computers ensure that the control response is such that the aircraft will always remain in a safe operating envelope. Thus, for example, if the pilot was to attempt to overbank in a turn at low speed, a conventional aircraft would stall and possibly enter a spin whereas the A320 would

automatically limit the angle of bank and, if necessary, automatically increase the engine thrust to maintain a safe flying attitude. All flight instrumentation, navigational information and systems status is shown on six interchangeable electronic display screens and the aircraft's sophisticated flight management system takes care of almost all the routine tasks associated with a flight.

Although the A320 has been a technical success, British Airways remains committed to standardising on an all-Boeing fleet and it is unlikely that further Airbus variants will be ordered although in the past very serious consideration was given to the A330 and A340 before orders were eventually placed for the Boeing 777. It is possible that the British Airways A320s will eventually be passed over to one of the airline's many subsidiaries and partners, with the French carrier TAT European being the most likely candidate. Worldwide, a total of 787 A320s had been ordered by August 1996, along with 273 of the derivative A319 and A321.

British Airways A320s are named after British offshore islands.

Previous page: **The A320 flightdeck is fully automated and all necessary information is shown on the six EFIS displays. Although this arrangement is common today, it was pioneered by Airbus in the 1980s. Note the sidestick controllers which have replaced the conventional control columns found on other aircraft.** *Airbus Industrie*

Below: **The A320 remains the only Airbus product in the British Airways fleet. The 10 aircraft were originally ordered by British Caledonian, but were taken over by British Airways in 1988.** *ASM Photo*

Boeing 737-200

Dimensions and Weight

Length:	100ft (30.5m)	Max Take-off Weight:	116,300lb (52,750kg)
Span:	93ft (28.4m)	Operating Empty Weight:	61,000lb (27,670kg)
Height:	37ft (11.3m)	Max Fuel:	18,000kg
Wing Area:	980sq ft (91.04sq m)		

Powerplant

Two Pratt & Whitney JT8D-15. 15,300lb thrust

Performance and Payload

Max Cruising Speed:	500kt at 22,500ft	Economic Cruising Speed:	430kt at 30,000ft
Range (Max Fuel):	2,000nm	Range (Max Payload):	1,680nm
Passenger Capacity:	106/116	Cargo Capacity:	2.4 tonnes

The Boeing 737 lays claim to being the most successful airliner ever built and over 3,000 had been ordered by the end of 1992. The original 737-100 first flew in 1967, sometime after its contemporary rivals, the DC-9 and BAC-111. Whereas the other aircraft opted for tail-mounted engines, the 737 retained the traditional wing-mounted configuration mated to a fuselage with the same cross-section as the earlier 707 and 727 which allowed a generous six-abreast seating arrangement.

The 737-100 was replaced by the 737-200 after only 30 of the former had been built and the new version featured a 6ft fuselage stretch to accommodate up to a maximum of 130 passengers. The aircraft rapidly became a

Below: **The Boeing 737-236 was ordered by British Airways in 1978 as a replacement for the fuel-thirsty Tridents. G-BKYH was originally named *River Dart* when delivered in 1984, but more recently has been allocated to BA Regional at Birmingham and renamed *Hotspur*.** *ASM Photo*

best-seller and a common sight around the world but it was not until 1978 that British Airways placed an order, initially for 19 aircraft, as part of a deal also involving the 757. Both aircraft were intended as replacements for the large fleet of Tridents inherited from BEA and which would be withdrawn from service during the 1980s.

The version chosen by British Airways was known as the 737-200 Advanced and featured several improvements as a result of in-service experience with the earlier models. These included lengthened engine nacelles incorporating improved thrust reversers, improved aerodynamics giving increased range, an automatic braking system and changes to the flaps and slats to improve landing and take-off performance. In addition, the aircraft were fitted with the optional uprated JT8D-15 engines. The first 737-236 was delivered in early 1981 and a further 43 followed over the next few years, with the last being accepted in April 1985. Most were configured for scheduled services in a variable two-class layout for up to 106 passengers but several were initially allocated to British Airtours for IT work and featured a high-density 116-seat interior.

The 737-236 fleet is now being slowly reduced as more modern aircraft become available. Currently there are 33 remaining in British Airways services, and these are based at Birmingham or Manchester, operated by BA Regional where they have replaced the BAC-111s previously used on services from these airports. A few are operated by the European division at Gatwick. Others no longer in the British Airways fleet are leased out to other airlines including Transavia and GB Airways. When first delivered, the 737s were named after British rivers but those based at Manchester have now been given titles with local connections (eg Pride of Manchester), while those at Birmingham carry the names of characters from Shakespeare's plays.

Below: **Almost all the remaining Boeing 737-236s have been transferred to the British Airways Regional subsidiary and are based at Manchester or Birmingham, most of them carrying the appropriate titles as shown by G-BKYE (*Hippolyta*) at its home base.** *ASM Photo*

Boeing 737-400

Dimensions and Weight

Length:	119ft 7in (36.45m)	Max Take-off Weight:	150,000lb (68,000kg)
Span:	94ft 9in (28.88m)	Operating Empty Weight:	73,790lb (33,470kg)
Height:	36ft 6in (11.13m)	Maximum Fuel:	16,680kg
Wing Area:	1.135sq ft (105.4sq m)		

Powerplant

Two CFM International CFM56-3C-1 turbofans. 23,500lb thrust

Performance and Payload

Max Cruising Speed:	492kt at 26,000ft	Economic Cruising Speed:	430kt at 35,000ft
Range (Max Fuel):	2,830nm	Range (Max Payload):	1,950nm (High Gross Weight version)
Passenger Capacity:	Up to 145		
Cargo Capacity:	3.1 tonnes (Series 300)		

Although superficially based on the earlier versions of the ubiquitous Boeing 737, the advanced 300/400 series features so many changes and improvements as to be almost a completely new aircraft. It was in 1981 that Boeing announced a new improved version of its best-selling airliner which was to be designated 737-300, and the main changes were the use of new CFM56 turbofan engines together with a 7ft fuselage stretch so that up to 149 passengers could be carried in a high-density configuration. Other refinements included a strengthened undercarriage for operation at higher weights, improvements to the aerodynamics of the wing and the use of new flight management systems and electronic flight information systems derived from those developed for the larger Boeing 757. The 737-300 first flew in 1984 and airline deliveries commenced at the end of the year. In the

Below: **The Boeing 737-436 entered service in 1991 and British Airways subsequently received 25 aircraft directly from Boeing, other similar aircraft entering the fleet through the takeover of Dan Air. This is G-DOCD (*River Aire*), one of the first to be delivered.** ASM *Photo*

meantime Boeing was considering a larger version which would be stretched by a further 10ft to seat up to 170 passengers and this became the 737-400 which flew in 1988. Subsequently Boeing has introduced the 737-500 which basically retains the short fuselage of the 737-200 (now no longer in production) but incorporates all the other features of the 300 and 400. Seating up to 132 passengers, this version first flew in 1989.

British Airways placed its first order for new generation Boeing 737s in October 1988 with a firm requirement for 24 aircraft and options on a further 11. This initial order was for the largest version, the 737-400, but at that stage the aircraft on option could be 300 or 500 series models as required, although neither of these variants has actually been specified to date. This order was of great significance to Boeing as it was won against strong competition from the Airbus A320 which was already in service with British Airways. The delivery of the first aircraft, in October 1991, was of further significance as it was the 1,000th new generation Boeing 737 to be delivered to an airline customer. Other deliveries quickly followed and all 25 were in service by the spring of 1993. In British Airways service the aircraft are configured in a flexible two-class 145-seat layout and, as with the other 737s, are named after British rivers. With the arrival of its own 737-400, British

Airways was able to begin returning six Boeing 737-300s which had been on long-term lease from the Danish airline Maersk since 1988, none of which remain in the current fleet. However, when British Airways took over Dan Air in 1992 it inherited a fleet of nine 737-400s and three 737-300s which were allocated to the Gatwick-based operation. In the interests of standardisation, the 300 series aircraft were not retained, although the expanding BA European operation at Gatwick continues to fly the ex-Dan Air aircraft (except for three which are sub-leased to GB Airways), supplemented by other leased 400 series aircraft and some from the original British Airways order.

Boeing has now developed a new 737 family comprising the 600, 700 and 800 series models. These all feature a redesigned wing, new avionics and quieter, more efficient engines as well as other detailed improvements. The 737-600 equates to the previous short fuselage 737-500, the 737-700 has the same fuselage size as the 737-300 which it replaces while the new 737-800 is based on the 737-400 but features a longer fuselage, stretched by 2.78m to increase seating capacity to a maximum of 189 passengers. As yet, British Airways has not ordered any of these variants, but, given its long relationship with Boeing, it may well do so in the future.

Below: **British Airways made a further acquisition in November 1992 when it took over Dan Air, until then Britain's oldest independent airline. While older aircraft were sold off, the ex-Dan Air fleet of modern Boeing 737-300/400 aircraft was integrated into British Airways' Gatwick operations. This takeover led to a considerable reorganisation at Gatwick which now has a substantial route network of its own based on the new North terminal.** *ASM Photo*

Boeing 747-100/200

(Data relates to Boeing 747-200)
Dimensions and Weight

Length:	231ft 11in (70.7m)	Max Take-off Weight: 820,000lb (371,940kg)	
Span:	195ft 9in (59.6m)	Operating Empty Weight: 380,800lb	
			(172,728kg)
Height:	63ft 4in (19.3m)	Maximum Fuel:	164,141kg
Wing Area:	5,500sq ft (511sq m)		

Powerplant

Four Rolls-Royce RB211-524C turbofans. 51,600lb thrust

Performance and Payload

Max Cruising Speed:	507kt at 35,000ft	Economic Cruising Speed: 490kt at 35,000ft
Range (Max Fuel):	Figures not released	Range (Max Payload): 6,900nm
Passenger Capacity:	373 or 425	Seating:14 First Class, 66 Club, 298 World
Cargo Capacity:	20.3 tonnes	Traveller or 47 Club World and 378 World
		Traveller

The mighty Boeing 747 was the first of the new generation of wide-bodied airliners when it took to the air in 1969, the same year as Concorde's maiden flight. The two aircraft could hardly be more different in shape and function, but, despite the technical excellence of the supersonic Concorde, it is the 747 which has changed the concept of air travel in a way which could not have been foreseen more than 20 years ago. The superb seat/mile cost of the large aircraft has brought long-haul air travel within reach of virtually everybody, with a

Below: **In 1977 British Airways took delivery of the first Rolls-Royce-powered Boeing 747-236. Increased maximum gross weight and improved engine efficiency gave almost 2,000 miles extra range compared to the earlier models. Shown just after take-off is G-BDXB (*City of Liverpool*).** *ASM Photo*

consequent staggering increase in the numbers of passengers being carried. British Airways' forerunner, BOAC, was one of the first major airlines to see the potential of the new aircraft and placed orders for six aircraft as early as 1966. The first was accepted in 1970, with scheduled services commencing in April 1971. A total of 18 747-136s had been delivered by 1976, although the current fleet stands at 15. All are powered by Pratt & Whitney JT9D-7 turbofans rated at 46,300lb thrust each. The initial configuration allowed for 358 passengers but current seating is for 14 First Class, 76 Club World and 266 World Traveller passengers, totalling 356 seats. As most of the 100 series are over 20 years old, they are being gradually replaced in service by the newer 400 series aircraft. At least one is leased to another operator and British Airways may convert them to an all-cargo configuration before putting them up for sale.

Following the early Pratt & Whitney-powered 747-136, British Airways placed orders for a Rolls-Royce-powered version of the 747-200 which, although dimensionally similar to the earlier variant, operated at much higher gross weights, allowing substantial increases in range and payload. The first Rolls-Royce-powered 747-236B flew in 1976 and deliveries to British Airways commenced in the following year. Of 19 aircraft ordered, two were sold to Malaysian Airlines before delivery and an all-freighter 747-236F was sold to Cathay Pacific in 1982. The last aircraft was delivered in 1988, one of three Combi versions in the current active fleet of 16 aircraft. With a higher maximum take-off weight, British Airways configures its aircraft for 378 passengers in a three-class layout, or 425 in a two-class layout, and the maximum range is almost 7,000 miles, nearly 2,000 miles more than can be achieved by the 747-136.

British Airways also acquired five 747-200s when it took over British Caledonian in 1987. However, these aircraft were powered by General Electric CF6 engines and consequently they were sold off at an early opportunity, although, in the process, British

Below: **The original Boeing 747-136 ordered by BOAC was powered by Pratt & Whitney JT9D-3 turbofans. Despite plans to convert them to freighters, they continue to give sterling service on long-haul passenger routes.** *ASM Photo*

Airways became one of the few airlines to have operated 747s powered by all three available engine marques.

Originally, many of the ex-BOAC 747-136s were named after British personalities and explorers of the Tudor and Elizabethan periods, but city names were adopted after British Airways took over. However, these were changed again to release the names of large cities for use on the new 747-400s and the original 100 series aircraft are now named after British lakes and inland waters, although the later 200 series are still named after major British cities (eg City of Edinburgh).

Boeing 747-400

Dimensions and Weight

Length:	231ft 11in (70.7m)		Max Take-off Weight:	870,000lb (394,625kg)
Span:	211ft (64.31m)		Operating Empty Weight:	390,700lb
Height:	63ft 4in (19.3m)			(177,218kg)
Max Fuel:	174,533kg		Wing Area:	5,650sq ft (525sq m)

Powerplant

Four Rolls-Royce RB211-524G turbofans. 58,000lb thrust

Performance and Payload

Max Cruising Speed:	507kt at 35,000ft		Economic Cruising Speed:	490kt at 35,000ft
Range (Max Fuel):	8,325nm		Range (Max Payload):	6,995nm
Passenger Capacity:	Up to 426		Cargo Capacity:	20.3 tonnes

Below: **A ceremony at Seattle was held to mark the handover of British Airways' first Boeing 747-436 on 29 July 1989.** *Boeing*

The next version of the 747 to be developed by Boeing was the 300 series which featured a distinctive extension to the upper-deck cabin to accommodate up to 44 extra passengers. This version first flew in October 1982 but was not ordered by British Airways which preferred to wait for the technically more advanced 747-400 which first took to the air in 1988. Externally this advanced variant can be distinguished by a lengthened upper deck and winglets fitted at the wingtips. However, many major improvements are apparent only on closer inspection and the most significant is the complete redesign of the flightdeck and control systems to incorporate the latest advances in digital avionics and automated flight management systems. Much of the aircraft structure has been redesigned to incorporate new advanced alloys and composite materials and, together with more powerful engines, the maximum operating weight has been increased to 870,800lb. British Airways aircraft are powered by Rolls-Royce RB211-524G engines which, taken with the aerodynamic and operating weight improvements, give the aircraft a maximum range of over 8,000 miles.

In 1986 British Airways signed an order for 16 747-400s (plus options on a further 12) and this order, valued at $4.3 million each, was the highest value aircraft order ever placed up to that time. In 1990, and again in 1991, further orders and options were placed to bring the total up to 50 (88 including options) — an indication of how important the 747-400 will be in the airline's fleet in the 21st century. The first aircraft from the original order were delivered in mid-1989 and by the end of 1995 no less than 35 were in service, making British Airways the largest operator of this variant, and second only to Japan Airlines as the largest 747 operator. Current orders will take the total to 66 aircraft with options on a further seven.

In British Airways service the 747-400 carries up to 426 passengers but the standard configuration is for 401 passengers in a three-class layout (14 First, 55 Club World, 332 World Traveller). The flightdeck crew is reduced to two pilots as the digital systems do away with the need for a flight engineer although additional pilots are carried on very long sectors to allow for crew rest periods in flight. The range of the 747-400 now permits British Airways to fly nonstop to destinations such as Singapore, Hong Kong and Tokyo where flight times can be in excess of 14 hours. As well as being among the most modern of the aircraft in the airline's fleet, the 747-400s are also the hardest working — each aircraft averaging around 4,900 hours utilisation per year. In common with many other 747s in the fleet, the latest aircraft are named after British cities.

Below: **Upswept winglets and a stretched upper deck distinguish the Boeing 747-436, now the most numerous wide body in the British Airways fleet.** *ASM Photo*

Boeing 757-200

Dimensions and Weight

Length:	155ft 3in (47.3m)	Max Take-off Weight:	220,460lb (100,000 kg)
Span:	124ft 6in (38m)	Operating Empty Weight:	126,000lb (57,155kg)
Height:	44ft 6in (13.6m)	Max Fuel:	34,150kg
Wing Area:	1,994sq ft (185.25sq m)		

Powerplant

Four Rolls-Royce RB211-535C turbofans. 37,400lb thrust

Performance and Payload

Max Cruising Speed:	505kt at 31,000ft	Economic Cruising Speed:	459kt at 39,000ft
Range (Max Fuel):	4,560nm	Range (Max Payload):	3,175nm
Passenger Capacity:	180/195 (Caledonian a/c 231)		
Cargo Capacity:	5.8 tonnes (3.9 tonnes, Caledonian a/c)		

The Boeing 757 was developed in the 1970s in response to the massive increases in fuel costs at the beginning of the decade and was intended as a replacement for the long-serving 727 trijet. The aircraft first flew in 1982 and, powered by Rolls-Royce RB-211s, it was the first time that Boeing had launched a new aircraft with non-American powerplants. The 757 was also one of the first aircraft to feature a 'glass cockpit' where the traditional rows of analogue instruments were replaced by a few electronic high-definition colour display screens and many of the routine pilot tasks were automated. British Airways was one of the launch customers (the other was Eastern Airlines) and placed firm orders for 19, with options on a further 18 in 1978. Following delivery of the first aircraft, commercial services began in 1983 and the last of the 42 aircraft ordered was accepted in mid-1992. All except four of these are standard 757-236 models and are used on a variety of domestic

Below: **G-BIKM (*Glamis Castle*) was one of the first batch of Boeing 757s to join the British Airways fleet, being delivered in March 1984.** *ASM Photo*

and European medium-density short-haul routes. They are normally configured in a variable two-class layout with 180 seats arranged for a minimum of 54 Club Europe and up to 126 Euro Traveller passengers. The arrival of the 757 in 1983 enabled British Airways to go ahead with plans to revamp and improve its shuttle services from Glasgow, Edinburgh, Belfast and Manchester to London Heathrow in reply to competition from independent carriers such as British Midland. Replacing Trident 3B aircraft previously used, the big and quiet 757s gave a much improved service on the now renamed 'Super Shuttle' and the aircraft dedicated to these routes have a one-class 195-seater layout. For Mainline European services, a flexible two-class layout carrying around 160 passengers is used, while those aircraft employed by BA Regional on long-haul routes to the US east coast carry 158 passengers (20 in Club World and 138 in World Traveller).

A feature of the 757's career has been its popularity in the IT market where several independent airlines have adopted the type. It was therefore a logical choice for British

Airways' charter operator, Caledonian Airways, whose fleet included four of the long-range 757-200ER leased directly from British Airways. This variant was powered by ETOPS-approved RB211-535E engines and could carry up to 231 passengers although cargo capacity was reduced to 3.9 tonnes compared to 5.8 tonnes on the Mainline aircraft. Caledonian later acquired two further 757-200ERs which had previously belonged to Air Europe. Although Caledonian is no longer part of British Airways, it occasionally leases some of the airline's 757s to fill capacity shortfalls. British Airways 757s are all named after British castles.

Below: **Boeing 757-236 G-BMRA (***Beaumaris Castle***) taxies at Heathrow.** *ASM Photo*

Opposite: **British Airways has a total of 25 Boeing 767-336ERs. Shown taxying at Heathrow is G-BNWE (***City of Lisbon***).** *ASM Photo*

Boeing 767-336ER

Dimensions and Weight

Length:	180ft 3in (54.94m)	Max Take-off Weight:	350,000lb (158,800kg)
Span:	156ft 1in (47.57m)	Operating Empty Weight:	179,400lb (81,374kg)
Height:	52ft (15.85m)	Maximum Fuel:	51,131kg
Wing Area:	3,050sq ft (283.3sq m)		

Powerplant

Two Rolls-Royce RB211-524H turbofans. 60,000lb thrust

Performance and Payload

Max Cruising Speed:	489kt at 39,000ft	Economic Cruising Speed:	460kt at 39,000ft
Range (Max Fuel):	7,180nm	Range (Max Payload):	4,900nm
Passenger Capacity:	193/247	Cargo Capacity:	Up to 12.3 tonnes

The wide-bodied Boeing 767 was developed in parallel with the smaller 757 and in fact was the first to fly, the prototype making its maiden flight in September 1981. This initial version was the 767-200 intended for medium-range routes up to 3,000nm and could carry a maximum of 290 passengers, although a more typical load was 216 in a two-class layout, and the lead customer was United Airlines. A 21ft 1in fuselage stretch resulted in the 767-300 version which flew in 1986 and was capable of accommodating up to 325 passengers although more realistic loads were 269 or 214 in two- or three-class configuration. However, the 767 really came into its own when Extended Range versions of both the -200 and -300 were produced in 1984 and late 1986

respectively. With higher gross weights permitting the carriage of more fuel, ETOPS-approved engines and other safety-related modifications, the ER versions have proved extremely popular and account for well over half of the 708 767s ordered up to August 1996.

Despite its early commitment to the 757, British Airways was a late customer for the 767 but was the first to order a Rolls-Royce-powered version of the 767-300ER. The initial order for 11 aircraft was placed in 1987 and since then firm orders have been increased to 28. Deliveries began in early 1990 and 25 are now in service, with the remainder due in 1998. British Airways employs the versatile 767 in two distinct roles. On high-density short-haul European routes such as London to

Left: **In the air it can be difficult to distinguish between the Boeing 757, 767 and the 777. This is one of the newest Boeing 767s in the fleet, G-BNWX (City of Bilbao), which was delivered in March 1994.** *ASM Photo*

Paris the aircraft are configured in a 247-seat variable two-class layout with accommodation for up to 154 Club Europe passengers and a minimum of 93 Euro Traveller passengers. On low-density long-haul routes such as to the Gulf and the east coast of the United States, when use of larger aircraft is not warranted, the 767 carries a total of 193 passengers in a three-class layout with 10 First Class, 42 Club World and 141 World Traveller seats. Those operated by BA Regional are configured to carry 215 passengers in a two-class layout, while all 767s flown on long-haul flights trade off cargo capacity and passenger numbers in order to carry more fuel on routes of over 5,000 miles.

The 767 is popular with passengers, particularly in World and Euro Traveller class where the unique 2-3-2 seating arrangement is much preferred to the more usual 3-4-3 on larger wide-bodied aircraft. British Airways 767s are named after European capitals and major cities.

Below: **Latest addition to the fleet is the twin-jet Boeing 777-236.** *British Airways*

Boeing 777-236

(Note: Figures refer to the IGW model. Dimensions are common to all versions)

Dimensions and Weight

Length:	209ft 1in (63.73m)	Max Take-off Weight:	590,000lb (267,600kg)
Span:	199ft 11in (60.90m)	Operating Empty Weight:301,400lb (136,713kg)	
Height:	60ft 6in (18.40m)	Max Fuel: 47,700US gal (166,500l)	
Wing Area:	4,605sq ft (427.8sq m)		

Powerplant

Two General Electric GE90-85B Turbofans

Performance and Payload

Max Cruising Speed: 499kt at 30,000ft | Economic Cruising Speed: 484kt at 35,000ft
Range (Max Fuel): Up to 8,000nm | Range (Max Payload): 5,500nmnm
Passenger Capacity: 267 (14 first class, 56 club world, 197 world traveller)
Cargo Capacity: Up to 18 tonnes

The latest addition to the British Airways fleet is the Boeing 777, a long-range wide-bodied twin jet which first flew in June 1994. British Airways was closely involved in drawing up the specification for the 777 and placed orders for 15 aircraft (plus 15 options) in August 1990, with deliveries scheduled to begin in 1995. Surprisingly, in view of the airline's long tradition of ordering Boeing aircraft powered by Rolls-Royce, it opted for the General Electric GE90 engine, although this choice was probably influenced by a simultaneous deal under which the engine manufacturer agreed to buy the British Airways engine overhaul facility in Wales for the sum of £272 million. In the event, problems with the GE90 test programme delayed delivery of the first aircraft to British Airways until 11 November 1995. In fact, the first five aircraft, all delivered by mid-1996, are the so-called A model with a standard take-off weight of 506,000lb and optional increases up to 535,000lb giving a maximum range of 4,900nm. The remaining 10 aircraft will be the Increased Gross Weight (IGW) model which, although having the same physical dimensions, will allow take-off weights up to 590,000lb and, using higher engine-thrust ratings and carrying more fuel, will enable up to 325 passengers to be carried over routes up to 6,600nm. These began to enter service from February 1997. Other likely developments include a stretched version, the 777-300, which may be available from 1998

onwards, and some of the options currently held by British Airways could be converted to orders for this variant. When the 777 entered service with United Airlines, Boeing proudly claimed that it was fully certificated by the world's airworthiness authorities for ETOPS long-range flights over the oceans. In the past, such status has only been awarded to airframe and engine combinations which have already shown the required level of reliability during actual airline service, but in the case of the 777, Boeing and the engine manufacturers carried out an intensive test and demonstration programme in order to obtain approval for ETOPS prior to service entry. All versions of the 777 are ETOPS capable and there will be no separate ER versions.

In the British Airways fleet, the 777 will bridge the gap between the 767 and the 747-400 and will eventually allow the DC-10s inherited from British Caledonian to be replaced. The A models currently in service are configured to carry 17 passengers in First Class, 70 in Club World and a further 148 in World Traveller making a total of 225, in addition to which up to 20 tonnes of cargo can be carried. These aircraft are used on low-volume long-haul routes to North America, the Caribbean and the Gulf. The aircraft are named after personalities and pioneers of aviation history such as the Wright brothers and Sir Charles Kingsford Smith, although the larger IGW versions remain unnamed.

British Aerospace ATP

Dimensions and Weight

Length:	85ft 4in (26m)	Max Take-off Weight:	50,550lb (22,930kg)
Span:	100ft 6in (30.63m)	Operating Empty Weight:	31,390lb (14,238kg)
Height:	23ft 5in (7.14m)	Max Fuel:	5,080kg
Wing Area:	843sq ft (78.3sq m)		

Powerplant

Two Pratt & Whitney Canada PW126A turboprops. 2,388shp

Performance and Payload

Max Cruising Speed:	266kt at 13,000ft	Economic Cruising Speed:	236kt at 18,000ft
Range (Max Fuel):	1,860nm	Range (Max Payload):	575nm
Passenger Capacity:	64	Cargo Capacity:	600kg

The ATP holds a unique position in the British Airways fleet as it is the airline's only propeller-driven aircraft and is flown exclusively by the Glasgow-based Highland division of BA Regional. Seating 64 passengers in a one-class layout, the ATP is derived from the older British Aerospace 748 which it has replaced in service. Compared to the older aircraft it has an 18ft longer fuselage, revised wingtips and tail, new Pratt & Whitney Canada PW126A turboprops driving quiet six-bladed propellers, and an all-new advanced flightdeck featuring electronic display systems. The lengthened fuselage means that the ATP is the only turboprop aircraft able to utilise the airbridge boarding gates now in common use at major airports.

Below: **The British Aerospace ATP fleet is based at Glasgow and is operated by the Regional division, concentrating on providing high-frequency services to Birmingham and Manchester, although examples are occasionally seen at other airports. G-BTPK (Strathrannoch) is shown about to depart from Newcastle on a summer scheduled flight to Jersey.** *ASM Photo*

Above: **A pleasing air-to-air study of a British Aerospace ATP. Despite its association with British Airways, this aircraft has made few export sales and production has now ceased.** *British Aerospace*

Below: **This is one of the early Boeing 747-136s (G-AWNO) delivered to BOAC and British Airways in the early 1970s.**
British Airways

British Airways originally ordered eight ATPs in 1988; four of these were based at Glasgow for use on domestic Scottish and other UK routes, while the others were based at Berlin where British Airways still provided some internal German services under an arrangement dating back to the end of World War 2. However, these traffic rights disappeared in the aftermath of German reunification and so the ATPs returned to Glasgow where they were joined by a further five aircraft ordered in August 1990, taking the total fleet to 13 aircraft, with options on a further six. Today the ATP has completely replaced the 748 in British Airways service and has also displaced the BAC-111 from many Glasgow intercity routes. Use of the smaller and more economical aircraft has enabled the airline to increase frequency on many services,

a typical example being Glasgow-Manchester which now has five services a day instead of the three previously operated, while Glasgow–Birmingham sees no less than eight daily rotations. The future of the ATP in the British Airways fleet is now uncertain following the reorganisation of its Scottish services and the allocation of many of its routes to British Airways Express franchisees. The next year or two may see these aircraft discarded or passed on to one of the partner airlines (Manx European/British Regional Airlines already operates this type). Maintaining a regional link, the 10 remaining ATPs are currently named after Scottish regions using the prefix 'Strath'.

McDonnell Douglas DC-10-30

Dimensions and Weight

Length:	182ft 1in (55.5m)	Max Take-off Weight:	572,000lb (259,450kg)
Span:	165ft 4in (50.4m)	Operating Empty Weight: 267,197lb (121,198kg)
Height:	58ft 1in (17.7m)	Max Fuel: 111,387kg
Wing Area: 3,959sq ft (367.7sq m)		

Powerplant

Three General Electric CF6-50C2 turbofans. 52,500lb thrust

Performance and Payload

Max Cruising Speed:	490kt at 30,000ft	Economic Cruising Speed:475kt at 31,000ft
Range (Max Fuel):	6,504nm	Range (Max Payload): 4,000nm
Passenger Capacity:	231	Cargo Capacity: 16 tonnes

In common with the rival Lockheed TriStar (now no longer flown by British Airways), the McDonnell Douglas DC-10 wide-bodied trijet was originally developed for use on relatively short-range high-density routes and first flew in August 1970, only three months ahead of the TriStar. However, McDonnell Douglas were quick to recognise the long-range potential of the aircraft and the CF6-50-powered long-range DC-10-30 became a best-seller. A determined attempt was made in the mid-1970s to obtain orders from British Airways for a proposed DC-10-50 powered by Rolls-Royce RB211 engines but the airline subsequently opted for the long-range TriStar 500 to retain

fleet commonality, although the Douglas proposal offered longer range and lower seat/mile costs.

The DC-10-30 finally wore British Airways colours as a result of the takeover of British Caledonian in 1987 when a fleet of eight aircraft was inherited, the latter company having operated the type since 1977. These were retained in service and used mostly on ex-BCAL routes to Africa and the Americas (north and south), achieving a very high utilisation of over 4,000 hours a year. Repainted in British Airways colours, the aircraft are normally configured in a three-class layout seating a total of 233 passengers (18

First Class, 35 Club World, 180 World Traveller), although this can be boosted to 311 in a high-density two-class layout. With the introduction of the long-range Boeing 767 and the larger 777, the DC-10's relatively short career with British Airways is drawing to a close: the aircraft have already been sold and are currently operated on lease. The DC-10s are presently used on services out of Gatwick to the US and the Caribbean and are occasionally sub-leased to other operators for IT charter work.

While in BCAL service the DC-10s were named after British forests and these titles were retained when the aircraft were taken over by British Airways. Although these were the only DC-10s to wear British Airways livery, it is interesting to note that the airline did operate some on short-term leases during the 1970s

Below: **The DC-10-30s were originally owned by British Caledonian and were absorbed into the British Airways fleet in 1987.** *ASM Collection*

Future Aircraft

Like all airlines, British Airways is constantly reviewing the size and composition of its fleet and, as well as placing additional orders for existing types, it is also in a continuing dialogue with the world's major airframe and aero engine manufacturers. In this way it can ensure that its own ideas and requirements are taken into account when new aircraft are being designed and developed. The continuing boom in air transport, particularly on long-haul routes, has led to an emerging requirement for an aircraft larger than the existing Boeing 747-400 capable of carrying around 600 passengers on transoceanic and intercontinental routes. To meet this demand Boeing for a while projected the 500X and the 600X series derivatives of its very successful Boeing 747 (but has subsequently cancelled these) while Airbus has responded with the all-new A3XX. British Airways is likely to order larger aircraft in the near future but the outcome is by no means decided.

In addition to the long-haul fleet, British Airways is also looking to rationalise its short-haul fleet and the replacement of the older Boeing 737-200s is high on the agenda. At the beginning of 1996 British Airways invited the major manufacturers to bid for a $1 billion order for no less than 60 regional jets, to be split into three distinct types or variants seating 80, 100 and 120 passengers respectively. However, this mouth-watering prospect was put on hold later in the year but a smaller order is now being considered. If it goes ahead,

Above: **The sole Saab 340 currently in BA colours is G-BNTE flown by British Regional. It was one of the first aircraft to carry Benyhone Tarten.** *Mike Barth*

Below: **The appropriately registered G-DCIO shown on the ground at Newcastle Airport after diverting from Gatwick due to weather problems. It is planned to dispose of these aircraft once sufficient long-range Boeing 777s are available.** *ASM Photo*

Right **Airbus may yet succeed in gaining a major British Airways order if it can convince the airline that the new double-deck A3XX can best meet the requirements of the 21st century.** *Airbus Industrie*

some of the aircraft will go to subsidiaries such as Deutsche BA and TAT, while others will go to British Airways Regional. Aircraft under review include the Airbus A319, Boeing 737-600, Avro RJ85/RJ100 and the McDonnell Douglas MD-95, although the Fokker 70 and 100 are almost certainly out of the running following the demise of the Dutch manufacturer. However, British Airways has not ruled out modernising its existing 737-200 fleet, particularly by applying hush-kits to the noisy Pratt & Whitney JT8D engines, if this can be shown to be a viable long-term financial proposition.

Finally, a new supersonic airliner to replace Concorde is still a possibility. Such an aircraft

is under active development by a consortium of major manufacturers led by Boeing and Aérospatiale but is unlikely to be available before 2015. If and when it does fly, it will be larger than Concorde, carrying some 250 passengers in order to substantially improve seat/mile costs, and because of environmental pressures it will be much more fuel-efficient and considerably less noisy. The difficulties of developing such an aircraft only serve to emphasise the technical success achieved by the British and French engineers in the 1960s when Concorde was developed and built. It is still therefore a matter of debate as to whether another supersonic aircraft will ever fly in British Airways colours.

Airbus A3XX-100

Dimensions and Weight

Length:	232ft (70.8)		Max Take-off Weight:	500,000kg
Span:	259ft (79m)		Operating Empty Weight:	N/A
Height:	79ft 8in		Maximum Fuel:	300,000kgh
Wing Area:	Figures not released			

Powerplant

Four 72–78,000lb/320-347kN thrust engines to be built by General Electric, Pratt & Whitney or Rolls-Royce (Trent 900)

Performance and Payload

Max Cruising Speed:	Mach 0.85		Economic Cruising Speed:	Figures not
Range:	7,500–8,500nm			released
	(13,900–15,750km)			
Passenger Capacity:	555 in a three-class layout. Over 800 in one-class economy configuration			
Cargo Capacity:	16 tonnes			

Airbus has developed the A3XX in order to ensure that its product range competes across the board with Boeing, the American company previously having a monopoly at the top end of the market with the ubiquitous 747. In launching the A3XX, Airbus had to face the fact that Boeing's rival 747 might have been available to customer airlines at an earlier date than the 2003 forecast for its own aircraft. However, Airbus maintains that there are significant advantages in the all-new design which will offer seat/mile costs at least 15% lower than the best available today. A double-deck fuselage layout has been chosen in order to keep overall length within criteria acceptable at today's airports and the wingspan is kept to less than 80m for the same reason. The data above relates to the initial A3XX-100, but already a stretched A3XX-200 is being offered which will further reduce seat/mile costs and will seat up to 990 passengers in all-economy seating, 550 on the main deck and a further

440 on the upper deck. In addition, the two-deck layout holds out the potential of a super-Combi freighter carrying around 400 passengers on the upper deck and a substantial cargo payload on a specially strengthened main deck.

Airbus forecasts a market for 1,380 airliners of 500 seats and above by the year 2014 and with the A3XX it is determined to take a substantial share of the $300 billion which this implies. Among its prime targets for a substantial order is British Airways and, as in the past, there will be substantial political pressure to buy a European aircraft rather than an American product, especially if it is powered by British Rolls-Royce engines. However, British Airways has shown in the past that it can resist such pressure in order to make a purely commercial decision and Airbus knows that it will have to fight hard to win an order from the British carrier.

Below: **Boeing's rival super-wide-body projects were based on the tried and tested Boeing 747, although the series 600X shown here in model form alongside the current 400 series would have featured new engines and a redesigned wing, as well as a stretched fuselage to increase capacity.** *ASM Photo.*

Aircraft Operated by British Airways Since 1974

Since its formation in 1974, British Airways has flown several aircraft types which are no longer represented in the current fleet. The following list gives brief details of all aircraft which have served with British Airways and its subsidiaries — British Airways Helicopters, British Airtours and Caledonian Airways — since 1974. Date of service entry and last commercial flights are given for each type. The list does not include aircraft which were operated on short-term leases from other airlines, nor those aircraft operated by BEA and BOAC but retired before the formation of British Airways. The helicopter fleet was transferred to new owners, British International Helicopters, in 1986.

Aircraft Type	In Service	Last Flown	Notes
Airbus A320	1988	In service	Ex-BCAL order
Aérospatiale Super Puma	1983 (BAH)	1986	
Augusta Bell Jet Ranger	1968 (BEAH)	1984	
BAC111-400/500	1968 (BEA)	1993	
BAC/Aérospatiale Concorde	1976	In service	
BAe ATP	1989	In service	
BAe/HS.748	1975	1992	Highland Division
Bell 212	1978 (BAH)	1983	
Boeing 707	1960 (BOAC)	1983	
Boeing 737-200	1980	In service	
Boeing 737-300 (i)	1988	1991	Leased from Maersk
Boeing 737-300 (ii)	1992	1993	Ex-Dan Air aircraft
Boeing 737-400	1991	In service	
Boeing 747-100	1971 (BOAC)	In service	
Boeing 747-200	1977	In service	
Boeing 747-400	1989	In service	
Boeing 757-200	1983	In service	
Boeing 767-300	1990	In service	
Boeing 777-200	1995	In service	
Boeing Vertol 234 Chinook	1981	1986	
Hawker Siddeley Trident 1	1964 (BEA)	1983	
Hawker Siddeley Trident 2E	1968 (BEA)	1985	
Hawker Siddeley Trident 3B	1971 (BEA)	1985	
Lockheed L.1011 TriStar	1976	1995	
McDonnell Douglas DC-10-30	1988	In Service	Ex-BCAL
Shorts SC7 Skyliner	1973	1975	
Sikorsky S.58ET	1974	1981	
Sikorsky S.61N	1964 (BEAH)	1986	
Sikorsky S.76	1980	1986	
Vickers Merchantman	1969 (BEA)	1980	Cargo version of Vanguard
Vickers Vanguard	1960 (BEA)	1976	
Vickers VC-10	1964 (BOAC)	1976	
Vickers Super VC-10	1965 (BOAC)	1981	
Vickers Viscount	1953 (BEA)	1982	
Westland WG.30	1982	1986	

Above: **One of the British Aerospace ATP fleet is unveiled in the new British Airway's livery at Manchester in June 1997. It carries the 'Blue Poole' design on the tail.** *Allan Jones*

Below: **Concorde G-BOAF displays the new Union Flag design on the tail. This is reserved exclusively for use on the Concorde fleet.** *John Dibbs*

Above: **British Airways Express G-BMAR, one of five Shorts 360s flown by Loganair, now part of British Regional Airlines.** *Malcolm Bradbury*

Below: **This TAT European Fokker 100 (D-ADFC) is on a temporary lease to Deutsche BA, both airlines being part of the British Airways global network.** *Deutsche BA*

Aircraft Flown by UK-based British Airways Express Airlines

The advent of the British Airways Express franchise operation has led to a massive increase in the variety of aircraft types now to be seen wearing British Airways colours and these are briefly described here.

Air International (Regional) ATR42
Span:80ft 7in (24.57m)   Length: 74ft 4in (22.67m)
Max Weight: 34,725lb (15,750kg)
Powerplant: Two 1,800/1,950shp Pratt & Whitney PW120 or PW121 turboprops
Cruising Speed:268kt (max)   Range: 1,050nm with max payload
Passenger Capacity:48   Flown by: CityFlyer Express

ATR72
Span: 88ft 9in (27.05m)   Length: 89ft 1in (27.17m)
Max Weight:44,070lb (19,990kg)
Powerplant: Two 2,400shp Pratt & Whitney PW124B turboprops
Cruising Speed: 286kt (max)   Range: 645nm with max payload
Passenger Capacity:66   Flown by: CityFlyer Express

Avro RJ100
Span: 86ft 5in (26.34m)   Length: 101ft 8in (30.99m)
Max Weight:97,500lb (44,226kg)
Powerplant: Four 7,000lb thrust Allied Signal LF507-1F turbofans
Cruising Speed: 426kt   Range: 1,507nm with max payload
Passenger Capacity: 100–120   Flown by: CityFlyer Express

Boeing 737-200
See main fleet section for details   Flown by: Maersk Air (UK) and GB Airways

Boeing 737-400
See main fleet section for details   Flown by: GB Airways

Boeing 737-500
See main fleet section for details   Flown by: Maersk Air (UK)

British Aerospace ATP
See main fleet section for details   Flown by: British Regional Airways
                                              (Manx European)

British Aerospace BAe146-200
Span: 86ft 5in (26.34m)   Length: 93ft 10in (28.60m)
Max Weight: 93,000lb (42,184kg)
Powerplant: Four 6,700lb thrust Allied Signal ALF502R-5 Turbofans
Cruising Speed: 423kt max   Range:1,176nm with max payload
Passenger Capacity: 95   Flown by: British Regional Airways
                                              (Manx European)

British Aerospace Jetstream 41
Span: 60ft 0in (18.29m) Length: 63ft 2in (19.25m)
Max Weight: 22,377lb (10.150kg)
Powerplant: Two 1,500shp Garret TPE331-14GR/HR turboprops
Cruising Speed: 292kt (max) Range: 590nm with max payload
Passenger Capacity: 29 Flown by: British Regional Airlines
(Manx European), Maersk Air (UK)

British Aerospace/British Aircraft Corporation BAC111-400/500
Span: 93ft 6in (28.50m) Length: 107ft 0in (32.61m)
Max Weight: 104,500lb (47,400 kg)
Powerplant: Two 12,500lb thrust Rolls Royce Spey 512DW turbofans
Cruising Speed :440kt (Max) Range: 1,480nm (with max payload)
Passenger Capacity: 86 Flown by: Maersk Air (UK) Ltd.

de Havilland Canada DHC-6-310 Twin Otter
Span: 65ft (19.8m) Length: 51ft 9in (15.8m)
Max Weight:1 2,500lb (5,670kg)
Powerplant: Two 652shp Pratt & Whitney PT6A-27 turboprops
Cruising Speed:182kt (max) Range: 160nm max payload
Passenger Capacity:18 Flown by: British Regional Airlines (Loganair)

de Havilland Canada DHC-8-300
Span:90ft (27.43m) Length: 84ft 3in (25.68m)
Max Weight: 43,000lb (19,505kg)
Powerplant: Two 2,380shp Pratt & Whitney PW123 turboprops
Cruising Speed: 285kt (max) Range: 800nm max payload
Passenger Capacity: 48 Flown by: Brymon Airways

Embraer EMB-145
Span: 65ft 9in (20.04m) Length: 98ft 0in (29.87m)
Max Weight: 42,382lb (19,200kg)
Powerplant: Two 7,000lb thrust Allison AE3007A turbofans
Cruising Speed: 400kt Range: 1,350nm (with max payload)
Passenger Capacity: 50 Flown by: British Regional Airlines
(Manx European)

Pilatus Britten Norman BN-2A Islander
Span: 49ft (14.94m) Length: 35ft 8in (10.86m)
Max Weight: 6,600lb (2,994kg)
Powerplant: Two Lycoming O-540-E4C5 piston engines
Cruising Speed: 140kt Range: 250nm
Passenger Capacity: 8 Flown by: British Regional Airlines (Loganair)

Saab 340A
Span: 70ft 4in (21.44m) Length: 64ft 8in (19.72m)
Max Weight: 28,500lb (12,700kg)
Powerplants: Two 1735shp General Electric CT7-5A2 turboprops
Cruising Speed: 282kt (max) Range: 643nm (with max payload)
Passenger Capacity: 34 Flown by:-British Regional Airlines
(Business Air)

Shorts 360

Span: 74ft 10in (22.81m)　　　　　　　　　Length: 70ft 10in (21.59m)
Max Weight: 27,100lb (12,292kg)
Powerplant: Two 1,424shp Pratt & Whitney PT6A-65AR turboprops
Cruising Speed: M21kt (max)　　　　　　　Range: 225nm with max payload
Passenger Capacity: 36　　　　　　　　　　Flown by: British Regional Airlines (Loganair)

Notes: The de Havilland Canada DHC-7 was flown by Brymon Airways in BA Express colours but these have now been replaced by the new Dash 8s. Brymon still retains two Dash 7s for use on oil-related contracts but these are not painted in BA colours. At one stage the CityFlyer Express fleet included a Shorts 360 in BA Express colours but this aircraft has now been sold. Maersk Air (UK) has replaced its former Jetstream 31 with the current Jetstream 41 and its BAC-111s, also painted in BA Colours, will be replaced by Boeing 737s.

Aircraft Liveries

When the formation of British Airways was announced in September 1972 there was naturally much discussion concerning the livery which would be worn by the aircraft of the merged fleet. There was a great desire for traditional elements of the former BOAC and BEA liveries to be retained and design consultants Negus and Negus drew up a scheme which used the British national colours, red, white and blue, with a stylised predominantly red segment of the union flag on the tail. The lower half of the fuselage was blue and the title 'British Airways' appeared on the

forward cabin roof together with a modernised version of the BOAC Speedbird insignia. Wings were left natural metal although ex-BEA staff had mounted a campaign to retain the red wings which were a feature of their aircraft prior to the merger. Although one or two aircraft were painted in trial colour schemes, the first aircraft to be painted in the new official livery, in 1973, was a BOAC Boeing 707 (G-AXXY) and this was followed by a BEA Trident 3 (G-AWZC) at the end of the year. Following this, all aircraft were gradually repainted in the new scheme, although, as a temporary measure, several merely substituted the title 'British Airways' for BEA or BOAC on the cabin roof.

Below: **This Vickers Vanguard displays the final livery used by BEA before it become part of British Airways. The Union Flag motif on the tail was echoed in the initial British Airways livery, and freighter versions of the Vanguard soldiered on until 1980.** *Ian James Collection*

The basic livery was retained for almost 10 years with no significant change. Aircraft of the charter subsidiary adopted the same colour scheme except that they bore the title 'British Airtours' on the cabin roof. In the early 1980s there was a short-lived revision when the word 'Airways' was dropped from the titles painted on the aircraft, leaving the rather truncated 'British' in place. The rationale behind this was never fully explained and it was not favourably received.

However, a major change of livery took place at the end of 1984 following almost two years' work by the American design consultants Landor Associates. Working in co-operation with Chester Jones, a British design bureau, they devised a new livery which is still in use today. Although loosely based on the old colour scheme, the new design introduced a pearl grey tone instead of white for the upper fuselage, while the lower fuselage and engine nacelles were finished in a rich midnight blue. The stylised union flag on the tail was retained, although blue became the predominant colour, and the British Airways coat of arms was superimposed. The speedbird insignia was abandoned but its shape was echoed in a diagonal slash of red forming the head of a red cheat line running down the lower fuselage.

The new livery was part of a multi-million pound revamp of the British Airways corporate image and was extended to the fleet of vehicles and to the new uniforms and workwear for all grades of staff. The uniforms were designed by Roland Klein and the workwear, worn by engineers and ground handlers, by the House of Andre Peters. In addition, all ticketing, labelling, stationery, letterheads, logos, advertising and other details were redesigned in the new pattern which, with its combination of rich and co-ordinated colours, exuded an indefinable air of quality.

The current livery has stood the test of time and is admired and respected around the world. Originally British Airtours adopted the same colours but with the takeover of British Caledonian in 1987, a new livery was adopted together with the name Caledonian. Aircraft were basically finished in the same pearl grey and midnight blue colour scheme but the fuselage cheat line was yellow and the word 'Caledonian' replaced 'British Airways' on the cabin roof, although the same Optima Bold typescript was used. The tail was all blue with the Caledonian lion rampant painted in yellow. When Caledonian was sold at the end of 1994, the new owners retained this livery which can still be seen today.

Below: **A Boeing 737-236 demonstrates the 'British' livery adopted in the early 1980s.** *ASM Photo*

The main variation to both tthese British Airways liveries was the Concorde fleet where the requirements of supersonic flight led to reduced colouring. In both cases the aircraft sported an all-white fuselage relieved originally by a thin blue cheat line and the airline title, and then by a red line and the words 'British Airways' on the forward fuselage. In both cases the standard tail markings were carried.

Other variations have related to particular marketing promotions and perhaps the best known of these was 'The World's Biggest Offer' where these words, together with a representation of the Eiffel Tower and the Statue of Liberty, were painted in blue on the upper fuselage. This logo was carried by several aircraft in 1991 to publicise a marketing campaign to stimulate traffic after the downturn caused by the Gulf War. Another similar campaign was mounted in 1995 to publicise the revamp of the various brands of customer service in which the slogan 'Fly New Club World' appeared on several aircraft. Other variations have included temporary marking for special flights and events, including the annual 'Dreamworld' flights to Florida organised by British Airways staff for disabled children and, in 1996, a Boeing 757 had a huge poppy painted on its tail as a mark of respect for Remembrance Day on 11 November.

Since 1993 a substantial number of regional aircraft have appeared in the British Airways Express livery. This was basically identical to the standard British Airways colour scheme except that the logo 'British Airway Express' was carried with the word 'Express' in normal rather than bold text. In addition, the name of the franchised airline was carried in small white letters on the nose, below the flightdeck windows.

There is an old saying that imitation is the sincerest form of flattery and it is interesting to look at the livery announced at the beginning of 1993 for the world's largest airline, United Airlines. This features a pearl grey upper fuselage, a blue lower fuselage and tail, and a red fuselage cheat line!

In fact, the use of similar liveries by other airlines was one of the factors which prompted British Airways to introduce a new and radically different colour scheme in June 1997 as part of a far reaching review of the airline's corporate image. Within the airline industry it

Below: **A Lockheed Tristar 500 wearing the original British Airways livery. The tail markings were predominantly red with a blue triangular insert. Note the BOAC Speedbird symbol on the flightdeck roof.** *Rolls-Royce*

was an open secret during 1996 that a new British Airways livery would be introduced and confirmation came at the start of 1997 when newly delivered aircraft and those emerging from major overhauls appeared in what was dubbed an 'interim livery'. In this scheme a pure white replaced the previous pearl grey on the upper fuselage while the blue used for the lower fuselage and engine nacelles was lighter and warmer in tone. The dividing line between the two colours was lower down the fuselage side and the red 'Speedline' was omitted. The words 'British Airways', now on the lower forward fuselage instead of the cabin top, were in a slightly modified typeface in which all letters were of uniform size and the leading 'B' and 'A' were not picked out in upper case lettering. The tail still carried the standard stylised Union Flag but the blue and white portions were picked out in the new lighter colours.

Despite the clues given by the interim livery, the final revised colour scheme revealed on 10 June 1997 still caused considerable surprise and interest — not to mention considerable controversy. Instead of one design applied across all aircraft in the fleet, it was planned to introduce a new concept in which the basic colour scheme revealed as the interim livery would be complemented by specially commissioned works of art which would replace the previous standard union flag tail design. The red 'Speedline' was replaced by a new 'Speedmarque' in the form of a twisted red ribbon, the shape of which vaguely echoed the original speedbird symbol inherited from BOAC.

Naturally, most interest rests on the tail artwork which initially comprised some 15 different images with a further 12 to be announced each year up to and including the millennium year 2000. The designs so far announced are the work of artists representing the traditions and culture of ethnic groups from around the world, although at least four relate to areas of the United Kingdom and are mainly, but not exclusively, intended for use on the fleets of the various British Airways Express partners. At least three works will be of German origin and will be used by the Deutsche BA fleet. Details of the designs and patterns announced to date are given in the following table.

Below: **The British Airtours subsidiary carried the standard livery with appropriate logos.** *I. MacFarlane*

Design: Union Flag
A red, white and blue design based on the design of the Union Flag of 1805 at the time of Nelson's famous victory at Trafalgar. Reserved exclusively for use on the Concorde Fleet.

Design: Colum
Artist or Originator: Timothy O'Neill
Area of Origin: Ireland.
The artist is a well known Celtic Calligrapher and his design echoes the colourful intertwining designs found on illuminated manuscripts of the 6th century.

Design: Benyhone
Artist or Originator: Peter MacDonald
Area of Origin: Scotland
This a traditional-style Scottish tartan design. The artist is one of the last traditional hand weavers in Scotland. Initially applied to some Scottish-based British Regional Airlines aircraft.

Design: Colour on the side
Artist or Originator: Terry Frost
Area of Origin: Cornwall, UK
An abstract design inspired by a Cornish artist, this design was unusual in that it was not specifically commissioned by British Airways but was originally painted in 1968. First seen on southwest-based aircraft of Brymon Airways.

Design: Blue Poole
Artist or Originator: -
Area of Origin: Midlands, UK
A design inspired by the traditions of quality and craftsmanship of the potteries in and around Staffordshire and features stylised fish and seabirds against a turquoise background. First applied to a Manchester-based ATP.

Design: Rendezvous
Artist or Originator: Yip Man-Yam
Area of Origin: China and Hong Kong
The artist has combined traditional Chinese calligraphic techniques with modern styling and the complete design is a scroll carrying one of his favourite poems. The design appears as black calligraphic symbols with a small but intricate red counterpoint.

Design: Delft Blue Daybreak
Artist or Originator: Hugo Kaagman
Area of Origin: The Netherlands
Showing that there is nothing highbrow about the tail art, this piece was commissioned from an artist who originally came to prominence as a graffiti painter in Amsterdam! His design in blue and white represents the more traditional virtues of Holland's famous Delftware.

Design: Sterntaler
Artist or Originator: Antje Brüggeman
Area of Origin: Germany
The artist is a leading German ceramicist and she has created a bold geometric pattern reflecting the German national colours of black, red and yellow. Her design will be used by aircraft of Deutsche BA and has also appeared on a aircraft of Comair in South Africa.

Design: Nami Tsuru
Artist or Originator: Matazo Kayama
Area of Origin: Japan
A swirling design in blue and grey in a traditional Japanese art form known as 'Nihon-Ga'. The original painting on which the design is based is entitled 'Waves and Cranes'.

Design: Ndebele
Artist or Originator: Emmly & Martha Masanabo
Area of Origin: South Africa
These twin sisters have produced two decorated panels in bright primary colours using beadwork and mural style painting as a basis. The resulting geometric patterns echo those which the Ndebele people apply to the exterior of their own home at regular intervals.

Design: Animals and Trees
Artist or Originator: Cg'ose Ntcox'o
Area of Origin: Botswana
Inspired by the flora and fauna of the Kalahari Desert, the artist has produced a semi-abstract design in black, red, blue and ochre depicting jackals resting under trees around an oasis.

Design: Koguty Lowickie
Artist or Originator: Danuta Wojda
Area of Origin: Poland
The tail design features a section of an intricate and colourful paper cut, originally in a circular format, and featuring birds and flowers

in a symmetrical arrangement. Such works were traditionally produced by the people of central Poland to decorate their homes at Christmas.

Design: Whale Rider
Artist or Originator: Joe David
Area of Origin: West Canada
Based on a coloured wood carving in the traditional style of the Tla O Qui Aht People of Canada's western seaboard, this design draws on images of the region's environment and the way in which its indigenous people are part of it. A stylised figure rides aback a the black outline of a whale, almost like a surfer on a board.

Design: Floating
Artist or Originator: Jennifer Kobylarz
Area of Origin: New York, USA
An abstract oil painting by a New York artist which features a wavelike pattern in red, blue, white and black.

Design: Crossing Borders
Artist or Originator: Chant Avedissan
Area of Origin: Egypt
The artist lives and works in Egypt and has created a design inspired by the traditional multicoloured hangings which are used to decorate the interiors of large tents. The design in muted natural pigments incorporates various ancient Islamic and Pharonic elements.

As can be seen, British Airways and their design consultants, London-based Newell and Sorrell, have literally painted a broad canvas in order to reflect images from around the world. This is intended to portray British Airways as a world airline and to encourage people from all over the globe to identify with the airline and not be alienated by any sense that it is an exclusively British affair. The new livery and artwork will not only adorn aircraft but will

Below: **Boeing 777 G-RAES displays the new livery with 'Delft Blue Daybreak' design on the tail.** *John Dibbs*

increasingly appear on ground vehicles, check in areas, signage, stationary, timetables, baggage tags and ticketing. The cost of commissioning the artwork and applying the overall design is in the region of £2 million and the total cost of the new image will approach a staggering £60 million although, in fairness, it should be pointed out that a significant proportion of this sum would have been spent in any case on the routine repainting of aircraft and the replacement and restocking of other items. It should also be remembered that the paint does not only decorate the aircraft but also performs a useful function, providing essential protection against corrosion, hydraulic and de-icing-icing fluids aviation fuel, the weather and the effects of powerful ultra violet rays at high altitudes.

The application of the new livery to aircraft is a complex affair. It typically takes four days and some 560 man hours to paint a Boeing 747 with the world images on the tail being applied in stencilled layers, each of which takes 12hr to dry. Given the scale of the task, it will be at least three years before all aircraft

of the British Airways fleet and those of its partners and subsidiaries are repainted. It would appear that British Airways Express aircraft repainted in the new livery will drop the word 'Express' from their titles, more readily identifying a commonality with the British Airways corporate body.

The adoption of this striking new scheme must be regarded as a bold and adventurous step by British Airways. Inevitably there has been some criticism of the new colours, particularly in respect of the apparent abandoning of the Union Flag motif on all aircraft except Concorde. However the previous livery, now held up as being essentially British, was heavily criticised when it first appeared as owing too much to the American taste of its designers! It may well be that British Airways have correctly anticipated the trends and requirements of its customers and perhaps in another 15 years or so commentators will be mourning the loss of the current contentious new livery when the airline will be possibly unveiling an even more dramatic change. Time will tell.

Below: **British Airways Express operator Brymon Airways retains two Dash 7s which are flown by its subsidiary Brymon Offshore on oil industry related contracts. The aircraft are finished in an eye-catching colour scheme representing a puffin flying over the sea.** *L. Marriott*

3. British Airways Fleet List

The following list gives details of aircraft flown by British Airways Mainline, European and Regional Divisions. Aircraft flown by British Airways Express airlines are listed separately. Note: Information concerning the location and basing of aircraft was current at 1 July 1997 although individual aircraft may be relocated at short notice and not all the aircraft allocated to Manchester and Birmingham carry the appropriate logo. Similarly, long haul aircaft (Boeing 747/7657/767) listed as being based at Gatwick may be exchanged with other Heathrow based aircraft.

Reg	Type	Name	Notes
G-BUSB	Airbus A320-111	*Isle of Jersey*	
G-BUSC	Airbus A320-111	*Isle of Skye*	
G-BUSD	Airbus A320-111	*Isle of Mull*	
G-BUSE	Airbus A320-111	*Isle of Scilly*	
G-BUSF	Airbus A320-111	*Isle of Man*	
G-BUSG	Airbus A320-211	*Isle of Wight*	
G-BUSH	Airbus A320-211	*Isle of Jura*	
G-BUSI	Airbus A320-211	*Isle of Anglesey*	
G-BUSJ	Airbus A320-211	*Isle of Sark*	
G-BUSK	Airbus A320-211	*Isle of Guernsey*	
G-BTPA	BAe. ATP	*Strathblane*	
G-BTPC	BAe. ATP	*Strathallan*	
G-BTPD	BAe. ATP	*Strathconon*	
G-BTPE	BAe. ATP	*Strathdon*	
G-BTPF	BAe. ATP	*Strathlarn*	
G-BTPG	BAe. ATP	*Strathfillan*	
G-BTPH	BAe. ATP	*Strathnaver*	
G-BTPJ	BAe. ATP	*Strathpeffer*	
G-BTPO	BAe. ATP	*Strathclyde*	
G-BUWP	BAe.ATP	*Strathisia*	
G-BOAA	BAe./Aerospatiale Concorde 102		
G-BOAB	BAe./Aerospatiale Concorde 102		
G-BOAC	BAe./Aerospatiale Concorde 102		
G-BOAD	BAe./Aerospatiale Concorde 102		
G-BOAE	BAe./Aerospatiale Concorde 102		
G-BOAF	BAe./Aerospatiale Concorde 102		1st of type in new livery
G-BOAG	BAe./Aerospatiale Concorde 102		
G-BGDA	Boeing 737-236	*Bridgwater*	BA Regional (Manchester)
G-BGDB	Boeing 737-236	*River Tweed*	BA European (Gatwick)
G-BGDE	Boeing 737-236	*Pride of Manchester*	BA European (Gatwick)
G-BGDF	Boeing 737-236	*Rivington Pike*	BA European (Gatwick)
G-BGDG	Boeing 737-236	*Trough of Bowland*	BA Regional (Manchester)
G-BGDI	Boeing 737-236	*Pennine Way*	BA Regional (Manchester)
G-BGDJ	Boeing 737-236	*Delamere Forest*	BA Regional (Manchester)
G-BGDK	Boeing 737-236	*Ribble Valley*	BA Regional (Manchester)
G-BGDL	Boeing 737-236	*Vale of Lune*	BA Regional (Gatwick)
G-BGDO	Boeing 737-236	*River Usk*	BA Regional (Birmingham)
G-BGDP	Boeing 737-236	*River Taff*	BA European (Gatwick)
G-BGDR	Boeing 737-236	*River Bann*	BA European (Gatwick)

Reg	Type	Name	Notes
G-BGDT	Boeing 737-236	*Wirral Penninsula*	BA Regional (Manchester)
G-BGJE	Boeing 737-236	*River Wear*	BA European(Gatwick)
G-BGJF	Boeing 737-236	*River Axe*	BA European (Gatwick)
G-BGJH	Boeing 737-236	*River Lyne*	BA European(Gatwick)
G-BGJI	Boeing 737-236	*River Wey*	BA European (Gatwick)
G-BGJJ	Boeing 737-236	*River Swale*	BA European (Gatwick)
G-BKYA	Boeing 737-236	*Ariel*	BA Regional (Birmingham)
G-BKYB	Boeing 737-236	*Portia*	BA Regional (Birmingham)
G-BKYC	Boeing 737-236	*River Wye*	BA European (Gatwick)
G-BKYE	Boeing 737-236	*Hippolyta*	BA Regional (Manchester)
G-BKYF	Boeing 737-236	*Mistress Quickly*	BA European (Gatwick)
G-BKYG	Boeing 737-236	*Prospero*	BA Regional (Birmingham)
G-BKYH	Boeing 737-236	*Hotspur*	BA Regional (Birmingham)
G-BKYI	Boeing 737-236	*River Waveney*	BA Regional (Birmingham)
G-BKYJ	Boeing 737-236	*Touchstone*	BA European (Gatwick)
G-BKYK	Boeing 737-236	*River Foyle*	BA Regional (Birmingham)
G-BKYL	Boeing 737-236	*Titania*	BA European (Gatwick))
G-BKYM	Boeing 737-236	*Moonshine*	BA Regional (Birmingham)
G-BKYN	Boeing 737-236	*Prince Hal*	BA Regional (Manchester)
G-BKYO	Boeing 737-236	*Oberon*	BA Regional (Manchester)
G-BKYP	Boeing 737-236	*River Ystwyth*	BA Regional (Manchester)
G-DOCA	Boeing 737-436	*River Ballinderry*	BA Regional (Manchester)
G-DOCB	Boeing 737-436	*River Bush*	
G-DOCC	Boeing 737-436	*River Aafric*	
G-DOCD	Boeing 737-436	*River Aire*	
G-DOCE	Boeing 737-436	*River Alness*	
G-DOCF	Boeing 737-436	*River Beaully*	
G-DOCG	Boeing 737-436	*River Blackwater*	
G-DOCH	Boeing 737-436	*River Brue*	

Below: **This Dash 8, G-BRYT, flown by British Airways Express operator Brymon Airways was one of the first aircraft to receive the new livery in June 1997.** *L. Marriott*

Reg	Type	Name	Notes
G-DOCI	Boeing 737-436	*River Carron*	
G-DOCJ	Boeing 737-436	*River Glass*	
G-DOCK	Boeing 737-436	*River Lochay*	
G-DOCL	Boeing 737-436	*River Lune*	BA European (Gatwick)
G-DOCM	Boeing 737-436	*River Meon*	BA European (Gatwick)
G-DOCN	Boeing 737-436	*River Ottery*	BA European (Gatwick)
G-DOCO	Boeing 737-436	*River Parrett*	BA European (Gatwick)
G-DOCP	Boeing 737-436	*River Quode*	BA European (Gatwick)
G-DOCR	Boeing 737-436	*River Tavy*	BA European (Gatwick)
G-DOCS	Boeing 737-436	*River Teifi*	BA European (Gatwick)
G-DOCT	Boeing 737-436	*River Tene*	
G-DOCU	Boeing 737-436	*River Teviot*	
G-DOCV	Boeing 737-436	*River Thurso*	
G-DOCW	Boeing 737-436	*River Till*	
G-DOCX	Boeing 737-436	*River Tirry*	
G-DOCY	Boeing 737-436	*River Weaver*	
G-DOCZ	Boeing 737-436	*River Wharfe*	BA European (Gatwick)
G-BSNV	Boeing 737-4Q8		BA European (Gatwick)
G-BSNW	Boeing 737-4Q8		BA European (Gatwick)
G-BUHJ	Boeing 737-4Q8		BA European (Gatwick)
G-BUHK	Boeing 737-4Q8		BA European (Gatwick)
G-BVNM	Boeing 737-4S3		BA European (Gatwick)
G-BVNN	Boeing 737-4S3		BA European (Gatwick)
G-BVNO	Boeing 737-4S3		BA European (Gatwick)
G-GBTA	Boeing 737-436	*County of Middlesex*	BA European (Gatwick)
G-GBTB	Boeing 737-436		

Below: **CityFlyer Express was the pioneer British Airways Express operator, adopting the franchise in 1993. Its current fleet includes seven ATR42-300s (G-BVED is shown here) and four ATR 72s. It will shortly be upgrading to jet equipment in the form of two Avro RJ100s due to enter service in 1997.** *ASM Photo*

Reg	Type	Name	Notes
G-AWNA	Boeing 747-136	*Colliford Lake*	
G-AWNB	Boeing 747-136	*Llangorse Lake*	
G-AWNC	Boeing 747-136	*Lake Windemere*	
G-AWNE	Boeing 747-136	*Derwent Water*	
G-AWNF	Boeing 747-136	*Blagdon Lake*	
G-AWNG	Boeing 747-136	*Rutland Water*	
G-AWNH	Boeing 747-136	*Devoke Water*	
G-AWNJ	Boeing 747-136	*Bassenthwaite Lake*	
G-AWNL	Boeing 747-136	*Ennerdale Water*	
G-AWNM	Boeing 747-136	*Ullswater*	
G-AWNN	Boeing 747-136	*Loweswater*	
G-AWNO	Boeing 747-136	*Grafham Water*	
G-AWNP	Boeing 747-136	*Hanningfield Water*	
G-BBPU	Boeing 747-136	*Virginia Water*	
G-BBPV	Boeing 747-136	*Blea Water*	
G-BDXA	Boeing 747-236B	*City of Peterborough*	
G-BDXB	Boeing 747-236B	*City of Liverpool*	Based at Gatwick
G-BDXC	Boeing 747-236B	*City of Manchester*	
G-BDXD	Boeing 747-236B	*City of Plymouth*	Based at Gatwick
G-BDXE	Boeing 747-236B	*City of Glasgow*	Based at Gatwick
G-BDXF	Boeing 747-236B	*City of York*	Based at Gatwick
G-BDXG	Boeing 747-236B	*City of Oxford*	Based at Gatwick
G-BDXH	Boeing 747-236B	*City of Elgin*	Based at Gatwick
G-BDXI	Boeing 747-236B	*City of Cambridge*	
G-BDXJ	Boeing 747-236B	*City of Birmingham*	Based at Gatwick
G-BDXK	Boeing 747-236B	*City of Canterbury*	Based at Gatwick
G-BDXL	Boeing 747-236B	*City of Winchester*	Based at Gatwick
G-BDXM	Boeing 747-236B	*City of Derby*	
G-BDXN	Boeing 747-236B	*City of Stoke on Trent*	
G-BDXO	Boeing 747-236B	*City of Bath*	
G-BDXP	Boeing 747-236B	*City of Salisbury*	
G-BNLA	Boeing 747-436	*City of London*	
G-BNLB	Boeing 747-436	*City of Edinburgh*	
G-BNLC	Boeing 747-436	*City of Cardiff/Dinas Caerdydd*	
G-BNLD	Boeing 747-436	*City of Belfast*	
G-BNLE	Boeing 747-436	*City of Newcastle*	
G-BNLF	Boeing 747-436	*City of Leeds*	
G-BNLG	Boeing 747-436	*City of Southampton*	
G-BNLH	Boeing 747-436	*City of Westminster*	
G-BNLI	Boeing 747-436	*City of Sheffield*	
G-BNLJ	Boeing 747-436	*City of Nottingham*	
G-BNLK	Boeing 747-436	*City of Bristol*	
G-BNLL	Boeing 747-436	*City of Leicester*	
G-BNLM	Boeing 747-436	*City of Durham*	
G-BNLN	Boeing 747-436	*City of Portsmouth*	
G-BNLO	Boeing 747-436	*City of Dundee*	lst of type in new livery
G-BNLP	Boeing 747-436	*City of Aberdeen*	
G-BNLR	Boeing 747-436	*City of Hull*	
G-BNLS	Boeing 747-436	*City of Chester*	
G-BNLT	Boeing 747-436	*City of Lincoln*	
G-BNLU	Boeing 747-436	*City of Bangor*	

Reg	Type	Name	Notes
G-BNLV	Boeing 747-436	*City of Exeter*	
G-BNLW	Boeing 747-436	*City of Norwich*	
G-BNLX	Boeing 747-436	*City of Worcester*	
G-BNLY	Boeing 747-436	*City of Swansea*	
G-BNLZ	Boeing 747-436	*City of Perth*	
G-CIVA	Boeing 747-436	*City of St.Davids*	British Asia Airways
G-CIVB	Boeing 747-436	*City of Lichfield*	
G-CIVC	Boeing 747-436	*City of St.Andrews*	
G-CIVD	Boeing 747-436	*City of Coventry*	
G-CIVE	Boeing 747-436	*City of Sunderland*	British Asia Airways
G-CIVF	Boeing 747-436	*City of St.Albans*	
G-CIVG	Boeing 747-436	*City of Wells*	
G-CIVH	Boeing 747-436	*City of Hereford*	
G-CIVI	Boeing 747-436	*City of Gloucester*	
G-CIVJ	Boeing 747-436		
G-CIVK	Boeing 747-436		
G-CIVL	Boeing 747-436		
G-CIVM	Boeing 747-436		
G-CIVN	Boeing 747-436		Delivery Nov 97
G-CIVO	Boeing 747-436		Delivery Dec 97
G-CIVP	Boeing 747-436		Delivery Jan 98
G-CIVR	Boeing 747-436		Delivery Apr 98
G-CIVS	Boeing 747-436		Delivery 2000
G-CIVT	Boeing 747-436		Delivery 2000
G-CIVU	Boeing 747-436		Delivery 2000
G-CIVV	Boeing 747-436		Delivery 2001
G-CIVW	Boeing 747-436		Delivery 2001
G-CIVX	Boeing 747-436		Delivery 2001
G-CIVY	Boeing 747-436		Delivery 2002
G-CIVZ	Boeing 747-436		Delivery 2002

(Note: A further 12 Boeing 747-436 are on order)

Below: **Boeing 747-436 G-BNLS (*City of Chester*).** *ASM Photo*

Above: **The first British Aerospace BAe-146 (G-MANS) to wear full British Airways Express colours belongs to British Regional Airlines and is shown taxying at Birmingham in April 1997.** *L. Marriott*

Below: **G-AWYR, operated by franchisee Maersk UK, is one of four BAC-111s still to be seen in British Airways colours.** *L. Marriott*

Reg	Type	Name	Notes
G-BIKA	Boeing 757-236	*Dover Castle*	
G-BIKB	Boeing 757-236	*Windsor Castle*	
G-BIKC	Boeing 757-236	*Edinburgh Castle*	
G-BIKD	Boeing 757-236	*Caernafon Castle*	
G-BIKF	Boeing 757-236	*Carrickfergus Castle*	
G-BIKG	Boeing 757-236	*Stirling Castle*	
G-BIKH	Boeing 757-236	*Richmond Castle*	
G-BIKI	Boeing 757-236	*Tintagel Castle*	
G-BIKJ	Boeing 757-236	*Conwy Castle*	
G-BIKK	Boeing 757-236	*Eilean Donan Castle*	
G-BIKL	Boeing 757-236	*Nottingham Castle*	
G-BIKM	Boeing 757-236	*Glamis Castle*	
G-BIKN	Boeing 757-236	*Bodiam Castle*	
G-BIKO	Boeing 757-236	*Harlech Castle*	
G-BIKP	Boeing 757-236	*Enniskillen Castle*	
G-BIKR	Boeing 757-236	*Bamburgh Castle*	
G-BIKS	Boeing 757-236	*Corfe Castle*	
G-BIKT	Boeing 757-236	*Carisbrooke Castle*	
G-BIKU	Boeing 757-236	*Inveraray Castle*	
G-BIKV	Boeing 757-236	*Ragaln Castle*	
G-BIKW	Boeing 757-236	*Belvoir Castle*	
G-BIKX	Boeing 757-236	*Warwick Castle*	
G-BIKY	Boeing 757-236	*Leeds Castle*	
G-BIKZ	Boeing 757-236	*Kenilworth Castle*	
G-BMRA	Boeing 757-236	*Beaumaris Castle*	
G-BMRB	Boeing 757-236	*Colchester Castle*	
G-BMRC	Boeing 757-236	*Rochester Castle*	
G-BMRD	Boeing 757-236	*Bothwell Castle*	
G-BMRE	Boeing 757-236	*Killyleagh Castle*	
G-BMRF	Boeing 757-236	*Hever Castle*	
G-BMRG	Boeing 757-236	*Caerphilly Castle*	

Below: **A Maersk UK Jetstream 41 displays the interim livery adopted early in 1997 prior to the unveiling of the new BA identity in June of that year.** *L. Marriott*

Reg	Type	Name	Notes
G-BMRH	Boeing 757-236	*Norwich Castle*	
G-BMRI	Boeing 757-236	*Tonbridge Castle*	
G-BMRJ	Boeing 757-236	*Old Wardour Castle*	
G-BPEA	Boeing 757-236	*Kidwelly Castle*	BA European (Gatwick)
G-BPEB	Boeing 757-236		BA European (Gatwick)
G-BPEC	Boeing 757-236	*Sir Simon Rattle*	BA Regional
G-BPED	Boeing 757-236	*Blair Castle*	
G-BPEE	Boeing 757-236	*Robert Louis Stevenson*	BA Regional
G-BPEF	Boeing 757-236		BA European (Gatwick)
G-BPEI	Boeing 757-236	*Winchester Castle*	
G-BPEJ	Boeing 757-236	*Llangollen Castle*	
G-BPEK	Boeing 757-236	*Cardew Castle*	
G-CPEL	Boeing 757-236	*Walmer Castle*	
G-CPEM	Boeing 757-236		
G-CPEN	Boeing 757-236		
G-CPEO	Boeing 757-236		Delivery Jul 97
G-CPEP	Boeing 757-236		Delivery Aug 97
G-BNWA	Boeing 767-336ER	*City of Brussels*	
G-BNWB	Boeing 767-336ER	*City of Paris*	
G-BNWC	Boeing 767-336ER	*City of Frankfurt*	
G-BNWD	Boeing 767-336ER	*City of Copenhagen*	
G-BNWE	Boeing 767-336ER	*City of Lisbon*	
G-BNWF	Boeing 767-336ER	*City of Milan*	
G-BNWG	Boeing 767-336ER	*City of Strasbourg*	
G-BNWH	Boeing 767-336ER	*City of Rome*	
G-BNWI	Boeing 767-336ER	*City of Madrid*	Based at Gatwick
G-BNWJ	Boeing 767-336ER	*City of Athens*	
G-BNWK	Boeing 767-336ER	*City of Amsterdam*	
G-BNWL	Boeing 767-336ER	*City of Luxembourg*	
G-BNWM	Boeing 767-336ER	*City of Toulouse*	Based at Gatwick
G-BNWN	Boeing 767-336ER	*City of Berlin*	
G-BNWO	Boeing 767-336ER	*City of Barcelona*	Based at Gatwick
G-BNWP	Boeing 767-336ER	*City of Dublin*	
G-BNWR	Boeing 767-336ER	*City of Hamburg*	Based at Gatwick
G-BNWS	Boeing 767-336ER	*City of Oporto*	
G-BNWT	Boeing 767-336ER	*City of Cork*	
G-BNWU	Boeing 767-336ER	*Robert Burns*	Based at Gatwick
G-BNWV	Boeing 767-336ER	*City of Bonn*	
G-BNWW	Boeing 767-336ER	*City of Bordeaux*	
G-BNWX	Boeing 767-336ER	*City of Bilbao*	
G-BNWY	Boeing 767-336ER	*City of Helsinki*	
G-BNWZ	Boeing 767-336ER		
G-	Boeing 767-336ER		Delivery Apr 98
G-	Boeing 767-336ER		Delivery May 98
G-	Boeing 767-336ER		Delivery May 98
G-RAES	Boeing 777-236(IGW)		
G-VIIA	Boeing 777-236(IGW)		
G-VIIB	Boeing 777-236(IGW)		
G-VIIC	Boeing 777-236(IGW)		

Reg	Type	Name	Notes
G-VIID	Boeing 777-236(IGW)		
G-VIIE	Boeing 777-236(IGW)		
G-VIIF	Boeing 777-236(IGW)		
G-VIIG	Boeing 777-236(IGW)		
G-VIIH	Boeing 777-236(IGW)		
G-VIIJ	Boeing 777-236(IGW)		Delivery Jan 98
G-VIIK	Boeing 777-236(IGW)		Delivery Feb 98
G-VIIL	Boeing 777-236(IGW)		Delivery Mar 98
G-VIIM	Boeing 777-236(IGW)		Delivery Mar 98
G-VIIN	Boeing 777-236(IGW)		Delivery Sep 98
G-VIIO	Boeing 777-236(IGW)		Delivery Jan 99
G-VIIP	Boeing 777-236(IGW)		Delivery Feb 99
G-VIIR	Boeing 777-236(IGW)		Delivery Mar 99
G-VIIS	Boeing 777-236(IGW)		Delivery Apr 99
G-ZZZA	Boeing 777-236		
G-ZZZB	Boeing 777-236	*Sir William Sefton Brancker*	
G-ZZZC	Boeing 777-236	*Sir Charles Edward Kingsford Smith*	
G-ZZZD	Boeing 777-236	*Orville Wright/Wilbur Wright*	
G-ZZZE	Boeing 777-236	*Sir John Alcock/Sir Arthur Whitten Brown*	
G-BEBL	McDonnell Douglas DC-10-30	*Forest of Dean*	
G-BEBM	McDonnell Douglas DC-10-30	*Sherwood Forest*	
G-BHDH	McDonnell Douglas DC-10-30	*Benmore Forest*	
G-BHDI	McDonnell Douglas DC-10-30	*Forest of Ae*	
G-BHDJ	McDonnell Douglas DC-10-30	*Glen Cap Forest*	
G-DCIO	McDonnell Douglas DC-10-30	*Epping Forest*	
G-MULL	McDonnell Douglas DC-10-30	*New Forest*	
G-NUIK	McDonnell Douglas DC-10-30	*Cairn Edward Forest* Leased to Caledonian	

Below: **This Boeing 757-236 (G-BPEE) is assigned to British Airways Regional at Birmingham where it is shown taxying for a departure to New York.** *L. Marriott*

59

Above: **This air-to-air shot of a de Havilland Canada Dash 8 Series 300 belonging to Brymon Airways emphasises the stretched fuselage which distinguishes it from the earlier Series 100.** *Bombardier*

Below left: **British Airways uses the Boeing 767 on short-range high-density routes as well as long-haul flights to the US east coast and the Arabian Gulf area.** *British Airways*

Above: **Airbus A320 (G-BUSC) on approach at Heathrow.** *ASM Photo*

Below: **The Boeing 737-436 has replaced the older 200 series aircraft in the Mainline fleet.** *British Airways*

British Airways Franchise Fleet Lists

The following lists show details of all aircaft operated under the British Airways Express franchise with the exception of the South Africa based Comair, these being unlikely to be seen in Europe. All aircraft listed are painted in BA Express livery.

British Mediterranean Airways

Reg	Type	Name	Notes
G-MEDA	Airbus A320-200		
G-MEDB	Airbus A320-200		Leased from Regionair (Singapore)
G-MEDC	Airbus A320-200		Leased from Regionair (Singapore)

British Regional Airlines
(ex Manx European, Loganair and Business Air fleets)

G-BRLY	BAe. ATP		Leased from BAe.
G-BUUP	BAe. ATP		Leased from BAe.
G-MANE	BAe. ATP		
G-MANF	BAe. ATP		
G-MANG	BAe. ATP		
G-MANH	BAe. ATP		
G-MANJ	BAe. ATP		
G-MANL	BAe. ATP		
G-MANM	BAe. ATP		
G-MANP	BAe. ATP		
G-MAUD	BAe. ATP		1st of type in new livery
G-MAJA	BAe. Jetstream 41		
G-MAJB	BAe. Jetstream 41		
G-MAJC	BAe. Jetstream 41		
G-MAJD	BAe. Jetstream 41		
G-MAJE	BAe. Jetstream 41		
G-MAJF	BAe. Jetstream 41		
G-MAJG	BAe. Jetstream 41		
G-MAJH	BAe. Jetstream 41		
G-MAJI	BAe. Jetstream 41		
G-MAJJ	BAe. Jetstream 41		
G-MAJK	BAe. Jetstream 41		
G-MAJL	BAe. Jetstream 41		
G-MAJM	BAe. Jetstream 41		
G-MANS	BAe.146-200		
G-BJOP	BN-2B-26 Islander		
G-BLNJ	BN-2B-26 Islander		
G-BLNW	BN-2B-26 Islander		
G-BPCA	BN-2B-26 Islander		
G-BVVK	DHC-6 Twin Otter 310		
G-EMBA	Embraer EMB-145		
G-EMBB	Embraer EMB-145		
G-EMBC	Embraer EMB-145		
G-GNTE	Saab 340		(Business Air)
G-BKMX	Shorts 360-100		

Reg	Type	Name	Notes
G-BLGB	Shorts 360-100		
G-BMAR	Shorts 360-100		
G-BMLC	Shorts 360-100		
G-ISLE	Shorts 360-100		
G-LEGS	Shorts 360-100		
G-WACK	Shorts 360-100		
G-BVMY	Shorts 360-300		

Brymon Airways

Reg	Type	Name	Notes
G-BRYA	DHC Dash 7 Series 100		Brymon Offshore
G-BRYD	DHC Dash 7 Series 100		Bryman Offshore
G-BRYG	DHC Dash 8 Series 100	Lothian/Lodainn	
G-BRYI	DHC Dash 8 Series 300	Northumberland/Drigantes	
G-BRYJ	DHC Dash 8 Series 300	Somerset/Gwaid Yr Haf	
G-BRYK	DHC Dash 8 Series 300		
G-BRYM	DHC Dash 8 Series 300		
G-BRYO	DHC Dash 8 Series 300		
G-BRYP	DHC Dash 8 Series 300		
G-BRYR	DHC Dash 8 Series 300		
G-BRYS	DHC Dash 8 Series 300		
G-BRYT	DHC Dash 8 Series 300		1st of type in new livery

CityFlyer Express

Reg	Type	Name	Notes
G-BUEA	ATR42-300		
G-BUEB	ATR42-300		
G-BVEC	ATR42-300		
G-BVED	ATR42-300		
G-BVEF	ATR42-300		
G-BXEG	ATR42-300		
G-BXEH	ATR42-320		
G-BVTJ	ATR72-202		
G-BVTK	ATR72-202		
G-BWTL	ATR72-202		
G-BWTM	ATR72-202		
G-BXAR	Avro RJ100		
G-BXAS	Avro RJ100		

GB Airways

Reg	Type	Name	Notes
G-BGDS	Boeing 737-236		Leased from BA
G-BGDU	Boeing 737-236		Leased from BA
G-BNNK	Boeing 737-4Q8		Leased from BA
G-BNNL	Boeing 737-4Q8		Leased from BA
G-BUHL	Boeing 737-4Q8		Leased from BA
G-TREN	Boeing 737-4S3		Leased from BA
G-	Boeing 737-300		Delivery 1998
G-	Boeing 737-300		Delivery 1998

Above: **Latest newcomer to the British Airways stable is the French independent airline Air Liberté. Its fleet includes eight MD83s, one of which (F-GHED) is shown here.** *ASM Photo*

Below: **Deutsche BA is a strong force in the German domestic market and rivals Lufthansa on many routes. It is in the process of becoming an all-Boeing 737 operator and one of its aircraft is shown at Düsseldorf.** *ASM photo*

64

Reg	Type	Name	Notes

Maersk UK

G-WMCC	Jetstream 31		
G-MSKJ	Jetsream 41		
G-BBMG	BAC.111-408EF		
G-AWYR	BAC.111-501X		
G-AWYS	BAC.111-501X		
G-AWYV	BAC.111-501X		
G-MSKA	Boeing 737-5L9		
G-MSKB	Boeing 737-5L9		
G-MSKC	Boeing 737-5L9		1st of type in new livery

Sun-Air of Scandinavia

OY-EDA	BAe. Jetstream 31		
OY-EDB	BAe. Jetstream 31		
OY-SVF	BAe. Jetstream 31	*City of Aarhus*	
OY-SVJ	BAe. Jetstream 31	*Skien*	
OY-SVK	BAe. Jetstream 31		
OY-SVO	BAe. Jetstream 31		
OY-SVP	BAe. Jetstream 31	*City of Skive*	
OY-SVR	BAe. Jetstream 31		
OY-SVY	BAe. Jetstream 31		
OY-SVZ	BAe. Jetstream 31		
OY-SVS	BAe. Jetstream 41	*Spirit of Aarhus*	
OY-SVW	BAe. Jetstream 41	*Port of Aarhus*	

Below: **Boeing 737-5L9 of Maersk UK based at Birmingham. The tail art is 'Waves of the City'.** *Mike Barth*

British Airway's Subsidiaries fleet lists

The following lists give details of aircraft flown by non British airlines which are wholly or partly owned by British Airways. It is expected that all these aircraft will eventually be painted in the new British Airways colour scheme with minor variations and appropriate titles added.

Reg	Type	Notes

Air Liberté

Reg	Type
F-GCJL	Boeing 737-200
F-GCLL	Boeing 737-200
F-GCSL	Boeing 737-200
F-GFYL	Boeing 737-200
F-GFZB	McDonnell Douglas MD-83
F-GHEB	McDonnell Douglas MD-83
F-GHED	McDonnell Douglas MD-83
F-GHEI	McDonnell Douglas MD-83
F-GHEK	McDonnell Douglas MD-83
F-GHHO	McDonnell Douglas MD-83
F-GHHP	McDonnell Douglas MD-83
F-GPVB	McDonnell Douglas DC-10-30
F-GPVD	McDonnell Douglas DC-10-30
F-GPVE	McDonnell Douglas DC-10-30

Deutsche BA

Reg	Type
D-ADBA	Boeing 737-300
D-ADBB	Boeing 737-300
D-ADBC	Boeing 737-300

Below: **Many of the aircraft operated by the Regional divisions carry the words 'Birmingham' or 'Manchester' after the airline title.** *ASM Photo*

Reg	Type	Notes
D-ADBD	Boeing 737-300	
D-ADBE	Boeing 737-300	
D-ADBF	Boeing 737-300	
D-ADBG	Boeing 737-300	
D-ADBH	Boeing 737-300	
D-ADBI	Boeing 737-300	
D-ADBJ	Boeing 737-300	
D-ADFA	Fokker 100	Leased from TAT
D-ADFB	Fokker 100	Leased from TAT
D-ADFC	Fokker 100	Leased from TAT
D-ADFD	Fokker 100	Leased from TAT

(Note. Boeing 737 fleet is planned to increase to 18 aircraft by the end of 1997. Remaining Fokker 100s will be returned to TAT)

TAT European (Jet a/c only)

Reg	Type	Notes
F-BUTI	Fokker F28 Fellowship 1000	
F-GBBR	Fokker F28 Fellowship 1000	
F-GBBS	Fokker F28 Fellowship 1000	
F-GBBT	Fokker F28 Fellowship 1000	
F-GBBX	Fokker F28 Fellowship 1000	
F-GDFC	Fokker F28 Fellowship 4000	
F-GDFD	Fokker F28 Fellowship 4000	
F-GDSK	Fokker F28 Fellowship 4000	
F-GDUS	Fokker F28 Fellowship 2000	
F-GDUT	Fokker F28 Fellowship 2000	
F-GDUU	Fokker F28 Fellowship 2000	BA Colours
F-GDUV	Fokker F28 Fellowship 2000	
F-GDUY	Fokker F28 Fellowship 4000	
F-GDUZ	Fokker F28 Fellowship 4000	
F-GECK	Fokker F28 Fellowship 1000	
F-GIAI	Fokker F28 Fellowship 1000	
F-GIMH	Fokker F28 Fellowship 1000	
F-GNZB	Fokker F28 Fellowship 1000C	
F-GIOA	Fokker 100	BA Colours
F-GIOG	Fokker 100	
F-GIOH	Fokker 100	BA Colours
F-GIOI	Fokker 100	
F-GIOJ	Fokker 100	BA Colours
F-GIOK	Fokker 100	
F-GMPG	Fokker 100	

(Fokker 100s F-GIOB to F-GIOE leased to Deutsche BA)

Reg	Type	Notes
F-GGFI	Boeing 737-200	
F-GGFJ	Boeing 737-200	
F-GGPA	Boeing 737-200	
F-GGPB	Boeing 737-200	
F-GGPC	Boeing 737-200	
F-GLLD	Boeing 737-300	BA Colours
F-GLLE	Boeing 737-300	BA Colours

(Note: Initially only TAT European aircraft used on international routes carried BA livery, although all will eventually wear the new colours introduced in June 1997.)

Above: **Eight Shorts 360s flown by the Scottish airline Loganair (now absorbed into British Regional Airlines) wear the British Airways Express colours. Another example was operated by CityFlyer Express but is now no longer in service.**
British Regional Airlines

Below: **The other partner in British Regional Airlines is Manx Airlines Europe which operates a fleet of ATPs, Jetstreams and a single BAe146. This Jetstream 41 was photographed at Newcastle in mid-1996 still bearing the Manx logo on the nose.**
ASM Photo

Below right: **Brymon Airways is an exception to the normal franchise arrangement and is in fact wholly owned by British Airways. It has recently standardised on the Dash 8-300 Series, one of which is shown on approach at Heathrow after a flight from Newquay and Plymouth.** *ASM Photo*

4. British Airways Franchise Airlines

British Airways Express is not a company in its own right, but a franchise operation for other airlines which provides both domestic and European services, many of which link with British Airways mainline services. Franchisees' aircraft are painted in BA livery with BA Express titles, crews wear BA uniforms and cabin staff receive training in BA standards of service. All flights are listed as BA services in timetables and computer reservation systems, bringing substantial benefits in increased passengers and revenues. The concept of this type of operation is not new and has been practised by major airlines in the United States where small regional airlines have operated under the wing of the majors using such titles as United Express (United Airlines), Delta Connection (Delta Airlines) and American Eagle (American Airlines). In fact, the idea has been tried before in the UK during the late 1970s when British Caledonian established the BCAL Commuter network which included airlines such as Humberside-based Eastern Airlines and Plymouth-based Brymon Airways, whose aircraft bore the BCAL colours together with the Commuter logo. However, the project was not particularly successful due to the lack of suitable aircraft and the fact that the British traveller at that time was not really prepared to consider air transport as a substitute for road and rail when travelling relatively short distances within the UK. More recently, the thrusting Air Europe set up a Commuter

subsidiary under the title Air Europe Express, although this was not a true franchise operation and, in any event, came to nothing when Air Europe suddenly ceased operations in 1991.

Today, however, the situation has changed dramatically. Many small airlines are using the new range of pressurised regional turboprops such as the ATR42, British Aerospace Jetstream 41 and the de Havilland Canada Dash 8 to carry a growing number of passengers who now see air travel as a viable alternative to frustrating journeys on crowded roads and find the break-up of rail services creating more problems than it solves. British Airways saw this increasing traffic as potential customers for its own route network but avoided the expense of operating a diverse fleet of regional aircraft by introducing its own franchise scheme. The first airline to join the BA Express system was Gatwick-based CityFlyer Express in 1993 which, interestingly, could trace its origins back to the original Air Europe Express. In 1994 Maersk and Brymon also joined the scheme following the split-up of Birmingham European Airways the previous year. Latest recruits are Loganair and Manx European Airlines (now grouped together as British Regional Airlines), although the latter two still remain part of the rival Airlines of Britain Group owned by British Midland, thus emphasising that the franchised airlines are not necessarily owned by British Airways. In

addition, the franchise concept has now spread to airlines in which British Airways already had a shareholding, such as GB Airways which now operates a series of scheduled flights to Spanish and Mediterranean destinations. In 1996 it was hoped to extend this principle to some of the Near East routes, such as Beirut, Damascus and Amman, by franchising British Mediterranean Airways to operate these routes on behalf of British Airways instead of in competition with them. However, this agreement fell through at the last moment but was revived for the 1997 summer timetable.

In the meantime, the franchise scheme continued to grow and two other non-British airlines joined the British Airways Express network — Sun Air of Denmark and Comair in South Africa. In both cases these airlines' aircraft are painted in BA Express colours and provide feeder services to their respective major national airports where they connect with British Airways International routes. Details of these two airlines are in the following section 'A World Airline'.

There is no doubt that the British Airways Express concept offers considerable advantages to all parties. For example, CityFlyer Express reported an immediate and substantial passenger increase on its Gatwick to Newcastle route which now sustains five return flights each weekday with ATR42s and 72s, soon to be upgraded to Avro RJ100s. In the year ending March 1995, British Airways reported that its franchise operators had provided 124,000 connecting passengers for its Mainline and European services, generating an additional £21 million in revenue.

Details of all airlines operating in British Airways Express colours are set out below and details of the relevant British airline fleets are appended to the main British Airways fleet list.

British Mediterranean Airways

This airline started operations under the Chairmanship of Lord Hesketh in October 1994 with a five times a week service from London to Beirut using a single Airbus A320. Expansion of services to other Mediterranean and Middle East destinations including Amman and Damascus occurred in 1995 and subsequently there was a certain amount of duplication of effort between British Mediterranean and British Airways. In 1996 it was announced that the former would become a British Airways franchise airline and that British Airways would withdraw its own services from Beirut, Amman and Damascus. For various technical and administrative reasons, this was not implemented, as originally planned, for the 1996/97 winter season but was delayed until the beginning of the summer 1997 timetable. In order to meet its new commitments, British Mediterranean has expanded its fleet to a total of three Airbus A320s by leasing two ex-China Airways aircraft. In addition to the services already listed, the airline will also commence flights to

Below: **The British Aerospace 146 finally got to wear British Airways colours when Manx European joined the British Airways Express scheme in 1994. It has now been joined by the Avro RJ100 flown by CityFlyer Express.** *British Regional Airlines*

Tibilisi in Georgia and Alexandria in Egypt during April 1997.

British Regional Airlines

This is the title adopted by Manx Airlines (Europe) as from September 1996. Aircraft are finished in British Airways Express livery and carry the British Regional Airlines title on the nose. The change of name was partly implemented in order to provide a separate corporate image and avoid confusion with sister company Manx Airlines which continues to operate independently under its own colours from its Ronaldsway base. At its inception, the British Regional fleet comprised a single BAe146 (the only example currently in British Airways colours), nine BAe ATPs, 12 Jetstream 41s and two Jetstream 31s. In October 1996, the Scottish BA Express operator, Loganair, was absorbed into British Regional Airlines which then became responsible for the operation of all British Airways internal Scottish services.

Also now forming part of British Regional Airlines is the Aberdeen-based Business Air which operates a fleet of 11 Saab 340s and a single BAe.146-200. Most of these aircraft operate services under contract to British Midland, but a single Saab 340 is flown on British Airways Express services and was actually one of the first aircraft to be seen in the new livery.

Brymon Airways

Brymon Airways is the odd man out in the British Airways Express operation as it is the only one which is actually wholly owned by British Airways. It began operations in 1972 with an Islander aircraft flying services between Newquay and the Isles of Scilly. British Airways first took a share in Brymon around 1980 when the airline began a steady expansion of services from its Plymouth base and was the first UK operator to acquire the DHC-7 with its spectacular STOL performance. In 1981, Brymon became involved in oil contract services based in Aberdeen, flying industry workers to Unst and other island destinations and during the 1980s a Shorts

330 was acquired for a short period to operate a Birmingham–Gatwick service as part of the BCAL Commuter network. The Dash 7s were put to good use in the development of London City Airport where the airline began operations in October 1987. Continuing its association with de Havilland Canada, Brymon became the first UK airline to fly the twin-engined Dash 8 in 1990 when it took delivery of two 100 series aircraft. In the meantime, the ownership of Brymon was vested in a company called TPL (The Plimsoll Line) of which British Airways and Maersk, a Danish transport conglomerate, each held a 40% shareholding. TPL also owned Birmingham European Airways and it was decided to merge the two companies in October 1992, under the title Brymon European. The Brymon fleet was briefly repainted in a new livery, but, within 12 months the merger was dissolved and Brymon reverted to its original title, although now 100% owned by British Airways and the aircraft adopted BA livery from late 1993 onwards. In January 1995 it forged even closer ties, becoming formally a British Airways Express operator. Early in 1996 it was announced that some of its Dash 7s and Dash 8-100s would be replaced by five new Dash 8-300 series. Two Dash 7s are now retained for oil industry support operations in Scotland, wearing a new house livery and not BA Express colours. Today, Brymon operates a substantial domestic network linking Plymouth, Bristol, Newcastle, Aberdeen and Southampton as well as services to the Channel Islands, Eire and Paris.

CityFlyer Express

This airline was formed in 1991 by management staff from the defunct Air Europe Express which was forced to cease operations when Air Europe collapsed. Initially, the title Euroworld was adopted, but in February 1992 the name was changed to CityFlyer Express. In April of that year the airline became the first British operator of the successful ATR42 turboprop airliner, and was also the first with the larger ATR72, in October 1994. Following a successful marketing agreement with British

Above: **The Air International (Regional) ATR42 was the first aircraft to wear the British Airways Express livery when CityFlyer Express pioneered the franchise agreement in 1993.** *AI(R) Photo*

Airways, CityFlyer became the first British Airways Express operator, in August 1993, and the aircraft were repainted in BA livery. The current route network includes domestic scheduled services from London Gatwick to Newcastle, Leeds, Jersey, Guernsey and international services to Antwerp, Dublin, Düsseldorf and Rotterdam. Other services are flown from Leeds, but a Luton–Paris route was short-lived and abandoned after a few months. The last Shorts 360 was phased out of service at the end of 1995, following orders for further ATR72s. Routes to Amsterdam and Cologne/Bonn were started in 1996 and a substantial increase in traffic, partly due to the success of the BA Express franchise, led to an order in mid-1996 for two Avro RJ100s, which entered service in 1997.

GB Airways

This airline was originally formed as Gibraltar Airways in 1930 as a subsidiary of the Bland shipping company and was based on the rock after which it was named. Services ceased in 1932 and the company lay dormant until 1947 when BEA took over a 51% shareholding and adopted the name Gibair. In this form the airline flew services from Gibraltar to the UK and also to North Africa. When BEA was absorbed into British Airways, the Gibair shareholding was reduced to 49% but services continued as before. The title GB Airways was adopted in 1980 and since then traffic has

increased considerably, necessitating the introduction of jets. In 1994 all services to North Africa were transferred to Heathrow, while Gibraltar and Madeira were served from Gatwick. GB Airways became a BA Express operator in 1995 and the aircraft, including a pair of modern 737-400s leased from British Airways, adopted BA livery. GB Airways now plays an important role alongside the British Airways European operation at Gatwick and has introduced several routes to Spain including Valencia, Nurcia, Jerez and Seville, as well as a new service to Malta. Two new 737-300s are on order.

Loganair

Loganair was formed in 1962 and became part of the Airlines of Britain Group (ABG) in December 1983. Early services concentrated on routes from Glasgow and Edinburgh to the Scottish Highlands and Islands and since 1973 it has been responsible for the Scottish Air Ambulance service. In the 1980s the airline considerably expanded its route network and flew several UK domestic routes including the Channel Islands and Manchester. However, a reorganisation in 1994 led to many services, and its fleet of ATPs and BAe146s, being transferred to Manx Airlines (Europe) while Loganair became a British Airways Express operator, although still part of the ABG. The remaining fleet consisted of five Islanders and eight Shorts 360s which are now painted in BA

Express colours and operate an extensive network of services around Scotland, including the socially important Highlands and Islands routes. From October 1996 Loganair was absorbed into British Regional Airlines and lost its separate identity.

Manx Airlines (Europe)

Originally formed as a joint venture between Air UK and British Midland to operate scheduled services between the Isle of Man and the UK mainland, Manx Airlines also operated services from Blackpool and in 1986 took over the Liverpool–Heathrow route from British Midland, initially using a Saab 340. As part of the Airlines of Britain Group it expanded rapidly and in 1990 it was split into two separate divisions: Manx Airlines based at Ronaldsway on the Isle of Man and Manx Airlines (Europe) which intended to expand regional operations from its Cardiff base. The fleet was boosted in 1993 by the addition of new Jetstream 41s and also by the takeover of many Loganair routes in March 1994. Manx European now has an extensive network of scheduled services within the UK and Europe. Main UK hubs are Belfast, Ronaldsway, Cardiff, East Midlands, Manchester, Edinburgh and Southampton. In January 1995, Manx Airlines Europe became part of the British Airways Express network, serving mainly UK destinations, and early in 1996 it took over Knight Air's scheduled routes based on Leeds

Airport, acquiring that airline's two Jetstream 31s. As part of a major reorganisation within the Airlines of Britain Group, Manx Airlines (Europe) was renamed British Regional Airlines on 1 September 1996.

Maersk Air (UK)

Maersk Air (UK) was formed in 1993 to take over the former assets of Birmingham European Airlines (BEA) which had been merged in 1992 with Brymon Airways to form Brymon European. When this airline was demerged in 1993, Maersk Air (a Danish airline) took over the 100% shareholding in the former BEA in which it had previously been only a 40% shareholder. After being painted briefly in Maersk colours, the aircraft were repainted yet again in 1994 when Maersk Air (UK) became a BA Express operator. Apart from a Birmingham–Newcastle service flown by the Jetstream, the rest of the route network consisted of international flights to European destinations initially flown by a fleet of six ex-British Airways BAC-111s which, no doubt, were surprised to find themselves back in their former owner's livery! The long-lived BAC-111s will remain in service until replaced by more Boeing 737-500s leased from parent Maersk. The sole Jetstream 31 to be repainted in BA Express colours for the Newcastle route has now been replaced by a larger Jetstream 41 to increase capacity on this sector.

Below: **GB Airways operates a substantial route network to Madeira, Malta, Spain and North Africa and its services are now fully integrated with the British Airways timetable. It adopted the BA Express franchise in 1995 and its aircraft, including this Boeing 737-4S3 (G-BUHL, leased from British Airways) seen at Madeira's Funchal airport, are now painted in BA colours.** *ASM Photo*

5. A World Airline

As part of a declared policy to become the world's best and most successful airline, British Airways has bought or negotiated significant holdings in a number of airlines around the world. Some commentators have forecast that within a decade there will only be around 10 major carriers in the world, with many of today's national airlines having been taken over or forced out of business as the so-called mega-carriers continually expand and fight for an even larger share of the world's passenger traffic. British Airways has every intention of being one of the leaders and, as one of the few major airlines to return consistent profits, is in a position to build on its success by the acquisition of shares in a variety of other carriers. National pride being what it is, most countries will not permit the outright purchase of one of their airlines by a foreign company, but, at the same time, the purchase of a shareholding in another airline normally gives British Airways access to the market and traffic rights in the country concerned. Despite the establishment of a so-called 'Open Skies' policy within the European Community in 1993, governments are still reluctant to see their national carriers lose identity or status and in the past this has forced British Airways to withdraw from proposed deals with Sabena and KLM. However, other deals and arrangements have been more successful and today British Airways is spreading its name and influence throughout the world (a list of British Airways' involvement and alliances with other airlines follows below). At home, a network of domestic and short-range European services are increasingly being flown by British Airways' franchise partners under the British Airways Express scheme and these airlines have been described in the previous chapter.

Air Liberté

British Airways' latest acquisition, in November 1996, is this French independent airline which operates a variety of scheduled and charter flights with a fleet of eight MD83s, three Boeing 737s, and four DC-10-30s. Initially, it will maintain a separate identity from TAT European (see below) but a single holding company will be set up to co-ordinate the

Below: **British Airways Express. Sun Air of Scandinavia is one of the latest recruits to the franchise operation, and its fleet of Jetstream 31s and 41s is being repainted in British Airways Express livery.** *ASM Photo*

Above: **G-CIVA (*City of St David*) is one of two Boeing 747-436s assigned to British Asia Airways.** *Malcolm Bradbury*

operation. Fortuitously the route networks of the two airlines do not overlap to any substantial degree and the combination of both will give British Airways 22% of the landing slots at Paris Orly. Air Liberté's international routes to North Africa and Portugal will be cut back in order to concentrate on domestic services and this will probably result in the disposal of the DC-10s. Inevitably the two French airlines will be merged to provide a single corporate entity, but, according to BA sources, this will not happen for at least three years.

British Asia Airways

A subsidiary created in 1993 to operate services to Taipei, the capital of Taiwan. The fleet consists of two Boeing 747-436s (G-BNLZ and G-CIVA) painted in basic British Airways livery with British Asia Airways logos and titles. As British Airways already flew to Beijing, the capital of mainland China, the new airline was partly financed by Taiwan business interests because political pressures prevent any single carrier operating services to both mainland China and Taiwan (Republic of China).

Comair

This South African domestic airline joined the British Airways Express franchise scheme in 1996 and passengers using British Airway's long-haul flights between London and South Africa can now benefit from Comair's extensive network for connections to and from other destinations which include Cape Town, Durban, Harare (Zimbabwe) and Windhoek (Namibia). Based at Johannesburg International airport, its fleet comprises eight 737-200 twinjets, four Fokker Friendships and two ATR42s and these are currently being repainted in the BA Express livery. The airline was originally formed in 1949.

Deutsche BA

At the end of World War 2 the victorious Allied powers allocated the rights to provide internal air services between Berlin and West Germany to British, US and French airlines. Although the latter soon dropped out, BEA (and later British Airways) together with Pan American continued to operate a comprehensive German route network until the German unification in the early 1990s rendered the arrangement out of date. For many years BA used a fleet of BAC-111s based at Berlin, but these were eventually replaced with quieter Boeing 737s and, in the final years, by ATPs belonging to the airline's Highland Division. However, British Airways was keen to maintain the valuable connections it had built up in the German market and was able to achieve this by purchasing a 49% shareholding in Delta Air Regionalflugverkehr, a regional airline based at Friedrichshafen and flying scheduled services with a fleet of Saab 340s. The remaining 51% is held by a consortium of German banks and the airline has been renamed as Deutsche BA.

British Airways is planning a substantial development programme for the new airline which is re-equipping with new Boeing 737-300s. The first of these was delivered in June 1992 and the airline's first commercial jet service as Deutsche BA, from Berlin to Stuttgart and Munich, took place on 29 June that year. Since then the jet fleet has expanded to include nine Boeing 737-300s, most of which are leased from Maersk which has also leased aircraft to British Airways in the past. In addition, there are now five Fokker 100s which are leased from the French airline TAT, now a wholly-owned British Airways subsidiary. The first Fokker 100 was added to the fleet in March 1993, and the other four arrived 12 months later; this movement of aircraft allowed a rationalisation of both airlines' fleets and illustrates one of the advantages enjoyed by the airlines grouped under the British Airways banner. Deutsche BA originally incorporated a fleet of Saab 340 turboprop airliners which were gradually being replaced by the faster and larger Saab 2000 Deutsche BA, the first of which was delivered in March 1995. This remarkable aircraft had a cruising speed of 360kt and, among other routes, was used to operate a Gatwick to Bremen service, taking only 5min longer than the Boeing 737 which it had replaced. However, in October 1996 it was announced that the airline was selling its turboprop operations, including both the aircraft and the access to the routes they served, to the

Nantes-based Regional Airlines so that it could concentrate on building up its jet routes.

Deutsche BA's aircraft were painted in a colour scheme very similar to BA's own with a dark blue lower fuselage and pearl white upper surfaces. The tailfin was finished in a similar style to British Airways' aircraft but incorporated the German national colours of red, yellow and black, while a thin yellow and red cheat line ran down the fuselage. With the introduction of the new livery in 1997, Deutsche BA aircraft will adopt the new colours with the artwork of German origin on the tail. Now based at Munich, the airline is a major force in the German domestic market where it serves 10 destinations, and also flies to 13 European destinations including London Gatwick and Jersey. Additional services are now being flown from Berlin and other new routes include Munich to Paris and Madrid, and Berlin to Oslo. Eventually, the leased Fokker 100s will be returned and Deutsche BA will become an all-Boeing 737 fleet.

QANTAS.

The Australian national flag carrier can trace its history back to 1920 and the formation of the Queensland and Northern Territory Aerial Service (QANTAS). After World War 2 the airline was nationalised in 1947 and developed an extensive worldwide network. It was the first airline outside the US to operate the Boeing 707 (in 1959) and was an early customer for the Boeing 747. Its current fleet consists of 24 Boeing 767-300ERs and around 30 Boeing 747s, including 18 of the latest 400 series which are replacing some of the older 200 series aircraft. From the end of World War 2 QANTAS was a state-owned airline which mainly operated international services, domestic flights being operated by a number of airlines including Australian Airlines. Prior to the privatisation of QANTAS in 1995, the airline took a 100% holding in Australian Airlines which maintained a comprehensive domestic network with a fleet of almost 39 Boeing 737-400s and subsequently the two airlines were merged. In 1992, in preparation for the deregulation of Australian air services and the privatisation of both QANTAS and

Australian Airlines, the Australian government invited bids for a 25% stake in QANTAS and the British Airways offer of £296 million was accepted at the end of 1992. This shareholding gave the British airline a welcome access to the Australian market as well as strengthening links in the important southeast Asia and Pacific regions and BA will have the opportunity to bid for a further share in the future. There is also a degree of fleet commonality as QANTAS's 747-400s are the same Rolls-Royce-powered version used by British Airways, and since 1995 the two airlines have rationalised their schedules on the so-called 'Kangaroo Route' between the UK and Australia with mutual advantage to both organisations.

QANTAS also operates extensive regional services throughout Australia by means of wholly-owned subsidiaries Airlink, Eastern Australia Airlines, Southern Australia Airlines and Sunstate Airlines. These operate a variety of commuter and regional airliners including the BAe146 and Jetstream, DHC Dash 8s and Twin Otters, and Shorts 330/360s. These aircraft are all painted in QANTAS livery.

Sun-Air of Scandinavia

Early in 1996 Sun-Air of Scandinavia became the first non-UK independent airline to adopt the British Airways Express franchise. It flies a fleet of Jetstream 31s and 41s on commuter services throughout Denmark and southern Scandinavia centred mainly on Copenhagen airport, although the airline's headquarters is at Billund in the west of Denmark. Sun-Air was formed in 1977 and currently operates a number of executive jets and turboprops for charter work in addition to its scheduled service fleet of Jetstreams. Sun-Air also operates a twice daily service from Billund to Manchester and as a result of healthy load factors it has ordered two British Aerospace ATPs for delivery in September 1997 to replace the Jetstream 41s currently used on this route. The Jetstream 31 fleet will be reduced and jet equipment may be introduced around the year 2000.

TAT European Airlines

Formerly known as Transport Aérien Transrégional from which the abbreviation TAT is derived, this French regional airline was founded in 1968 and by 1990 was carrying

Below: **British Airways owns a 25% stake in the Australian airline QANTAS and both airlines co-operate on the important UK–Australia route. QANTAS also operates a substantial domestic network.** *ASM Photo*

over three million passengers a year on an extensive route network covering French domestic and other European destinations. Following the merger of Air France, UTA and Air Inter, TAT is now the second largest French airline with a fleet of over 50 aircraft, including seven Boeing 737-200/300s, 12 Fokker 100s, 18 Fokker F28s, 10 ATR42s and six ATR72s. A fleet of Fairchild FH-227s (licence-built Fokker F27s) is up for sale.

In September 1992 British Airways announced that it had taken a 49.5% share in TAT for a reported £17.5 million and the cash provided enabled new routes awarded as a result of the Air France mergers to be developed to their full potential. In addition, there was conditional approval for British Airways' to purchase the remaining shareholding by 1997, and this option was exercised in April 1997. Under British Airways' management, TAT has undergone a major restructuring and, apart from services to London Heathrow and Gatwick which feed into British Airways international network, the French airline now concentrates almost exclusively on the difficult domestic market where there is extensive competition not only from other airlines such as Air France but also from the efficient and popular TGV high-speed

rail network. Since 1992, the airline has had a troubled financial history, partly caused by the problems associated with restructuring but it is expected to break even in 1996/97 and move into profit thereafter.

Unlike Deutsche BA, the majority of the TAT fleet retains its original blue and yellow colour scheme and only those aircraft employed on routes directly associated with British Airways are painted in the standard BA livery with the words 'in association with TAT' painted on the nose. The aircraft concerned are those Fokker 28s and 100s not already leased to Deutsche BA and two Boeing 737-400s operated on services to Heathrow. However, the fleet will probably adopt the new livery but the tail art having some French associations.

Below: **US Air was one of British Airways' longest standing partners and it brought substantial numbers of passengers to the British Airways route network. However, the partnership was dissolved at the start of 1997.** *ASM Photo*

carried to ensure the very best of service. The normal schedule leaves London at 10.30am and arrives in New York at 09.20am (New York time).

First Class

While other airlines have thought it necessary to give their best level of service rather confusing names such as Royal, Presidential and Upper, British Airways has stayed with the title which has a traditional and unambiguous meaning — First Class. The current product and service features date from 1996 when the airline's First Class service was completely overhauled and introduced some completely new concepts, including a specially commissioned seating system which by means of subtle screening gives the impression of a private cabin. Single or double seats are available, the former incorporating a visitor's seat so that two people can conduct business or dine together as they wish. All of these seats convert, at the touch of a button, to a full-length flat bed and a personal video and entertainment centre is naturally incorporated. Food from a delicious à la carte menu can be enjoyed at any stage of the flight and for those passengers who do not wish their rest to be disturbed, a similar meal can be served prior to take-off at the airport and a sleeper suit and duvet cover are provided to ensure a good night's rest once aboard the aircraft. At Heathrow and Gatwick dedicated First Class lounges are available in the Pavilions and these can also be used to freshen up after arrival. In addition, First Class passengers have access to over 180 lounges worldwide and receive priority transfers, if required, between Terminals 1 and 4 at Heathrow. First Class is available on all British Airways intercontinental flights, which are mainly operated by Boeing 747s where the accommodation is in the nose cabin on the maindeck, or by the new Boeing 777 which has 17 seats in the forward part of the passenger cabin. The new First Class seating is not available on the Boeing 767 and DC-10 fleets which retain the more traditional but still extremely comfortable arrangements.

Club World

This is the title of British Airways' business class brand on intercontinental flights and has just undergone a major upgrade which is being progressively introduced in 1996, replacing the previous standard which dated from 1988. The emphasis is on making life as relaxed as possible for the business traveller and there are exclusive check-in desks and separate lounges offering business facilities. At Heathrow there is a car parking service which allows the passenger to drive up to the terminal and hand the car over to an attendant who will see to its parking. On board the aircraft the Club World cabin has a 2-3-2 seating configuration set at a new 50in pitch, less than First Class but still giving plenty of room, and capacity varies from 74 seats on the 747 to 42 on the 767. The seats themselves are of a new 'cradle' design with a unique tilting action and are fitted with head-rests, lumbar supports and leg-rests for complete comfort. Catering is of a high standard, featuring a five-course meal with a choice of menus, and a new feature called 'Raid the Larder' allows passengers to help themselves to snacks and other treats after the main meal has been served. On arrival there is a priority delivery of baggage, assisted at London Gatwick and Heathrow by access to a Fast Track arrivals channel allowing a speedy passage through airport controls, as well as the facility of Arrivals Lounges.

Club Europe

As the name implies, this is the Club Class level of service as applied to the European route network where many business travellers are regular customers, often making return flights in the same day. With this in mind, flights are arranged to facilitate business requirements and passengers can check in for their return flight on departure, thus saving time and hassle at the end of the day. Naturally, there are separate desks and access to the Club Europe lounge in Terminal 4 at Heathrow. This can seat up to 400 and is comprehensively equipped with desks, phones and fax machines as well as having access to

a spa facility where travellers can change and have a shower. British Airways Club Class passengers benefit from access to 30 similar lounges at other European airports. Also available is the express car parking service and priority baggage handling. The airline's short-haul aircraft do not have separate Club cabins but Club Europe passengers are allocated seats at the forward part of the aircraft which, in flight, is curtained off by a movable divider and this allows considerable flexibility in booking and ticketing. Normally the centre seat in each row of three is left vacant to give passengers more space and the seating is set at a 34in pitch. A high standard of catering is offered and there is usually a choice of main courses.

World Traveller, Euro Traveller

These are the names applied to British Airways' basic level of service on long- and short-haul international flights and were introduced in 1991 as part of a general improvement to the Economy class. Despite being the least expensive class, high standards of service and catering are maintained and little touches such as newspapers, orange juice, hot towels and comfort packs, as well as a complimentary bar service help to relax the passenger. World Traveller cabins feature an in-flight television and audio entertainment system while Euro Travellers are provided with an audio system. Seating pitch is 32in, less than Club but still adequate and greater than that offered by many rival airlines.

Above: **Separate check-in facilities are provided for different categories of passengers.** *ASM Photo*

Super Shuttle

The intensive high-frequency shuttle operations serving Manchester, Glasgow, Belfast and Edinburgh from Heathrow have their own special brand of service and facilities for passengers. Originally started in 1983, it has been continuously improved over the years and now carries over 3.5 million passengers a year. The emphasis is on convenience of use together with guaranteed seats, although there are now alternative fare structures for business and leisure travellers. The former is called Super Shuttle Executive and retains fully flexible ticketing and the turn-up-and-take-off guarantee which is the concept's hallmark, while leisure travellers can take advantage of Super Shuttle Savers which offer low fares but with less flexibility. A popular innovation has been the introduction of automated ticketing machines which can be accessed using British Airways' own credit cards and other machines allow self check-in on arrival at the airport. In-flight there is a one-class service with hot meals at appropriate times of the day except on the Manchester run where cold meals are served due to the short flight time.

Skyflyers

British Airways recognises the problems

encountered by children when travelling, whether alone or as part of a family group, and has arranged extra facilities and services for them under the Skyflyers brand name. These include special lounges at Heathrow and Gatwick with staff on hand to assist, while on longer flights there is a special member of the cabin crew to give extra care to children and families. In addition, there are packs of baby-care items, magazines and games, and special meals are provided.

Executive Club

Membership of the British Airways Executive Club offers substantial benefits, particularly to business travellers who fly regularly. There are three levels of membership (Blue, Silver and Gold) but all offer priority seat allocation on busy flights, dedicated reservation and service centres, and worldwide discount rates on hotels, car hire and travel insurance. Gold and Silver members have access to Executive lounges at many airports.

The prospective passenger will often look to an airline to provide more than just the flight, no matter how pleasant it may be, and so all operators have connections in other aspects of the travel business including car rental, hotels and holidays. British Airways is no exception and has marketing agreements with such concerns around the world. In addition, it owns British Airways Holidays, Air Miles Travel Promotions Ltd and Travel Automation Services Ltd, the latter better known as the Galileo computer reservations system, while it also owns a small stake in Hogg Robinson, a travel agency chain specialising in business travel arrangements.

Below:
World Traveller passengers check in at Heathrow's spacious Terminal 4 where British Airways' long-haul services are concentrated. *ASM Photo*

7. Support Services

Catering

British Airways places great stress on the quality of its cabin service and an integral part of this is the provision of in-flight meals. These can vary from a simple coffee and biscuits to the elaborate multi-course menus offered to First Class passengers. Apart from having to be interesting and pleasant to eat, each meal must meet exacting technical standards covering presentation, taste, storage and hygiene as well as meeting the dietary, ethnic and religious requirements of a wide cross-section of travellers. Little wonder then that catering is given a high priority within British Airways which takes great pride in the results. The investment involved is exemplified by its new 180,000sq ft European Catering Centre at Heathrow which became fully operational in January 1992 and provides up to 29,000 meals a day for short-haul services operating out of London. Other establishments cover the long-haul operation where more than one meal is served on each flight, and there are extensive contractual arrangements with other airlines and catering organisations to provide meals to British Airways' specifications at overseas departure points. The airline recently carried out a complex exercise to compare the costs and quality of its in-house organisation with products bought in from contract caterers, resulting in a significant improvement in the performance of its own unit, but the long-term aim is to sell off this area of operations.

Cabin Crews

To the average passenger the face of British Airways is represented by the steward or stewardess who looks after them during a flight. The airline employs almost 11,000 cabin staff who are all trained at the Heathrow Cabin Services Training Centre where, in addition to learning how to look after passengers and their requirements, they are also taught the vital procedures to be used in the event of any emergency such as a fire or a ditching. They are also taught the correct use and operation of safety-related equipment such as emergency exits, escape slides and life-jackets as well as basic first aid procedures.

Out of the total number of cabin staff, some 700 are recruited from overseas and are assigned to various long-haul flights in order to provide a point of reference for passengers from abroad who may not speak English and whose culture may require a slightly amended type of service. Out of these 700, approximately 120 are Portuguese or Spanish speakers for the South American routes, another 150 are Japanese and a further 100 are Chinese, based at Honk Kong. On a typical 747 flight there will be a cabin crew of 15, of which four or five may be overseas staff. On the long-haul 767s there are usually two overseas staff out of a complement of nine. Additional Hispanic staff are being recruited to cover new direct services to Mexico and to cater for the increasing numbers of Spanish speaking passengers on flights to and from the southern United States.

World Cargo

Unusually for a major airline, British Airways operates no dedicated cargo aircraft and almost all freight is carried in the underfloor holds of aircraft on regular scheduled services, although the Boeing 747 fleet does include three Combi variants which can also carry freight on a section of the maindeck. Despite this, the airline carried 666,000 tonnes of freight in the operating year 1994/95, the highest figure of any airline not operating specialist cargo aircraft, and is seventh overall in terms of freight tonne/kilometre and freight tonnes carried according to IATA figures. When it is considered that a 747-400 can carry up to 20 tonnes of cargo in addition to its passenger load, it can be understood where the capacity comes from. A 767 carries 12.3 or 11 tonnes depending on configuration and the 757 on scheduled services carries up to 5.8 tonnes. Occasionally, the airline will lease additional capacity or part purchase capacity on other specialist freight services. In addition, British Airways maintains four European road haulage hubs which feed cargo from the

Continent into the Heathrow- and Gatwick-based intercontinental services. The first of these was established at Maastricht in 1986 and others are at Helsingborg in Sweden and Lyons, France.

British Airways Cargo has 2,500 staff and is run as a separate profit centre responsible for its own strategic planning, marketing, budgeting and financial affairs — the first British Airways department to be accorded this status. Although mostly concentrated at the main cargo freight terminals at Heathrow and Gatwick, there is also a major cargo facility at Manchester, opened in 1986 at a cost of £7 million. Much of the handling has been automated and up-to-date information on any item or consignment is maintained using the advanced CARAT (Cargo Agents Reservations and Air-waybill issuance and Tracking) system. This is the biggest project of its kind in the UK and uses radio data terminals which transmit barcode readouts from consignments to the airline's central cargo computer. Thus the progress of a particular item of cargo can be monitored throughout its journey and this information is readily available to the customer, his agents and the airline when required.

Cargo is a global business, over 80% of revenues earned being in foreign currencies, and total income from this source generates profits in excess of £10 million a year. To maintain the efficiency of the cargo network, British Airways has recently invested £23 million in new warehouse and handling systems, as well as further computer systems.

Since becoming an independant British Airways' subsidiary, World Cargo has launched a new Service Development Strategy and some of the fruits of this programme can be observed already. A £2 million Premium Products building opened at Heathrow in April 1997 and this 24,000sq ft facility is dedicated to handling express and courier operations on a 24hr basis. Another new facility, also opened in 1995, was the 23,000sq ft unit operated by World Cargo Handling and specifically designed for the efficient movement of perishable fruit and vegetable cargoes and features over 4,000sq ft of refrigerated storage space. Traffic in this market sector currently

runs at 500 tonnes per week and has been growing at 10% a year.

The most significant future development will be the opening in 1998 of the new World Cargocentre, presently under construction on the south side at Heathrow. This massive new facility will be over 300m long and will have a floor area of 33 acres spread over four levels. Initially it will handle up to 800,000 tonnes of cargo each year, but this will quickly grow to over 1 million tonnes. It will be British Airway's largest ever single real estate investment at Heathrow.

British Airways Engineering

In 1996 the British Airways fleet consisted of over 250 aircraft, ranging from the turboprop ATP to the supersonic Concorde and the high-technology Boeing 747-400, powered by a total of almost 700 engines (excluding spares). Each aircraft is equipped with a variety of complex electrical, hydraulic and pneumatic systems as well as increasingly sophisticated avionics, including navigation and communications equipment. To keep these aircraft flying reliably and safely British Airways has a maintenance and overhaul workforce of 9,700 staff, almost exactly 20% of the total staff numbers, and the Engineering division also earns a valuable £70 million a year through the overhaul of aircraft belonging to other airlines such as Canadian Airlines International, Continental Airlines and Cathay Pacific. Indeed such is the size and complexity of the engineering task, that in April 1995 British Airways Engineering became an operating division and profit centre run as a separate business within the British Airways Group and has its own Board of Directors and marketing department. Its projected turnover in the first five years is predicted to reach £1,000 million.

Once established in its new format, British Airways Engineering is now setting in place a major reorganisation of its staff and facilities in order to improve efficiency, reduce costs and attract new business. Basically, this involves the establishment of three 'Fleet Streams', each dedicated to supporting specific aircraft types. Fleets 1 and 2 utilise the massive engineering base occupying a 220-acre site at

Above: **British Airways World Cargo carries almost 700,000 tonnes of freight every year.** *British Airways*

Hatton Cross on the eastern edge of Heathrow where the former BEA and BOAC facilities were established during the early 1950s. Since then new hangars, workshops, stores and offices have been added to make it one of the largest complexes of its type in the world. Fleet 1 will look after the Airbus A320, Boeing 757 and Boeing 767 fleets, while Fleet 2 will be concerned with Boeing 747, Boeing 777 and Concorde fleets. At Gatwick, Fleet 3 will look after the entire Boeing 737 fleet, including both 200 and 400 series, as well as McDonnell Douglas DC-10s and the British Aerospace ATPs (based at Glasgow). In addition, Fleet 3 provides the engineering support for the ex-British Airways Tristars now flown by Caledonian Airways. All three Fleets already provide maintenance facilities for third party airlines at the various bases and British Airways Engineering is now actively marketing its skills, facilities and expertise to significantly increase such business.

In addition to the three Fleet Streams at Heathrow and Gatwick, British Airways Engineering also opened a major complex at Cardiff Airport in April 1993 which is dedicated solely to the overhaul and maintenance of the airline's fleet of Boeing 747s of all variants. Originally known as project Dragonfly (an oblique reference to the Welsh location), this 70-acre development employs around 850 staff

and now operates under the title of British Airways Maintenance Cardiff (BAMC). The purpose-built facility can accommodate three 747s simultaneously and every major check and modification can be carried out here. In the three years since starting operations, BAMC has already turned round some 120 aircraft including some from airlines such as Canadian Airlines International, Southern Air Transport, Evergreen, American International Airlines, Corsair and Tower Air as well as British Airways' own aircraft.

Wales is also the home of another British Airways Engineering subsidiary, British Airways Avionic Engineering Ltd (BAAE) which is based at a purpose-built 13,000sq m facility situated near Llantrisant, Mid Glamorgan. Also opened in 1993, this organisation actively markets its expertise to other operators as well as taking care of British Airways' own requirements. The spread of work carried out is quite amazing and includes servicing and repairing a vast range of avionic equipment from radio and radar, through air data computers and navigation equipment to the increasingly sophisticated in-flight entertainment and communication facilities now finding their way into modern airliners. Until December 1991 British Airways maintained a comprehensive engine-overhaul facility, also in Wales, but this was sold to the

Above **A Boeing 747-436 enters the BAMC hangar for a major service.**
Malcolm Bradbury

American company General Electric which continues to carry out work for the airline under contract. Situated at Nantgarw, it replaced the previous facility at nearby Treforest and the complete range of British Airways engines is overhauled here with the exception of the Pratt & Whitney Canada PW126s for the ATP.

To give some idea of the work involved in maintaining a modern airliner, the following inspection and maintenance schedule for a long-haul Boeing 747-400 provides a fascinating insight. Basically it is organised into a series of increasingly complex checks as the aircraft passes various milestones based on accumulated flying hours. The following table also gives an indication of the manpower requirements at each stage.

Transit check. Before every flight.
Two engineers and a flightcrew member. Exterior check of the aircraft and engines for damage or leakage. Specific checks on listed items such as brake and tyre wear.

Ramp 1 check. Daily. Four engineers. Transit check plus additional checks on engine oil levels, tyre pressures, aircraft external lighting, cabin emergency equipment, engine health monitoring systems and assessment of technical log entries.

Ramp 2 check. Every 190 flying hours. Four engineers.
Transit and Ramp 1 checks plus checks on APU and component oil levels, engine component oil levels, cabin interior condition and windows.

Ramp 3 check. Every 540 flying hours. Six engineers.
Transit, Ramp 1 and 2 checks plus replacement of hydraulic-systems filters, checks on cockpit and cabin seats and attachments, sterilisation of water system and detailed inspection of system filters. More detailed inspections on items covered in previous checks including avionic systems and standby power systems. Batteries changed.

Above: **British Regional Airlines are the first British operator of the Brazilian-built Embraer EMB-145 twin turbofan regional jet. Three aircraft will be delivered in 1997 with the airline taking options on a further two. This photograph shows one of the manufacturer's prototypes at Farnborough in September 1996.** *ASM Photo*

Service check 1. Every 1,060 flying hours during overnight stopovers at a maintenance base. Fifty engineers.
All previous checks plus partial stripdown of structure and engines for detailed inspection. Replacement of worn components and soiled or damaged cabin equipment and furnishings. Servicing of undercarriage struts. Total service check takes around two shifts (approximately 16hr) to complete.

Service check 2. Every 2,120 flying hours. Fifty engineers.
All above checks plus additional and more detailed inspections of specific areas. External wash of aircraft, system clarification function checks, and deep cleaning of cabin water and waste systems. Requires three shifts to complete.

Service check 3. Every 3,875 flying hours. Fifty engineers.
All the above plus detailed inspection of flying controls, structure and engines. Fluid levels drained and refilled in major mechanical components. Aircraft washed, avionics systems integrated checks. Cabin condition assessed and repaired in depth. Requires four shifts.

Inter check 1. Every 6,360 hours. 160 engineers.

Detailed inspection and repair of aircraft, engines, components, systems and cabin, including operating mechanisms, flight controls, structural tolerances. Takes between seven and eight days.

Inter check 2. Every 12,720 hours. 160 engineers.
All the above plus additional system function checks. Takes eight to nine days.

Major service. Every 24,000 hours or every five years if sooner. 180 engineers.
A very intensive inspection taking between 20 and 25 days. Involves major structural inspections including attention to fatigue corrosion. The aircraft is virtually dismantled, repaired and rebuilt as required, with systems and parts tested and repaired or replaced as necessary. Corrosion prevention and control tasks carried out.

It is interesting to compare the information above with that contained in the first edition of this book published in 1993. Although the schedule of work to be carried out remains much the same, in almost every case the time taken and the number of engineers required has been significantly reduced — an indication of the sort of staff productivity required to maintain the airline's profitability.

Simulator Centre

British Airways has a fleet of over 250 aircraft which carry passengers all over the world but it also owns another fleet which is in constant operation, can fly anywhere and do anything, but which never carries a single passenger and never leaves the ground. This is, of course, the 17-strong fleet of aircraft simulators housed in the British Airways Cranebank centre on the eastern side of Heathrow. These amazing electronic devices are realistic reproductions of the flightdeck of a specific aircraft and in most cases they have a six-axis motion system to give absolute realism during the course of simulated flights. In addition, the more modern simulators are fitted with advanced computer-generated visual systems which give a realistic wide-angled view over areas of terrain and airports for use when simulating landings and take-offs.

The fleet at Cranebank includes modern simulators for the newest aircraft types such as the 737-400, the 747-400 (2) and the 767-300. In addition, there are also 757 simulators as well as another dual-purpose 757/767 example. There are also a number of simulators for older types such as the early versions of the 747 (100 and 200 series), the 737-200, BAC-111 and the Lockheed TriStar. In addition to flight simulation, the Cranebank centre also offers a variety of other training courses both for British Airways staff and for those of other airlines. These include Safety Equipment and Procedures for cabin crews, Aviation Medicine, Aviation Fire Management and Crew Resource Management training. When British Airways took over British Caledonian in 1987 it gained a second simulator training centre at Gatwick and this continued in business as British Caledonian Flight Training. Its current simulator fleet includes examples for the Airbus A320, Boeing 737-200/300, Boeing 757/767, McDonnell Douglas DC-10-30, MD11 and MD83. With these it has trained pilots from airlines all over the world as well as British Airways, and a significant contract was for the training of some American Airlines crews on the MD11 simulator. However, in March 1992 British Airways disposed of its remaining 50% shareholding in British Caledonian Flight Training which now continues in being as an independent company, although still providing services to British Airways under contract.

Below: **Pilots undergoing continuation training on a Boeing 747-400 simulator, one of many at British Airways' Cranebank centre.** *British Airways*

Appendix 1

British Airways Route Network

The extensive British Airways route network serves over 150 destinations in 69 countries and at Heathrow the airline accounts for some 45% of the scheduled passengers using the airport. A number of European and intercontinental destinations are also served from other UK airports, notably Gatwick where activity has expanded greatly in recent years to the extent that more destinations are served than from Heathrow. A complete list of destinations served by direct flights from UK airports is listed below.

1. Scheduled destinations served from Heathrow by direct nonstop flights. Many other destinations such as Sydney, Melbourne and San Diego are served by flights making one stopover.

Aberdeen	Bologna	Dubai
Abu Dhabi	Bombay	Düsseldorf
Amsterdam	Boston	Edinburgh
Athens	Brussels	Frankfurt
Bahrain	Cairo	Geneva
Bangkok	Calgary	Gibraltar
Barbados	Cape Town	Glasgow
Barcelona	Casablanca	Gothenburg
Basle	Chicago	Hamburg
Beijing	Cologne	Hannover
Beirut	Copenhagen	Helsinki
Belfast	Delhi	Hong Kong
Berlin	Detroit	Inverness
Bilbao	Dhahran	Istanbul

Above: **The 64-seater British Aerospace ATP is the last prop-driven aircraft in the British Airways inventory and is flown by the Regional division based at Glasgow.** *ASM Photo*

Right: **The futuristic Compass Centre on Heathrow's north side contains the airline's operations centre. The strange shape of the building ensures that it does not reflect unwanted signals back to Air Traffic Control radars.** *British Airways*

Jeddah
Jersey
Johannesburg
Kuala Lumpur
Kuwait
Larnaca
Leipzig
Lisbon
Los Angeles
Luxembourg
Lyon
Madras
Madrid
Manchester
Miami
Milan
Montreal
Moscow
Munich
Muscat
Nagoya
Nairobi
New York (JFK)
New York (Newark)
Newcastle
Nice
Osaka
Oslo
Paris (CDG)
Paris (Orly)
Philadelphia
Prague
Riyadh
Rome

San Francisco
Seattle
Seoul
Singapore
Stockholm
Stuttgart
Tangier
Tel Aviv
Tokyo
Toronto
Vancouver
Venice
Vienna
Warsaw
Washington
Zürich

Total destinations 91

**2. Scheduled destinations
served directly from
Gatwick**

Aberdeen
Accra
Amsterdam
Antigua
Antwerp
Athens
Atlanta
Baku
Baltimore
Barbados
Barcelona
Belgrade

Berlin
Bermuda
Bordeaux
Bremen
Brussels
Bucharest
Buenos Aires
Caracas
Charlotte
Cologne
Copenhagen
Cork
Dallas
Dubai
Dublin
Düsseldorf
Edinburgh
Faro
Frankfurt
Funchal
Geneva
Genoa
Gibraltar
Glasgow
Gothenburg
Grand Cayman
Guernsey
Hamburg
Harare
Houston
Jerez
Jersey
Kano
Kiev

Kingston
Krakow
Lagos
Leeds/Bradford
Lisbon
Lusaka
Luxembourg
Lyon
Madrid
Malaga
Malta
Manchester
Marrakech
Marseille
Mexico City
Miami
Milan
Montpelier
Moscow
Munich
Murcia
Nairobi
Naples
Nassau
New York (JFK)
New York (Newark)
Newcastle
Newquay
Orlando
Oslo
Paris (CDG)
Perpignan
Phoenix
Pisa
Pittsburgh
Plymouth
Porto
Riga
Rome
Rotterdam
St Petersburg
San Juan
São Paolo
Seychelles
Sofia
Stavanger
Stockholm
Tampa
Tel Aviv
Toulouse
Tunis
Valencia
Verona

Vienna
Zagreb
Zürich

Total destinations 102

3. Scheduled destinations from Manchester (direct flights)

Aberdeen
Amsterdam
Belfast (City)
Belfast (International)
Billand
Brussels
Cardiff
Connaught/Knock
Cork
Dublin
Düsseldorf
Edinburgh
Frankfurt
Geneva
Gibraltar
Glasgow
Guernsey
Islamabad
Jersey
London (Gatwick)
London (Heathrow)
Londonderry
Madrid
Milan
New York (JFK)
Paris (CDG)
Shannon
Southampton
Warsaw
Waterford

Total destinations 30

4. Scheduled destinations from Birmingham (direct flights)

Aberdeen
Amsterdam
Barcelona
Belfast
Berlin
Brussels
Copenhagen
Dublin

Düsseldorf
Edinburgh
Frankfurt
Glasgow
Hannover
Lyon
Milan
Malaga
Munich
New York (JFK)
Newcastle
Paris (CDG)
Stuttgart

Total destinations 21

5. Scheduled destinations from Glasgow

Aberdeen
Barra
Belfast (City)
Belfast (International)
Benbecula
Birmingham
Bristol
Campbeltown
Cardiff
Donegal
Guernsey
Inverness
Islay
Kirkwall
London (Heathrow)
Londonderry
Manchester
New York (JFK)
Southampton
Stornoway
Tiree

Total Destinations: 22

Note: Above lists apply to British Airways scheduled flights, including destinations served by associated British Airways Express companies such as Brymon and GB Airways.

Appendix 2

BRITISH AIRWAYS FACTS AND FIGURES (Year to 31st March in each case)

1.Scheduled services	1992	1993	1994	1995	1996
Revenue passenger km (m)	65,896	73,996	81,907	87,395	100,274
Available seat km (m)	93,877	104,507	116,974	122,063	n/a
Passenger load factor (%)	70.2	70.8	70.0	71.6	70.8
Cargo tonne km (m)	2510	2691	2991	3349	3506
Passengers carried (000)	23,788	25,905	28,656	30,552	32,900
Cargo tonnes carried (000)	502	532	607	666	n/a

2.BA Group operations (inc Deutsche BA and TAT European))

Passengers carried (000)	25,422	28,100	32,749	35,643	n/a
Average total staff	50,409	48,960	51,350	53,060	n/a
Aircraft in service	230	241	294	283	n/a
A/c utilisation (hrs/day)	7.42	8.02	8.04	8.20	n/a

TOP TEN WORLD AIRLINES - COMPARATIVE DATA 1996

Airline	RPKs (Million)	Total Pax (000s)	FTKs (000s)
1 . United	187,786	81,945	2,607,296
2 . American	168,141	79,261	2,949,200
3. Delta	151,130	97,345	1,724,260
4. Northwest	110,440	52,682	3,279,621
5. British Airways	100,274	32,900	3,506,787
6. Japan Airlines	77,229	30,198	4,170,959
7. Continental	67,439	38,232	524,350
8. US Airways	63,104	56,640	221,781
9. Lufthansa	60,775	31,760	6,448,000
10.Air France	57,558	16,425	4,659,388

(RPK - Revenue Passenger Kilometres. FTK - Freight Tonnes Kilometres.)

Comparative Data 1996

	British Airways	United Airlines	Lufthansa
Fleet Size (a/c)	249	564	194
Staff	55,296	86,315	57,740
Passengers	32,900,000	81,945,000	31,760,000
Net profit ($ Million)	895.86	533.00	404.00

The UK's fastest growing aviation magazine . . .

AIRCRAFT ILLUSTRATED

- **INCORPORATING** —
  Air Display International
- **BIGGER, BUMPER ISSUES** —
  96 pages of solid aviation
- **UNBEATABLE COVERAGE** —
  of the aviation scene – military,
  civil, past and present
- **STUNNING IMAGES** —
  from the top aviation
  photographers, including many
  exclusives from JOHN DIBBS
- **UNRIVALLED COVERAGE** —
  of the airshow scene – news,
  previews, interviews, 'in cockpit'
  reports and much more

*Subscribe today to **THE** magazine
for the aviation enthusiast.*

For details of subscriptions please contact:
Ian Allan Subscriptions, Coombelands House, Coombelands Lane,
Addlestone, Surrey KT15 1HY. Tel: 01932 857257.
Fax/Overnight Answerphone: 01932 828769.

Be assured of your copy by ordering now!
Publishing